PLANET OF THE APES

OMNIBUS 3

PLANET OF THE APES

OMNIBUS 3

GEORGE ALEC EFFINGER

TITAN BOOKS

Planet of the Apes Omnibus 3
Print edition ISBN: 9781785653933
E-book edition ISBN: 9781785653940

Published by Titan Books
A division of Titan Publishing Group Ltd
144 Southwark Street, London SE1 0UP

First edition: September 2017
1 3 5 7 9 10 8 6 4 2

George Alec Effinger asserts the moral right to be
identified as the author of this work.

A CIP catalogue record for this title is available from the British Library.

Printed and bound in the United States.

PLANET
OF THE APES

OMNIBUS 3

MAN THE FUGITIVE

"The Cure"
based on the teleplay by Edward J. Lasko.

"The Good Seeds"
based on the teleplay by Robert W. Lenski

Based on characters from *Planet of the Apes*

For Sherry Gottlieb and Jim Fenkel, my cavalry.

THE CURE

1

The village of the humans was called Trion. It was a small village, even by the standards of the other human communities that ringed the inner zone. Ape society and the ape power was at its strongest in the inner zone and the human population meant no more than the size of a potential slave force. The humans who lived in Trion did not live as poorly as the humans who lived in the central ape city; the people of Trion had some degree of freedom: a tiny, half-forgotten shred of pride and dignity. That slight bit of freedom could easily be lost, at the vaguest whim of one of the ape leaders. They could never forget that fact, not while the soldiers of the gorilla army patrolled the boundaries of the village, and watched with contempt while the humans sweated in the fields.

Life was hard for the humans of Trion, but life was... life. The people had learned many years before that to resist the vast number of apes could only bring death. No single man was a match for one of the awesomely powerful gorillas, or even the less brutal, more intellectual orangutans and chimpanzees. Where resistance and rebellion meant death, the only thing that meant life and relative peace was work for the ape masters. This the humans understood and accepted. They labored, and the apes permitted them to live.

Sometimes, the humans could almost believe that they were happy.

"I almost wish you hadn't come here," said Amy, a bright, pretty girl of fourteen years. She was walking slowly with a man, a stranger to Trion, a strangely secretive visitor who had arrived in the village with his two companions, another man and a chimpanzee. Now Amy and her friend, Alan Virdon, were approaching the village, walking through the fields that surrounded it. The two had spent the morning exploring the forest and marsh lands just beyond the cultivated area.

Virdon stopped and looked around at the cluster of mud brick huts, and the poor handful of people working silently in their fields. On the far side of the village, beyond the fields, was a low hill. On the top of the rise was a barracks built of wood and stone, where two gorilla guards were tending to their arsenal of weapons. Virdon looked down from the hill and saw another gorilla carrying a rifle, walking along the perimeter of the far fields. The man turned and saw more thatched huts, more fields, and another gorilla, this one watching Virdon and Amy suspiciously.

"I'm sorry we have to go, Amy," said Virdon, his eyes still on the gorilla. The gorilla stared back for a moment, gave a derisive snort and turned away, continuing his rounds. Virdon laughed softly to himself, what a pitiable victory that had been for humankind.

"Why did you tell me who you are?" asked Amy. "Why me and no one else?"

Virdon seemed to be startled from some deep thought. He studied Amy's young face for a moment before he answered. His voice was low and filled with emotion. "I don't know, exactly," he said. "Maybe because you re special. Because I look at you and I see how it was when I was young. And I wanted you to know—life wasn't always like this."

It hurt Virdon to say those words, more than he thought it would. Just telling Amy brought back a flood of memories, thoughts which Virdon had to bury in his mind or else they threatened to overwhelm him. Before he and his fellow astronaut Pete Burke had been squeezed through time, into this upside-down, nightmare world, Virdon had a pleasant home in Houston, Texas. He had a wife whom he loved more than any person in the world, and he had children. One daughter was just about Amy's age—except that his daughter, and his wife, and everyone Virdon knew in his former life had been dead for two thousand years. Their world was dead. Everything they had built together had crumbled, and this mad dictatorship of the apes had somehow arisen to fill the gap. The insignificant bits of the old ways that Virdon and Pete Burke witnessed on their travels only made them more homesick.

"Life wasn't always like this," said Virdon again, grimly.

"But if I'd never known," said Amy, her expression thoughtful, "then I... I mean... She looked up at Virdon and shook her head. "You shouldn't have told me."

Virdon touched the girl's hair. It was exactly the same color... he forced the thought from his mind. "Amy," he said, "knowledge, is a lot like love. You get some pleasure from it, sometimes some pain. Like taking a trip to an unknown place." He looked up at the central meeting area of Trion, where he stood with Amy. His words were harsh against the gentle, distant sounds of the humans working. "Once you arrive at the unknown place, it's too late to wish you'd never started."

Amy smiled, trying to understand. Virdon gestured, and the two walked toward the hut of Amy's father.

Outside the crude shack, Talbert, Amy's father, was helping Virdon's companions slip into their backpacks. Talbert was a large man in his forties, browned by the harsh sun, built solid and hardened by long years of endless labor. Talbert held a backpack for Pete Burke, hesitated for a moment, shook his head, and picked up a second backpack. This one belonged to Galen, the chimpanzee who accompanied Virdon and Burke and shared in their changing fortunes. The chimpanzee shrugged his broad shoulders and settled the pack in place. Virdon joined his friends, swung his own backpack up, and waited while Burke thanked their host. Amy, her expression sad and thoughtful, stood a few yards away, listening in silence.

"Well," said Burke, a tall, handsome, dark-haired man, "thanks for putting us up."

"Why don't you stay, make your home here?" asked Talbert.

"That's a good question," said Burke with a short laugh. "I guess the answer is—" he jerked his thumb toward Virdon, "—he's got an itch in his feet, and I've got rocks in my head."

Talbert frowned, the lines in his deeply-tanned face falling into sharply outlined creases Like his daughter, Talbert had difficulty understanding what Burke and Virdon meant most of the time. The two strangers often referred to people and things that made no sense to him, and they used phrases and figures of speech that conveyed even less.

Burke, seeing Talbert's puzzlement, tried to give him a better explanation. "We're taking a survey of the far side of every hill on the horizon." Burke sounded rueful but he was cheerfully resigned to Virdon's consuming urge to explore their new home. Burke smiled, and Talbert only sighed. He still didn't quite get what Burke was driving at; after all, there wasn't anything better for a human, any where on the planet of the apes. He shook hands with Burke, and then, solemnly, with Galen.

"I'd try to give you a better answer," said the chimpanzee, "but I don't know what it is myself. Thank you for everything."

Talbert nodded. Pete Burke looked at Virdon. "Ready?" he asked.

Virdon, signalling he was, walked over to Talbert and shook his hand. "She's very special," said Virdon, nodding toward Amy. "Take care of her "

Talbert didn't reply. Galen, Burke, and Virdon, their equipment secure, their supplies replenished from the sparse rations of the generous people of Trion, moved away along the narrow road through the village. They passed Amy; the girl glanced at her father, but Talbert's expression was unreadable. The two astronauts and the chimpanzee paused for a moment to say goodbye to Amy.

"Will you ever pass by this way again?" asked the girl.

"Anything's possible," said Virdon, as gently as he could.

Amy gestured that Virdon should bend down. He did so, and she whispered in his ear. I'll keep your, secrets," she said, "even from my father."

"I may come back just to witness *that* miracle," said Pete Burke. Virdon jerked himself upright in surprise, and Amy stared at the darker man, obviously displeased that Burke had overheard.

"Miracle?" she asked.

"Oh," said Burke in a careless manner, "a woman keeping a secret."

"Women keep secrets," said Amy defiantly.

"I know, I know," said Burke, smiling. "I was joking… It makes the goodbyes easier." After a moment, Amy managed a smile herself. Virdon bent again and kissed her forehead.

"Goodbye, Amy," he said.

Now Amy could only nod. Virdon joined his companions, and the three fugitives started off down the road. Amy stood and watched, struggling to hold back the tears suddenly welling up in her eyes.

The three travelers had already given their attention to the problems that would soon be facing them in their trek through the unmapped territory. Amy watched them go. Talbert, too, watched the three strangers who he had quickly learned to call friends. Standing behind his daughter, unseen, his thoughts were melancholy. The daily life in Trion would be the poorer without Virdon, Burke, and Galen. The strange feeling which filled his body must have something to do with the departure of his guests. He felt a little faint, a little uncertain. He wiped his sweating face, blinked the drops of salty moisture from his eyes. The feeling did not pass away. He shook his head slightly to clear his thoughts.

On the edge of the village, Burke, Virdon, and Galen stopped, turned and waved. Talbert and Amy waved back. The Talberts watched as Neesa, one of the huge gorilla perimeter guards, paused in his rounds and waited for the three to approach him. Virdon saw Neesa, and put out a restraining hand, holding Burke from getting any closer. Galen would have to handle the situation. Neesa raised his rifle.

"I am transferring these two to the work force in the next village," said Galen, stepping forward between the humans and the gorilla.

Neesa looked Virdon and Burke over carefully, studying their faces. Reluctantly, the powerful but slow-witted gorilla lowered his rifle. Galen smiled and nodded, walked past the guard, paying no more attention to the gorilla, as though he and the two humans had every right in the world to travel about freely. Virdon and Burke acted their parts, the roles of two unhappy but docile slaves. Neesa watched them disappear out of sight, scowling and muttering under his breath. At last, he took up his rifle and started his rounds again.

The day passed slowly for the three travelers. They talked infrequently, saving their strength for the arduous march. Each was occupied with different thoughts: Virdon wondered if their next stop might give them the necessary clue they sought, some vital bit of information that would return them to their own time and their homes. Burke, on the other hand, was not so concerned with escaping back to the world he had been born into. He had a suspicion that he and Virdon were stranded in the ape world forever and that the main thing for them to do was build a new life in the best way possible. He was not unhappy with that prospect. He had no wife and family. He accepted what fate had given him, and he was prepared to make the most of it. Galen, the sympathetic chimpanzee, observed the two humans with a kind of scientific detachment. He wondered about their stories of technological marvels created by their human culture, and, while bound with them in common flight from the head of the gorilla police and military forces, a cunning gorilla named Urko, Galen wanted to learn as much as possible from the astronauts.

They climbed through rocky wastes beneath a pitiless sun. They waded through foul-smelling swamps. They helped each other along with a guiding hand or a few words of encouragement; but beneath it all, they shared a curiosity and fear of what dangers their journey might present them with.

The afternoon waned. Back in the village of Trion, Talbert rested on his straw-filled mattress. His face expressed an unaccustomed fear. As he lay, his body convulsed. His face was streaked with sweat. Again, his body shook spasmodically. Trying to raise himself up, the effort proved too great, and Talbert fell back down, swearing softly.

At that moment, Amy came through the door, a basket of freshly picked vegetables on her arm. Her intended lighthearted greeting was stopped short when she saw her father. Hurrying to the side of his bed, she looked down at him, worried and frightened. "Daddy," she said, "what's wrong?"

Talbert forced a smile to his lips to help remove the fear in her voice. "It's nothing," he said weakly. "I'm just a little tired. Little tired…"

"I'll get you some water," said Amy uncertainly. She left the bedside to do so.

Alan Virdon, Pete Burke, and Galen had found a pleasant clearing near a fresh-running stream. It was early evening, and they decided to call a halt to the day's march. Already, the memories of Trion and the people they had grown to like there were beginning to fade, to blur with the memories of so many other places and people they had met since their unlucky arrival in this undreamed-of future. The rigors of their new life were too difficult to allow the three adventurers the luxury of entertaining fond memories; that only weakened their attention, distracted their alertness. In this alien world, if Virdon, Burke, and Galen weren't alert, they were dead.

Swinging his backpack off with a loud sigh, Burke knelt by the stream and splashed the cool water on his face. Virdon set his pack down and began looking through it for their supper rations. Galen stood a little apart, deliberately excluding himself from the activities of the two humans, watching, observing, making mental notes with his shrewd, scientifically trained mind.

Burke took a long drink of the water, then turned to Virdon. "When we were in training a mere two thousand years ago," he said, "I used to hate all those hours we spent running on that treadmill. I hated that the most. Upward and onward to nowhere! So we get accidentally pushed twenty centuries into our own future, and do you know what? Nothing's changed."

Virdon gave a little laugh. "Except the world," he said. Irony hung heavy in his voice.

"Well, yeah," said Burke, "there's that. The old world was the nicest world I knew. Still is; was, I mean. Whatever."

"I wish you could have seen it, Galen," said Virdon. "The way it was…"

The chimpanzee waved the idea away. "Obviously I can't," he said.

"Maybe you'll get a chance," said Virdon. "I still hope

that somewhere, somehow, we'll find a way back."

Burke pointed to Virdon. "I'd be ready to certify that guy's bananas, but I'm going along with him, so what does that make me?"

Virdon smiled. "An optimist. What are you complaining about? When you were a kid, didn't you always dream about camping out, roughing it, even if it was only in your backyard? Well, here's your chance." Virdon continued to make camp for the night.

"This isn't exactly what I had in mind," said Burke, grumbling just a little. Taking Virdon's example, he opened his backpack and rummaged through it. He continued to mutter under his breath. "*He's* okay. Everybody else is crazy."

Virdon broke up small sticks and built a pile of kindling for their evening fire. Burke gathered the larger logs that would be needed. They worked together in silence: the routine they established during their travels, had become more habit than necessity.

Galen, in the meantime had moved to the edge of the clearing and stood motionless, listening intently. At this time of the day, his normal chore was to break up the larger logs into usable sizes; with his greater strength, Galen wedged the limbs into the fork of a tree and pushed. Virdon and Burke were always amazed at the great power of the chimpanzee. They knew that the chimpanzees were, on the whole, smaller than the orangutans, the ruling class of the ape world, who were in turn dwarfed by the massive gorillas. It was no wonder that the human population, now shrunken into insignificance in both physical strength and number, had little hope of regaining its former dominance.

But now, Galen did not join the humans in the work.

Every few seconds he cocked his head, or turned it a few inches, his expression showing deep concentration. Virdon noticed this and was immediately concerned. "Do you hear something?"

"Not yet," said Galen, waving to Virdon to be silent.

Burke, however, was startled by Galen's strange reply. Why would the chimpanzee be listening so hard, if he hadn't yet heard anything? Burke and Virdon stood up, and both men walked slowly and quietly to join Galen. "What are you expecting, then?" asked Burke.

"Trouble," said the chimpanzee.

Burke looked annoyed. "What is this, crystal ball time?"

Virdon gave Burke a quick glance, then tried to hold off any resentment between his fellow astronaut and Galen. "All right," he said to Galen, "what's bothering you?"

Galen's answer was simple. "You," he said.

"Say it," said Virdon.

"When I joined you two," said the chimpanzee, without any sign of anger or bitterness in his voice; he was merely reciting facts, "I knew I'd be facing the same danger you face, being recaptured. In fact, Urko may even have told his gorillas that I'm the first priority on his death list. I'm a renegade in the eyes of my own people. I accept that. But I did think that, under the circumstances, *we'd* try to protect each other."

Burke chewed his lip thoughtfully. He wondered what Galen could mean. Certainly, the three oddly matched friends had been joined by bonds of more than scientific curiosity; they recognized that they shared common enemies, and that their association might work to their mutual benefit. But this was true, just as Galen said, only as long as all three worked carefully for their joint protection. "Who isn't protecting what?" asked Burke. "Or did I miss something?"

Virdon knew immediately what the chimpanzee was referring to. "Hold it, Pete," he said to his friend. He turned to Galen. "I've done something you object to Galen. I'm not sure that I know what it is. If you tell me, I'll apologize or try to correct it. You know that I wouldn't deliberately jeopardize you. That would be cutting my own throat. Let's get this out into the open and settled."

Galen grunted. "You can't pour water back into a broken bottle. You've said yourself, so many times, how careful we must be, how we mustn't tell anyone about ourselves, who we are, where you've come from—"

"Amy," said Virdon flatly.

"A child," said Galen. "You trust her not only with your life and Burke's, but with mine, also. Can you see my point of view?"

"Yes," said Virdon, "yes, of course. But you know that I never would have said anything unless I was certain that she would never talk."

"As sure as if you had not told her?" asked Galen.

Virdon was silent. There wasn't an answer to that. The chimpanzee was right; Virdon had needlessly and foolishly endangered not only himself, but also two others who were counting on him. He felt a little ashamed that he had failed their trust. His mental anguish was obvious from his expression; Pete Burke tried to salve it. "Knock it off," he said. "Maybe the bottle's broken, like Galen said, but arguing won't paste it back together. Anyway, nobody's come after us, yet—"

Virdon recognized that Burke's words were beside the point. He waved at Burke to be silent. Virdon turned to Galen. "You're right, of course. I'm wrong. I should not have told her. She… well, I have a couple of children of my own. My daughter was… is about Amy's age. Sure, I know that's not an excuse, it's only an explanation. I'm sorry, Galen."

There was silence for a moment in the forest clearing. No one spoke; the sound of the rushing stream grew louder, and the pleasant night noises of birds and insects made the scene seem more peaceful than it was. Perhaps that lulled Galen's fears, at least for the time being. He raised a hand and spoke softly. He was evidently moved by Virdon's sincere emotion and candor. "I didn't think you *meant* any harm," he said, "but why did you take the risk?"

Burke clucked his tongue. "It's getting late," he said. "We have a stack of firewood to collect. We have our canteens to refill before it gets too dark. We ought to scout the area a little better before we settle down to supper. We have to clean up after we eat, in order to get an early start in the morning. We have all these things to occupy our time, and our friend Galen wants to get into psychoanalysis."

"Into what?" asked Galen.

"Nothing," said Burke, with a sigh. "You're lucky. It's something your ape culture hasn't developed. It was a kind of ritual magic. Purification rites. Things like that."

"You humans continue to astound me," said the chimpanzee. "Such things existing in the same society with the scientific wonders you always speak of. It must have been an odd time to live."

Burke and Virdon exchanged amused looks, but neither answered Galen. Burke went back to his wood gathering; Galen insisted on an answer from Virdon. The tall blond man thought for a few seconds. "It's hard to say just why I told Amy," he said at last. "Perhaps just a need to talk, to confide, to relate to someone who brought back the past for me. I can't really explain it. Maybe you could just chalk it up to the fact that, despite all my expensive training, I'm still only human."

Galen nodded. He spoke with genuine sympathy. "Yes," he said, "I forget now and then that you can't help some of the weaknesses you have. As you say, you *are* only human."

Burke slapped his forehead. "Oh, brother," he said. Virdon laughed. Galen looked puzzled. Then all three began to get their camp ready for the night.

The first evening stars were coming out in the sky over Trion. The sun had set, and a few clouds were blazing a bright carmine color in the west: Slowly the red left the sky, and the evening deepened. Along the main road that ran through the village, torches on poles were lit. Candles and oil lamps provided, light in the small huts, and bright squares of light marked the windows of the gorilla barracks on the hill over the village.

Amy Talbert was carrying two pails of water from the village's well to her home. The water splashed and fell on the ground about her as she walked; her father usually took care of carrying the heavy pails, but tonight he felt too tired to do it. Amy moved carefully through the door of the hut; when she saw her father, she put the pails down and hurried to him. He seemed worse than he had been earlier in the day. Now he was only semiconscious. His body convulsed often, and his face was shiny with sweat. His delirious mutterings were often interrupted by gasping attempts to fill his lungs with air. Amy, terrified, knelt beside him. "Daddy," she said.

There was no response.

"Daddy!" Amy watched in horror for a few moments,

then ran out of the hut. In the evening gloom she stumbled over the rough ground, her eyes almost blind with tears. She ran to a nearby hut, tripped, and caught the edge of the door with one hand. With her other hand she opened the door. She was crying when she half stepped, half fell into the hut. "Help me!" she said desperately. "Help me, please! My father!"

The hut was very much like the Talbert hut. The furniture was rough, hand-made, with few decorative touches. Indeed, there was little in the entire hut that was not purely functional; ornamentation was a luxury that the human race could no longer afford. Amy did not fear that her abrupt entrance into the home of her neighbors would cause any anger: the humans had long ago learned that they had to band together for their mutual support. No one ever knew when he might have to rely on the aid of his neighbor; therefore, a request for help was never refused. In any event, Amy was so worried about her father's condition that she never gave her loud intrusion a thought.

Amy stood in the doorway, looking wildly about the hut. No one seemed to be home. At dinner time, where could the people be? It was too late to be still working in the fields. The gorilla guards would certainly prevent anyone from strolling about after sunset. Becoming aware of strange sounds, Amy investigated, moving around the heavy wooden table in the center of the room.

An elderly couple, their faces pallid and sweating, were lying helplessly on the ground. They murmured incoherently, and the sound was chilling. Amy stared in horror. Backing away, she reached behind her with one hand. She knocked over a chair, and the loud bang startled her. Still she backed away from the stricken couple. Amy ran out of the hut, then stopped uncertainly.

After a moment's hesitation, she ran back to her own hut.

Her father was still in the same condition. Amy went to his side slowly. She knelt by him, cradling his feverish head in her arms. "Daddy," she whispered. He did not respond. Amy began to sob uncontrollably. She looked up, pleading. "Oh, please," she said, and her tears mingled with the rivulets of sweat that ran down her father's wan face.

2

It was a warm day in the central city of the apes. It was not yet noon, but already the temperature was so high that the air seemed stifling. Chimpanzees and orangutans bustled about their private business, under the watchful, somewhat bored gaze of the gorilla police. Almost as numerous as the apes themselves were the human slaves, who worked without respite from the broiling sun.

Inside one of the important buildings of the ape government, a meeting was in progress that would lead to serious consequences for many human beings, people who did not even know they were being discussed by their ape masters.

A wooden gavel slammed loudly on a table. The sudden noise quieted the murmur of angry voices that had filled the council chamber. Zaius, an intelligent, mature orangutan, was the presiding officer of the Council of Elders, the wielder of the gavel. He pounded it again for order. The meeting was officially in session.

"Please," said Zaius, "please, let us keep order here. You're babbling like a group of frightened humans."

One of the orangutan representatives on the council spoke up, greatly agitated. "There is much at stake here, Zaius," he said. "We have reason to be concerned. Our historians have brought this to my attention. If I may be permitted to read—"

"Go ahead," said Zaius.

The orangutan nodded and opened a large, crudely formed book. "'In the early part of the Oman period'," read the orangutan, "'several hundred humans were found in a section of the outlying rural zone—all dead from a fever of this description. The entire sector became barren for *years* afterward'…"

There was an immediate and violent response from the other members of the council. The chimpanzees, more curious than the other members, wanted to take the opportunity to experiment. The orangutans, the rulers, were concerned chiefly with the administrative problems the crisis presented. And the gorillas, led by General Urko, did not care at all about the more refined implications. The gorillas always met problems in the simplest way possible, generally the most violent as well.

Zaius banged his gavel over and over until order was restored. When he could make himself heard, he spoke. "I am aware of the potential loss of goods and labor," he said. "That is why I have ordered Trion quarantined. Pending investigation, that is." There was no concern for the safety and welfare of the humans in the village, not beyond what the people might mean economically to the apes.

General Urko leaped up angrily. "Quarantined?" he shouted. "Burn it!"

"Before we consider such measures, Urko," said Zaius,

"our Chief Medical Officer, Zoran, has a few words."

Zaius indicated a large chimpanzee, an intelligent medical expert. Zoran had a very self-assured manner, even in the face of hostile reactions from the gorillas. With Zoran was his assistant, another chimpanzee, though one of a more retiring nature, named Inta. Zoran thanked Zaius for the opportunity to speak, rose from his seat, and paced back and forth before the assembly. "I have done considerable research with diseases of the lower species," he said, "and I have developed certain... theories of treatment. Including such afflictions as this fever."

Once more General Urko jumped up, shouting and waving his great, brawny arms. He was the undisputed leader of all the gorilla forces, all the police and military might of the ape world. At times, this power and responsibility made him act in ways the other apes thought ruthless. It was not only the human slaves and workers who feared Urko. "Theories?" he screamed. "Theories, Dr. Zoran? Just an excuse for you to waste our time and resources on your intellectual games and guesses."

Zoran stared at Urko calmly. While the others in the council might react with fear to Urko's fierce behavior, Zoran wanted to make it clear, particularly before Zaius, that he was not easily intimidated. He waited until Urko had calmed down and then continued. "I intend to test my theories in Trion," he said simply. This announcement, seemingly admitting the truth of Urko's accusation, set the whole council to murmuring again.

Urko was greatly annoyed. He pounded on the desk in front of him with his great fists. "The entire labor force of a sector is threatened and he wants to test *theories*?" Zaius had a good deal more difficulty restoring the council to order. "Trion is quite isolated," he said finally. "And with the quarantine, the risk is greatly reduced."

Zoran spoke quickly, unwilling to let Urko seize the initiative. "If I can save Trion." he said, "we need never fear the fever again—ever! And that means zero loss of labor or goods in the future."

"All right, Zoran," said Zaius quietly, trying to keep order by the calm tone of his voice and the hint of authority behind it. "I believe that we've heard enough to form our opinions on the matter. Let us vote. Those *for* allowing Chief Medical Officer Zoran to proceed to Trion—"

The members of the council engaged in several debates among themselves. Finally, every member nodded yes in turn—every member except Urko.

"So be it," said Zaius.

Urko would not let the matter conclude so reasonably. He rose slowly and ponderously to his feet. Everyone in the council chamber looked toward him, wondering what he could say or do, after the legal vote had been taken. Urko walked slowly toward Zoran, still silent. The other members of the council began to file out of the chamber. Zoran ignored Urko and followed his colleagues. Urko grabbed Zoran by one arm. "I'll be there at Trion to enforce the quarantine, Zoran," said the gorilla general. "And if you fail..." Urko, leaving the threat unspoken, turned abruptly and marched out of the room. Zoran stared after the gorilla, contemplating Urko's words. The other chimpanzees and orangutans had stopped at the sound of Urko's voice. Now Zoran addressed them.

"You will not regret your faith in me," he said. Then he, too, walked confidently from the council chamber. His assistant, Inta, followed him nervously.

At the forest clearing where Virdon, Burke, and Galen had

spent the night, the three companions were finishing their morning chores. The few utensils that had been used for breakfast were washed in water from the stream. Burke used a knife to dig a wide hole; the ashes and embers from their cooking fire were scraped into the shallow pit and covered over. The area was carefully disguised with dead tree limbs and leaves. When they had finished, it was impossible to see that anyone had been there at all. Everything was repacked, and the backpacks were hoisted into place on the three well-muscled backs. Virdon and Burke were ready to take up the journey again; they waited for Galen, who was at the stream, taking a last mouthful of the fresh, sparkling water.

The chimpanzee stared in surprise at the sound of a heavy cart coming through the trees into the clearing. Burke and Virdon slipped behind the boles of large trees, out of sight. They waited a moment, and at last saw a single itinerant human, wheeling a cart full of roughly made implements. He looked over his shoulder, and was not aware of the presence of Virdon and Burke, who stepped out from their concealed places. Galen remained motionless by the stream. The stranger was clearly afraid of something; he had been hurrying, fleeing something, and now he rested in the clearing, panting, his face and body sweating profusely. He walked by Virdon, still without saying a word, and went to the stream. He was about to dip his face in the water when he noticed Galen for the first time. In the silent forest his gasp of surprise seemed almost like a scream.

"Your permission—?" he asked.

Galen only nodded.

"Thank you," said the man. He splashed water on his face. Galen left the edge of the stream and walked toward

Virdon. The stranger paid no attention.

"Ready?" asked Galen.

Before Virdon or Burke could answer, the stranger jumped up and came toward them. "You're not going to Trion, are you?" he asked.

"No," said Virdon. "Shouldn't we? Who are you? What are you running away from?"

"My name is Mason," said the stranger. "The village is quarantined. A plague. Many are dead and more will die. Many more." Mason looked from Virdon to Burke, pride filled his face: he had been the bearer of important news. It was the first time in his meager life that he had ever done anything like it.

Burke was not so easily satisfied. "Were you there?" he asked curtly.

Mason was taken aback by Burke's attitude. He might expect a dubious response from an ape, but he did not anticipate it from another human being. "No," he said slowly, "not in the village, thanks be. The guards let no one in, and no one out. A man was shot trying to run—"

Virdon couldn't stand the man's vague gossip any longer. "Do you know any more?" he asked heatedly. "The names of any who died?"

Mason stared at Virdon in surprise. He shook his head. "Nothing, nothing. I was spared. Even a name might carry the fever. Who knows?" He shrugged. Mason turned to Galen "Your permission—?" he asked.

Once again, Galen nodded. Mason went back to his cart, checked its contents, and hurriedly pulled it out of the clearing, away from Trion. Virdon and Burke silently watched the man go. Galen laughed softly, perhaps amused by the man's strange behavior and the contrast between his evident panic and the coolness of the two astronauts. All humans were different, and the chimpanzee was only beginning to realize how much he had yet to learn.

"Well," said Burke, "there he goes. A prime example of what our fellow man has turned into." Burke shook his head.

"I would hazard the guess," said Galen equitably, "that a people may not become what is not in them from the beginning."

"Now, wait a minute, Galen," said Burke. "Just because—"

"Wait a minute, yourself," said Virdon suddenly. Both Burke and Galen turned, waiting for him to continue. He didn't. After a moment, Burke sighed.

"A guy doesn't have to be a mind reader to know what you're thinking," he said.

"Maybe we can help," said Virdon.

Pete Burke turned to Galen with an expression of mock anguish on his face. "Will you tell this guy that it makes zero sense to try to bust into a plague village?"

Galen nodded in agreement. "If we *could* get in, what good would it do?"

Virdon thought for a moment. The strength of his original impulse weakened a little as he realized that Galen and Burke had a valid point. "I don't know," he said. "What if we were the ones who started it, carrying in some virus that was harmless to us, but ended up being murderous to them?"

"That kind of reasoning is typically human," said Galen.

"What's that supposed to mean?" asked Burke.

"Only that even if what Virdon says is true, there still is no logical reason for returning to Trion. Isn't it just as possible that you'd catch the fever if you went back there?"

Burke lost some of his defensiveness. Once again, the chimpanzee had struck right to the sensible heart of the matter. "Yes, you're right," said Burke. "Of course it is That is, if somebody doesn't shoot us for trying to get in, in the first place." The dark haired man looked at Virdon. "Of all the goofed-up ideas, this particular one takes the platinum cake knife."

"Pete," said Virdon, "don't you think we *should* at least try to help?"

Burke chewed his lip for a few seconds. "Did I say I didn't think that? Come on." He took a few steps across the clearing, back in the direction they had come the previous day.

"Just a minute." Galen's voice stopped Burke and Virdon in their tracks.

"What is it, Galen?" asked Burke. "Are we acting typically human again? Or are we acting not typically human, and you want to know why?"

"Were you planning to include me in this trip back to Trion?" Galen ignored Burke's pointed comments.

Burke looked at Virdon, unwilling to make any reply.

"I assumed we'd stay together," said Virdon uncertainly.

Galen walked slowly toward them, gesturing as he spoke as though he were lecturing a particularly difficult pupil. "We went through this only last night," said the chimpanzee. "Just because the girl reminds you of your daughter is no reason that I should run the risk of going back."

"No, no reason," said Virdon glumly.

"I just wanted to be sure that you understood that fact," said Galen. "You can appreciate my position. In the first place, the young human girl has no emotional attachment for me at all. Indeed, the entire human settlement means little to me, in other than the merest intellectual ways."

"Sure; Galen," said Burke. "But we'd do the same—" The Chimpanzee cut off Burke's words with a sharp gesture.

"And, further," said Galen, "you see that there is actually little reason for you two to go, either."

"No," said Virdon.

Galen cocked his gruff simian head to one side and stared into Virdon's eyes. "But yet, you stubbornly insist, upon returning."

Virdon looked at Burke. Burke shrugged, but did not say a word. After a moment, both men nodded.

Galen looked up into the clear sky. He spoke as if to some great watchful being above them. "I'm getting to be no better than a human!" he said. "All right, let's go."

Virdon and Burke grinned at each other. Burke slapped Galen's shoulder, a motion of gratitude and comradeship that Galen did not understand for a moment. Virdon was on the point of explaining it, but then he just shook his head and turned away. The three started the long walk back to Trion.

In the village, there was already more activity than the humans had ever seen. Unfortunately, everyone was too involved with the sudden epidemic to appreciate the attention they had drawn from their ape masters. Nearly every human was either sick or tending to the helpless victims. No one watched the gorilla forces that were enforcing the quarantine. There was no time to think about Trion's future, as far as the relative freedom of the humans was concerned. The fever occupied everyone's thoughts, and the gorillas went about their business virtually unobserved.

General Urko and his armed gorillas had surrounded the village in full force. Urko rode on his horse all along the village's perimeter, giving orders, stationing his forces to their best advantage. His headquarters, set up well away from the town, fitted Urko's rough style, being little more than a large tent that served as his command post.

Within the village, men, women, and children alike were in terror. They had no idea of what was striking them down. There was nothing to fight, nothing that they could see, nothing that they could grasp hold of. Grown men shrank in fear from the corpses of the dead around them. Children, crying, found no one to soothe their panic. The people of Trion huddled near their homes, terrified.

Some, though, continued to do their best to help the poor people who were stricken by the unknown disease. Amy Talbert tended to a dying old woman, putting wet cloths on her face and arms. Amy, knowing that it did no good, barely eased the woman's pain. The woman would die and Amy would nurse another person. The girl wondered how much longer she could continue, until she broke from the growing hysteria within her. Or until she was claimed by the sickness herself.

On the edge of Trion, Neesa, the gorilla guard, was tired and agitated by the unusual activity in the village. He did not like the nearby presence of General Urko. Before the epidemic, Neesa and his comrades lived under a relaxed discipline. Now times were harsher for the gorillas, as well as for the humans.

Neesa heard a sound behind him. He turned, half expecting to see the guard who was due to relieve him. Instead, he saw Galen, Virdon, and Burke. He was startled to see them step out of the forest area beyond the fields. As they approached, he called to them. "What are you doing back here?" he asked. "Haven't you heard? There's fever."

"We are somewhat familiar with this problem," said Galen smoothly. "We would like to go in and help."

Neesa sneered. "The council has sent the Chief Physician. So turn around and go back where you came from."

Virdon stepped forward, not willing to be so easily blocked by this infuriating obstacle. He wanted to be reasonable, but he knew that reason was a quality totally foreign to Neesa and his kind. "Look," said the man, "we just want to—"

Virdon was stopped short by Neesa's rifle which the gorilla pointed squarely at his chest. "I have orders to kill anyone who tries to cross the quarantine line."

Burke pushed his way forward. "Look," he said angrily, "I'm not going to take anything from some refugee from the Bronx Zoo."

Galen made a grunting noise; Virdon, fearful of what Burke's words and actions might cause Neesa to do, grabbed his friend by the arm. "Wait a minute," said Virdon. "That kind of thing isn't going to get us anywhere. Perhaps the guard is right. After all, he's only following his orders."

"Yes," said, Neesa, with a warning edge to his voice, "now go."

"We seem to have no choice," said Galen. The three adventurers walked back the way they had come.

Northeast of Trion was a small area of wooded growth, where, earlier, Virdon and Amy had walked. The forest area gradually merged with a wet marshy region. The three moved through the tangled vegetation for a few minutes. Water was standing over the ground, still and stagnant. There was no motion anywhere, nothing to be heard but the buzzing and ticking of insects. After a short while they stopped and looked back. Neesa, who had been watching them, had grown bored and had continued his slow rounds. Burke pointed, and the other two followed him, returning to the village the long way around through the marshy area.

The splashing noises they made wading through the brackish water went unheard by the gorilla guards, who were too concerned with their own business to post sentries that far from the village. All at once Burke stopped. He held up his hand, signalling the others not to move. Before them was a large pool, somewhat deeper than the water they had been walking through. The pool was thick and ugly, and the breeding ground for mosquitoes. Burke studied the area, then suddenly slapped at mosquitoes buzzing near him. He turned to Virdon, pulling his friend and Galen back.

"Stagnant water and mosquitoes," said Burke. "What does that make you think of?"

The two men and the chimpanzee moved quickly away from the place. Galen did not understand what Burke meant; he followed curiously, turning often to throw puzzled glances at the pool.

After some time, and frequent detours around more stagnant pools, the three travelers came out into one of the outlying farms of the village. They stood on the edge of the field and watched carefully. There did not seem to be any gorilla forces nearby. They started forward again, crossing the open field cautiously. When they reached the hut area, they stopped short, stunned.

Never before had Burke or Virdon, or Galen for that

matter, seen such desolation and hopelessness. The entire village had been reduced to a mass of frightened, sick people, helpless to save themselves from the strange curse that had attacked them. As Virdon, Burke, and Galen walked along the main street, they saw only terrified people, huddled together, with sick and dying people lying unattended among them. The bodies of the corpses remained where they had fallen; the survivors were too afraid to move them.

They walked through the center of the village. One of the sick men saw them and struggled to raise himself up on one elbow. His face was streaked with sweat and dirt, and his hand shook as he reached out toward them. His pained cry was the sound of a dying animal. He tried to wave, but could not control his movements; he ended up clawing the air in an attitude of desperate supplication. The sight tore at the hearts of Virdon and Burke, and even Galen was moved to pity. Virdon and Burke stopped and knelt by the man, examining him.

"Help... me..." whispered the man in a hoarse croaking voice.

Virdon tried to make the man lie down, but the hopeless man clung to Virdon's arms. He had little strength left, and Virdon forced him down; after a brief struggle, the man heaved a thick, rattling sigh and fell back to the ground, his body convulsing and his eyes staring unfocused before him. Virdon looked up at Burke. "You read it like I do?" he asked.

"Malaria," said Burke sadly.

Standing up, Virdon surveyed the village. It was a scene from some demented painter's vision of Hell. "God," he whispered, "God, what do we do now?"

A few huts away, Amy Talbert came through a door.

Stopping in the hot sun, she wiped the sweat from her forehead. She looked around, trying to decide where she could be of use. Suddenly seeing her three friends, she rubbed her eyes. "Virdon!" she cried.

At the sound of her voice, Virdon, Burke, and Galen turned. Stumbling toward them, she stopped, exhausted; her face suddenly lost the expression of hope it had carried, and her features went slack. Virdon ran to her quickly, caught her by her shoulders before she fell, and studied her face.

"My father," she said slowly, "my father is... dead..."

Virdon felt a moment of wrenching emotion. At first he did not know what to say. "Amy," he said at last, as gently as he could, "I'm so sorry." But even that sounded inadequate to him.

Burke joined them. Together, he and Virdon helped Amy over to the shade of one of the huts. "Amy," said Burke, "how do *you* feel?"

Amy tried to speak, but her throat was so dry that she couldn't make the words come out. She swallowed hard and tried again. "I'm... tired," she said, "but I'm not... sick..."

Virdon looked at the girl for a few seconds. He ran his hand through his hair. Things had to be done, but the measures that he could advise would be so pitifully ineffective without the proper medications. Still, a start had to be made, or else the situation would only deteriorate that much more quickly. And the situation would then be not just desperate. It would be final.

Virdon moved to the center of the village's meeting area. "Listen to me," he called. "All of you. If you can, come here and listen."

A cluster of frightened people stared at him from the

small scrap of shade next to a hut. They were uncertain: in their weakened condition, with sickness raging in their bodies, with the haunting memories of family and friends dying before their eyes, they did not know whom or what to trust.

Virdon turned his attention to another group, hanging back by another hut. Like the first group, they did not seem anxious to put their faith in this stranger, even though they had gotten to know him well in his stay in their village. There had been no such plague before the arrival of the three fugitives.

Something had to be done. Virdon realized that he was getting nowhere. "Please," he said, "time is against us. We've got to act quickly."

A few of the people, not as hopelessly ill as the others, caught the note of hope in Virdon's voice. They had learned from experience that to do nothing would lead surely and quickly to death. Virdon promised action which might mean life. They moved slowly and painfully toward him.

Following the first group, another group decided that Virdon was their best hope in their desperate situation. They moved away from the side of their hut and walked slowly across the hard-baked dirt toward the astronaut.

Anyone who could still walk or help another person gathered in the meeting area. They clustered about Virdon as though he brought news of their salvation. They had put their last hope in Virdon, and the blond realizing just how much he had promised with his encouraging words, wondered if he could possibly deliver on that promise.

"We must bury the dead," he said. "Immediately. You can't realize how important that is. If we don't, we'll be fighting the fever, and complications, and *worse*."

His words were interrupted briefly by the sound of

hoofbeats, rapidly approaching the village along the road. The crowd of people turned away from Virdon to look; no one was yet in sight. Virdon spoke out again, to regain his audience's attention. "A treatment center must be set up," he urged.

Chief Medical Officer Zoran rode into the village, followed by his assistant, Inta. They stopped their horses and dismounted, and hurried to where Virdon was standing. Virdon tried to continue. "Work teams must be organized," he said.

"Silence!" commanded Zoran.

Virdon stopped. All eyes, those in the crowd and those of Virdon, Burke, and Galen as well, turned to Zoran and Inta. The two chimpanzees studied Virdon closely.

"You seem to be a leader here," said Zoran curiously. "I wonder how General Urko would feel if he knew that a human was attempting to organize the other workers."

"I am no leader," said Virdon hastily. "What I said just makes good sense."

"Who are you?" asked Zoran.

"Just a… man, trying to help his fellow men," said Virdon cautiously.

"I am Zoran, Chief Medical Officer of the Supreme Council. This is my assistant, Inta. I have come to assume full authority here now."

Burke, Amy, and Galen moved forward to stand beside Virdon. Neither Zoran nor Inta paid the humans or their chimpanzee friend any attention. Zoran walked slowly across the street to examine one of the helplessly sick men who was lying in the middle of the road, too weak to move himself out of the way of whatever traffic might happen by.

Burke held Virdon's arm, stopping his friend from following

too closely. "What are you going to do?" asked Burke.

"It's obvious that the apes have no idea what malaria really means," said Virdon. "They don't know what causes it, they don't know how to cure it."

Burke looked worried. "We have to be careful here," he said. "We can't look like we have all the answers. The apes won't like that at all. Still, we have to do what we can. I don't have an answer. Do you?"

Virdon shrugged. He hurried after Zoran, assuming a deferential attitude. "We're very glad to see you," he said. "Perhaps we can work together."

Zoran gave Virdon a dubious look. "I can very well understand how you might want to work with me. After all, that would certainly increase your status among your fellow laborers, wouldn't it? But why in the world would I want to work with *you*?"

"He has a point," said Galen. Burke only gave their chimpanzee friend a warning look.

Zoran finished his examination of the dying man, then stood up, brushing his gauntleted hands together and nodding confidently.

"A pit will be dug at once," said the Medical Officer. "It will be filled with water I will add certain medications— ground nuts and roots, and specific natural chemicals. You will all disrobe and immerse yourselves. Then each of you will have an incision made on your upper arm, and you will be carefully bled—the amount depending of course on your size and age. There will be no physical contact among you until I have this disease under control." Zoran turned to speak directly to Virdon. "You," said the chimpanzee, "with the evident talent for organizing. You will supervise the digging of the pit."

Virdon was stunned, left speechless by the inanity of

Zoran's prescription. He stood unable to respond. He just stared in disbelief. Burke stepped forward angrily. "Look, Doc," he said through clenched teeth, "you're whistling Dixie!"

Now it was Zoran's turn to stare in shocked amazement. When he spoke, it was first with bewilderment, then annoyance. "I'm whistling? I... will... speak... clearly. Do you still hear whistling? Is there some structural malfunction in your ears?"

Galen sensed that the two humans were putting themselves in a position that could easily lead to trouble. It was another case of the astronauts' ignorance of the way things worked in this world, their refusal to accept the natural order of life, the perfectly reasonable superiority of apes over men. Galen took a deep breath; he was well-known in his own society, a fugitive. He hoped that Zoran would not recognize him. He had never had any conversations with the Chief Medical Officer before, and there was no reason to think that there would be any risk now. But Galen knew, perhaps in a way that Virdon and Burke never could, that *every* situation they found themselves in held its own latent dangers. "What he is suggesting, sir," he said, in a reassuring manner, "is that this... *particular*... disease, with which he is familiar, demands special treatment."

"Who are you?" asked Zoran irritably. "Why are you here in this village?"

Galen sighed. He was safe. "I was taking these two humans to another farm. Listen to them. They are more intelligent than most."

Zoran stared at Galen thoughtfully, weighing the chimpanzee's words. The doctor looked around him at the dying wrecks that once was the labor force of the village of

Trion. The problem of the disease was certainly bad enough; but Zoran had staked a lot of his personal ambitions on his being able to come up with a solution. He had risked his own future, in front of the Supreme Council, in front of Zaius, in front of General Urko. When Zoran thought of the gorilla chieftain, his lip curled angrily. It was all because of that monstrous Urko that Zoran was here at all. He certainly didn't especially want to be—of what remarkable value were these dismal looking human beings? There were always plenty more, breeding away in some other village. And the sun was hot—

Zoran realized that his attention was wandering. He looked at Burke. "So *you*, too, are familiar with this disease."

Burke did not hesitate in his reply. "It's malaria," he said.

Zoran laughed out loud. He turned to Inta, his assistant. "How clever," said Zoran. "He's even given it a name. Oh, call the guards, Inta. I haven't time for this fool."

Inta nodded, mounted his horse, and rode off toward the barracks of the gorillas.

Galen was alarmed. "Sir," he said quickly, "the guards won't be necessary."

Virdon had stopped worrying about his own safety. He knew that he had to convince this Zoran of the truth of his knowledge, or the people of Trion were as good as sentenced to death. Virdon would not have much time, or much chance of success, but he knew that he had to try. "Listen to me, sir," he said, hating the term of respect even as he uttered it, "malaria means 'foul air'. Like the kind you find around stagnant pools, like the kind we saw on our way into this village, not far away. You see, *sir*, the mosquitoes around this stagnant water carry the disease, and it's communicated by their sting."

Zoran had just about all he could stand. He was not used to talking with human beings—whenever that became necessary in his job, it was usually taken care of by Inta—and he definitely did not find it pleasant to be contradicted by one. Zoran was glad that Inta had gone, so that the assistant could not see what, to Zoran, was a horrible embarrassment. The Chief Medical Officer exploded. "That is enough!" he screamed. "I don't know whether to have you shot for plain stupidity, or hanged for insolence. Plagues flying through the air on the backs of *insects*! Diseases of the lower species are communicated by bodily contact."

Burke ignored Zoran's words "the lower species". He spoke as calmly as he could. "This one isn't," he said.

Zoran was even more furious. "You *are* challenging my word!"

Galen grew even more agitated. It seemed that Virdon and Burke were deliberately trying to get themselves further and further into trouble! Didn't these humans realize that they couldn't risk antagonizing someone as powerful as Zoran? It made no difference who was right in this matter; all that was important was that Zoran had the authority, and that Virdon and Burke were, after all, only humans.

"Believe me, sir," said Galen in a conciliatory tone, "he does not mean to be insolent. As with all humans, fear has put foolish words in his mouth."

The sound of returning hoofbeats caused Galen to look around nervously. Virdon and Burke watched the road carefully; they realized that, perhaps, they had gotten themselves into a situation that no amount of talking could get them out of. It might be, as much as they didn't like the idea, that they might have to fight their way out of Trion.

Zoran noticed their discomfort. "Fear, eh?" he said. "Is

that what causes their foolish words? I have a certain cure for that disease."

Galen tried one last time to convince Zoran. "These men do know something of medicine."

Zoran waved the suggestion away. "Impossible," he said.

Meanwhile Neesa rode into the village, roughly knocking several humans aside with his horse. With him rode Inta and another gorilla guard. Virdon noticed that Neesa was sweating profusely—the gorilla was on the very edge of exhaustion. It seemed that only the blond astronaut saw Neesa's condition. Zoran pointed at the two humans. "Arrest those two!" he cried.

At first, it looked as if Zoran's angry demand would go ignored by Neesa, who was having difficulty controlling his horse. Neesa rubbed his heavy brow with a gloved hand. The horse, feeling the gorilla's unsteadiness, began to prance around. Neesa shook his head to clear his dizziness, then reined in tightly. The horse quieted down; after a moment Neesa spoke as though nothing were bothering him. He glared at Virdon, Burke, and Galen. "Arrest them?" he said angrily. "I'll *shoot* them. They've crossed the quarantine line against my orders."

Zoran looked thoughtfully at the gorilla guard. Such bloodthirstiness still did not sit well with the more intellectually inclined chimpanzee. Nevertheless, Neesa represented the gorilla guards, who were the apes' only protection against whatever dangers might develop in these outlying areas. They probably knew what was best in these matters; it was not Zoran's position to countermand the gorillas' orders. After all, Zoran had a difficult enough time as it was. He shrugged. "Do as you please," he said, turning away.

Virdon and Burke started to protest. Galen held them back, knowing that their interference would only make things worse, and hasten their execution at the hands of Neesa and the second gorilla guard. The two astronauts exchanged helpless glances. Galen stepped in front of them and spoke to Zoran, who had turned his back and was walking away. "Sir," said Galen, "I must protest your actions here—"

Galen's argument went unnoticed by Zoran, who continued across the road. Neesa. however, was happy to have the situation in his control; he raised his rifle and tried to aim it at Virdon. At the same time, the second gorilla raised his own rifle and pointed it at Burke. Before either could fire, though, Neesa's strength finally failed him. He dropped his rifle and fell from his horse. "Kava," called Neesa hoarsely. Kava, the other gorilla, was too startled to answer. He grabbed the reins of Neesa's horse to prevent the animal from trampling its master. While Neesa rolled in the dust of the road, Kava struggled to control the riderless horse.

The commotion behind him caused Zoran to turn and watch the scene for a moment; he saw Neesa convulsing on the ground. Virdon and Burke knelt, examining the gorilla. After a moment of silence, Burke stood and addressed Zoran. "Shove this up your theory," said Burke. "Has he had 'bodily contact' with any of the lower species? He *has* malaria!"

Kava, Neesa's companion, was frightened. Even with the gorilla's rigid military framing with its Spartan emphasis on discipline and restraint, fear showed on his face. Rising in his saddle, he urged his horse closer to Zoran. Burke's words had gone straight to Kava's heart. Now Kava exploded with indignant rage. "What is he saying?" he demanded, "How could this be? Explain!"

Zoran stared at the writhing Neesa. He did not seem to hear Kava's desperate questions, or his peremptory command for an explanation. Zoran was as frightened as Kava but on top of it was the sudden insight that there was a good deal more to the situation than anyone yet suspected. Perhaps these puny humans were correct, after a fashion. Perhaps the apes did not have such a complete grasp of medical science, after all. In a way, that idea was more disturbing to Zoran. He studied the dying Neesa and shook his head in disbelief. All logic seemed to desert him. "I… I can't explain…" he said.

Kava glared at Zoran with contempt. "You fool," said Kava. "Will you dare tell that to Urko?"

Zoran had no answer.

3

The next day was as hot and clear as the previous one. In the village of Trion, more humans died. Outside the village, in Urko's command tent, a hastily assembled meeting of the Supreme Council was trying to reach a decision. The meeting was going much less smoothly than the one before. Now the emotions of all the members seemed to interfere with the coldly logical reasoning on which they prided themselves. Outside the tent, two gorillas stood guard. Watching the horses of the council members, they tried in vain to hear some of the progress of the meeting. All that they heard were the sounds of angry voices, and an occasional word that was shouted above the raucous clamor.

"Fire!" cried Urko. "Purification by fire! It is the only course left to pursue."

One orangutan tried to speak. He started several times, each time drowned out by the excited arguing of the others. At last Zaius came to the orangutan's aid, banging his gavel over and over until everyone settled down. Then the orangutan proceeded. "The situation *is* different now, Zaius," he said. "*Apes* are being threatened."

Zaius did not appear to be moved. "Please," he said calmly, "we must quiet ourselves and think rationally."

The orangutan pounded his fist on a table. "But an *ape* is dead, Zaius. An ape! It's no longer a minor problem."

Almost every member of the council took the opportunity to demonstrate the intensity of his feelings. Unfortunately, the cumulative effect of so many simultaneous demonstrations was complete and uncontrollable chaos.

Zaius banged his gavel, but this time there was no quieting the apes. At last Zaius gave a sigh and stopped; his gavel-banging was only adding to the noise and confusion, After a few moments, realizing that they were making no progress at all, the council members returned to their seats.

Zoran conspicuously took no part in the loud display and sat silently in his seat, a shaken and doubtful chimpanzee. Urko noticed Zoran's frightened manner and took advantage of it. "You," he cried, pointing his hugely muscled arm at Zoran, closing his fingers into a threatening fist, "you and your 'theories'." Urko turned from the Medical Officer and addressed the rest of the council. "He should be burned with the others."

Zaius pounded his gavel to stop the uproar that greeted Urko's words. "I do believe that suggestion is a little extreme, even for this situation," said Zaius. "In any event, you are out of order, Urko. I suggest that we hear Zoran's appraisal of the circumstances."

A member of the council, an orangutan, shouted out his approval. "I agree," he said. "He promises us success." It was a challenge to Zoran's professional abilities.

Everyone in the command tent looked at Zoran. There

was a sudden, deep, and unnerving quiet. Zoran took a breath. He understood the importance of what he would have to do in the next few days. It was possible that he might emerge from this dilemma a discredited and broken ape. It had all begun so simply! He almost wished that he had let Urko have his way at the previous council meeting. Still, the possibility remained that Zoran might yet wrest a victory from these unpromising events. Zoran rose from his seat, his thoughts racing. Everyone waited for him to speak. "Upon… my arrival in Trion," he said, considering each word carefully, "I discovered that the fever… was of a different type than I had assumed. It is of a… rare variety… called… Malaria… and it is obviously fatal to apes as well as humans. This leads me to conclude… that it is… obviously… not transmitted by bodily contact…"

"Then in what other way *could* it be communicated?" asked Zaius.

Zoran wondered if he believed what he was going to say, himself. "I have reason to suspect… the disease grows in… stagnant pools of water… and is carried into the bloodstream by the sting… of… mosquitoes." The council members stared at Zoran in amazement. They had never before heard such a preposterous statement, and they surely didn't expect such a thing from so noted an authority as Zoran.

"You can't be serious," said one of the orangutans.

Urko laughed harshly. "He's got the fever himself."

There was a great deal of unpleasant muttering from the council members. Zaius rapped his gavel for order. "Zoran," he said, "are you aware of what you are asking us to believe?"

"There are such stagnant pools in Trion," said Zoran. "Both the humans and," he addressed Urko, "your soldiers have been exposed to these areas."

"And what action do you propose we take now?" asked Zaius.

That was the question that Zoran dreaded. He had thought about the matter until his mind refused to consider it any more; he had gone over everything the two humans had told him, and it still made no sense. He had to stall. Perhaps something would happen, or some idea would occur to him in the meantime. "I will need a few hours to... further appraise the situation," said Zoran, in his best bureaucratic manner.

General Urko took the opportunity to take another swipe at Zoran; the difference was that this time he voiced sentiments that were shared by almost all the other members of the council. "I'll be damned if I'll back down to a mosquito!" he roared.

Zoran knew that he had to defend his shaky position. The problem was in finding a way to do it. He had little sympathy left among his colleagues; Urko was gaining more and more influence. Zoran's reasonable talk was sounding increasingly like vague and unfulfillable promises. "Urko," said the Medical Officer, "since this disease is fatal to our people, too we should use this... this situation to develop a cure. Can't you understand that?"

"Yes," said Zaius, to Zoran's great relief, "perhaps there's a positive side to this. We can experiment with the humans. Even if we lost the entire village—as long as an ape cure were developed—it would be worth it. Historically, medicine has progressed because of such experimentation. Yes. I believe we should seize this opportunity."

One by one, thanks to the backing of Zaius, the other members of the council nodded agreement.

"So be it," said Zaius. He turned directly to Zoran.

"You'll report to us."

"Yes, sir," said Zoran.

Urko did not voice his disapproval. He merely rose ponderously to his feet and pushed through the others. He left the command tent unaware of the nervous looks the members of the council gave him as he passed.

The day was getting hotter. Urko shielded his eyes when he emerged into the bright sunlight. He stood motionless for a moment, then signalled to one of his guards to prepare a horse for him. The young gorilla brought Urko's mount, and the general, still fuming at the council's foolish delays swung up into the saddle and rode away. A few moments later Zoran came out of the tent. Now more shaken than before the meeting, he felt trapped.

In the village of Trion work groups had been organized. Parties of men still strong enough buried the dead. Those who had been weakened by the disease were carried into one of the largest huts. More people carried water from the village well into the hospital hut.

In other parts of the village, women and children were fashioning crude gloves and cloth headpieces with narrow eyeslits. Virdon went from group to group, inspecting their work. He gave them all encouragement; he knew that, even if this labor didn't actually stave off the attacks of the fever, it at least absorbed the attention of the survivors. It substituted a positive plan for panic and hysteria.

Burke felt differently; he thought that the very fact that they knew what was striking down the people of Trion was a tremendous advantage in fighting it. At least, they weren't digging pits and filling them with water. At least, they weren't bleeding the people. What simple things they *could* do were along the right lines. He thought for a moment about how the scientists of his own time had fought malaria and yellow fever. A bacteria had been developed that attacked the particular mosquito that spread these diseases. When the bacteria was introduced into the pools where the mosquito bred, the mosquito larvae died in a few days. The method, harmless to man, was much safer to the ecology of the area than spraying with insecticides. But Burke, wiping the sweat from his brow, would more happily settle now for an elementary medical textbook of his own era, one that would direct him and Virdon with more authority.

The sick were being placed on cots arranged in rows inside the large hut. Burke directed this operation; Amy and Galen bathed the sick with well water that was carried in for their use. These tasks ceased at the sound of hoof-beats; Burke looked out of the hut window and then went outside.

Virdon heard the sound, too, and looked up, shielding his eyes with one hand. He waited for Burke to join him from the hut. Zoran rode into the village and dismounted. The Medical Officer walked about the village, examining the activities that the astronauts had organized. They picked up a pair of gloves and a mask that the women were making. "What are they doing?" he asked.

"Protective masks and gloves," said Burke. "We've got to send a work crew to drain off the stagnant water."

Zoran considered Burke's words. Now he did not attack their suggestions: his personal situation was so desperate that he had to accept whatever help was available, no matter how unorthodox it seemed. He had committed himself this far; the only reasonable thing was to see the thing through to the end, whatever that might prove to be. "I am in a most difficult position with the council," he said. "I have related your... mosquito theory." Zoran paused, studying the faces of the men. He took a deep breath. "Of course, in order to save you from punishment—should we fail—I told them it was *my* own…"

Virdon and Burke exchanged wondering looks. This benevolent attitude they rarely encountered among the apes. Usually, the masters were all too willing to let the blame for failures fall upon the "inferior" human beings. "You're very generous," said Virdon.

Zoran looked at the humans curiously. He wondered if they were,, after all, just as simple as the other humans of Trion. Surely, they ought to be able to understand how he, personally, was involved with the situation now, and how he *had* to come up with a solution to save his own career and, possibly, his own life. He sneered; any of the other human beings would see that. He wondered how Virdon and Burke could overlook it. If they were that unsophisticated, how could he put any faith in their medical advice? "I'm not entirely generous," he said, baiting them. "If I told the council that I heard it from two humans, they would have asked questions: who you were, how you came by this information. Urko, particularly, would have been more than curious about humans who know more than they should. I hope, for *all* our sakes, that you do know about this disease."

The mention of Urko's name drew concerned looks from Virdon and Burke. There was no one in the world that more wanted to see the astronauts dead than General Urko: the gorilla feared that the humans might bring knowledge to their oppressed people. But worse, in Urko's eyes, was the possibility of the astronauts' leading a slave revolt against the ape masters. Zoran caught the exchange of silent glances and misinterpreted it. "Have we been wrong up to now?" asked Burke.

This only made Zoran grow more suspicious; the humans seemed to be unusually defensive. While Zoran considered the matter, Galen came out of hut to see if his friends had gotten themselves into trouble again.

Zoran hit a fist into the gloved palm of his other hand. "You've provided a theory," he said to Burke. "A name for the disease, a diagnosis. Right or wrong, it adds up to very little. What about *treatment*?"

Burke shrugged. He was wondering how long it would take the Medical Officer to think of that.

"There's one known treatment for malaria," said Virdon. "Quinine. It's extracted from the bark of a semi-tropical tree called the cinchona."

Zoran looked suddenly very weary. He rubbed his eyes and sighed. "I've never even heard of such a tree," he said. It was obvious that he thought the humans really didn't know what they were talking about.

"Just beyond the marsh there's a heavily wooded area," said Burke. "It's fairly tropical growth. If we're lucky, you'll get to see one."

Virdon walked to the shaded area of one of the huts, where women and children had finished a number of protective garments. He picked out a pair of gloves and a headpiece for himself, tried them on. then nodded his approval. He picked up another set and offered it to Zoran. The chimpanzee nodded and accepted the articles. Virdon, Burke, and Galen smiled to themselves.

Properly attired, the two men and two apes started off toward the marshy area. They took along several men, who also wore the gloves and headpieces. The sun was very hot, and inside the masks, the party grew more uncomfortable. Still, they all understood the importance of not removing the headpieces.

The stagnant pools surprised Zoran with their size. He bent down and studied the water, a little fearfully. He saw the small, tadpole-like larvae of the mosquitoes, swimming around in great numbers. Great numbers of the adult mosquitoes settled on the protected areas of the party's bodies. "Are you sure we're adequately guarded?" asked Zoran.

"If they can't bite you, they can't hurt you," said Burke.

Virdon turned to the work party that had come with them, some carrying crudely made shovels and other digging tools. "Remember," he said, "no part of your body can be exposed." The blond man turned to Galen, who was to supervise the draining operation. "Good luck, my friend," said Virdon.

Galen nodded and began organizing his crew. Burke, Virdon, and Zoran moved away, followed by half of the men.

After a few minutes of walking, the group approached the edge of the heavily wooded area. "Listen," asked Zoran, "do we still have to wear these things? We've come a good distance from the danger region."

"I think we'll be all right," said Virdon. They pulled off the headpieces in order to see better and be more comfortable. The sound of hoofbeats announced the arrival of an unwelcome, interruption.

Virdon, Burke, and Zoran turned to see who was coming. The sight was unpleasant for all three, although it meant much more to the astronauts than to the chimpanzee. It was Urko and several of his armed soldiers riding toward them. The gorillas shouted as they rode, making an awesome spectacle of military might. Zoran found it distasteful; Virdon and Burke found it potentially fatal.

"Uh oh," whispered Burke.

Virdon thought hastily. He pulled the headpiece back over his face, to hide his identity from Urko. Burke followed his friend's lead. Together they waited, anxious and concerned, not only for their own safety, but also for what their recapture would mean to the people of Trion.

Urko and his gorilla guards pulled their horses to a halt a few yards from the small party. The gorillas laughed and insulted the humans, pointing at the bulky protective gear and making foolish comments. Urko quieted them by raising one hand. He walked his horse in front of Zoran, blocking the path of the party.

Urko leaned over in his saddle and spoke menacingly.

"What's wrong? Running away from the village, *doctor*?" he asked.

Zoran suddenly realized that it looked to Urko as if the Medical Officer were trying to escape, to flee for his own life. If Urko could convince the Supreme Council of that, everything would have been for nothing, and Zoran's life might end in disgrace. "The cure is in the bark of a certain tree," he said. "We believe such a tree can be found in those woods."

Urko laughed; it seemed that Zoran was doing everything he could to back himself into a corner. "*We* believe?" asked Urko cheerfully. "What do you mean, *we*? I was under the impression that *you* had sole authority here."

Zoran realized that he had set a trap for himself. But he had not risen to his high position within the council without learning the same kind of verbal agility that Urko was using. His voice was steady when he replied. "I have sole authority. But I have described the tree and *we*," Zoran turned indicating Virdon, Burke, and the others, "*they* believe such a tree might be found in there." Zoran nodded to the nearby wooded area.

Urko grunted. He prodded his horse even closer to the group of humans. He noticed that the workmen had removed their headpieces, but that Virdon and Burke still wore theirs. Urko, more intelligent than the usual gorilla, turned this idea over in his mind. "What are you two afraid of?" he asked.

Burke answered, trying to disguise his voice from Urko. From within the headpiece, the sound of Burke's voice was further muffled. "Mosquitoes," he said.

Urko started and without a word he wheeled his horse around. The gorilla general looked about him worriedly, but saw nothing suspicious. Although there were no mosquitoes in the immediate area, Urko rode off at great speed, his soldiers close behind.

Zoran watched Urko's departure for several moments. Then, when the gorillas had ridden safely away, he turned to Virdon and Burke, suspiciously. Walking slowly toward them, fingering his own headpiece thoughtfully, he tried to seem casual, but the effect failed.

"You two," he said. "I notice that you are wearing your protective headgear again. I remember that you took them off shortly before General Urko arrived. And because you have been of such great assistance up until now, and because you seem to have so deep an understanding of this situation. I'd like to know why you think it necessary to cover your faces." He looked at them, and he was unable to keep the suspicion out of his expression. "There are no mosquitoes here," he said.

Burke clapped his hands at an imaginary mosquito. He held his palms closely together; Zoran watched closely as Burke slowly opened a gap between his hands. "Missed!" said Burke disgustedly. "It was an albino mosquito. All white, with pink eyes. Very hard to see."

Zoran snorted derisively, but when Burke did not react, the Medical Officer raised his eyebrows. He did not know whether to believe Burke. An albino mosquito! But, still, the humans *had* been correct about things so far. Zoran continued to stare at Burke, whose innocent expression seemed to reassure the chimpanzee. A small hint of suspicion remained on Zoran's face, but Burke ignored it. He and Virdon moved on. Zoran and the others followed.

In the large hospital hut, Amy Talbert was carrying fresh water and bathing her fevered patients. As she knelt to rinse the sweating face of one old man, she suddenly felt faint. Recovering, she shook her head to clear it; and forced the gnawing fear that she, too, might be showing the first symptoms of the fever out of her mind. She continued to work among the dying people, while near her, Inta, Zoran's assistant, followed his superior's instructions and aided the sick humans as well as he could.

In the wooded area, Virdon, Burke, and Zoran searched among the trees, looking for the particular growth that would yield a medicine for the fever. Burke was pessimistic: how many people would know what to look for, and recognize it when they found it? Virdon was more confident; he remembered the astronauts' survival courses for various climates. A thorough study of animal and plant types had been given to them, along with a survey of native cures. The cinchona had been one of the things they had studied. Even if Burke hadn't paid close enough attention, Virdon had. He described the tree and its bark to the others. "It's more like a large shrub," he said, "although there are several types we can use."

"I don't think these guys would know a cinchona if it

bit them on the leg," said Burke.

"Would you?" asked Zoran.

"Sure," said Burke hurriedly. "Oh, sure. Of course." The party split up to search the area more thoroughly.

They worked all the rest of that day, the men in the group getting more and more frustrated and hopeless as they brought scraps of bark to Virdon for identification. Nothing looked even vaguely like what Virdon was searching for. Then, while Virdon was looking for Burke, near sunset, he went through a portion of the forest that had been assigned to Zoran. The first thing the blond man noticed was a grove of what seemed to be cinchona trees. He stopped in his tracks and stared. Then slowly, muttering a short prayer, he walked to one of the trees to look at it closer. He pulled off a small, flat, brown piece of bark. He bit into it; the bitterness of the bark made Virdon wince.

"Is it—?" asked Burke, who had come up behind Virdon.

Virdon turned around, too hopeful to be startled. "Looks like it could be, and it sure tastes bad enough."

"I'd feel a lot better if you were sure," said Burke.

Virdon laughed. "To tell you the truth," he said, "so would I."

Zoran joined them. He saw the bark in Virdon's hands. "Have you found it?" he asked.

"I think so," said Virdon.

Zoran reached out and took a small piece. He put it in his mouth and tasted it. "Ugh!" he said, making a face and spitting out the rest of the bark. "Terrible."

Virdon and Burke laughed at the sight the pompous Medical Officer made. "All good medicine tastes awful," said Burke. "That was one of the first things I learned when I was a kid:"

Zoran didn't deign to reply to Burke. Instead, he turned his attention to Virdon. "But will it cure the fever?" he asked.

"Not if we just stand here," said Virdon. He began pulling off the bark. Zoran helped him, and Burke called the other men to come and join them. The work went quickly; the men had no idea of what the bark could be good for, and Zoran had only a vague notion. Burke was ignorant of the procedure for turning the raw bark into a usable medicine. Virdon spent the hour rehearsing in his mind the steps that had to be followed. In the preparation of quinine, the alkaloids in the bark had to be separated out, the natural lime in the bark neutralized, and the resulting crystals dissolved in an oil or alcohol base. None of the steps would be too difficult; that is, assuming that the humans of Trion had stores of the necessary substances.

It was nearly dark when they finished peeling off a good supply of bark, and Virdon was satisfied that it was a sufficient quantity. They bundled it up as well as they could, and the humans, Zoran and Galen, began the march back to Trion.

Torches were being lit along the main road that connected Trion with other nearby villages. The party entered the town wearily, throwing down the loads of bark in front of the hospital hut. Virdon looked around to see what had been accomplished during their absence. Most of the dead had been buried. Water was being fetched from the well and carried into the hospital in a steady operation. Some people were preparing food, and distributing it among those too ill to feed themselves, or too busy to fix their own meal. These people looked up when the astronauts and their helpers entered the village. There was a light of hope in their eyes, one that Virdon or

Burke had not seen before. Each of the men wondered if they could be worthy of the faith the people of Trion had placed in them. The villagers gathered around Virdon and Burke, anxious to know what would happen next.

"Here," said Virdon to them, "we've got to work quickly. Get stones, flat stones, grind this bark into powder." As the villagers began to take up, this new chore, Virdon turned to Inta, who had come out of the hospital hut. "Any more deaths?" asked Virdon.

"One more," said Inta. "And two more sick."

At this news, Virdon, Burke, and Zoran hurried into the hospital hut.

They were met by a shocking sight, one that caused Virdon to gasp out loud. Burke swore softly. They ignored the pleadings of the other patients in the hospital hut; their attention was drawn to one small form, lying on one of the poor straw-filled mattresses. Amy's face was bright with sweat, gleaming in the flickering light from candles and oil lamps. She jerked, spasmodically and cried out in pain. Even Zoran was moved at the sight of the heroic young girl who had been made so helpless by the rampaging fever.

Burke was stunned. He moved slowly to Amy's side and knelt by her. He took her hand, and he was amazed by how pale it was, and how soaked with perspiration. Amy turned slowly, trying to see him through the haze of her delirium. "I'm sorry," she murmured.

Her words brought Burke nearly to the edge of tears. "What the hell for?" he asked, his voice almost choked with emotion. Virdon knelt down on the other side of her mattress.

"I... wanted to... help," said Amy.

"We got what we went for," said Virdon. "So you

hang in there. You just hang in." Amy nodded, then the effort was too great for her, and she was swallowed up by the sickness. Moaning, while her body twisted uncontrollably on the pallet. Virdon rose and walked sadly away. He was joined by Burke. They spoke together in hushed tones.

"I'm sorry, Alan," said Burke somberly.

"About what?" asked Virdon.

"A few things I've said and even more things that I've thought." Burke jerked his head toward Amy. "This is rough on you."

"It's not easy on anybody."

"When I look at her," said Burke thoughtfully, "I don't see a little girl who used to call me 'Daddy'. I guess I'm lucky. No one back there to remember, really."

Virdon smiled. "Is that lucky?" he asked.

"Absolutely," said Burke. "I think. But, if we ever *could* make it back, you know, where we came from, I'd maybe start looking hard for someone soft, and permanent."

Virdon laughed ironically. "Then all of this hasn't been in vain," he said.

Burke looked hurt. "I only said 'maybe', remember," he said.

"In that case," said Virdon, "if I find a way back, I'll think about taking you along."

Burke laughed. "You be sure to do that," he said. Together the two friends moved outside.

Throughout the night, Virdon directed the preparation of the medicine. The bark was ground into a fine powder by the work crew that had earlier made the headpieces and gloves. Powdered lime was added to the bark, and water, and the paste was dried in an oven for nearly an hour. Burke chafed at the passage of time, recalling the frightening aspect of Amy's suffering. Nevertheless, there was nothing else to do. The manufacturing of the medicine couldn't be hurried. The dried result of the baking was mixed with the only alcohol available, a kind of local whiskey made by the people of Trion from corn. The powder was allowed to settle to the bottom of the alcoholic mixture. The whiskey was discarded, and the powder was mixed with water and boiled. Virdon watched each step closely; everything had to be done at the right time, and only he understood the process. The powdered bark was purified several more times, redissolved in various solvents, and boiled with a large quantity of water. At last, near morning, Virdon judged that the bark had been transformed into usable quinine.

Burke made Virdon sleep; the blond astronaut was nearly exhausted. Burke, who had rested fitfully during the night, now took over the supervising. He saw to it that each patient in the hospital hut was dosed with the quinine. Zoran and Inta watched curiously, then began to help in the treatment when it became obvious that there weren't enough humans who were both well and awake, to tend to the sick.

In the spare moments, when things seemed to be going smoothly, Burke nursed Amy, who seemed to be slipping further into delirium. The huge burden of work she had taken upon herself in the last few days had badly weakened her resistance.

Galen resumed his work with the human crew, draining the last of the stagnant pools near the village. Near noon, the chimpanzee, covered with mud and more tired than he had ever been before, led his party back into the village.

And General Urko, sitting astride his horse on a nearby

hill, watched the activity with ill-concealed displeasure. He saw Galen leading the work party and was startled: as far as he knew, the only apes in the village were Zoran and Inta. From the distance he could not recognize Galen. But he was impatient, and the gorilla felt a nameless, growing fear within him.

In the center of the meeting area, Burke and Virdon, once again awake and working, walked out to meet Galen, who looked every bit as tired as he felt.

"Are you all right?" asked Virdon.

Galen nodded. Around him, the work crew threw down their rough implements. They, too, were exhausted and glad to be back in the village. They didn't understand the urgency of their work. They knew only that their labor, the hot summer sun, and Virdon's protective gear, had, combined, been more unpleasant than anything they had ever had to endure from the apes. Galen pointed out of town, toward the area where he had been working. "It's done," he said. Then, as an afterthought, he added, "Urko is here."

Virdon looked where Galen indicated. He saw the silhouette of the gorilla general, sitting on his horse, on the top of a low hill outside the village. Virdon nodded grimly.

In the hospital, Amy Talbert cried out in her delirium. Her voice was filled with pain and fear. It attracted Zoran's attention; the chimpanzee turned from the patient on the mattress beside Amy.

"Don't leave me… tell me… she murmured. "Other place… the other place…"

Zoran moved closer to Amy, wondering what she could be talking about. He took a piece of cloth, rinsed it in some fresh water, and softly wiped her sweating face.

"Tell me again…" she said. She smiled. Zoran's quick

mind told him that the girl was not merely reciting her wandering fantasies. "Tell me again…" she said, "how it was… before…"

Zoran raised his eyebrows. He spoke softly, encouraging her. "Before *what*?" he asked.

"This," whispered Amy, "all… this…"

Zoran opened his mouth to ask another question, but before he could speak, distant shouts made him stand up and go to the door of the hospital hut.

Out in the afternoon sunlight, Galen, Virdon, and Burke were running with the other villagers toward the central area, where they could get a better view of the disturbance. Zoran was curious; something terrible must have happened, but the Medical Officer had no ideas what it could possibly be. He arrived with the others, puffing and wheezing from the short run. He looked up to the gorillas' hill.

Several gorilla guards were running away from something. Although their words were not distinguishable, the note of terror was clear. Virdon and Burke started running toward them, with Galen following uncertainly behind.

Zoran stayed where he was for a moment. He watched the disturbance on the hill. He saw Urko riding toward the frightened, scattering gorilla guards. Suddenly, Zoran made a decision.

The chimpanzee ran to his horse, mounted quickly, and rode out of the village as hastily as the horse could carry him. He had an idea what the trouble might be, and Urko would certainly interfere. Zoran wanted to reach the soldiers first.

Burke and Virdon stopped on the edge of the town, watching the gorillas uncertainly. Burke made a motion that they should continue up the gorillas' hill, but Galen grabbed his arm and pointed to the right. "Urko," said the chimpanzee.

Indeed, the gorilla general was riding toward his troops. The men heard the sound of another set of hooves, and saw Zoran, also riding toward the same place. It was apparent that Urko would arrive before the doctor. Virdon, Burke, and Galen had to remain where they were, or else risk being recognized by Urko. They watched as several terrified gorillas pushed past Zoran's horse, as the Medical Officer urged his mount up the hill.

Urko rode into the middle of the area, accompanied by a few gorilla troopers. Urko reined in and took a quick survey of the situation. He saw Kava, the gorilla guard, prostrate on the ground, his body twisting and rolling in the grass, his face contorted with pain. Kava's breath was coming in short, pained gasps.

Zoran arrived, stopped his horse, and stared down at the ground, at Kava.

Urko turned to Zoran, his gigantic rage fairly spilling out of him. "Now we'll see... *doctor!*" he shouted. "Now we'll see if the council still believes in you. The village will burn—and everyone in it! Everyone!"

4

Kava's condition was obviously serious. The gorilla was barely conscious; the disease must have progressed in him for quite a while, and only his trained sense of self-control had prevented him from showing the signs of weakness before this. Unfortunately, malaria does not respond to mere acts of will, and sooner or later the victim is conquered.

"Urko," said Zoran forcefully, as the Medical Officer dismounted and handed the reins to one of the gorilla guards, "I promise you—"

Urko still sat on his horse, observing the entire scene, his expression impassive until Zoran began to speak. Then his face became so grim and threatening that Zoran's words faltered and he became silent. Zoran was concerned by Kava's illness, but he was equally fearful of Urko's rage. His concern and his responsibility as a doctor won. "I promise you that I will give him every care," he said.

Urko slammed a fist against the side of his saddle,

making his horse jump nervously. Urko gave the reins a short jerk, quieting the horse almost without thinking about it. His attention was entirely somewhere else. "You make empty promises while my soldiers die!" he said fiercely.

Zoran went to his horse and took a small canteen that was looped over the saddle's pommel. He walked back quickly to Kava's side, but turned to face Urko. "Believe me," said Zoran, "I have the means now to cure him." He held up the canteen and shook it. Inside was a quantity of Virdon's distilled quinine. "This is a new medication. It is made from the bark of a tree I looked for and, luckily, found in time."

Zoran opened the canteen and knelt down to give Kava a drink of the medicine. Urko spurred his horse forward, enraged, and kicked the canteen from Zoran's hand. The chimpanzee looked up in surprise; the usually even-tempered Zoran was now becoming very angry himself. He was not used to treatment like this, and he would not accept it, even from Urko. Before he could say a word, however, Urko's horse brushed against Zoran and knocked the Medical Officer sprawling in the dirt.

"You will not experiment with my men!" said Urko. With a quick movement, he wheeled his horse and rode off toward his command tent. The other gorillas followed, leaving Zoran alone on the hill; two of the guards had put Kava on Zoran's horse and were leading it away. Another gorilla carried the canteen of quinine and was splashing it out as he rode after his leader. Zoran could only watch resentfully. After a few moments he picked himself up, brushed off his clothing, and began the long walk back to the village.

Later that day Zaius called another meeting of the Supreme Council of Elders in Urko's command tent. They were meeting to evaluate the progress Zoran had made, and to decide what further action should be taken. Zoran sat in his usual place, his manner not at all hinting at the furious doubts and worries that boiled in his mind. Urko stalked impatiently back and forth, as he addressed the group in awesome fury. "Burn the village!" he demanded. "Now—before we are all destroyed!"

The members of the council reacted with fearful chattering. Urko was doing a good job of stirring them up. Zoran realized that he would have to fight to continue his work. "No," he shouted over the uproar. "We are making progress!"

Zaius banged his gavel until there was quiet. "This medication, Zoran," he said calmly. "Is it effective?"

Zoran had to consider his answers carefully; he knew that Zaius would treat the matter fairly, but even so, if Zoran sounded the least bit uncertain, it would be a sure victory for Urko. "Yes," said Zoran. "Yes, it *will* be, soon. Of course, it takes a certain amount of time. A few hours."

Urko responded quickly. It was developing into more than the usual council debate. It was a battle between two different and irreconcilable means of governing apes and humans. To Urko, the issue of the disease was only, a secondary matter. The real question was *power.* "There *is* no more time!" he shouted. The gorilla turned to the rest of the council. "How many must die—how many of *you* must die—before you do what must be done?" Urko turned back to Zaius. "I demand a vote!" he cried.

Zaius would not permit himself to be drawn into the growing uneasiness of the council, or the grotesque struggle for dominance that Urko was so obviously initiating. "You will have your vote, Urko," he said.

"Now!" shouted Urko, ready to do anything he had to

in order to force, the issue. "No more *talk!*"

Zaius sighed wearily. No one in the council ever seemed to appreciate what an emotional drain it was, to sit in the chair of the presiding officer. "I wonder what you fear most, Urko," he said softly, "death, or a few words of reason."

"I fear *you*," said Urko angrily, "all of you, listening to this fool!"

"Enough, Urko," said Zaius. Urko quieted down at the note of authority in Zaius' voice. There was absolute silence in the command tent for a moment. The noise of the bustling gorilla soldiers and their horses came in, along with the soft peaceful chirp of a nearby bird. Zaius wondered how such a pleasant place could be the scene of so much turmoil and anxiety. Slowly he rose from his chair. He would have to override both Urko's emotional appeal and Zoran's vehemence. He would have to present the case to the council now in a brief but equitable summary. "Zoran has found a medication," he said, looking at each member of the council in turn. "Zoran is our chief Medical Officer. It is his word, and his *alone,* that we must accept on the effectiveness of the medication. Perhaps it will cure... perhaps not. What Urko says is also true, that with delay... there *is* risk."

There was an undercurrent of uncertain murmurings from the council members. When stated simply, the problem resolved itself into a greater dilemma. Stripped of Urko's fiery rhetoric, the problem revealed itself worthy of the most serious consideration.

"We've come this far," Zoran urged, "the answer, right or wrong, is only a few hours away."

"That is up to the council to decide," said Zaius. "The time for debate has ended. Urko has asked for a vote, and we shall have it now." Zaius turned to the council. "Those for letting Zoran continue," he said.

Three of the seven council members raised their hands, including Zoran. Urko muttered inaudible curses at the others who voted with the Medical Officer.

"Those against?" asked Zaius.

Urko and two others raised their hands. A tie. Zaius guessed that the vote would end up that way, as it so often did. The two men who voted with Urko almost always agreed with him on other matters. The three apes were a kind of party faction in the council. Zoran and the other two sometimes voted together, sometimes not. Zaius could remember too many occasions when he had to cast the deciding vote. Sometimes it got to be too great a responsibility. "Very well," he said slowly. "The decision is mine."

Zaius studied Zoran, who sat in his chair quietly, completely motionless. Perhaps the Medical Officer truly had no idea of the validity of his theories. Perhaps Urko was correct, and Zoran was using the situation as a readymade laboratory for his private use, disregarding the danger it meant to the rest of his fellows. But then, there was always the chance…

Zaius nodded. "You have until noon tomorrow," he said.

Urko turned to Zoran and the other two apes who had voted against the gorilla. His look was mean and hateful. "Fools," he said. "In a few hours when you are dying in your own sweat—like him—remember what I told you." The council broke up. Some members walked toward their horses, discussing the situation in low voices. There was an almost unbearable tension; the apes gave Zoran many a quick and doubtful look. Urko mounted his horse, but did not ride off. The others mounted and left the command area as quickly as possible.

Zaius and Zoran walked toward their horses together. Zoran was thanking the presiding officer for his generosity, but Zaius cut him off, "Noon, tomorrow," he said, climbing on his horse. Zoran nodded, and Zaius rode off.

Urko prodded his horse closer to Zoran, who backed away. He remembered how Urko had nearly trampled him. Urko pointed to Kara, who was lying in pain in the shade of a large tree. "Stay away from him," said Urko. If you touch him again, I'll kill you." Zoran did not reply. While the chimpanzee was getting on his own horse, Urko wheeled and rode off to inspect his perimeter guards. Zoran turned his horse and rode back to the village, his thoughts muddled and discouraged.

The afternoon wore on, and the people of Trion worked to prevent the fever from spreading. Some villagers made more quinine; some gathered more cinchona bark; others kept up the daily routines of food distribution and water carrying; everyone took turns ministering to the sick. The regular work in the fields had to be tended to, but only a minimum effort was made to this, however, for the immediate problems outweighed the long range considerations in the minds of the humans. When night fell, enough medicine had been made to last for the next two days. Everyone in the village drank a regular dose of the foul-tasting stuff. The people who had been making the quinine were given a short rest period, and then reassigned to other duties.

The night was quiet, except for the moaning of the sick from the hospital hut. Torches along the single road lit the scene with flickering patches of light. Shadows grew and jumped with the changes in the blazing torches. Some of the huts showed little beams from candles and oil lamps. As best they could, the survivors of Trion were trying to return to normal life amid the horrors of the epidemic. The most light came from the hospital hut.

Virdon walked among the beds of the sick in the hospital, studying the faces, hoping for a sign that the medicine he had devised was having its proper effect. He joined Zoran at the bedside of a young woman, who was lying bathed in sweat, unconscious. Zoran finished giving her a drink of the medicine. "She drank enough, just before she collapsed," said the ape.

Virdon only nodded, his thoughts elsewhere. "Noon, tomorrow," he said worriedly. He rubbed his forehead. "I don't know…"

Zoran looked up, startled. "You said the medication worked quickly."

Virdon shrugged. "Yes, it does," he said tiredly. "But there could be… extenuating factors. A mutation of the germ. A different variety of malaria. So many intangibles. So many unknowns…"

Virdon's words, and the note of doubt that had been so evident in his words, made Zoran suspicious. The chimpanzee stood and looked at Virdon closely. "I have put myself in a difficult position," he said. "Because I trusted your advice, that is. I was not in a position to bargain with the council today."

Virdon was appreciative of what Zoran had done, and of the personal dangers the ape faced. He spoke gently. "I know," he said. "I understand." There was little more to be said. The two walked slowly among their patients. "We'll give them another dose in the morning," said Virdon. "All we can do for the moment is—wait…"

Zoran nodded his head in agreement. "That's always

the most difficult part in these cases," he said. "You'd better sleep. You're getting less rest than anyone in the village."

Virdon tried to reply, but found to his dismay that he was just too fatigued to speak any further. He nodded and staggered to an empty mattress. He lay down. Burke was already asleep on a nearby mattress. Zoran watched the two humans. After several moments, he was satisfied that they were both in deep sleep. Then the chimpanzee moved quickly and quietly to Amy's cot.

Zoran stood for several seconds, staring down at the young girl. He wondered what this seemingly unimportant, example of a lower species might be able to tell him. It would be ironic indeed if this human child would provide information that would shake up the ape establishment. Amy Talbert might be the key Zoran needed to regain whatever lost esteem he would suffer should Virdon's magical cure fail to perform its advertised miracle.

Zoran knelt by the girl's side. He took a wet rag, squeezed out the excess water, and wiped her fevered face. Amy tossed uncomfortably on her mattress. Zoran saw that she had half wakened. "Amy," he whispered.

Either the girl had not heard him, or, if she had, she had been unable to reply. Zoran tried again. "Amy?"

"Yes…" The word sounded brittle and dry to Zoran's ears. The girl's voice sounded like the voice of a dying person. Zoran swallowed and forced himself to continue. "Your friend," he said brightly, "from the… 'other place'…"

"Yes… said Amy.

Zoran tried to sound like an interested friend. He hoped that in Amy's delirium, she would imagine that she was talking to one of the other people of Trion, to her father, perhaps. "Where *is* that 'other place'?" he asked, trying not to sound like he was interrogating her.

"Where did he come from?"

Amy answered, but Zoran had to bend close to her lips to catch her words. "Here…" she said.

Zoran was puzzled and disappointed. "Here?" he asked.

"From… *before*."

Suddenly Zoran caught a glimmer of the truth. It was more important and more startling than he had even dared to hope. "Another time," he suggested.

"Yes…" said Amy weakly.

"A long time ago?"

This was the critical bit of information. Zoran listened closely, but all that he could hear was his own heart beating, the blood rushing in his ears. Amy did not respond. "A long time ago, Amy?" asked Zoran forcefully.

"Yes…" she said at last.

Zoran's eyebrows went up. Zaius would be impressed. Even General Urko would have to admit that Zoran had made a significant contribution, if the tall blond human with the blue-green eyes, and the tall dark-haired human with the brown eyes were whom Zoran suspected they were. "An 'astronaut'," asked Zoran, not really understanding the word, but recalling it from a council meeting some months before, when Urko and Zaius had gotten into a more heated argument than usual. "Is your friend an 'astronaut'?"

Amy drifted off again into sleep. Cursing in frustration, Zoran tried to hold himself in control. "Amy," he said, almost pleading with the human girl, "listen to me, Amy."

Zoran tried to revive her. After a time he realized that it was useless to try any further. Cursing again, he stood up. As he turned to leave the hospital, he stopped short.

Standing a few feet away, studying him, was Galen.

Despite pulling himself up to his full height, Zoran

was not imposing; he was defensive, uncertain. "Why are you sneaking up behind me?" demanded Zoran.

Galen kept a casual manner. Here he was not dealing with simple human beings; he was confronting another ape, another chimpanzee. Zoran had quite a few years more learning and more experience than he. If they came to any kind of struggle, it would be one of wits, not, force. Zoran was certainly no exponent of Urko's kind of tactics. "I was just coming to look at the girl," said Galen. "Is she… talking strangely again?"

Zoran looked at Galen closely, trying to understand the chimpanzee's connection with the girl and with the two strange humans. "Yes," he said vaguely, "strangely."

Galen knelt beside Amy's mattress, and wiped her face. The young chimpanzee felt a curious attachment to this human girl, perhaps because of her intelligence, her devotion, her courage. These were qualities which Galen had thought to be all but nonexistent in the human race. Of course, Virdon and Burke had taught him differently, but then, of course, Virdon and Burke were actually from a different human race. Galen looked at the girl's face and wondered if that was exactly true.

"Have you heard her speaking strangely?" asked Zoran.

"Yes," said Galen, remembering what he had recently witnessed. "The fever. It makes her say… impossible things. She has a very good imagination. For a human."

"Yes," said Zoran airily. "I could make no sense of it." The Medical Officer turned and walked away, apparently giving no further thought to the girl and her delirious ravings.

Nonetheless, Galen was worried. He watched the departure of Zoran with growing fear, wondering if the village of Trion might yet turn out to be the death trap he had first imagined.

The long night passed. On the edge of Trion, gorilla guards marched the perimeter, just as they had before the fever came to the small village. Only now, the four gorillas garrisoned near the town had been reinforced by dozens of other troops, and the situation had attracted the attention of General Urko himself. The pale light of the moon flickered on the metal uniforms as gorillas moved slowly through the night.

Nothing moved in the fields outside the village. In the huts, the candles and lamps had long since been extinguished, except those in the hospital hut. No one moved on the road, no one disturbed the deep stillness of the night. Only the occasional sound of one of the sick people in the hospital broke the tense quiet. About an hour before dawn, Virdon awoke and rubbed the sleep from his eyes. He looked about himself; for a moment he couldn't recall where he was. Lately, that happened to him often. It came from moving around too much, waking up too many mornings in too many different, unknown places. His weariness only made his mind foggier: he had not slept well.

Virdon came to the door of the hospital hut and looked out across the village, up toward the hill where the gorilla guard was stationed. Inta, Zoran's assistant, was seated by the entrance to the hut, evidently taking a break from his job as night attendant. Virdon greeted him, and Inta grunted a tired reply. They both fell silent again, and once more Virdon's attention wandered to the hill beyond the fields. A single torch burned brightly there; from the village it looked like a huge, flickering star.

The light from the torch was almost hypnotic in its effect on Virdon. He stared at it for a long while. For a moment, he could not remember why that torch might have been put there, but then he recalled what Zoran had told him earlier, about what had happened on that hill between Zoran and Urko. Virdon took a deep breath and let it out. He shrugged helplessly—how could he hope to fight the obstinacy of the gorillas? He turned to go back into the hospital, to return to his mattress and his interrupted night's sleep; he stopped, struck by an idea. He continued on into the hospital hut, and emerged with one of the small canteens. He swung the strap of the canteen over his head and then hurried off into the darkness.

On the hill, the torch had been stuck into the ground next to Kava, who was otherwise unattended. It would be considered ungorillalike to have one of the troops watch the dying Kava through the night. No one volunteered to do so, and it was certain that Kava would have been humiliated if he knew that anyone had. The only gorilla guard near him was the regular sentry, who was many yards away, watching for what only the gorillas could imagine. Perhaps the sentry himself did not know exactly what he was watching for, but he could not take the risk of questioning one of General Urko's orders.

Virdon cautiously approached the area. He had slipped through the gorillas' defenses easily, giving the lie to their claims of military invulnerability. He could see Kava from his place of concealment. Virdon stopped for a few minutes to study his next move.

The sentry moved restlessly at his post. Every once in a while, he looked at Kava. He knew that it was unmilitary for him to show any emotional response to Kava's trouble; but Kava was, after all, a comrade. Perhaps, thought the sentry, perhaps Urko was being too strict in his orders. The sentry shook his head to rid himself of these thoughts; it was late, and he had been on guard duty for several hours. One was bound to be troubled by crazy thoughts after a while...

Virdon picked up a large stone and tossed it down the loose shale face of the hill. The stone set up an ominous noise, as the loose rock rattled down the incline.

The guard was immediately alarmed. He brought his rifle up. "Who's there?" he called loudly. There was no answer. The sentry was certain that he had not imagined the noise. He moved away to investigate. "Who's there?" he called again, his voice growing softer in the distance. Virdon smiled to himself. The gorillas really had a very subjective view of their strengths. They actually weren't very bright.

The blond astronaut took advantage of the situation to sneak closer to Kava. He moved in quickly, opened the canteen, and gave Kava a long drink of the quinine medicine within. Kava tried to protest; he raised one hand, but he was too weak.

Meanwhile, the gorilla guard had gone as far as he thought wise, and was returning to his post. It was not wise, he knew, to be caught away from his station. If General Urko saw him wandering around, and asked for a reason, saying that he had "heard a noise" would not be very good for the guard's career.

As he returned, he saw a dark form bending over Kava. He was startled; his first thought was to shoot, but even his slow-witted gorilla mind realized that it might not be wise. He didn't know who the intruder was. It might even be Urko, himself; the general might have had a change of heart. The guard stumbled forward, calling out "Who goes there?" he shouted.

Virdon cursed under his breath. He had counted on the gorilla's being gone a little longer. The trouble with the soldiers was that they were so stupid, and their attention span was so short, that they couldn't be relied on to keep anything in mind for more than a couple of minutes at a time. The gorilla couldn't have made a very thorough search of the area. But it was too late to worry about that. Virdon was forced to drop the canteen and run for his life. Some of the liquid splashed on Kava's face.

When the stranger did not answer, and began to run away, the gorilla raised his rifle and fired.

Virdon heard the bullet rip through the leaves of a tree not far to his right. He heaved a sigh; he was glad that the gorillas were as bad marksmen as they were sentries.

Virdon ran like he had never run before. The gorilla's shot would soon have the rest of the gorilla garrison aroused; there was a good distance back to the village to cover before Virdon could relax and think that he was safe. And every step of the way, he imagined that there were gorilla soldiers riding murderously after him, ready to shoot him down in his tracks.

The sentry did not try to follow, however. It was very rare that the soldiers actually got to do anything; they had received quite a bit of training, and, for the most part, saw no action. After the guard fired his first shot, he was so excited that he kept firing, blindly into the darkness.

The shots tore wildly through the foliage on both sides of Virdon. The man crouched low as he ran. When he got to the fields, losing the cover of the trees, he ran along the edge of the small farms, all the way around the village, approaching Trion from the side opposite the gorillas' hill. Then he slowed down and walked calmly into the town. It would be best to establish some kind of alibi, in case General Urko investigated the identity of the mysterious intruder.

About the time that Virdon was arriving at Trion, the gorilla guard heard the reassuring sound of hoofbeats. His comrades had arrived at last! Reinforcements! They would see what a splendid job he had done of routing the enemy. He stopped firing and turned to see General Urko riding up. Urko hurriedly dismounted and ran to the sentry. "What is it?" he asked.

The guard was a little dismayed to be face to face with the general himself. "I heard a sound, sir," said the sentry. With those words, the gorilla remembered the thought he had had earlier, and he knew that his worst fears were being realized. "I went to see. When I came back, there was someone with Kava."

"Who?" asked Urko. The tone of voice indicated that the guard had better have a good explanation.

"I... I couldn't see, sir," said the gorilla weakly.

Urko knelt by Kava. The general examined the unconscious soldier and the ground nearby. Immediately, Urko saw the abandoned canteen. The general was alarmed; he shook Kava until the gorilla regained consciousness. "Who was here?" Urko demanded.

There was no response from Kava.

Urko shook him again, and slapped the suffering gorilla's face. "Who was it?" asked Urko. "Was it Zoran?" Urko shook the canteen. "Did you drink this?"

Kava managed to give an affirmative nod. "Yes," he whispered hoarsely.

Urko let Kava's head fall heavily back to the ground. Kava's face showed frustration and anger at his weakness; but the emotions there did not come close to matching the strength of Urko's rage.

Urko stood slowly and walked to where the sentry was watching. With one vicious blow, Urko knocked the gorilla guard to the ground. "If Kava dies," said Urko with real hatred in his voice, "if they've poisoned him with this 'medicine', I'll have you shot!"

Urko walked to his horse and mounted. He pulled on the

reins and turned the horse in the direction of his tent, leaving the stunned and bewildered sentry where he had fallen.

The shooting attracted the attention of the villagers. They poured out of their huts, awakened by the unaccustomed clamor. Galen, Burke, and Zoran stumbled out of the hospital, blearily looking for some kind of explanation in the morning's light. There was no longer anything to be seen on the gorillas' hill. They turned, shrugging, to go back into the hospital, when a voice stopped them. "Looks like it'll be a nice day, doesn't it?"

Burke and the two chimpanzees turned around in surprise. Virdon was approaching along the road, from the other direction. "A nice day, for sure," said Burke wonderingly. "And where have you been taking a pleasant morning stroll?"

"We heard shots," said Galen, watching Virdon curiously. The chimpanzee had his head cocked to one side, as he usually did when he was faced with something he couldn't completely comprehend. "What happened? Where have you been?"

Virdon smiled. He answered casually. "Oh," he said, "a small mission of mercy."

Zoran was surprised. He could hardly believe what Virdon was suggesting. "You treated Kava?" he asked.

"Yes," said Virdon.

"You risked your life," said Zoran in amazement. "For an ape?"

"I'm sure his pain hurts as much as those in there," said Virdon, indicating the hospital hut. "Unfortunately, I left the evidence behind when I ran."

Burke was suddenly fearful. "Could anyone up there identify you?" he asked.

Suddenly Virdon became serious. He realized that his, simple act of compassion could have grave consequences, not only for himself and his two companions, but also for Zoran and the townspeople. "It was dark. I... I can't be sure," he said.

Galen and Burke exchanged worried looks: Their concern did not go unnoticed by Zoran. He looked back up at the hill. "I wonder if it really matters," he said thoughtfully.

Virdon didn't know what the chimpanzee was talking about. "What do you mean?" he asked.

"Whether Urko thinks it was you... or me... the result is the same," said Zoran.

Virdon, Burke, and Galen turn to look. There was considerable activity around Urko's command tent. They could see campfires blazing. Gorilla troopers could be seen fashioning torches, attending to their horses, and bustling back and forth from Urko's tent to the large group of gorilla soldiers that was assembling.

The most frightening aspect of the soldiers' activity was the stockpile of torches that had been made. "If Zoran loses," said Galen, "Urko wins. More authority, more freedom to run things the way he wants. Urko wants power to do things *his* way, and it's not a very nice way." No one could come up with a simple answer to that for several moments.

"We'd better pull something out of our hat soon," said Burke. "Or else this village will be nothing but ashes." Silently, the two men and the two chimpanzees watched the preparations being made on the gorillas' hill.

There didn't seem to be anything that they could do. Not far away, according to Urko's instructions, torches were lit and horses were saddled. Things would begin to happen very soon.

5

East of Trion, the road seemed to run directly into the rising sun. The morning's natural elements were as unhurried and peaceful as ever. Birds were in the cultivated fields, robbing the villagers of an early breakfast. A couple of chipmunks were chewing on some dried kernels of corn in the shade of a hut. A gray squirrel, standing on its hind legs, peered over the edge of an empty bucket left beside the village well. Everything was well and normal with nature. It was only with the human and the simian communities that one could find fault; it was there that one had to look for disturbing factors.

On the outskirts of the village, the gorillas' preparations were nearly complete. Urko sat astride his horse and shouted the final orders. His followers shouted back; they raised rifles and torches and shook them. It would not be long before the huge gorilla soldiers worked themselves into the proper mood of warlike hysteria, and the headlong charge would begin, one that would mean the end of the village of Trion.

Inside the hospital hut, Burke sat beside Amy. It was his turn to watch the sick in the room. Although Burke never neglected any of the others, he spent most of his time beside the young girl. She had come to represent everything that he denied himself in his old life. Burke was bathing Amy's face and arms when Virdon and Zoran came into the hospital, conversing in worried and uncertain tones.

"Hello, Pete," said Virdon. "Still working?"

"Sure," said Burke gloomily. "Aren't you? Isn't everybody?"

"What do you think?"

Burke looked down at the peaceful face of the young girl. "She's resting," he said. "Her fever seems to be down some."

Virdon seized upon his words ferociously. "The others, too?"

"Well," said Burke, "when they wake up, we'll give them another dose." He paused and stared levelly into Virdon's eyes. "We need time, Alan," he said.

Zoran shook his shaggy head. "Zaius gave us until noon," he said. "*If* he can keep control of the situation."

Even as Zoran spoke these words, there came the sound of shouting from outside. The clamor was great, but it sounded too distant to be coming from any of the villagers. Zoran and the two astronauts stepped outside.

In front of the hospital, Galen was supervising the preparation of cinchona bark, in the way he learned from Virdon. He did not greet the men and the chimpanzee when they came out of the hospital. He was too occupied with the horrible sight beyond the village.

Urko and every available gorilla soldier were riding

down on Trion, waving their rifles and burning torches, screaming as though they were engaged in the greatest battle imaginable.

Burke affected a false calmness. He watched the gorillas approaching for a moment, spat in the dust, and laughed softly to himself. "Seems the situation is *already* out of hand, if you ask me. Is anybody asking me?"

Virdon only stared helplessly. Galen looked to his two human friends; they did not seem as though a plan of action had been made, and he did not know what to do. Only Zoran was roused to anger.

"Urko cannot do this!" cried the Medical Officer. "He is acting against the wishes of the council."

"You may only think that he can't do it," said Burke acidly. "It certainly looks to me like he *is* doing it."

Zoran ignored Burke's comments. The chimpanzee turned to his assistant, Inta. "Get my horse!" He ordered. Zoran chafed at the delay, while the gorilla horde rode ever closer. "I came here for a victory of my own," said Zoran, his voice firmer than the others had ever heard. "Urko will not take it away from me. Not when I'm this close…"

Virdon had a sudden, unpleasant thought. "Maybe the council changed its mind," he said.

Zoran did not take his eyes off Urko's army. "I think not," he said. He paused meaningfully. "This is between Urko and myself."

Inta led Zoran's horse to him. Zoran mounted and prodded the animal into a gallop. Burke and Galen wished him luck as he left. Virdon remained silent. Zoran rode out to meet his rival.

"Well," said Burke, "things are moving rapidly toward a climax, aren't they?"

"Sure," said Virdon. "Aren't they always?"

"I guess so," said Burke. "It gets a little tiresome, sometimes... I mean, we could have just kept going, but no, we had to come back. We could have just kept going into the beautiful unmessed-up sunset. Or sunrise. Or whatever it was."

"Are you really sorry we came back?" asked Virdon quietly.

Burke watched the gorillas, now so close that he could hear their strange battle cries. "No," he said. "Why would you think that? Just because we're about to be engulfed by a bunch of refugees from an old two-reel silent film? What ever gave you that idea?"

Galen interrupted Burke's sarcastic musings. "What *do* we do now, my friends?" he asked. "Do we take Amy and try to get away?"

Virdon nodded in the direction of the gorillas. "I'm afraid it was too late for that quite a while ago," he said reflectively.

Galen looked around and saw that gorilla soldiers had completely surrounded the village. They had obviously been there for some time, preventing any escape, and only a small percentage of Urko's forces were riding with him in the main attack. This explained why Burke and Virdon had so resignedly discussed the matter, without making an attempt to flee. Galen appreciated once again that the two astronauts were a good deal more aware of their surroundings than any ape ever was. Perhaps apes had grown too complacent in their world. These two men were always alert. If he were to contribute to their association, if he had any hopes of the fugitive life that had been forced upon him, Galen knew that their talent was well worth cultivating.

Burke and Virdon watched the gorillas on horseback,

and stared at the soldiers that ringed the town. There was no weakness in the apes' formation; there was no place to break through. The only thing to do was wait.

Virdon spoke quietly. "It seems our future is in the hands of the Chief Medical Officer," he said.

Burke said cynically, "Watch closely," he said. "You may see the future come to a very quick end."

"We're helpless," said Galen, wondering why the humans did nothing but watch. "We can't run and… and we have no weapons."

Virdon shook his head. "We have *one*," he said.

Virdon turned and walked into the hospital hut. Galen and Burke exchanged puzzled glances; neither knew what Virdon's last words meant, but they knew that he was planning something. Both knew that at times like this it did no good to question the blond man. Virdon hated to talk about his plans prematurely.

Galen and Burke shrugged and returned their attention to Urko and his soldiers, who had ridden down to the bottom of the hill and had reached the road. The mounted warriors turned onto the road; they would make good speed, now. For good or ill, things would soon be over. The two friends watched, both feeling a little helpless, a little afraid.

"You know what this feels like?" asked Burke.

"Yes," said Galen. "But if I told you, you wouldn't understand."

"This feels like the last quarter of the Michigan—Michigan State game, my senior year. The score was fourteen to fourteen. I can remember it like it only happened yesterday."

"What?" asked Galen.

Burke paid no attention. "The State punter kicked this real cloud-hanger, man, I thought it would take forever to come down. I just stood there watching the ball sailing toward me, end over end, and listening to those gigantic linemen coming after my neck."

"I don't understand," said Galen.

"It felt just like this," said Burke. "Well, maybe not as bad as this. But, come to think of it, there was a time in the Ohio State game, my junior year."

"Burke," said Galen, exasperated, "I don't understand. I purposely didn't tell you my experience, because I knew that you wouldn't understand *me*."

"Huh?" said Burke, suddenly recalled to the present He realized what he had been doing. "Oh, I'm sorry, Galen."

"That's all right, my friend," said Galen. "I am beginning to realize how much you human beings have to live in the past."

Burke stared out along the road. "I'll tell you, my boy, I sure do wish we could."

Kava still lay where he fell, in the grass on the hill. The torch that had lighted the area around him had burned out. The sentry had left, gone with Urko to attack the village. Kava was the only one of the gorilla forces who hadn't accompanied the general. Kava was all alone.

He was calmer, but he was still feverish and weak. He rolled over and raised himself up on his arms. From that position he could look down and see the village of Trion, and the marauding gorillas led by General Urko, who had almost reached the town. Confusion overwhelmed Kava; he was filled with regret, an emotion he had consciously subdued during the last few years. He tried to get up, not precisely sure what he could do. He failed to stand. He rolled back in the grass and stared into the sky.

* * *

Zoran pulled his horse to a halt squarely in front of the onrushing Urko. Urko had to pull up, also, or risk a collision that might seriously injure both apes. The other gorillas with Urko halted when the general did.

"You have great courage, *doctor*," said Urko. "Move your horse aside." His tone was one of intense scorn.

"It is several hours yet until noon, Urko," said Zoran.

"Stand aside or you will die with those in the village."

Zoran could hardly control his anger. The only thing that kept him in check was the knowledge that his behavior here would affect the remainder of his life. "The council voted," he said simply.

Urko stood in his stirrups, as if to swat the chimpanzee aside like some troublesome gnat "The council be damned!" he said.

A third voice answered Urko. "That is treason, General," said the new party.

Both Zoran and Urko turned to see Zaius, who had ridden up while the two apes argued. Behind Zaius was the remainder of the council, prodding their horses forward uncertainly.

Urko would not be stopped this close to his goal. He defied even the council. "Better treason than madness!" he shouted.

Zaius would not be moved by Urko's display of might "I *command* you to withdraw, Urko," he said. His voice was level and completely without fear.

Urko laughed harshly. He turned to see what effect Zaius' words had on his subordinates. The gorillas all sat expressionless, just as Urko had trained them. The general turned back to Zaius, confident that his men would follow him anywhere, even against the dictates of the Supreme Council. "*You* command?" asked Urko.

"You have words. I have weapons."

One member of the council, an orangutan, spoke up wearily. "Perhaps another vote," he suggested.

Other voices were raised, agreeing. "Yes! Another vote!"

Zaius gave only the slightest shake of his head. "The vote was taken," he said. "We shall stand by the decision!"

Urko lifted his rifle. "Remove yourself, old man!" he said, grunting.

"Would you kill *me*, Urko?" asked Zaius quietly.

"Before you allow him," he indicated Zoran, "to kill my men. Yes!"

There was a loud mutter of approval from the gorillas, who heard in Urko's words a loyalty and feeling of brotherhood that they never received from the chimpanzees and the orangutans. None of the other apes had such a clannish attitude, and now it looked to the gorillas as if Zaius and the council were attacking them, all, through Urko. The soldiers leveled their weapons at Zaius and the other members of the council.

Zoran turned to the gorillas. "Listen to me!" he pleaded. "Urko doesn't care for you! He thinks only of his own position. He wouldn't let me help Kava. He would let Kava *die*, just to discredit me and strengthen himself."

Urko was shaken by just how close to the truth Zoran had come. "No," said the general, "Zoran is the one who thinks only of himself! He could not help Kava. He could not help *anyone*!"

Zaius laughed softly. He saw something that Urko could not. "It would appear that you are misinformed, Urko," he said.

The eyes of the soldiers, of Urko and Zoran, and of the remaining members of the council turned to where Zaius was looking.

The sick human beings of Trion, who a couple of days before had been wracked with fever and virtually given up for dead, were walking out of the hospital hut. They were obviously still weak, but even more obviously they were greatly improved, a visual tribute to Zoran's success.

Zoran, Urko, and the council watched silently. There was some murmuring among the gorilla soldiers.

Along the narrow road walked the sick of the village. The old men and women, so close to complete collapse the day before, were now well enough to take part in this demonstration. Each formerly dying person was supported by one of the healthy villagers, and they all moved in a slow line toward the position of the shocked gorillas. Behind them came the rest of the villagers, those who had worked such long hours to make this recovery possible.

Leading the weak, walking in the very front of the bold exodus of human beings, was Amy Talbert. Behind her was a line of stumbling, but definitely improved men, women, and children. It was obvious even to the gorillas, even to Urko, that the fever had been beaten down. It was more obvious to Zaius and the council members. Alongside Amy walked Inta, Zoran's assistant, who smiled, evidently relieved.

Virdon and Burke stood by a window and watched the march. Despite all they had done for the people of Triori, this was not their show. This was a blow against the tyranny that Urko and his kind were trying to establish; men, throughout their relatively brief ascendency in the world, had made this fight time after time. It seemed that the two astronauts had taught a valuable lesson, one from which other apes could benefit just as much.

There was also no good reason to be recognized by either Urko or Zaius.

"This rather changes the picture, then, does it not, Zaius?" asked Zoran, a note of gloating in his voice.

"Yes," said Zaius, "it is certainly a quite different situation than that which we expected to witness this morning. Nevertheless, we still cannot be completely certain of its significance. We must still wait."

"But the people—" said Zoran.

"I will admit that it seems to be a victory for your new theories," said Zaius. "But it only *seems* to be. We must be certain."

Urko and, his gorillas were still trying to understand what was happening, why they were being prevented from carrying out the actions they had worked so hard to prepare. The general himself, who understood what those cursed people of Trion were trying to do, was caught off-guard. He turned in his saddle to speak, but he had nothing very remarkable to say. He had lost a lot of his usual fire and swagger. "It's a trick!" he shouted. "A lie!"

"No!"

All eyes shifted to see who had spoken. Kava, still weak, fevered, but very much improved, stumbled forward to address himself to Zaius.

"Last night," said Kava, glancing at his general nervously, but determined to do what he felt to be his duty, despite the consequences, "last night, someone from the village… came to me… I was dying."

Urko was enraged at this act of insubordination from one of his trusted soldiers. Besides the simple act of betrayal, as Urko saw it, Kava's actions might entirely undermine the authority of the gorillas. Urko glared at Kava, then rose one arm as if to strike him. "Silence!" he shouted. "That is an order."

For a moment, Kava was confused. His general, whom

he had followed without question since Kava had been a young gorilla, represented the only way of life that Kava had known or desired. He had been given a direct order by his supreme commander. Nevertheless, there was a person to whom Kava owed even greater allegiance, and that was Zaius, in the latter's function as presiding officer of the council. Kava wavered in his mind. After all, it was as Urko had said: Zaius had the words, but Urko had the weapons. If the circumstances were not settled quickly, Zaius and the council would be dead, and Urko would assume all the powers and privileges of dictator. The gorillas would receive the special status they had sought for hundreds of years. All of the gorillas, except Kava. Kava would be dead.

"They gave me something to drink," said Kava anxiously. "Bitter medicine. Urko, you are wrong. The medicine made me better. It saved my life."

The gorillas studied Kava. They had all seen him as he lay on the grass of the hill, helplessly convulsed by the fever, suffering indescribable pain, delirious with the sickness. Now the gorilla was coherent again, although weak. He stood before them and spoke sanely and calmly. Beside him, Urko seemed like a rash and thoughtless child. The soldiers turned wondering looks on their general.

Although more intelligent than his men, Urko could feel his grip on them loosening. His mind raced to find an answer. His power was being taken away. The more he thought, the more he realized he was helpless.

Zaius considered the situation. It was much more difficult than any he had had to face in his long tenure as presiding officer of the council. A wrong word here, a misinterpreted gesture, and the whole thing might yet blow up into tragic bloodshed. Zaius did not have any personal attachment to the people of Trion, nor did he overly worry about his own death at the hands of Urko's enraged followers. Even the murder of the council was not so disastrous: each of the members could simply be replaced by apes equally as competent. The real horror lurking behind the scenes here was the potential of Urko wresting *all* power and *all* control of the lives of apes and human beings everywhere. And that was an event that Zaius had sworn to guard against.

"I tell you again, Urko," said Zaius. "Take your troops and withdraw, while you still have them to command."

Urko stared at Zaius with impotent fury. Then he turned to face his soldiers. The gorillas, who were all stupid enough to be easily swayed by the arguments of anyone with a scrap of authority, were all watching their general with growing insolence. It was apparent that it would be quite a while before rigid military discipline could be imposed again upon this company. Urko sneered at them, but said nothing. He wheeled his horse and rode away. For a moment the gorilla soldiers hesitated, but they all realized that they had no other life than with Urko. They too shouldered their weapons and followed him.

The thunder of the hoofbeats filled the air and shook the ground. Zaius and the council sat impassively while the gorilla horde charged away. Once again Kava had been left behind; now it seemed that Urko considered him a traitor. Kava was not worried about that as yet. Like the humans of a few days before, he had more immediate concerns. "Would you treat me," he asked Zoran, "in the village... with the others... until I am better?"

Zoran smiled. He had bluffed Urko. The arrival of Zaius, and the remarkable showing of the humans had rescued him from the gravest situation of his career. He could afford to be generous. He helped Kava up on his horse; the gorilla sat unsteadily behind Zoran. Together they rode slowly along the dusty street toward Trion.

Zaius turned his horse and studied the members of the council. They all looked subdued and embarrassed, recalling the less than honorable way they had behaved during the showdown between Urko and Zaius. The presiding officer spoke with unconcealed disgust. "How quickly compromise becomes attractive," he said. "You, who are charged with fashioning the edicts by which our entire culture must survive, would gladly have granted Urko anything if he had spared your worthless lives." Then he, too, prodded his horse and rode off. Entirely ashamed, the council members followed at a distance.

In the village, things were getting back to normal for the first time since the disease first came to the town. Men who had been preparing medicine and tending to the sick were now able to return to their fields. Women and children were in the street visiting with neighbors and helping each other restore their huts to normal.

A little while later, in the hospital hut, Zoran moved down the narrow aisle that separated the rows of mattresses. He checked the patients, all of whom were greatly improved, thanks to the quinine that Virdon had taught them to make. The men and women were eating again, smiling, talking among themselves, relaxing after the long ordeal. Inta was tending a human child's needs. Zoran was intrigued by the situation, and by the change in attitude his assistant had made. The Chief Medical Officer was obviously very pleased at the progress. He stopped by one end of the hut and looked back.

Burke, Virdon, and Galen were talking and laughing with Amy at the other end of the room. The young girl seemed to be almost entirely recovered, her young, strong body reacting quickly with the medicine to throw off the last ravages of the fever. The scene gladdened Zoran's heart; it was unusual for him, too. Before this situation had occurred, he always felt uneasy even being in the same room with a human being.

Zoran walked to the small group. Amy, Burke, Virdon, and Galen were laughing when he approached, and they did not hear him until he spoke up. Zoran's voice was uneasy and disturbed. "I would like to speak to you two a moment," he said, indicating the two human astronauts. The laughter died around Amy's cot. There was a moment of awkward silence.

Zoran turned and left the hospital hut. Puzzled by Zoran's sober tones, Virdon, Burke, and Galen looked at each other worriedly. Then Galen shrugged and turned back to Amy. He was learning a great deal about the daily life in the village. Virdon and Burke stood up and followed Zoran outside.

Amy looked at Galen, not suspecting anything out of the ordinary. "Is something wrong?" she asked.

"I don't know," answered the chimpanzee; He stood up and followed his friends, more out of curiosity than concern.

Zoran, Virdon, and Burke walked slowly along the street, away from the hospital and the hearing of the others. "I suppose you'll want to be leaving soon," said Zoran, his voice shaking just a little.

Virdon nodded. "Yes," he said. "We thought we'd be going later today."

Zoran looked as uneasy as he felt. His voice was developing a nervous quality that neither of the astronauts liked.

"I'm afraid… that won't be possible."

Burke was puzzled by the chimpanzee's words. "Why not?" he asked.

Zoran took a deep breath. He had had to do a number of difficult things in the last few days, but this was the worst of them. "Well," he said, "I just can't let you go."

"But everything's under control," said Virdon. "You can handle it without us."

Zoran cursed the denseness of these humans. They insisted on making the situation more difficult than it had to be. "No," he said, "you don't understand. I mean, I must tell Zaius and the others about you."

At this point in the conversation Galen came out of the hut and caught up with his friends. He overheard what Zoran had just said. Virdon and Burke exchanged alarmed looks.

"You see," said Zoran regretfully, "I *know* who you are."

Burke decided to adopt a blithe ignorance. It was a simple plan, and one that did not have much chance of success, but Burke was beginning to feel desperate. "I don't know what you're talking about," he said.

"Please," said Zoran, almost begging. "This is difficult enough. Your knowledge of medicine. Things the girl said in her fever. I know that you are the two 'astronauts'. And this must be Galen with you."

Burke and Virdon looked at each other. Burke sighed. There was no point in arguing.

"Understand," said Zoran with genuine feeling, "I deeply appreciate what you've done here, what I have learned from you."

Burke had had just about enough. "Then how the hell can you turn us in?" he demanded.

Zoran would not be dissuaded. "Because you are fugitives. Zaius wants you. And I am loyal to Zaius."

"I thought what we did here," said Virdon, "I thought what we shared here… meant something."

Zoran turned away. The situation was too much for him. "It does. It does. But—"

Burke spoke bitterly. "But we're a lower species."

"Yes."

"Well, then," said Burke, with a vicious edge to his voice, "if we're lower—how come we're smarter?"

Zoran still had his back turned. His words came muffled. "I… I can't explain that."

Galen took the opportunity to mention something that only another ape might think of, that only another ape could appreciate. "How will you explain that your 'victory' here was really *theirs*?"

Galen's words made Zoran turn around again. His expression was fearful and cautious. Galen stepped forward.

"Or do you intend to take full credit for yourself?" asked Galen, making a casual question out of it, letting the real meaning of what Galen was driving at develop slowly in Zoran's mind.

"Well," said Zoran falteringly, "I, well, I have no choice. I have my… my position to uphold."

Burke knew immediately what Galen had meant, and what Zoran either had missed or was consciously ignoring. "You turn us in," he said, "you think we won't tell Zaius?"

Zoran was outraged. "He wouldn't believe you! Not the word of a… a human against that of an ape. And I am a member of the Supreme Council!" Zoran drew himself to his full height and tried to look imposing.

Galen paid no attention. "He'd believe me," he said calmly.

"Very well," said a deflated Zoran. "I won't turn you in. You may leave."

Galen nodded toward his two companions. "Where *they* go," he said, "I go."

Zoran was stunned. This was unheard of behavior for an ape. "You can't be serious," he said.

"Try me," said Galen.

"But... but..." said Zoran, stammering in his astonishment, "they are..."

"Yes," said Galen, disgusted at Zoran's outmoded attitude, "I know. They're... lower species."

Zoran had to lean against a hut for support. He was shaken. The very basis of his life, his beliefs had been weakened, time and again during the last few days. This last development was the final blow.

"You've got a decision," Virdon said. "Your loyalty... or your own selfish ego."

"Ego?" asked Zoran, his voice but a hollow echo of its former strength. "I am not familiar with that word."

"How will you feel, Doctor," asked Burke, "when Zaius learns that you were advised by humans... every move you made... every word you said?"

Zoran sat down heavily in the dust by the side of the hut. Suddenly he had a great deal to think about. He had planned the ending of this experience with great economy and benefit to his career. Now, though, it seemed that he would emerge with nothing to show for it but a great weariness and the bitter taste of quinine still in his mouth. Zoran considered the words of Virdon, Burke, and Galen. At last he nodded. "I would suggest, then," he said, "that you leave under cover of darkness."

Galen, Virdon, and Burke smiled.

Late that night, the village had returned almost completely to normal. No one was any longer in danger from the fever. Families, mourning their lost members, were joined together again and celebrating all the blessings that they still had. From the huts came cheerful lights, and more cheerful voices.

Outside of the hut that had been used as a hospital Galen and Virdon were preparing their backpacks again, ready to make another attempt at leaving the village of Trion; the last attempt, only a few days before, now seemed shrouded in the haze of a greater length of time. It was a moment of some sadness for the man and the chimpanzee; they had learned to like the citizens of Trion, and the people there had made it clear that they would hate the thought of the companions' leaving. But, as so often happened to the two men and Galen, their personal preferences mattered very little. It would only be a matter of time before Zaius or Urko learned of their identities.

Only three humans were still in their cots in the hospital, those who had been stricken late in the course of the disease, and who still needed a small amount of medical attention. One of these was Amy. She was almost completely recovered, but Virdon prescribed another day's rest, just to be certain. He moved to her mattress and sat down beside her. The young girl looked up at him and smiled.

"You know," she said, "it's just as bad the second time. Saying goodbye, I mean."

Virdon laughed softly. "You're going to be all right."

"Sure," said Amy.

There was an empty moment, a painful pause.

Then Virdon said, "Maybe we'll find a way to get back. Someday, back where we came from. Maybe, somehow, you could come with us."

Amy looked at Virdon seriously, then nodded, smiling. She did not really believe him. "Sure," she said, "maybe." She paused. "Meanwhile, some of the things you've told me, maybe I can use them. You know, to make things better here. That's something, isn't it?" There was a strong note of hope in her voice.

Her words tore Virdon up inside. She was the most courageous, strong girl he had ever known; he corrected that in his mind. She was one of the strongest *people* he had ever known. "Yes," he said sadly, "that's surely something." He leaned over and kissed her forehead. "Goodbye, Amy," he said.

"Goodbye," she said.

Virdon turned and walked quickly out of the room without looking back. Tears were beginning to come into his eyes; he forced his mind to suppress the melancholy that had sprung up unbidden. He walked over to where his friends were waiting. It was more than likely that he would never see Amy again. He hoped that her life would be happy, and that she would, indeed, use some of the things he had taught her to make her own days and those of her fellow humans easier.

The two astronauts and their chimpanzee friend shouldered their packs and headed back out the road. People in huts came to their doors and shouted their farewells. A couple of people ran up with gifts of food and clothing. Virdon, Burke, and Galen accepted with some embarrassment and thanked the people.

As the travelers passed by, Inta and Zoran watched them go. At last Zoran waved slightly, a small and final token of friendship. But Virdon, Burke, and Galen did not see; he had been too late. Already the men and their chimpanzee friend were disappearing into the shadows.

Zoran looked at his assistant. Inta glanced at Zoran's still-raised hand. Zoran noticed what Inta was looking at and, slowly, sadly, lowered his hand to his side. Then, when Virdon, Burke, and Galen had completely vanished from sight, Zoran turned and went back into the hut.

THE GOOD SEEDS

6

Summer had its way with the field; things that bore early promise of beauty and bounty either fulfilled that promise or died. Most of the wild flowers had opened to the sun, had thrilled to live for their short period, and already were dead brown husks among the undergrowth. Some bushes still held their gift of berries, providing small feasts for the birds and insects. These, too, would be gone. Soon, autumn would begin its brilliant reign, and winter would follow with spirit-killing frosts. But everywhere, locked into the everlasting and ever-mysterious cycle that was life and death in the field, was the implicit promise of continuation. Spring would return the melting field to vibrant fife.

There was very little to distinguish this field from many others in the vicinity. It was neither large nor so lushly overgrown that it would attract attention. Beyond its limits were gently rolling hills. The skies above the field had been bright blue, the very deepest blue that happens only once during the year; now, however, mounds of cumulus clouds were beginning to pile themselves up at the horizon, and the first hints of a fresh wind pushed the clouds overhead, obscuring the sky and the hot sun. The air smelled fresh and the sound of the field was the gentle noise of insects and bird calls.

There was no movement to be seen by an idle observer. But the same hypothetical audience would be aware of a swelling, growing racket of approaching horses. Beginning as a light, rhythmic pounding felt on the ground, the vibrations swelled, until the sound of thundering hooves was almost deafening.

Three mounted gorilla police rode by at a gallop, oblivious to the field's subtle beauties. The gorillas, entrusted with keeping the security and safety of the other ape citizens, had no time for what they termed effete foolishness: the appreciation of beauty would be expected from the intellectual chimpanzees, or possibly even the governing orangutans. But a gorilla was trained from birth to a Spartan life, and each gorilla gloried in it, for there was little else to do with the results of the drills and training. There were no wars and no enemies—there was only watchfulness.

At the leader's signal, the gorillas pulled to a halt. As the leader peered into the distance, frowning and unhappy, a second gorilla swung down from his horse to the ground, the metal clasps and buckles of his uniform jangling even more than the metal of his horse's gear. The second gorilla studied the ground intently. At last, spotting something, he knelt to look more closely, and stood up with a triumphant expression on his face. "They were here," said the second gorilla. "And the track is still fresh!"

Remounting his horse, he pointed in the direction they

should follow. The leader nodded wearily and signalled the advance. With a crashing of hooves, the three horses rode off.

As the year was in its last glorious moments, so was this day. The sun was low in the western sky, lighting the cloud-covered sky with a glowing band of brightness, colors which rivaled even the summer flowers for intensity. Not a great distance from the field, on the side of a brush-covered hill, three strange figures struggled. The figures neither fit in with the unspoiled landscape about them, nor, in a greater sense, with the social environment that encompassed their world.

There were two human beings and a chimpanzee. They labored up the hill as though they had been marching for many long hours, for many uncountable days. This, indeed, was true, and though they had traveled a great distance since early the morning before, still they kept going. They were fugitives, and there was not a place in the world that was safe for them to rest. Nevertheless, they had to keep looking; to stop would admit defeat. And that, as always, would mean death.

The two human beings were named Alan Virdon and Pete Burke. Although they had not been born in this world, in this time, they had known its loveliness in another context. The chimpanzee was called Galen, and he was a contemporary of the gorilla police. These three oddly matched comrades had been bound together by the chains of mutual need, mutual respect, and a growing and unprecedented friendship.

They panted and fought the fatigue that threatened to engulf them. At last, reaching the crest of the hill, they stopped briefly. Burke, tall, handsome, with dark hair and dark eyes, looked back the way they had come.

"What's the matter?" asked his friend Virdon.

"I don't see them," said Burke hopefully.

Virdon ran a hand through his blond hair. "If you did," he said, "it would already be too late. Come on." Burke took a couple of deep breaths. "Galen can't keep up this pace."

"I'm not tired," said the chimpanzee.

Burke laughed. "The iron man over here," he said, indicating Galen. "Oh, excuse me. Iron *ape*."

"Sure," said Virdon, joining in the moment of relaxation, "you have room to talk. Michigan's great running back."

"Well," said Burke, with a mock tone of outrage, "you have to remember that that was two thousand years ago."

Virdon laughed. For once he was able to forget their immediate situation and respond to Burke's sarcastic wit. "Two thousand years," he said, his eyes wide with imitation surprise, "why, that's the prime of life." He suddenly got very serious. "Move it! No telling how close Urko's men are. We'd better make that forest down there before it gets dark."

Burke sighed. "Coming, Mother," he said. Galen wheezed a little as he trotted to catch up to his human friends, but otherwise he said nothing. Together the three began climbing as rapidly as they could down the hill, in the failing light.

The forest was pleasantly cool, the damp smell of the trees like a tonic to their drooping spirits. They slowed a little in the woods, knowing that the gorilla guards trailing them would have a difficult time tracking them on horseback in the dense growth. They came into a small clearing and stopped while Virdon looked around. It was silently agreed that Virdon was the leader, at least at this particular time, under these particular conditions. The leadership often changed and rotated among the three friends, depending upon whose gifts and abilities were best suited to circumstances.

Burke looked at his blond fellow human hopefully. "Sack time?" he asked.

Virdon gave a little snort. "No way," he said. "*Now's* our chance to get clear." He took something from his pocket and gave it close scrutiny. It was a compass, small, utilitarian, crudely made by Virdon when chance had provided the materials and the opportunity. In an ape world, such objects were disdained, even feared: the old knowledge had fallen into disuse when the apes took over the mastery of the world from its former rulers.

"We know what direction we're going in," said Virdon thoughtfully. "They don't. That gives us an edge they won't be able to make up with speed alone."

Burke was frustrated; it was clear that he had had enough running for one day. "When there's nothing in any direction," he said, a note of disgust entering his usually cheerful voice, "what difference does it make?"

Galen the chimpanzee looked at Virdon curiously. One of the reasons he had decided to stay with the humans in his flight from General Urko and his soldier gorillas was the opportunity to scientifically observe Virdon and Burke, to learn from them scraps of the knowledge which was forbidden and deliberately buried in his own society. "I have seen you look at that object on several occasions," said Galen. "I have always thought that it was another of your curious amulets. You can tell direction from that? Without being able to see the stars?"

Virdon showed the object to Galen. "It's a compass, Galen," he said patiently, understanding the chimpanzee's great love of learning. "It always points north."

The chimpanzee took the compass and experimented for a moment, turning around in the small clearing, walking short distances in several directions in turn; his expression grew more and more wondering, as he saw that the home-made compass did exactly what Virdon claimed.

"With this cloud cover," said Virdon, "Urko's men don't know what direction they're going in. They'll go around in circles. We can go straight ahead. That's what your superior ape world has done for you, Galen. Or so you say."

The chimpanzee paid no attention to this remark. "A 'compass' you called it. It's amazing. Is it witchcraft?"

Virdon laughed at the idea. "Just handicraft," he said, taking the compass back from his shaggy friend. "I made it." He turned to lead the way out of the clearing. Burke took a step after him; it was a great effort for the darkhaired man. "Well, Alan," he said, "I'll tell you what you do. Next handicraft class, why don't you make me a trail bike. A twin jet." Virdon didn't answer, saving his breath for the remainder of the day's travel. Galen was bewildered: there were so many words in Burke's remark that he didn't understand, like "trail bike" and "jet". But this was something he had come to accept. Burke and Virdon had been accidentally forced two thousand years into their planet's future, and they, had brought with them a wealth of knowledge and odd ways that Galen wanted to investigate. Often it led to pure puzzlement, particularly with the cynical Burke; but at other times he learned valuable things, as with the compass.

The night deepened, and the three disappeared into the thickness of the forest, passing a gnarled, lightning-split tree trunk as they abandoned the pleasant clearing.

Finally after another hour and a half, Virdon called a halt. They all stood around for a moment, listening to the stillness and feeling the cool night air on their sweat-soaked bodies.

"This isn't just another rest stop, is it?" asked Burke. "I don't want my poor legs to get all excited for nothing. This isn't a false alarm, is it?"

"Just a rest stop," said Virdon. "I'm sorry, Pete," he said. "I don't think we can stop safely for the night yet."

"Hear that, legs?" asked Burke. "Ten minutes you get, then up and at 'em again. Don't blame me. Blame the mechanical man, here."

"Save it," said Virdon. The three rested in silence.

Hooves thundering like the most violent of great storms, broke the gentle quiet of the night. The three gorilla guards rode into the small clearing where Virdon had demonstrated the compass to Galen. Now the trees were lit by blazing torches carried by the mounted apes. Strange, sinister shadows leaped among the branches, and the place that had been so friendly to Burke, Virdon, and Galen, now looked sinister. The gorilla police reined their horses to stop, but the lathered animals wheeled and pranced, their energies difficult to control. They had been ridden hard all day and night, and now they stomped the ground impatiently. The first gorilla leaped to the ground, his torch in his hand. He walked back and forth over the clearing, scanning the area for any sign of the fugitives. After a time, he spotted what were obviously tracks. "Through here," he shouted. "They've been this way!"

The gorilla climbed back on his horse and the three charged into the night, their torches and the sound of their horses creating an eerie sense of lightning and thunder among the trees. They passed by the same lightning-rent tree trunk, and the garish light from the torches made it look like some wizened, grasping monster of the night.

Virdon, Burke, and Galen ran through the night as well, unaware of how far behind their trackers might be.

The three gorillas, intent on closing the distance between themselves and their quarry, urged their tiring horses on into the darkness. The forest through which they were riding seemed to go on forever; each of the gorillas wished for the woods to end, for the landscape to become clear and open once again. They might be able to see the fugitives silhouetted against the sky as the two men and the single ape climbed some rise in the distance. But the gorillas did not get their wish. They rode into a clearing and pausing once again, reined in. They held up their torches, searching the ground for signs. With exasperation, the leader recognized the same gnarled tree trunk on the edge of the clearing. He leaped down and shouted in his anger. "Clouds!" he cried, looking up. "Blasted clouds!"

The other two gorillas slid from their saddles. "It's forbidden to travel without the stars to guide us," said the second gorilla.

The first gorilla looked at his subordinate with unconcealed scorn. "Nothing's forbidden when you ride for Urko," he said, taking out his frustration on his dim-witted soldier.

The seconds gorilla had little to say in defense. "Then how come the spirits have pulled our horses' tails in a circle?" he asked.

There was a pause. Once more the night smoothed itself with silence in the small clearing. Then the leader of the gorilla force realized the futility of going on any further. He was completely frustrated. He never had to deal with a situation like this before; if it weren't for the fact that his orders came from General Urko himself, he would have gone back to the rural garrison and forgotten the whole matter. After all, who really cared about two runaway humans and a renegade chimpanzee? But what General Urko wants, he gets! Even if it meant getting lost in the forest, he had his orders. But without the stars to guide them…

"All right," barked the leader, "all right! We'll camp here for the night. Get some wood together and make a fire." He looked up. "Stand watch to see if it chases the clouds. If not," he said to the second gorilla, "first sight of where the sun rises… you ride back to General Urko and report that we are going on. We're going on until we catch those three!"

"Yes, sir," said the second gorilla, impressed with the responsibility his leader was entrusting to him. The poor soldier did not have the imagination to picture what General Urko would say and do when he learned how his three troops had wasted the night and let the fugitives widen the distance between them.

Virdon, Burke, and Galen were running no longer. It was the middle of the night, and they had come a very long way. The terrain had become very hilly, and there was no light from the sky; the three walked on through the blackest of nights, barely able to see a few feet in front of them. Burke temporarily took the lead, and after a while he stopped, exhausted, to lean against a tree. His breath came in short, painful gasps. "You know," he said mildly, "I should have bought that nice, quiet little bar in Galveston…"

Virdon walked quickly past him, continuing the journey, and then Galen went by.

"Come on, Burke," said the chimpanzee, "we're following the 'handicraft'." Galen ran to catch up with Virdon. Burke watched the ape; they were all so tired that they had to pretend that they had boundless energy; it shamed the others into keeping up. Now it was Virdon's turn to lead, and Galen was playing the role of the fresh, rested wanderer. Burke couldn't be fooled. He had seen Galen, just a moment before, panting and clutching a tree to keep from falling in his tracks. The chimpanzee had courage, though, Burke thought; and if Galen and Virdon could keep going, well, then, so could he. Galen's act *was* effective. The three of them made a great team.

"Watch yourself in here, Galen," called out Burke.

Galen cavorted around a tree to display how much enthusiasm he still had. He wanted to catch up to Virdon and get ahead of the blond man. Suddenly, Galen slipped.

Burke saw the dark form of the chimpanzee disappear over the edge of a precipice. He hurried to the edge and looked down. There was a sheer drop down to ragged rocks below. Burke couldn't see Galen anywhere; Virdon turned back at Burke's anxious call. All of a sudden they heard a scream of terror from the startled chimpanzee. Burke and Virdon glanced briefly at each other, then they began scrambling down to Galen's aid.

Galen, still conscious, moaned in extreme pain. Virdon and Burke half-slid, half-fell the remaining distance to the bottom of the cliff and arrived near their injured friend. They were greatly worried when they heard Galen's cries; there was a deep and profound note of unbearable agony in the chimpanzee's voice. He was holding his leg. They picked their way to Galen's side. "Just take it easy," said Burke. "Easy there, Galen. We're here now. Everything will be okay if you just don't move."

"Burke, my friend," said Galen, still trying to make light of the situation, "I can't think of a single place I'd like to go right now. I'm very much in favor of staying very still. Ohhh…"

Virdon knelt in the damp ground near him and quickly inspected the chimpanzee. He moved Galen's arms and the other leg, but they seemed to be uninjured. Then, cautiously, slowly, Virdon inspected the injured leg. There was a look of shock on Virdon's face when he saw the extent of the wound. The leg had been badly torn on a jagged rock, and the shaggy hair of the ape's leg was matted with blood. "Lie still," said Virdon. He turned to Burke. "Need a tourniquet. Hurry!"

Burke quickly tore a long strip of cloth from the bottom of his roughly knit shirt, rolling up the swath to make a pliable, ropelike tourniquet.

"Ohhh!" said Galen, moaning. "I'm sorry…"

Burke was very worried, more for his friend the chimpanzee than for what Galen's injury meant to their chances for escape. In fact, that thought hadn't occurred yet to either Burke or Virdon. "Hey," said Burke anxiously. "Be quiet, will you? I'm giving you the shirt off my back, buddy. Just be quiet, there."

Burke handed the tourniquet to Virdon, who wrapped it expertly though hastily around the leg above the wound and started twisting. Meanwhile, Burke looked around in the darkness for a strong stick that Virdon could use as a lever. Finding one, he tested it quickly, and broke off a length. He handed it to Virdon, who muttered something that Burke couldn't hear. The blond man slipped the stick through the knot of the tourniquet and twisted even tighter. Galen clutched one of Virdon's arms, but he did not cry out.

"You have a fractured leg," said Virdon. "A simple fracture, you don't have to worry about a compound fracture unless you do something dumb right now. I was afraid the broken bone might have pierced your leg when

I saw all the blood, but that's a surface wound caused by the rocks."

"Compound?" asked Galen weakly. "I don't know what that means."

"Your ape medicine is a little behind," said Burke. "Some time when you're feeling lazy, have Dr. Virdon here explain it to you. It's something no home should be without."

"What?" said Virdon. "An Alan Virdon or a compound fracture?"

"This is getting us nowhere," said Burke, sighing.

"You should be glad," said the other human.

"I'm not," said Burke.

"Rest easy," Virdon said to Galen, who was already trying to get up. "We've got to be sure that we've stopped the bleeding."

"It was dark," said Galen. "I... I fell—"

Burke decided that the best approach was humor. "It wasn't your fault, Galen," he said. "That old magic compass is great for back and forth, but it ain't worth a hoot for up and down."

After a time the chimpanzee fell asleep from exhaustion. Burke lay down and made a rough bed for himself from leaves and grass. Virdon, because of his knowledge of first aid, waited up until dawn, in case of some emergency. The remainder of the night passed uneventfully, fortunately enough. When the sun began to rise, Virdon shook Burke awake. Together they gathered strong tree limbs and, tying them together with plaited vines and strips of their clothing, built a crude litter.

Galen's face was contorted with pain while the two men lifted the heavy ape onto the litter. Burke had had only two hours of sleep while Virdon had had none; still, they knew that with daylight, their danger increased a hundredfold. They made the best time they could through the forest, carrying their chimpanzee companion. The burden, coupled with the strain of the night's efforts, had brought the two former astronauts to the point of collapse.

"Sun's been... up for... half hour," murmured Virdon.

"Feel like... *I've* been up... half a year," answered Burke.

"Got to... keep moving," said Virdon. "Sitting ducks."

"Sitting?" asked Burke. "What's that? I... seem... to remember..."

"Need a place... to hole up... or...*hey!*" said Virdon. It was obvious that he had spotted something. He stopped, so Burke had to, also. The darker man looked in the direction that Virdon indicated.

Through the trees, in a clearing, there was a cabin. It was better constructed than the mud-brick huts that humans lived in throughout the rural sector away from the central ape city. A good many apes, of course, chose to live away from the city; but, as the rural, outlying districts and the humans and apes who lived there were considered somehow inferior, Burke, Virdon, and Galen often discovered that the country dwellers had, in fact, a saner, more reasonable approach to life. The two astronauts hoped that this would hold true with the farmers here.

Behind the cabin were outbuildings, and beyond, tilled fields. "An isolated farm," said Virdon. "Just exactly what the doctor ordered."

"Yes, doctor," said Burke.

"Will you kindly stop calling me that?" asked Virdon.

"Yes," said Burke, "sir."

Their conversation was broken up by the distant, mournful mooing of a cow.

Virdon and Burke raised their eyebrows at the sound. They looked at each other, then turned their attention back to the farm. Burke could almost taste the sight. "Oh, man," he said, "would you look at that. Chicken and dumplings… mashed potatoes and gravy… honey-cured ham… and steak and eggs for breakfast. You hear that, Galen? Just what you need. Fix you up like *that*."

Galen, like every other ape in his world, was a strict vegetarian; it was one thing that set the apes and humans apart, and always made the apes feel a little superior. "Meat," said Galen, for a moment forgetting even the intense pain of his leg. "Ugh!"

"This may be it at last, Pete," said Virdon wistfully. "Show me a couple of nice, rackety diesel tractors, and it's home sweet home all over again. Come on." They laboriously carried the litter with Galen in it closer to the cabin.

Closer, the hope of a modern farm like those in the world from which Virdon and Burke had come, vanished. The cabin itself was very primitive, and the rest of the farm showed little of the everyday farming sense that even the poorest human farmer had known in the astronauts' own day. Virdon and Burke came into the yard and paused. They weren't quite certain how to proceed.

They set the litter down carefully. Galen was able to raise himself slowly on one arm, in order to watch what happened. Virdon went to the door of the cabin, but Galen couldn't see. Tiredly, the chimpanzee let himself fall back down.

Virdon looked back over his shoulder at Burke, who stood to one side. After a moment of hesitation, Virdon shrugged his brawny shoulders. They had come this far and, after all, they *did* have a badly injured companion. Filled with expectancy, Virdon knocked on the door.

There was no reply. Virdon tried again, knocking louder. There was only silence.

Virdon tried once more. He knocked loudly, so that if there had been anyone in the cabin who had not heard the first two knocks, it was very unlikely that they wouldn't hear the third. There was a pause... and the door was opened slowly, just wide enough to reveal the face of a large ape. He had to study Virdon's face only a moment "Get away from here!" he said. "Now!"

Virdon didn't move. He was disappointed that the farm wasn't run by humans, but the ape's threatening tone wouldn't make him flinch.

"I'm warning you," said the ape, "we have clubs and corn knives."

Virdon took a deep breath. He hadn't said a word, and already he was deep in the hole. "We need help," he said quietly. "Our friend has been hurt."

The ape was adamant. "We don't help humans," he said.

Virdon hesitated briefly, unsure of how to continue. Then he stepped back and gestured toward Galen, who was invisible from the door of the cabin. The large farmer, evidently the head of the farm family, opened the door wider and cautiously looked beyond Virdon. He saw the two other figures waiting in the yard. The ape turned back into the cabin and spoke to someone there. "Stay back," he said.

As the ape stepped from the house, more figures pressed themselves against the door. Virdon gave them only a glance as he followed the ape to where Galen rested. The farmer walked the few steps to Galen and Burke with caution, as though he expected to be ambushed and pounced on. He stopped at the litter and took a quick look at Galen.

Meanwhile, the four other figures came out of the door and stood outside the cabin. The force of curiosity had been irresistible. There was a woman, evidently the farmer's wife, a large and strong son, carrying a corn knife, a younger son, and a daughter somewhere between the two males in age. All four came to stand near the litter. "What is it, Polar?" asked the farmer's wife.

Polar turned around, startled to find his family standing so near. "Jillia," he said to his daughter, "go back in the house. You, too, Zantes." He gruffly pushed his wife toward the cabin.

Jillia, the daughter, retreated a slight distance toward the house, but Zantes, Polar's wife, knelt quickly at Galen's litter. She saw immediately how badly hurt the young chimpanzee was. She glanced curiously at the tourniquet, but did not touch it. Polar stood helpless, the failure of his authority noticed only by him.

"Oh dear!" said Zantes. "This is terrible." She turned to her daughter. "Jillia, put a kettle of water on the stove. This will have to be cleaned better, at least."

Polar tried to reassert his control of the situation. "Just a minute," he said to Galen. "Who are you?"

Galen could only answer weakly. "My name is Galen," he said. "These are my friends…"

The elder son stepped forward. He brandished his machete-like knife aggressively. "Anto," said Zantes, "stay back. You're only blocking my light."

The youthful ape paid no attention. "Are you their prisoner?" he asked Galen. "Have they captured you?"

Galen's voice was growing weaker with the effort needed to deal with Polar and his family. "No… no…" he murmured. "Please… help us…"

The younger son pushed forward curiously. "Are you

rich?" he asked. "They're your bonded humans. Aren't I right? Aren't I, Mom?"

Zantes looked up at her son. "I don't know, Remus," she said. "Why don't you and Anto go into the house, like your father says?"

"Why don't *you* go into the house," said Polar to his wife. "This poor ape may be at the mercy of these bonded humans. They may even have hurt him, and they might do the same to you."

"No... no..." said Galen.

Virdon was on the point of saying something, but Galen suddenly sunk back down, unconscious now from the exertion and his loss of blood. Burke reacted to this serious sign of Galen's worsening condition.

"Look," said Burke angrily, addressing Anto, the elder son, "put that knife away and help him." Burke turned to the others. "Will you? We're no danger to you. Do something for him!"

Zantes looked up at Polar and Anto. "Take him inside. I'll do what I can."

Neither her husband nor her elder son moved; they were both certain that they didn't want the human friends of the injured ape anywhere near the farm, let alone in their very house. For a moment there was silence.

During the seconds of strained tension, Zantes had grown angry at her husband's stubbornness which was only making the poor injured Galen suffer the more. She wondered how her husband, basically a good-hearted ape, could be so blinded by his prejudice of humans to include Galen. "Ask all your questions later," said Zantes, an unanswerable edge to her voice. "This chimpanzee needs help."

Polar was still reluctant, although he could see the

sense of his wife's words. Nevertheless, he genuinely didn't want the humans around his house, around his wife and daughter. He had only the vaguest, illogical reasons, but to him they were strong. And he was supported by the presence of Anto, who shared his father's dislike of the humans. Polar had made some loud declarations, which had been ignored; now he tried again to assert his authority. "Don't order me around, woman," he said. "I've already made up my mind that we should help this unfortunate ape."

Virdon and Burke were relieved; for a while it looked as though they might be turned away. Then, they would have had to take up their journey again, carrying Galen to the next farm house. They didn't welcome that thought. They started to pick up the litter, to carry Galen into the house, but Polar shoved them both away. Virdon and Burke were startled, but they knew that they didn't dare object.

"Not you two," said Polar. "Anto and I will carry him in." There was no disagreement from the humans. Polar motioned toward another building, a good distance from the house. "You two can wait in the barn," said the ape. His voice took on a stern tone. "Don't touch anything or steal anything, or I'll put the Patrol on you." '

Virdon and Burke exchanged amused looks. They were being treated like the slaves of a bad film or novel from their own time. With a shudder the two humans realized that here, two thousand years in the future, in a world ruled by apes, that was precisely what they were. It was so easy to overlook the fact, especially when they were only with Galen. It was when they had to deal with other apes that the difference in social position was underlined.

"Just take care of him," Virdon said softly.

The younger of Polar's two sons looked at the humans

thoughtfully. "What'd you do to him?" he asked.

Zantes stood as Anto and Polar hefted the litter. She gave Remus a warning look. "You're as bad as your father," she said. "Now go inside." Virdon and Burke, realizing that the situation was now completely out of their control, began heading for the barn that Polar had indicated. With a grunt, the ape farmer and his elder son moved toward the house, carrying the heavy litter. Galen was unconscious.

The barn was a simple, functional structure. There was a stall with a cow. Nearby, a pile of straw stood somewhat in disarray. The humans could imagine that Remus spent a good amount of time playing in it. Virdon looked around. Burke, with no hesitation, went straight for the pile of straw. The cow mooed softly; a cricket started chirping somewhere in the barn; the steps of the humans sounded loud and foreign in the peaceful quiet. They were grateful for the respite, and for the first time in many hours they allowed themselves the luxury of relaxation.

Burke just collapsed on the straw. "Man," he said, sighing, "I could sleep standing up, balanced on the tip of an icicle. You want to see some serious sleeping, you just watch me. Some people just sleep, without any appreciation or technique. Me, man, I'm a *serious* sleeper." He stretched his arms but and yawned, looking around the barn. "Diesel tractors, hah! If Columbus had landed here, he wouldn't have got off the boat!"

Virdon laughed. He let himself fall down on the other side of the straw pile. "If you're so tired," he said mockingly, "try closing your mouth and see if the rest of you'll go to sleep."

Outside of the barn, unknown to either Burke or Virdon, Anto was approaching with a pitchfork in his hands. His expression was murderous.

Burke and Virdon were already dozing when they were jerked awake by the creaking of the barn door. They looked up in surprise, curious about what might have happened. They expected that there was some news about Galen. Instead, they saw Anto coming closer, his pitchfork held in a menacing manner. The young ape jabbed at Burke with it.

"Ouch!" cried Burke. "Hey!" Anto's expression of hate did not change. Burke tapped Virdon's shoulder. "What now, boss?" he asked in a hoarse whisper.

"I'm not sure," said Virdon. "I have this feeling that our host's strapping son has taken an instant dislike to us. That is, if you want my opinion, and immediate analysis of the situation."

"Thank you, Alan Virdon," said Burke. "And now—" Anto jabbed at Burke again. "Okay, Sarge," said the astronaut. "Take it easy. I didn't hear reveille…"

Virdon scrambled to his feet. Burke, more cautiously, arose and kept a wary eye on the pitchfork. Virdon attempted to look cheerful and unafraid; he nodded a pleasant greeting to Anto. It had no effect. Anto continued to hold the pitchfork in a threatening aspect.

The young ape spoke through clenched teeth. "Why did you sleep so close to the cow?"

"Oh, *that*," said Burke. "Well, you see, we both figured that the straw would be a good place to sack out, and the straw, as you can see, was put very near the cow. Now, we thought about moving the pile of straw but, as you remember, your father warned us not to touch anything." This speech only made Anto more confused. He could not believe that Burke was serious, yet there was no reason for the human to be otherwise.

"You would move a pile of straw?" asked Anto. He shook his head and repeated his first question. "Why did you sleep so close to the cow?"

"Does she seem to object?" asked Burke. "We've gotten along very nicely, I think."

Virdon realized that Burke's bantering was only getting them deeper into trouble. He interrupted his friend. "We meant your cow no harm," he said.

"Ha!" snorted Anto contemptuously. "Humans are a curse to cows! Everyone knows that."

The cow mooed again. All three turned to it. The sound seemed to come at an ill-timed moment; it made Anto increasingly angry. Neither Burke nor Virdon could understand the significance of the situation.

Anto regarded the cow with a look which the humans found difficult to interpret. "Five years," said Anto musingly. "Five years I've waited for the bull calf! My own bull... to start my own farm. And nothing but female calves... *heifers*. For the landlord!"

Burke still didn't quite understand, but he thought it was time that Anto stopped being so threatening. "Well, look," said Burke in mild tones, "put the hay stabber down, eh? Maybe this'll be your lucky year."

Virdon was completely lost. He didn't know what to say or do to extricate them from an obviously serious circumstance. It was a feeling he didn't enjoy. "I don't understand," he said.

"Hah," said Anto, in a distrustful voice. "You understand. When a son becomes of age, he must wait for a bull calf to be born before he can start his own farm. Five years I've waited for the bull calf. And the signs were against me, nothing but female calves. This year I knew the signs were right... until you came."

Virdon nodded. "A kind of rite of passage," he whispered to Burke. "These back-country apes must have many local customs. Superstitions, really. Initiation rites."

The cow mooed again. There was an anxious quality to the sound.

"You hear?" asked Anto. "You are a bad omen. If you have put a curse on her, I may *kill* you…"

"Hey," said Virdon desperately, "wait a minute."

"Remove the curse," said Anto. "Go away. Today!"

The door creaked again. All three turned to look. It was Remus, the younger son, running in to them, excited and showing undisguised curiosity. But also on his face was a look that said he had information… and, what was rare for him, *authority*. "Hey, you two!" he said, panting a little, "Galen is awake and asking to see you. He's awake—"

Virdon and Burke headed for the door, but Anto stopped them momentarily with the fork. "Wait a minute," said the ape with disgust. "Wash first. It's bad enough having humans in the house. But wash first. You carry a smell with you."

Virdon and Burke looked at each other, first with amusement, then with a stifled outrage. There was nothing that they could say or do.

Inside the farmhouse it was bright and clean. Galen had been quartered in Remus' room. The chimpanzee rested on a crude bunk, awake and very pleased just to be alive. His spirits had lifted a good deal from the depression he had entered immediately after his fall. Zantes was finishing the application of a new dressing to Galen's wound. Behind her, stood Polar, watching in silence.

It was some time since Galen had been able to relax in such comfort; the great pain in his leg could almost be ignored in the atmosphere of hospitality and friendliness that the household of Polar and Zantes had shown him. He had no reason to believe that things had gone any differently with his human friends. Galen smiled at Zantes. "That's very good," he said. "You've done this before."

Zantes looked up, a little embarrassed. "Once, a long time ago, I trained to be a nurse. Until I met Polar..."

Polar grunted. It was obvious that he thought that Zantes' meeting him was the best luck she had ever had. "Humph!" he said. "The city. No place to raise a family."

This was obviously an old, old argument. "Not even to visit?" asked Zantes wistfully.

"Some day," said Polar with finality.

"Every time," said Zantes, "every time, the same answer."

"Well," said Polar with what he believed to be reasonableness, "Anto needs his bull calf. Remus is barely out of rompers."

Jillia, the daughter, entered, carrying a freshly fluffed new pillow to place under Galen's head. She did it coyly; she was evidently pleased with the presence of this handsome young chimpanzee. Polar did not miss the look she gave Galen.

"Jillia hasn't even sought out a husband," he said.

"Daddy—!" cried Jillia in embarrassment. She stepped back, shocked by her father's lack of tact. Galen laughed softly. He was a city ape himself, and he prided himself on a certain sophistication which was lacking in everyone except, possibly, Zantes. He observed Polar with a kind of innocent condescension.

"You're young and strong," said Zantes to Galen. "You will heal more quickly than an older ape. Still, you won't be able to stand on that leg for some time."

Zantes' words worried Polar. He did not like the idea

of Galen and his companions staying around his house that long. "How long do you mean?" he asked.

"Why, several days at least," said Zantes, wiping her face with her apron. "Possibly a couple of weeks. There's no definite amount of time to these things. We can only let nature take its course."

"I can't have those humans hanging around," said Polar loudly. "It's dangerous. They've been known to kill cows—just for the meat!"

Galen spoke up soothingly. "Virdon and Burke won't kill your cows," he said.

"Where are they from?" asked Jillia. "Those humans, I mean? Why are they with you?"

There was an uncomfortable moment; Galen hesitated, unwilling to answer Jillia's innocent question. "You must let them stay," he said at last, avoiding the matter. "They'll work for their keep."

Polar snorted derisively. "Work?" he said. "Of course they'll work! That's what humans are for!"

Zantes stood up. "Well?" she said.

Polar was uneasy. He didn't like the situation at all, but he was always helpless to go against the strong will of his wife. "I'll see," he said at last. He strode quickly from the room.

Zantes turned back to Galen. "He means well. You'll see," she said.

Galen had a sudden thought. "Did you send for my friends?" he asked.

There was a look of mild revulsion on Jillia's face. She was a bright young ape woman, but she shared many of the same beliefs and prejudices that her father and brothers accepted. "How can you keep calling them... friends?" she asked softly.

Outside, at the side of the barn, a tub of water sat on a bench. Burke took off his roughly knit shirt and began washing himself. Virdon had already finished and was drying himself on a rough towel. He put his own shirt back on; as he did so, he gazed thoughtfully toward Polar's farmhouse. "I think we've got to stand inspection," he said. "Are you ready?" He tossed the towel to Burke, who dried himself and began putting his shirt back on.

The two men watched as Polar walked toward them. With his father was Remus, while Anto, still very angry, stood a few feet away. "I have decided," said Polar, trying to project an image of paternal prerogative. "You can stay until your... friend... is well. Or able to walk." Polar stood, his arms folded. He had made his pronouncement. Burke and Virdon said nothing. It was clear to them who had made that decision. It had *not* been Polar.

Anto advanced, his expression full of hate and fear. "No!" he cried.

Polar gave his elder son a quick, warning look. His voice, when he spoke, was stern, the voice of a patriarch in a family dependent on the earth for its living. "Enough!" he said. "I have said what my word on this is. I do not change my word." Anto had been given his orders.

The young ape did not accept the state of affairs with good grace. He was not in the least mollified; his face darkened with fury. "The cow is *my* say," he said, his lip curling in a hateful sneer. "They must stay away from the cow!" With those words Anto strode angrily away. Polar gazed after his son silently. Burke and Virdon, still mystified by the peculiar ways of these country people, did not know how to placate their host. They decided that the best thing to do was to remain silent.

Polar watched Anto disappear behind the barn. "He's

right about that," he said. "The cow is his say until the calf is born."

Virdon and Burke exchanged curious glances. The situation here was strange, even for the oftentimes illogical world of the apes. "Anything you say," said Virdon, trying to demonstrate his good will.

Polar had not finished delivering his decision. "But you will work," he said, in the tones of the boss of a road gang. "Every day, you will work! Just as though I could afford you!"

Burke laughed, although there was no humor in the sound. "Sure," he said. "We come cheap."

Polar glared. "Just as though I owned you!" he said. Neither Burke nor Virdon liked the sound of that, but there was nothing they could do except hope that Galen would recover quickly.

Remus looked up at his father. His expression was suddenly excited. Here were two human slaves, just like the rich apes owned. No one near Polar's farm was wealthy enough to afford human slaves. Polar and the farmers like him were all tenant farmers, giving most of what they grew and earned from their meager harvest to their landlord. Indeed, one of the principal reasons that Virdon and Burke had encountered so much prejudice and bad treatment from Polar and his family was that the apes had only rarely even seen a human being. Zantes alone, having spent a large amount of time before her marriage in the central city, was accustomed to seeing humans.

Remus was delighted at the idea of having slaves, of having one for his very own. "I get one of them," he said, his eyes wide with the prospect. "One of them's mine."

Polar looked down fondly at his younger son. "We'll see," he said, in the ageless manner of the devoted but sometimes helpless parent. "We'll see, Remus."

In the distance, during this conversation, Virdon watched a cloud of dust rising on the road; a rider on horseback was approaching, riding hard and fast toward Polar's farm. There was no possible way that a stranger could be good news for the fugitives. Virdon watched the approaching rider with growing anxiety. He pointed toward the road. "Who's that?" he asked.

Polar turned to look where Virdon was pointing. The ape shielded his eyes with one hand and stared for a moment. It became apparent after a while that he didn't like what he was seeing. He, too, watched the rider coming closer. Virdon and Burke fidgeted nervously. They wanted to hide from the stranger's arrival, but they couldn't think of a way to do so without unnecessarily arousing Polar's suspicions.

The rider's identity did that unpleasant job for them. He turned back to the humans, a worried expression on his face. "It's the mounted Patrol," he said. There was a tense pause. "Are you sure you are not escaped bonded slaves?" he asked at last.

Virdon was in a hurry to reassure Polar and to find a quick place of concealment. "No, sir. I pledge you that,"' he said. "We are free humans."

Polar saw something in Virdon's speech that the human had not intended. The ape's expression grew sly. "You will work for me!" he said, reminding Virdon and Burke of their promise.

"Yes," said Virdon hastily. The rider was very close.

Polar thought for a brief instant. "All right," he said, the lure of free labor too much for him. "Hide back there. I'll talk to him."

Burke and Virdon hurried to find a hiding place back toward the small farm's outbuildings. As they ran, Polar and Remus started walking, slowly and casually back toward the front of their house.

The horseman, an official-looking, uniformed mounted Patrolman, came thundering up in front of the farmhouse. About the same time, Polar and Remus arrived to meet the Patrolman. The farmer and the young ape were genuinely curious about what the uniformed gorilla had to say: it was not often that the tenant farmers were involved in the mysterious, vaguely sinister activities of the police and the military. The gorillas had a kind of native excitement about them. The farmers privately held the gorillas in contempt, just as the gorillas held the other members of the ape culture, the orangutans and the chimpanzees, in similar contempt.

The gorilla Patrolman did not dismount. He took advantage of the respect his uniform demanded and the superior psychological position of his mounted posture. This particular gorilla's manner was even more surly than usual. "Whose farm is this?" he demanded.

"This is Polar's farm. I am Polar."

The front door of the house opened, and Zantes walked toward her husband, as curious about the Patrolman as she had been earlier with the arrival of Burke, Virdon, and Galen.

The gorilla gave a derisive snort. He did not want to spend more time in the company of inferior farmers than he had to. "Listen well, Polar," he said, in a voice both bored and scornful. "I am from the Patrol post. I am rounding up escaped bonded slaves. Have you seen any?"

Just at that moment, Anto walked up curiously to hear what the mounted gorilla was saying. The Patrolman's words made the young ape think. Possibilities opened up in his imagination that seemed likely to solve all of the problems he had learned to live with.

Anto wondered what he ought to do. If he kept silent,

he might be throwing away an opportunity to bypass the rigid code that tied him to his father's farm and kept Anto from starting his own life. But if he did speak up, he would blatantly defy his father, something that Anto, for all his impatience to be independent, did not wish to do. He loved and respected his father too much.

His conflict resolved itself. He seemed to be on the verge of saying something when his mother noticed what was evidently happening in her son's mind. She forestalled a potentially unpleasant scene by speaking up herself. "Humans?" she asked innocently, in the heavy rural dialect of a country wife.

"The gorilla laughed at the stupidity of the woman. "Of course, humans," he said. "What else?"

Zantes shrugged. "We are just poor tenant farmers," she said. "What would we be doing with bonded humans?"

The Patrol gorilla glanced around. The answer to that deceptively naive question was simple: concealing them. "If you see them," said the gorilla slowly, "report immediately. You know the penalty."

Polar nodded gravely. "We know the penalty," he said.

The gorilla turned to Anto. He had noticed the young ape's anxious expression of a moment before. "Are you dumb?" asked the Patrolman. "Do you know the penalty?"

Anto hesitated. He saw his mother and his father staring at him, waiting for him to answer. "I know," he said at last. "Yes, I know the penalty."

The gorilla reveled in his authority. "If you see a stray human," he said, "report at once." The Patrolman gave each member of Polar's family a searching look. They stared back with idle curiosity, showing no sign that they comprehended what the soldier told them. The gorilla shook his huge, shaggy head resignedly. How he hated these stupid farmers!

The family watched as the Patrol gorilla spurred his horse ahead and galloped away. Remus waved. Anto stared after the uniformed gorilla. "I wonder if there's a reward," he said. The elder son glanced at his father, who gave him a stern look back. Then Polar turned away.

Virdon and Burke watched the scene anxiously from the barn, peering through the door as the horseman left.

Since the two astronauts had crashed back on Earth, although an Earth nightmarishly different than any they had known, they had spent many unpleasant hours hiding to protect themselves. They had lied to conceal their identities, and stolen when forced to in order to feed themselves. There were only two choices for Virdon and Burke, the same two choices that were available to the other humans living in the ape-dominated world: docile subservience to the apes, which meant soul-numbing slavery, or death. To make the situation worse, Virdon and Burke carried with them the additional worry that they were unlike other humans. The Supreme Council of Elders, the governing body of the apes, wanted the two astronauts, to extract information from them. Urko, the gorilla leader of all police and military forces, wanted them, he wanted them *dead,* before the two men could stir up the human slave revolt Urko feared so deeply.

And so, like so many times before, Virdon and Burke watched quietly while others determined their fates. "That didn't look like one of Urko's men," said Burke.

Virdon shook his head. "Don't kid yourself," he said. "He was some kind of local patrol. But they're *all* Urko's men."

Both men wore expressions of deep concern. Behind them, the cow that Anto guarded so jealously mooed uncomfortably. Burke turned to her. "Don't tell *me* your troubles," he said. "We've got our own problems."

7

The fields that adjoined Polar's farmhouse were planted in several different crops. The chief money crop was corn: corn fed the vegetarian apes and the animals. Corn was ground for meal, and was fermented into an alcoholic beverage. A large percentage of the corn was paid to the landowner. Most of the rest of the acreage was planted with vegetables and fruit trees to feed the farm family. There was rarely enough surplus to bring in extra money. Polar's family scraped by, year after year, just enough in debt to the landlord to keep them under his control.

The tilled land was a scene of heavy farmwork during the day. Everyone in the family helped, and now, with Virdon and Burke to join in, the burden of labor was eased a little for the apes. For Burke and Virdon, however, there was more physical work than they had been called upon to perform in a very long time.

Anto, with an ox hitched to a crudely manufactured plow, was making a long furrow. He came down a sloping hill parallel to several other vertical tracks. The elder son of Polar came closer to where his father and Virdon were carrying unearthed boulders from the rugged field to a fencerow of rocks that had been plow-breakers over the years.

The adult ape and the blond astronaut heaved their boulders onto the growing pile. Polar watched Virdon from the corner of his eye, nodding with satisfaction: this human was, as Virdon had claimed, good help. He was help that was much needed around the farm.

"Rocks," said Virdon, wiping the dripping sweat from his face. "There's no end to them. The earth keeps turning them up, the plow keeps banging into a fresh supply every year."

Polar glanced at Virdon with curiosity. "How do you know?" he asked.

"Oh, I know," said Virdon, looking at the pile of boulders with genuine resentment. "I lifted half the rocks in Jackson County when I was a boy."

Polar shook his head. "You keep talking strange," he said. "There is no such place."

Virdon paused and wiped his face again. "There was," he said quietly.

Polar shook his head again. He turned a little to watch Anto's plowing as the ape youth came down the hill toward them. "It's a bad field," said Polar resignedly. "But we need it. We need every square foot."

Virdon looked with Polar at the badly eroded hillside, deep gullies cutting into it, carved by the passage of running water.

"It's going to get worse every year," said Virdon. It was obvious to him that the apes knew as little about farming technology as they did about other facets of their lives. "The field will just keep deteriorating as long as you plow it like that."

Polar was amazed to hear a human being offering advice on farming techniques to a farmer who had worked the soil his entire life. "What?" asked the ape.

Virdon walked to the rock pile without another word and picked up a large earthen jug of drinking water that Polar had carried with him from, the house. Then he turned back to the ape. "Come on," said Virdon, "I'll show you."

Virdon led Polar to the plowed area that Anto had just finished, at the bottom of the hill. Anto was sweating profusely, and he paused for a moment to rest. He leaned against the plow, ignoring the pull of the ox, watching his father and the human curiously. He half expected to get a reprimand for his laziness from Polar, but his father said nothing. Polar seemed intent on what Virdon was doing. Anto waited, letting the rest of the plowing go until later.

Virdon stopped at the freshly turned earth. Anto noticed, and thought that the human was going to criticize the job he had done. Anto layed the reins on the plow and walked up next to Virdon; the ape youth certainly wasn't about to take any kind of judgment from a human being.

Virdon knelt in the moist dirt, smoothing out a piece of the fresh earth. With a forefinger he made vertical lines in it. He set the jug of water down on the ground beside him. Then he looked up at Polar, who was watching in bewilderment; it seemed to the ape that Virdon was playing in the dirt like any child.

"Look," said Virdon, indicating the miniature hill he had built, "when you plow up and down that hill, like you're doing now—" He poured water from the jug onto his model. "—Every time it rains, the water washes more of your topsoil off." Virdon pointed at the effect the water was having on his small hill. "Look, see? You start getting gullies." Virdon looked up at the plowed hill above him.

"They get so deep. They steal your land. You have to work around the gullies."

Anto did not understand what Virdon was driving at. He snorted contemptuously. "Playing in mud!" he said.

Virdon moved over in the dirt a little. He smoothed out another small hill, like the first. "Now," he said, "if you'd plow *around* the hill instead… like this…" He made a series of small horizontal furrows circling the model hill. "Now, every time it rains—" He poured more water from the jug. "—the furrows would hold the water, saving it for your crops, and preventing the rain from running off with the rich soil on top. And you don't get the gullies. See?" Virdon looked up at Polar, waiting to see if his lecture had impressed the farmer.

Polar glared down for a long moment, naturally not trusting anything that Virdon had to say. But the thought that the human might actually have a way to save them all work, and increase the productivity of the farm finally won him over. He knelt and scrutinized the results of Virdon's two experiments. He was amazed by the simple demonstration. "Look!" he cried to Anto. "See, it's true! Just like he says."

Virdon realized that the admission was a difficult one for the ape farmer to make. He was not only allowing that someone might teach him something new about his own life's work, but taking that the knowledge from a *human*. That Polar could admit this made Virdon respect him even more.

Anto was not so impressed. The elder son spat on the ground beside Virdon. He was bewildered that his father could be so easily and quickly tricked by the human, especially after all the years of mistrusting the creatures. Anto knew better; Anto would not be so gullible. "It's foolishness," he said. "Everyone knows that plowing *down* the hill is the ox's rest from plowing up it. Any other way is foolishness. Going around the hill makes it hard work the entire time."

Polar stood up, smiling at Virdon. It was apparent that he had not put much store in his son's words. He was pleased with the discovery; it promised much for Polar and his family, and that was what the ape cared about. It was the overriding factor, submerging even the source of the new wisdom.

Anto walked over to Virdon's two small hills and stamped them flat. He snorted in disgust. Polar paid no attention. He still had some doubt of his own, but that was more about Virdon's background than about the science he taught. "You learned this where?" asked the ape.

Virdon gazed wistfully across the rows of crops. "My family owned a farm. When I was young."

Virdon's words brought a quizzical look from Polar, a look that the blond astronaut did not see. Virdon was seeing in his mind's eye the farm where he had grown up; he saw his family again, each person dead now, dead for so long…

Polar interrupted Virdon's musings. The ape farmer spoke to his elder son with determination. "We'll do it," he said. "We'll plow around, like the human says."

The reaction from Anto was predictable. The young ape made his large hands into fists and pounded the air. He kicked at clods of newly-plowed earth. His rage was directed at more than simply the novelty of Virdon's idea; somehow, Virdon realized, Polar's acceptance of the plowing innovation represented a threat to Anto.

"Then *he'll* plow around," shouted Anto. "I'll have no part of it."

Virdon looked at Polar, who shrugged helplessly.

Anto stormed away from them in anger. Virdon looked disappointed; he had tried to give the apes a gift of knowledge, and he was treated with suspicion.

"Don't mind him," said Polar, sighing. "He's just worried about his bull calf. He is tied to this farm and to his childhood until he gets that bull. It is much on his mind." The ape was silent for a while, and Virdon didn't wish to intrude on Polar's thoughts. At last Polar jerked a hand toward the field. "Show me," he said. "I'll try."

Virdon smiled. "There's nothing to it," he said. "It's easy."

Polar looked around at Virdon quickly. "But you lie, don't you?" he asked slyly.

Virdon was puzzled. "Lie?" he said, not understanding what Polar could mean. "No. You'll see."

Polar shook his head. "No," he said, "I don't mean about the furrows." The ape stepped closer to Virdon, curious about where the human had come from, where he *had* learned this thing. Polar liked Virdon, despite his life-long aversion to human beings. He wanted Virdon to realize that Polar was willing to accept the astronaut if the false pretenses were dropped. He spoke in confidential tones. "I mean about your family owning a farm," he said. "Only apes ever *own* farms. Then it's only the rich ones who have friends in the government…"

Virdon stared out over the cultivated lands, toward the hills standing gray-green in the distance. His expression was resigned: there was nothing that he could say or do that could change what had come to pass.

During the time that Virdon had been showing Polar and Anto his idea about plowing, Burke was busy building a fence, supervised by Remus. Burke had split timbers into rails, and was now constructing a sturdy rail barrier from them. He carried a long length of rail from the pile he had made and inserted it on top of the previous interlocking section. Remus had watched for some time, and now began jumping around vehemently behind Burke, protesting. "No, no, no!" shouted the younger son of Polar. "Stop! I order you to stop!"

Burke carried the rails to their positions, ignoring for the moment the ranting of the young ape. Finally he had enough. He set the rail in position and turned around. His face was dripping with sweat and he was too tired to put up with any more of Remus' tirade. "Look, lieutenant," said Burke, "I can't work with you shouting at me all the time."

Remus was amazed at just how stupid this human being was. Everything that Remus' father and brother had said was true—only apes could do things right. That was said, because slaves should give the masters more time to do the things that apes *liked* to do. Now it seemed to Remus that he would have to undo all of Burke's foolishness and fix the fence himself. "That's the wrong kind of fence," said Remus disgustedly.

"You show me a bale of barbed wire and I'll build you a proper one. Right how, this is the best that I can do."

"Poles!" said Remus, wondering how long it would take Burke to catch on to the idea. "You set poles up and down, stuck in the ground, next to each other. Like that."

He pointed to a fence on the far side of the field where Burke had been working. It was a fence as Remus described, constructed of poles cut to a uniform length, buried partially in the ground and standing up close together. It was half fallen, like a flimsy miniature fort.

"Come on, Remus," said Burke. "You'll work a month of Sundays to put up a stick fence like that. And the first time old Bessie rubs against it, it falls in."

Burke pointed back to the fence he was building. "Now look here," he said. He bent down and grabbed a lower rail. Remus turned from the sapling fence to watch what Burke was doing. "You take a rail fence like this," said the dark-haired astronaut, "it's locked tight. Strong as a bull. It'll last a lifetime. And, besides, it's pleasing on the eye."

Remus eyed the rail fence suspiciously. He would not be convinced so quickly by Burke's simple salesmanship. There were too many new ideas for him to grasp all at once. "Fences never last long," he said. "They're not supposed to."

"That's where you're wrong, lieutenant," said Burke, smiling.

Remus took quick exception. "I'm not wrong," he said fiercely. "I'm the boss. You can't talk to me like that."

Burke realized that behind Remus' childish pouting lurked the real danger of Burke's being punished for the insolence of a slave to a master. He swallowed hard. "Sorry, Boss," he said. "I just think this kind of a fence will grow on you." He paused for a moment, then spoke up as if he had come up with another idea. "For instance," he said, "if you ever want to move it, say if your father wants it over there,' say, you just take it apart… and put it together over there again."

"Is that right?" asked Remus, beginning to be intrigued. The younger son of Polar walked to Burke's fence and kicked a lower rail. It was solid; it didn't even move in its place. Remus tested it again. After that, he lifted the top rail from its position easily. What Burke had said about portability was true! Burke watched the youngster, himself interested in Remus' reaction to this "modern" fence. The ape was very pleased, but he still had to assert his authority over it. Remus backed away from the fence. "You could just take it down and put it up somewhere else?" he asked.

"Would I lie to you?" asked Burke.

Remus thought for a moment. "I've decided," he said finally. "It's a good job."

Burke smiled. "Thank you, Boss," he said. The apes were simple enough, and the astronauts' sophistication gave the humans an intangible advantage. Still, Burke realized with a sigh, that sophistication and its alleged advantage often came in conflict with the apes' crazy, strongly defended beliefs.

Remus ended the moment's respite. "Get back at it," he ordered.

Burke started wearily back for the pile of rails, with the young ape tagging along after him. The human picked up a rail from the pile; Remus disdained to help. "Who taught you to build a fence like that?" asked Remus.

Burke paused for a few seconds. He decided to take two rails at once, to hasten the end of the job. He grunted with the effort. "Abraham Lincoln," he said.

Remus considered this answer; the name was definitely unapelike. "I'd like to meet this Abraham Lincoln," he said reflectively.

Burke's face was streaked with sweat. His expression showed the strain of his load. His eyes turned heavenward. "So would I, Massa," he said wistfully. "So would I."

Not a great distance away was the central city of the apes. Around it, the farming communities were arranged like satellite rings of subservient humans and indentured apes. In the city, the more fortunate and independent apes went about their daily affairs. Orangutans, the rulers of the ape world, oversaw the legal and executive administrations.

Chimpanzees, the intellectuals, performed as doctors, teachers, and philosophers. The gorillas, weakest according to intellectual standards, but the strongest in physical strength, lived only for the clash of battle and conflict.

The leader of the gorilla forces, General Urko, sat behind the rough wooden desk in his office. The room was big, with large windows providing light and ventilation. Nevertheless, the air was still and hot, and the gorillas chafed in their heavy uniforms under the contemptuous stare of their mighty leader.

The gorilla from the pursuit team arrived at Urko's office to make the report his superior had instructed him to deliver. While the rural patrol gorilla related the events, Urko paced back and forth with authoritarian anger. Urko finally had enough. He barked at the bewildered gorilla, "The point is, you let them get away!"

The gorilla was shaken, bearing such evidently bad news, in Urko's headquarters. "It became cloudy," he said weakly. "We could not follow them at night."

Urko slammed one great hand on his desktop. "Virdon... Burke... and that traitor, Galen," he said, his eyes wide and his face contorted with hatred. "They can see through the clouds to the stars, I suppose?"

The gorilla was very frightened. "It's like their eyes had arrows, sir," he said defensively.

"Garbage!" shouted Urko. "They're ignorant, hairless savages!"

"Yes, sir," said the gorilla.

Urko walked to a large colored map on one wall of his office. He studied it in silence for a long time. Although sounds of the busy city came in through the open windows, no one dared disturb the leader's concentration. "How long?" he asked.

"Four days' hard riding, sir," said the gorilla patrolman.

Urko indicated a spot only vaguely mapped. "That's all farm country. Tenant farms. A few big plantations."

"Yes, sir."

"Some horses in that area," said Urko thoughtfully. "They could steal horses."

The gorilla spoke up, trying to prove that he could be of use. "It's death for a peasant or a human to ride a horse there, sir," he said.

Urko turned to the unlucky ape. The General was smiling in a sinister way. "Yes," he said. "I know." There was a brief pause. "Do you know the way back?"

"Yes," said the patrolman, "but it will be slow. The weather is covering the stars again. Many nights in a row."

Urko would not be denied. "Then the gods themselves will take time to guide us," he said in a thunderous voice. "These humans are dangerous, don't you understand that? They think that they're as good as we are. They stir up trouble."

Outside the barn on Polar's farm, Anto and his father, both outfitted with pitchforks, stood near a hay-filled wagon. The wagon itself was a crude vehicle, not very large, with solid round wooden wheels. Anto and Polar watched as Virdon put the finishing touches on a mysterious machine that he had built that day. His final operation was to rig a sling around the entire load of hay. Anto couldn't stand any more of the human's foolishness; he started for the wagon with his pitchfork, ready to begin tossing the hay up into the loft. Virdon was delaying the chore: the sooner they started, the sooner they'd finish. Polar restrained his scornful son. Anto would not wait. "Make an *ox* pitch hay into the barn?" asked Anto with a sneer. "Isn't that enough to convince you that he's not right in the mind?"

"Wait," said Polar, recalling how Virdon had been right about the contour plowing. "Watch."

Meanwhile, at the wagon, Virdon tightened the rope of the sling; the sling itself had been hastily sewn together and arranged beneath the load of hay. Virdon looked up at the other rope hanging from a specially rigged roller pulley he had fastened at the peak of the barn, over the large open door to the loft.

The ox waited patiently, unaware of its part in the proceedings, standing a few feet away from the load, one end of the lift rope already fastened to its yoke.

Virdon climbed down the wagon to secure the other end of the lift rope to the top of the gathered sling. He tied a quick knot, jumped down, and came to join Polar and Anto. He inspected the load from the different perspective; it seemed to be well balanced. The pulley was mounted strongly. The only variable seemed to be the ox, and Virdon had no control of the beast. "Okay," announced the astronaut, "I think we're ready."

Anto still rebelled. "Work is meant to be work!" he said. "Hay is meant to be pitched! By the *forkful*!"

Virdon smiled at Anto's attitude. "Drive the ox ahead," he said.

There was a slight pause, and Polar studied the face of Virdon for any sign of deceit. He saw none, and he was satisfied. Polar walked to the ox, picking up a switch stick. Before, getting the ox in motion, he looked back dubiously at the load of hay. Virdon knew what Polar was thinking; the ape was picturing the entire load spilled out over the farmyard. Virdon was having the same ugly vision. Then it was too late; Polar tapped the ox lightly on the flank…

"Ho there," called Polar, goading the ox. "Ho there."

The ox moved slowly ahead, and the entire load of hay raised slowly, slowly, up from the wagon, up into the air, slowly up toward the open door of the hayloft. Virdon helped it into the opening; Polar looked at the feat as though it were magic. He hurried back to congratulate Virdon, slapping the human on the back and laughing. "Very good!" said Polar. "Hah! Very, very good! Show me how to make the trick work."

Virdon nodded. "Easy," he said. "I'll show you."

Polar turned to his son. "You saw!" he said. "Isn't that better than forking a whole load of hay one throw at a time? Eh? Come on, Anto, isn't it?"

Anto continued to stare at the opening to the hayloft; he was on the verge of agreeing with his father. The moving of the hay had been a big success for Virdon, even greater than the plowing instructions that he had given to Polar. But the possibility of Anto joining in the celebration was short-lived. The sound of painful mooing came from the barn, and Anto, so sensitive to every change in the cow's condition, ran toward the building, fearful of the sound from his prize animal. Virdon and Polar followed.

Anto arrived to see the cow lying down in the stall, her head drooping as though she were ill. The cow let out another low moo, as though she were hurting. Virdon and Polar arrived at the stall not long after Anto, who was already kneeling, holding the head of the cow, the special animal: the source of his independence. Anto glared up angrily at Virdon.

"You see," he said accusingly, "she must have already eaten some of that hay that fell in here from that... that evil device! You see? She's dying. I know it. The humans, they're a curse. I told you!"

Polar looked at Virdon for some explanation of why this

might not be so. After all, it was common knowledge among the ape farmers that human beings were dangerous to cattle. "Anto makes a strong argument," he said equitably.

Virdon did not answer; there was no verbal reply possible. In this situation, the conflict was futile, too easily resolving itself into a "Yes, you are," "No, I'm not," kind of fight. That surely wouldn't strengthen the humans' position and definitely would do no good at all for the suffering cow. The blond man, understanding more about the situation than either Polar or Anto, stepped by them and into the cow's stall. He knelt and made a thorough, nearly professional examination. He gently pushed the cow's extended belly with his closed fist. He held his hand in and then quickly pulled it away. He tried the same maneuver in other places; the cow did not try to stop him. She just lay on the hay-strewn floor and mooed softly. At last, after looking at the cow's eyes and mouth, Virdon seemed satisfied. He stood up and turned to Polar. "How soon is she expected to calf?" he asked.

Polar rubbed his aching head. "Three weeks," he said. "Three weeks, I think."

Virdon gave Polar a reassuring smile. "I think your calendar might be a little off," he said. "It's more like two or three days. She'll be off her feed for a while, that's all."

Polar squinted and looked at Virdon closely. The calving of cows, the gathering of hay, the planting and harvesting of crops, all these things were governed and predicted by the moon and the stars. They were often just a little wrong, a fact that could easily be accepted; but it was not often that something like a cow's calving could be off by as much as almost three weeks. "Are you sure?" asked Polar, his faith in Virdon once again reduced by the human's contradiction of established custom.

Anto was not just doubtful. The cow and her calf were the single most important thing in his young life. He would not take the chance. He would stay with the long-held traditions of the ape farmers. "It's a lie!" he cried. "Throw them all out now, or she will die!" His voice was tinged with desperation.

Virdon sighed. He would have to win Anto over again, but this time the process would be infinitely more difficult than on the previous occasions. This time, Anto had an intensely personal interest in the crisis! Virdon tried to use reason. "The cow is not going to die, Anto," he said. Anto continued to glare with almost insane fury. "Look, Anto, we can't leave until Galen can walk. You know that. You can see how badly his leg is hurt. But by that time, your cow here will be a happy mother. We'll be just as happy to be on our way again."

Anto would not hear the logic of Virdon's words. Logic had no value, when he felt his future and his acceptance, into adult life threatened. He spoke to his father. "No!" he said. "I am the eldest! The cow is in my charge!"

Virdon tried to reinforce his statements. "Have we shown you anything evil yet?" he asked Polar. "Tell me, Polar. If we have, well, then send us away."

There was silence in the barn for almost a full minute. He had grown to respect the words of Virdon and Burke in the few days that they had been staying at the farm. Nevertheless, what they suggested now went against generations of experience and folklore. And there was Anto to think of. Polar could recall the time when he Polar, had waited for the birth of the bull calf that gave him his freedom. He knew what Anto was going through and Anto had had such bad luck. It was a big decision to have to make.

"The farm seems to profit from them," he said to Anto, almost apologetically. Polar turned to Virdon. "You may stay," he said. "But if anything happens to the cow, as Anto fears, your fate will be up to him."

Anto was beside himself with rage at this verdict. His last chance for his future was disappearing, killed by the evil, loathsome curse that humans invariably brought to all cattle. He couldn't understand why his father did not see. "By then it will be too late," he said, nearly on the point of crying. "What good will *that* do?"

"Enough!" said Polar sternly, and walked away, having given his final world on the matter. Anto, in complete frustration, gave Virdon a threatening look. Virdon only looked back mildly. Anto stomped off in another direction, leaving the human alone in the barn with the quietly mooing cow.

Several hours later, night had fallen, and the family of Polar the farmer were gathered in the living room, around the glowing fireplace in the rough-hewn but comfortable room, Burke sat near the hearth, sketching something on a rough board. As the lines filled in more and more of his picture, it began to look like a design for a windmill, a mechanical device that had not been seen in the world for over twenty centuries. Zantes was helping her daughter, Jillia, make a garment of cloth, sitting in a chair near the fire. Across from her, Polar was mending a harness rope, weaving the loose ends together. Remus sat near his mother's side, shelling corn from small ears, dumping the kernels into a clay pot. Virdon walked from the cot on the far side of the room, where Galen was lying; the blond human sat near Remus, watching.

"Where is Anto?" asked Zantes suddenly.

Polar thought for a moment. "I think he has some things to work out in his mind," he said.

Virdon interrupted the younger son's work. "Remus," he said, somewhat puzzled, "I thought you said you were shelling corn for *seed*?"

Remus looked up, surprised. "I am," he said. "Of course, Burke should be doing it."

Burke looked up from his sketching with an expression of mock horror. "Hey," he said, "have a heart. Even convicts get time off for good behavior, eh?"

Polar made another pronouncement; he did that quite a bit since the arrival of the humans. This time he did not even bother to look up from his work. "Remus will shell the corn," he said. "The youngest son prepares the seed."

Virdon reached into the corn bag, probed around for a moment, and brought out an ear twice the size of the ear Remus was holding. "Here," he said, "you should always use seed from the best ears, not the smallest."

Remus laughed. He glanced around the room to see if anyone else had heard this absurdity. It made him laugh again. He was glad that the humans weren't *always* right. It proved that they were, after all, only human.

Polar had stopped his work and looked at Virdon with a kind of patient amusement. Perhaps the human had gotten so confident or swell-headed about his successes that he believed that he could criticize every aspect of their farm life. Well, thought Polar, perhaps it was time to show Virdon that the apes knew a thing or two about farming themselves. Zantes did not look up from her sewing, but she had a large smile on her face. Jillia paid little attention. Remus laughed again. "Did you hear that?" he asked, to no one in particular.

Everyone went back to his chore. Remus looked up at

Virdon. "The best ears are for feed and flour," he said. "That's what we *eat*, Virdon. That's why we grow the corn in the first place. The little ears are for seed."

Virdon nodded, understanding the apes' objection to his comment. "Oh," he said, "I see. Then it's the, uh, the bad spirits who have been making the stalks in the field smaller and smaller every year?"

Remus exchanged a look with his father. "How did you know about that?" he asked Virdon. The human had hit the truth, and Remus was confused. Everyone knew that fields of corn were often susceptible to the spirits, but how had Virdon known that had been the case in Polar's field? Virdon detected that his wild supposition was precisely what the apes believed.

Galen filled the silence, trying to avoid any unpleasant suspicions, thoughts that had been put to rest during the previous days. "Virdon used to be a farmer when he was young. You remember. He's said that before himself." Remus snorted. Even another ape like Galen could not help to defend Virdon in this case. Besides, Galen was a little suspect himself, just from his association with two human beings. "He couldn't have been much of a farmer," said the younger son. "Not wasting his big corn on seed."

Virdon laughed and waved at Galen to be quiet for a minute. He would have to convince Remus and Polar through logic and example. "Do you expect to be big and strong like your father some day?" he asked Remus.

The young ape smiled broadly. It was evident that he loved and admired his father. "Of course," he said enthusiastically.

"Ah," said Virdon, drawing a parallel between the family and the com, "that's because Polar came from good seed. If your father were small and puny, *you* probably wouldn't grow big enough to wrestle a calf—let alone an ox. Right?" Remus nodded dubiously, seeing what Virdon was hinting at. The blond man handed the ape the large ear of corn. "Each year," he said, "if you use the biggest, best ears for seed, the crop will get bigger and better. You'll see."

Virdon watched Remus, as the young ape studied the ear of corn. Meanwhile, the man's thoughts traveled back to nights very much like this, when he sat around his own living room, with his own son. If he closed his eyes, Virdon might almost pretend that he was back home, listening to the sounds of his contented family. It was a strong, melancholy feeling, something that he couldn't share with his friend Burke who had not left any family ties behind. Tears began to well up in Virdon's eyes, and he stood up to go by the fire. Zantes noticed his discomfort.

"Is something the matter?" she asked.

Virdon brushed a single tear away, in an offhand manner so that no one might suspect. But Remus did notice, and he watched Virdon silently, bewildered.

"I… I was just remembering," said Virdon. His voice was heavy and mournful. "I remembered how I once… sat around a fire something like this… telling my own son almost the same thing." He swallowed, and was unable to continue for a moment. "Chris," he said finally, softly. "I wonder whatever became… of the little guy…"

Remus had gone quietly to stand by his mother and tugged at her sleeve. Virdon, who was staring blankly into space, did not notice being consumed for the moment by his memories. Zantes bent to hear her son's whispered words. "Is he *crying*?" he asked.

"Well," said Zantes, studying Virdon with pity, "they have feelings, too… just like us. Now hush."

Remus looked at the large man and shook his head. He couldn't understand why Virdon suddenly broke up their discussion. The ape child looked again at the ear of corn he held and thought about that, instead.

At night, the headquarters of the gorilla mounted Patrol seemed peaceful enough. A weak yellow light beamed through the windows. There was no movement except the slow wandering of the horses in the corral.

A gorilla Patrol rider, coming off duty, tried to urge his horse into the corral. He gave the animal a whack on its flank. The horse jumped forward, and the ape closed the gate behind it.

The ape adjusted his uniform and pulled his heavy gauntlets tighter, a nervous habit that he repeated every few minutes. He turned to speak to someone behind him. "Why are you so interested in runaway bonded humans?" asked the gorilla. "You couldn't afford to buy one, anyway."

Beside him stood a nearly exhausted Anto. The sweat dripped from his face and his shaggy hair was matted with twigs and leaves. He had run most of the night.

"Oh, no," said Anto quickly. He wanted to avoid arousing the gorilla's suspicions until Anto had the information he sought. "I was just wondering if there was a… a reward for helping you find one… or maybe two."

The Patrol gorilla looked at Anto closely. It didn't seem likely to him that the young ape would run so frantically at *night* just to ask that question. Not unless there was more to the story than he was revealing. "Reward?" said the gorilla scornfully. "Of course not. Why? Do you know where some humans are?"

Anto jerked as if startled. "Why, no," he said. "I just thought that you might tell me what a couple of escaped humans looked like. If you had some descriptions of some recently escaped humans, maybe I could stay on the lookout for them."

The gorilla thought that this was particularly stupid. He waved the notion away. "All humans look alike," he said. "You know that."

Anto tried to strengthen his flimsy story. "Maybe... I would go hunting for them. I mean, if it would pay enough to... well, to buy a new bull calf."

The Patrol rider's lip curled in contempt. "You peasants are all the same," he said. "You want to get paid for doing your duty."

Another uniformed gorilla was walking slowly toward them from the Patrol-area headquarters. The first gorilla turned away from Anto and began pulling his gauntlets tight again. Anto guessed that their conversation had come to an end; he had learned little, but there was nothing more he could say or do without giving everything away to the dull-witted gorillas.

The Patrol rider with whom Anto had the discussion moved away to meet his companion. He spoke to Anto without turning around. "Now go on," he said. "Unless you want to be arrested for loitering around horses."

The first gorilla met his comrade on the path and stopped. The new gorilla was the same one who had ridden into Polar's farm so boldly, inquiring after escaped human slaves. He looks questioningly toward Anto. "Who is that?" he asked the first gorilla.

"Some back country farmer," said the Patrol rider. "He thinks we ought to be giving a bounty on bonded humans this year."

The second gorilla stared at Anto. "He looks familiar. I've seen him in the last few days. Where is he from?"

While he spoke, Anto moved away, off into the darkness.

"Some distance, I'd say," said the first gorilla. He looked like he'd been running half the night."

The second gorilla looked suspicious. "Hmmm. Looking for bounty, you say?" he mused.

"Reward, he said."

The second gorilla slapped one fist into the palm of his other hand. "I think that it just might pay to have him followed."

8

The next morning, the sky was covered with heavy black clouds threatening a storm by day's end; the atmosphere at Polar's farm was similarly charged with a nameless anxiety. All attention was focused on the stall in which Anto's cow still lay, making low grunting sounds of pain. Anto was extremely worried. He knew that no one understood the seriousness of the situation as well as he. Polar was as concerned as his son, but Anto was so nearly out of his mind with worry he could not admit it. "She'll die," he said, his voice choked with impotent anger. "Then what will I do? Wait another three years for another heifer to freshen? Another three years, another four years?"

Polar had nothing constructive to do or say. All that he could say was a helpless, "Virdon says that she'll be all right."

Anto glared. "Sure," he said, between clenched teeth, "Virdon! Who's helped you plow the fields and harvest the crops all these years? *Virdon*?"

Polar knew that his elder son could not be answered. Anto had shared the successes and failures of the farm since he had been of age to help. Virdon had only been around several days. And… Virdon was a human being. "He does seem to know about these things," said Polar weakly.

"He's turned your mind," said Anto aggressively. "He's won you with clever talk and tricks." Anto paused for effect. "This cow is dying from their curse. She started dying the day they walked in here. Remember? They came in here, carrying that human-lover, Galen."

Polar did not answer immediately. Anto's words had a great persuasion especially when Polar didn't have the counsel of Virdon or Burke to offset it. And the coincidence that Anto mentioned was also too great for Polar's superstitious mind. "I'll have a talk with them."

Anto had another trump to play. "Galen can stand," he said evilly. "I've seen him."

Polar looked surprised. Were the humans and their "master", Galen, out to trick Polar, after all? It did not seem likely, but if what Anto had said was true, then…

"They're just staying so the cow will die, I tell you," said the young ape. "Humans burn the flesh and eat it, you've heard that!"

Polar was revolted, but he nodded his head. There were stories of human beings eating the cooked meat of cows. But Polar wanted to be fair to everyone concerned. "Are you sure that Galen can stand?" he asked.

In Remus' brightly lit room, Galen was standing, weakly, with the aid of a crutch. His mind swam dizzily with the effort, but he was determined to hasten his recovery; every hour that he remained in one place endangered not only himself, but also the two human beings he had come to trust and admire. He experimented a few moments at a time. He took a step or two, and then had to stop. The sweat stood out on his young face in large droplets and his hands shook in a disconcerting manner. Galen had to fight off faintness.

While he was exercising his injured leg, Jillia entered the room, carrying a water jug. "Not too much at one time," she said. "You'll, break open the wound, Mother says."

Galen smiled at the young female ape. He was glad to see her. He had spent many long months in the company of the human beings or among hostile apes. It was an unexpected pleasure to meet someone as lovely and sensitive as Jillia. In many ways she was like her mother, Zantes, and that was a high compliment indeed. "It's feeling better," he said lightly. "The pain has turned to itching. That's supposed to be a good sign. Virdon and Burke will be surprised... when I walk right out to them."

"Not quite yet," said Jillia. There was a moment of silence, while Jillia set the jug of water by Galen's bed. When she looked up, there was a curious, concerned look on her face. "I don't understand you anyway," she said. "You must have come from a good family... your manner... your speech. And now you're running with... with... *humans.* And they've filled your mind with mad ideas."

Galen laughed. He enjoyed his conversations with Jillia. Like Zantes, she showed an innate brightness and cheerfulness of spirit. Galen was saddened at the thought that, also like her mother, Jillia might well be buried by the hard life of a farmer's wife. Nevertheless, it was a good life, though a wearing one; as well Jillia had never seen the city, as her mother had, so the young ape woman would not miss its excitements. "I'm not mad, Jillia," he said. "Now, you know that I can't tell you any more, so please stop asking."

"Why don't you just let them go on by themselves?" she asked.

Galen sat down on his bed, sighing loudly. He passed a hand over his sweating brow. These country apes…! He caught himself quickly. One of the things that he had begun to learn from his association with Virdon and Burke was the stupidity of prejudice and indiscriminate hatred. The gods themselves knew how much of that he had suffered himself! "I can't let them go," he said. "You keep asking the same question in different ways! Before I learned better, that's just the way I thought *every* female was born to behave."

Jillia spoke wryly. "I thought that you might never notice." She turned and left the room, unaware of Galen's raised eyebrows and amusement.

Later, in a field at the bottom of a hill on the farm, Burke stood watching water pour from a trough that he had built. His rough-knit clothes were soaking wet and filthy. He had labored without rest all during the day, and although Polar occasionally stopped his own work to watch, the ape had no idea what Burke was doing. The field that interested Burke was a virtual swamp, of no use to anyone, and Burke's interest in it seemed a waste of valuable time.

Burke had constructed the trough with split bamboo-like reeds. He was draining the water from the marsh land into a ditch that he had dug for the purpose. Now, after many hours labor, Burke could rest. He stood with a very pleased look on his face. Remus standing near him, applauded the sight. Polar approached again with Anto. Burke could hardly wait for them to arrive, so that he could show off his newest engineering feat.

Polar kept silent until he came very close to Burke. He

did not notice what Burke had accomplished, so intent was he on his own mission. He gestured for Remus to leave them alone in order to speak privately. "Burke," he said, "I must talk with you and Virdon." Then he noticed the water pouring from the bamboo trough. "What is this?" he asked.

Remus had not left, and instead, began jumping up and down excitedly, proud himself to be a part of Burke's new success. "See," he said loudly, "Burke is making us a whole new field. We'll have a whole new field!" His enthusiasm had robbed him of his articulateness.

Polar had had just about enough of the two astronauts and their bizarre creations. Soon, everything on the farm and everything in the house would bear the mark of the humans' meddling; then what would the neighbors say? How could Polar dare to face them? "Silence!" he commanded his younger son.

"Well," said Burke, wiping his muddy hands on his torn trousers, "it isn't exactly the Panama Canal, but I'm draining the water off that low marshy field for you."

Polar turned to look at the swamp that had always been a source of frustration to him. It was part of his homestead, but there had never been the least chance that it could be made productive.

Anto was just as belligerent as usual. He looked at Burke and wrinkled his nose in disgust. The human reeked from the work he had been doing. "That field is no good for anything but a hiding place for snakes," he said.

Burke laughed. "I suppose that's what it's been for generations," he said. He knew that the best way to get to Polar was to suggest some way for the family to make a little more honest money, to improve the condition of life for Polar's wife and children. Burke nodded out toward the draining marsh. "It will be useful, though," he said. "Probably the best field on your farm as soon as it's drained, dry enough to plow and plant. That's good rich soil that you've never used before."

Polar knelt near the flowing water. He touched the water running from the bamboo pipe. He was genuinely amazed. The prospect was overwhelming. A new field... more crops... *better* crops. Could Burke be right, again?

"Is this some new... magic?" asked Polar.

Burke shook his head. How long would it be before Polar would grasp the simple principles behind what the astronauts had been doing? Would the ape cling forever to the dictates that he had received from his father, from his grandfather, from his predecessors, generation upon generation?

Remus spoke up importantly, as though he had a momentous secret. "Wait'll you see," he said. "Wait'll you see!"

"Be still," said Polar absently, still wondering over Burke's drainage work.

Burke noticed that Polar was showing obvious interest in his recent invention. He knew that, sooner or later, there would come the inevitable discussion of how Burke had come by the knowledge. He tried to forestall that. "Just a little... engineering... I learned once," he said.

Anto did not understand the word at all. It created just the reaction that Burke was trying to avoid. Anto was trying to start a row on any pretext. "You see," he said insolently, "he admits it! 'Engineering'..."

Remus tried to intercede for Burke. The younger son had watched the entire job, and knew that nothing supernatural was involved. "No, no," he said. He began tugging excitedly at his father's sleeve, trying to get Polar to follow him.

"Father, Father," he cried, "you have to see what Burke

has been doing. There's nothing magic about it. I know, I was guarding him the whole time. Anto doesn't know. He wasn't even there. Wait'll you see the rest, Father! Come on! Come on!"

Polar was bewildered and a little annoyed. He was tugged along by his son toward an area on the other side of the ditch. They walked toward higher ground, behind some trees. Polar turned to glance back over his shoulder, at the mysterious water flow. Behind him, a proud Burke and an angry Anto followed.

In the field, behind the grove of maple and birch trees, Virdon was hard at work. He was just fastening the last slat in a windmill wheel. He sat on the ground, beside the base of a windmill tower that he and Burke had set up. The tower was constructed of saplings bound together with tough vines and spare lengths of rope. He looked up when he heard the approaching voices.

When the group came close enough, Virdon rose slowly, holding the windmill wheel in both hands. He nodded to Polar and smiled to Burke. Virdon did not care to notice Anto's glares.

"Tell them, Virdon," said Remus, "tell them what you're making. A *windy* mill."

Virdon tossed the wheel to Remus, who caught the contraption easily and laughed. "A windmill," corrected Virdon.

"That's what I said," said Remus. "A windmill."

Burke pointed up at the windmill tower. "This will be the other half of your irrigation system, Polar," said Burke.

Polar was growing weary of these mysteries. Virdon and Burke had, in all truthfulness, wrought some beneficial changes on the farm but why did they always have to proceed with such mystery? "Speak plain," said Polar.

"Well," said Burke, "when Virdon's through with that wheel, it goes up there." The dark-haired astronaut pointed to the top of the makeshift windmill tower. Everyone glanced up with him, each with a different emotion on his face. "And then," said Burke, pointing back to the ditch that had followed the same route they had taken, "we'll pump that water out of the ditch, and onto the dry ground up here where you need it when it doesn't rain."

Burke's words were too much for Anto. Once more, he had reached the limit of his patience and credence. He flew into the rage that became all too common in the last few days. "You see!" he shouted. "Making oxen lift hay that should be pitched. Now, conjuring the wind to... to make water pour where it shouldn't. It's unnatural! No wonder my cow is dying! Tell them!"

Polar was utterly confused. He had a duty to Anto to help him through his difficult time. But Virdon and Burke promised the reclamation of a swampy field, and the watering of an arid one. He avoided the matter for the moment. "Anto has seen your... friend, Galen, stand," he said.

Virdon and Burke exchanged looks of surprise. It was obvious that this was news to them. They wondered why Galen would conceal his recovery from them. The only effect of that would be mutual endangerment.

Polar knew, or at least he could guess, what it meant. "If this is so," he said, "you must go."

Anto was perfectly happy to accept this dictum. "Yes!" he cried. "It's true! He stands."

Remus took the opportunity to voice his own protest. He hated the thought of losing Burke now: the slave had become a friend. "They can't go now," he said, whining just a little. "Not until they finish, so I can see it work. No, no!"

Polar looked down at Remus, wondering how the

young ape could so quickly become attached to the two humans. Remus had had pets before, but…

"It's not for you to say," said Polar. "The youngest has no say in this matter."

Remus kicked at a nonexistent stone. "I *do* have a say," he muttered. His mind was on more important things than his father or brother could imagine. "I have a say. Anto is only worrying about a bull calf."

Anto gave a short, derisive laugh. Remus may have been right, but the youngster did not understand the seriousness of what he had said. "Wait until *your* time comes to worry," he said.

Remus wasn't convinced. A bull calf… did that equal the many wonderful things that Burke and Virdon had shown him? "I want to, learn about bigger things, like this." Remus indicated the windmill. "They can't leave now. Not until I see it work. Please? Please?"

Polar looked at the strange structure of the windmill, the oddest thing he had seen in his many years. This, and the mystery of the youngest son rebelling against him; the constant, wearing pressure from Anto, it had suddenly all become too much for Polar. He threw up his hands in defeat and started walking away.

"Stay… leave… stay… go," he said to himself, shaking his head. "I made one mistake, one bad mistake. That was being a father in the first place." He turned to his sons. "Do what you want," he said. "I just live here from now on."

As he walked away, Anto joined him. Burke and Virdon watched, helpless in the middle of the family dispute. They vaguely heard the protests from Anto and the noncommittal refusals from Polar. Meanwhile, Remus was still jumping up and down. "Yes, yes," he shouted, "stay, stay."

Burke looked at his friend and sighed. He didn't

especially like the way things had gone, but there was no other alternative. "I think we've got ourselves in the middle of a family brawl, buddy," he said.

"Anto could be trouble," said Virdon thoughtfully.

"*Real* trouble. That mounted patrol was looking for escaped laborers. But that gorilla didn't look too fussy about whom he turned in, as long as they were human."

Burke's eyes opened wide. It was apparent to his friend that Burke remembered something, thinking back to the innocent days of their old lives, in the old world, the life two thousand years ago that had seemed so normal, so permanent. "Sitting in some hick country ape jail ain't my idea of a good way to spend my old age," said Burke at last.

"I think we'd better have a talk with Galen," said Virdon, recalling Anto's challenge. "So he can stand, can he?"

Shortly, Virdon and Burke joined their chimpanzee friend in Polar's house. When the humans entered the farmhouse, they saw Galen standing on his crude crutch. They gave him a friendly, accusing look. Galen was happy at his progress, but a little disappointed that his surprise was spoiled. "I stood for several minutes today," he said.

Burke turned to Virdon. "Several minutes," he said. "How do you like that? And we're supposed to be friends."

"Well, I wanted to surprise you," said Galen, unaware of all that had been transpiring outside.

"Anto is chomping at the bit to get us out of here—" began Virdon. Galen cut him off with a quick gesture.

"Apes do not chomp at bits!" he said, with a slight but noticeable hint of coldness to his voice.

"I'm sorry," said Virdon. "Anto is *anxious* that we leave. And I think that we'd better accommodate him, or he may get some idea of turning us in, just to be rid of us."

Burke laughed shortly. "Maybe we should have some

words with that doggone cow. Give her a dose of Epsom salts and get this whole business cleared up."

Virdon was thoughtful. Neither Galen nor Burke seemed to understand how potentially volatile the situation was.

"If the calf isn't a bull," he said, "we'll still be blamed for it."

"If the cow dies," said Galen, "Anto is entitled to kill you."

"It's too late to burn incense to the right people," said Burke. "Or apes. Or whatever. Have you noticed how much trouble I have with that?"

No one answered him. "It's hopeless," said Galen. "Anto is just looking for the chance to get us, and there's no authority that we can turn to "

"Well," said Burke, "I'm glad that he knows his rights."

"If you could just give me three days, maybe two... I'm healing fast, now" said Galen.

Virdon considered their plight. While they worked, showing the farm family a variety of new and better ways to do everyday things, they all tended to forget, despite Anto, the grave threat that remained wherever they went. "We could carry you," said the blond astronaut, "But as soon as we leave here, Urko or that mounted patrol is going to pick up our trail. We'll be chased. If we could only get to some horses. I take it that this isn't horse country."

Galen wondered how someone as knowledgable and quick as Virdon could be so ignorant of the world's ways. Even though Virdon and Burke did not belong to this world, the chimpanzee thought that they *ought* to understand the most self-evident features. "Only landed apes and police can ride horses here," he said. "Farmers must walk, or ride cows and oxen."

"Keep 'em poor," said Burke, nodding thoughtfully. He with his more cynical attitude, could often see the reasoning behind what the apes in the government were doing. And just as often, despite Galen's defense of his people, Burke was close to the mark "Keep 'em poor, and keep 'em too busy to know they're getting the dirty end of the stick."

Virdon sat down on a chair. His expression was perplexed; they were caught in a genuine dilemma, this time. Finally, with both Galen and Burke looking to him for leadership, he said, "We'll just have to sit it out, I guess. See whether that cow... or Galen here... makes it first."

Early the next morning, Zantes and Polar were tending to their chores in a covered work area outside the farmhouse. Zantes pulled two freshly-baked loaves of bread from a brick oven, setting them on a table where Polar sat brooding. There was an earthen jug on the table before him, filled with some strange yellow stuff.

"You know," he said softly, his thoughts evidently somewhere else than his farm and the work he would shortly have to begin for the day, "I'll be glad when they're all grown up and gone."

Zantes reacted with surprise. "That's no way for a father to talk," she said. But she stopped and imagined what it would be like to be alone with Polar again, when they were first married, before Anto was born...

Polar looked at the slippery yellow stuff that coated the finger he had stuck into the jug. "What's this?" he asked.

Zantes glanced at her husband. "Oh," she said, "Virdon called it 'butter'. You put milk in a barrel, and churn it and churn it, and it comes out like that."

Polar sighed. Virdon... Burke... Burke... Virdon. Every day, the two human beings did something else to change the life that Polar had always rather enjoyed, just the way it was. Perhaps some of their tricks made the work a little easier and promised better, more profitable days in the future, but it wasn't the old life. "Milk is to drink," said Polar, "Not to eat."

Zantes knew better than to try to answer her husband with words. In any event, those were the same words that she said to Virdon when he had shown her how to make butter. Now she tore a heel from a loaf of warm bread, went to the table, and scooped the bread across the top of the butter crock. "Taste it," she said. "That's all you have to do. Then tell me if Polar the farmer is so smart, after all."

Polar held the bread dubiously. He loved the freshness and taste of his wife's bread, just the way it always was. But this new, *human* stuff was going to spoil that taste. He took a small bite; he liked it. He took another bite, while Zantes watched. "Mmmm," said Polar.

"See?" said his wife.

Polar's expression changed from pleasure to the doubtful, pensive look he had worn a few moments before. This newest discovery just underlined what he had been thinking about. "Since they came," he said sadly, "I don't know *anything* anymore. You know, I used to be Polar the farmer. I never made any show of being as educated or as cultured as those city apes you used to know. You realized that when you married me. You knew what kind of a life I had to offer you."

Zantes took her husband's hand. "I knew then, and I've never regretted it for an instant," she said.

"But now," said Polar, "even the things I thought that I knew, things that the city apes didn't even know, turn out to be wrong. I suppose that Virdon and Burke will be turning your head, by making milk turn the color of those gold necklaces the wives of the rich farmers wear."

Zantes laughed softly. Sometimes her husband had to be treated as gently as a baby. "Don't be silly," she said. "My head doesn't turn so easily. Besides, there must be *some* good in them, to work so hard in exchange for the care we're giving Galen."

That idea made Polar thoughtful again. There were some things about the three that he still didn't grasp. "Galen. You see, that's what happens when you grow up in the central city. You start running with humans."

Zantes sighed, recalling her days in the city, and wondering for the millionth time whether she would ever see it again. "These humans are not a bad sort. Not like some I've heard about."

That sign of Zantes' sympathy might be dangerous. Perhaps she was being drawn into some strange trap of the humans. "Maybe they don't seem so bad," said Polar. "But, still, I don't want Jillia around them. Do you hear?"

Zantes was sympathetic, perhaps, but she was still the mother of an impressionable young girl. "Well, of course I won't," she said. What do you take me for?"

At the side of the barn, a clumsy but operable shower had been constructed, consisting of a tub raised on a simple scaffold, a modesty screen of rough homespun material, and a pull-cord to release the water. Burke reveled in the shower while Virdon dressed.

"You know," said Burke, in a happier voice than Virdon had heard in a long while, "I don't mind being a peasant as long as I have all the conveniences of the rich."

Virdon laughed. "In this world, even the rich don't have showers," he said. "And I'll tell you what. As long as you're adding conveniences, maybe tomorrow you can put in the hot water."

Burke snorted. "How about a cinder track around the

farm, for a little jogging?" he asked. "And a steam room and modest gym. Lockers for members and guests only. Would that be enough?"

"Well," said Virdon, "it's all right for openers."

The two men had no idea that they were being observed: from one of the rolling hills on the limits of Polar's land, the suspicious Patrol gorilla watched. To view the farm below, he had to look toward the sun. He squinted, shielding his eyes with one huge hand. From this vantage point Burke was faintly visible, moving behind the shower screen beside the barn.

The Patrol gorilla had seen enough. He stood and wiped his hands on his uniform trousers. He was confident that he had seen what he had come for. He walked slowly and thoughtfully to his horse, mounted, and galloped off.

About noon, while Virdon and Burke were busy helping Polar with the day's tasks around the farmyard, there came a loud shout from Anto in the barn. "No!" cried Polar's elder son. "No, no!" Then, following this yell, there started the eerie sound of a low, hollow bell being rung.

In the barn, Anto was on his knees near the cow's stall. The ape was filled with grief. He was striking a ceramic bell with a wooden mallet, fulfilling some other strange rural tradition. The cow was lying on her side, barely moving. Anto rocked himself back and forth, moaning with almost unbearable sorrow.

This was the scene that met the eyes of Virdon and Burke, when the two men rushed into the barn. Following them were Polar and Remus, Zantes and Jillia. They all had a fairly good idea of what to expect. "It's her time," said Polar flatly. "The tolling of the bell…"

Anto paid little attention to the others. "She's dying," he kept repeating. "She's dying."

The members of the family held back, knowing that they had no part in the drama that was soon to take place. Even Burke was too unsure of the situation to offer any help. But Virdon rushed into the stall, alarmed by the condition of the cow.

Virdon made a quick diagnosis; this was something that was not new to him. Although he wasn't an expert, he had grown up with a few more head of cattle on his farm than Polar could afford. He turned back to Burke with a very worried look on his face. Burke came to join him, and the two men conversed in whispers.

"Trouble, Doc?" asked Burke.

"If I could only remember exactly what the vet used to do in this situation," said Virdon, frowning. He ran a hand through his blond hair and stared at the floor while he thought.

"Try hard," said Burke, suddenly realizing the seriousness of their plight. "I've got a feeling that we don't want to lose this patient. Not at all."

Polar and Zantes, meanwhile, had walked past the two humans and were trying to comfort their son, but he pushed them away. Parents played no role in this trial; Anto was alone, with the suffering cow. Anto continued to toll the bell, underscoring the moment with a mournful tone that the two humans found almost petrifying. The tolling of the bell had a sad futility about it, an impotence mirrored in the faces of Polar and Zantes.

"Dying," whispered Anto. "Dying… dying… dying…"

Virdon knew that absolutely nothing would be accomplished if they all just stood around and listened to Anto's moaning and his bell-ringing. "Look, Anto," said Virdon urgently, as he knelt beside the ape youth, "listen to me."

Anto had hypnotized himself with his own rhythmic chanting. "Dying… he whispered. "She's dying…"

Virdon tried harder to break through Anton's psychological impenetrability. "The cow is giving premature birth," he said. "You've seen that before, haven't you? Sure. And she's suffering now because her calf is turned. Do you hear me? She needs help."

As Anto looked slowly into Virdon's face, he exploded with rage, shoving Virdon backward. The ape jumped to his feet, dropping the bell, leaping for a pitchfork. The elder son now turned slowly, menacing Virdon with the implement.

"Anto!" cried Zantes, "Stop!"

Polar held his wife back. From now on, he was as helpless as she. The ruling factor was the cow, and the cow was Anto's hope and his responsibility. Where the cow was concerned, not even Anto's father could interfere. Remus and Jillia stepped back in fright. Burke moved forward to help his friend, but Virdon waved him away. Anto advanced on Virdon slowly, threatening him with the pitchfork. "You," said Anto, "you have done this." His voice was slow and full of malice.

Polar thought quickly. He desperately wanted to avoid any unnecessary violence. Virdon had become a friend to him, a benefactor of the whole family. Anto's accusation might well be true, but it had yet to be proven. "Wait!" called Polar in a stern tone of command. "The cow is not dead. You cannot claim a life yet."

Anto remembered the rule, long established by custom and rustic superstition. He was caught in a dilemma, but he restrained his impulse to kill Virdon with the pitchfork. If Anto's judgment were correct, then the humans were causing the cow's troubles In that event, merely having the human beings nearby would be enough to insure a disaster for Anto. But, on the other hand, it was possible that there would be no disaster unless Anto first killed Virdon. The ape youth compromised by holding the pitchfork threateningly close to Virdon's neck, and awaiting developments.

"The cow needn't die," said Virdon, forcing his voice to be calm. "I can help. It's just a matter of turning the calf around."

"No!" cried Anto. "You've worked your last trick here. When she dies, you will die!"

There was a creaking sound from the barn door. Everyone except Anto turned to see what was happening. It was Galen, entering the barn with great effort, hobbling on his single crutch. "Anto," he said, evidently still in some pain, "stop."

For reply, Anto jabbed the pitchfork at Virdon, who jumped back just enough to avoid it. Burke stood by helplessly, not knowing what he could do that wouldn't endanger Virdon even more. In the silence, the cow's mooing came strained and pitiable. "Come in, you human-lover," said Anto, disdaining to turn around. "Come see what you've done."

Galen hobbled forward a few steps, a quick survey of the situation filling in the important details for him. The intelligent young chimpanzee understood that, at the moment, he was the only hope for Virdon, for Burke, and, possibly, for his own life. "Blame me, then," said Galen. "It was my wound that brought them here. We'll leave. Now. We'll all leave."

Polar tried to second Galen's reasoning. He indicated to Zantes that she should stay back with Jillia; Anto's father took a few steps forward. "You hear, Anto?" he asked. "They'll leave."

Anto would not listen to reason. He still didn't know if the humans' leaving was a good thing for the cow or not. "No one will leave," he said. "Not until this is all over, one way or another. Toll the bell, Remus. It is probably too late for that, but toll the bell."

Remus cautiously walked over and picked up the ceramic bell; he started to strike it slowly, making the strange, alien sound. Anto kept Virdon pinned in place with the pitchfork. No one else said anything. All that could be heard was the slow rhythm of the bell and the awful noises of the cow. No one moved.

9

The Patrol gorilla, riding hard from his spy mission above Polar's farm, arrived back at his rural outpost exhausted but excited by the news he carried. He hurried into the headquarters and reported to the officer in charge, a grim-looking gorilla named Barga. "If you saw one," Barga asked, drumming his fingers against the rough wood of his desk, "why didn't you bring him in?"

The Patrol rider didn't have a good reason for this. In fact, the idea hadn't even occurred to him before now. He stammered, fidgeting with his heavy gauntlets. There was a tense silence in the Patrol headquarters. "I thought that there might be more," said the rider lamely.

The officer roared his disapproval. "Since when are a few humans too much for a single mounted Patrolman?" he asked.

Again, the Patrol gorilla didn't have a good answer. Barga watched him impatiently. He wished that his own superiors would send him better men; sure, they were stationed far from the central city, in a region where the need for gorilla forces was small. Still, when the need arose, Barga found himself equipped with troops like this poor replica of a soldier. "Maybe *many* more," said the rider at last. This was just the excuse that Barga expected to hear. "A good catch, maybe," said the rider to save face.

Barga had to go over every detail in the Patrolman's report. There were just too many odd things about it. "Standing beneath a stream of water, you say," he mused. "Are you sure you haven't been gulping down the fermented apple juice again?"

"Not a drop," said the Patrol rider defensively. "It's just as I say."

"All right," said Barga, trying to keep the discussion going before all the important features blurred irrevocably in his soldier's weak mind. "I believe that I'll return with you. How far?"

The rider was proud of his accomplishment. His officer had taken official notice. "Two hours' ride," he said. "The Polar farm. But shouldn't we wait until dark? If they try to run, humans are easier to see in the dark."

Barga stared aimlessly past the rider's shoulder. "Well," he said, yawning, "if you're too tired—"

"No, sir," said the soldier, dismissing that possibility from his leader's mind.

"Prepare the mounts," said Barga decisively. "What is your name again?"

The rider was crestfallen. "Lupuk, sir," he said.

"Very good, Lupuk. If farmer... Polar... has been hiding humans, well, I'd like to see him hanging while it's still daylight!"

The sun had passed zenith and had dropped about

halfway down the sky, toward sunset. The Polar farmyard was deserted. No one was bustling about, doing his daily chores; dinner was not being prepared in the farmhouse; the animals had gone unfed. There was no motion to be seen other than the wind-blown leaves in the trees. There were no baking smells from the oven, only the brisk tang of newly-cut hay still hanging in the air. Birds chirped, but other than that the only sound was the slow, steady, almost eternal tolling of the ceramic bell. That chilling sound announced that the tense vigil was still going on inside the barn. Remus kept up the tolling, as his elder brother had ordered.

The younger son of Polar knelt in the open area of the barn floor, gently ringing the roughly made bell. Galen had hobbled closer to the cow's stall, near where Anto still held Virdon uncomfortably pinned with the menacing pitchfork. Polar and his wife and his daughter stood back, mute witnesses to the scene of fear, tradition, superstition…

Virdon, without moving, without antagonizing Anto into a sudden, fatal lunge, spoke out. "Polar," he said, his voice almost cracked with the strain, "talk sense to him." Polar, helpless in the situation, waiting with Anto to see what happened with the cow, did not answer. Zantes grasped her husband's arm tighter, but neither dared speak.

Burke was the only one who was able to think and act without restraint. It became clearer as the minutes passed slowly by that his friend's life was in his hands alone; Galen, another ape, closer to Anto than Burke ever could hope to be, had failed in his attempt to reason with the ape youth. Burke spoke to Virdon in a jargon both could understand, but which was completely unintelligible to Polar and his family.

"Say the word," said Burke, measuring his words and

tone like Virdon had, to preclude the possibility of Anto's panicking into foolish action. "Just let me know, and I'll commit such a clipping penalty, we'll clear the fifteen yards and out the tunnel to the clubhouse."

Virdon understood exactly what Burke meant, but there were other things to think about. "What about the line judge?" he asked, meaning Galen.

Burke thought for a moment. Polar stared at the two of them. The ape's thoughts were puzzled; how could they carry on such gibberish, while one of them stood until the very real threat of death?

"*Between* us," said Burke. "The old five-legged race."

Virdon shook his head very slightly. "No," he said. "What good is that going to do the cow?"

Burke could barely believe his ears. He had always admired Virdon's integrity, sure, but there were limits… "You're six inches from being skewered, buddy," said Burke, "I'd let the cow worry about herself."

At this point, Polar stepped slowly forward, one hand raised in a calming gesture. Remus stopped tolling the bell at his father's movement. "Anto," said Polar, his voice neither as strict as he had been before, nor yet completely acquiescent, "I don't think that there's a need for the fork. They will not run." Polar had comprehended enough of the astronauts' conversation, particularly the last few exchanges.

Anto did not share his father's confidence. "Why won't they run?" he demanded, not moving the pitchfork away from Virdon.

Polar indicated the still-injured Galen; the chimpanzee leaned heavily and painfully on his home-made crutch. "Because Galen can't run with them," said Polar. "They have a strong feeling for him. Or they would have left him to die."

Galen made a weak sign with one hand. "That's right," he said. "I'm their… friend."

Anto was caught in an intellectual puzzle. Every new development just made his condition worse, his ability to reason more cloudy with doubt and hopelessness. "Very well," he said, pulling the fork away from Virdon's throat, stepping back. He spoke with a firm new intent. He turned to Galen, who now looked worried that Anto's murderous intentions would be directed toward him. Galen's brow sweated as he imagined the devilishly sharp tines of the pitchfork stabbing the shaggy hide of his own throat…

"Very well," said Anto again, "let them run. If anything happens, *you* will answer for it." He jabbed at the chimpanzee. Galen-breathed more shallowly, but Virdon sighed with relief. Anto's change of mind indicated that the ape youth's thoughts were not organized. With that knowledge, Virdon knew that he could have an insurmountable advantage against Anto. Nevertheless, there was still a good deal of work to do.

Virdon, freed by Anto's change of position, took the opportunity to debate with the ape youth once more. He had very little time left. "Look, Anto," he said, pleading, "I can help the cow live. I've seen veterinarians do it a dozen times. If you'll only let me help."

Anto roared his answer. "No!" No one, not Virdon, not Galen, not even Anto's own family, would come close to the cow, now.

Virdon turned to Polar, appealing to the father's sense and his ideals of fairness. "Polar," said Virdon, "do you want this cow to die?"

Polar shook his head; of course he didn't. Besides its sudden symbolic meaning, the cow represented food and money to the family the remainder of the year. "At birthing time, however," he said sadly, "the fate of the cow is in the hands of the eldest son. I have no say, now."

Polar's wife, Zantes, had listened to about all she wanted to hear. She stepped forward angrily. "Who says that you have no say?" she asked. "Those are old words, words of fathers' fathers. They have been passed down so long that we don't even know if they're right any longer."

Polar was amazed to hear what his wife had said. She was not merely questioning, as Virdon, Burke, and Galen had done. Zantes had *denied*. "Be still," he said to her. "Don't say such things in front of the young ones!"

Zantes, usually so quiet and restrained in front of her husband, was driven by the desperation of the circumstances to behavior peculiar for her. "I won't be still," she said. "And it *is* Remus and Jillia that I'm thinking of." She turned to Anto. "Listen. You are my firstborn. You have seen these humans show how to keep hills from washing away in the rain. You have seen them create… cropland… from fields an ox would drown in. You want this calf, and the bell asks that it be a bull. Let Virdon help you."

Virdon made a turn toward the stall, but once again Anto would have none of it. He raised the fork again. There was nothing that had been said that could get through Anto's overwhelming fear. "No!" he cried. "They've loosened my mother's tongue with that yellow salve they make by casting spells on milk. You will not do the same to me. You will not touch the cow." Anto took up a position between the moaning cow and the rest of the group in the barn. He pointed his pitchfork at whomever seemed to threaten him next, human, Galen, or member of his own family.

Zantes realized that her word had had no effect on Anto, and that, in any case, a woman's word was useless here. Burke stepped closer to Virdon and conferred with His companion. "Alan," he said, "what are the odds that you can do it? Are you sure that you can pull this off?"

Virdon stared at Anto for a moment, considering. In the many weeks since their space vehicle had crashed back on Earth, but so far in their own future, the two humans had been called upon to live by their wits, to recreate so much that they had taken for granted in their own lives before. "No," said Virdon slowly, "I'm not sure. But I *am* sure that this expectant mother will die if she isn't helped."

"I like the odds better your way," said Burke. "Get ready to operate, Doc, I'm taking a hostage…"

Before Virdon could reply, Burke whirled around. Anto swiveled uncertainly, pointing his fork first at Virdon, then at Burke. Burke spun and grabbed young Remus off the floor in one quick motion. "Come on, *bellboy*," said Burke to the young ape. And the dark-haired human lunged to the far side of the area with him, grabbing a corn knife from the wall where he saw it hanging. Burke held the knife to Remus' throat. There were shrieks of protest from Zantes and Jillia, who were uncertain still of Burke's intent. Anto started toward Burke with his pitchfork, then held back for fear of his young brother's life.

"Good boy, Pete," said Virdon, wondering whether the ploy would work or not. There were only two of them— Galen was still too weak to be helpful in a fight—against a family of angry apes, each of whom was no doubt stronger than a single human being. If nothing else, Burke had bought some precious time, at least until Polar and Anto realized that there was no genuine threat.

"Now you just put that pitchfork down, Anto," said Burke, holding Remus up off the floor, the corn knife pressed tightly against the young ape's throat. "Or your baby brother is never going to live to see his own baby bull born." Burke turned to Virdon and nodded. "Get to work, Doc," he said. "I can't hold the lieutenant here all night."

Anto dropped the fork in temporary defeat, almost numb with anguish. He stumbled back to the bell that Remus had dropped during Burke's sudden attack; Anto fell to his knees, and picked up the ceramic object. Virdon took a quick survey of the scene; Polar, Zantes, and Jillia were concerned only with Remus' safety. No one at all was watching the blond human. Virdon hurried into the stall with the cow.

Galen wiped the sweat from his brow, stinging droplets of which had fallen into his large, intelligent eyes. He felt as though he were about to fall any second, but then Anto or Polar would capture him, and each side would have a prisoner, weakening the chances of the humans and himself. He forced himself to stay erect. He hobbled the few steps to Anto and looked down. "You want it to be a bull, Anto," he said kindly. "Ring the bell."

Galen's idea was that the rhythmic action would remove hostile thoughts from the young ape's mind, that Anto would be so caught up in his hopes that he would not do anything to disturb Virdon's desperate work. Galen discovered that Anto was not so easily distracted. "You won't get away," said Anto through clenched teeth. "When this is over, if I don't kill you, the police will. I won't lie to them again."

And then, slowly, regularly, Anto began the ringing of the bell.

* * *

Outside the barn, beyond the limits of Polar's farm, along a rural road, the galloping horses of the mounted Patrol gorillas, Barga the officer, and Lupuk the soldier, came closer and closer to their goal, riding at ominous speed. They knew what was waiting for them at the end of their journey, and they both knew that it was a rare opportunity for rustically posted guards such as themselves.

Inside the barn, Virdon was discussing the problem with the cow. He pushed gently on both sides of the animal; each time, Virdon received a pain-filled grunt in reply. "I'm sorry, girl," he said. "Okay, sweetheart, now I'm going to do my best for you. And I want you to do your best for me, eh?"

Burke held Remus in a bear-hug grasp with arms strong by human standards, but terribly weak according to the physical prowess of the average ape. Even Remus, only half-grown, might well have bested Burke in a wrestling match, if the young ape had thought of it. Only the corn knife at his throat prevented Remus from trying to escape. He did not know that Burke was not actually threatening. "Hey," said Burke, "come on. Forget the bedside manner. Get to work."

Virdon looked up, realizing that everyone else in the barn was involved in the situation, in one way or another. Even worse for the others, they could do nothing but watch and pray.

Remus looked up at Burke protestingly. He spoke in a soft voice. "Don't hold me so tight!" he said. "I'm not going anywhere. I want to see!"

Burke looked down at his young captive with surprise. Remus was much like Burke himself had been as a boy; of course, Burke had forgotten exactly what that had meant, and it made him feel strange to see himself reflected in this shaggy ape youth. "Huh?" asked Burke.

"I'm on your side, you dumb human," said Remus in a whisper. "I want to *see*…"

Burke felt a sense of guilt over the way he had manhandled Remus just a few moments before; but then, he told himself, at the time it was the only move open to them. Now he felt some responsibility, particularly at the display of trust that Remus had evidenced in him. He tried to cover his emotions with brusqueness. "All right, lieutenant," he said, "you watch." Burke turned his own head away. "I get a little queasy in the operating room."

Polar motioned for Zantes and Jillia to stay back; he walked to the cow's stall with cautious curiosity. Virdon was already working. Polar turned to Galen with a worried question. "Do you know if he can do this?" asked the farmer. "Can he instruct the cow in the birthing of her calf?"

There was a pause; even Galen was a little uncertain about the possibility. But he was wise enough to realize that the thing that was most needed was a little reassurance. "He's made a needle that can see directions, even on a cloudy night. I think he can… direct a calf into the world."

On the road that ran by Polar's farm, in the opposite direction from Barga and Lupuk, two more gorillas, uniformed and fierce, were traveling on horseback at an easy walk. One of these gorillas noticed something interesting ahead of them on the road. He stood in his stirrups for a better look, then pointed one gloved hand. Both gorillas reined up.

"A mounted Patrol," said one of the gorillas. "They must be from some outpost nearby." He was about to kick up his horse to ride to meet the other two gorillas.

"Stay!" barked the other gorilla, evidently the first soldier's superior. "Sit erect! You are from headquarters."

The soldier was shamefaced. "Yes, sir," he said.

The headquarters officer studied the Patrol gorillas as they approached. "Field troops," he said, musing to himself. "Stupid sort." He turned to his junior companion. "Straighten that mane," he ordered. "Hold those reins up."

The soldier wanted to say something. but there was nothing to be said—nothing safely, that is, except, "Yes, sir."

And then Urko, for that was who the officer from headquarters was, started slowly ahead, followed by his gorilla guardsman. The two moved with a certain air of a general and his aide about to strut commandingly into an infantry outpost at the front.

By this time, Remus was standing a pace *away* from Burke; the ape youngster was watching the scene in the cow stall intently, craning his head to see better. Suddenly Burke realized that their younger son was holding the corn knife, idly, harmlessly.

Zantes and Jillia noticed that Remus was free. They sensed that he was never really in danger from Burke. They smiled to each other but said nothing to disturb the uneasy truce. They glanced at Anto, who did not yet realize that his brother was no longer a hostage.

"How is it?" asked Burke anxiously.

Virdon's face was drenched with perspiration, as he labored with his task. "Worse, than I thought at first," he said.

"Well, for crying out loud," said Burke in some exasperation, "how bad is *that*?"

"Settle for *twice* as bad," said Virdon.

Burke's face twisted with his own inner pain. He looked like a survivor trapped on a mid-ocean raft that was slowly, inexorably sinking. "Just a quiet little bar in Galveston," he whispered to himself. He stole a look at Anto. "With a bell over the door…"

Urko and his soldier sat astride their mounts, haughtily awaiting the arrival of the two Patrol riders, who were approaching at a fast gallop.

As they met, the rural Patrol gorillas reined up, ready with angry words at the two gorillas who dared to block their road. Before their harsh words could be uttered, they recognized the uniforms of their superiors. All at once, they who had almost autonomous control over the country district, became submissive.

"Sir!" cried Barga.

"I am Urko," said the general. "Headquarters."

Both of the rural Patrol gorillas became almost rigid with military respect. Their surprise at meeting the supreme commander of all gorilla military and police forces was so great that all they could do was repeat, "Sir!" Urko's junior officer basked in the reflected glory which was his solely because of his propinquity to the great Urko.

"Your horses are lathered," said Urko quietly. "For what reason have they been worked so hard?"

Barga took the initiative in answering. "Escaped bonded humans, sir," he said. He nodded to Lupuk. "The Patrol rider here thinks that he spotted one on a farm near here."

"Yes, sir," said Lupuk proudly. "Standing under a stream of water." A quick glance from Barga told Lupuk that he had spoken out of turn, and Lupuk quieted again, chastened.

"How far?" asked Urko.

"We're almost there now, sir," said Barga.

"We're hunting two escaped humans and a defector," said Urko casually. "The defector is an enemy of the state, and the humans are dangerous."

"Well, sir," said Barga doubtfully, "I can't be certain that—"

Urko interrupted the local officer with a haughty sneer. "If there are doubts," he said, "I will have them. After we've had a look. Lead the way."

"Yes, sir," said Barga. With the local Patrol gorillas in the lead, the four galloped off in the direction of Polar's farm.

Inside Polar's barn, Virdon's face was completely covered with perspiration. He had worked continuously for a long time, but now he wore a large smile. The others crowded around to see the reason.

Polar came to the cow's stall first, his heart beating loudly, the blood rushing in his ears. It was the first time in many years that the ape farmer felt anything close to fear. When he saw what Virdon had done, his eyes widened with disbelief.

Galen struggled with his weakened leg and his crutch, and stood next to Polar by the stall. He, too, looked at the result of Virdon's pressure operation. His reaction, though he knew Virdon well and understood the blond astronaut's facility with areas of science unknown to the ape culture, was also one of amazement.

Burke did not step as close as the others. He stood slightly apart, his eyes closed, as he rehearsed in his imagination the worst that could have happened.

Maaaaaah!

The sound of a baby calf. Burke opened his eyes; at that moment, the stillness of the barn was broken by a second *maaaaaahh* of a different pitch, the sound of a *second* calf!

No one moved for the briefest of instants, too astounded and too awestruck to react. Then, one by one, they all rushed to the stall, in delight and wonder. All, that is, except Anto, who hung back, too frightened and too nervous to see for himself.

In the stall, one calf was lying, the other was already just trying to stand—two baby bull calves, *twins*! Zantes and Jillia were half-crying, half-giggling in relieved amazement. Remus stared with wide-eyed wonder. Polar and Galen exchanged pleased looks as Virdon, exhausted, stood and wiped his hands on a piece of the homespun material that Zantes handed to him.

Slowly, everyone turned to look at Anto, who had stopped tolling his bell. The ape youth still looked down at it, not yet venturing a look toward the stall. "Come on, Anto," said Burke in a friendly manner, "take a look. It's all yours."

Anto stood cautiously, his body obviously weary from the long days of sustained grief. He staggered slowly toward the stall.

As the others backed away, for this was Anto's big moment, he pushed through them. Polar, Zantes, Jillia, and Remus were indescribably happy for him. The bull calves meant the start of his own, independent life, something that, through the whim of fate, had been denied to him for too long a time. Anto looked at the twin bull calves, and he blinked in disbelief. Then, as ecstatic delight swept over him, he cried. "He looks like he found a sweepstakes ticket stuck in the bottom of a sugar bowl," said Burke happily. "Well, go on, Anto, cash it in. It's a winner." The elder son of Polar fell on his knees near his calves, holding first one small head then the other, crying, laughing, moaning with the greatest single pleasure of his entire life…

Burke turned to Virdon, taking advantage of this moment of relative solitude amongst the scene of confusion. "When you said that it was twice as bad," he began. Then he just shook his head. "You're a genius, Virdon. I'll never knock a farm boy, again. Twins! I hear that it's all in the wrist."

Virdon laughed; it was so much easier for all of them now. He shuddered to think what would have happened if he had worked as hard, and the calves had been heifers. Virdon's life, surely, would have been forfeit, and probably Burke's as well, and Galen's, and the matter would have simply been one of chromosome matching many months before… "They're both bulls," said Virdon, suppressing a shudder. "I think the bell ringing may have had something to do with it."

Outside the barn, independent of the jubilation within, the four gorilla horsemen came stomping and shouting into the area of the farmyard at a gallop, shaking the very ground with the thunder of their arrival.

Jillia ran to the door of the barn and peered out. As her family and friends looked up, frozen momentarily at the sound of pounding hooves and the snorting of horses, Jillia turned from the door. There was only fear on her face.

"Police," said Jillia, her voice constricted with anxiety. "All kinds of police."

Polar thought quickly. There was not much time. "Hide," he said to Burke and Virdon. "Hurry, back there." He turned to his family. "Come outside, quickly." Anto hesitated, the intense emotions of the previous moments still dulling his thoughts. "Anto," said Polar urgently, "come."

Polar, Remus, Zantes, and Jillia headed out of the barn door, into the farmyard, while Galen, hobbling, was helped by Burke and Virdon into a back, hay-filled area of the barn.

Polar and his family, all except Anto, now walked with the best expressions and whispered conversations of surprise that they could muster. They met the mounted gorillas in the farmyard.

Barga, the chief of the rural mounted Patrol gorillas, took charge of the situation. After all, until Urko's arrival, this had been a local affair. Even now, Urko's reasons had remained secret. Barga shrugged. "Polar!" he commanded in a louder voice than necessary: he wanted to impress Urko.

Lupuk, the Patrol rider, pointed at the head of the household. "That is Polar," he said. Barga gave his soldier a brief look of scorn; of *course* the ape was Polar; who else could be the patriarch of this farm family?

Urko and his junior officer sat stiffly a few yards back on their horses with supreme authority, while the regional gorillas put on their display of toughness.

Zantes spoke first, though Polar had been summoned. "Why do you come riding through here?" she asked, in the tones of the eternally put-upon female, a role that ill-suited her, but which her quickness of mind told her was correct in this situation. "Enough racket to shake the turnips from the ground!"

"Shut up, female!" shouted Barga.

The now-familiar creak of the barn door interrupted the bewildering confrontation for a moment. The family and the mounted gorillas turned their attention to the barn. Anto emerged and joined Polar and the family.

Barga sighed inaudibly. He knew that, in front of so august a personage as General Urko, the important thing was to conclude the affair with efficiency and dispatch.

"You," said Barga, pointing unwaveringly at Polar, "you are hiding escaped bonded humans, Polar!"

"No! That's a lie," said Polar, not raising his voice. "*He* was through here before." Polar pointed to Lupuk.

Barga saw that the circumstance could quickly get out of hand. *If* Lupuk were correct, and there was no definite proof that he was, then Polar would act precisely the way he was acting. If Lupuk were incorrect, then there were no escaped humans, and Polar would behave the same way. "Silence!" shouted Barga. That single word was a great method for restoring order, but not for restoring reason.

Lupuk spoke up again, diffidently this time. He pointed to the shower by the side of the barn. "He was standing there, under that... thing."

Slowly Barga turned his attention to the contraption that the rider indicated. Urko and his officer deigned to look that way, also. Polar and family worried: the shower was definitely an unapelike device. It clearly seemed to prove the presence of humans.

Anto stared at the shower thoughtfully, realizing that the Patrol rider must have spied on them when Burke or Virdon would have been clearly visible. He knew that if Lupuk's word were believed, then Polar and his family were in grave danger.

Lupuk reinforced his statement. He pointed again toward the shower, this time urging his horse toward the shower stall. "One of them was standing under there," he said, "in a kind of rain."

At this point, at this most tense of crises, Anto cracked the brittle atmosphere with a doubled-up laugh! His laughter not only caught the mounted gorillas by surprise, but his own family as well. There was a moment when the family didn't really understand Anto's unleashed feelings of amusement—was it a delayed reaction to the birth of the bull calves?

Barga frowned. Nothing like this had been covered in his training period in the central ape city. No one had ever hinted that his command would include humiliation in front of the commander-in-chief. "What's so funny, farmer?" he asked. "You won't laugh when Polar is hanging from the end of a rope."

Anto tried to explain, but his laughter was so intense and so unrelenting that he couldn't explain for a moment. "It was *me!*" he said at last, gasping for breath. "He saw me!"

And Anto laughed again. He walked to a large tub of freshly stone-ground flour near the wall of the small granary. "We are a poor family," he said, indicating the other members of Polar's tribe. He looked calmly from Barga to Lupuk, and then to Urko himself, whom Anto did not recognize. "Would you deny us what little fun we can make for ourselves?"

Anto reached into the tub of flour for the large wooden scoop buried in deep. He started dousing himself with the flour, covering his shaggy ape body and upper torso, then even his head with the flour. Loads of it puffed over him, making him almost white.

Then Anto put the scoop back in the tub and walked into the very center of the farmyard. "See?" he asked. "See? I make the family laugh. I'm white, like a human, see?"

Polar and his family laughed, obliging their son's plan and, even, with genuine amusement at the ridiculous sight.

Anto strutted in front of the frowning, uniformed gorillas, oblivious to the danger he was putting himself in. "Then I walk around," he said. "Like a straight-necked goose... like a human, see?"

Anto started his parade, his neck and back straight

like he had seen humans walk. It was uncomfortable. But even the mounted gorillas started to laugh.

Anto was encouraged by his performance and by the reaction it was getting. It brought the natural comedian in him, a quality that had been long submerged by the rigors of his farm existence. "I think I'll have some meat," he said, mimicking the speech of a human being. "I'll cook it *good*! Ha, ha, ha!"

As the gorillas laughed at this imitation, along with Polar and his family, Anto sought to nail down the one last piece of evidence. He walked slowly to the shower, while the laughter of the gorillas and his family echoed in the otherwise still afternoon. "See," he said, "this is what he saw. My dressing room, where I take the makeup off…"

Anto hurried into the shower, realizing that if he failed here, the whole episode would have gone for nothing. He was a little chagrined to realize that he wasn't sure how to work the shower. He saw the cord, and pulled it. With a gasp of surprise, he stood beneath a sudden shower of cold water, drenched. He was, as Lupuk had reported, standing under a kind of "stream".

Everyone in the farmyard had stopped laughing, except the lowest ranked Patrol gorilla, who continued his foolish giggling until his officer shouted at him. "Fool!" cried Barga.

The Patrol gorilla stopped immediately, embarrassment and anxiety evident in his expression. The two Patrol gorillas began to ride off as they saw the now normal but soaking wet Anto step from the shower. But Urko was always the thorough policeman. He turned to his own junior officer.

"Search the barn!" he ordered. "Eyes that deceive once… can deceive twice." The General directed a scathing glance at the horrified Lupuk.

The junior officer jumped from his horse and strode officially by the Polar family into the barn. Anto, wiping his face with one of the rough towels, looked worriedly at Polar. The father only shrugged.

Urko, always a menacing figure in his uniform and on his obviously valuable thoroughbred horse, rode around the meek Polar family in a circle, waiting. He watched the ape family in a superior, threatening way. "A clown, eh?" he said to Anto with a sneer. "We'll see."

Just as the sound of two "maaaaas" from the young calves came from the barn, all eyes turned to the door. There was a tense, expectant hush. The junior officer emerged from the barn, shaking his head. "No humans here, sir," he announced. "Two brand new calves, though. They would have been eaten if there were humans around." The subordinate remounted his horse.

Urko rode up to Barga and spoke in low tones to the officer of the rural Patrol. Both gorillas eyes were on Lupuk, and it was evident to everyone what the subject of their conversation was. "Demote that Patrolman," said Urko gruffly. "He has made fools of authority."

"Yes, sir," said Barga, glad at least that General Urko had let him off without any punishment.

Urko and his officer rode off at a high gallop, turning onto the narrow rode that ran by Polar's farm. This time, they took the lead, followed by the Patrol riders. As the huge, pounding sound of the hoofbeats died away, Barga was heard cursing the stupidity of his subordinate, Lupuk.

The Polar family gave a collective sigh of relief when the gorilla force departed. Meanwhile, Burke, Virdon, and Galen appeared from the barn to join them, the clinging stray straws revealing where they had hidden.

Anto walked toward Virdon, his head hung in shame

for his earlier actions, he said, "Virdon, I… I'm sorry for how I acted to you in there. I just couldn't… I just couldn't *believe*." There was a painful pause. "Thank you," he said at last. "Thank you very much."

Virdon waved Anto's apology away. "I watched through a knothole, Anto," he said, smiling. "And if I hadn't seen it for myself, I wouldn't have believed that, either." Virdon clapped the young ape on a shoulder: "I'd say we're about even," he said.

Remus, the precocious youngster, walked boldly up to Virdon. Anto continued speaking. "Will you show me," he asked, "you know, what I must do, in case some day… when you are not around."

Remus laughed. He had watched the entire operation, and he considered himself an expert. "Just ask me, Anto. I know. I memorized the entire thing."

Anto and Virdon glanced down at the young Remus. Neither of them had been aware at the time of Remus's place in the crisis. Soon, both Anto and Virdon broke out into big, astonished smiles. Remus walked about proudly.

Many days later, a quite spry Galen, accompanied by Virdon and Burke, was bidding goodbye to the Polar family. Burke carried a sack which had been given him by Zantes.

"I put some bread in there," she said. "With that solid gold milk on it."

It was an awkward moment for all of them, as farewells so often are. Burke, Virdon, and Galen had had certainly enough practice in the last few months. How Burke would have liked to find some nice place to settle, and how Virdon would like to find some nice place that offered a clue to returning to his own time and his own family. And Galen? Galen just wanted to *learn*, and this alone made him an enemy of the ape society.

Jillia turned to Galen. "Be careful of the leg," she said solicitously. "I don't want you coming back here and laying around... for me to wait on."

Galen smiled. "Oh?" he said. Jillia couldn't meet his look. She lowered her eyes, but a small smile played on her lips, too.

Virdon, Burke, and Polar stood aside, while Virdon checked his pocket compass. "Polar," said Burke, looking at the blisters that had grown on his hands, "you've been an interesting host, *interesting,* that's the word. Better than the most expensive Florida health resort. Worked off those spare pounds and inches."

"Not many of those to start with," said Virdon dryly.

"Where will you go?" asked Polar, knowing that the humans' words were not supposed to be understood, at least not by him.

Virdon looked at the compass. "We don't really know." he said. "West. That used to be a good direction. We'll try it again." He put the compass in his pocket.

Anto joined the small group, his left hand stuck out in imitation of the gesture that humans performed at moments like these. Virdon did not correct Anto: whether the ape offered the left hand or the right, the meaning was clear. Virdon grasped it warmly. Then Anto shook hands with Burke and Galen. "Thank you, Virdon," said Anto. "I will never forget you."

Virdon gave Anto a friendly smile. "I'm not going to forget you right away either, Anto," he said.

Virdon put a hand on Anto's shoulder, pleased that the ape didn't shrink from this contact any longer. Then, over the peaceful though somewhat sad scene, came the sound of two "maaaaaas", distantly, from the barn.

"I've named my bulls," announced Anto. "One is

named Virdon, the other Burke."

Burke cleared his throat, the prelude to a mock-serious revelation. Virdon laughed and waited to hear what his fellow astronaut would say. "Just one thing," said Burke. "Be careful of that bull named Burke around the females. Those heifers won't get a moment's rest."

Virdon, Galen, Anto, and Polar laughed. Burke tried to keep a straight face, but he, too, joined in the laughter. "Goodbye," said Virdon solemnly, "goodbye."

Burke and Galen added their goodbyes now, and the three fugitives walked away from the front of the small farmhouse where they had first come for help so many days before.

On one of the fields behind the house, early the next day, the first bright spears of sunlight picked out the turning blades of the windmill's wheel. Polar and Remus stood watching it, wondering how far away the two humans and their chimpanzee companion had traveled since the evening before.

Polar and Remus were pleased by the sight of the strange device that was malting the wind work for them. As their attention turned from the windmill to the house, where Zantes had finished cooking breakfast, they heard the familiar pounding of horses' hooves on the hard-packed dirt road.

Lupuk, the Patrol gorilla, rode up to them and stopped. The uniformed ape did not exchange any words of greeting with Polar and his younger son; indeed, the Patrol rider glared down with his superiority restored from the beating it had taken the day before. Polar, too, offered no words of pleasantry; he had won out over this emblem of their oppression by the gorilla forces. Lupuk looked up at the odd structure that towered over them.

"What's this?" he asked, in a voice that threatened nothing specific.

"A windmill," said Polar.

"Where did it come from?" asked the Patrol gorilla.

Remus looked smug. "I built it," he said.

The Patrol rider gave the youngster a disbelieving look. Polar noticed. "He's very bright," said the ape farmer.

The rider took another look at the thing and snorted. "Humph! If *you* were bright, old farmer," he said, "you'd keep him at work in the fields, not building these... these toys to play in the wind."

With this admonition, feeling even more superior, the Patrol rider spurred his horse and hurried off.

Polar waited until Lupuk had gone. Then he pointed to the low-lying field that had been drained to feed the ditch the windmill was pumping from. "Next spring," said Polar thoughtfully, "we'll plant that new field the humans made for us. It will be good, rich earth, as they said."

"And we'll plant the best seeds... Like Virdon said... huh?" said Remus.

"Yes," said Polar slowly. "We'll try it. The best seeds this time."

For a few moments more, the two apes stood staring over their tiny domain. The windmill would remind them forever of the bizarre experience they had with those strange humans. As Polar and Remus began walking toward the farmhouse. Polar realized that the corn was not the only "best seeds" to be planted. Already a different kind of seed had been cultivated. It had sprouted, and grown, and flowered within their minds and hearts. Virdon, Burke, and Galen had done their work well.

ESCAPE TO TOMORROW

"The Surgeon"
based on the teleplay by Barry Oringer

"The Deception"
based on the teleplay by Anthony Lawrence
& Joe Ruby & Ken Spears

Based on characters from *Planet of the Apes*

For Milkwood, Trout, and Fish, my best friends among the non-hominoid chordates.

THE SURGEON

1

It was a day in late spring, when the light green of the trees had already changed to the dark, healthy color that would remain through the summer. During the early part of the morning the sky was covered with haze, but that burned off quickly, and the sun beamed down unobstructed for many days in succession. Rain fell infrequently, and when it did, it was a welcome relief from the temperatures which were already climbing steadily toward the upper limits of tolerance.

In this pleasant season, two men and a chimpanzee were hurrying along the dry bed of a stream, between steeply eroded banks. The bottom on which they walked was embedded with many large stones, which made their progress difficult and painful; still, they continued in the path of the now-dead rivulet, out of sight of anyone who might be watching from a distance.

The men were tall and strong, darkly tanned by the sun and their constant exposure to it. It was evident from their appearance that they had traveled long. They wore roughly made clothing, completely utilitarian, without a thought for style or decoration. Their companion, the chimpanzee, was shorter than they, but heavier and stockier. His movements and his great arms and shoulders indicated strength superior to the humans, yet he followed them, well behind the pace set by the men.

The two humans were distinguished between themselves: one was tall, with dark hair and brown eyes; the other was broader with blond hair and blue eyes. At this moment, the blond man was leading the way. He looked up at the banks of the stream, which rose above his head on both sides. Beyond the lip was a dense forest. Everything seemed peaceful, calm and harmless; the blond man shook his head. He had had that same feeling before...

Ahead of the trio, perhaps a quarter of a mile along their route, two uniformed gorillas sat waiting on horseback. They were back a short distance from the gully, near the trees; they could easily watch the progress of the men and the ape without being seen. They waited in silence as their quarry hurried nearer and nearer.

The sun rose above the tops of the trees and began to beat down on the backs of the three fugitives. The blond man stopped and wiped the back of his hand across his brow. The dark-haired man caught up to him and stood, panting. Neither spoke for a moment. The only sound was the raucous cry of a jay. The chimpanzee, his face drenched with sweat, joined them. "You know something, Alan?" said the angular, dark man. "We've been following this stream long enough to win a merit badge. Where are we supposed to be going?"

The blond man chewed his lip for a few seconds. He sighed. "Galen says there's a secret hiding place somewhere along one of these gullies." The human nodded toward Galen, the chimpanzee. "He used to hide there when he was playing hooky from school."

"That's great," said the dark-haired man sarcastically. "It's terrific, except that the truant officers weren't coming after him armed with rifles." He dug his heel in the dry, hard-packed dirt of the stream bed. "At least, there could be a taco stand along the way here."

The chimpanzee stared at the human, perplexed. At last he shook his head. "Burke," he said, "you know, I have difficulty sometimes understanding these cultural references. 'Taco stand.' Is that some sort of emergency aid station?" He looked at the dark man, Burke, who just stared, repressing a smile. Galen turned to the blond man, who also refused to answer. At last, Galen gave up in frustration. Sometimes, these humans acted just like the inferior animals the apes believed them to be. There was nothing more to be said. The three moved on, the two men laughing quietly over their private joke, Galen following slowly and clumsily.

A few minutes passed silently as the trio picked its way along the dry watercourse. About a hundred yards ahead of them, still undiscovered and invisible to the fugitives, the two gorillas waited, their rifles at the ready, as their unknowing quarry approached. As the mounted apes waited for their targets to come into closer range, one of the horses, groping for a surer foothold near the edge of the cliff, danced around and unloosed some gravel, which slid down the embankment with a rattle that seemed desperately loud to the gorillas. They urged their horses to the very edge, in case the two humans and the chimpanzee tried to run away; then the gorillas would at least have a better shot at them. The horses moved nervously near the edge.

The rattle of the stones went unnoticed by the trio. It was a sound completely in harmony with the surroundings; they moved on along the stream bed, still unaware of their ambushers.

One of the gorillas began to prepare for the coming conflict. It would be short, he knew, particularly if he and his partner shot quickly and accurately. He raised his rifle with one hand, steadying his horse with the other. The horse settled down a little, and the gorilla dropped the reins. Now, if the stupid animal would just remain still... The gorilla aimed the rifle at the blond human's chest and began to tighten his finger in the final, fatal squeeze.

While the uniformed gorilla prepared to fire, his horse shied away from the precipice. One hoof slipped as the gravel gave way beneath it. The gorilla lurched to one side, suddenly fearful of being thrown and falling down the steep cliff. His rifle fired accidentally; the bullet went wild, tearing through the dense foliage across the gully with a thunderous crash.

The humans and the chimpanzee looked fearfully around, trying to find their attackers. Galen, the chimpanzee, reacted first. "This way!" he cried. The two humans saw the gorillas at the same moment and ran after the scurrying chimpanzee.

They turned and raced for a narrow, brush-covered gully that opened into the stream bed. The gorillas tried to follow on horseback, but their horses shied away from the steep drop. The animals had become almost completely uncontrollable, and the apes jerked the reins roughly, muttering curses. Burke and Galen reached the small tributary gully first, and the blond man brought up the rear. The gorillas, seeing their quarry escaping, fired from the edge of the bank. The blond man cried out, stumbled and fell. Burke turned at his friend's cry; he saw what had happened, and rushed to help his fellow human. Arduously, Burke dragged the blond man into the narrow, concealed gully, out of line of the gorillas' fire. Once safely there, Burke helped his friend to his feet, but the blond man's legs buckled beneath him.

"It's my back," said the man hoarsely. "I can't move."

"Come on, Virdon," said Burke, "you can do it." He spoke without conviction, as he watched Virdon writhe in pain on the ground. Galen pointed back the way they had come; Burke could see the gorillas dismounting and following on foot. He bent down and picked up Virdon, slinging the blond man over his shoulder in a fireman's carry. Galen, who had been frantically searching the nearby terrain, pointed to a steep brush and rock-covered rise.

"Up there," said the chimpanzee.

Panting from exertion and anxiety, Burke and Galen struggled to the top of the rise. Burke supported Virdon, and Galen looked around, trying to remember the details of the surrounding landscape.

"All right, Galen," said Burke worriedly, "what do we do now?"

The chimpanzee did not answer immediately, but continued his scrutiny of the neighborhood. His apparent disregard of their danger infuriated the short-tempered human. "Come on, Galen," said Burke, "this isn't a post-prom picnic, you know."

"What do you want me to do?" asked the chimpanzee. "Shall I panic?" Burke did not answer; he knew the chimpanzee was right. "Keep going down the path as far as you can," said Galen. "I'll catch up."

The tall, slender human slung Virdon more comfortably across his shoulder. Burke said nothing to Galen; they had been together for a long while, and had gone through too many dangerous situations, too many times when each depended on the other, for an apology to be necessary. Galen understood Burke's attitude and his real feelings. The human's actions and words were one of the chief reasons that Galen remained a member of the party, instead of striking off on his own; Burke's odd ways piqued Galen's scientific curiosity.

Burke carried Virdon, disappearing with him into the dense growth. Galen poked at some boulders, using a thick branch as a lever. Just then, the gorillas appeared in the gully below him. They spotted Galen, and began firing at him. The chimpanzee crouched behind one of the larger boulders until the shots stopped, and the gorillas had to reload. Then Galen replied by sending the boulder toppling down toward them, creating a miniature rockslide. Galen turned and ran away, not waiting to see the result of his strategy; but he was satisfied by the gorillas' panicky cries that he had been successful.

Later, when Galen had rejoined Burke and Virdon, and they had hurried on, away from the gorilla patrol to safety, they stopped and rested. They built a small cooking fire near a stream of fresh water. There was a rocky cliff above them, protecting one side, and the running water protected another. The only remaining approach was through a dense forest, and Galen and Burke agreed that it would be difficult for the mounted gorillas to sneak up on them from that direction.

Galen crouched by the fire, lifting a small pot of water off the fire. He stirred some herbs into the water. Near him, in a sheltered spot outside a cave in the cliff wall, Virdon was being tended to by Burk. Virdon's back was bandaged with cloth, but none of the three friends had much confidence in the efficacy of their treatment so far.

Each had ideas about what to do next. Burke left Virdon and went to the fire. He squatted down and looked at the herbs Galen had used to make his tea.

"This looks familiar," he said. Burke crushed some of the dried flowers in his hand and smelled them. "This looks like chamomile," he said.

Galen looked up from the tea that he was brewing. He shrugged. "I don't know what it is," said the chimpanzee. "It grows wild all over the countryside. My mother used to give it to us when we were sick. It was very effective, as I recall."

Burke shook his head wonderingly. Sometimes he couldn't understand how the world had lost so much knowledge since the days when humans had ruled it. Burke and Virdon had crashed back to Earth from their mission of space exploration, and found themselves two thousand years in the future; so much had changed that the world was completely unrecognizable. It wasn't only that apes were now dominant. There were other differences, too, and almost invariably, they were for the worse.

"Chamomile for a bullet wound!" said Burke dubiously. "That's like prescribing chicken soup for a broken leg."

Galen paid no attention. The ape gave Virdon the drink; the blond man took a few sips. Burke stood and turned to watch his friend. "How's the pain?" asked Burke.

"Not too bad," said Virdon. "Except when I try to stand up. The bullet must be pressing on a nerve."

"Well," said Burke thoughtfully, "we both had pretty good training in emergency first aid during our astronaut indoctrination. Maybe I can dig the bullet out."

Galen looked up at Burke, a curious look on his

face. He had seen both Burke and Virdon do many unexplainable and wonderful things, but he knew that there was a limit to their knowledge. "That sounds dangerous," said the chimpanzee.

Burke looked thoughtful. He realized the gravity of his previous suggestion, and he knew that there was indeed a very definite limit to his abilities. He suddenly didn't like the idea of having to perform surgery on his best friend, especially when he had neither training nor aptitude for such an operation. "He's right," said Burke to Virdon. "We're going to have to get you to a hospital."

Virdon moved slowly, trying to change position so that he'd rest more comfortably. The effort made him wince with the pain. "What hospital?" he asked. "Our Blue Cross expired twenty centuries ago."

Galen realized that Burke had come close to the true solution, although the human didn't have any idea of how to proceed. "There *is* a medical center on the outskirts of Central City," said the chimpanzee.

Virdon looked up at Burke and shook his head. The idea was too fantastic. They had spent many months trying to evade the clutches of the apes. Now Galen was suggesting that they return the way they had come.

"That chamomile must be going to your head," said Burke. "If we walk into an ape hospital, we can forget about reading any more continued stories. The gorillas would be all over the place before we filled out the registration forms."

Galen listened to Burke's words, and then raised one hand impatiently. "I don't think that this is the time to indulge your humor," he said. "Not with Virdon hurt. After all, he is not the only one in danger. We are all threatened by the possibility of recapture."

"I wasn't being funny," said Burke sourly. "How do you expect us to get into an ape hospital without the apes noticing?"

Galen spoke softly. "I know the chief surgeon at the Center. She'll help us."

"But Galen," said Virdon, his voice filled with suppressed agony, "we're well-known as dangerous enemies of the state."

Galen shook his head. How often had they made suggestions or planned a course of action, and he had bowed to their decisions? And now, when Galen knew the best thing, they joined together to deprecate his judgment. How like a human being that was! "Kira will not know," he said. "She's a physician, she doesn't care about politics. Most of the people at the Center probably never heard of you. And even if Kira knew, she wouldn't turn her back on someone in trouble."

Virdon tried to raise himself up, interested in the possibility. The effort was too much, and he fell back against the rock wall with a grunt. "What makes you so sure?" he asked.

"We were very close once," said Galen hesitantly. He did not like to disclose the details of his private past. "In fact, we were going to be married. Things didn't work out. But we're still the best of friends."

Neither Virdon nor Burke spoke for a long moment. The crackling of the fire and the evening noises of birds and insects filled the small camp area. There was a feeling of peace about the place, a feeling that each of the three companions knew was entirely false, one that could explode with lethal suddenness, with the bellowing, booming attack of a patrol of General Urko's gorillas. Burke looked at Galen, who waited for the humans' decision. At last the dark-haired astronaut spoke up. "It's worth a chance, I guess," he said.

Galen smiled broadly and started speaking before Virdon had a chance to protest; after all, it was Virdon who would be helpless in the situation, and it should be he who made the final choice. Nevertheless, Galen took Burke's words as the binding agreement in the matter. "I know a way back to the Center, along little-used roads," said the chimpanzee. "I won't have any trouble traveling alone. I will consult with Kira, and then we will plan for your arrival. Don't worry. I happen to be an expert in female psychology. I know Kira won't let me down."

"I know we're in trouble, now," said Burke. "Any time any male claims to be an expert with females, I know the situation's hopeless." But before either man could veto the plan, Galen had disappeared into the darkening shadows of the woods.

The next day, Galen arrived at the medical center. It was a compound of buildings on the outskirts of the Central City of the apes. Over the entrance to the main gate, a red and white flag with an ape's head and a row of three red circles fluttered in the warm breeze. The head and the circles symbolized a hospital; the circles represented the three varieties of apes that ruled the world, the orangutans of the governmental bodies, the chimpanzees of the more intellectual positions, and the brutish, warlike gorillas. The same symbol was everywhere about the hospital— on the uniforms of the staff, and on the ambulance carts.

Inside the main building, in a scrub room just off the main surgical theater, Kira, the young female chimpanzee, was washing her hands beneath a running faucet. She was still dressed in her surgical gown. Behind her, other apes on the medical staff were washing up after surgery.

The door to the scrub room opened and a chimpanzee entered. This male chimpanzee was middle-aged, with an easy, confident, subtly arrogant manner. He was sure of his authority and the way he carried himself indicated that he felt there was no interpretation of the world other than his. Kira did not see him as he came in; she was preoccupied and somewhat depressed. The male chimpanzee called her by name. "Kira."

She stopped washing and turned. She was briefly startled, but then she seemed obviously gratified to see the chimpanzee, despite her depression. "Director Leander," she said. "How kind of you to come by." Her voice was glad at his presence, but still worried about something else.

"I watched the operation," said Leander. "You did a brilliant job. I have to congratulate you again on your technique. You are an inspiration to all of us."

"It is an old joke, and a very bad one," said Kira. "Unfortunately, the patient died." She turned away to finish her washing.

Leander crossed the room, smiling indulgently, and put one arm around Kira's shoulders. The female surgeon did not react to his intimate gesture, even though such a show of affection was quite out of place in the hospital. Leander was too wrapped up in his own thoughts to notice that Kira had not responded. "The patient may well have died, but the operation itself was a success," he said. "Look at it this way. The surgical knowledge we learn from these failures will someday help other patients, and other surgeons."

Kira finished washing and turned off the water. She dried her hands and arms on a stiff white towel. "That's not a particularly satisfying philosophy," she said. "Try to comfort the patient's family with that. I'll have to use the conventional apology, and, believe me, it is never easy. It may be a long time since you had to tell someone that their loved one has died on the operating table. Maybe it's been too long."

"Are you angling for my position already, Kira?" asked Leander with a smile. Kira only sighed. There was no way that she was going to get through to him.

"No, of course not," she said. "I just think that you may have lost touch with the personal side of medicine. Everything is a cold and mechanical experiment with you."

Leander smiled again. "Do you think I'm cruel? You can tell me the truth."

"Tell the truth to my employer?" asked Kira with mock astonishment. "I could be fired for such recklessness."

Leander removed his arm from Kira's shoulders. "Only a fool would fire his best and most beautiful surgeon," he said. There was a short pause. "I'll see you at the conference tonight, won't I?" he asked at last.

Kira looked at him, a little confused. "What conference?" she asked. There were always so many meetings to attend, and so much paper work to claim her attention, besides her regular rounds and surgical work, that she often had to be reminded by her secretary of appointments. But the secretary had said nothing about a departmental conference for that evening.

Leander tried to look serious as he answered her question. It was apparent to Kira that Leander was playing one of his transparent jokes. "It's just a private lecture I'm giving," he said. "On the therapeutic virtues of vegetable casserole and apricot wine. I'm holding it in my apartment, at eight."

"Is attendance mandatory?" asked Kira.

Leander laughed softly. As far as he knew, she had not guessed the truth yet. "Only for you," he said, and laughed again.

"Well," said Kira, laughing to let Leander know that she finally understood, "in that case, I'll be there." Silently, she wondered how such a likable chimpanzee as Leander could still be as insufferable as he was at times. She touched his arm in a small gesture of affection, and left the scrub room. Leander watched her go with a look of even greater emotion, mingled with self-congratulation about what a witty and sophisticated fellow he was.

Kira headed down the corridor, past numerous bustling hospital personnel. There was the regular ape staff in white uniforms, and a human or two doing menial chores as sweepers and orderlies. Kira did not acknowledge the greetings that she received from them; her thoughts were on the patient she had just lost, and on her duty to the patient's family. She reached a door at the end of the corridor, opened it, and stepped into her office.

When Kira entered the room, it was dark. She crossed to the windows, opened the curtains and let in the light. She stood gazing out of the windows thoughtfully, thinking about many things, thinking about her position, her responsibilities, the honor her success brought her, the pain her failures represented. She thought about Leander, and about others in her life, and about the normal home life she had forsaken for her career. She glanced around her office, at the symbols of that lifestyle she had chosen: desk, table, chairs, cabinets, shelves of primitive medical instruments, books. Kira took off her surgical gown and turned toward the small cupboard. She jumped and uttered a shocked cry when she saw Galen standing in a dimly lit corner.

"Hello, Kira," he said. He did not move. His voice was soft. Kira did hot know whether that was because of his emotions or his fear of discovery.

Kira was still too stunned by Galen's sudden presence to speak. She stared at him for several seconds, holding her gown, one hand still reaching for the door to the cupboard. "Galen!" she said at last. "What are you doing here?"

Galen, too, was overcome by his feelings. He did not know what to do, now that he had accomplished the difficult part of his journey, getting into the hospital compound unrecognized. "I thought that it might be time for my annual checkup," he said in a poor attempt to make light conversation.

"Are you insane?" asked Kira. "You're a criminal—a traitor!"

Kira's words, and the tone of her voice, made Galen uncomfortable. This was certainly not the welcome he had hoped for and he was visibly shaken. "I didn't expect to hear that from you," he said sadly.

Kira shook her head. It was plain to her that Galen hadn't changed much in the long time since their earlier relationship. He hadn't yet learned to accept the consequences of his actions. "What *did* you expect?" she asked, her voice hard and uncompromising.

Galen took a deep breath. He realized that he wouldn't be able to appeal to her as a former friend. He would have to approach her in her capacity as one of the best and most renowned doctors in the ape world. "I need help," he said. There was an uncomfortable pause. "One of my friends is hurt."

Kira looked even more startled than before. She closed the cupboard door after hanging up the surgical gown.

She looked steadily at Galen. "Your friends!" she said. "Don't you think that I know who your friends are? The only friends you have are renegade humans!"

"They're as good as we are, Kira," said Galen quietly.

Kira was even more shocked. "Is that what you've come to?" she asked, outraged. "Putting us on the same level as animals? I shouldn't even be listening to you. I should be calling the police."

Galen pointed to the door, at the gorilla police that lurked beyond it, everywhere in the ape world, under the orders of General Urko, to punish the slightest misstep by citizen or human slave. "They'd kill me," said Galen simply.

Kira moved her mouth, but no words came. She was in the grip of a terrible conflict. She had once been extremely fond of Galen, but she understood that there was a point at which loyalty ended and duty began. Still, she couldn't quite bring herself to summon the gorilla guards. She knew how brutal they were, and how unlucky were the apes and humans who fell into their charge, no matter what the offense. But long years of indoctrination controlled her mind. "They'd be doing justice," she said.

There was a long silence; the hatred in her words hung heavy in the air. Kira had tried to mask that feeling, but it had shone through nonetheless. Her previous affection had been conquered by her revulsion to Galen's notorious behavior.

Galen thought for a few moments, and memories of the happiness he had shared with Kira were prominent in his mind. "I loved you once," he said in a quiet voice. "To hear these words from you now... I'm sorry I came."

Galen shrugged his broad shoulders and turned to leave through the window. Kira called to him, afraid to let him leave, afraid, too, to let him stay. "Galen," she said.

Galen turned around again and waited. He said

nothing. Kira continued, making nervous gestures, her mind in a turmoil of conflict. "You were a decent, law-abiding ape once," she said somberly. "What happened to you?"

Galen remained silent again for several seconds. How could he outline for her all the things he had seen, all the things he had learned, since he had first begun his acquaintance with Virdon and Burke? Could he convince her that the astronauts were as educated—more importantly, as intelligent—as any ape in Central City? Could he hope to tell her of the wonders he had helped the two men perform, of the spirit of comradeship that had grown among them? Because only if he could, could he have the slightest hope of winning Kira's aid. "I had a terrible accident," he said at last. "I collided with the truth: that apes and humans are meant to be equals, not masters and slaves."

Kira's face formed an involuntary frown. She still considered human beings to be less than slaves, to be a form of trainable animal. To her mind Galen was not suggesting that apes raise humans to their level. She thought that he wanted to lower apes to their level. And this idea was entirely repugnant to her. She saw human beings every day, working servile jobs about the hospital. She had not the slightest feeling of fellowship with the creatures, and no desire to extend a benevolent hand to them. "You really believe that?" she asked incredulously.

"Yes," said Galen.

"And to help you, I must help them?"

Galen nodded. "They are my brothers now."

There was another long silence. Then, in a voice filled with anguish and despair Kira said, "I thought I had forgotten you, that I had a chance to find new happiness. I should have known you'd come back to destroy me."

Galen could only stare, the force of her bitter words still stinging his mind. How things had changed, to bring Kira to say such a thing. Galen had had no idea he was so hated by his people and that Kira would share that hatred. He could only stare.

It was growing dark in the wooded area by the stream where Burke and Virdon were camping, waiting for Galen's return. The night was clear, and the stars began to come out; Burke noticed again that the familiar constellations of his former life had changed slightly but noticeably. It was only another reminder that a great deal of time had passed since the fateful day when he and Virdon embarked on their interstellar mission of discovery. He shrugged; he could make a new life in this strange world. It was Virdon who remembered the strong ties that bound him to the old days. Burke thought gratefully that he had no family and few friends to call to him across the vast chasm of millennia.

Burke tended the embers of their cooking fire. Virdon, meanwhile, was still awake, resting uncomfortably on a bed of leaves and pine needles. Suddenly, there was a noise. Burke whirled, grabbing for the thick tree limb that he had chosen for a weapon. While thoughts of accidental discovery chased through Burke's mind, Galen stepped forward into the dim light of the clearing, carrying a sack over his shoulder. Burke relaxed. "What took so long?" he asked.

"I had to pick up a medical degree," said Galen lightly. He took a medical uniform from the sack. "This is for the renowned specialist, Dr. Adrian." From the sack he took out a human's orderly uniform. Both suits were marked with the ape's head and three red circles. "And this is for his faithful servant. Under the circumstances, it was the best position available."

"As long as the job offers me opportunities for advancement," said Burke.

"We'll, be lucky to end up where we started from," said Galen soberly.

Virdon watched Galen's proud display with some misgivings. He felt completely helpless; this was one time when all their combined cleverness could not get them out of their difficulty. They needed help from a qualified doctor, and, he realized, all of those were apes. Virdon did not wait to hear Galen's plan. He had learned from experience that the well-intentioned chimpanzee's schemes were always a little extravagant and a bit unorthodox. "Look," said Virdon, "even if this crazy masquerade works, the hospital is miles away, isn't it? I can't even stand, much less walk that far."

Galen walked closer to the blond astronaut, shaking his shaggy head. "Oh, my dear Alan, a patient of your importance should not have to walk at all." The ape turned to Burke, who stood nearby with a perplexed expression. "Right, Pete?" asked Galen.

Burke looked up, startled. "Huh? Oh, yeah, right. Sure," he said.

Later that night, on a country road not far from their campsite, Burke, Virdon, and Galen waited. None of them spoke; this was a critical part of Galen's plan. Virdon did not hold out a good deal of hope that it would work, but he had no alternative to offer. After a while they saw the blaze of a torch approaching along the road. Galen carried Virdon into the shrubbery along the edge of the road, and Burke stood silently where he was.

The torch was carried by a uniformed gorilla, who was carrying a rifle in his other hand. He rode alongside a human driver on a horse-drawn food cart. They both caught sight of Burke at the same moment. The human looked questioningly at the gorilla, but the ape made no sign for a few seconds. Then, having reached a decision in his slow mind, he signalled for the driver to stop the cart. The gorilla raised his rifle and shouted. "You," he cried. "What are you doing out after curfew?"

"My cart broke down," said Burke plaintively. "I was going on to the village to get some help."

The gorilla considered Burke's words for several seconds. His low intelligence made him suspicious of everyone, because he had been tricked often in his life. The gorilla came to the conclusion at last that there was no way of proving the matter by discussion. The gorilla's human driver never made an attempt to say anything. "Let me see your identity card," said the gorilla, still pointing the rifle squarely at Burke's chest.

Burke nodded and began reaching into a pocket. As he did so, he looked past the gorilla, to the opposite side of the road. There was movement in the dense undergrowth, but there was no noise. The gorilla was unaware of anything but Burke and his slowness to comply.

"All right," said the gorilla, "let's have it."

"Just a second," said Burke, putting a fearful edge on his voice. "I just may have left my papers in the cart."

The gorilla snorted. "That's a stupid thing to do. Just like a human, eh?" he asked his driver. The silent human only shrugged.

Meanwhile, Burke watched as Galen sneaked out of the bushes behind the cart. Suddenly, Burke pointed away from Galen and shouted in sudden alarm. "That comet," he cried, "it's headed right for us!"

The gorilla turned to look; Burke knocked the rifle from the ape's hand, then picked it up and clouted the gorilla with it. Galen jumped the human driver and knocked him from the cart, and pinned the man to the ground. Burke checked on the gorilla; the ape was unconscious. Burke emptied the gorilla's rifle, then tossed the gun into the bushes. He walked up to the terrified driver. "You're not a slave any longer," he said. "Get going. You'll discover that there are places where you can live a free life, unbothered by the apes and their gorilla stooges. But not around here."

"They'll hunt me down," said the man in horror. "Do you know what they do to runaway slaves?"

"You do what you want," said Burke, sighing. "Goodbye and good luck."

Burke motioned to Galen, and the chimpanzee let the driver go. Burke and Galen watched silently as the man ran off down the road, back in the direction he came from. "Well," said Galen, "perhaps it is as our schoolbooks always said. That some creatures—humans—did not deserve freedom, because they did not know what to do with it and are not prepared to risk anything to gain it."

"It does seem as though most humans have lost the desire to fight for their freedom," said Burke slowly. "But that might not be their fault. And everyone deserves freedom. It's an inalienable right."

"What?" asked Galen.

"Something we wrote a long time ago, Galen," said Burke. "In the Declaration of Independence. A piece of paper that seems to have gotten lost in the shuffle." The chimpanzee did not answer. Burke roused himself from his thoughts and hurried with Galen to the bushes, behind which Virdon was still lying. Together, man and chimpanzee lifted the blond astronaut onto the cart, and pulled a tarpaulin over him. Virdon winced with pain, but he did not cry out. Galen took the gorilla's seat, and Burke took the reins; the cart started to move off along the road.

The room was softly lit by candles. The drapes were tied open, and the lights in other chambers across the courtyard shone as bright yellow points of light. The stars burned steadily in the black sky. Leander and Kira, at opposite ends of a table, were having dinner in the director's quarters. He looked at Kira, who seemed distracted and lost in thoughts of her own. "You don't seem very excited about my vegetable casserole," said Leander. "Did I put in too much honey?"

Kira looked up, embarrassed to be caught so plainly wandering. "It's delicious," she said. "Really. I'm just not very hungry tonight."

Leander understood that something serious must be troubling Kira. She was not at all her cheerful self. Her depressed mood had put a ceiling of unpleasantness on the entire evening. "It can't still be the patient you lost today," he said.

"No," said Kira, "I've taken care of that. I'll write the report in the morning, and you'll have it tomorrow afternoon."

"No, no," said Leander, waving a hand. "I'm not concerned about that at all. But if it isn't the patient, then there's something else worrying you."

"I was thinking about that orderly we sent to disciplinary camp for not obeying orders. I wonder, was it really necessary to treat him so harshly?"

Leander laughed to discover that the matter was so simple. He had been afraid that Kira was growing tired of him. "He behaved like an unruly beast; he needed punishment. Where is the harshness?"

Kira toyed with her food for a few seconds before she

spoke. Her thinking was indirect contradiction to the very basis of the apes' society. "But are humans nothing but beasts?" she asked finally.

"At their best, they're useful animals. At their worst, they are carriers of hatred and destruction."

Kira followed Leander's chain of reasoning in her own mind. The conclusion she came to was not pleasant. "In that case, it is our duty to stamp them out?" she said.

Leander sat back in his chair and nodded. "Like the plague," he said.

The comparison was especially unpleasant to Kira. It brought to mind the only way the apes had of controlling plague: by slaughtering every human and ape who had come in contact with it, sometimes whole villages; mercilessly hunting down anyone who might have escaped, and then killing all those innocent people who had been unfortunate enough to come across the path of the fugitives. Kira's innate sense of compassion revolted, but before she could reply to Leander, there was a knock at the director's door.

"Come in," said Leander.

The door opened and a young chimpanzee intern entered. Kira recognized him as Dr. Stole, a bright young ape whom Leander had assigned to his own personal staff. That was a practice that Kira secretly disfavored. Leander consistently took the best of the new doctors to do his own administrative work, leaving the least qualified surgeons to perform the actual operations. Kira, as chief surgeon, often had her hands full, consulting and correcting the work of her juniors.

"I'm sorry for interrupting, Director," said Dr. Stole. "There's a new arrival, a Dr. Adrian. He says that Dr. Kira is expecting him."

"Quite all right, Stole," said Leander, yawning. He turned to look at Kira.

"That's the new visiting physician," she said. "I'd better show him to his quarters. I'm sorry that I have to leave, Leander. Thank you for a lovely evening."

Leander frowned, but he tried to make his reply pleasant. "The loveliness was in you, not the evening," he said. Kira nodded gratefully, got up, and followed Dr. Stole out of the room. Behind them, Leander still sat in his chair, brooding, pensive.

Outside, in the courtyard that faced the main gate, Kira walked toward the security booth. The air had cooled since sunset, and the breeze was very pleasant, but Kira did not notice. Her thoughts were on what she had consented to do, and on what Leander had said over dinner. At the front gates the cart with Burke and Galen waited. There was another human being there, a slave kept by the hospital staff, about forty-five years old, named Travin. Kira nodded at Travin's greeting. Seeing Kira, Galen called out to her. "Ah, Dr. Kira," he said. "I'm sorry that I'm late. We had an accident. One of my orderlies has been injured."

Galen pulled back the tarpaulin to reveal Virdon lying in the back of the cart. Kira looked at him briefly, trying to conceal the fear that grew steadily within her. "Is that your treatment, Dr. Adrian?" asked Kira. "Throwing a tarpaulin over the creature?"

Galen was startled, but realized that Kira's words would do more to cement his identity with the witnesses, Travin and the gorillas at the gate, than all the effusive greetings in the world. "Shock, Doctor," said Galen. "I was afraid that the human would go into shock, so I wrapped him well. It was the best that I could do on the road, without the resources you have at your disposal here." Kira only grunted in reply.

"Travin," she said, "find room for these two in the humans' quarters.'" Kira turned to Galen. "I'll show you to your room, Doctor," she said.

Travin helped Burke carry Virdon toward the humans' quarters, a low building at the edge of the compound. Galen went with Kira toward the main hospital building.

High above them, staring down at the torch-lit scene, Leander stood, his expression unreadable. His thoughts were confused for the first time in a long while, and his usually unshakable self-confidence was weakened. Couldn't Kira have sent the intern to show the new doctor to his quarters? Why did Kira take the opportunity to leave? Leander let out his breath in a loud sigh. He couldn't deduce her reasons, but there would be time enough to find the answers. He turned away from the window, his mind already burying his worry beneath smooth, comforting layers of assurance.

Meanwhile, Travin led Virdon and Burke to the humans' barracks. Travin and Burke half-carried, half-dragged the wounded man slowly and arduously across the hard dirt yard. Travin studied the two newcomers distrustfully. He didn't like anyone whom he didn't know, anyone who might present a threat to his small scrap of authority among the other humans. Before they entered the barracks, Travin spoke to Burke. "I'm not even going to ask how your friend here got a bullet in him," he said. "Your ape friend said you had an accident on the road. It must have been some accident."

Burke looked calmly at Travin. "I'm glad you're not going to ask about the bullet," he said. "Let's get him inside." Travin muttered under his breath, but said nothing.

The humans' quarters consisted of a large central room, little more than a hovel, that served as entrance hall, dining room and, for the humans of the lowest status, sleeping place. Several humans were about; one of them, a plain-looking, timid, withdrawn girl of about eighteen years, was cleaning up after supper. She stopped her work and stared as Travin and Burke carried Virdon across the threshold. The two men carefully rested Virdon on one of the straw pallets that lined the perimeter of the room; Travin started to leave. Burke caught the man by one arm. "Not here," said Burke. "He'll need his own room."

Travin stared in astonishment.

"I have my own room," he said with a sneer. "All the other humans sleep here."

Burke chewed his lip. Virdon often argued that their common enemy was not the apes; it was power and the individuals who abused it, whether simian or human. Here was an instance that proved Virdon right.

"He's sick," said Burke at last. "He needs special care." Travin snorted. "We don't provide special care for sick humans," he said. He said *humans* as though it meant a kind of creature he had never himself seen. "If a man is sick, he rests. If he lives, he returns to work."

Burke frowned; he noticed that both of his hands were clenched into fists. He forced himself to relax, to think through the situation carefully. The tiniest misstep would land Virdon and himself, and Galen, too, in the hands of the gorillas and General Urko. And then they'd be dead. "That's a very progressive system you have there," said Burke, "but it doesn't apply to us."

"It applies to everyone," said Travin angrily.

Burke laughed, putting on an air of confidence he didn't feel at all. "Sorry, Mac," he said. "We work exclusively for Dr. Adrian. And he gets very nervous when his servants get pushed around. So whatever passes for the luxury accommodations around here, that's where my friend goes. Can you understand that? It's really not all that difficult." And without waiting for an answer from Travin, Burke turned to Virdon and started to help him to his feet.

Virdon grunted and did his best to stand, but he just couldn't. His face twisted with agony. "Come on, pal," urged Burke, "I've just arranged for the Presidential suite."

"Maybe I ought to stay put," said Virdon. "We shouldn't cause trouble." Once more he tried to stand, and again the exertion proved too painful.

"Your friend is making sense," said Travin. "You really oughtn't to make trouble. You don't know the way things work around here. You don't know who can make trouble for you—if you understand me."

"I think you'd be amazed how well I understand you," said Burke contemptuously. He turned to Virdon again. "There won't be any problems, Alan. He won't tangle with, uh, Dr. Adrian." Without turning around again, Burke spoke to Travin. "Give me a hand," he said.

Travin scowled; he was frustrated and angry, but Burke had been right about one thing. The invocation of a chimpanzee doctor's authority had stopped him. Reluctantly Travin helped Burke lift Virdon and carry him toward the interior of the building.

Later that night, after they got Virdon settled comfortably in Travin's own quarters, Burke sat at a dining table, trying to dig into a plate of some unrecognizable food. Behind him, at the fire, was the same girl who had been cleaning up when Burke and Virdon had arrived. Next to Burke, Travin was eating his own meal in glowering silence; half a dozen other humans, all men, sat at the table, no one making any conversation. Burke took a bite of the food, chewed, it several times, and made a disgusted face.

"This is really terrific," he said. "I've been all over, and, believe me, this is the lousiest food I've ever eaten. What is it, dried mule hooves? I've had better food when I got a mouthful of sand at the beach." Burke looked around him, but there was no answer. None of the others even looked at him. "Yeah," said Burke, "and remind me when, the time comes to make a few comments on the ambience of this place, too. It reminds me of a lot of traffic courts I've been in. But the food tops that. I can't believe the food."

There was still no answer. The others continued eating without reacting to Burke at all.

"You wouldn't happen to have some chili sauce for this, would you?" he asked. "Anything. Just to kill the taste."

Travin did not look up from his own dish. He spoke in a quiet voice, his tone filled with scorn. "We have what we have," he said.

Burke realized that his comments weren't making him very popular with the local humans. He was sounding like the pampered servant of an ape, one who had become used to fine living while Travin and the others passed their lifetimes as slaves. Burke was playing his role well, but he got an inkling that he might be going too far for his own welfare. "Well," he said, "that's okay. They probably didn't have great food camping out with Attila the Hun, either. All that paprika had to be covering *something* up."

The girl came up to the table and set some bread down before each man. Nobody said anything to her, until she placed a piece of bread before Burke. He smiled at her; she either didn't or wouldn't notice. "Thanks," he said.

"What's your name?"

There was a heavy silence, for a brief interval. Then, suddenly, Travin exploded with outrage and anger. "Don't talk to her!" he shouted. He slammed his hand on the table next to Burke, almost upsetting the dark-haired astronaut's plate.

"You almost spilled my food," said Burke. "That would have been a real shame. Then you would have killed off all those bugs on the floor."

"Did you hear me, you fool?" shouted Travin, still standing over Burke threateningly.

"I heard you," said Burke softly. "I just asked her name."

Travin's brows drew together, and his face flushed red with rage. Slowly he let out his breath and sat down. When he spoke again, it was from between clenched teeth. "She has no name," he said.

Burke leaned back and looked calmly at Travin. He picked at a piece of food lodged between his teeth. After he had let Travin stew for a few moments, he said, "Everybody has a name. That's kind of a tradition among us folk. That's so we don't get confused who we are."

Travin looked like he was about to throw a punch at Burke's jaw, but the memory of what the man had said about Dr. Adrian stopped him. "Her name has been taken from her," he Said. "She is no one."

Burke looked up at the ceiling and shook his head. "I really can't believe you people. Her name was taken away? What did she do, run a red light?"

Travin glowered at Burke, but did not answer. After a few seconds he got up and left the table in anger. One of the other humans cleared his throat and spoke.

"The girl is his daughter," said the man.

"What?" said Burke, not sure that he had heard correctly.

There was no further conversation. The man who had answered him returned his attention to his bowl of food. The room was once more sunken in silence. "That's terrific," muttered Burke. "It's really great being here with you guys. I think I'd almost rather have the bullet in the back." But he didn't say it loudly enough for anyone to hear; he had the definite feeling that what he said could easily be arranged.

A few hours later, when the day had ended and the men had chosen their sleeping places on the floor of the main room, a figure entered, illuminated only by the light of a flickering lantern in the adjacent kitchen area. Travin, for that was who was walking carefully and stealthily among the sleeping men, checked that Burke was among them, and that he was sound asleep. Then he walked on through to the interior of the building.

He stood on the threshold of his own room, in which Virdon lay, asleep. Virdon was on a crude cot in a corner of the small room. Travin entered, put down the lantern which he had taken from the kitchen, and sat down on the floor. For a long time he stared at the sleeping man. Satisfied that Virdon was sound asleep, Travin got up slowly and quietly and went to the bedside. Carefully, he began to search Virdon's pocket.

Virdon awoke suddenly, startled. The motion was painful, but he forced himself to grab Travin's arm. "All right," he said, grimacing in the dim, flickering light, "Who are you and what are you doing?"

Travin fought down the panic that was rising in him. He knew that Virdon didn't know who he was as well as Burke did; he knew that Virdon was probably half-asleep and partially delirious from his wound. He forced himself to calm down, and in a firm voice he said,

"They told me to look in on you. I wanted to make sure that you were all right."

Virdon nodded. His face was dripping with perspiration. "I'm all right," he said in a hoarse voice. "Thank you."

Virdon closed his eyes again and slowly lowered his head to the cot. Travin watched him and saw the twinges of pain that stabbed through Virdon's body. "I wish it was that other guy," muttered Travin, as he turned to leave.

Outside, alone in the compound under the black night sky, Travin slowly opened his fist to examine the object that he had found in Virdon's pocket and had concealed from the man.

It was Virdon's compass, a crudely made model fashioned from a few scraps that the astronaut had picked up in his travels. Still, it was something that had not been seen in the world in many centuries. The gorillas and the other apes, dependent upon the stars for navigation at night, were often hindered by clouds. It was the compass that enabled Virdon, Burke, and Galen to outrun their pursuers on many occasions, for the three always knew in which direction they were traveling. In the hospital compound's yard, Travin turned the compass around in his hand, and wondered at the needle that always pointed in the same direction. His limited imagination couldn't figure a reason for such a thing; as a matter of fact, he thought that having a needle that wouldn't turn was a definite disadvantage. He looked off toward the north, toward which the compass needle pointed. He looked up at the stars in that part of the sky; a faint glimmering of the value of the compass began to spark in his mind.

Suddenly he stared at the strange object in awe and terror—who were these strangers? What magic did they know?

2

Kira sat at her desk. Her office was clean and, because of its distance from the operating rooms, quiet. The sun poured in through the windows, shining brightly on the polished wood of the desk and cupboards. Kira frowned as she studied a large book. After a long moment of silence she looked up, tense and unhappy. "It's no good," she said.

Galen sighed. It was going to be difficult after all, even though he had Kira's full cooperation. She had such a highly developed sense of ethics that she wouldn't proceed until she had completely researched the case. "All the medical texts deal with apes," she said. "There's nothing in any of them on humans."

"But you know where the bullet is," insisted Galen.

Kira answered him impatiently. "We know the bullet is lying near a nerve. We don't know what that nerve looks like or where it runs. And there could be major blood vessels in the area. If we just went in blindly, we could kill him."

Galen was surprised by her words. "Which means that you care what happens to him," he said:

"I'm a surgeon," said Kira bluntly. "I'm not a butcher who goes blundering in with a knife, just to see what will happen. And to operate in ignorance *is* butchery."

Galen considered what Kira said for a moment; the situation was a genuine dilemma. All the good will in the world would do Virdon no good; but Kira had a sound argument, as well. "All right," said Galen at last, "If I found a book on human anatomy, would that help you?"

Kira nodded, but her voice sounded hopeless. "There are no books on human anatomy," she said. "What ape would have wanted to write one?"

Galen shook his head. "I was thinking of a human book," he said.

Kira was astonished by the notion. "What are you talking about?" she asked. "Humans don't write medical books."

"They did once," said Galen with conviction. He didn't have the time to convince Kira of all that he had learned from Virdon and Burke, but he had to persuade her of this particular point. "A long time ago they did, when *they* ruled the earth."

"You're really mad," said Kira, her voice shaken, almost a whisper.

"No," said Galen forcefully. There was a pause, during which Galen licked his lips, wondering how to continue. Kira stared at him, truly convinced that Galen was insane. "I've seen such books."

"Only in the fantasies of your deranged mind."

Galen took a deep breath. "In the house of the President of the Supreme Council. In the house of Zaius." Galen made the statement with such powerful assurance that Kira could not help but stare at him in shock, her vision of the world suddenly turned upside down. She couldn't accept the idea—yet, looking at Galen, she couldn't completely deny its possibility. Before she could find an adequate response, the door of the office opened and Leander entered.

"Good day, Kira," said Leander. "I hope I'm not intruding. You will forgive me for not knocking, but I thought that you were scheduled to give a lecture to the staff this morning." His tone was abrupt and businesslike, although his thoughts were still partially on their interrupted dinner of the night before.

Kira answered Shakily. "I postponed it until tomorrow," she said. "I... I wanted to show Dr. Adrian our facilities."

Leander turned to Galen. "And what is your impression, Doctor?" he asked.

Galen smiled and nodded. "Fantastic!" he said. "Certainly far beyond anything I've seen. Of course, I'm not sure I would agree with *all* your procedures."

Kira stared in mute horror at Galen's acting. Was he, after all, crazy? It certainly seemed that he had little connection with reality. Leander took up the challenge. "Oh?" said the director of the medical center. "And what quarrel do you have with our procedures, Doctor?"

"I don't wish to cause any offense—" said Galen.

"Come, come, Doctor," said Leander, interrupting. "I'd be glad to hear your learned opinions. Wouldn't you, Kira?"

The female chimpanzee was almost ready to collapse. "Yes," she said. "Yes, of course. Dr. Adrian is quite renowned in his field."

"Well," said Galen pompously, playing his part well beyond the call of duty, "as I see it, there's altogether too much emphasis these days on surgery, for everything from a broken leg to the vapors. While surgery is necessary in some cases, I myself prefer a more conservative approach."

Leander laughed softly. "I have heard the same thing before, generally from provincial doctors," he said. "You mean some kind of herbal remedy for every ailment?"

Galen kept a deadpan expression. "Except colds, of course. That illness still has our best minds stumped, and the wisdom of our elders has this peculiar gap in it."

Behind Leander's back Kira was signalling to Galen to stop. Galen acknowledged her motion and quit his small evaluation. Kira waited for Leander's outraged reaction, but to her surprise the director laughed. "I like our visitor," he said. "I hope you'll do your best to keep him here."

"And I look forward to working with you, Doctor," said Galen.

"Good, good," said Leander. He slapped Galen's shoulder, made a short bow to Kira, and, still smiling, turned and left the room. Galen looked at Kira, who was almost hysterical.

"'I look forward to working with you'!" she mimicked. "Do you think he's a fool? This whole thing is impossible. This crazy imposture, that non-existent book in Zaius' library—"

"Kira," said Galen, suddenly sober, "I'll find the book. And you'll have in your hands the power to advance our medicine. That book means life!"

Kira shook her head. "It means death, if we're caught."

"If we're caught," said Galen, "I'll confess that I forced you into this by threatening your life."

Kira's shoulders sagged in despair. "Do you think that I want *you* to die?"

"No one wants to die," said Galen. "Ape or human. But we can't turn back now."

Kira was silent; Galen took that for a sign that her resistance to his scheme was diminishing. That, at least, was something. Feeling hopefully, he turned and left Kira alone in her office.

The young ape looked in on Virdon briefly. The blond man was lying on his cot, feverish and only semi-conscious. With Galen was Pete Burke. They spoke together in quiet, urgent tones.

"He's still running a fever," said Galen.

Burke stared down at his friend, who was now so helpless. Galen was doing everything he could, but Burke felt useless in the situation. He wanted to do something for Virdon, something constructive. "I think that the bullet might be causing some kind of toxic reaction," he said. "That medicine that Kira gave us should start to work soon. If it doesn't…"

"Shhh," whispered Galen.

Burke looked up to see Travin come in with some ice packs, which he handed to Burke. The astronaut took them, thanking Travin. Burke put the ice packs on Virdon's forehead. Suddenly, Virdon began to rave, deliriously.

"Oh, no!" he cried out in his fevered nightmare. "The instruments! What does it mean? It can't be… it doesn't look like… This isn't Earth! What is it?" Then, even more terrified, he said, "They're apes, Pete! Oh, no, this world is run by apes!"

Travin edged closer, listening to Virdon's ravings. "What is he saying? Everyone *knows* the world is run by apes. And what did he mean, 'This isn't Earth'?"

Galen looked at Travin coldly. He put out a hand to prevent the man from approaching any nearer. "I didn't realize the orderlies here did psychological studies of the patients," he said.

Travin was obviously chastened. "I only meant—"

Galen cut in sharply. "He's having a fever hallucination. It's your job to take care of him. If he dies and I have to break in a new orderly, I'll hold you responsible."

Travin was suddenly submissive before Galen's hollow show of authority. "Yes, Doctor," he said. The man turned and walked out of the small room. Galen and Burke watched him go. Then Burke turned to Galen. His expression was twisted with a strong emotion that the chimpanzee was unable to identify immediately. Galen wondered what had happened in the humans' quarters in all the time he had spent in relative luxury with Kira and Leander. Evidently this man Travin was one to avoid. It seemed that there always was at least one, whether human or ape.

"That guy worries me," said Burke simply.

"That's obvious," said Galen. "I don't like him, either, and I don't even know him. Is there any particular reason for your distrust?"

"No, nothing definite," said Burke. "But the situation here is really strange."

"Strange to you, perhaps, but if it were explained, I think that you might be better able to understand it. In any event, he wouldn't think of challenging my authority."

Burke laughed softly. Sometimes Galen, despite his experience and the new things he had learned from the astronauts, could be astoundingly naive. "That's exactly what many human governments said about their neighbors, just the day before the neighbors marched across the borders. Sure, you're an ape, he'll obey you as long as he thinks you're a real doctor. But if Virdon keeps on raving like this, he's bound to give us away sooner or later."

Galen nodded thoughtfully. "You know, that's a new concept to me. Borders. Here, we have one community, the ape community, that spreads out in a circle around Central City. There are no other communities, no borders. That's just another example of how we've improved on the old human ways. Just think of the time and resources that were thrown away, nervously watching those borders."

"Galen," said Burke, "I have to admit it. I think you're right. It's really tough for me to say it, though."

"You're coming along fine," said Galen.

"Sure," said Burke, laughing, "you'll make an ape out of me yet.

"I wouldn't go that far," said Galen. They both laughed. Then Galen spoke seriously. "We'll have to get that book from Zaius' house. I'll tell Kira to prepare for the surgery." The two friends parted company, and Burke started off across the courtyard adjacent to the humans' quarter. He had walked a few yards when he was stopped by a woman's scream behind him. The noise was so shrill and so full of pain that he stopped and looked back. What he saw made his short temper flare uncontrollably. The girl, Travin's daughter, was lying in the dry dust of the courtyard, writhing and twisting in pain. Her cries were enough to make Burke sick to his stomach. Standing over her was a man Burke knew to be called Lafer; the man was beating the girl with a heavy rod. The poor girl could do nothing to avoid the man's blows. Blood ran from her nose and her eyes were both blackened. Large bruises had appeared on her arms and legs. Burke realized that Lafer could easily kill the girl. Other humans in the area were going about their business as though nothing at all unusual were happening. The whole scene was incredible to Burke; these were not people. Perhaps the apes were right, after all. Perhaps the human beings *were* only animals, fit only for slavish duties. Burke felt a kind of revulsion at being one of their number.

Lafer prepared to give the girl another clout with his rod. Burke ran toward them, shouting at Lafer to stop. He knocked the man's arm away and pulled the stick out of his grasp. Lafer, infuriated, turned on Burke and threw a punch at the astronaut's head. Burke easily avoided the blow, and replied with a sharp kick to the man's solar plexus. Lafer doubled up, but before Burke could follow up his attack, the man recovered. They struggled in the courtyard, Burke's skill matched by Lafer's superior strength.

Meanwhile, summoned by the commotion in the courtyard, Travin emerged from the humans' building. He stopped when he saw what was happening. For a moment he watched, hoping that Lafer would beat Burke senseless. But after a short while, Travin realized that Burke was holding his own, and that he apparently could do so indefinitely.

Then an accident occurred which changed the picture. Lafer grabbed Burke, and in the astronaut's attempts to free himself, his shirt was ripped, exposing the knife that he carried beneath it. Travin and the other humans saw it and reacted with a fear more extreme than the situation seemed to warrant. One of the humans, a woman named Brigid, her voice trembling, could only stand and point at Burke. "He has a weapon," she said shrilly.

Burke heard the woman's words while he grappled with Lafer. Her tone told him that having a weapon here was a dangerous thing. He filed that away in his memory, in order to be more careful around the apes: He hoped that Virdon's knife had not yet been discovered; if either weapon were reported to the gorilla guards, it could mean the end of their history.

Travin finally ran to the scene of the fight across the

courtyard, just as Burke delivered a solid blow to Lafer's jaw. Before the struggle could continue, however, Travin stepped between, the two men:

"All right, all right, that's enough," he said, holding back Lafer, who did not want to stop. His pride was wounded more than his body, and that was motivation enough to continue, even after his leader commanded a halt. Burke, for his part, was perfectly willing to stop. His hands were cut and bleeding, and he was out of breath. He knew that Lafer would begin to get an insurmountable edge on him very soon. Lafer cooled down after his leader's repeated order. In a few seconds, only Travin was still angry. "What do you think you're doing?" he cried. "You could have had the entire gorilla garrison here in another couple of minutes. That would have been just fine, you dumb clods. Every one of us, the whole human population, could have been confined to quarters for a month. You've had that happen before—staring at those filthy walls for a month. Do you like it, or something? Do you enjoy a month of dull conversation?"

Lafer just pointed at the girl, who was still rolling back and forth on the ground in pain. "She spilled the water," said the man.

Burke was incredulous. "And that's why you were beating the daylights out of her?" he asked furiously.

Travin put a restraining hand on Burke's chest. "All of us are required to discipline the girl," he said calmly. "It's our duty, to keep us safe from her curse."

"She's your own daughter," insisted Burke.

Travin just stared back. "I have no daughter," he said in a flat voice.

Burke looked back at Travin, the astronaut's mind a bewildering mixture of thoughts and feelings. Travin just stared blankly. Burke turned his attention to the girl, whom no one yet had come to aid. The girl sat up, holding her arms around her knees and rocking back and forth. She did not return Burke's gaze. Frustrated, still angry, and not quite comprehending the circumstances, Burke kicked at a pebble, sending it several yards across the courtyard, in the direction of the other humans. He looked at them disgustedly.

Travin turned to Lafer. "I believe she's been punished enough for now," he said.

Lafer nodded glumly, still looking hatefully at Burke. Finally, though, he turned and left. Travin stared after him and gave the girl a meaningful look. She whimpered slightly, then stopped, the effects of years of discipline dictating her actions. She picked up her water pail and hurried back toward the building. The other humans dispersed, leaving Travin alone in the courtyard with Burke. Travin took a deep breath. He did not like this man, but he knew that he had to establish some kind of control over him, or risk bringing down the wrath of the apes on the rest of the human crew. "I saw your knife," he said, expecting that to be enough of a warning for Burke.

"So?" said Burke, without interest.

"Humans are forbidden to carry weapons," said Travin. There was a short pause. "Who are you?" asked Travin.

Burke sighed. This man Travin was really too stupid to be believed. If Burke was who he said he was, the matter was settled. If he wasn't, did Travin really think that Burke would reveal the truth? Human beings couldn't have become *that* stupid. Burke looked at Travin's cruel face again and decided that the last statement might well be an unwarranted assumption. "I'm Dr. Adrian's servant," he said. It was the same story that Travin had heard upon their arrival, and the only story he was likely, hopefully, to hear. Travin could take it or leave it.

The invocation of Dr. Adrian's name stopped Travin again; his fear of all apes and their total power over human beings prevented him from saying anything further. Burke waited a moment, then turned around and walked, away. Travin watched him go, then reached into his pocket and took out the compass that he had stolen from Virdon's pocket. He looked at it again, then, with a gesture of finality, closed his fists on it, a hard glint of suspicion in his eyes.

The Central City of the apes was just that: the metropolitan and cultural nexus of the entire society. There was nothing else like it anywhere in the ape world. All administrative and social functions were located in Central City; smaller communities, mere satellite stations and agricultural towns, were grouped in an almost circular band around the city. Beyond these was an uncharted wilderness, a strange and deadly area that was forbidden to apes and human beings alike.

One of the busiest addresses in Central City was the office building of General Urko, the gorilla chief of all police and military forces in the ape empire. Urko was a fierce, huge gorilla, dedicated to keeping an iron grasp on the daily lives of all citizens and slaves. He desired above all things an orderly world, and the only way that he could see to maintain it was by force and fear. That he also greatly enjoyed the privileges and swaggering power was another forceful reason for keeping things as they were.

On this particular day, Urko was interrogating a human being, something that he generally delegated to his junior officers. But General Urko had a suspicion that this human being might be able to give him information about the location of two human astronauts—whatever that word meant—and a chimpanzee traitor named Galen. Urko hated these three with a passion that far transcended rationality; he would stop at nothing to get them back in his power, and so demonstrate in front of the entire ape world that no one could evade his might for long. The two humans were an embarrassment to him; of course, they had the mind of a chimpanzee to aid them, but Galen was known publicly as a rash, impulsive youth, and an ape not especially given to planning stratagems. That Urko had not yet recaptured the three was a fact that nagged at him day and night.

The human being whom the general was questioning was the same driver that Burke and Galen had overpowered on the road to the medical center. The gorilla guard who had been with him was also present.

"The one who attacked you, Asher," said Urko quietly, "what did he look like?"

Asher, the human, was frightened to be in the offices of the notorious General Urko. His answer was given in a voice that fairly wobbled with terror. "I don't know," he said. "I couldn't tell. It was dark." He was almost whining with fear.

Urko pretended that the matter was of little consequence, ignoring the fact that if it *were* so unimportant, Urko would not be pursuing it himself. "Was it a gorilla or a chimpanzee? You certainly could tell that much."

There was a long silence. Urko played with a letter opener shaped like a sword, that lay on his desk. He looked up again, waiting patiently for an answer from this typically ignorant creature. Then Asher, trembling with fear, said in a low voice, "There were two of them. I already told you. A chimpanzee and…" Asher paused, "and a human."

The gorilla that had been with Asher, who had not seen Galen, reacted with fury. "You're saying that an ape helped a human to commit a crime?" he cried.

Urko interrupted coldly. "I'm handling this, Officer Haman," he said. Haman nodded dutifully and said nothing more. Urko turned again to Asher, and spoke in a friendly, reassuring voice. "You are aware that you could be flogged for spreading such dangerous fantasies, aren't you? Oh, I'm not trying to frighten you. Quite the contrary. I'm trying to apprise you of the legal precedents here. I could have one of my secretaries look it up for you, if you didn't want to take my word for it."

"I believe you," said Asher hoarsely.

"Fine, fine," said Urko absently. "But I'm not going to have you flogged. I just mentioned it so that you'd understand how lenient I'm being."

"Thank you," said Asher, his voice almost disgustingly obsequious. "Thank you, General."

Urko waved Asher's gratitude away. "What you're trying to say is, you were frightened, it was dark; you couldn't tell who attacked you, isn't that so?"

By this time, Asher would have agreed with anything that General Urko said. "Yes, sir," he said, his eyes directed to the floor.

Urko studied the abject human being before him; the general's lip curled in a sneer of hatred and loathing. He wished that he didn't have to deal with such filth. What he really desired was to rid the entire ape world of all human beings, but he realized what a devastating blow that would be to the economy, which depended on the slave labor force. Still, things would be much simpler without such creatures as Asher. And those blasted astronauts! "Good," said Urko wearily. "You've done your duty. You can go now."

Asher, grateful, bowed and left the office, glad to be still in one piece and functioning. When he had left, Urko turned to the gorilla, Haman. "Return to your post," said the general. "And on your way out, tell my aide to come in."

The gorilla saluted. "Yes, sir," he said. Then he, too, turned and left the office.

Urko crossed the room and went up to a large wall map. In the center of the map was Central City; surrounding it were the names of various villages and farming communities. The roads were drawn boldly, in straight lines linking the various towns. Urko cursed under his breath; he wished that he had the confidence of the mapmaker. Half the towns on the map hadn't been in existence for two generations. Half the towns that *did* exist weren't anywhere on the map. And the roads... Sometimes what was represented on the map by a wide, firm black line turned out to be a beaten-down path through high weeds. The map was almost useless, and it was the best in the ape world. Urko studied it for a moment. The door opened and the general's aide entered. Urko turned and nodded. Then he pointed at the map. "Cleon," he said, "that patrol that claimed to have sighted the astronauts the day before yesterday. How sure are they of the identification?"

Cleon considered his words before answering. He had learned from experience that Urko demanded clear and concise information, not opinions. "The men in that patrol belonged to one of our best units, sir," he said. "They're absolutely certain that the astronauts were headed into the Northern Mountains, away from Central City."

Urko thought about this for a few seconds, staring at the map. "Could they have reversed their route and come back toward Central City?" he said.

Cleon looked at the map. The Northern Mountains were drawn in only sketchily, and the entire territory was labeled "Unmapped." It seemed to General Urko's aide that it would be a reasonable assumption that the astronauts and their chimpanzee friend would head for the area. "This city is the most heavily patrolled region in the world," said Cleon. "It just isn't logical that they'd take such a risk, leaving a relatively unpopulated area to return right into our hands, so to speak."

General Urko slapped one gauntleted fist into the palm on his other hand. He had been chasing these humans in circles long enough. He swore to himself that he would catch them, and to do that, he would have to learn to think as they did. "We know that they're not always logical creatures," said Urko thoughtfully. "Humans are often driven by odd impulses." Urko considered the problem for a little while longer; Cleon knew enough not to say anything while the general was thinking. At last Urko spoke. "Cancel my trip to the New Territory," he said. "I think I'll stay on here for a few more days."

Cleon nodded silently, saluted, and departed. General Urko turned to the map again and studied it with deep concentration. In his eyes was the look of a hunter closing in on his prey.

3

The sun was already touching the western horizon, and the first pale flush of stars had begun to spread across the sky. The streets of Central City were not as crowded with bustling pedestrians as earlier in the day, but there was still a number of apes strolling along, looking at merchandise in shop windows, or deciding on a restaurant or theater. Many human slaves hurried about, on errands for their masters. In the streets themselves there were few vehicles, for it was expensive and inconvenient to maintain the horses needed to draw them in the city.

And so, when the sound of horses galloping along the main street of Central City echoed among the low buildings, many apes and humans stopped what they were doing to look. A covered horse-drawn cart sped by briskly. On its side was the red and white apes' head flag above three circles to indicate it was a hospital vehicle. The pedestrians watched it with mild curiosity, wondering what had happened to summon the emergency cart.

The hospital cart was driven by a figure in a hospital uniform, covered by a hooded garment that seemed to be drawn tightly against the cold; if anyone had thought about the matter, he would have realized that it wasn't that cool, even aboard a racing ambulance. The figure hiding in the cloak was Pete Burke, and beside him sat Galen. They drove quickly and surely through the city; before they reached their goal, however, the racket of horses' hooves sounded from behind. Galen looked around and saw a patrol of two mounted gorillas overtaking them. The first gorilla rode abreast of the cart and signalled for Galen to stop.

"What's wrong, officer?" asked Galen.

"I'm sorry," said the gorilla. "That's a restricted quarter. What are you doing here?" His voice was without the usual contempt that gorillas had for anyone not of their number; he was merely doing what he had been ordered to do: question anyone who crossed the line into his area of responsibility.

"It's an emergency," said Galen impatiently. "We've been called to the house of Zaius."

The officer looked doubtful. He had heard of nothing unusual that evening; Zaius' house was one of the buildings he had been charged to protect. The gorilla thought that if anything had happened to Zaius, the police would have learned of it. "Zaius?" asked the gorilla. "I saw him earlier in the day. He seemed to be in excellent condition."

"He's had a heart attack since then," said Galen irritably. "Shall we spend the rest of the day discussing it?"

The gorilla's eyebrows rose at Galen's angry retort. So did Burke's. But once again, Galen's aggressive bluffing carried him through the danger. "Zaius!" said the gorilla.

"I'll give you an escort." He turned to his fellow officer and instructed the gorillas to continue their rounds. Then the first gorilla kicked up his horse and rode on beside the ambulance.

"Terrific," muttered Burke to Galen. "We need him for an escort about as much as we need a case of cholera. What do we do when we get there? Tell him that Zaius changed himself into a medical textbook?"

"Don't be foolish, Burke," said Galen calmly. "We're playing this all as it happens, step by step. Why worry about it now?"

"Somebody has to," muttered Burke gloomily. They rode on into the growing darkness.

There was no time to communicate any further plans as the danger of having them overheard by the gorilla was too great. At last, guarded and guided by the officer, the ambulance arrived at the house of Zaius. It was a large, airy, open building, like most ape homes and offices, reflecting the apes' longing for nature and their desire to avoid anything that might divide them from their simple past—a past which they remembered, subconsciously at least, to be governed by human beings. That was a thought which every ape either did not know or suppressed.

The next moment, both cart and officer's mount came to a halt outside the house of the President of the Supreme Council. Galen and Burke jumped off the cart, taking a stretcher and a blanket with them; Galen carried a black medical bag. They started for the front of the house. The gorilla officer followed them, hoping to be of help. Galen turned to him before they reached the door. He did not smile or frown at the gorilla, but spoke in a businesslike manner, trying to avoid arousing the officer's suspicions. "Where are you going?" he asked.

The officer was startled. He had assumed that the medical team would require his services. Like most gorillas, he did not believe that chimpanzees or orangutans were really capable of action without gorilla supervision. He was wrong. "Into the house," he said. "If Zaius needs help—"

Galen cut him off with a sharp wave of his hand. He had had lots of practice in bluffing authority lately and, to be truthful, he rather enjoyed it. Once again he adopted a tone of voice that would allow no contradiction. "My dear fellow," he said soothingly but firmly, "Zaius has had a heart attack. That's a medical condition, not a criminal offense. I believe that you'd be more use guarding the ambulance; one of my colleagues had the wheels stolen off his cart almost within sight of the police garrison."

Without waiting for an answer from the startled gorilla, Galen and Burke followed the path that led toward the front of the house. There were lights burning behind pulled drapes. No one in the house had yet become aware of what was happening outside. When Galen and Burke had moved out of sight of the gorilla, they changed direction and headed around toward the back of the house, where Zaius' study was located. They left the stretcher on the ground, and climbed through a window that had been left open there.

Galen entered first; it would look better if anyone were around, to have an ape discovered. There just might be the slightest chance of an explanation. If a human were found creeping into the house of an ape, and such a prestigious ape as Zaius at that, there would be no questioning. The human would be taken away and shot, simply and quickly. Galen grunted a little as he forced himself over the window sill; he stood up in Zaius' study and satisfied himself that they were safe. He signalled to Burke, who joined him in the room. The human was more nervous. Galen whispered that Zaius had probably retired to his bedroom to study matters of state with his usual nighttime glass of vegetable juice.

"Well, draw the curtain anyway," said Burke, still thinking about the gorilla police officer outside.

Galen nodded and did so. The room was shrouded in darkness, its furniture and decorations hidden in the dense shadows. Galen realized that if they were to find what they had come for, and speedily enough to prevent any suspicious doubts in the gorilla, they needed light. Galen crossed the room and lit an oil lantern hanging on the wall, illuminating the cool, dark room. The chimpanzee recoiled in shock and horror—the first thing the light shone upon was the face of an orangutan, glaring at him, frowning with an expression of seriousness and intelligence. Then Galen relaxed. He saw that the face belonged to a sculptured bust on a platform. He examined it quickly, thoughtfully. The bust was of Doswa, one of the greatest of the apes' executive officers, one of Zaius' most renowned predecessors. After a moment, he and Burke turned their attention to the other objects in the room.

There was the usual collection of sentimental things from days and accomplishments long gone by; curious shells and pieces of wood on the desk, which could have meaning to no one other than Zaius; framed citations and testimonials from many groups in the ape city; and everywhere heavy, black, handbound books. Their search ended as their gaze fell upon a glass-doored cabinet, also filled with books. Burke tried the cabinet door. If was locked. He tried his knife, and after some nervous moments, he jimmied the door open and scanned the titles printed—unlike the usual ape-manufactured volume—on the spines. He found one book and took it out.

Both Burke and Galen looked for a long moment at the book. It was smaller than the ape-made books, bound tightly and permanently by some machine process. The print was regular and legible. But the most important thing, the thing that would prove most startling to Kira and her associates, was simply the title and the author: *Principles of Surgery*, by Walter Mather, M.D., F.A.C.S.

Burke thumbed through the book excitedly; he recognized the illustrations from his high school and college days, the red and blue drawings of veins and arteries. The apes had no such accurate mappings of body systems, either ape or human. That was what Galen had meant when he told Kira that the book meant life; there were enough revolutionary ideas in the simple medical text to cause arguments for the next hundred years. The book itself was ancient now, having lasted since human domination of the world, since the days of Burke and Virdon's own era. The pages were brown and crumbling; Burke handled it carefully, almost reverently. There hadn't been much to see in the ape world that was directly connected with the almost-forgotten human world. It gave Burke a little emotional lift, a feeling of justification, followed by depression. The book had no place in the present except hidden and locked away. General Urko or any of his subordinates would have destroyed it in a matter of seconds, without another thought. "Well, this is it," said Burke. There was a slight pause before he spoke again. "But how do we get it past that gorilla?" he asked finally.

Galen looked around. His eyes strayed to the bust of Doswa, the orangutan leader. He went over and picked up the life-size piece of statuary. It was of light clay with a hollow interior; Galen carried it with ease. Holding it up to Burke, Galen said with mock pomposity, "Offhand, I'd diagnose this case as a severe heart attack." The young chimpanzee looked at the bust and murmured, "Doswa, you led us well, according to the history teachers. Now, please, you'll have to lead us out of here."

With that, he scooped up some pillows lying on a sofa. Burke closed the cabinet, and they went to the window. Suddenly Galen remembered the lamp; he crossed back to it and extinguished the flame. Once again the room was plunged into blackness. Galen joined Burke at the window and together they climbed down.

They clambered to the ground, where they had left the stretcher only minutes before and looked around, anxiously for the gorilla, but he was evidently following his orders and guarding the ambulance cart. All at once, Burke thought of something. "What if Zaius goes to his front door, or looks through a window?" he asked.

Galen gave Burke a short look. "Do you mean that you're just thinking of that now? Sometimes I wonder about you two fellows. Sometimes I think that you're not all that you say you are."

"I was trusting you," said Burke.

"Well," said Galen with a brief laugh, "that ought to teach you better."

They arranged the pillows on the stretcher and put the sculptured head of Doswa at the top. Then they carefully put the blanket over it, leaving just the clay head exposed. Burke went to the medical bag for the final touch. He rummaged around in it for a few seconds, and finally took out a sterile mask, which he put over the mouth and nose of the sculptured bust, completely disguising its identity. He and Galen carried the stretcher back out to where the ambulance wagon was parked. The gorilla watched them, but Galen signalled to him that they could load their precious cargo without his aid. Besides, Galen didn't want the gorilla officer to discover how light the stretcher was. When they had finished, Galen turned to the gorilla. "Can I talk with you in private?" he asked solemnly.

The officer nodded and walked off a few paces with Galen. The chimpanzee spoke in hushed, confidential tones. "When an ape like Zaius falls ill, it's more than a medical problem. Affairs of state are involved. Do you follow my meaning?"

The gorilla was awed by Galen's words. "Yes," he said, "I think so."

Galen paused. He thought suddenly about what he was so blithely trying to do. For a few moments, speaking with the gorilla, he had enjoyed his role-playing. Now, though, he had a quick glimpse of Burke's worried expression. And then Galen remembered the reason for the entire masquerade: Virdon, who lay helpless and crippled in an ape hospital, who might at any time be identified and turned over to General Urko and his hateful colleagues. Both astronauts were counting on Galen to keep the scheme simple, for only in simplicity was there any hope of success. Already their quick escape had been held up by Galen's desire to push his phony authority as far as he could. He was jeopardizing their safety, the very thing he had accused Burke and Virdon of in times past. He had to save them all now, he had to speak carefully.

"The Prime Minister is in there. Zaius, the President of the Supreme Council," said Galen, jerking one thumb over his shoulder toward the hospital wagon. "He told me to keep this quiet. We surely don't want to start a panic, do we? I know I can count on your cooperation. *He* trusts in your ability, also. He is a very ill man, but the situation is by no means hopeless. He was still conscious and speaking coherently when we found him. We'll take, uh, the patient to the hospital, and you will resume your normal patrol as if nothing happened. Is that all quite clear?"

The gorilla looked proud at being involved in such a momentous event. He saluted Galen. "Yes, sir," he said.

Galen only nodded in reply and walked back to the wagon. The gorilla remounted his horse and rode off. Galen joined Burke on the cart and they, too, drove away from the house of Zaius.

Although it was night, Kira still sat in her office. Before he left, Leander ducked in briefly to say goodnight and ask why Kira had not yet gone home. She answered that she had some work to catch up on. When he closed the door, she went back to worrying about Galen. The young chimpanzee hadn't told her the details of his plan. All that she knew was that he intended to break into the house of Zaius himself, and steal some hypothetical book. The whole scheme made her nervous, just to think about what might happen to Galen. How long would he be gone? How much longer did she have to worry?

Finally, when she thought she could stand it no more, her office door opened slowly, and Galen and his human friend, Burke, entered. They carried a thick book, much different from the books Kira was used to seeing. "You did it, then," she said.

"Of course we did," said Galen. "Here, look."

Kira took the volume from him and glanced at it. As she leafed through the pages at her desk, her expression grew more and more stunned. Galen and Burke waited patiently on the opposite side of her desk.

Kira looked up at them incredulously. "Diagrams of the circulatory system," she said. "Surgical procedures. Is this a medical text? Or a work of fiction?"

Galen stared back at her, realizing that the book represented an entire change in her thinking. He recalled when he had had to make the same change. "You knew the answer to that as soon as you saw it," he said.

"I can't believe that a human wrote this!" said Kira, slamming one hand on her desk.

"Dr. Mather *was* one of our greatest surgeons," said Burke, trying to be helpful. "He worked at the Hanson Clinic when I was in college."

Kira turned back to Galen, astonished. "If Zaius knew about this, why weren't *we* allowed to know?"

Galen sighed. "Well," he said slowly, "for political reasons. If humans could write books like this, why should they be content to be slaves? He was afraid it would mean the end of our civilization."

There was a long pause, a frightened silence, during which Kira searched Galen's face for some sign of reassurance. She had thought at first that Galen had made his remark facetiously. The idea of human beings ruling the world was ridiculous to her. The thought of one being intelligent enough now to be her equal—or perhaps, her superior!—could not be borne. Surely Galen must be joking. But there was nothing in his expression to indicate that. Kira took a deep breath. "What if Zaius is *right*?" she asked fearfully.

Burke laughed softly at the anxiety the concept was causing Kira. He felt like a pet poodle that had just displayed talents for the piano and expressionistic painting. Meanwhile, Kira's question hung heavily and ominously in the air. Before Galen could respond, there was an urgent knock on the door.

Galen, being nearest to the door, opened it. Travin stood there, evidently agitated. He spoke directly to Kira, ignoring Galen and Burke. "The stranger," he said excitedly, "he's very sick."

Suddenly, Kira jerked her head toward Galen. In their discussion of the world and the role of human beings, in their curiosity and fear of the human medical book, they had forgotten about Virdon. All that time, he had grown steadily worse under the insufficient attention of the rest of the medical staff and the human slaves. Kira just pointed, and followed Travin, Burke, and Galen out the door.

They hurried across the hospital compound, to the shabby building that housed the human servants. Travin led the way through the large central room where they drew mildly curious looks from the slaves and human orderlies who sat around the edges of the meeting hall, passing the hours in fatigue and frustration.

Virdon was in the throes of a convulsion. Burke went to his side, anxious and not exactly sure what to do. "Hold him down," said Kira softly. She tore a strip of cloth from the rough covering on the pallet and pressed it between his teeth. After a few moments, the convulsion subsided. Virdon opened his eyes wearily. Burke tried to disguise his fear and smiled at his friend.

"Easy, buddy," said the dark-haired man. "Are you okay? How are they treating you? The food okay? Of course not. Anyway, you wouldn't believe what your good pals have done for you tonight."

Virdon was dazed; he stared at Burke, as though he were trying to make out shapes in a fog. "Okay?" he murmured, like a faint echo of Burke's words. "I'll let you know as soon as the room stops moving. What happened?"

Kira pushed in front of Burke, trying to resume control of the situation. Her medical training and her compassion came to the fore, drowning her fear and her conditioned loathing of humans. "You had a convulsion," she said, in an impersonal, somewhat cold voice. "The bullet must have moved slightly, closer to a nerve."

Virdon seemed to notice Kira for the first time. He looked into her face, frowning, trying to focus his eyes. "You're Dr. Kira, aren't you?" he said at last.

Kira would not be drawn into anything other than a professional conversation. If what Galen had hinted were true, then it might mean hard times in the future for all of the ape society. Kira found herself caught in the dilemma, and the only solution that she could see was to remain businesslike. "It's no concern of yours who I am. Take this medicine," she said. She brought out a small bottle, opened it, and gave it to Virdon. Nevertheless, the blond human hesitated. He held the bottle near his lips; everyone was silent, watching, but Virdon did not drink.

"Go ahead," said Kira softly. "I'm not trying to poison you. It's just a mild sedative."

"Come on, pal," said Burke, "you've swallowed worse things in the line of duty. Think of that banana sundae they gave us on that trip to Titan." Burke smiled when he saw Virdon shudder. Virdon swallowed the medicine and grimaced. After a moment he closed his eyes, surrendering to the effects of the drug. Burke stood up and joined Kira and Galen in a conference in a corner of the room. "He's in bad shape," said Burke, looking back toward his now unconscious friend. The two men had always been close, but now, in a strange world, they had been brought even closer. Burke's concern was as great as though he himself were lying wounded on the bed. "We just can't delay that operation anymore."

Kira looked thoughtfully at the still form of Virdon, then at the book of human surgery which Galen held. "We may not be able to operate, after all," she said.

Burke looked at her incredulously—especially after all the trouble and danger they had gone through, bringing Virdon to the hospital and stealing the book. "What are you talking about?" he demanded.

Kira took a deep breath. She had had to deal with many families before and to deliver the worst news on many occasions. That was part of her job. Now, though, it was a little different. "That seizure," she said. "I've seen it very often in gunshot cases. The bullet may have migrated into a region of dense blood vessels. If we go into that area, it's almost certain to touch off massive internal bleeding. And in his condition, he couldn't survive a heavy loss of blood."

Burke understood Dr. Kira's objection, but the answer was so routine and obvious that he was perplexed. "We could transfuse blood during surgery," he said, wondering why he had to remind a senior surgeon of such a commonplace fact. "Surely there are enough humans here to come up with some donors."

Dr. Kira waved the suggestion away impatiently. "Blood transfer is impossible," she said, a note of finality in her voice.

"Are you speaking from the vast tradition of ape medicine," Burke said sarcastically, "or from scientific experience?"

Kira looked at Burke. She couldn't believe that a human being could speak in such a manner, especially to an ape—a chimpanzee of authority. Whether what Galen had said about these two astronauts was true or not, this man Burke had better learn to respect the limits of propriety. He wasn't in his own time any longer. "We tried it once, a few years ago," she said coldly.

"On apes?" asked Galen.

Kira turned and gave her former suitor a tired look. It seemed to her that Galen's association with humans had somewhat damaged his promising intellect. "On humans," she said bluntly. "We wouldn't consider trying such a radical procedure without testing it on animals first."

"Naturally," said Burke, his voice filled with scorn. "What happened?"

Kira was growing tired of this interrogation. She was used to giving orders and being obeyed. She didn't like having to explain every step of every procedure she ordered. "The patient suffered a severe reaction and died within minutes of the blood transfer. Dr. Leander concluded that transferring blood from one being to another was against the laws of nature."

Burke chewed his lip as he thought. It had been demonstrated time and again that the apes had yet to discover what used to be termed "the scientific method," something which every school child accepted as plain common sense. The scientific mood dictated that one began with a hypothesis, made experiments, collected data, examined the information obtained and compared it with the expected results, and then came to a conclusion. It was understood that the experiments were to be conducted in a rational atmosphere, and in such a way as to exclude the influences of all other factors beyond the one under study. The apes, on the other hand, seemed to come to speedy and generally erroneous conclusions, based simply on a quick examination of a single event. That was the kind of thinking that many centuries ago had determined that the Earth was the center of the universe.

And, of course, the majority of apes believed that, too.

"You must have tried the transfusion with a mismatched donor," said Burke at last. It was the only explanation that he could find. "There's a simple blood test we can do to find a compatible donor. We're bound to find one among all the humans here."

"What will you tell them?" asked Kira. "You said yourself that Travin is getting suspicious."

"Don't worry," said Burke with a laugh, with more lightheartedness than he felt, "I'll handle Travin."

"How?" asked Galen. Galen could always be counted on to ask that. He called it intellectual probing. Burke called it quibbling.

"We have something in common," said Burke, thinking of the chief human in the hospital compound. "We hate each other."

Virdon moaned in his sleep, but the drug kept him from awakening and suffering. The long night passed with Burke, Galen, and Dr. Kira always nearby, watching. When the sun rose and filled the main room of the humans' quarters, there was frantic activity already going on. Travin entered the building, ready for a full day of hard work; he glowered at what he saw inside. He stood for a moment, brooding. There was a line of humans, already dressed in their orderly uniforms; the last in the line was holding his hand out so that Burke, under the nominal supervision of Dr. Adrian, could take a blood sample. When he finished, Burke turned to Travin. "Come on," said the astronaut, "it's your turn."

"No," said Travin.

"Yes," said Galen.

Travin looked at Burke, then at the chimpanzee. Travin shrugged and held out his hand. Burke carefully and quickly took his sample. Travin did not change expression or say a word.

"We've got eleven samples here," said Burke. "I was told that there are twelve humans here."

"There are only eleven," said Travin in a cold, hostile voice.

Burke thought for a moment, his expression somber. Then he remembered. "Where's the girl?" he asked.

Travin reacted with hot anger. "She is not a person!" he cried.

Burke ignored Travin's words. "I think you'd better get her," he said calmly.

Before Travin could make any kind of response, Galen looked at him and said, "One moment." Then the chimpanzee pulled Burke aside. "It could be dangerous to tamper with these people's taboos," he said. "Do we really need the girl?"

Burke looked past Galen's massive shoulder to where Travin stood. The human's expression was threatening; it was obvious that Travin was just waiting for an opportunity to break up Burke's and Galen's entire show. "We might need her," said Burke thoughtfully. "Virdon's blood type is labeled O. Statistically, there's about one chance in ten of finding a compatible donor."

Galen considered Burke's reasoning. He had never before heard of such a thing as blood types. The words "AB negative" meant little to him, about as much as the terms "propulsion units" or "flight command center." But he had accepted these things as parts of Burke's old world, and he assumed that in this case, too, the astronaut knew what he was talking about. For the sake of their blond friend, he'd *better* know what he was talking about. Galen turned back to Travin. "Where is the girl?" he asked.

"By the well," said Travin sulkily.

Galen turned again and nodded to Burke, who left without another word. Travin watched him go, then asked Galen, "These blood samples. Is it permissible to ask what they're for?"

"It is not permissible," said Galen, drawing himself up to his full height.

Galen stared at Travin until the human had to look away. It made no difference what Galen's identity really was; even if he were the lowliest farmer or peasant, his status as an ape would make him master of all humans in any situation. Travin nodded, acquiescent. But when Galen turned away, it was Travin who adopted the sneering attitude and his look of suspicion was directed at Galen himself.

The morning sun was already warm on Burke's back as he left the dark building that housed the human slaves. The apes and human beings of the medical compound were scurrying about on their early errands, and Burke walked among them unnoticed. He crossed the hard-packed dirt of the courtyard, spotting the solitary figure of the girl, who was seated by the well. Burke went up to her and smiled. She ignored him.

He stood for a moment, looking down at her. "Hello," he said, smiling again.

She looked up at him, squinting against the sun; she was startled that anyone would speak to her. She reacted suddenly, turning away in conditioned fear.

Burke realized that he would have to proceed with great care. "Don't be afraid," he said. "I just want to talk to you."

Burke's friendly overture didn't change the girl's attitude. Her wariness had been developed through years of punishment. She stared away from Burke, looking at nothing in particular in the dusty distance. "No one may speak to me except through my father," she said in a dull voice.

Burke frowned, wondering how to proceed. He knew that Virdon would know the right way; Virdon, who left children of his own back where they came from. Burke felt a rare feeling, a sudden longing for family and friends, a growing loneliness. He shrugged the feeling off; there was nothing to be done about it. Not here. Not now. Fate had seen to that—even Virdon's beautiful family had been dead for two thousand years, a fact that the blond man could never escape. Now, Burke had to find the key to these people's traditions, or the blond man himself would soon join his family under less happy circumstances. "Your father said that it's all right," said Burke. "I need your help."

"What kind of help can I give you?" asked the girl flatly.

Burke tried to make his voice light and cheerful. "We're running a medical test," he said. "It's an experiment Dr. Adrian is conducting. That's why we're here. He wants a sample of everyone's blood."

The girl shivered, fearful. She turned around for the first time and looked at Burke. "What for?" she asked.

"Just to help in some lab work. It's nothing to worry about. Please. Trust me."

She thought for a moment, recalling how Burke had stopped the human, Lafer, from beating her. She looked at Burke, torn between her fear and her feeling for this one person who had been kind to her. After a few seconds she said, "I trust you."

A while later, inside the laboratory of the apes' medical compound, Burke worked over the samples of blood that he had obtained through the false authority of

"Dr. Adrian." Dr. Kira had her normal responsibilities to attend to, so Burke and Galen were alone in the lab.

"We had studied blood types for almost a hundred years before I was shot into this ape world," said Burke. "We were learning more and more about blood every year. There are dozens of different things that go into making up blood. Somebody once suggested that a list of all the specific things or absence of things might identify a person better than a fingerprint."

"Fingerprint?" asked Galen. The apes, of course, had not made that discovery yet.

"Never mind. Look. You see what happens here. We can divide blood into four types: A, B, AB, and O. If you mix A with B, it will get all clotted up. The same thing happens if you mix A with O, if the A is coming from a donor. We can work out a chart of blood types, based on which types are compatible. A simple rule is that a person with O blood can give his blood safely to anyone else, and a person with AB blood can receive safely from anyone else. That's ignoring the existence of the Rh factor and a few other things. We don't have the time or the equipment to be that sophisticated. We know that Alan has type O blood. That means that he can receive blood only from another type O person;"

"Who?"

"Well," said Burke, "I've typed all of the humans in the compound, and we have two choices." The astronaut sounded hesitant. "One of them is that guy I clobbered. Lafer. He seems like the best choice. Let's hope his blood is in better shape than his brain."

It was not long before Lafer was seated in a chair in the lab. Galen and Burke looked at the man meditatively. He was pale and sick-looking; Dr. Kira was giving him an examination, to which he reacted in a listless fashion, totally unlike his usual bullying manner. Burke and Galen waited until Kira turned from Lafer and went to Burke and Galen. She spoke softly. "He has a fever. I believe he has a bad-water illness," she said.

Burke chewed his lip at this piece of news. "That figures," he said glumly. "Of all the times to pick, too. This guy Lafer gets my vote for Crumb of the Year."

"Crumb?" asked Kira.

"Archaic," said Burke. "Pejorative slang. Forget it."

"Certainly," said Kira.

"What it means is that we can't transfuse his blood," said Burke.

Galen looked over his shoulder; Lafer looked very ill. The chimpanzee shuddered at the thought of taking unclean blood from the human and transferring it to Virdon. "You said that there was another eligible donor," he said to Burke.

The dark-haired astronaut hesitated a moment. He realized that Virdon only had one chance left, and all the ancient rituals and folkways of these strange apes and strange humans would have to be bent for his sake. "I'll get her," he said.

Burke hurried outside. He assumed correctly that he could find the girl somewhere in the courtyard before the quarters of the human' slaves. When he approached her, she seemed to panic. Burke guessed that her father had been talking to her. "Listen to me," he said. "My friend, the blond man, will die unless you help us."

"I know what you want," said the girl, horrified. "You want me to give him my blood."

"He'll die," said Burke. He held out one hand to her, but she didn't come closer. Burke silently prayed to his long-neglected God and began pleading with the girl. "The procedure is safe. And you'll help to save his life. Doesn't that mean anything at all to you?"

The girl became hysterical. "No!" she cried in a hysterical voice. "I'll kill him! The curse will kill me, too. It'll kill all of us!"

She made her hands into small fists and flailed the air around her. Tears streaked her red cheeks. Then she bolted and ran toward the exit of the courtyard. Burke, alarmed, ran after her.

Meanwhile, Lafer had come out of the laboratory building and had begun walking unsteadily back to the humans' quarters. He witnessed the entire scene. Travin, curious about the girl's shouting, emerged from the, humans' building; Lafer met him, and explained. "The girl ran away; the stranger wanted to take her blood."

Lafer stared across the courtyard; Burke was still chasing the girl. The astronaut's cries seemed to float back over the dusty ground to Lafer and Travin. Travin reacted with a terror that seemed to go far beyond what was called for by the situation. "No, no," he said in a trembling voice. "It mustn't happen!"

The girl saw the gorilla in the guard post by the main gate and turned away, parallel to the wire fence that bounded the medical compound. Soon she came to a place that evidently had been used before: she lifted the wire fence and slid beneath it. Burke was only a few yards behind. No apes witnessed their peculiar chase. The girl ran out into a broad street that served the suburban neighborhood as a main street. Burke followed in pursuit, without a thought as to what might happen if they were caught by any of the ape citizens. After a few more yards he overtook the girl. She struggled in his grasp, crying hysterically. Burke did his best to calm her down.

"Please," he said, "listen to me."

"No, no!" she said, sobbing. "My blood is evil. I'll kill him. Please, please!" The girl collapsed, crying. "I don't want to kill again," she said, almost incoherently.

Burke was puzzled by the girl's words. "Again?" he asked. "What do you mean?"

The girl just continued to cry, her fists pressed against her eyes, and her whole body shaking. Burke swore softly at this delay. Before she could answer his question, Travin's voice came from behind them. "She's a murderer," he said, in a cold, hate-filled tone.

Burke turned around to face the man who had followed him and the girl. The astronaut was astonished to see, besides Travin, Lafer and several other men from the compound. "Don't you think you're endangering your secret exit like this?" asked Burke contemptuously.

"Shut up," said Travin. The man turned to his daughter. "Tell him," he said.

"No," begged the girl, looking up wildly at the circle of men, searching for a friendly face among them. "Please—"

Travin put a firm grip on the girl's shoulder and tightened it. "Tell him!" he said, between clenched teeth.

There was a long silence. Then the girl, sobbing, tears running down her cheeks, told her story. "My brother," she said mournfully. "I murdered him."

Burke looked startled. "Come on," he said. "Let's get back to the humans' building. We look like we're out trick-or-treating."

"What?" asked Lafer.

"I get that reaction a lot, lately," said Burke to himself. "I wonder if I *do* have a southern accent, after all."

A short time later, when the humans had successfully

re-entered the compound and gone back to their quarters, Travin began explaining the girl's story. "My only son," he said, in a voice filled with pain. "He was sixteen."

Burke stood near the chair in which Travin sat. At her father's feet sat the girl, still crying.

"There was a hunting accident," said Travin, taking a deep breath. "They brought him back to the medical center. The doctors there were doing experiments with blood transfers. It was the only time they ever tried such a thing. I told them that they could use my son in the experiment." He looked up at Burke. Travin raised his eyebrows and continued hastily. "I wasn't putting his life in danger. He was dying. This was a way to save him. At least, that was what those ape doctors told me."

Burke nodded, not willing to antagonize Travin further. "What happened?" he asked.

"My daughter gave him her blood," said Travin bitterly. "The boy died. The doctors said her blood was no good... no good!" Travin seemed on the point of tears. His voice was anguished. "My only son... *she* killed him with her evil blood!"

Burke knew that he had to stop what was becoming an ugly scene. "Listen to me," he said loudly. "Her blood wasn't evil. The blood was incompatible. It was of a different chemical type, that's why your son died. This girl has type O blood. She is, generally speaking, a universal donor. But there are other factors. The doctors ought to have tested the blood before they tried transfusing it. If they had, the transfusion never would have taken place."

"Are you saying that I killed my son?" asked Travin hotly. "I was trying to save him! *She* killed him. If she gives her blood to your friend, he'll die just like my son!"

Burke made a fist and shook it before Travin's face. He

was growing angry with Travin, and he caught himself before he completely ruined any chance to save Virdon. "You're not worried that my friend might die," he said. "You're worried that he might live, aren't you?"

Travin stared at Burke, unable to answer for a few seconds, stunned by the audacity of the astronaut's accusation: Travin started to speak, then stopped. He took a deep breath. Suddenly, for the first time in many years, Travin was in a defensive situation, his authority questioned and crumbling. He had to do something to save himself in front of the other humans whom he had ruled for so long.

Before he could begin his defense, Burke continued. "Dr. Kira told me the doctors had their doubts about the blood transfer experiment," said the astronaut. "They were afraid to try it, even on humans. But Dr. Kira says that you insisted."

Travin's face fell when Burke confronted him with this condemning bit of evidence. The others crowded closer, to hear if it were true. "To save my son!" cried Travin.

Burke would not be put off by this simple excuse. He had formed his own ideas and, for Virdon's sake as well as the future welfare of the humans of the compound, he pressed the matter. "Was that the only reason?" he asked. "Or were you trying to get in good graces with the apes, so they'd reward you, promote you?"

Travin was now in tears. He knew what Burke was leading up to and, as it was the truth, there was little that Travin could do. "My son was dying!" he said, sobbing. "Can't you understand that? There was no other way to save him."

Burke began to feel a little pity for the man. In a way, he had traded his own son for a position of security. Given the same situation, who was to say that Burke wouldn't have done the same? "You'll never know for sure," he said. "All you know is, your way failed. And the guilt's been tearing you apart ever since. So you made up this story about a curse, and eventually you even came to believe it yourself. It was easier to believe *she* was cursed than that you had killed your only son."

Travin was falling apart before Burke's eyes. He was just a helpless old man now. "No, no!" he cried, but his voice did not carry the same force it had before. Travin turned to the girl, his daughter. "Don't listen to him," he pleaded. "If you give him your blood, you'll spread the curse. The people will kill you!"

The girl looked at her father in silence for a tense moment. New understanding, seeded by Burke's arguments, began to dawn on her. When she spoke, her voice was quiet, full of despair. "What would they be taking from me by killing me?" she asked. "I died long ago."

Travin opened his mouth to reply, but no words came out. He looked at her, unable to respond in any way to the simple truth of her words. He turned away, angry, frustrated; then Travin rushed out of the room. Burke took the girl's hand; she held on to it tightly.

One of the operating rooms in the medical center's main building had been prepared in haste and secrecy. Operations upon human subjects were rare, and when they did happen they were for the purpose of scientific experimentation only. Repairs were hardly ever undertaken upon humans, because slaves were easy to replace.

Now, though, Virdon lay on the operating table. Dr. Kira was getting ready to operate, and Galen and Burke stood nearby to help.

The girl was lying on an operating table close by, ready

to transfuse blood if the need arose, through a simple gravity-operated transfusion apparatus. The medical book which Galen and Burke had stolen from Zaius' home was propped up where Burke had easy access to it. Various instruments were laid out on an adjacent table. Just before the operation began, Burke turned to Kira. "Do you have any cloth masks?" he asked.

Dr. Kira was puzzled by the question. "Yes," she said. "We use them for going into the room of the dead. But what do *we* need them for?"

Burke wondered again at the large gaps in the knowledge of the apes concerning medical procedures. Apparently they hadn't developed a germ theory, or the practice of disinfecting all operating room equipment that would follow such a theory. "It's a long story," said Burke wearily. "It has to do with keeping the operating room as clean as possible."

Dr. Kira was beginning to think that there was something clinically wrong with Burke's mind. He always had something new and odd to say. "We already scrubbed our hands with soap and alcohol, as you instructed. However, if you think it's necessary…"

Shaking her head, Dr. Kira walked across the room to a small wooden cabinet. She pulled open a drawer and took out some cloth masks. She put one on herself, and gave the others to Burke and Galen. Burke put the mask over his nose and mouth; then he bent down to speak to Virdon. "Dr. Kira says we're going to use a liquid anesthetic," he said. "All you have to do is breathe naturally through the cloth. You won't feel a thing."

"At least not until I get the bill," said Virdon weakly.

Burke smiled and nodded to Galen, who took the chloroform-soaked towel from a closed container and laid it across Virdon's face. Virdon breathed deeply several times. His eyelids drooped closed, and then he was asleep.

Outside the operating room, in one of the corridors of the main building, Dr. Leander walked slowly toward Kira's office. Toward him came another chimpanzee, Dr. Stole. "Good evening, Doctor," said Dr. Leander.

"Good evening," said Dr. Stole. "Is there some kind of emergency that brought you out this late after your regular office hours?"

"No," said Dr. Leander in a genial voice. "I was just looking for Dr. Kira. I couldn't find her in her quarters, and no one has seen her for several hours. I thought that she might be working in her office."

"Ah," said Dr. Stole. "No, she isn't in her office."

Dr. Leander thought that this Dr. Stole must be, after all, a pretty stupid fellow. "Well, then," said Leander, disguising his irritation, "do you know where she is?"

"Certainly, sir," said Dr. Stole. "She's in surgery."

Leander reacted with surprise and consternation. "Surgery?" he said. "But I'm quite sure that we don't have any surgery scheduled for tonight. I made up the assignments myself."

"It was just posted, Doctor."

"Who is the patient?"

Dr. Stole paused. "Dr. Adrian's orderly," he said finally.

Back in the operating room, the team was running through the final stages of its preparations. Virdon rested unconscious on the table. Burke watched him anxiously. Galen watched Dr. Kira, unable to do more than fetch things as she ordered. Kira instructed Burke to check Virdon's pulse a final time before they began. He did and reported, "Pulse and respiration are normal, Doctor."

"Well, then," said Dr. Kira, drawing a deep breath, "I suppose that we can begin." She seemed nervous and uncertain, and she certainly had good enough reason. Her brows creased over her sterile mask. She looked up at Burke. "What if there are complications?" she asked.

Burke did his best to reassure her. He tried to sound confident, but he was afraid that he failed in that miserably. "I've got the book right here," he said. But he knew that Kira still didn't have complete faith in the ancient human medical text.

Kira picked up a scalpel and held it motionless over Virdon's body. There wasn't any way that she could avoid doing the job, now. She shook off her fears and became her cool, professional self. Just before she could make the first incision, however, she was stopped by a voice. "Kira," said someone who had just entered the operating room.

Kira stopped, holding her hand frozen above Virdon. She turned with the others to see Leander at the door. Burke muttered something unintelligible under his breath.

Leander took a few steps toward them. Galen and Burke exchanged worried glances. "Why didn't you tell me you were operating tonight?" asked Leander.

Galen decided that he would have to continue his bluffing act if the situation were to be saved. He adopted a know-it-all attitude and spoke up. "My fault, Doctor," he said heartily. "I was supposed to notify you. Dr. Kira must be held blameless."

Dr. Leander waved the explanation away, suddenly curious about the patient and the technical aspects of the planned surgery. "What kind of operation is this?" he asked.

"A bullet wound," said Dr. Kira. "It is very possible that the nervous system may be affected."

Dr. Leander looked up suddenly at Kira, then turned his

gaze on Galen and Burke. "That's very interesting," he said. He tried to keep his voice impersonal, but the danger of the situation was obvious to everyone. "In what way did the human get this bullet wound in the back?"

"My colleagues and I were hunting," said Galen, unable to think of anything more convincing on the spur of the moment. "My orderly was retrieving the game, and he was shot by accident. Dr. Kira is going to try a new technique in experimental surgery. If it works, it is likely that it can then be applied to apes."

For the first time, Dr. Leander seemed to notice the girl on the other table. "This girl," he said. "Why is *she* here?" He examined the transfusion apparatus. "Surely you're not planning a blood transfer?"

Dr. Kira wiped her sweating forehead. "There could be extensive bleeding," she said, her voice hoarse and strained.

Leander walked closer to Kira. His expression was unreadable, except that Galen and Burke knew whatever the ape was thinking, it was unpleasant for them. "We tried a blood transfer before," said Leander to Kira. "If you will recall, I believe I proved that it can't work."

Galen interrupted; he couldn't count on Kira's maintaining her resolve in the face of this pressure from her supervisor. "We're trying a new process, as I said," declared the chimpanzee. "I've been working on it, uh, at my clinic."

Dr. Leander looked at Galen closely, torn between his sincere scientific curiosity and a sense that things were not quite right. The whole operation seemed to have been planned and almost carried out with a view to avoiding his official attention.

"In that case, Doctor," said Leander in an ironic tone of

voice, "we may be on the threshold of a breakthrough in medicine. May I join you?"

Kira looked at Galen, expecting him to continue the imposture that had so far brought them all into such a dangerous situation. Galen said nothing for a moment. Burke stood motionless, waiting to see how Galen would react to Leander's unexpected challenge. Then Galen, handing one of the sterile masks to Leander, said, "It's our pleasure and honor to have you with us, Doctor. Would you mind wearing one of these masks during the operation? We've found it useful at our clinic to wear them as protection against the vapors."

Leander looked at Galen suspiciously, but accepted the mask. "And you don't think these masks interfere with your technique at all?" he asked.

"Not at all," said Galen authoritatively. "Dr. Kira has already become accustomed to its presence, isn't that right?" Kira only nodded.

"You practice a fascinating kind of medicine, Dr. Adrian," said Leander with a wry smile. There was no humor in the expression, and the director's implied threat was easy to interpret. "I'm quite eager to watch you in action."

"I'll bet you are," murmured Burke. Leander didn't hear him. Galen swallowed nervously but didn't answer. Dr. Kira could only look helplessly at Galen. They had all come to the final crisis.

4

The operation proceeded. The team of Dr. Kira, Galen, and Burke was grouped around the table, working under the extreme pressure of Leander's ominous presence. Compared to it, the danger inherent in the surgery itself lessened somewhat, but not so much that any of the three were not continually reminded that they were entering territory in medical knowledge that had been unexplored for hundreds of years. Kira, who had done most of the work, flashed another quick look at the medical text, but it was on Burke's side of the table. Burke had to help her and block Leander's view of the book at the same time. Leander stood behind Galen, peering over the young chimpanzee's shoulder.

"I think you've neglected to see that a clamp is necessary on that bleeding vessel, Doctor," said Leander.

Galen looked up at Kira. How did he do that? Burke slowly handed Galen the clamp, without saying a word. Galen took the thing and looked at it for a few seconds.

He didn't know what in the world to do with it. Suddenly he got an idea and turned to Leander. "It's rare that a country doctor like me gets a chance to see a well-known surgical authority at work," said Galen. "I'd like to watch you do it."

"It's just some minor bleeding, Doctor," said Leander, his brows contracting above his mask. "However…"

Leander reached forward and took the clamp from Galen's hands. Galen quickly and agilely slipped past Leander and let the medical director get to the operating table. Galen pantomimed a sigh of relief behind Leander's back, and Burke nodded in reply, to show that he understood what Galen hoped to do. Now involved in the surgery, it was possible that Dr. Leander might forget about Galen's presence, and that Virdon would have the benefit of two top surgeons, rather than a single expert and a puzzled fugitive chimpanzee. Leander applied the clamp and stopped the bleeding. Galen relaxed for a moment.

"The bullet," said Kira anxiously. "I can't reach it."

Her words cut through the tense atmosphere of the operating room like a shrill siren in the quiet of night. "It's trapped," she said. "Here, between the nerve cluster and a large blood vessel."

Leander looked where Kira's probe was pulling some tissue aside. The dull glint of a portion of the bullet was visible. Leander shook his head and said with cool detachment, "There's no way of removing that safely. You'd better just close up."

But Burke, who had been dreading this very moment, turned to the book and said in a steady voice, "Make a second incision, about three inches below the first. We'll try to get at the bullet from below the entry point."

Burke's words caused an immediate and diverse

reaction among the apes in the operating room. Dr. Kira thought about the suggestion for a brief instant, then nodded her agreement. Galen had nothing to suggest, and he still wanted to avoid Dr. Leander's notice. The latter, though, responded much more violently. The very idea of a human being speaking at such a time, in such a tone of authority, made the chimpanzee director of the medical center furious.

"What is he saying?" cried Leander. He turned to Galen and shook a fist at the young ape. "Who is he?"

Galen kept his voice as steady as he could as he answered, "He's my orderly." Galen hoped that Leander would not question him any closer than that, because it would be terribly easy to establish that Galen wasn't, in fact, Dr. Adrian, but Galen, the renegade chimpanzee, and that his two human companions were the astronauts, whom General Urko never tired of warning the citizens of Central City about.

"I cannot believe what I've heard here tonight," said Leander. "An orderly giving instructions to Dr. Kira?" He pushed past Burke—and saw the medical text. All activity in the operating room ceased. There was a suffocating hush. If Galen and Burke had thought that things could not have gotten worse, they were wrong. Things had become infinitely worse.

Leander picked up the book slowly, staring at it. Then, slowly, deliberately, he set it down and said in a calm voice, "It's obvious to me that you have things well in hand, Doctors. I think that I can return to my other duties now."

Leander turned and started to move to the door of the operating room. To any observer who had not witnessed the preceding angry explosion, Dr. Leander might have seemed completely unconcerned with what was happening. But

Galen knew better; he barred Leander's way. "You'd better stay here, at least for a while," said Galen.

"Are you feeling unwell?" asked Leander quietly. "Forcing me to stay here could be defined as kidnapping. I'm certain that our guards would define it that way."

"I'm not completely convinced that your guards will have the chance," said Galen.

"Besides,", said Burke, "I don't think they could define anything, anyway."

"Let's not talk about the gorillas," said Galen. He pressed something against Dr. Leander's throat. It was a scalpel.

"You are holding me captive, against my will," said Leander. He exhibited not the slightest sign of nervousness. "You're foolish, but you're not insane. Dr. Adrian, whoever you are, you wouldn't use that scalpel." Leander ignored Galen from that point on. He turned his attention to Kira. "Did he force you to do this?" he asked.

The question was vital to Leander's authority in the situation. Dr. Kira understood what her answer might mean. There was silence for a moment, and then, simply, Kira said, "No."

"Then why are you going along with these brutes?" asked Leander.

"Because I'm a doctor," said Kira. To her mind, uncluttered with the bureaucratic methods that Dr. Leander lived by, that seemed reason enough. "I have no right to reject the truth," she said.

Leander was furious once more. "The truth!" he cried. "That book is not truth! It is treason; madness!"

Dr. Kira looked calmly at her director. 'The book exists," she said quietly. "To deny what exists *is* madness." Then she looked at Burke. "Scalpel," she said. Burke handed her the instrument.

Some distance from the medical center, the quiet warm night was broken by the blazing torches of a squad of gorilla police. Their heavy leather uniforms gleamed in the flickering firelight, and bright beams glanced from the metal of their buckles and rifles. Horses pranced and snorted in the street; the gorillas were on guard in front of the house of Zaius, the Prime Minister of the ape world and the President of its Supreme Council.

Inside the house, Zaius stood in his study, conferring with his rival for power, the fierce General Urko. Zaius represented the rational forces which governed the apes, and Urko embodied all the raw, animal strength which lay beneath the thin veneer of civilization. Now, though, instead of vying for political influence, Urko was investigating a burglary. He walked about the room, frowning. Zaius had been of little help, and Urko could discover few clues to help him further. The rest of the house had been left alone; only this room, a study, with obviously little of value in it, had been disturbed. General Urko was puzzled.

"There are a few things that I just can't fit together, Minister," said Urko thoughtfully. "You suggest that a burglar broke into your house—into the home of the Prime Minister, directly into your study—ignored valuable objects of art throughout your house, and made off into the night with an old piece of sculpture worth, according to you, roughly about the price of a loaf of bread."

"I am presenting the facts to you, whether I can draw conclusions or not." Zaius shrugged. "After all, all critics are not thieves. We may surmise that all thieves are not critics."

Urko would not be deterred from his investigation. The circumstances were cloudy enough without Zaius' word-playing. "I admire your sense of humor,

Minister," he said gruffly. "But don't you think this is a serious matter?"

Zaius laughed quietly. There were occasions when he and Urko agreed, but they were rare indeed. "You told *me* that it was serious, remember? I don't think that it's serious enough to keep us from our business. Had I been here instead of at a meeting of the Council, I would not have thought it necessary to call the police over such a minor burglary."

"That is one of the main differences between gorillas and other apes," said Urko defiantly. "In my opinion, Minister, no crime is minor. So let me ask my questions, and possibly we can come to a closer idea of what actually happened. Is there a key to that cabinet?" Urko indicated the cabinet from which Galen and Burke had taken the medical book. The space where the book had come from had been closed up by pushing the remaining books together. But the door to the cabinet stood open, and the marks around the lock indicated to Urko that someone had forced it open.

"Why do you ask?" said Zaius.

"Nothing serious, possibly," said Urko. "In the course of investigating your study here, that cabinet door swung open. It seemed to me that it should have been locked, but that the lock had recently been forced. Call it an intellectual curiosity, but if you have a key nearby, it would show that I was at least partly correct. Even a brutish policeman is entitled to expand the potential of his limited mind." Urko uttered these words with an unpleasant sneer.

Zaius stared at him. Then he went to his desk and took out a key from one of the drawers. He handed the key to the gorilla who opened the cabinet and scanned the row of books within. He noticed a place where the dust had been disturbed. He moved the books to the left and right, exposing a place that fit the width of a full-sized book. Urko turned back to Zaius.

"You know, you do have an impressive collection, Zaius," he said. "I can't think of anyone in all of Central City that might have anything to rival it. That's because I don't know anyone but you who might be so reckless. It is an impressive collection, and dangerous. You should have burned them as I warned you when they were first discovered."

Zaius shrugged. "I did what I thought was best. One day these books will serve us," he said.

"They will enslave us!" cried Urko. "And the process already has begun. Look, here. Your burglar was a more clever critic than we supposed, it seems. One of your volumes is missing. What does your burglar have? A text on human politics? A manual of war?"

Zaius shook his head. He knew how deeply ran Urko's hatred and fear of the humans. Only these two apes had a genuine appreciation of the fact that the human slaves might once have been—and, even worse, might still be—the intellectual equals of the apes. Zaius saw this as a hopeful sign for the future. General Urko, however, could only see death and destruction at the hands of a human revolt.

"The burglar took a book of surgery," said Zaius.

"You knew it all along, didn't you?" said Urko. "When will you trust me, Minister? We can't afford to play games when our civilization might well be in danger at this very moment. I suppose you have an idea who your mysterious burglar might be."

"Yes," said Zaius, "and if I am correct, they are welcome to the book."

"They?" said Urko. "Ah, yes. Our astronauts and their

chimpanzee friend. Danger, Zaius, our civilization may be in danger."

Zaius sighed. "I agree, General, there might be danger. I don't agree on hysteria as a means of dealing with it. Is there anything else?"

Urko looked at him, then said quietly, his own plan forming in his mind, "No, Minister. You've given me all the information I need." And on that cryptic, ominous note, Urko turned and left the room.

The operation on Virdon continued. Beads of perspiration stood out on Kira's brow, as well as on Galen's and Burke's. Only Dr. Leander did not seem to be overly concerned with the outcome of the crucial experimental procedures.

A transfusion bottle stood on its stand; the bottle was now only half-full, and emptying through a tube in the direction of the surgical table. Kira continued to work over Virdon, who might already have died on the operating table without the transfusion. Burke gave her all the assistance he could; Galen still guarded Leander with his scalpel. Leander watched Dr. Kira's technique, impressed despite himself by the curious work that was going on before him. "It's quite fascinating," he said. "The blood transfer seems to be working."

"Then you'd be willing to admit that your pronouncement banning them on the basis of a single experiment might have been premature?" asked Kira without looking up.

Leander made a noncommittal sound. On the other side of the table, lying tense and still, was the girl. She gave a sigh of relief when she heard Leander's words and Kara's reply. The girl relaxed a little.

"Now maybe you'll change your mind about us backward humans, too," said Burke.

"That's not as likely," said Galen.

"Very astute, Dr. Adrian," said Leander. "On the contrary, this whole exercise demonstrates the low level of your intelligence. Even if your friend lives, he can only hinder your escape. He will need postoperative care. He won't even be conscious for a long while, and then he will be weak and in pain. You would have done better to let him die in the forest."

"Ah," said Burke, "but then several important things wouldn't have occurred. I wouldn't have had the opportunity to sharpen my breaking and entering skills. And we wouldn't have had the chance to meet you. That would really have been too bad."

Leander laughed loudly. "You show remarkable calmness under pressure," he said. "I would have to guess that was an act. I suppose that what I said has you genuinely disturbed, but you're too prideful to let me see. If I shut my eyes, I'd almost think you were an ape."

Burke grinned. "Almost, but not quite, huh? Doc, you've made my whole day!"

Galen interrupted the bantering conversation. "Is that supposed to be doing what it's doing?" he asked, pointing to the respiration bladder. It was, actually, an animal bladder that expanded and contracted with Virdon's breathing. Now, though, it fluttered weakly, then stopped. "Kira!" cried Galen.

Kira and Burke both looked up and saw Galen pointing at the unmoving bladder. Burke hurried around the corner of the table on which the book rested and picked up one of Virdon's limp arms. "I can't get any pulse," he said frantically.

The girl lifted her head up a little. "I killed him, too!" she said in a mournful voice.

"Don't be silly," said Galen.

"Yes," said Leander. "I think the problem is that the amount of anesthetic might have been too much for his heart. We have this problem frequently, because operations on humans are generally carried out without anesthetic. The proper dosage is not yet determined." Burke gave Leander an ugly look. Leander didn't appear to notice. "There's a stimulant in the cabinet," said the ape.

Burke stared at Leander, not knowing precisely what to do. Leander continued with impatient sarcasm. "What's the matter? Don't you trust an ape surgeon? Or are you waiting for verification from your great Dr. Mather?"

Burke turned and went to the cabinet, muttering dark sentiments under his breath. If Leander was telling the truth, there was no time to waste. If he wasn't telling the truth, Virdon was a dead man. But Burke didn't want to think about that last alternative. He took out the bottle of medicine Kira was pointing to. Leander took the bottle from Burke, opened it, and poured some of the medicine onto a rag. Then the ape forced Virdon's mouth open and squeezed some of the medicine down the blond man's throat. There was a long, tense silence.

"I suppose you don't how know much of *that* to give him, either," said Burke.

Leander was unruffled by the remark. He just handed Burke the rag and stepped away from the table.

"I'm sorry," said Burke. Leander said nothing.

The respiration bladder began its expansion and contraction. A short moment later, Burke announced, "We're getting a pulse again!"

Galen and Burke both relaxed. As Kira continued to

work at her difficult surgery, Burke turned to Leander. "Thank you, Doctor," he said.

Leander shrugged. "I don't like patients dying in my operating room. It's bad for morale."

Dr. Kira had been working wordlessly through the entire episode. Now she made a final, tiny cut with a small scalpel and pulled aside some tissue. Then, carefully, slowly, she lowered a pair of long-nosed tweezers into the incision. "There it is," she said, "the bullet." She closed the tweezers on it, withdrew the bullet and held it up.

"It's funny how much trouble a little piece of lead like that can cause," said Galen.

"It isn't funny at all," said Burke. "I don't remember it being funny."

Kira turned triumphantly to Burke. "Let's close up," she said.

They returned to their work, which from that point on was routine and relatively simple. The wound was packed and stitched closed, the outside was cleaned and sterilized, and the entire area was bandaged over. "There isn't a great deal of time left," said Galen, indicating the transfusion bottle, which was almost empty. Even as he spoke, the last of the blood sputtered and gurgled through the tube.

"We're done," said Kira, her voice suddenly full of the tiredness she had repressed throughout the long evening.

Outside, the night had grown even quieter. All through the medical complex lights went out in windows as apes and humans turned in for the night. But the peace of the evening was shattered by the sound of galloping hooves. Travin was awakened by the racket as it grew louder. He carried a lantern from the humans' quarters and crossed the courtyard to investigate. As Travin arrived at the main gates, a squad of mounted and armed gorillas, led by Urko, pulled up at the entrance.

"Come on, come on, open the gates!" shouted Urko to the sleepy gorilla guards stationed at the sentry box. Before the gorillas could move, Travin rushed up and opened the gates, then fell back in fear as the gorillas rode in.

"We're looking for two humans and a renegade ape," said Urko to Travin. "One of the humans was wounded. We think they came to one of the hospitals for help. Have any strangers come here in the last two days?"

Travin thought for a moment before he answered. "We see many people all the time," he said evasively.

Urko was quickly irritated. "These people are traitors," he said, leaning down closer to Travin's fearful face. "The penalty for helping them is death."

Travin stared up at the gorilla's fierce expression, torn between his conditioned docility to the apes and a newer, still-unresolved attachment to his fellow humans. Then, in a quiet, tormented voice, Travin said, "I haven't seen them." He was a man whose sense of certainty and authority had both been shattered.

Urko considered what Travin said. Before either could speak again, a voice interrupted them. "He's lying!" said a human, whose identity was still shrouded by the darkness. Urko raised the lantern which he took from Travin's grasp. Lafer hurried up to the gorillas and pointed accusingly at Travin. "They're here," cried Lafer, still a little ill and unsteady. "Right here in the hospital."

Urko glanced first at Travin, then back to Lafer, who was fumbling something out of his pocket. Urko shone the light of the lantern on the object in Lafer's hand. It was the compass which Travin had stolen from Virdon.

"I found this among Travin's things," said Lafer.

"He got it from the stranger. And his own daughter is helping them!"

Urko looked back to Travin. "Your daughter helps them?" he said, raising his eyebrows. "Then she can die with them."

"No!" cried Travin. He grabbed at Urko's arm, then tried to catch the reins of the gorilla chieftain's horse. One of the guards knocked Travin aside with the butt of his rifle. The gorillas paid the humans no more attention, but rode hastily into the courtyard.

In the operating room, the tense scene had ended. Kira was dismantling the transfusion apparatus as Burke watched over Virdon. The girl looked up weakly and made a motion, catching Burke's attention. "Is he dead?" she asked.

"No," said Burke in a kindly manner, "he's just sleeping. He'll live now, thanks to you. The curse is gone."

"Thank goodness," said the girl.

"I don't know," said Dr. Leander, who stood at a window. The ape surgeon was still covered by Galen and the scalpel. Leander looked out at the courtyard. "Not quite," he said quietly.

Burke, Galen, and Kira reacted to Leander's words. They hurried to join him and looked down at the scene below. In the courtyard, illuminated by the dancing light of torches and lanterns, the gorillas were fanning out, moving closer to the hospital buildings, to cover all the exits.

Leander turned to the others. "You came here to use the operating room. Perhaps the room of the dead would have been more appropriate," he said. His grim humor was not appreciated.

Urko, accompanied by two other gorillas, headed down the main corridor of the building, only a few moments later. Their rifles were held at the ready, and they checked each door as they came to it, offices, storerooms, operating theaters, every niche that might serve as a place of concealment for the fugitives. Leander and Kira came around a corner, acting surprised to see the gorillas.

"We're looking for some escapees," said Urko. 'Two humans and a chimpanzee. We understand they're here."

Dr. Leander did not seem to be the least bit cowed by the presence of General Urko. "Was one of the humans wounded?" he asked.

"Yes," said Urko. "Where are they?"

"I don't know," said Leander.

"What do you mean?"

"They're gone," said Leander, spreading his hands and smiling, as though he wished that he could be more help. "And I'd suggest you go too, as quickly as possible."

Urko stared, unbelieving. "Are you giving *me* orders?" he asked.

"Not orders. Just a medical warning."

Urko looked across the corridor, where Leander pointed. The room there had a flag draped over its doors; the flag showed a white ape's skull on a red background, with an X over the skull. It was clear to Urko what the hospital used that room for.

"The room of the dead," said Dr. Leander. "Our busiest room, the last few days, since the coming of the plague."

Urko recoiled in horror. "Plague?" he said.

"The Black Death. Seven cases in the last forty-eight hours. When the strangers learned of it, they fled. Of course, if your duty compels you to search the hospital, please, don't let me stand in your way. I have a very good record with the police. I always try to be as helpful as I can."

Urko stared at Dr. Leander as though the surgeon was the very embodiment of death. Then the gorilla turned and hurried back down the corridor, his aides following him. Leander's final words still hung in the air, ignored by the armed gorillas.

Inside the morgue, Galen and the girl crouched against the cold, white-tiled wall. Virdon lay on the wheeled table near the rear of the room, tended by Burke. Galen peered out through the small window in the door; as the gorillas retreated down the hallway, he sighed in relief.

Later that day, Kira walked with Leander from room to room, on her regular rounds. She took his arm as they went down the corridor. "Why did you help them?" she asked.

"I was afraid you'd be taken in along with them," said Leander. "Purely selfish reasons, to be sure. After all, we were to have dinner again tonight." Dr. Kira looked up at him and smiled. Leander smiled, too, something rare for the medical director. "Besides," he said, "if the police had arrested them, they might have found this." He reached beneath his tunic and pulled out the surgical manual. Kira laughed out loud. Leander tucked the book back under his arm and he and Kira stopped to read the day's patients' reports.

A few days later, after Virdon had been nursed back to an ambulatory condition, able to travel without making a dangerous situation for his companions, the three friends made plans to strike out across the country again, heading possibly for the ocean, where the cool, clean air would be a welcome change from the loud and bustling atmosphere of the city. The stitches had been removed from Virdon's back, and he was only slightly weaker than normal. Dr. Kira announced that he was well enough to leave.

That afternoon saw Burke, Virdon, Galen, Travin, and the latter's daughter walking slowly along a mountain path, some distance from the hospital compound. They stopped and Travin pointed. "This path will take you over the mountains," he said.

"I still think you'd be safer coming with us," said Burke.

"No," said Travin thoughtfully, "My people need me. You've shown me the truth. Now I must share it with them."

"You will be in danger," said Virdon.

Travin laughed softly. "The police won't be back for a long while. When they do come, Dr. Leander and Dr. Kira will protect us, thanks to you."

"I'm the one who has to say thanks," said Virdon.

"Not to me," said Travin, sadly. "In my ignorance and cowardice, I almost killed you. My daughter was wiser and braver than any of us."

Virdon turned to the girl. "I shouldn't leave without knowing the name of the girl who saved my life," he said.

The girl hesitated, looking at her father. Travin nodded. The girl smiled. "It's just an ordinary name around here," she said. "Prunella Alexandrina."

Virdon's eyebrows raised a bit. "Now that was worth waiting for!" he said. Burke, Galen, and Travin laughed, and the girl only looked puzzled. Then she, too, laughed.

THE DECEPTION

5

Many miles and many days from the medical compound of Dr. Leander, there was a quiet farming community of apes. The settlement was almost completely independent of the Central City, in that its inhabitants lived a self-sufficient existence. They needed nothing in trade from the Central City, because their little world was simple and unambitious. And, in return, Central City had almost forgotten them, because what the apes there could not exploit, they did not care about.

It was about the middle of the summer, on a bright, clear day, that a large group of apes from this village had gathered on a hillside just outside their town. The grass smelled sweet, the air was clean and refreshing, and the breeze which came from the ocean was pleasant. The sound of waves breaking against the shore could be heard faintly in the distance.

The apes were staring at a simple grave marker; upon its smooth surface were carved the words LUCIAN,

FATHER OF FAUNA. Some of the apes wiped tears from their cheeks. Others stood stoically, however much they may have been moved by their emotions. They listened to an ape named Sestus, who was delivering a eulogy.

"As for the ape," said Sestus, "his days are like grass… like a flower of the field he flourishes…"

Sestus was a serious, brooding chimpanzee. He was reading from a small, clumsily-bound manual. Near him stood a young female chimpanzee, Fauna, the daughter of the dead Lucian; she held a kerchief to her face, sobbing uncontrollably in her grief. On the other side of the grave, a gorilla police chief named Perdix stood, grimly watching the proceedings. Next to him, Zon, his deputy, stood with a rifle in his hands. Zon did not show any symptom of compassion or pity, unlike his superior.

Behind the gorillas were a dozen or so ape villagers, a mixture of chimpanzees and gorillas, all looking on with an attitude of proper solemnity.

Sestus paused in his reading and passed one of his large hands through his hair, which was already streaked with gray; he gazed thoughtfully across the assembled crowd, but he gave no indication of his thoughts. After a few seconds, he returned to his reading.

"For the wind passes over the field and is gone," he said. "And the place knows it no more. Rest forever, O Lucian, Father of Fauna…"

Behind Sestus the gentle grassy slope abruptly ended at the edge of an ocean cliff, and beyond that was the sprawling blue expanse of the sea. Sestus slowly closed the book and put his arm around Fauna, trying to comfort the grieving young female chimpanzee. Suddenly, she broke down completely. "Why?" she cried. "Why? How could they do it?"

Sestus patted the young chimpanzee's shoulder. Lucian had been his brother, and Fauna was his niece. She would be his ward, now, and the elder chimpanzee was a little concerned about doing the right thing for her. He knew that he wouldn't always be sure what was right. "Savages, child," he said softly. "They're just savages. They don't know any better."

Fauna cried some more. "That's no reason. That isn't any kind of an excuse. He said that he trusted them..." Sestus took a deep breath and exhaled slowly. "You can't trust humans, Fauna," he said. "I warned him. You remember that, don't you? You were there several times when I warned him of the trouble he was asking for. It doesn't do any good now. Oh, I wish he had listened to me!"

Fauna's expression turned to one of hatred. "I hate them!" she said bitterly. "I hate them!"

Perdix, the gorilla chief of police, listened to Fauna's declaration and walked to join her and Sestus. His expression was fierce and determined, but softened somewhat with a more rational approach to the problem. Although he shared the apes' general loathing and mistrust of humans, he always desired to proceed in a lawful and civilized way. "We will capture them, Fauna," he said. "I make this promise to you on the grave of your father. The humans will be caught and punished for what they have done. Our laws and traditions prescribe the ways we must go about this, and we will do so tirelessly until we have captured the murderers of Lucian."

Fauna could only nod gratefully in response to Perdix's words. His announcement signalled that the funeral services were over, and other members of the crowd began to make their feelings known.

From the crowd, three apes stepped forward. They were

well-known in the village, and their hatred of humans was as great as anyone else's. They were a chimpanzee named Chilot, and two gorillas, Macor and Krono. Their mood was ugly, and it served as a model for the others. Chilot raised a fist and shook it at the police chief. "How, Perdix?" he demanded. His voice almost broke with the weight of hostility it carried. "Are you and Zon going to arrest every human being in this entire district?"

Perdix stared at Chilot. The chimpanzee had caused him a great deal of trouble in the past, with his disregard for law. "If necessary," said Perdix in a steady voice.

"A hundred humans for every ape!" shouted Macor. "They will hide the killers among themselves! They will lie for their killers!"

Krono grunted in agreement. "And now that they have tasted ape blood," he said, his lip curling in a disgusted sneer, "they will kill again!" He pointed at the other members of the crowd, indicating that the next victim could be anyone—anyone at all. The frenzied apes returned his challenge with shouts of alarm, concern, and anger.

Perdix tried to control the crowd; they had been put in a vengeful frame of mind by the murder of Lucian, and now the words of Chilot, Macor, and Krono were urging the simple villagers to take matters into their own hands. Perdix had no desire to see the crowd turn into a raging mob. "You don't know any of that!" he shouted.

He was answered by angry shouts from the crowd. "And you," said Chilot, pointing at Perdix, "do *you* know that?" Perdix was at a loss for an answer. His sympathies might well have been with the outraged apes, but his responsibility was to keep order.

Chilot took Perdix's silence for tacit approval. He turned again to the crowd. He raised both arms above his head; the others quieted down when they saw that he wished to speak. "The time has come, fellow apes, Perdix, everyone! The time has come to unite!" There was applause and cheering; Chilot was appealing to both pride and fear. "Let us drive the humans out!"

The shouts of approval from the crowd drowned out any further arguments for several moments. Chilot looked around and was pleased at the reaction he was getting. Perdix was growing more and more unhappy.

"No!" said Perdix, when the noise had settled down a little. "This matter will be handled within the law. We have always been proud that we have been independent from the government in Central City, at least as far as our internal affairs go. If Zaius and the Supreme Council hear that we have resorted to murder, even of mere humans, we will attract their attention. We must keep to the law. And I am the law!"

There was a moment of silence. Behind Perdix, Zon, the gorilla deputy, raised his rifle, not as a threat, but as a symbol of the gorillas' authority. "You have heard," said Zon. "All of you return to your homes. Now!"

There was another pause, during which the apes of the rural village were undecided. They had rather enjoyed indulging themselves in an outpouring of hate; but, after all, Perdix and Zon did have the authority, and it *was* a funeral for poor Lucian. The angry crowd turned and headed back to the town, out of respect more for Lucian's memory than for Perdix's authority. Krono stopped suddenly and turned around to face the gorillas. "We will drive them out!" he shouted threateningly.

Once more the crowd erupted into excited sounds of approval. Perdix stared coldly at the departing group. His thoughts were his own, and he didn't bother to answer Krono's challenge.

Meanwhile, Sestus moved closer to Fauna and put his arm around the young female chimpanzee. She was crying, almost totally oblivious to the conflict that had just occurred. All she knew was that her father, whom she had loved more than anyone else in the world, was dead.

A small gray squirrel stopped its frantic gathering of food as it heard the rapid approach of an enemy. The squirrel was not certain just who the enemy was, of course. But the heavy, lumbering tread that crashed through the forest's thick undergrowth *had* to be an enemy. Everything that wasn't a squirrel was an enemy. Even most squirrels were enemies.

The tiny creature climbed part way up a giant oak tree, and ran around to the side opposite the approaching noises. It peered around the curve of the tree and saw a pair of large, smooth feet moving through the grassy space among the trees. Another pair of human feet was close behind. Then came ape feet, larger and more irregularly shaped. The squirrel stared, frightened for a moment, then ran up the tree to safety.

At the top of a grassy knoll, Alan Virdon, Pete Burke, and Galen came to a stop. They rested for a moment before they started down the other side. All three were weary, but Galen was doing the worst. When they started up again, Galen waved and tried to cry out to Virdon, who was leading; the chimpanzee's voice wouldn't leave his throat. Virdon raised a hand, seeing something ahead. Burke stopped behind him, and Galen stumbled up to meet them. He, too, looked down the hill at where Virdon was pointing. He saw no danger.

"What is it?" asked Galen.

"Nothing threatening," said Virdon. "I just recognized our position."

"How much farther?" asked Galen. His words were almost pitiably fatigued. "I'm about to collapse from this awful heat."

Virdon didn't laugh. He knew that the shaggy-haired chimpanzee in his heavy clothing was less accustomed to extremes of temperature. Even though Galen had been forced to lead the life of an outlaw, he still clung to many of his old ways and beliefs. He would never have considered trading his clothing for the lighter, more comfortable apparel of the humans.

"It isn't much farther at all," said Virdon. "Another mile, maybe."

Galen groaned at the news and settled to the ground, where he rubbed his aching feet. Burke gave him a reassuring pat on the back as he, too, crouched down and handed the chimpanzee their canteen.

"Cheer up," said Burke, grinning. "Once we get to Jasko's you can take a nice cool swim. I hear he's got a lake in his backyard."

"Swim?" asked Galen, giving Burke a sideways look. "Very funny. You know that apes can't swim."

Burke was all set to make one of his devastating replies, but Virdon stopped him with a quick motion. Virdon raised a finger to his lips and nodded toward Galen; the chimpanzee was suddenly alert. He heard something off in the distance, and now he was looking in that direction. "Listen," said Galen. "Horses!" Each of them knew that only apes could own horses, and that apes meant a threat to their lives.

Galen stared into the distance, one large hand shading his eyes from the afternoon sun. Below them a road ran through the greenery. The sound of hoofbeats grew louder and louder. Galen thought that he could make out the movement of horses along the road further off, but he couldn't yet decide whether the flickering of shadows among the trees was caused by the movement of the horses or the shifting of branches in the wind.

All at once, a racing troop of mounted apes broke from the cover of the trees several hundred yards along the road. Galen counted six horses. The riders were a mixture of four gorillas and two chimpanzees. Each ape carried a blazing torch; their identities were hidden behind fearful leather masks that covered the riders' eyes and noses. "These provincial apes," murmured Galen with a certain amount of condescension.

Virdon indicated with a short gesture that they should move back over the hilltop, and quickly. They were open to discovery in their present position, outlined against the sky. Galen scampered briefly on all fours, then rose to his feet, and was in the lead as they dashed back over the top of the knoll.

The mounted apes pounded along the road, shouting and waving rifles. They left the cover of the trees and galloped out into the open. One of the gang looked in the direction of the fugitives and was surprised at what he saw. Virdon and Burke stood out on the crest, in plain view. He shouted to his leader. "Humans!" he cried.

The leader of the strangely costumed apes pulled up and waited for the excited follower to catch up. "Where?" he asked.

"There, there!" cried the ape. He pointed with his rifle, up the slope of the hill. Without waiting for his leader the ape turned his mount away from the group and charged off toward the grassy knoll. The rest of the apes reined up, regrouped, and rode after him, the horses laboring uphill among the rocks and stones.

Burke and Virdon heard the commotion behind them. They turned briefly to look back, and they saw the one masked ape in the lead, the rest not far behind. They hurried ahead and began scrambling down the ridge's farther side.

Virdon, Burke, and Galen raced madly ahead for the cover of the underbrush and boulders they had left behind only a few minutes before. From the sounds of the horses behind them, it would be close; none of the three friends could tell whether or not they would be overtaken before they reached safety.

The leading ape crested the knoll and spurred his horse down the back side. The horse ramped a little and the ape pulled sharply on the reins. The horse slipped and stumbled awkwardly down the slope.

Burke and Galen had already reached the safety of the underbrush and were hidden from the apes' sight. They tried to urge Virdon on, but there was no way that they could help him. He had plainly been sighted by the ape. Burke and Galen exchanged worried looks.

The ape charged Virdon, holding his torch at the ready like a flaming mace. Virdon stood his ground before the bellowing rider. The ape thundered on, aiming straight for the yellow-haired man. At the last possible instant, Virdon side stepped and, grabbing the shaft of the swinging torch, he pulled the ape from his horse in a wide, crashing arc.

The ape landed hard. The dull thud his head made when it hit the ground made Virdon wince. He checked, and the ape was indeed unconscious. Virdon hurried to the underbrush, joining Burke and Galen; the three bent low to the ground and disappeared from view as the rest of the mounted apes galloped over the ridge.

One of the apes dismounted to tend to his fallen comrade. The others fanned out, searching for any sign of the humans.

Virdon, Burke, and Galen peered out from their hiding place, well-concealed by the heavy underbrush, confident that they could not be spotted by the apes. A mounted gorilla passed close by; he was evidently the leader, judging from the way he gave orders to the others. He rode back and forth across the small clearing impatiently, while his troops failed to find their quarry.

The leader of the mounted apes reined in his horse and raised his hand. Behind him, the other five horses were pulled to a snorting, stamping halt. The frightening mask hid the rider's identity, but his broad, powerful physique marked him as a gorilla. He looked around at the others scornfully. "They're gone," he said. "Forget those two humans. There are plenty more."

He spurred his horse on, the others following him. They rode down to the bottom of the ridge and back out toward the rough trail they had been following when they had first spotted Burke and Virdon. The three fugitives watched them disappear from sight.

When they had gone, Galen spoke up. "Did you see that?" he asked. "They were wearing masks!"

"This is your world, remember," said Burke. "Tell us what they were. Bandits?"

"I don't know everything," said Galen.

"You're a big man to admit that," said Burke.

Galen looked at him, shocked. "Watch what you call me," he said. "Man, indeed."

"Well," said Burke, "you're kind of a medium-sized ape. Anyway, I didn't think you had to worry about ape bandits."

"They might be bandits," said Virdon thoughtfully.

"But why the torches?"

Galen and Burke could offer no explanation. They looked at Virdon, all three puzzled. They watched the cloud of dust the apes had raised as it settled back slowly, covering everything, returning the area to its quiet, peaceful, secretly treacherous landscape.

Later that day, Virdon, Burke, and Galen stumbled wearily up to Jasko's house. It was a crudely built, small one-room cabin. On one side was a small open shed that served as a storeroom for feed and grain. Several chickens and a small goat meandered about the yard. In back of the house was the lake that Burke had mentioned.

Jasko came out to welcome his two human visitors and their chimpanzee companion. The three travelers were tired and hungry, and Jasko brought them inside, where a vegetable stew was bubbling in a small kettle over an open hearth fire. Jasko removed the kettle from the fire and placed it on a nearby table where Virdon, Burke, and Galen were sitting. There was little conversation; each was too tired to do more than mutter a reply to Jasko's friendly questions. Still, they managed to learn a little about their pursuers, the masked apes.

"You're lucky to have escaped," said Jasko, a man in his fifties, with strong features and a stocky build. He was a man of the soil, born and raised in this very cabin. He spoke as he ladled each of his guests a bowlful of stew.

"They are the Dragoons. They've driven off many humans, burned their homes, killed several. The past weeks have been bad—very bad."

Virdon and Burke ate some of the stew while Jasko talked. Burke looked up and shook his head. "This is a real nice friendly community you've got here, Jasko," he said.

"I'll bet you have some terrific Little League games."

"It's hard to believe that even apes would go to all this trouble and violence over the killing of a single ape," said Virdon.

"That killing caused the kettle to boil over," said Jasko. "It's really nothing new. It's just grown out of proportion. The apes here hate the humans, just like in many other places. But here they think that there are too many of us. It's understandable, I guess."

Jasko seated himself at the table and helped himself to the stew. Galen hadn't yet tasted the meal. He listened to Jasko and the two astronauts, staring at his dish.

"Sure, sure," said Virdon. "It's the same old story. Somebody gets hot under the collar and decides to take the law into his own hands. It always turns out that a lot of innocent people suffer."

"I think the whole matter is terrifying," said Galen, still staring somewhat forlornly at his bowl.

Burke noticed that Galen wasn't eating, which, for the young chimpanzee, was a rare enough occasion to require some explanation. Burke knew that one of the main points of conflict between the apes and humans was eating habits; the apes never ate meat, and they were disgusted by humans who did.

"Chow down," said Burke. "It's good."

Galen looked up at Burke and frowned. The ape returned his attention to the food, playing around in it a little with his spoon. He was still reluctant to taste some of this human food.

"It's meatless," said Burke, grinning at Galen's change of expression.

Burke's words were welcome news to the chimpanzee. He smiled and lifted a spoonful of the vegetable stew to his mouth. He tasted the human creation. "Yes," he said happily, "yes, it *is* good."

"Thank you," said Jasko. "I knew that you'd be accompanying Virdon and Burke. I'm sorry if you thought that I'd serve you a meat dish."

"No, no, it's my fault," said Galen. "Consideration is a quality that I was taught is completely absent in human beings. I now have to learn exactly the opposite. But I have better teachers, now." Virdon and Burke exchanged smiles.

Galen ate another spoonful. Then he looked up thoughtfully. "These Dragoons, as you call them. Surely they're illegal," he said. "I mean, even apes must abide by laws which forbid such actions against humans."

"He is sometimes very naive," said Burke in an apologetic tone.

"He led a very sheltered life," said Virdon.

"Sometimes I think that's all they have here," said Burke. "For the apes, anyway."

Jasko waved aside their comments. He looked serious. "We are far from any kind of forceful authority," he said. "The village where you met my brother has enough police to deal with such things. But here…" Jasko's voice trailed off into a despondent sigh. "Perdix and Zon try, but they cannot be everywhere. No, my friends. Humans are in grave jeopardy. Especially strangers like yourselves. Take my advice. It would be better for you to move on as soon as you have rested."

"There's no need to try to convince me," said Burke. "I've grown rather fond of living."

Virdon glanced at Jasko. "Will you come with us?" he asked.

Jasko shook his head, slowly and sadly. "I've lived here my whole life. To start over again? No. I will take my chances. This terror cannot last forever."

Virdon and Burke looked at each other again, but this time their expressions were deeply concerned.

Early the next day, the leader of the Dragoons sat astride his horse. His eyes were ablaze with a raging lust for blood. Around him, the sounds of horses' hooves and the yells of frightened humans mingled. He had to shout to be heard above them. "Drive them out!" he cried.

The Dragoon leader spurred his horse on toward the scene of terror which was taking place. A man and his wife were running for their lives into the countryside. The man stopped to scoop up his small child, who was crying in fear. Behind them, the Dragoons were wreaking havoc on the humans' small hut.

After breakfast, Burke and Virdon went for a swim in the small lake behind Jasko's house. They were thoroughly enjoying and refreshing themselves. Burke kicked over on his back and sent up a fountain of water from his mouth. Meanwhile, Galen sat at the shore and filled a bucket with water. He dipped a cloth in die water and wiped off his face.

Virdon made a surface dive and swam under the water until he couldn't hold his breath any longer. Then he broke back up and gasped air into his aching lungs. He laughed with pleasure. "I sure haven't had much time to do this since—well—since I was a boy back in Jackson County."

Burke splashed some water toward his friend. "Like I said before, there's nothing like a lake in your backyard."

Galen watched the two astronauts cavorting in the water; he shook his head dubiously. He wondered how humans could stand getting all wet, having their hair matted and heavy on their bodies. Of course, humans didn't have the thick hair that apes had, but still... Galen decided it was just another basic difference between apes and humans, one that he could find it easy to forgive.

"Backyard?" asked Galen. He looked off toward the cabin. "Jasko's house must be a half mile away."

Burke stood up in a shallow part of the water near the shore. He looked away toward Jasko's house. "Well," he said, "so he has a *big* backyard!"

"Yes, certainly," said Galen. "And the next thing you'll say, Pete, is that it goes from here, across the lake, across the hills, right up into Central City to the doorstep of Zaius."

"Haven't you ever seen Zaius and Jasko leaning over the back fence in the morning?" asked Burke. "They swap recipes and show each other pictures of their kids."

Galen frowned. "There are some things that you shouldn't make jokes about," he said. "Zaius and Jasko, indeed."

"You started it," said Burke, flicking a few drops of water toward their chimpanzee friend. Galen ducked away. "You know," said Virdon, "you should let us teach you to swim sometime, Galen."

"Yeah," said Burke, "who knows? You might even learn to like it."

"It *is* a useful thing to know," said Virdon.

"No, thank you," said Galen. "I get all of the water I want out of a bucket." The chimpanzee smiled. Virdon and Burke returned his smile. There was a moment of lazy peace. Then Galen seemed to freeze; he had heard something again. "Look!" he cried, pointing toward Jasko's house.

Virdon and Burke followed Galen's gesture and saw a group of ape horsemen moving down the road toward Jasko's house. Though barely distinguishable at that distance to the human astronauts, Galen muttered "Dragoons!"

Virdon watched the mounted apes for a few seconds.

Finally he could make out the horrible leather masks, and the rifles the apes carried. "Dragoons," he repeated. He and Burke moved as quickly as they could to the shore. Galen edged behind a bush, keeping his eyes riveted on the attackers.

The Dragoons stopped for a moment about a hundred yards down the road from Jasko's house. The leader leaned over the flank of his horse to give instructions to his followers; neither Burke nor Virdon, nor even Galen, could hear his words. The Dragoons lit the torches they carried, kicked up their horses, and rode steadfastly toward Jasko's house. They shouted as they came closer, and they held their blazing torches high. The pounding hoofbeats, the clatter of rifles, and the metal parts of their gear made a fearsome racket.

The noise brought Jasko to his door. He had been washing, and water still dripped from his face. He dried his hands on a coarse towel, staring for a moment at the mounted apes. Then Jasko reached for a wooden pitchfork that leaned against the house. The Dragoons paid little attention, but galloped menacingly into his yard.

Jasko called out to them, but his words were drowned out by the apes. He took a step toward them, his pitchfork held out defiantly. He showed no sign at all of cowering. He was defending his home and his life, and he would not be robbed of either without a fight.

Burke and Virdon were at the edge of the lake, still wet and donning quickly their rough-woven trousers. As soon as they had dressed, they raced madly for the house. Galen came out from his place of concealment and followed them.

The Dragoons were stamping about the yard on their horses, doing petty and insulting things. One Dragoon was scattering Jasko's few animals; the ape's horse shied away from a chicken and accidentally killed another. The ape, who hated humans principally for their bloodthirsty ways among themselves, with apes, and with other animals, never noticed what he had done. Another Dragoon used the butt of his rifle to smash Jasko's small shed, spilling the seed and grain across the yard.

The leader of the Dragoons reined up to face the defiant Jasko. "You have one minute to clear out, human!" shouted the masked ape.

Jasko spat at the Dragoon leader. "No!" he said gruffly. "I will not leave. This is my home!"

"Then watch it burn!" The Dragoon leader signalled with his hand. A Dragoon spurred his horse forward, closer to the house, and stood in his stirrups to toss his torch onto the roof.

"No!" cried Jasko, horrified at what the ape was about to do, but still unafraid to accept the consequences of his actions. He charged the Dragoon and knocked him from his saddle. The torch hit the ground. While the Dragoon and Jasko struggled in the dust, the leader of the masked apes whirled a rope and lassoed Jasko. Then, spurring his horse, the Dragoon leader dragged Jasko across the ground. The leader's actions caused his followers to compete in a flurry of terror tactics. A torch was thrown onto the roof, another tossed inside the house. A cart was pulled over, broken up, and thrown into the growing fire. Flames erupted, consuming the entire structure in a matter of moments. Jasko was dragged back and forth through the melee.

Virdon, Burke, and Galen reached the house. The horror of the situation registered quickly. "Jasko!" shouted Virdon. His cry was drowned out by the raucous and chaotic destruction that was happening.

Slowly, the Dragoons regrouped a little way from the blazing cabin. Their energies had been spent, and there was nothing left to be broken. The totality of their fury had been spent. The Dragoon leader reined up with Jasko still in tow. The human did not move. The leader dragged the still body once more across the yard, then raised his rifle to the sky. "This is a lesson for all humans!" he shouted. His voice was almost choked with hatred.

Then, abruptly, with a laugh, the Dragoon leader tossed the rope aside. He spurred his horse and galloped off, followed by his troops; one chimpanzee Dragoon, however, wheeled his horse and surveyed the scene before he thundered off in pursuit of his leader. Virdon thought that the Dragoon might have caught his eye, but if that had been the case, the chimpanzee Dragoon would have signalled his comrades to return. Instead, the Dragoon shook his rifle at the still-burning cabin and rode away.

The dust of the departing Dragoons had not yet settled when Virdon, Burke, and Galen ran into the yard. They stopped short when they saw Jasko lying in the dirt a few yards away. Virdon went to the man and knelt by him.

"How is he?" asked Burke.

Virdon glanced up. "He's dead, Pete," he said quietly.

Burke and Galen stood over him, their faces wearing expressions of grief and frustration. Virdon looked up at them; there was no need to say anything.

"We've got to stop all of this," said Virdon grimly. "Somehow there must be a way."

Burke nodded. There was a painful silence. "This whole thing started when that ape girl's father was murdered," said Burke, trying to put the situation in perspective, trying to find a key to its solution. "Alan, I don't know. It's a long shot, but suppose we try to find the killers and get the whole thing back into a framework of justice, instead of vigilantism. That could do it."

Virdon considered the idea for a moment. He stood up and took a long, deep breath. "It's a chance, Pete," he said, staring down at Jasko's corpse.

"But where?" asked Galen, "How? What do we do first?"

"We only have one lead," said Virdon. "The girl, herself. Maybe she could be of help to us. That's the only thing we have to turn to now."

Virdon and Burke crouched in hiding behind the cover of some large boulders. While they hid, Galen talked to an ape farmer in an open field a short distance from the farmer's house. Galen had interrupted the farmer's plowing; an ox and a crude plow waited nearby. The farmer pointed off behind Galen. The chimpanzee thanked the farmer and left; the farmer went back to his work, forgetting about Galen almost instantly. Galen joined his human companions behind the boulders.

Burke turned to him. "Any luck?" he asked urgently.

"I think so," said Galen, nodding. "At least, he told me where we can find her."

"Well," said Virdon, "that's a start. I wish I had a better idea of what we're going to do after we *do* find her."

They moved away from their place of concealment, silently and carefully, without arousing the attention of the ape farmer. Galen led the way in the direction the farmer had indicated.

They walked up a path along the side of a grassy hill. At the top was a lone grave. The ape girl, Fauna, was kneeling at the gravesite with some flowers in her hand. Virdon, Burke, and Galen crested the hill and stopped when they caught sight of her. Virdon and Burke ducked back down out of sight. "Wait here," said Galen. "I'll talk to her." He took a step forward; his foot snapped a twig. The cracking sound was magnified by the silence of the place.

Virdon and Burke watched as Galen approached the girl. The noise of the breaking stick made them recoil as though it had been a cannon shot. "Oh, boy," said Burke quietly. "Here we go."

"That's pretty much the idea," said Virdon. "I just wish Galen had more experience in these things."

"I wish *we* did, too," said Burke.

"I don't think we can help but get it," said Virdon.

"We should live so long."

Galen stopped where he was; he didn't want Fauna to think that he was sneaking up on her. He waited for her to turn around and look at him; for a moment it seemed to Galen that the young ape girl was concentrating on her prayers or was too involved with her grief to have heard him. He coughed slightly to let her know that he was there.

Fauna reacted to the sound. Her head tilted slightly as she listened. She turned around, alarm beginning to show in her expression. But it was clear that she was not looking directly at Galen. Virdon and Burke realized at the same moment that Fauna was blind.

"Who is it?" she asked hesitantly, warily. "Who's there?" She turned her head from side to side, trying to catch another sound. Galen felt a sudden upwelling of pity for the young ape girl; he turned back to Virdon and Burke, not certain of his next move. Virdon waved, indicating that Galen should just go on with their plan. Burke and Virdon realized with some relief that Fauna had not actually seen them, that she could see nothing. They moved slightly forward, behind Galen.

"We are strangers here," said Galen. "I hope that we didn't frighten you. We mean you no harm."

Fauna's voice was still uncertain. "You are... apes?" she asked.

There was a moment's pause, while Galen considered the best reply. Whatever he answered would determine how they would continue through the entire situation. "Of course," he said at last. He probed a little at her feelings. "You are frightened of humans?"

Fauna indicated the grave. "They killed my father," she said bitterly.

"I'm sorry to hear that," said Galen. "I did not think they dared to kill apes."

"They're savages," said Fauna, the hate in her words sounding incongruous with her otherwise innocent manner. "I hate them. I shall always hate them for what they did."

There was another uncomfortable pause. "My name is, uh, Phoebus," said Galen. "And these are my two friends, Alar and Pago."

"I am Fauna." She turned, trying to locate the others. "Where are you?"

"We're right here," said Burk hesitantly, glancing at Galen, wondering if he had done the right thing, after all.

Fauna tilted her head again, listening to Burke's voice. She smiled wistfully and shook her head. "Your voice," she said curiously, "it's familiar. Which one are you?"

Virdon looked at Burke, wondering how Fauna could have thought that Burke's voice was familiar. Burke shrugged. "I am Pago," he said. "I don't think that you know me. I'm from a very distant section. This is the first time I have ever been to your village."

"We were lost along the way," said Galen. "We stopped

for directions from a farmer nearby, and he told us that your community was nearby."

"Yes," said Virdon. "We've been traveling a long way."

Fauna took a deep breath. "Well, then," she said, "in that case, you must be tired and hungry. Even though this terrible thing has happened, I cannot forget the ways of hospitality that my father taught me. Will you come with me to my house? You can rest there, and I have food and drink."

Galen was about to reply, but Virdon cut him short with a curt gesture. "Do you live alone?" asked the blond man warily. They couldn't let their sense of urgency or their physical discomfort persuade them into a dangerous relaxation of their guard.

"I live with my Uncle Sestus," said Fauna. "He has ridden into the village for supplies, but he will be back by nightfall."

Burke and Virdon looked at Galen, who merely shrugged. A decision was needed, and quickly; but there wasn't enough information on which to base it. Could they trust this ape girl's uncle? There was no way of telling. And the girl thought that all three travelers were apes; the uncle would immediately see that they weren't. The evident lie would cause instant mistrust.

But, on the other hand, they *were* hungry and tired.

"Well," said Burke, looking to Virdon for advice but getting only a shrug of the blond astronaut's shoulders, "we haven't much time to spare, but we haven't eaten in quite a long time."

"Good, good," said Fauna delightedly. "Then follow me." The ape girl walked slowly back toward the grave, carrying some flowers she had brought when the three fugitives had interrupted her. Virdon and Burke backed quickly away from her as she passed, to avoid discovery if she accidentally touched their skin. She knelt again and placed the flowers on the grave, feeling it gently with her sensitive fingers. Then she rose and walked off with easy, sure steps, using only a stick to guide her. The two humans and the chimpanzee watched her, feeling a sense of admiration for Fauna's courage and self-control. When she had passed, they followed.

"I hope you will stay to meet Uncle Sestus," she said. "You will like him."

"That may be," whispered Burke, so that only Virdon and Galen could hear. "But the problem is, will *he* like us?"

"Galen," whispered Virdon, "you may have to be really charming tonight."

Galen only raised his eyebrows. "No problem," he said. "No problem at all."

A couple of miles away, on the road that led past Jasko's house toward Fauna's village, the Dragoons galloped, tired from their raid, but exulting in their power and success. They were a fearsome group, although for the most part their only audience was themselves. They shouted to each other as they rode and waved their rifles fiercely above their heads. They reined up at a crossroad. One of the group, the same Dragoon chimpanzee who had watched the destruction of Jasko's home with such emotion, pulled over to a wagon parked off the road beneath a shady oak tree.

The Dragoon leader watched the chimpanzee as he harnessed his horse to pull the wagon. "You will be notified when we raid again," said the leader.

The Dragoon chimpanzee nodded that he understood. He climbed up on his wagon, and the rest of the Dragoons galloped off. The last Dragoon in the party turned and waved. "See you then, Sestus!" he called.

The chimpanzee on the wagon removed his leather mask; beneath it, the graying hair and beard of Sestus, Fauna's uncle, lay matted with sweat. He watched the Dragoons as they disappeared around a bend in the road. Then he turned and flicked the reins. The horse started walking slowly back to the village, and the wagon made a lonely creaking sound in the afternoon stillness.

6

The atmosphere of stillness and peace was so intensive that it seemed unbreakable to Virdon, Burke, and Galen. But that same feeling had been shattered on previous occasions, and the fugitives knew that this situation was potentially just as explosive. Nevertheless, listening to the singing of the birds and the sighing of boughs in the fresh ocean breeze, they could almost pretend that they were safe and secure. They could *almost* pretend happiness; it was as close as they ever got.

They saw a simple frame house built of wood and stone with a small barn toward the rear. This was the house of Fauna's uncle. The young female ape led them to the front porch and into the house. Before they entered, the humans and their chimpanzee friend searched carefully for any sign of the uncle, but he was nowhere to be seen.

"Please sit down and be comfortable," said Fauna when they had all come in.

"This is a very nice home," said Galen. "Bright, airy, and very clean."

"Thank you," said Fauna.

"Can we help you with something?" asked the chimpanzee.

Fauna turned to face him. She smiled. "Why do you ask?" she said lightly. "Because I'm blind? Don't be silly. I manage quite well."

She went about the room, setting the table with wooden utensils and ceramic dishes. Then she prepared a simple but refreshing vegetarian meal and set that, too, on the table. Finally she made some lemonade, a special treat. The lemons had been a gift to Fauna from Lucian, her father, shortly before he was murdered. She paused while squeezing the lemons; to the humans it seemed that she might cry. But she quickly got control of herself and finished setting out the meal.

"Being unable to see has really changed very little," she said in a soft, poignant voice. "I know the farm and most of the area for some distance around; and I am so familiar with it that I don't really need my eyes."

Burke, Virdon, and Galen sat at the table and hungrily began to eat the food.

"Of course, there are some things that I miss," she said wistfully. "The sun setting. The colors of the flowers. And, most of all, reading. My father collected many books and, though I read them all when I was still young, he would read them to me over and over. Every night, by the fire, my father—" She broke off, tears at last spilling out and running down her cheeks.

Burke watched Fauna, his expression sympathetic and pitying. He wanted to comfort her, but his false identity had built a wall between him and the chimpanzee girl. He wondered at his own feelings; after all, he had never felt such strong compassion before, not for an ape. Even

Galen, who had become a genuine friend, did not create in Burke so strong an attachment. Burke looked at Galen, who was occupied primarily in emptying his plate. He was not paying close attention to what Fauna was saying. Virdon, like Burke, was struck by the depth of the female ape's feelings.

"You must have loved your father very much," said Virdon gently. He understood what she felt, perhaps better than Burke, because Virdon had left his own wife and children behind. Burke had always been more of a lone spirit; Virdon reacted to displays of familial love with his own painful memories.

"Yes," said Fauna, nodding.

"These humans who, uh, who..." Virdon's voice trailed off. He couldn't bring himself to finish the sentence. "Do you know who they were?"

"No," said Fauna, wiping the tears from her face. "But my Uncle Sestus saw it happen. He was there. He told me everything."

"I hate to seem like I'm prying," said Burke. "But we traveled here as soon as we heard the news about your father. We thought that we might be of some help."

"I appreciate your kindness," said Fauna. "Perhaps it would be good for me to talk about it. Especially to such sympathetic apes as you. It helps to remind me that we are not as the humans. We are apes, and they are savages." Again, as she said those words, her expression twisted into a startling mask of hatred. Burke turned a helpless face to Virdon.

"How did it happen?" asked Burke.

"There were two of them," said Fauna, her voice soft and aching. "They came here asking for food, and my father gave it to them. He tried to make friends with them.

Uncle Sestus warned him that humans were treacherous, but Father didn't listen. Then, down by the river, the humans attacked my father and killed him."

A few seconds elapsed during which none of the three travelers wished to say anything. "But there must have been a reason why they did it," said Burke. "There must have been some kind of motive."

Fauna frowned. "They're savages," she said bitterly. "They don't need reasons to kill."

Once again there was a pause; Burke looked at Virdon. The situation was less promising than they had first imagined. A solution seemed further off than ever. And Fauna would be unlikely to help them; it was only a matter of time before their disguise was penetrated.

"Fauna," said Burke, "please tell me if you don't feel like answering my questions. But I think we can help bring whoever is responsible for your father's death to justice."

"That is all that I want," said Fauna. "Now that I know nothing can ever bring back my father."

"Did your uncle get a description of them?" asked Burke. "How tall? What they were wearing, anything that could help us?"

"No," she said. "It was dark, early in the evening. Under the shadows of the trees, on the bank of the river, it was difficult to see clearly. Uncle Sestus said that he saw very little of the humans; he did not know what was happening until it was too late. Besides, who can tell one human from another? When I could see, they all looked alike to me."

Galen had finished his meal and sat back in his chair. He smiled at Burke and Virdon. "I have the same problem," he said. Virdon just shook his head in disbelief.

"Let me get some milk for you," said Fauna. She stood

up from the seat she had taken at the table and went into the kitchen area again. She returned with a pitcher of milk. She started to pour a cupful, then paused thoughtfully. "Pago," she said, "where are you?"

"Here," said Burke warily. He had an idea what she was going to say next.

She finished pouring the milk and moved very close to him. She put the cup of milk down and, as she drew back, she made a slight attempt to touch his hand. "I'd like to—" she said.

Burke, frightened, snapped his hand away quickly, knocking over the milk which spilled across the table. This moment gave Burke a chance to move away from the table, and away from Fauna's touch. "I'm sorry, Fauna," he said. "I'm afraid that I've spilled your milk."

"It's all right, Pago," she said. "Sit down. Don't worry about it. I'll clean it up. Pour yourself some more."

Fauna started to get a cloth to clean up the spilled milk, but she stopped. She seemed to be listening to a sound that her acute hearing had picked up. "I think that I hear Uncle Sestus' wagon," she said happily. "He must be coming back early."

The fugitives reacted in alarm. Galen rose and went to a window. He glanced out. "I don't see anyone yet," he said, trying to make his voice calm and unworried. "I don't hear a wagon, either."

"My hearing is sharper, perhaps," said Fauna. "I have come to depend on it. I can recognize sounds that most people can't even hear."

"Ah, yes," said Galen evenly. "I see a wagon coming along the road in the distance. It's drawn by a single horse. A single chimpanzee is riding in it. That would be your uncle. The back of the wagon is filled with supplies."

Galen turned around. Burke and Virdon had gotten to their feet; the three stood motionless, trying to decide the best course now. It was plain that they couldn't stay to be discovered by Fauna's Uncle Sestus. But they couldn't run out without arousing the ape girl's suspicions.

"Fauna," said Burke quietly, "there's something I think we'd better tell you—"

Virdon and Galen showed alarm at the dark-haired man's words. Burke just waved for them to be silent. Fauna turned toward Burke curiously. He spoke to her quickly and confidently. Everything depended on their elaborating the original lie without alienating Fauna. Burke got a sudden inspiration; he did not have much time.

"What could it be?" asked Fauna, her face creased with a frown of surprise. "Surely you're not going to tell me that you're human beings, after all."

Burke gave a strained laugh. He held up his hand again to signal to his friends that he knew what he was doing, and that they ought to play along. "Oh, no," he said. "Nothing like that. You said that you miss reading, most of all. Well, the love of books is something that we share with you. But unfortunately it's gotten us into trouble with the Ministry of Knowledge."

Fauna's frown deepened. She did not understand the ways of the apes in Central City or the workings of the government. "Trouble?" she said. "What kind of trouble?"

"There were certain books which we didn't know had been banned," said Burke. "The police found those books in our house. Rather than be tossed into prison just because we like to read, we chose to run."

Fauna was astonished. She had never heard of anything so terrible happening among apes. "You mean, they were going to punish you for reading?" she asked.

Virdon picked up on Burke's idea and added a supporting argument. "Well," he said, "it's a matter of those ideas in books which some people find threatening to their way of life."

Galen peered out of the window again. Sestus was drawing closer; he was only a couple of hundred yards down the road. Whatever Burke was leading up to, it had better reach its conclusion soon.

"But surely it can't be against the law to think," said Fauna.

"Your uncle might not be as understanding as you are," said Burke. "We better leave now, before he comes. You can see why we have to be careful."

Fauna seemed disturbed. She considered what Burke said. "Yes," she said, "I'm afraid Uncle Sestus doesn't feel quite the same way as I do about books. He used to quarrel about them with my father." Fauna fell silent. Galen looked at Burke, trying to convey a thought of "what now?" Virdon wore the same expression. Unfortunately for all of them, Burke had arrived at the same empty conclusion. "I have an idea," said Fauna. "I know a place where you can hide safely. You can rest there as long as you like. It's not far from here."

Galen was uncertain. He preferred just making a run for it and leaving the territory altogether. "I don't think that's a very—" he said.

"Oh, please," interrupted Fauna. "Let me do this for you. It would give me great pleasure."

Virdon, Burke, and Galen exchanged glances. A silent vote was taken.

Sestus drove the loaded wagon into the yard in front of his house. The wagon and the horse made a noisy alarm for the two humans and two chimpanzees inside. The wagon passed the front door and went around the corner of the house to the small barn. When the wagon had passed, Fauna led the astronauts and their chimpanzee ally out of the house and toward the sea cliffs beyond. Galen carried a basket of food and drink. They walked quickly across the yard, as quietly as they could manage.

Sestus got down from the wagon. He was tired from the day's excitement; he was thinking about unloading the wagon, and then eating dinner and taking a nap. He unhitched the horse from the wagon, completely unaware of the group leaving the house.

Fauna cautiously led the fugitives toward the cliffs. The farther they marched, the better were their chances of escaping without detection by Sestus. They entered the cool shade of the nearby wood, and followed a stream as it ran toward the sea. Finally, Fauna found the path she was looking for, and they followed it down between high banks, to a narrow beach lapped by ocean waves.

Fauna led them to a cave cut into the side of the cliffs; above the water. The cave could be reached only by a narrow ledge which ran from the sand upward at a steep angle. The cave was safe from discovery from above; only if someone followed Fauna's secret path could it be seen at all. The entrance was obscured by foliage. Fauna moved forward, her stick touching trees and rocks, making her way quite surely, with obvious familiarity of each thing she touched.

Fauna moved to the cave entrance with Virdon, Burke, and Galen following at a safe distance. She swept back the foliage and led them inside the cave. Virdon was about to enter, when he stopped and looked around at the cave, the beach, and the ocean.

"Wait a minute, Pete," he said. "I have the strangest feeling."

"Do you think we're in danger here?" asked Burke.

"No, no, it isn't that. Does this place look familiar to you?"

Burke paused and looked around him. "Oh, good grief," he said in hushed tones: "Hanson Point. We spent a couple of days here after the preflight indoctrination. I remember the cave. It didn't have all that stuff growing in front of it. In fact, it wasn't so high above the water then. And the beach was only a few feet wide at this point."

"That was two thousand years ago, buddy," said Virdon.

"Oh, man," said Burke. He just stared at the cave mouth.

"See," said Virdon, "it can hit you, too. You weren't as alone in our world as you wanted to pretend. You had a date with that redhead, the same afternoon we got yelled at by that colonel."

"I remember," said Burke. "I remember that redhead. Two thousand years has done nothing to hurt my memory. Jan Adams. We carved our initials in this same cave. She may be the only woman I ever carved my initials with."

"I wonder if they're still in there?" said Virdon, smiling sadly.

"I'm almost afraid to look," said Burke. "I wish *she* was still there."

The two men looked out to sea, at the constant, yet ever-changing waves. After a moment of silent thought, they entered the cave.

They saw Galen standing just inside, and Fauna bustling about the small room. She was wiping off dust from chairs and table, dust which she couldn't see but which she knew must be there. She reached up to a small shelf and brought down some small candles. She found some of the large, clumsy matches used by the apes, and lit a couple of the candles. "Ah," she said. "I'm glad these are still here. I haven't needed them for a long time. I don't suppose this place would make a comfortable home for three apes, but it will do temporarily. It has a lot of wonderful memories for me."

Burke was about to say something, about the cave and about memories, but something made him keep quiet.

Fauna took the rest of the candles down from the shelf. Galen took these from her and then lit them. The yellowish glow from the small flames illuminated the interior of the cave. It was larger than Galen had at first estimated. Even Virdon and Burke had forgotten just how large the cave was. There were chairs made of wood and carved from stone. There was a clutter of articles on the table, things which Fauna had made use of since childhood, plates, cups, bowls, and so on. Galen put the basket of food on the table while the others looked around.

"I used to come here with someone I grew up with," she said, thinking back. "Someone I cared for very much. It was our secret place where we could hide and play and shut out the grown-up world."

"You just can't, shut out the grown-up world," said Virdon. "No matter how hard you try. It's always waiting, and it pounces on you, sometimes when you least expect it."

Fauna was lost in her own thoughts; she didn't seem to have heard Virdon. "He left here long ago," she said in a melancholy voice. "When I became blind…"

There was a quiet moment, during which Fauna reached out her hands. "Pago…?" she whispered.

Burke didn't recognize his assumed name for a few seconds. He, too, was lost in the surge of memories that the cave brought back; memories that, while different for Fauna, Burke, and Virdon, were equally strong in their poignancy. Only Galen had never seen the cave before. Only he had been spared its sentimental pull. Burke was tracing the initials P.B. and J.A. carved in the side of the cave. There were other initials carved there, too, most of which hadn't been there before; he wondered whether human or ape hands had made them.

"Pago?" asked Fauna again.

"I'm here, Fauna," said Burke.

She turned to the sound of his voice and moved closer to him. He backed instinctively to avoid the close contact, but quickly he found himself against the damp stone wall of the cave.

"Your voice reminded me," said Fauna. "It's so much like his…" She moved closer to Burke; the man sank down against the wall a little, but there was no chance that he could escape this time.

"I wonder," she said awkwardly, but almost imperatively, "I wonder if I might touch your face…"

Virdon and Galen were alarmed almost beyond the breaking point. Perhaps Galen had been right—that the entire situation had been a mistake from the beginning. But now it was too late to back out gracefully. If there had been an error in judgment, and the humans were not certain, merely admitting to it would not save them now.

Fauna was not aware of the confusion and panic she was causing; "It would help me to know what you look like," she said.

Slowly, she lifted her hand, moving it toward him. Burke was shaken, knowing that he couldn't allow her to touch him without giving away the fact that he was human, and that he had wilfully deceived her. He was at the point of guiltily revealing his ruse when Galen moved noiselessly beside him and took Fauna's hand. The chimpanzee guided the young female's hand up to his own shaggy ape face, giving her the impression that she was actually touching Burke. Fauna examined the features of Galen's face as Burke moved slightly out of the way. Fauna seemed to be very happy with the impressions she received. "It's… very much as I thought," she said. "A strong, handsome face."

Her fingers touched Galen's coarse simian features for a moment; Galen began to perspire nervously, hoping that Fauna wouldn't ask "Pago" to speak. That would only necessitate another round of shuffling. Sooner or later, they would be trapped; and, as far as Galen was concerned, later was always better.

Slowly Fauna dropped her hand. Slowly Galen backed away *sliding* along the rough rock wall. After a few steps, he turned and walked somewhat noisily, indicating that he had joined his companions. For all intents and purposes, they had all reassumed their proper false identities. Fauna went to the entrance of the cave. She turned to face her new friends. "Please stay," she said. "It's been so long since I've felt that I could be useful. You'll be safe here. I'll come back in the morning with more food, after Uncle Sestus leaves for the village."

She turned and went out of the cave. They could hear her steps fading away along the narrow ledge outside. There was a moment's silence, while they waited for Fauna to get out of hearing range. Then Burke turned to Galen. "That was really close, buddy," he said. "All she had to do was find out I'm a human."

Galen nodded, but his expression was somewhat upset.

"I didn't like doing that," he said. "It wasn't right to deceive her, no matter what our reasons were."

Burke nodded his understanding. "Yeah," he said. They stood looking at each other. "Well," said Burke, "where do we go from here? From what Fauna said, our chances of finding the killers are next to zip."

"So we do the next best thing," said Virdon. "We go after the Dragoons."

"Wait a minute, Alan," said Burke. "Chasing down two human criminals is one thing, but taking on the Dragoons? They're not the Campfire Girls, pal. They don't *like* us."

"How on earth do you intend to accomplish that?" asked Galen.

Virdon chewed his lip thoughtfully. "One of the great accomplishments of human civilization was the vast stockpile of ancient wisdom we accumulated. For instance, an old human proverb: cut off the head of a snake and the body dies. Great old proverb."

Burke grinned. "An all-purpose saying. It works for anything. That's the trouble with you apes. You're too specialized."

"You just told me last week that we weren't specialized enough," said Galen. "Wait a minute. You're both confusing me!"

Virdon thought for a few seconds more, straightening out the details of his scheme in his own mind. "Look, Galen," he said, "if we can expose the Dragoon leader, or even maybe capture him, then Perdix will be forced to arrest him."

Galen looked puzzled and doubtful. It wasn't clear to him precisely why Perdix would be compelled to arrest the leader of the Dragoons; after all, while the Dragoons were an illegal group, apes rarely arrested other apes. The police were there to control the human population, generally speaking.

"The point is, Galen," said Burke, "no leader, no Dragoons."

"All right," said the chimpanzee, "that sounds reasonable." In his mind, though, the idea was still slightly less than that. "But, granted the logic of your plan, how do you propose to reveal his identity?"

"From the inside," said Virdon. "Somebody will have to join the Dragoons and find out who he is. Once he's exposed, the group will fall apart and this crazy killing will stop."

Something in Virdon's words struck unpleasantly. "Somebody?" asked Galen. "Who is *somebody*?"

There was an amused silence. After all, Galen had answered his own question.

"Me?" he cried. Virdon and Burke laughed; they had never seen quite so astonished an expression on the poor chimpanzee's face.

The rest of the day passed slowly. Virdon, Burke, and Galen spent the hours trying to coordinate their roles in the plan to end the vigilante movement. There were so many variables: how long could their deception hold? Could they keep themselves hidden, even while they worked toward their goal? Would the apes of the Dragoons trust and accept Galen? And, the same question that disturbed their sleep, the same possibility they faced each day, but which they never discussed—what if Perdix or one of the gorillas recognized Virdon, Burke, and Galen from General Urko's dispatches? It was possible that Urko had ordered them shot on sight.

After a little thought, the three friends began to realize that the odds against their success were piling up faster than any one could count.

They ate the food that Fauna had left them, and when it began to get dark, they closed up the entrance to the cave with branches and boughs. They talked for a while later, then blew out the candles and went to sleep.

The sun rose an hour after the chimpanzee, Sestus,

had risen to tend to his chores the next morning. After finishing his work and eating a quick breakfast, Sestus prepared to leave for the village. Fauna walked with him to the wagon. Sestus gave the girl ape a kiss on the cheek, boarded his wagon, and drove it out around the house and toward the small community. Fauna waited a few seconds, then returned to the house. She was unaware that Galen had watched the scene from the safety of some nearby trees. He waited nervously as Sestus' wagon approached him. Galen looked up toward Virdon and Burke, who had climbed a hillside overlooking Sestus' house. They were concealed behind a low growth of bushes, with a good view of the scene below. They waved to Galen to get out into the middle of the road.

Galen looked away from Virdon and Burke, back toward the approaching wagon. He was glad to realize that the two humans couldn't see how afraid he was.

Sestus was still unaware that anything unusual was happening. He drove with his chin sunk against his chest, his eyes half-closed. Suddenly he was brought completely awake as Galen jumped out, waving and shouting. "Stop! Stop!" shouted the chimpanzee.

"Who is this?" muttered Sestus to himself. Nevertheless, he reined up the horse and stopped the wagon. "What is it?" he asked. "What's the matter?"

Galen took a deep breath. It was too late to back out now. He was committed to seeing the charade through. "Two humans," he cried. "They attacked me! Took my horse!"

Sestus was instantly alert. "Where?" he asked, shocked.

Yes, thought Galen, where? "Uh, over that way, that way!" He pointed off in what he hoped was a likely direction. He wished that he could remember the geography of the area better; he might be pointing directly at the ocean. Well, if he wanted to go riding in the surf, that was his business. Sestus would believe him. After all, they were both apes. "Is there a village nearby where I can report this to the police?"

"Climb aboard," said Sestus. "I will take you there."

Galen climbed up on the wagon, and it rambled off down the road. When it rounded a bend, Burke and Virdon lost sight of it.

Virdon and Burke felt much the same as Galen, although their parts didn't require them to become so intimately involved with the Dragoons. The wagon carrying the two chimpanzees was gone, its sound muffled by the distance and the foliage. Quickly the area regained its peaceful and serene mask.

"I never knew that there was so much ham in an ape," said Burke thoughtfully. "It's amazing how good an actor he is."

"He thinks of it as lying," said Virdon. "It makes him feel adventurous. Whatever it is, let's hope it works."

They turned and moved quickly along the hillside, keeping as low as possible to avoid detection.

Virdon and Burke began jogging on a narrow trail parallel to the road. They said nothing, but conserved their energy for the tiring job ahead. They had covered perhaps half a mile; each had relaxed a little, lulled by the stillness of the woods and the pleasant weather. Suddenly Virdon saw something moving ahead of them. He dropped to his stomach, lying flat on the ground. "Down, Pete!" he said urgently. Burke dropped to the ground before the words even left Virdon's mouth.

Burke moved his head slightly, so that he could watch ahead of him. There was a gorilla on horseback moving at a steady pace along a path leading toward the woods. He didn't seem to be aware that the two humans were nearby; Virdon and Burke did nothing to attract his attention. After a short while they felt that they had not been spotted, and that they could safely continue. They sat up in the prickly grass.

"Okay," said Burke. "Hitch number one in our plans. Was that a Dragoon? Or was that Perdix, the police officer here? Or, what was his deputy's name? Zon?"

Virdon shook his head. "I don't know," he said. "There's no way of telling. He could be a Dragoon. We have to realize that we're operating completely in the dark. Our plans have to be flexible."

"Yeah," said Burke. "Flex us right into a firing squad. I suppose that we could follow him. Maybe we could find out something useful. We don't have anything to lose. At least it would be a positive action."

"All right," said Virdon.

"We could tail him until—"

"Not *we*," said Virdon. "Me. I saw him first. Anyway, you have to keep an eye on the store. We can't let Fauna get suspicious."

"Terrific," said Burke. "This is the hardest thing I've had to do since we landed in this left-handed world. I have to spend the whole day waltzing away from that ape girl. I get tired."

"It'll get your legs back in shape," said Virdon.

"Sure," said Burke, frowning. "Don't be gone long." He gave Virdon a quick slap on the back and smiled. Then he got up and started running, back to the cave. Virdon watched him for a moment, then he got up and started running after the gorilla.

* * *

The branches hung heavily above the road. The sun glared through the dark leaves, making bright, jewel-like beads of light that passed above Galen's head as he rode along in Sestus' cart. The birds and insects, whose sounds had cheered Galen earlier, were inaudible now beneath the racket of the horse's hooves and the rumbling of the solid wooden wheels. The noise of the wagon was so loud that Sestus and Galen conversed in voices that grew hoarse from shouting.

Sestus was excited and disturbed by Galen's story. The thing that he desired more than anything else was for things to stay the same; he hated interfering factors that created changes in his life. Still, Galen's bad news was offset by Sestus' acquaintance with the pleasant young ape. "You say that you were thinking about settling here, Phoebus?" he asked.

Galen made a wry face. "I was," he said. "But if, as you say, the area is overrun with humans," here Galen's voice took on a strong overlay of disgust, so noticeable. that Sestus turned to glance at him with eyebrows raised, "I will definitely have to reconsider."

"Oh, the community has its good points, too," said Sestus.

"No doubt, no doubt," said Galen. "I'm not trying to say anything negative about this area. After all, I haven't yet seen the village or met your fellow residents. But just the smell of so many humans about must be overwhelming!"

Sestus laughed at the vehemence of Galen's words. But after a moment he grunted his agreement. "What can you expect?" he said, shaking his head. "They're nothing but animals."

"That's what I mean, precisely," said Galen. "I take it that you have no liking for humans, either, Sestus?"

"I would rather keep company with a rattlesnake!" said the graying Sestus. "They're not half as treacherous and at least the snakes rattle before they strike."

"I know exactly what you mean," said Galen, amused.

"Perhaps you don't know how far my feelings go," said Sestus. "Only a short time ago, my own brother was murdered by humans."

Galen acted stunned by the news. "Murdered!" he said. "Oh, I'm terribly sorry to hear that. I can safely assume that the humans responsible were dealt with unmercifully," Sestus laughed derisively. "They haven't even been caught yet," he said. "I doubt that they ever will be."

There was something in Sestus' tone, more than in his words themselves, which indicated to Galen that now was as good a time as any to take a chance. Perhaps Sestus was only a mourning, angry, and helpless adult ape; but, perhaps, he was something more. If he were, then things might begin to happen on schedule; if not, he might give Galen a clue about what had to be done to meet a representative of the Dragoons.

"What an amazing and unhappy coincidence," said Galen sadly. "You know, where I just came from we had a similar killing. I can tell you, none of us apes was at all prepared for such savagery. We had been lulled into a kind of false sense of security, because in our generous and foolish hearts, we had assumed that humans might possess our own feelings of revulsion toward murder. But, mark my words, once the horrible deed was done, we got together. Our eyes had been opened concerning the true nature of humans. And the only way we could deal with the problem was by—no. No, I'm sorry. I swore secrecy never to reveal—"

Sestus' interest was aroused more and more during Galen's bit of play-acting. Of course, Galen had invented a situation that closely paralleled what had happened here with the Dragoons; that way, Sestus would quickly discover that this Phoebus was an ape with interests similar to his own. Or else, Sestus would be outraged, and Galen, with some careful probing, would learn who the ringleaders of the Dragoons were. "Go on," said Sestus. "You can trust me."

"Of course, of course," said Galen, showing the initial reluctance that Sestus would expect to see. "Still, I'm not sure…"

Galen waited a moment, letting Sestus become more curious. "A group of us apes banded together," said Galen at last. "We ran about fifty humans off and burned their homes. We even killed a few. It did wonders as far as keeping the rest in line."

"Ah, fine, fine!" cried Sestus, elated. "You know, the entire ape world would be much better off if it were without humans altogether."

"My sentiments, exactly," said Galen. "In fact, if I had my way, we'd drive them all out and ship them back to the Forbidden Zone where they all came from."

Both apes laughed at the thought. Galen realized that with a few well-placed lies and exaggerations, he had completely won over Sestus' confidence and admiration. Galen felt a glow of pride; he wished that Virdon and Burke could see him now.

"You know, Phoebus," said the elder chimpanzee, "I think you will enjoy meeting some special friends of mine."

"Special friends?" asked Galen innocently.

Sestus nodded. He lowered his voice, although they still drove through a green and tangled forest. "Have you ever heard of the Dragoons?" he asked.

Galen pretended to think for a moment. "Dragoons?"

he said musingly. "Why, no, I don't believe I have. Tell me about them." He turned toward Sestus with his sincerest look of interest...

Krono the gorilla, one of the three young militant apes who had caused such a scene during Lucian's funeral, prodded his horse on, moving at a walk up a steep trail. His thoughts were elsewhere, and he didn't pay much attention to his surroundings; the horse was familiar enough with the path. Behind Krono, Virdon followed stealthily, half-running, at a distance that prevented Krono from hearing the sounds of his pursuer. For some reason, when Krono topped the small hill, he halted the horse and turned in the saddle, surveying the path behind him. Virdon ducked into the underbrush on one side of the trail, out of sight. Krono, confident that he wasn't being followed, continued on. A short time later, so did Virdon.

While Galen rode with Sestus and Virdon trailed Krono, Pete Burke had climbed down to the cave. He made a snack out of the remnants of the food Fauna had given them. Then he idly explored the cave again, feeling yet another shiver of strange emotion when he saw the carved initials. He forced himself to forget the past, at least for the moment; he set about cleaning the wooden and rock furniture in the cave, for want of anything better to do. Who had made the furniture? Ape or human? Burke would never know. He wished only that Virdon would forget the gorilla on horseback and return to the cave. He started to go toward the entrance of the cave, with a vague notion of climbing up and looking for his friend, when he heard something. "Alar?" he called.

It was Fauna. She stepped into the cave toward Burke. He reacted in surprise when he saw her, retreating a little to avoid contact, disturbed at being alone with her, without Galen to help him out in case of a crisis. Fauna didn't seem to be at all concerned; she was still unaware of the larger situation in which she was playing such an important part. She carried another basket of food for Burke and his friends. "It's Fauna, Pago," she said. "Isn't Alar here? I've brought food. I suppose it isn't much for three healthy chimpanzees, but I have to be careful with my uncle's supplies."

"Thank you, Fauna," said Burke. "Alar and, uh, Phoebus went to get some fresh water from the stream."

Fauna brushed on past him. "I'm glad," she said. "I like talking with you."

"Same here," said Burke worriedly.

"I'm glad that we can talk now, just the two of us." Burke did not reply. Fauna settled to the ground and uncovered the basket. She put out some fruit on a cloth napkin. There was a strained silence; finally Fauna said, "Pago?"

Burke sighed and closed his eyes. Here it comes again, Pete thought, Fauna's lonely and dangerous prying. He couldn't help being fond of her, even though she was an ape; but his own feelings had to be repressed, even his natural tendency toward kindness. There were lives at stake, the lives of the humans in the area, like Jasko. And, Burke reminded himself, also the lives of Virdon and Galen. And Pete Burke's, as well.

"Pago?"

"Yeah?" said Burke. "I'm sorry, Fauna. I was just thinking about the homes we left behind. My *family*. My friends." There, thought Burke. That ought to cement the old identity a little better.

"Can you tell me about the books you've read?" she asked. Burke sighed again; he was glad the question wasn't more personal. Everything would be all right if he could keep things on an intellectual level until help arrived. But Fauna would have to cooperate. "Could you tell me some of the stories?" she said.

"I suppose that I could," he said. "You know that those books were what got us into trouble. And if I tell you about them, they may get you into trouble, too. I'm not sure that I ought to do that."

"Oh, don't worry," said Fauna. "I can say that my father showed the books to me."

"Well, I just wanted to be certain that you understood. In case some of the gorilla police came and started asking questions. Then you wouldn't think less of me."

"I'd never do that, Pago," said Fauna breathlessly. "I understand."

Burke rubbed his eyes. It hurt him to keep adding to the deception, but it was all for the best he kept telling himself. How often had people done things, all for the best, and had them turn out just the opposite?

"All right, then," he said. "I suppose it wouldn't do any harm." Fauna found a chair and Burke sat down across from her. "Well," he said hesitantly, "there was one I always liked. It was about a ma—I mean, an ape. An ape who became stranded on an island in the middle of a great ocean. His name was 'Robinson Crusoe.'"

"Robinson Crusoe?" asked Fauna. "What a strange name."

"It was long ago," said Burke. "When apes had two names."

"What kind of an ape was he? Was he a gorilla?"

"No," said Burke. "He was a chimpanzee. I think that he might have been very much like your father." Fauna said nothing to this, but her expression wavered for a moment, on the brink of tears. Burke saw this and hurried on. "One day he was walking on the beach of this island, and he saw a footprint in the sand. It was the footprint of a human."

Fauna listened, fascinated despite the cold shudder that passed through her at the mention of the human. "What happened to the poor chimpanzee?" she asked.

Sestus and Galen arrived in the village of the apes while Burke was entertaining Fauna with the story. The citizens of the village were going about their day's business, shopping, visiting, and delivering mail and business orders. The activity was mild compared to what Galen had become accustomed to in Central City, but he was growing fond of the slow pace and the friendly atmosphere of the rural towns. One difference between this village and others Galen had visited during his forced exile was the complete absence of humans on the streets. It was a rare thing; even in the humblest ape communities, there were a number of humans used for slave labor. But, considering the mood of the apes in this town, it wasn't difficult to understand.

As they drove down the main street of the village, they saw two uniformed mounted gorillas riding slowly toward them. When the gorillas saw Sestus, they reined up close by the wagon. Sestus pulled his horse to a halt and greeted the apes. Galen took a deep breath; here was the first test of their improvised scheme.

"Good morning, Perdix," said Sestus. "Good day, Zon." Perdix, whom Galen had already tentatively identified from his police uniform, nodded.

"Sestus," he said by way of a curt greeting. Zon did not say anything. "We were about to begin our afternoon rounds," said Perdix. "Have you heard of anything out of the ordinary in the area today?"

"Strange that we should meet you like this," said Sestus. He nodded toward Galen. "This is my friend Phoebus. I met him on the road, perhaps a mile or two from the village, shortly after I left my house. He was attacked by two humans. He was left alone, helpless. They took his horse. He was lucky that I happened by. Another outrage, Perdix. I hope it hasn't dissuaded Phoebus from settling in our community."

Perdix looked at Phoebus with narrowed eyes. "Two humans, you say."

"Yes," said Galen, warming to the task of being Phoebus, the traveling chimpanzee. "It happened just as my benefactor, Sestus, told it. Do you think that you can get my horse back? It was given to me by my father, and it would hurt the poor old ape to hear that it was stolen. It isn't worth much, but—"

Galen was interrupted by a curt gesture from Perdix. The young chimpanzee was happy; he had learned that a style of run-on embroidery of facts and outright lies often made a false story seem more real. It was much more fun than studying had been, back when he was a promising scholar in Central City.

Perdix turned to his deputy, nodding absently to Galen. "Perhaps the two humans are the very same killers we are looking for already."

Zon nodded in agreement and looked at Galen. "Rest assured, Phoebus," he said. "These human criminals will be hunted down."

"They will be found, captured, and disposed of, *within* the law," said Perdix. *"We* will bring them in."

"That's very reassuring," said Galen. Perdix and Zon each gave a kind of half-salute to Sestus, nodded to Galen, and turned their horses in the direction Sestus' wagon had come from. They rode out at a brisk gallop. Sestus jerked on his reins, and the wagon continued on down the street, to the first of the old ape's stops for that day.

In the secret cave, Burke was still elaborating on the story of Robinson Crusoe; it had never occurred to him before how much his own situation was like that of Defoe's hero. But, in a way, in a much more complete and hopeless way, Burke and Virdon were shipwrecked, too. The astronauts would gladly have traded places with Crusoe, just to have the knowledge that they were somewhere—*anywhere*, in their old, human world again. But, like Crusoe, they were learning to make the best of what happened to be handy. And, like Crusoe, they had to do it without much in the way of help from other people.

Fauna had sat through the entire tale without saying a word. Burke had done his best to salt the narrative with what he hoped were subtle but pointed comments about brotherhood and the need for apes and humans to learn to live together in peace. He wondered if Fauna had understood. "And so," concluded Burke, "after thirty-five years, Crusoe and his human friend, Friday, were rescued and taken to Crusoe's home to live." There was a pause after he finished; Burke looked anxiously toward the cave entrance.

"Alar and Phoebus haven't come back," he said, getting up and pacing across the cave's dim interior. "I'm getting a little concerned."

"I'm sure they'll be all right," said Fauna, dismissing the subject. "I love the story of Robinson Crusoe, even though the human frightened me. I don't trust him." Burke grimaced but said nothing. "I wish that I could read those books," said the young ape girl. "Are you sure this story came from one of the old books?"

"I'm sure," said Burke. "Does it sound like anything we apes write? That's why I was so interested. But the Ministry of Knowledge says that it knows what is best for apes to read and know and think."

"That can't be right," said Fauna. "You must have misunderstood what they said. Or they must have misunderstood what you did. Our governing council wouldn't be so silly."

"I've heard stories that those old books, the ones that are so different than ours, were written by humans, a long time ago," said Burke.

Fauna was silent for a moment. "Now," she said, "that was worse than silly. I'll pretend you didn't say it at all." She got up from where she was sitting and moved toward a shelf where some loose rocks covered a small opening. "I want to show you something, Pago," she said. She put her hand into' the opening, reaching inside and trying to locate something purely by touch. She moved the rocks to make the opening larger and took a dusty journal from the hiding place. She wiped it off and handed it to Burke. He looked at it curiously. It was roughly made and bound together, the kind of heavy, inefficient construction that marked the apes' published works.

"What is it?" asked Burke.

"It is something I would like you to read to me," said Fauna, her voice a little choked with emotion. "It's something my father left me, something he wrote himself. He told me that I should never show it to Sestus, that my uncle would not understand."

Burke opened the journal carefully and began to read on the first page. "'I came into the woods because I wanted to live only with the essential facts of life,'" he recited.

Fauna listened to the words in rapt attention. Burke

could not decide whether this was the first time that she had heard what Lucian had written in his journal, or if the words were ones that Fauna had listened to often, read by her beloved father. Burke was impressed by what he was reading, too; unlike almost everything he had ever read by ape authors, the contents of the journal had a sensitivity that was almost—*human* was the only word that Burke could come up with.

He knew it wasn't fair, that saying apes weren't human only perpetuated the kind of thinking that had caused so much trouble in his own time and in this time. But Burke knew that he was a product of his environment, for good and for bad. And, as far as the bad was concerned, it would take a great effort to overcome its influence. Burke almost thought *superhuman* effort instead of great; but he caught himself. No sense in making the same mistake twice in one thought.

"'You see, nearest the bone is where life is sweetest…'" he read. The words had a familiar ring to them.

The room was dark, made darker by heavy, coarse curtains which had been drawn across the two windows in the back wall. The small storeroom was crowded and hot; chimpanzees and gorillas, even a couple of orangutans, stood about the back room of one of the village's buildings. Ceramic mugs filled with fermented apple juice clattered together, as the apes raised them in a ceremonial toast.

The talking and joking stopped with the knocking together of the mugs. This was no mere joyful celebration; it was a cold and serious initiation. The solemn voice of Sestus broke through the gloom. "A toast to our Dragoon-to-be," he called. "To Phoebus!"

Around the room, small points of candlelight, symbolic of the wicked torches the Dragoons wielded, picked off points in the bright eyes and perspiring brows of the assembled apes. In the crowd, besides Sestus and Galen, were Macor, Chilot, and others to whom Galen had been introduced, but whose names he had already forgotten.

Galen pretended to be surprised and pleased at the meaning of the ceremony and the acceptance he had won. The truth was that the young chimpanzee was almost ready to collapse from fear. The apes drank a gulp of their liquor. Then two torches were lit and placed on either side of a broad banner that symbolized the might and unity of all apes.

"To all apes!" cried a Dragoon. The apes raised their mugs again, and Galen joined them. They took another drink.

"To the Dragoons!"

They drank a third time. This concluded the ceremony, and the apes shouted their approval. They laughed and drank up the rest of the liquor and clapped Galen on the back.

"Congratulations, Phoebus," said Sestus, filling up their mugs again. "You are soon to be one of us."

"Words cannot describe my feelings, Sestus," said Galen. That was probably a very accurate statement, but Galen figured that Sestus wouldn't know how he meant it; he was correct on that point.

"And at the meeting later, you will get our leader's *final* approval," said Sestus proudly.

"I do hope he accepts me," said Galen.

"Nothing to worry about," said Sestus reassuringly. "Afterwards, you will ride with us in a raid on the humans!"

Galen smiled weakly and tried to appear happy about the situation. He was glad that it was dark, that his companions were getting a little drunk, and that, actually, no one was paying very close attention to him.

Virdon wondered about his friends; he hoped that Galen didn't run into any serious snags in the village. The chimpanzee had a dangerous job to do. And Burke did, too; he had to stay alone in the cave, perhaps with Fauna. Virdon decided to stay with the gorilla he was following for just a short while longer. Then the astronaut wanted to head back to the cave; he knew that Burke would be getting edgy, all alone.

Krono, the gorilla, walked his horse through the woods and into a small clearing. The open area was well-hidden from view, protected by dense woods and rock-studded hills on two sides. The clearing was well marked with hoof prints; the grass and undergrowth had long since been trampled down. Sawed tree stumps served in places as seats around a small fire pit. From his place of concealment, Virdon could see that it was clearly some kind of secret meeting area. Krono walked his horse across the clearing and tied it up to a small sapling. He looked nervously about the area, as though he had the idea that he was being watched.

Virdon tried to move silently to a better position. He was hiding behind one of the large boulders on the small hill that guarded a side of the clearing. He watched Krono carefully as he slowly moved across the hillside.

Krono removed a canteen of water and sat on one of the stumps, oblivious of Virdon's presence nearby.

Virdon studied the clearing and Krono, so that he could lead the police chief back to the place. He then started to move away, back to the cave and Burke. In so doing, however, he knocked loose a rock that clattered down the hillside. Virdon didn't wait to see what Krono would do; the blond man started running.

Krono looked up suddenly at the sound of the falling stones. The clearing had weighed him down heavily in mood; he had fallen completely under the spell of its solitude and peace. The rattle of dislodged rocks intruded sharply.

There was a glimpse of movement, a few quick motions blurred by the dim light of the forest and the distance. But Krono was nonetheless certain of what he saw: a human, running away as fast as he could. That made sense, too; an ape would not be afraid and would not behave in such a way.

Krono didn't go through all of this reasoning while he stood and watched, though. It happened in the back of his mind, even as he dashed across the short distance that separated him from his tethered horse. He mounted as quickly as he could and spurred his horse on in pursuit of Virdon.

Virdon skirted the far side of the hill and followed a rutted trail, overgrown in places, dangerously guarded by roots that made him stumble. All that he could think about was losing the gorilla somehow, and getting back safely to the cave. There had to be a way that a man on foot could lose an ape on horseback; surely the gorilla wouldn't dare to follow through dense trees, where at the speed the horse was traveling a low branch could kill an unwary rider. The problem was getting to the woods before he was overtaken.

Virdon's mind raced on ahead of him, making and discarding plans as he ran. Suddenly, though, half-stumbling along the path, he came to a halt. His plans were as good as dead; he had reached an impasse. The trail ended at the foot of a sheer rocky slope. Behind him, the sound of the mounted ape came ever closer. Virdon searched with diminishing hope for cover.

Krono galloped up to the end of the path. As he saw the rock wall ahead, he slowed his horse to a walk and eased it forward cautiously. The gorilla held his rifle at the ready. His eyes scanned the countryside; he looked up the rocky slope. There was no sign that a human had passed by.

Krono examined the surroundings, carefully, cautiously, a little fearfully. He looked over to a tree, drawn by the rustling of branches; the noise hadn't seemed like the soughing of leaves in the wind...

He looked up slowly until he saw Virdon, crouching on a limb, half-hidden in the foliage. The human was a beautiful target as he clung shakily to the tree.

Krono smiled as he raised his rifle and pulled back the hammer. He sighted along the weapon's length. There was a raised sight on the end of the barrel, and Virdon's terrified face was centered just above it.

7

Virdon stared down at the gorilla. The ape's left eye squinted close as he took sight along the barrel of his rifle. Virdon crouched desperately on the tree limb, his mind racing. There was nowhere to go; there were no branches above him that he could leap to easily. Besides, he would be just as much a target in the process as he was now.

Well, thought the blond man, if there was nowhere to go, he'd have to go there. He acted quickly. Virdon sprang from the tree, worrying only slightly about the injuries he might sustain; after all, if he didn't jump, he could have the rest of eternity to try and recover from a bullet through the heart.

Krono fired just as Virdon hit the gorilla, feet-first, in the ape's massive chest. The shot went wild, and the booming of the rifle reverberated through the small canyon. Virdon and Krono fell heavily to the ground together. They wrestled, thrashing around the small bit of ground. It was a matter of the gorilla's vastly superior size and strength against Virdon's knowledge of self-defense. The battle was bitter and brief. At first, Virdon seemed to be a match for Krono; but the ape's strength made him more than enough for Virdon to handle. Krono took the advantage and landed on top of Virdon. The gorilla's huge hands locked together in a death hold on the human's throat.

It would not take Krono long to strangle him, Virdon knew. He had to act while he still had some strength left. With a final effort, he brought his legs up and over Krono's head, crossed his ankles below the ape's chin, and pushed the gorilla over backwards.

Krono staggered quickly to his feet, grabbing a thick piece of tree limb as a club. Virdon watched him carefully, meanwhile finding himself a similar weapon. The two antagonists circled each other briefly. Then Krono charged, swinging his club in a roundhouse blow aimed at Virdon's head. Virdon ducked under the swing and jabbed his branch into Krono's midsection. Krono doubled over painfully, the wind knocked from him. Virdon stepped in closer and delivered a sharp uppercut to the gorilla's chin. Krono dropped to the ground. Virdon stood for a few seconds, gasping for breath, staring down at his unconscious enemy. Disgustedly, Virdon threw away his wooden weapon.

The blond man looked around him, wondering what to do with Krono, where to go, what effect this unexpected discovery and confrontation might have on the success of their plans. Virdon saw the gorilla's horse, idly standing nearby, as though the violent scene had been a common occurrence in the animal's life. It no doubt was. Virdon staggered wearily to the horse and opened one of Krono's saddle bags. He rummaged through its contents and pulled out a Dragoon's mask. Virdon looked at the leather mask with an expression of distaste. Then he tossed it aside, left the horse and Krono where they were, and started walking back to the cave.

Burke continued to read from Lucian's journal. He had not noticed that he had ceased to read aloud, though; so interested was he in the handwritten manuscript that he read silently, his face reflecting his amazement and curiosity. After several moments, Fauna interrupted his concentration. "Why did you stop?" she asked. "Don't you like my father's ideas?"

Burke looked up, startled. He realized what had happened and laughed. "Oh, no, nothing like that, Fauna," he said. "I'm sorry; your father wrote very beautifully. I hadn't realized that I wasn't reading to you."

"Yes, I'm glad that you like my father's writing. I had no idea myself. He was very secretive about his work in the book. I think he was afraid to let anyone know what was in it, even me. But there isn't anything to be ashamed of, is there? It's lovely."

Lucian the chimpanzee had filled his notebook with thoughts that had come to him over many years. He detailed his reasons for living as he did, a kind of recluse, living even farther from the village than his brother Sestus. He explained why he liked the rough weeks he spent in relative discomfort, camping at the cave, experiencing the peace and quiet. His sensitive nature had led him to think thoughts that went ignored by the great masses of apes; this was the reason that not even Fauna had been allowed access to them while Lucian was still alive. These thoughts were what interested Burke, because they echoed thoughts that he had believed almost entirely extinct, among humans as well as their ape masters.

"I'd like to read you some more," said Burke, "but I'm going to have to put it away now. I'd better see what's keeping Alar and Phoebus. They should have been back awhile ago. I'm worried about them."

Fauna sighed. "You'll read to me some more later?"

"I promise," said Burke.

Burke stood and went to the shelf. He bumped the rocks about to make noise; he wanted to give Fauna the impression that he was hiding the journal back in the hidden recess. But when he finished, he hid the book inside his shirt. "Will you be all right here?" he asked her.

"Of course," she said. "I'll get the rest of the food ready while you're gone."

"Fine," said Burke. "Thanks." He turned and moved past her, out of the cave.

After he left, Fauna turned her head, tilting it slightly as she listened to him climb down the narrow ledge. She waited a moment, then silently followed him. She could not hear him ahead of her; after a short while she realized that she had lost him. Sadly, she found her way back to her uncle's house, to begin her chores there. She would return to the cave later.

Burke moved away from the shore cliffs toward the wooded area up ahead. He was unaware that Fauna had tried to follow him, and he would have been disconcerted to know that she had. Now his only thought was for Virdon's safety; he had been gone a long time, which was unlike Virdon. The blond man did not take unnecessary chances. He ought to have spied on the ape and then come directly back to the cave. The only reason that Burke could think of for Virdon's absence was trouble.

At the top of a hill he stopped to survey the area. There

was no sign of Virdon at all. Burke turned and saw Fauna in the distance, walking quickly toward her uncle's cabin. He shrugged and continued on.

He walked almost three miles farther, not knowing in what direction to search. He made some large circular explorations of the countryside. When Burke had almost decided to give up, return to the cave and wait for Galen, Virdon appeared ahead.

"Alan!" cried Burke.

"Pete!"

"I was just about to give up. Are you okay?"

"Give up?" asked Virdon. "Some search party you are."

"I didn't see any reason for all of us being picked off, one by one. I figured that you'd either get back to the cave, and want to meet me there, or something had happened. In that case, me and Galen would be a lot better than just plain me."

"I know, I know," said Virdon. "I wasn't serious. I'm all right, except for almost getting myself killed."

"Well," said Burke, with a surprised look, "what kind of a day would it be if we didn't do that?"

"That ape that I was following led me to the Dragoons' meeting place," said Virdon. "It's about a mile from here, if I can remember how to get there."

"Good going," said Burke. "Now if Galen has any luck, we could be in business." He reached inside his shirt and took out Lucian's journal.

"Let's hope so, anyway," said Virdon. "But next time, it's your turn for death and danger."

"You asked for it," said Burke. "Anyway, I wasn't aware that we were keeping score."

"That's why you're losing. What's that, Pete?"

Burke riffled a few pages of the journal, staring at it

thoughtfully. "Fauna gave me this journal. Her father wrote it, but she never knew what was in it. I was reading it to her when I got to a part that really interested me. I guess I stopped reading aloud, and it was probably a good thing. Lucian was talking about meeting some humans. They were humans he seems to have liked and respected."

"Fauna might not have liked that," said Virdon. "Go on."

"Well," said Burke, "he knew the apes in this area hated the humans, even more than in most of the rest of the world. But Lucian started to meet with them in secret, anyway. He was his own man—his own ape, I guess—and he was persuaded only by his own convictions. He wanted to share with the underprivileged humans the knowledge he had learned."

"Teaching humans," mused Virdon. "Being friendly to them. That's a subversive idea around these parts." There was a pause, during which both men tried to understand what had happened. "Then why would the humans kill him, their benefactor?" asked Virdon at last. "It doesn't make any sense."

"When did it ever?" asked Burke. The two men exchanged puzzled looks.

Galen and Sestus declined the drinks that the other Dragoons offered them. As Sestus had explained, Galen's initiation was not yet complete, although the final acceptance was usually only a formality. Nevertheless, Galen decided that he would prefer to face it as clearheaded as possible and Sestus agreed.

After Sestus finished his rounds and bought the supplies that he needed, they looked in on the Dragoons' celebration again. It was still going on. "It seems to me that besides the useful work the Dragoons do," said Galen, "the organization is a kind of social club as well."

"I'm glad that you see it that way," said Sestus, once more turning down a mug of fermented fruit juice. "A lot of our members get very few opportunities to see each other and relax."

Galen frowned slightly. He thought about the kind of relaxation the Dragoons enjoyed: killing and burning, looting and destroying. It wasn't his idea of a pleasant way to spend an evening.

As the afternoon waned, the two apes walked slowly back to Sestus' wagon. They climbed aboard and stowed the supplies securely. Then Sestus flicked the reins at his horse, and they began the journey back to the cabin. They made the trip without incident and with little conversation; as the wagon neared the small trail into the yard, Sestus reined up and stopped the wagon. Galen climbed down, then reached up to shake Sestus' hand.

"Are you sure that you won't change your mind?" asked Sestus. "It would be an easy way for you to meet the other Dragoons who weren't at the initiation today. Why don't you come with me? It will only take an hour or so. It's my duty to drive, around and inform them all of the meeting tonight."

"No," said Galen. "I really am. very tired. It's been a busy day for me. I'm not used to all this excitement. I think a little nap would do me good."

"My niece, Fauna, will see to you," said Sestus. "Tell her you will be staying with us; I'll return shortly."

"Fauna," said Galen. "A pretty name."

Sestus remained silent for a moment, thinking of Fauna and her dead father, Lucian. "She is a gentle girl," he said softly. "She's blind. And Phoebus, she knows nothing of my, uh, activities. I would like it kept that way."

Galen nodded his head. That fit in very well with his own plans. "Of course," he said.

"When I return, I'll bring a horse for you," said Sestus, suddenly remembering. "You'll be needing it." Sestus smiled, and Galen tried to return it. The young chimpanzee couldn't tell whether he succeeded.

Sestus waved and said goodbye; then he shouted at his horse, and the wagon creaked and rumbled out of the yard again. Galen stood watching it until it rounded the first bend in the road. He wondered if he had to accompany the Dragoons on a genuine raid. If he did, would he be able to bring himself to do what the Dragoons expected of him? Was he that good an actor?

And then, what would Burke and Virdon think? They were so clannish about the treatment of humans. All humans, every one of them, whether the astronauts had ever met them before or not. Sometimes Galen felt that Burke and Virdon carried brotherhood to unreasonable limits. It was certainly impractical—look what it had done to them now!

Galen turned and headed for the farmhouse, thinking these weary thoughts. He glanced away from the path, making sure that no one was watching, that Fauna or Sestus had not returned. Instead of going to the house, Galen headed for the cave. As he passed the cabin, however, he saw Fauna gathering some wood at a small shed at the side of the house. She looked up, sensing or hearing Galen's presence. "Phoebus?" she asked.

Galen stopped in his tracks, disappointed that Fauna had heard him sneaking by, a little amazed that she knew who he was. "Oh, hello, Fauna," he said, adopting a startled tone that would sound as though he hadn't seen her before. He went to join her. "How are you today?

I came by here, but I didn't think that anyone was home. Uh, how could you tell that it was me?"

Fauna laughed. "I've had to use my hearing the way I used to use my eyes. How can you tell one person from another when you see them? Because they have distinguishing features. But your ears can do the same for you, if you listen correctly. Your feet gave you away. The blind can tell someone from the way he walks."

Galen was genuinely interested. This was a problem he had never before considered; he was, after all, an ape with a considerable background and interest in science. He loved learning things, and, whatever else she might be in the peculiar circumstances, Fauna was also a source of interesting information. "That's very fascinating," said Galen. He bent to take some of her load of wood. "Here," he said, "let me help you." He took the firewood and followed her as she walked into Sestus' house.

Fauna dropped her part of the load in a woven basket near the fireplace. She moved aside so that Galen could do the same. When they stood up, Fauna brushed bits of wood and dry leaves from her clothing. "Did you get your water?" she asked.

Galen, of course, didn't have any idea what she was talking about. "Water?" he said. His voice was hollow and a little apprehensive. One of the difficulties with Virdon's plan was that Galen would be out of touch with the humans for great amounts of time. Neither he nor they would know what had happened in their separate situations.

"Pago said that you and Alar went to get some," said Fauna. "He was very worried because you hadn't returned on time. In fact, he went out looking for you. You didn't run into trouble, did you? I told Pago that you were probably splashing in the stream with Alar or something, and that he didn't really need to be concerned."

"Oh, yes, yes!" said Galen quickly, recovering and playing along with Burke's story. But something disturbed Galen. "You were with Pago earlier today, then?" he asked.

"At the cave," said Fauna, not catching Galen's sudden change in tone. "He told me a story about an ape named Robinson Crusoe."

Galen stared off into the distance, his expression unseen by Fauna, but his audible movements conveying anxiety and distrust. "Pago has a way with females," he said.

Fauna did not seem to hear Galen's last comment. "I think I'm in love with him," she said hesitantly.

Galen reacted with a burst of outraged anger. "Isn't that kind of sudden?" he asked, trying to keep his voice under control.

"I know that he reminds me of someone else," said Fauna, pacing across her uncle's living room. "But it isn't just that. It's a gentleness in his voice. A warmth all his own that makes me feel more alive than I've felt in a long time."

Galen was becoming deeply disturbed. This was something that no one had counted on. It was something that Galen had to quench. "Fauna, you must be careful," he said. "You can't trust love that happens so quickly."

She laughed delightedly. "That's nonsense, Phoebus," she said. "Is time any guarantee that love will be binding? Oh, surely I know that it's asking a lot for him to love someone who is blind. But do you think it's possible?"

Galen looked at her pityingly. "Do you want an honest answer?" he asked in a solemn tone of voice.

"Of course I do," said Fauna.

"No, I don't think it is possible."

Fauna answered proudly. "I can do anything a female with sight can do," she said.

The matter was growing beyond a dangerous point. Galen flared furiously again. "Except to recognize the truth, Fauna. Can't you see? Pago is not an ape—" Galen was amazed at what his emotions had made him say. He coughed, as though to clear his throat. "Not an ape you can *trust*," he finished lamely.

Fauna turned to face Galen. She could hardly believe what she heard. She had been fond of Pago; now, Galen's words forced her to defend Pago, making her attachment that much stronger. She identified herself with Pago against what she felt to be unwarranted attacks by a false friend.

"I don't believe that," she said. "I think you're the one who can't be trusted. He's supposed to be your friend, yet you talk about him like an enemy."

Galen realized that he had made an error in judgment. Burke and Virdon had cautioned him many times that anger was their greatest enemy. Now, glumly, he realized that they had been right. He would have to work hard to restore the breach he had made. "He *is* my friend," he said, trying to soothe her. "But I know him better than you do. I'm concerned about *you*."

Fauna flared into rage. She wouldn't listen to any of Galen's improbable explanations. "I don't want to hear any more from you," she said in a tight, even voice. "Leave me alone."

Fauna turned around abruptly, leaving Galen standing in the room, his mouth open, ready to make another reply. He saw her sad form, shaking a little as though she were crying; he recalled that she had kept the tears back, even at her father's graveside. Galen blamed Burke for this gloomy affair; but there was little that anyone could do now. Angry, and at a loss for words, Galen left Sestus' house.

The walk back gave Galen awhile to collect his thoughts. The entire matter of the Dragoons and what they would expect of him later that same day was pushed to the background. As he walked, Galen's imagination worked quickly, building more and more unlikely scenes involving Fauna and Burke. Even though the need for deception prevented the most harmless kiss, Burke still might not be trusted to avoid feeding his own ego at Fauna's expense. Might he not lead her on, knowing that eventually there would be no harm in the situation—for him? Would he be so callous, so cruel, as to play with, the affections of a blind, orphaned ape girl?

Galen thought that he knew Burke well enough to answer "no" to these questions. And, certainly, he wanted to. But what he had heard from Fauna, and what his own active mind invented, had him convinced of the opposite before he arrived at the cave.

As he entered, he was still grim and furious. "You were right, Alar," he said. "Sestus not only knew all about the Dragoons, he's one of them himself."

Burke and Virdon laughed. "How about that!" said Burke.

"I've won their confidence," said Galen in short, clipped words. "They're bringing me up for membership at a meeting later tonight."

"Good work, Galen," said Virdon.

"Yeah," said Burke, "we knew you could pull it off."

Galen looked at him caustically. "We should all be proud of ourselves." His brows contracted in a deep frown. "Right, Pete?" he asked pointedly.

Burke, of course, had no idea what Galen was talking about. But he could sense that something was bothering the chimpanzee. "Well," he said, thinking that Galen must mean something about the matter of the Dragoons, "I can't take any of your credit. I haven't done anything."

Galen snorted at what he thought was Burke's coy answer. "Oh, but you have," he said. "Don't be so modest. You have, indeed."

Burke was tired of Galen's baiting. "Hey," he said, "stop it. I'm not up to game-playing right now. What's eating you, anyway?"

"I'll tell you," Galen snapped. "Here's what's eating me—what a disgusting figure of speech. I think you ought to stay away from Fauna!"

Burke was frankly puzzled. He was a human. Fauna was an ape. It was almost as though the parent of a tree had warned Burke to stay away from its child. "I'm sorry, officer," he said to Galen. "I just don't read you."

Galen glared at the bewildered astronaut. "She's in love with you!" he said resentfully.

Burke laughed aloud; but when he saw that neither Virdon nor Galen were joining him, he stopped. "Love?" he asked. "What are you talking about?"

"She told me. She wanted to know if I thought you could love *her*."

"Galen," said Burke, "let me remind you. I'm practically going steady with a nice young woman from Texas. She's dead, now, but I'll wait. Anyway, Fauna likes the ape she thinks I am, not me."

Galen did not answer. He just stared. Burke turned to Virdon for help. "It's ridiculous," he said.

"Ridiculous?" said Galen. "It's tragic! Can you imagine what it's going to do to her if she finds out you're a human?"

"Look," said Burke, starting to get angry himself, "*you*

were the one who made her think I was an ape."

Galen flared into self-righteous anger. "I didn't think you would become involved with her."

Burke's eyes widened; he was every bit as furious as Galen. "I'm not involved with her! It's the stupidest thing I ever heard! Somebody tell this guy to lay off before I forget that we're such good friends!"

Virdon was not amused. Like Burke, he didn't really understand what caused Galen's anxiety. But he could see that Galen's problem was real, at least to the chimpanzee. Galen had proven to be a trustworthy and intelligent companion, and Virdon had learned to respect his opinions. It was clear that Galen, at least, thought that there was something to worry about. "Okay, okay," said Virdon, interceding. "Cool off, you two. What happened, happened. Nobody planned it that way."

There was a long tense moment when no one in the cave spoke. Only Galen's hoarse breathing could be heard. Burke looked from Virdon to Galen. "Look," said the dark-haired man, "I don't want to hurt her any more than you do. And I'm not going to. I'll talk to her."

"I don't know if that's the best thing to do," said Virdon.

"I don't, either," said Burke. "I'll go anyway. Human beings had problems like this for millions of years. It looks like apes inherited them, too. And they're no better at solving them." He started to leave.

Galen blinked his large eyes several times quickly. Then he sighed. "Pete," he said softly, "be gentle with her."

Burke stopped by the entrance to the cave and turned around. He looked at Galen for a few seconds. Then, without saying a word, he nodded, turned, and disappeared from view.

Burke walked the distance to the house as quickly as he could. From what Galen had said, Fauna was alone; Sestus would not be home, or the conversation that Galen reported would not have taken place. Burke only hoped that he could get to the apes' cabin, do his painful duty, and leave before the human-hating Sestus returned. Because if he didn't he'd have the Dragoons out searching for him, with a tearful Fauna giving the vigilantes directions and descriptions.

Fauna was lifting a bucket of water from a well in front of Sestus' house. Burke saw her there, took a deep breath, and approached. "Fauna," he said gently. "It's Pago."

Fauna looked worried. "You shouldn't be here. Uncle Sestus will be here very soon."

"I had to talk to you," said Burke. "I was worried when I got back to the cave and you were gone. I thought it would be better if I came to speak to you here."

Fauna spoke breathlessly. "Did you want to talk about us?" she asked.

Burke was about to speak, but suddenly, seeing the expression on Fauna's face, he lost some of his courage. He delayed the crucial moment by pulling her father's journal from his shirt. "Actually, Fauna," he said hesitantly, "I wanted to ask you about your father's journal. I took it with me."

Fauna seemed a little disappointed. "I know," she said. "I didn't mind."

"I'm glad," said Burke. He couldn't think of anything else to say. He didn't know how to say what he had come to tell her.

Fauna guessed that Burke was disturbed about something. She tilted her head curiously, waiting. Burke did not seem ready to speak. They stood there in the dusky warmth.

Fauna sighed. "Did Phoebus talk to you after he left here?" she asked.

"Yes," said Burke. "That was one of the reasons I wanted to come now."

"I thought so," said Fauna. "You are a good and decent ape. Perhaps Phoebus *was* only thinking of my welfare, but I didn't like what he was saying about you."

"Fauna—" said Burke.

She stopped him with a gesture. "I hope you weren't too angry with him," she said.

"Phoebus has been a good friend of mine for a long time," said Burke.

"He is very lucky," said Fauna. "Anyway, it's all right if you don't care for me. I've done a lot of thinking. After all, we've only known each other a short time. I understand. It's too soon. Perhaps, though, perhaps in time…"

Burke knew that to let her think such a thing would be more cruel than anything Galen had accused him of. "I think you're a… lovely… gentle person, Fauna," he said, searching with difficulty for the proper words. "But there are things about me that you don't know."

Fauna laughed softly. "Now you're sounding like Phoebus," she said. "I've never heard someone attack a friend the way he did."

Burke was beginning to wonder just how venomous Galen had been. He made a mental note to ask the chimpanzee; some day when they were safely away from this place. "Maybe you should have listened to him," said Burke, a little upset. If Fauna *had* listened to Galen's arguments, then Burke wouldn't have to go through them all over again.

Fauna was undaunted by Burke's sad persuasion. "You tell me," she said. "You tell me what is so wrong about you that surpasses what is wrong with me."

Burke looked at her for almost a minute. "Fauna, this makes me remember another story. It was a story my mother used to tell me when I was very small."

"Will you tell it to me?" she asked.

"It's from a book called the Bible," said Burke.

Fauna thought for a moment. "I never heard of it," she said.

Burke licked his dry lips and began the story. "It's about a blind ape named Isaac, and his two sons, Jacob and Esau. Esau was strong and hairy, a hunter whom his father idolized. Well, Isaac was dying and on his deathbed he blessed Esau. That was something that meant a great deal in those days. The other son, Jacob, was soft and smooth of skin. He wanted the same blessing from his father. So he posed as his brother by covering his hand with a piece of goatskin. Old Isaac, fooled into thinking he was touching Esau, gave Jacob the same blessing."

Fauna's expression was puzzled. She did not speak for several seconds after Burke finished his story. "I am not sure that I understand the meaning of the story," she said.

"It was a deception born of desperate need, Fauna," said Burke, trying to lead into his disclosure. "It was not meant to harm anyone."

At that moment, Burke slowly reached out his hand toward Fauna in an attempt to make contact with her, so that she might feel his smooth skin and at last know the truth about him.

Slowly his hand moved closer to hers. Burke's face was shiny with perspiration; this was, indeed, one of the most difficult things he ever had to do. He only had to move his hand a few inches, but in his heart, it felt as though he were trying to move a mountain. He saw the contrast between his own smooth skin and the dense, shaggy wrist of Fauna. But as he almost touched, her, he hesitated.

"You could not deceive anyone, Pago," said Fauna, wondering what his message might be. "I have touched you. I have touched the strong features of your face. It is as strong as Esau's. If you were smooth and soft like Jacob, I would fear and despise you. But you must not worry about such a silly thing."

Her words made him falter. He slowly drew his hand back, without touching her.

Burke looked at her open, trusting face. He realized that he could not tell her the truth; that knowledge made him angry with himself, for lacking the courage, and for continuing the deception.

He had a difficult time even finding the words to cover his shame and his unhappiness. "Fauna," he said, "you must understand that there is nothing between us and there can never be. My friends and I are leaving here. And you will never hear my voice again."

Fauna almost collapsed beneath the terrible emotional weight of Burke's announcement. She began to cry softly. "No," she murmured. "No, no." Her voice was aching and lonely.

Burke was moved almost unbearably. "Goodbye, Fauna," he said. He wanted to be away from there, away from the painful scene that had become necessary. Certainly, it was the right thing to do; but it was also better to leave her quickly rather than let her try to cling to him with hopeless arguments.

Burke placed her father's journal in her hands as a final severing of the ties which had begun to bind their lives together. He turned suddenly and hurried away, still disturbed and angry with himself; he realized that there was no pleasant way to do what had to be done. Nevertheless, he blamed himself for Fauna's anguish.

Behind him, shaken, disbelieving, poignant as she stood and listened to the fading sound of Burke's steps, Fauna wept noiselessly. Limply she held her father's notebook in her hands. Her body trembled and the journal dropped to the ground. She did not notice. The wind rustled the pages, making a quiet, lonely sound, but Fauna didn't hear.

Sestus arrived at the farm a short time later. Galen was waiting for him in the small front yard. Fauna was nowhere to be seen; she was probably inside the house, nursing her grief. Sestus rode one horse and led another for Galen's use. Galen mounted the horse and followed Sestus along the road toward the secret meeting place in the woods. Virdon and Burke, concealed on the hill overlooking Sestus' house, watched the scene closely.

Virdon turned to Burke. "We haven't much time," he said. "We've got to get into the village and try to get Perdix to attend that meeting. If he doesn't, all of this will have been for nothing."

Burke smiled weakly. "I hate to be a killjoy," he said. "But I've got this terrible feeling in the pit of my stomach that is trying to tell me Perdix might not want to come with us. And if he doesn't, we're not going to be able to do much convincing."

"Well," said Virdon lightly, "since you're doing such a good job with all the convincing so far, you'll just have to find a way to persuade him."

Burke looked at his friend from the corner of his eye. "Thanks a lot," he said. They moved away from the house, keeping low to avoid being spotted. But they did not see

Macor, who watched the two humans from a distant rise. Macor watched them until Burke and Virdon disappeared from his view. Then he spurred his horse down into the forest, toward the Dragoons' meeting place.

It was still not quite evening; the sun was tinting the western clouds a bright pink. In the village of the apes , business was coming to an end for the day, as the citizens closed up their shops and went home for dinner. Virdon and Burke scrambled down a low slope behind the gorilla garrison and stealthily crept toward the back door. They noticed Perdix's and Zon's horses, saddled and tied up, ready for the evening patrol.

The two humans pressed themselves against the wall next to the rear door; they caught their breath and collected themselves for the next step. Virdon glanced through a window; he saw Perdix inside, reading a circular. A gorilla patrol guard was cleaning a rifle. Zon was about to leave the room.

"Are you going, Zon?" asked Perdix, looking up.

"For a while," said Zon. "I'll be back soon, Perdix."

Perdix nodded and followed Zon into another front room. Zon came around and mounted his horse after a few seconds, not noticing Burke or Virdon, who had hidden themselves in the deepening shadows only a few yards away.

Burke stared after Zon. "Well," he said, "we lost one. We'll need all the help we can get, against those Dragoons."

Virdon nodded toward the garrison, indicating Perdix who was still inside. "We only need one," he said. "Are you ready?"

"No," said Burke, "but that never stopped me before."

"I wish that someone was around to wish us well," said Virdon. "We're not doing this for any great cause, secret security reason, or scientific mission. We're doing it so that we can get out of this town alive."

"That's not a bad reason at all," said Burke. "My dad in New Jersey used to look at me and say, 'Son,' he'd say—I think he'd forgotten what my name was—'when the going gets tough, and the tough get going, what will you do?' I always figured that I'd be left standing all by myself."

Virdon gave a low laugh. Then he reached for the door knob, turned it, and both men burst into the garrison.

The gorilla guard inside jumped to his feet as he heard the loud crash of the door. Burke and Virdon stumbled across the threshold and stopped, with the guard's rifle pointed at them. "Take him," said Burke, and the two men jumped the gorilla and wrestled the ape to the ground.

Burke held the gorilla with an armlock; the man's free hand was clamped over the ape's mouth. Virdon pulled the rifle from the gorilla's grasp.

"Take it easy, Perdix," said Virdon. "We just want to talk."

The gorilla tried to say something, muffled by Burke's hand. "No yelling, okay?" asked Burke. "Let's be sensible."

The gorilla nodded. Burke released his hold on the ape's mouth. Virdon stood ready with the rifle, in case the gorilla decided after all to shout for help.

The ape was frightened and confused. "I... I'm not Perdix," he said. There was a sudden, tense silence in the room.

His words hit Burke and Virdon like sledgehammers. The whole careful scheme had already hit a large snag. This was the kind of accident that made disasters out of sure things. Burke and Virdon looked at one another. Something had to be done; they had to act quickly, and they had the ape guard to consider. Before they could decide, the sound of a rifle bolt turned them.

A uniformed gorilla stepped out of the anteroom, summoned by the scuffling sounds. Burke and Virdon knew immediately that this armed ape was the gorilla they had come to see. Perdix trained his rifle on Virdon and Burke. "Were you looking for me?" he asked sourly.

The gorilla guard retrieved his rifle from Virdon and stood behind the two astronauts. No one answered Perdix. Virdon and Burke wore defeated expressions. They had walked into a lions' den, and the lions had been more than ready for them.

8

Flames licked up into the air from the torches that circled the clearing in the forest. The Dragoon leader stood on a tall stump—the podium of the Dragoons' meeting place. Around him, the murmur of many ape voices sounded like the constant babbling of a fresh running stream. The Dragoon leader allowed the informal gathering to continue, until he felt that the time was right to assume control. He raised both hands over his head. Two masked Dragoons on either side of him raised their rifles over their heads as a symbolic gesture. The motion caught the attention of the apes in the clearing. "As leader of the high council," he said in a deep, resonant voice, "I now call the Dragoons to order."

The murmur subsided. Around the sweet-smelling clearing had gathered twelve apes—four chimpanzees, two orangutans, and six gorillas. All of them wore their fierce masks. Several of the apes carried blazing torches, the others held rifles. They were seated in a semi-circle before the Dragoon leader, Galen sitting nervously beside the masked Sestus.

The Dragoon leader paused, creating an atmosphere of importance and drama. "If no one objects at this time," he said, "we will not list the grievances the humans voiced concerning our last raid. The matter has been taken care of for us. It seems those complaining humans are now dead!"

There was a roar of laughter from the apes; Galen found the whole matter sickening, and he wished more than anything else to get away. He steeled himself with the knowledge that he was helping to end the Dragoons' unchallenged reign of fear. The delighted ovation from the audience continued. Galen realized that he had a part to play; he forced an unconvincing laugh himself.

As the sound of the laughter subsided, the Dragoon leader raised his arms again, taking control of the meeting. He paused and looked among his listeners. They knew that he was about to speak seriously to them. "I understand that we have a new prospect who wishes to join our ranks," he said. "Will he please stand?"

Sestus urged Galen up, and Galen stood, trembling slightly but not willing to let the other apes know how afraid he was. He looked around the masked-ape audience, feeling even more nervous and apprehensive. Then he thought about Fauna, and the life she could expect to live under the shadow of these apes.

The Dragoon leader's next two questions were a formality. Galen had been provided with the answers and coached. "Your name?" asked the Dragoon leader.

"I am Phoebus," said Galen as evenly as he could manage.

The Dragoon leader looked around his audience again. "And is there anyone here who vouches for Phoebus?"

Sestus stood up next to Galen. "I vouch for him. I, Sestus!"

The Dragoon leader was evidently pleased. "Sestus," he said. "Yes, good." The masked leader turned again to Galen. "Are you, Phoebus, familiar with the goals of the Dragoons?"

Galen decided that this was a very strategic time to make a good impression. He cleared his throat and spoke loudly. "Yes!" he said, with vigor. "We must drive every human from our lands. We cannot rest until this has been done!"

There was applause and cheers from the apes.

"And the humans who refused?" asked the Dragoon leader.

"Death to them," cried Galen with supreme enthusiasm. "Death to them all!"

There were more wild cheers and grunts from the apes. Galen had indeed won them over.

"It appears that Sestus has brought us a worthy prospect. Let us take the vote."

Before the actual decision was made, though, one ape stood up in the crowd. "Wait," he shouted, above the noise of the excited apes. "Before we go any further, I would like my say." It was Macor, one of the three trouble-makers, the gorilla who had seen Virdon and Burke only a short time before.

"Speak, Macor," said the Dragoon leader.

Macor looked around. "It may mean nothing," he said, suddenly-sorry he had brought attention to himself. "But then again, I would like to know what humans are doing on Sestus' farm!"

There was a startled and confused murmur from the other apes. Galen was horrified; Sestus was perplexed and worried. The Dragoon leader raised his hands for silence.

"On my farm?" asked Sestus, still trying to understand

what would make Macor say such a thing. "Humans?" He made a dismissing wave of one hand. "It's impossible."

"Two of them," said Macor doggedly. "One with yellow hair. They were hiding near a cave, not more than an hour ago. I was witness to the whole scene."

"You know me, fellow Dragoons!" cried Sestus, livid with rage. "I wouldn't allow it."

Krono the gorilla rose and addressed the gathering. "The one who attacked me," he said solemnly. "He was a human with yellow hair."

There were more whisperings from the apes. They had grown suspicious of Sestus. He turned and appealed to the Dragoon leader.

"You know my loyalty," he said, bewildered. "I swear, I know nothing of these humans!"

The Dragoon leader nodded. He was satisfied with Sestus. "And you, Phoebus, a stranger in our midst, do you know anything of these humans?"

Galen was highly indignant. "Me? What would I know of humans on *Sestus'* farm?"

The Dragoon leader stared down at him with a chilling look. "Yes," he said slowly, "what would you?" He gave a command to his followers. "We will go to this cave and find the humans!" he cried. All the apes in the clearing except Sestus and Phoebus joined in loud and frenzied cheers.

The noise continued, so loud and so vehement that the Dragoon leader could not stop it. The apes were getting themselves mentally ready to make a raid. Finally the leader signalled to his two subordinate officers; they moved among the crowd with their rifles, and soon the apes had almost settled down to docile attention. "Phoebus," said the Dragoon leader in a loud voice, "Phoebus, *you* will have the honor of killing these humans!" There was another ovation, this time for Galen. He could only stand in place and smile uncertainly, his mind a mixture of doubt and fear.

As the sun touched the western horizon and became a shrinking scarlet globe, Virdon and Burke trotted along the rough road. Although they were out of breath from their run, they still tried to speak to each other between gasps. "Stop worrying," said Virdon. "I tell you he's convinced we're telling the truth."

"That's a nice thing to believe," said Burke. "I'm sure that you find it very comforting. The only thing that I want to know is, why is he pointing that rifle at our backs?"

Perdix rode on horseback a few yards behind the running astronauts, his rifle at the ready.

Virdon panted for breath. "He probably has some kind of gun fetish," he said. "Look, he wants to nail those Dragoons as bad as we do. If we have a friend—he's it."

Perdix heard the faint sounds of their speech, although he couldn't make out their words. He spoke up loudly. "If you humans have lied to me," he said coldly, "I will execute you *personally*. It is within my right, and it is my duty.'"

Burke snorted. "You know, Alan, I hate to knock your friends. But for such a good buddy, Perdix gives me this slight feeling of insecurity. I don't know. It's probably not his fault. It's probably just me. Just me, and his rifle, that's all."

The Dragoons went to their horses and mounted. They checked their masks and armed themselves with torches or rifles. Then they waited for the Dragoon leader to give the instructions to move out. They thundered out of the forest clearing, Galen riding among the leaders of the gang.

After a short time, Galen became aware of the sound

of waves rolling in to a rocky beach, and the roar of the water as it broke upon the sea cliffs. They were getting close to the critical moment.

Galen was not aware of the lonely, still form of a young female chimpanzee standing on the edge of those cliffs. He was still too far away to see Fauna, as she began wandering along the edge of the steep escarpment, aimless, lonely, uncaring where she was going. Fauna was an important part of the puzzle that was slowly beginning to draw together, but Galen had underestimated both Fauna's need for emotional support and her possible effect on all of their lives.

The Dragoons came pounding out of the woods, unaware of Fauna's presence, unaware of anyone in the world except themselves. They yelled and gesticulated in the deepening gloom, until their mood had become an insane craving for blood.

And Virdon and Burke trotted on ahead of Perdix, bound for the same destination as the Dragoons—the cave. When they neared the vicinity, the two humans pulled up suddenly and looked off down the road.

"Keep going!" cried Perdix. 'I'm not going to be played for one of your human tricks. As long as I'm riding behind you with this rifle, you'll keep running."

"Look," said Burke, pointing.

Ahead of them, the Dragoons galloped toward the cave area.

"There are your Dragoons, Perdix," said Virdon, winded from his long run. "Let's see you do something about them."

"Just the way we promised," said Burke.

Perdix hesitated for a moment. Faced now with the awesome responsibility of confronting the almost autonomous Dragoons, Perdix was beginning to show some timidity. Still, he urged the humans on and the small party came closer to the masked vigilantes.

The Dragoons thundered into the small open area at the top of the sea cliffs. They reined in and jumped down from their horses. Two of the apes were assigned to hold the reins, while the others waited to hear the leader's directions.

The leader dismounted and walked toward Macor. "Where did you see them?" asked the leader.

"I was on my horse, on my way to the meeting," said Macor. "I was crossing that ridge, there." He pointed across the wooded area to a bald spine of rock some distance away. "I could clearly see the humans here. They stood out against the bright sky. I know that there's a secret cave right below us. I used to play there when I was younger."

The Dragoon leader gestured, and three apes with rifles followed his pointing hand to the barely visible trail. They scrambled down the path toward the cave. Galen and Sestus waited to one side, neither sure how such a pleasant day had taken so bad a turn.

The three apes clambered down to the beach. After a moment, one of them found the narrow ledge that led back up to the concealed cave mouth. One ape waited outside, while the other two rushed in, ready for a battle. After a quiet moment, the apes emerged. They shouted up to their comrades.

"There's no one in the cave," called one. "It's been occupied," he said and held up some fruit. "Someone has been here very recently."

The Dragoon leader looked off into the distance. Sestus and a couple of other apes followed his gaze. "They can't be far," said the leader, thinking. "They may still have

Phoebus' horse." The leader shot Galen a distrustful look.

"There!" cried one of the apes.

The Dragoon leader jerked around and scrutinized the shadowy woods. Coming toward them on the road was a small group of figures. "It's Perdix!" said Sestus worriedly. "And he has the humans!"

Perdix led the two astronauts into the middle of the scene. Galen tried to ignore Virdon and Burke, but they caught his worried, almost hopeless expression. "Ah," said the Dragoon leader in a sinister welcome, "Perdix! You have saved us the trouble of hunting these humans down."

Perdix gave the leader a cold look. "And they have saved me the trouble of hunting *you* down." He turned to the other Dragoons. "All of you, throw down your weapons!"

The Dragoons hesitated; they recognized Perdix as the emblem of authority, directly from General Urko of Central City. But there was a great distance between the village and Central City, a distance measured more accurately in custom and temperament than miles.

"Throw them down!" cried Perdix. He stared unblinkingly into the eyes of the Dragoon leader.

The leader looked back through his mask. The two apes seemed to engage in a battle of wills. "No!" said the Dragoon leader, finally and irrevocably defying the authority of Urko and the Supreme Council.

Perdix suddenly recognized the voice of the Dragoon leader. "Don't be a fool, Zon!" he said, disappointed that his own deputy should be the leader of his enemies.

Zon, the leader of the Dragoons, ripped the mask from his face. His expression conveyed the hatred that the gorilla had fed for many years. There was also a terrible and frightening lust for the murder of Burke and Virdon.

"You are the fool, Perdix!" said Zon with an evil laugh.

"A fool not to side with us! Turn your back. Let us kill these humans!"

"No," said Perdix. "This killing and terrorizing will stop. This insane hatred will stop. Now throw down your weapons!"

Zon laughed again; Virdon thought that he heard a trace of psychopathic mania in the sound. "We have ten weapons to your one," said the Dragoon leader. "Are you willing to die with these humans?"

Perdix leveled his own rifle at Zon's chest. He spoke calmly, as though he were not actually near the brink of death. "Are you willing to die to kill me, Zon?" he asked.

The atmosphere had become unbearably tense. The Dragoons shuffled about uneasily, looking to Zon for leadership. Perdix held steady. Virdon and Burke glanced from one to the other; a bloodbath seemed almost inevitable.

Sestus cried out to Zon in an anguished tone of voice. "This has gone too far," he pleaded.

"Shut up, Sestus," said Zon, through clenched teeth. "We set out to do something, and we're going to finish it."

Sestus licked his lips. "I'm willing to shut up where the humans are concerned," he said. "But now we're endangering apes! We were formed to protect apes, not kill them!"

Zon gave Sestus a sharp look. "I'll kill anyone, human *or* ape, who tries to stop us!"

Zon slowly aimed his rifle at Perdix's chest and cocked the firing hammer back. The two gorillas stood that way for a maddening moment, their rifles pointed at each other.

Just out of sight along the bend of the sea cliff, Fauna wandered near the edge, involved in her own tumultuous thoughts. She did not hear the loud arguments of the Dragoons and Perdix; in her frame of mind, she might not have heard them if they had stood inches away from her. She stumbled at the brink of a cliff and slipped, grabbing blindly at some roots as she fell over the edge. She managed to catch something and did not fall to certain death below, but she was trapped. She knew that she couldn't hold on indefinitely. Very soon, her grasp would weaken... She cried out for help. Her shrill scream was wordless, but it conveyed her alarm.

The cry came muffled by the trees and the sound of the sea. Burke and Virdon reacted immediately, recognizing the ape girl's voice. Her scream echoed in the still air. "Fauna!" cried Burke. He bolted toward the sound. Zon jerked around, raising his rifle and taking aim at the dark-haired man. Sestus jumped in and knocked the Dragoon leader's rifle away.

"No," said Sestus. Zon glared at the chimpanzee in helpless rage.

Fauna still clung precariously to the roots that had broken her fall. She struggled vainly to climb back up the sheer face of the cliff. Burke was running rapidly toward her, shouting encouragement.

As the seconds passed, though, Fauna's hands cramped and weakened; she lost her grip on the roots and fell. She landed in the turbulent water below; her fall had been eased by her catching the roots. She was not killed by the fall; Burke looked over the edge of the cliff and saw her thrashing, panic-stricken, in the white foam below. He knew that while death had spared her momentarily, it would claim Fauna very soon. Without a moment's hesitation, without thinking about what might happen to him, Burke made a long, clean dive into the roaring, raging waves below. There might have been invisible rocks below the breaking surf; he might have dashed himself to instant death, but he never considered that possibility. All he knew was that Fauna had been swept under by a wave, and she had not surfaced again.

Perdix, Virdon, Galen, and the rest of the Dragoons came down toward the edge of the cliffs, watching Burke as he swam laboriously toward the spot where Fauna had gone under.

Burke reached her limp body, grabbed her, and began pulling her toward the shore. Fighting the heavy sea, the astronaut was near exhaustion himself; only his determination kept him swimming with his burden. He struggled toward a sandy beach, just away from the cliff where Fauna fell. Seeing where Burke was heading, the group above him on the cliff top hurried down a trail to the beach.

Burke carried Fauna in his arms out of the water. He stumbled in the sand, wearily trudging up the beach as the others drew near. Burke lowered Fauna slowly and carefully down on the sand. Then he, too, fell back in utter fatigue. Sestus came forward. Virdon took a blanket he had grabbed from a horse's saddlebag and covered Fauna with it. She began to recover consciousness and moaned slightly. The sound made Burke sit up and smile. "It's all right, Fauna," he said gently. "It's all right now."

"Pago?" asked Fauna in a weak, distant voice. "Pago... is that you?"

"Yes, Fauna."

She shivered, relieved and happy that he had come back to her, after all. She reached out and touched his face. There was an instant of contact with his human flesh; she pulled her hand back as though it had been burned. "No—no—" she cried, confused and horrified. "You're not Pago. You're..." she could barely bring herself to say it, "*human.*" She uttered the word as if she were spitting out poison.

Burke thought of the Biblical story he had told her. "It was a… deception born of desperate need, Fauna," he said imploringly. "It was not meant to harm."

But the combined shock of the near-fatal accident and the revelation of Burke's true identity were more than Fauna could take. She almost went into hysteria at the thought of being so close to a *human.* Shocked, revolted, she recoiled from him in abject terror. "Get away from me," she shrieked. "Get away!"

Burke was shaken. He retreated from her, not wanting to upset her further. Sestus stepped in to try and placate her. "Fauna," he said, "it's your uncle, it's Sestus. I'm here. There's nothing to be afraid of."

"He's human!" murmured Fauna. "Human!"

"But he isn't going to hurt you," said Sestus.

"Get him away, get him away," said Fauna angrily. "He tricked me, like the others tricked my father! They're treacherous, just as you said, Uncle Sestus. Like animals. They must be treated like animals…" She broke down into sobs, her body trembling violently.

"Fauna, listen to me," said Sestus pityingly. "The human saved your life, do you hear? It was not I who saved you from the ocean. It was the human."

"No," said Fauna, shaking her head, "I don't believe it."

"It's true, Fauna!" said Sestus, taking hold of the young female ape's shoulders. "I saw him! He risked his own life to save you!"

"I hate him! A human killed my father. *Killed* him!"

Virdon knelt beside Fauna and tried to speak with her. "Fauna, it's Alar," he said, as gently as he could. She did not respond. "Fauna. I don't know who killed your father. But even if it was a human, that doesn't mean all humans are bad. Just as all apes are not good."

"That's a lie!" said Fauna, snarling. "I hate humans!"

"Fauna," said Sestus, unable to keep his secret any longer, "this Alar speaks the truth. It was *not* a human who caused your father's death."

"Shut up, Sestus!" said Zon in a warning tone.

Perdix looked suddenly interested. "What are you saying, Sestus?" he asked.

Sestus turned back to Fauna; the aging chimpanzee was almost in tears, too. His voice was full of pain. "I... hated and feared humans, just as you do now. We all did. But your father... he was different. He didn't fear the humans. He trusted them. He believed in them." Sestus had to pause while he collected himself. "That night," he said falteringly, "I was with Zon..."

"No, Sestus!" shouted Zon.

Sestus ignored him. "We warned your father not to trust them as you are warning me now. But he was stubborn. Zon became angry. There was a fight. Zon hit your father. Lucian fell and struck his head on a rock. Zon said we were both responsible for his death." Sestus was overcome with anguish. "Fauna, I couldn't bring myself to tell you the truth. So I made an agreement with Zon; we would blame it on the humans. Then Zon used this lie as an excuse to drive off and kill humans. But I can't go on living like this any more. Not when I see how wrong I was in thinking they are all bad. This is a lie that we must not let continue. I have acted worse than any human." He held Fauna tightly to him as the ape girl slowly accepted and absorbed the meaning of his words.

Zon's frenzy was growing during Sestus' speech.

"Sestus is a coward," he said, trying to regain his swaggering dominance over the other apes. "What difference does it make who killed Lucian? The humans are our enemies. We must drive them from our land. We must rid ourselves of their evil!"

During this speech, the Dragoons, one by one, removed their masks and dropped them to the ground. With looks of scorn and pity for Zon they slowly rode away.

"Kill them!" screamed Zon. "Kill the humans!" He noticed that the Dragoons had left him behind. "Listen to me! *Listen to me!*" All the Dragoons were gone.

There was a long silence. Everyone left on the narrow beach was lost in his own thoughts. Perdix stepped forward and put a hand on Zon's shoulder. "Let's go," he said.

Perdix gestured with his rifle. Zon cast a long look to the others who had remained, then moved away, followed by Perdix, his captor. Night was closing in on them all.

The next morning began bright and clear. It was a new day, a clean and fresh morning. Virdon, Burke, and Galen prepared to venture on. Burke helped Galen with his backpack. Sestus had his arm around Fauna. "You're welcome to stay, of course," said the chimpanzee.

"No, thanks," said Virdon. "We have to move on."

Burke stepped up close to Fauna. He spoke to her gently. "Fauna," he said warmly, "I hope that you forgive me for deceiving you."

She was sheepish and uncertain. "I just can't understand," she said, her expression becoming even more confused. "How could I have thought that I loved... a human?"

Burke smiled, understanding her feelings. He managed to overcome his own inner feelings about Fauna's ugliness. He kissed her lightly, gently on the cheek. She was startled at the touch of his lips, her hand coming up to touch the spot.

Not long afterward, Burke, Virdon, and Galen were marching away from the house toward the crest of the hill. Fauna, her head tilted, her ears listening to the sound of the travelers' fading footsteps, waved gently to a man she could not see. Her eyes were bright and wet with tears.

She could not sort out the feelings inside her that had caused those tears. That was a question she would try to answer on many dark nights through many long years.

JOURNEY INTO TERROR

"The Legacy"
based on the teleplay by Robert Hamner

"The Horse Race"
based on the teleplay by David P. Lewis and Booker
Bradshaw

Based on characters from *Planet of the Apes*

For Carol Antosiak, a supplementary Muse.

THE LEGACY

1

Two human beings and a large chimpanzee moved slowly across the wilderness. The two human beings had once been astronauts. They had been, and still were, close friends. Their names were Pete Burke, a tall, lanky, dark-haired man, and Alan Virdon, who was more muscular, blond, and possessed of a drive and a will that motivated even his companions. The chimpanzee, whose name was Galen, followed the humans in a kind of hunched-over scuttle. He was better dressed—for the times—than the men, and, considering the times, he spoke the language better.

These were strange times.

Men had lost control of their world, and intelligent apes had taken their place. There were orangutans, the administrators; chimpanzees, the thinkers and doers; and gorillas, the brutish soldiers. Humans rated a mention in this list only by default of other types of ape, and by the fact that they were economically essential to the continued prosperity of the ape world. Humans were slaves, servants, or indigent village farmers. Every aspect of their lives was overseen by an ape in authority. There was no such thing as freedom for a human, nothing like dignity, either. That was why it was so odd that Burke, Virdon, and the chimpanzee Galen had become close allies. It was a thing that had never before happened in the ape world. It was a thing that would mean their deaths if they were ever recaptured by the gorillas.

They fled across miles of unmapped wasteland. Ancient human cities were forbidden to the apes; humans went there sometimes, to avoid the constant scrutiny of their masters. But the humans who lived in the forbidden areas led a harsher existence than their fellows who remained slaves. These city dwellers were the ones who could truly define the price of liberty, such as it was.

Burke and Virdon had crash-landed back on Earth some two thousand years after their takeoff on an interstellar mission. The Earth they found had nothing in common with the one they had left; their families, their friends, even their society, had all been dead for twenty centuries. Galen, a renegade ape who was guilty of thinking too much, had joined them, and the three fugitives had fashioned an interdependent life together. Each had things to learn and teach; this they did, but their primary concern was just staying alive. This they had done, also, but as for tomorrow...

The countryside they were crossing looked like much of the landscape they had seen in the many months of their adventures. They knew that they were in what had been North America, for occasionally a landmark was unmistakable. But the ape civilization centered in North America, and the two millennia that had passed, had effectively erased any vestige of their old lives. Galen listened with amazement and his eager scientific curiosity when Burke and Virdon described the land as they had known it. At first, Galen found it difficult to accept the premise that human beings had created a culture that was in many ways superior to his own. If that was true, where was it now? Why were human beings now slaves? To answer these questions, Galen would have to make certain assumptions about his own race, assumptions that were painful even for him to accept.

Low hills stretched ahead of them all the way to the horizon. The sky above was blue, with scattered tatters of clouds. The sun beat down upon them. They had been marching since before dawn, and the two humans and the chimpanzee were beginning to show the first signs of fatigue.

"We have to keep going," said Virdon.

"We always have to keep going," said Burke. "We all know that. But do we have to keep going now?"

"Let's get to the top of this next rise," said Virdon. "We can rest up there, and see the neighborhood without being spotted ourselves. We can take a break up there."

"That says a lot about you," said Burke tiredly. "You never suggest a rest stop down here. It's always up there."

"Good, sound strategy," said Galen. "I approve."

"Well, in theory, so do I," said Burke. "But I can't get the message across to my tired old bones."

"Come on, tired old bones," said Virdon, smiling. "One more rise, after all of the traveling we've done in the last couple of weeks. One more rise."

"Sure," said Burke, following his blond leader, "but that last rise... Isn't that where you always spot the next one?"

"I can't help that," said Virdon, not turning around.

"My guiding motto used to be, 'Let well enough alone'," said Burke with mock displeasure. "I had to fall in with a couple of scientific investigators. Remind me next time to get stranded with a few home-loving starlets."

"Starlet?" asked Galen, never having heard the word before.

"They were like, uh, beautiful works of art," said Burke. "They didn't do anything much, and they enjoyed sitting around. Unlike today's ambitious leader, Alan Virdon of the Mounties."

"But why 'starlets'?" asked Galen.

"Because they brightened up your life," said Virdon. Galen nodded; it seemed like a rational explanation. The three continued on in silence.

They climbed the hill. Before they reached the summit, Galen signalled that he was too weary to go on. He stopped abruptly. Virdon and Burke halted as a result. They were tired, too.

"I was just thinking," said Galen, smiling, "until I met you two, I had a comfortable house, I ate excellent food—every day—and I was living a good life. Now look at me!" He laughed softly to show his friends that he really had no regrets.

"You're hard to please," said Burke. "After all, don't you like being on the run with a fair chance of being killed by that gorilla General Urko? Out of all the apes in the world, you alone have that wonderful opportunity. I would have thought that you'd be humble."

Galen could not tell whether the dark-haired astronaut was serious or not. "I'd like a few minutes to think before I answer that question," he said.

"What about the excitement and stimulation we provide?" asked Virdon. "And all the fun things you've learned?"

Galen's eyebrows raised. "I've learned that the world is made up of a series of hills which I can climb up so I then get a chance of climbing down."

Burke laughed. "It isn't our fault," said the dark man. "You apes should have built your world with an eye for level ground. Anyway, you're jumping to conclusions. How can you be sure there's another hill on the far side of this one? There might be a river, a canyon, or a village with beautiful girls to welcome us."

"Want to bet?" asked Galen. "That kind of thing hasn't happened too frequently in our travels. If we had spent as much time going across the land as we have going up and down it, we'd be I don't know where by now."

"You're I don't know where right now," said Virdon. Galen only grimaced.

"I'll bet you," said Burke, turning back to the chimpanzee. "How about my back pay as an astronaut? The government owes me for two thousand, three hundred fifty years. Not even counting the interest on it all. Match that!"

"Your government owes you that," said Galen. "Your government doesn't have an embassy in Central City. Not even a tiny record that it ever existed. My government does exist."

"That's why we're climbing hills," said Burke softly. He stared at Galen, who suddenly felt that he had carried the joke too far.

"I know exactly how to tell what's on the other side of this hill," said Virdon, trying to break up the mood of depression and loneliness that was quickly forming.

Galen nodded and Burke laughed humorlessly. "We know," said the chimpanzee. "We know, we know. Climb to the top and see. With all your imaginative tricks, that's always the only way."

"Right," said Virdon.

Burke groaned aloud. The three companions

shouldered their packs and resumed the climb to the top of the hill. "It's marvelous the way you figure these things out!" said Burke. "I wish I had your talent for delving right to the solution of the world's mysteries."

Virdon was several paces ahead of the other two, hefting his heavy gear into a more comfortable position on his back. He did not reply or react to Burke's words; if he had to think up a clever retort to every one of Burke's sarcasms, they would still be standing beside their crashed spacecraft, prisoners of the gorilla army. When Virdon reached the top of the rise, he raised a hand, beckoning the others to join him quickly. Burke scrambled up the last few yards, and Galen brought up the rear, puffing and panting from the exertion. When they reached Virdon's position, they followed his gaze downward. "You lose," said Virdon.

Burke and Virdon stared off into the distance. Not far away, by their standards, within easy marching, were the blue-gray ruins of a city. A city of the human world, part of the forbidden area, a piece of Burke's and Virdon's lost lives.

Virdon and Burke were, of course, excited. Galen, too, felt a strange and unfamiliar thrill as he stared down at the mass of twisted architecture that filled the low-lying area. But the chimpanzee's feelings were scientifically detached, while the astronauts felt a resurgence of hope, an emotion that had served them cruelly in the months past, but which they could no more stifle than they could their breathing.

"Oh, man," said the usually unexcitable Burke, "I've forgotten what a city looked like!" No one moved for several moments more.

"It means that we'll be able to pinpoint our location exactly," said Burke thoughtfully. "For weeks now, we've been climbing hills blindly. Now we can proceed with a bit more sureness."

"I like that," said Galen. "I'm in favor of certainty."

They continued to stare toward the city for another few seconds. Then, without a signal from their nominal leader, Virdon, the two men and the chimpanzee moved forward down the far side of the hill, hurrying toward the city as quickly as their tired bodies could push them.

They reached the city itself about an hour later. They walked along its rubble-filled streets in awe and fear. Here had been one of the greatest communities of the human world, and it was now nothing more than a junkyard. They walked past ancient, crumbling department stores, all of which had long ago been looted of anything valuable or useful. In the ape world, those two words had become synonymous. Great display windows had shattered and even the shards had been scattered far away in the preceding two thousand years. Statues had corroded beyond recognition. Buildings had decayed and collapsed, falling upon their neighbors, causing avalanches of brick to fall into the highways and main streets. The smaller side streets were almost impossible to walk along, with their towering mounds of debris and the constant threat of more danger from above. Galen inspected everything with open-mouthed curiosity. Virdon's reaction was the same as Burke's: disappointment.

When the two astronauts, accompanied by a third man named Jones, had gotten into trouble on their interstellar flight, they had set an automatic recall which made the spacecraft find its way back to Earth. This it had done, killing Jones and stranding Burke and Virdon over two thousand years in their own future. But Virdon had saved the small recording disk that had kept a record of their flight, and he believed that it alone could help them return to their own time. But to do so, they had to find a computer resourceful and sophisticated enough to interpret the disk. Only in a city like this could they have any chance of success; the apes hated and feared almost anything that had to do with science. The apes knew what had happened to the humans. At least, the apes in charge of the others did.

The disappointment showed clearly on the faces of Burke, Virdon, and even Galen, as they began to realize they had little chance that the city would offer the kind of aid they sought. The streets were eerily deserted. Their footsteps were loud and echoed from the sheer walls of the buildings around them. The smell was old, stale, and foul. There was no active remnant of the human scientific community here, as Virdon had half-hoped.

They pushed over boulder-sized blocks of brick and mortar, skirted twisted, sharp chunks of steel girders that blocked their path. Virdon called for a rest stop, and the others halted. No one said anything for a while. Then Burke spoke up. "This is downtown nowhere," he said.

They continued along the street, their eyes glancing from left to right. They felt an odd elation; the city was so different from everything they had seen since their journeys began. But they carried with them the same nagging doubts. The city was a constant, ugly reminder that human beings had let the worst in their nature free to ruin the world. It was a kind of vindication of everything the apes had said about humans. There it was, for Burke, Virdon, and Galen to see. The human failure.

"Well," said Galen, trying to cheer his friends up, "it certainly must have been wonderful, living in times that could create such a city as this."

"It wasn't wonderful living in times that could knock it back down," said Burke, sourly. Galen did not reply.

They reached a cross street and stopped in the

intersection. Neither Virdon nor Burke knew where they were going—they did not yet even know which city this might have been. Their plans, which on the road always sounded so hopeful and confident, now seemed empty. What could they do?

"Wait a minute," said Galen softly. He touched Virdon's arm and motioned that the astronauts be silent. Then he pointed to the left. There was an old human standing in the doorway there, hiding, afraid. He was about fifty years old, dressed in tatters and rags. His hair and beard were filthy and matted with dirt. The old man, made older by the harshness of his existence, tried to press himself deeper into the doorway, out of range of the three companions' examination.

"Don't do or say anything to spook him," said Burke softly.

The man didn't need that kind of stimulus. He watched them in frozen surprise for a moment, then ran out of the doorway and down the street in the opposite direction. He ran with a heavy limp.

"We could catch him," said Galen.

Virdon just shook his head. "Hello," he called. The old man made no response, but kept up his shuffling progress down the street. "What do you call this city?"

There was still no answer from the man. He was almost a block away.

"We're friends," called Virdon. "We just want to talk to you."

"Are there any apes here?" shouted Burke. Neither man got even the slightest response from the human. Instead, he turned suddenly and darted into the doorway of another building.

"Well," said Burke, "there goes the welcoming

committee. It looks to me like—" He was interrupted by Galen, who raised a hand for him to be quiet. Galen's hearing was much more acute than the humans', and they had learned to trust his hunches. Slowly, Burke and Virdon, too, became aware of the sound. They listened hard. In the distance came the pounding of approaching hoofbeats. Generally speaking, horses meant apes; more importantly, horses meant members of Urko's gorilla army. The three fugitives looked around for hiding places. Twisted steel, broken glass, chunks of concrete...

Virdon pointed to a building that had once been an impressive and imposing edifice, and which still stood only barely damaged by time and catastrophe. They all ran quickly toward it. Galen was genuinely worried; he alone knew just how close the gorillas were. He shook his head. "No time!" he muttered.

Galen, Burke, and Virdon realized that they didn't have enough warning to hunt out a secure place of concealment. They would have to take their chances with what fate provided. They ducked behind a badly deteriorated wall that more closely resembled a pile of rubble without a building attached.

Just as they dropped their heads out of sight, a squad of mounted, armed gorillas rode around a corner and into the street. They were patrol gorillas, not looking for anything out of the ordinary, and their leisurely pace indicated that they hoped that they wouldn't find anything, either.

"I don't care if these gorillas grew up in Serbia-Croatia," said Burke, in a hoarse whisper. "They're part of Urko's force, and they all have descriptions of us."

"They have orders, too," said Galen with some amusement. "They're ordered to shoot to kill."

"We'll just stay here for a while, then," said Virdon. "The shade is restful."

The apes continued their patrol up the street. They drew abreast of the fugitives' hiding place. Burke and Virdon squeezed themselves closer to the mound of debris; Galen watched them curiously, then did the same thing. Occasionally it was difficult for the young chimpanzee to realize the horrifying consequences that his natural curiosity might bring. The patrol gorillas noticed nothing unusual and rode by, their view of the two men and the chimpanzee hidden by the rubble.

After the apes passed, Virdon, Burke, and Galen breathed a slight bit easier. Still, they waited for a moment to make sure that the patrol had passed out of hearing range. This was what their lives had become, and it wasn't something they enjoyed or had chosen; still, without their watchfulness, they might have been killed on many, many previous occasions. They waited.

After a time, Burke murmured, "Okay to get my heart started again?"

Galen snorted. He raised himself up so that just his eyes peered over the edge of the mound. The apes were nowhere to be seen.

"It seems to be all clear," said the chimpanzee.

"But we know it isn't," said Burke. "It never is."

"We'd better hole up for a while," said Virdon. "That's the wisest choice. This city has been here for a while. It'll keep another few hours."

Burke looked imploringly up at the sky. "Well," he said dryly, "another day, another hole."

Virdon surveyed the nearby buildings, looking for one that might offer them a good chance of combining safety with comfort. These buildings had been erected after the astronauts' departure from Earth; some gave Virdon trouble, merely identifying them. At last he chose the large, central building that had first caught his attention. "Let's try this one," he said. He scrambled over the rubble, hoping that the ape guard had not circled back within earshot. Behind him came Burke and Galen. Bending low to avoid being seen, the three ran for the entrance.

"Are we really going in there?" asked Galen, who, despite his good ape education, was still a little afraid of the forbidden areas.

"Unless you want to try out Urko's hospitality, you're coming in with us," said Burke. Galen shrugged.

"I wonder what this place was," said Virdon, looking up at its towering, almost unspoiled face.

Galen glanced around at the shabby, decayed buildings in the neighborhood. "I would guess that it was something important," he said. "It was built well." Virdon walked slowly up to the entrance.

"So was the Colosseum," said Burke, behind them.

Galen stopped and turned. He wrinkled his face in the quizzical look that so often initiated long question and answer sessions. "The Colosseum?" he asked.

"An arena," said Virdon. "Humans were forced to fight animals. It was a long time ago. Someone was trying to combine sporting events with social reform, of a strange type."

"The smart money was on the animals," said Burke.

Galen stared. The ideas were so chilling, and the astronauts' discussion so... unconcerned... that Galen could not decide whether this was another of their jokes or a cruel facet of human life he had never before encountered. He could think of nothing to say.

Meanwhile, Virdon had spotted something near the door, and had begun to brush away the dust and rubble.

Burke and Galen went to help him; after a moment they uncovered what Virdon had seen—a barely readable bronze plaque bolted to the building's front. Even though the sign had been damaged and corroded through the millenia, the three companions were able to read it. It said, OAKLAND SCIENCE INSTITUTE.

"Well, how about that?" asked Burke.

"'Oakland Science Institute,'" said Virdon. "If I remember right, that was one of those government think tanks. I wonder if this building is holding what those people thought up."

"So you think this is Oakland?" asked Burke.

"Why not?" asked Virdon. "It has to be someplace."

Burke looked around him with more interest. Before, the city had been nameless, without personality. Now the human tragedy of the place hit him. "Even George Blanda has gone to dust by now," he said.

"Who?" asked Galen. "Did he fight animals in the Colosseum?"

"He fought Lions, and Bears, and sometimes Saints," said Burke. The astronaut shook his head. Galen was completely confused by Burke's football references, but it wasn't a new feeling. The chimpanzee just shook his head, too, and looked at Virdon.

"Let's have a look inside," said the blond astronaut.

With him in the lead, the trio moved slowly through the empty doorway of the building. Piles of rubble and sections of walls inside littered the floor. The high, vaulted ceiling of the entranceway had collapsed a long time before, and the fugitives had to climb laboriously over the debris. The air inside was stifling and bad. There were no sounds, not even the faint rustling of vermin. It was as silent as an empty grave.

"Interesting decor," said Burke, looking around the main hall. "What would you call the style? Early American Disaster?"

"Close enough," said Virdon. He moved away from the other two in order to examine a section of broken wall. The part he was looking at seemed to jut out from the main hall's perimeter, destroying the rectangular spaciousness of the area. "I'll bet the original designer didn't put this here," said Virdon. "There could be something behind it."

Burke and Galen watched him curiously. Virdon was never one to let the unknown possibilities of a situation remain that way for long. He started to tug at something embedded in a section of the crumbling wall. The entire part of the wall immediately began to fall down upon them. "Be—" shouted Burke, but he was interrupted by the crash of stone, brick, and mortar all around them. The three desperately dived for cover.

"—careful," finished the dark-haired astronaut. They were out of the pile of debris that had toppled over, standing now in the protection of an archway. They watched the rest of the wall slip, tumble, and crash to the floor. The air was filled with dust. They choked while the dust settled once again to the floor.

"You're very good at that," said Burke, still coughing. "Have you ever considered taking it up as an occupation?"

The gray dust settled in Galen's thick, hairy coat and on the astronauts' heads and arms. They slapped as much of it off as they could. Virdon returned his attention to the wall, which had completely fallen down. He saw a wheeled vault lock and a steel door. He stepped carefully across the debris, making loud crunching sounds in the echoing chamber; he grasped the wheel and turned it. They were all startled by the loud whoosh of air. Virdon turned back to his friends. "Vacuum sealed," he said. Galen did not understand, but he was too curious to ask for an explanation. He wanted to see what was inside.

Beyond the swinging vault door was a small alcove. The back wall was the original wall of the Institute's lobby; this small place had been built afterward, to house the odd-looking machine that rested on a pedestal in the center, just behind the door. Virdon stepped in to look at the device. It was a rectangular box of clear plastic. There were no control knobs, buttons, or switches. "Pete," called Virdon, "here, look at this."

Galen and Burke joined Virdon in the alcove. The three looked over the machine, each as puzzled as the others. "It was made after our time," said Burke. "That's for sure."

Galen looked from Virdon to Burke. "What do you think it is?" he asked. The apes had avoided the technology that produced anything but the most primitive and utilitarian objects.

Virdon had been looking at the pedestal that the device rested on. It was apparent that there was a kind of storage battery and electrical connections behind a smooth gray metallic panel. With close scrutiny, Virdon could make out a confusing arrangement of lenses. But there didn't seem to be anything to focus, no film threader or slide feeder. "It could be some kind of projector," he said, "but what kind I don't know."

"Projector?" said Galen. "I don't understand. Not only do I not understand what *you* don't understand, I don't understand your explanations."

"Try to put yourself in our position," said Burke. "How do you think that makes *us* feel? We thought we'd done a good job of filling you in on the last two thousand years or so."

"Burke," said Galen coldly, "there are things about you which I will never understand. I can accept that. But there are things which I *should* understand, for the safety of all of us."

"I'm sorry, Galen," said Burke, truly apologetic. "I usually get that way when I don't know what's happening either."

"Whatever it is," said Virdon, "it was well protected and hidden."

"Yeah," said Burke. "It might even work."

"What's a projector?" asked Galen.

"It's a machine to reproduce—" Virdon was cut off by Galen's deepening look of puzzlement. Virdon sighed "Look," he said, "it takes little pictures and makes them look big by putting an enlarged image on a flat surface."

Galen still looked bewildered. "The basic thing that I don't understand," he said, "is how you take little pictures and make them look big. It's very easy to do the opposite. You just walk away."

"That's a thought," muttered Burke. He was glad that Galen could not hear him. Burke turned to Virdon. "This thing must have been important," he said. "Somebody sure wanted it to last. Who knows? Maybe it *will* work."

Virdon merely grunted in reply. He had removed part of the device's front panel and had discovered what were apparently the controls. He looked these over and traced the connections of wires and printed circuits. His engineer's training let him have some insight into the almost completely alien machine.

"Do you realize that I still don't understand?" asked Galen petulantly.

Virdon put his thumb in a small depression among the controls.

"Look," said Burke, "the thing is probably—"

"In the years to come..." The voice that spoke those words belonged neither to Burke nor Virdon. Both men jerked around. Galen looked up, his eyes wide, startled, frightened. The voice was deep and full of authority. The three companions each found his heart beating loud and fast. Each was afraid, but each for different reasons.

Besides the surprising suddenness of the voice, there were overtones to the situation that made it more dramatic than it might have been on another occasion. For Virdon, it was the first concrete clue to a way back to his wife and family, all of whom had been dead for many, many centuries; for Burke, it was the defeat of emotion at the hands of intellect, once more, and he pitied Virdon for the hope that it would stir in him; for Galen, it was the first real connection between what the astronauts had been telling him for so many months, and the truth.

Before them was the image of a gray-haired scientist, dressed in a loose white robe. The man was evidently in his eighties, but that was only his evident age; his voice was much younger, his eyes seemed much older. Who could tell what human medical skill had been able to accomplish after Burke and Virdon left their home world? The projection moved against the wall opposite the projector; even though Virdon tried blocking the device with his body, the image did not waver or disappear.

"Whoever finds our Institute," said the scientist, now long dead, as was his science, "we, the scientists, greet you. The destruction of our world, as we know it, is imminent..."

Galen stared, unblinking, at the projection. Here was truth and knowledge, the very things he had yearned for throughout his short life. Here were the answers that even Burke and Virdon did not know, answers that the ape leaders either did not know or kept suppressed.

"...but our civilization's great advances must not vanish," said the ancient scientist gravely. The man paused, as though waiting for his listeners of future generations to puzzle out the meaning of his words thus far.

Virdon looked at Burke; the latter was about to speak, but Virdon gestured for him to be silent. The scientist continued.

"We have therefore deposited the sum of all our scientific knowledge in a number of vaults which are located in various cities throughout the world."

Burke nudged Virdon. Included in that knowledge was the skill that had gotten them into space; with it, they might be able to trace the process backward and end up home again. With it, they might be able to liberate the human beings left in this ape-ruled world; Virdon, Burke, and Galen might be able to disprove the prejudice and cool the hate so that the species might live together in peace. It all depended on knowledge. The astronauts waited for the image to speak again.

"We want and hope this will be found by future generations," said the scientist. Now, however, the image began to flicker, and there was a strange slurring to the scientist's voice. "In this city, the vault is embedded—"

The sound faded abruptly, and the image of the old scientist mouthed unheard words for three or four seconds: Then the image, too, faded and the machine was dead. Virdon turned and hurried to the device, trying various connections and various combinations of the controls. Everything he did was useless.

"How are we supposed to know what's wrong?" asked Burke in frustration. "This thing was invented a long time after we left. It probably runs on flower power or something like that."

Virdon looked up suddenly, a dawning look of comprehension on his face.

"What did I say?" asked Burke, puzzled. "Power?"

"It just may be," said Virdon. He turned back to the machine, looking for a way to open the back of the device and examine the rest of its components. "This baby's been here a long, long time. Whatever kind of battery it runs on could have leaked off most of its charge by now. I don't think those scientists expected their descendants to wait this long before starting the climb back up."

Galen watched them in silence. He saw Virdon trying vainly to pry the back of the device off. The chimpanzee looked around himself and picked up a sharp-pointed piece of metal. He held it out to Virdon. "Will this help?" he asked.

"Thanks," said the blond man, taking it. He started to lever the panel open.

"You're welcome," said Galen. "About once every month or two I like to feel that I've contributed something. Then I don't feel so bad about asking for explanations all the time."

Burke looked at Galen, wondering just what the young ape was thinking. "If we understood anything, we'd tell you," said Burke. "But you saw and heard everything we did. If anything, I'd think your people would be able to explain things to us. We're the strangers here." Galen didn't answer.

"Uh," said Virdon. The back panel came off suddenly and he fell backward with it. Galen and Burke went around to the other side of the projector. Inside the machine was a tangled forest of strange circuits, utilizing components that neither Burke nor Virdon could even name. Galen moved to one side, although interested; he knew that he could be of no assistance.

"There," said Virdon, pointing to a small section of the wiring. "That's got to be the battery. But they sure didn't make units that looked like that when I was a kid."

"What did you expect?" asked Burke. "Did you want this whole thing to be run on two flashlight batteries, not included?"

Virdon thought for a moment. "Still, no matter how advanced it is, there will probably be zinc in the power unit. We should be able to find copper plumbing pipe nearby. All we need is a container and some sulphuric acid."

Burke was not quite as quick at technical solutions as his fellow astronaut, but after a moment's thought, he figured out Virdon's plan. "And we rig a battery and get this thing going again."

Galen was unsure what a battery was. He had no idea at all what the excitement was about. "Does it matter?" he asked.

"You heard the man on the wall," said Burke. "'The sum of all our scientific knowledge.' He meant everything from nuclear fusion to freeze-dried coffee."

"It could give us the answers we've been looking for, Galen," said Virdon. "For the apes as well as the humans." The blond man's mind turned to more practical thoughts. He looked at Burke. "We need some copper," he said.

At that, all three took a final look at the dormant projector and headed back toward the door.

After nearly an hour of searching, Burke and Virdon had located what they sought: a source of copper tubing which they had wrestled out of place and broken or sawed into small bits. The two men and Galen were carrying these pieces back toward the Institute, along a tortuous path among the hills of rubble. Burke spotted something else useful amid the junk around them. "Over there," he said. The three moved to the crumbling section of a building wall, which Burke had indicated. Virdon quickly tore off some of the insulation material from the interior of the wall, looked at it for a moment, then turned to Burke.

"Good job, Pete," said Virdon. "This insulation should do as well as anything else we might be able to dig up."

"Do what?" asked Galen, who was growing exasperated at being left out of everything except the carrying.

While Burke collected some of the insulation material and stuffed it under the waistband of his trousers, Virdon explained to the chimpanzee. "We burn this," he said, indicating the insulation that Burke had noticed. "Then we collect the fumes and we've got sulphur dioxide. Blend that at the right temperature with water and oxygen, and you have sulphuric acid."

"You two humans forget that I'm not exactly sure about why it's such a wonderful thing to have sulphuric acid," said Galen, as he, too, joined in ripping up pieces of the insulation.

Virdon answered while he worked. "First we melt down the copper we've got here. Then we can make a base conductor. With all of that, we'll have a battery. I hope." They continued stripping off the gypsum-based insulation material. No one said anything further. The sun climbed in the sky, and beads of sweat dropped from their faces. The city was peculiarly quiet. Except for the gorilla patrol and the old human, the trio hadn't seen a single living thing. But, of course, this was the forbidden zone...

When the sounds returned, they split the silence as completely as the explosion of a bomb. A captain of the ape guards and six of his soldiers had turned into the street from its opposite end, on their routine patrol. They had not spotted Virdon, Burke, or Galen yet, being still several hundred yards away.

The racket of the gorillas' horses was startling to Galen. He stood upright suddenly, fearfully; he wondered that Virdon and Burke did not react the same way. Then he remembered that the humans were afflicted with poor hearing. Galen took a final look at the gorillas coming nearer, then he spoke. "Soldiers," he said in a hissing whisper. The two astronauts looked up, suddenly alert.

As the Captain of the gorilla guard and his troops rode casually up the street, they affected an air of unhurried calm. But Galen could see that the Captain and his Sergeant beside him were carefully studying Virdon, Burke, and Galen.

"They're not like the other humans in the city," said the Captain. "They're too well-fed. No one in the city looks as healthy as these. Perhaps they are escaped slaves. But they are with an ape…"

The Sergeant thought for a moment. "Could it be that they're the outlaws General Urko has been searching for?"

"That thought appeals to me," said the Captain. He said nothing more.

Virdon, Burke, and Galen stood where they were, frozen in position. There was no point in trying to run. Still, they attempted to give the impression of being innocently casual. They stared up the street at the approaching Captain and the gorillas. Virdon turned to lead the others in an apparently unhurried stroll which angled away from the gorillas, trying to put a little more distance between them. He spoke to his friends in short, hushed, authoritative tones.

"All right, listen up," he said. "We don't have much time.

When I signal, we separate. Then run. We'll meet back at the Institute. Anybody that doesn't show up there in the next twenty-four hours, figure that he's not coming."

"Sure," said Burke. "Then we'll search for whoever—"

Virdon sighed. The pressures of being a leader sometimes overwhelmed him. He had to make his point, and make it quickly. Burke's notions, although courageous and laudable, were foolish. "No!" said Virdon. "That's an order. Don't wait at the Institute. Get the projector going, locate the tapes. That has top priority. It's much more important than any of us."

Burke glanced over his shoulder. He was about to say something; Virdon could guess what his friend's remark would be, and cut it off with a curt gesture. "This isn't any time for sentiment," he said. "Those gorillas aren't worried about it. We can't be, either, or we'll be taking on a huge disadvantage. Now! Scramble!"

Virdon, Burke, and Galen suddenly turned and ran back for the cross street. When they reached the smaller road they separated. They dashed in three different directions. The Captain of the gorillas rose up in his stirrups to see what was happening. He waved at his troops, and they charged after him, splitting up, too, in order to capture the three fugitives.

Burke, a former football player at the University of Michigan, put his head down and ran. He concentrated on speed: stretching his stride and quickening it. He did not think about his pursuers. It was like running back a punt; you just put your head down and charged. Behind him, he heard two or three gorillas turn into the street along which he was running. Then he heard the sound of gunfire behind him. That was enough to make Burke stop his flat-out sprint in favor of some good old-fashioned broken-field running.

Galen ran up another street, without Burke's experience and natural speed. But he did have a better idea of the motivations and techniques of the gorilla guards. Instead of trying to outrun them, he ducked into a crumbling, deteriorated building, just seconds before the Sergeant and several gorillas hurried into the street. The gorillas ran up the street, past the building that shielded Galen.

Virdon, too, was running up another street, hopefully one that would lead him away from the center of conflict. He trusted his instincts, because he had no knowledge to rely on. He was halfway up the street when he tangled his feet in a mass of cable. Virdon fell, taking a rough tumble on the ground.

He grimaced in pain; the cable had held his foot stationary while he twisted in his fall. He tried to stand, but his right ankle wouldn't bear his weight.

"Well," thought Virdon ironically, "that's it. I've had it. It's funny the way they never have chapters on being hopelessly captured in the instruction manuals. Three of us landed here in this crazy world. Me and Burke, well, we've managed so far. But old Jonesy never even got to see what happened. I wonder if the instruction book would have approved of the way he died. I'd like to have the guy who wrote that book here, right now, with his ankle twisted up like mine. I want to know how to get out of this."

The answer, of course, was obvious; if there were a chapter on it in the instruction book, Virdon would know just what to do. He desperately wanted to have the man or woman who wrote that manual here, in the astronaut's place. Then Virdon could watch from a safe, distant place. Virdon wouldn't mind even taking notes.

But there was no one else to help. It was only Virdon and the sharp, crippling pain in his leg as he tried to escape. He gave up running; his right leg was just so much dead weight. He would have to drag it behind if he could hope to make any kind of progress. He slowly limped across the street and out of sight down a narrow alley.

Just as Virdon entered the alley, two gorillas hurried into the main street, their shaggy heads moving from left to right, eliminating the potential hiding places in doorways and entrance halls. They moved methodically down the street, working in the cold, practical manner devised by General Urko for all of his subordinate teams.

The gorillas urged their horses slowly forward up the street, maneuvering slowly among the piles of rubble, searching for any signs of movement, of life. There were none. The empty windows had been gaping holes in the buildings since before the memory of anyone born into this planet of the apes. Nothing moved there, either. Slowly, the two mounted gorilla guards approached the place where Virdon had fallen. One of the gorillas continued to ride on past the spot. His eyes were directed to the roofs of the buildings, those that had not collapsed in upon themselves. The rooflines presented excellent protection for human snipers; of course, the humans' weapons were inferior to the apes' rifles and hand guns. But the chunks of rock, concrete, and brick that the humans threw was in much greater supply.

The second guard noticed something. His eyes caught the glinting of sunlight on pieces of copper which Virdon had been carrying and dropped when he fell. This metallic sparkle was not part of the natural scene. The gorilla stopped his horse and bent lower for a better view.

"Did you see something?" asked his fellow gorilla.

The first gorilla signalled for the other ape to be quiet. He drew his pistol carefully and slid noiselessly to the ground. He knelt by the pieces of copper; yes, it was obvious that someone had broken these bits. For what purpose? The slow-witted ape could not understand. But the evidence was enough for him. He stood up, very much on the alert. Before he said anything to his companion, he scanned the immediate area. He saw nothing suspicious.

Virdon, at the same time, grimaced with the great, throbbing pain in his ankle, and tried to hurry up the alley toward a safe place of concealment. He had been in greater pain, in worse situations, and his sharp, well-trained mind had always gotten him safely through. Now, though, there wasn't much for his superior wits to work with. He dragged himself further into the shadows of the alley.

In the same dark, littered inlet among the buildings, a small, thin street boy hid from the patrol of gorillas. The boy was about twelve or thirteen years old. His clothing was even more coarse and filthy than the clothes of the fugitives; the boy was a resident of the city, dependent on the city for the necessities of life. He hid himself now behind a pile of rubble through which he had been rummaging for food. He peered out from his hiding place and stared silently at Virdon.

The blond man continued to crawl up the alley for another dozen feet or so, looking around wildly for some place to hide. He came to a doorway at last and darted toward it.

The door would not open; a quick examination of the hinges told Virdon that the door would open outward, and it was blocked by a low mound of rubble. He fell to the ground, scrabbling at the shards and pieces of concrete, trying to scrape enough away to allow him to force the door open.

The rubble protected Virdon from observation from

the mouth of the alley; this fact only partially made up for the labor that he undertook. If he could open the door, he would be even better protected. As he scooped more and more of the debris aside, Virdon made an astonishing discovery: he was digging into a kind of nest, a hollow area that had been built and was now occupied by a young woman. Virdon felt a huge wave of pity and sadness overwhelm him. What had these people been reduced to? Living in piles of garbage and trash? Scrounging the offal and refuse for their daily meals? And now he, Virdon, an intruder, was casually destroying their only vestiges of civilization, of community life, of *humanity*.

The young woman stared at Virdon mutely. Her expression was not one of fear; she had outgrown that emotion many years before. Her face showed a great weariness, a life-long hunger—for food, for warmth, for human compassion, perhaps for the knowledge that as a human being she counted for something. She was not an unattractive woman by Virdon's standards, ideals which had died with his world but lived in his mind. She was in her late twenties, already an old person in this harsh world. Her hair was long and blonde, and her eyes were large, blue, and staring straight into Virdon's. He stopped his frantic burrowing for a moment and stared back at her. He did not know what to say, what to do.

The woman cowered deeper into the doorway. She had a bag with the few pitiful belongings she had gathered in her lifetime. Virdon slid down the rattling broken bits of concrete and brick. He got to his feet, but stayed bent over to prevent his being seen by the gorillas who were searching for him. His bad ankle still hobbled him. He spoke to the woman in hushed, urgent tones.

"Don't be afraid," he said. He wondered what effect

his words could have on her; *don't be afraid.* He felt the foolishness of the sentiment even as he spoke it. This woman had spent a lifetime afraid. She had every reason to be afraid, even before this strange blond man appeared, bringing with him a hostile search party of gorilla guards. "I'm not going to hurt you," said Virdon, trying to reassure her that, at least for the moment, at least as far as her physical well-being was concerned, she was in no danger. Whether or not she believed him, that was a matter Virdon had too little experience to predict.

While the astronaut sought to comfort the woman's anxiety, the boy was creeping behind them, moving closer toward the mouth of the alley, climbing up the back of a mound of rubble. From that vantage point, the boy could see what was happening in the main street, and he could look back to watch Virdon's speech with the blonde woman.

Virdon's apology had done nothing to ease the woman's terror. "Please," she said, her voice dull and empty of emotion—even her fear, so constant a factor in her life, failed to color her speech—"you have to leave."

The astronaut struggled to squeeze into the tight space between the shallow cover the woman had dug for herself and the doorway. His ankle still gave him trouble. "I can't leave," he said. "Those gorillas are looking for me."

"And you will bring them here," said the woman. "I have lived here all of my life, and I haven't found a place of safety. The only safety is in not making the apes angry. Then they leave me alone. If they found you here with me, they would think that I was trying to help you escape. You know what they would do with me then."

"Yes," said Virdon softly, painfully. The woman was not begging or pleading with him. She was simply reciting the facts of the matter. That she could so coldly accept things as they were made the horror even more intense for Virdon. While he stared at her lovely though dirt-streaked face, his ankle gave way. He fell, and the woman instinctively reached out to hold his arm, to catch him. Again, Virdon looked into her eyes. He could not tell if there was anything there beyond instinct, impulsive reactions, thoughtless actions based on need and want.

The woman waved Virdon back. The man pressed himself into the shallow cover of the doorway. The woman curled herself into the depression in the rubble. The Sergeant of the gorilla guards and his men, dismounted, ran through the alleyway. When they reached the mouth of the narrow passage, they had not spotted anything. Virdon let his breath out in a quiet sigh. The woman near him signalled that they were not safe yet. Neither human moved.

The boy, in plain view on the mound of rubble, turned to face the guards. "Sergeant," he said boldly.

The gorillas grabbed the boy roughly and pulled him down from his spy position. "A human boy," said one of the gorillas. "A filthy human boy, a stinking animal."

"If you let us have food, if you let us have decent homes, we wouldn't stink," said the boy. "If you let us have water."

"No one is holding you here against your will," said the ape sergeant. "You could journey to one of the farming communities and grow food for yourself and your ape masters. You could travel to Central City itself and become whatever the Supreme Council decided you were fit for."

"To travel, I have to have food," said the boy. "I couldn't live three days on the road. I don't have food, water, or even identification. If I left this forbidden zone, I would end up in an ape prison."

The Sergeant laughed, a harsh, raucous sound in the

stillness of the ruined city. "Then you would be fed," he said at last.

"Until I was executed," said the boy, with a wisdom that came from experience beyond his few years.

"Of course," said the Sergeant. "There is that to consider. But you still have a free choice."

"I could tell you something you'd like to know," said the boy.

"Your name," said the Sergeant. "I will conduct the interrogation."

"I am called Kraik," said the boy. "But you won't ask the right questions. I have something you'd really be interested in."

"Yes?" said the Sergeant.

Kraik hesitated for a moment, looking back toward the doorway where Virdon still hid, unable to hear the gorillas and the boy. "It's worth a lot," said Kraik.

"Your idea of what is worth a lot, and mine, are quite different," said the Sergeant. "Also, your idea of 'a lot' and mine, aren't the same, either."

"Well," said Kraik, smiling confidently, "let's start trading. This part is fun."

"This part will be short," said the Sergeant, suddenly angry for letting this human boy speak to him on equal terms. "This part will not be fun. And if you do not have anything very interesting, this part will be fatal. For you."

"Isn't it always?" said Kraik with a shrug. One of the gorilla guards slapped the young boy hard, across the face, for speaking with such disrespect to a sergeant of General Urko's guards.

"How much is what you have to tell me worth?" asked the Sergeant, his teeth clenched in hatred.

Kraik shrugged. He did not seem to have noticed

the blow from the gorilla guard, nor the atmosphere of potential danger that the interview had suddenly taken. "Two days' food," he said simply.

The Sergeant turned away, frowning. He would not be treated in so impudent a manner by any human. This young human could die before the Sergeant would give him two days' food, for any reason.

"One day, then?" came the response from Kraik, whose voice, for the first time, showed the hope and longing he had hidden in his expression.

The Sergeant turned back to face the boy.

"What's happening out there?" asked Virdon, pressed against the door, only slightly protected by the small entryway.

"Nothing that I didn't expect," said the woman, her voice flat and emotionless.

"What do you mean by that?" asked Virdon. Before the woman could reply, the man could hear the heavy steps of the gorillas running back up the alley toward them. "Did the boy—" He never finished the question. The gorillas saw the blond man and grabbed him, dragging him through the rubble. Virdon tried to fight them off; any single gorilla was more than a match for the astronaut. The gorillas had the strength of three men, and here was a sergeant and a squad of subordinates. It did not take them long to overwhelm Virdon.

A few moments later, the squad dragged Virdon and the woman to the mouth of the alley. "It's over," said the woman.

"I'm sorry," said Virdon, horrified at what he had brought on her.

"I'll be all right," said the woman. "These guards know

me. They know that I can't possibly be of any danger to them. But you're a stranger. And that's the worst thing in the world to be."

"It always is," murmured Virdon. "Any time. Any place."

"I'm sorry, too," said the woman. "I'm sorry for you."

"Thank you, uh," said Virdon, realizing that he didn't know her name.

"I am Arn," she said simply.

"I am Alan Virdon."

"Not for much longer," said the Sergeant. "Now shut up."

While the gorillas marched Virdon and Arn toward the main street, they were watched by Kraik. The boy stood to one side, not in the least remorseful about what he had done. Hunger is a powerful force. Kraik knew that there was a point when he would do anything for food—*anything*. He was starving; he was at that point now. He had always been at that point, on the verge of death by starvation.

As the Sergeant, the gorillas, and their prisoners passed the boy, the Sergeant took a leather pouch from his belt and tossed it to Kraik. The boy's eyes opened wide and he dove for the pouch, not minding the cuts and bruises he took as he scrambled down a mound of debris. He picked up the pouch eagerly and opened it to see what his reward was. The Sergeant directed his men to drag Arn and Virdon away. Arn was protesting that she had done nothing, that she had not helped this stranger, but the gorillas, in their stupid way, would not listen, although they very likely knew that what she said was the truth.

Kraik scurried up the street to find a new hiding place, in case other humans had seen what had happened and were planning to steal his find. He found one of his favorite places of concealment and settled down. He swept away some rubble and lay back contentedly. He opened the pouch, took out some dried vegetables, and eagerly, hungrily, began to cram his mouth full.

2

The day passed. Virdon and Arn had been taken into custody, and Galen and Burke had followed their own separate routes to safety. Now the sun had set, and the ruined city took on shadows and moonlit shapes from the tormented nightmares of crazed minds. Burke and Galen had worked their way back to the Institute, the assigned meeting place. They waited, during long, tense hours. They waited, but Virdon did not arrive.

The human and the chimpanzee sat on the floor, their backs against one of the Institute's crumbling walls. Neither moved for a long while, evidently lost in their separate trains of thought. Galen showed signs of irritability, however. Moonlight shone through a window opening and glinted on his leather gloves as he smacked a fist into his other palm.

"What are we supposed to do?" said Galen, breaking the long silence. "Sit here and wait? There's got to be something more we can do!"

Burke sighed. The chimpanzee did not feel any differently than Burke himself; but Galen had never taken training such as the astronauts had. Discipline was the most important thing, now. As much as he wanted to go out searching for Virdon, Burke knew that was the worst thing, the most impractical thing, to do. "There is something more we can do," he said to the impatient Galen. "We can sit and wait here some more."

Galen looked sharply over his shoulder and glared at the human. "That won't help Alan," he said angrily.

"Look at it this way, hotshot," said Burke, wearily closing his eyes and rubbing them with one hand, "when you joined this outfit, you got stuck with obeying orders from the officer in command. That's Alan Virdon. It's that simple."

Galen stood and went to the window, through which the moon was beaming brightly. He accidentally kicked a large chunk of masonry. The stone set up a loud, echoing clatter in the room. Galen swore softly under his breath. He turned around and faced Burke coldly. "I don't take orders," he said.

"Then why are you waiting around here?" asked Burke, laughing.

"There is a difference," said Galen, sulkily. "I wouldn't expect your human-educated mind to appreciate the difference. I accept suggestions."

"Your whole ape world is concerned with prestige," said Burke. "Urko and Zaius, right at the top. You and me, here at the bottom. It may be the one thing that keeps you from ever coming close to our level of civilization."

"This is your level of civilization," said Galen, indicating the ruined Institute and, beyond, the rotting, dead, crumbling city.

Burke had no answer for a moment. "Okay," he said

finally, "Alan suggested we sit tight and wait for twenty-four hours."

Galen began pacing across the littered chamber. "Think, Pete," he said. "This is Alan. He is my friend. He has been your friend for even longer. And now he's in the hands of the gorillas. He could be in a cell somewhere. They could be delivering him to General Urko. He could be wounded, badly hurt..."

"Or look at it the other way. He could have gotten away, the way we did. He could be laying low, waiting for a chance to get back here. Now, what would he do if he got here and we were gone, out looking for him?"

"Do you believe that?" asked Galen impatiently.

"No," said Burke softly. "But I'm trying. Galen, I got news for you. It's liable to be a long, cold night." The chimpanzee only nodded and sat down again, huddling against the rough, damp wall of the former Scientific Institute. Together, in silence, the oddly-matched friends waited.

Morning came to the Central City of the apes. Human slaves bustled on their ways to and from assignments. Middle class apes opened their shops for the day. The orangutans, the leaders, sat down for a day's bureaucratic shuffling. The chimpanzees, the thinkers of the ape world, took up their studies or began their office hours as professors, lawyers, or doctors. And the gorillas, the armed, hostile gorillas, patrolled and guarded against nothing. There were no dangers, none other than the ones that General Urko created to keep his minions sharp.

Morning saw the leader of the apes' Supreme Council of Elders, Dr. Zaius, and the leader of the gorilla forces, General Urko, leaving the Central City just as the sun tipped the eastern horizon. They rode with a few of Urko's underlings for protection. Some time later, they arrived at the forbidden city, the deserted, decaying buildings, the rubble-strewn streets, the awful stench, the paralyzing, total silence of the place. The face of death.

The guards who daily patrolled the area had their headquarters in a building that had not been as damaged as its neighbors. Outside, a gorilla stood sentry duty. Urko and Zaius rode up to the building, dismounted, and quickly moved to the main entrance of the gorilla headquarters. The sentry snapped to attention when he recognized his commanding general and the leader of the Supreme Council.

"I don't think we have to hurry so quickly," said Zaius, panting from the pace Urko had set. "Not if your guards are as good as you tell me they are."

"They are good," said Urko. "But why shouldn't we hurry? Isn't this the answer to our problems? Both of ours?"

"Perhaps," said Zaius.

"You say 'perhaps'," said Urko. "Gorillas say 'yes' or 'no'."

"You can't be wrong with 'perhaps'," said Zaius gently.

"You can't be right, either." Urko opened the door and moved past Zaius into the hallway inside. A gorilla guarded a door further along the hallway. He was lounging against the wall, sloppy in posture and uniform. In an open office, the Sergeant and his Captain were sitting around a small table, one drinking from a wooden cup, the other playing a curious ape game, a kind of solitaire requiring a wooden board with diagonal marks making diamond-shape spaces. The gorilla played with small pebbles, some dark-colored and some light. At the sound of Urko and Zaius' footsteps, the gorilla guard in the hallway turned to see who was coming. When he recognized the important visitors, he reacted visibly, snapping to attention. "Attention!" he called out, to alert the officers in the ward room. The guard briskly shouldered his rifle, which had been leaning against the wall. The Sergeant and the Captain hurried to rise, brushing the board and pebbles to the floor so they wouldn't be noticed. Before they had a chance to further correct the appearance of the office or their own uniforms, Zaius and Urko swept into the small room.

"Well," said Urko, "I'll wager that you weren't expecting a visit from the commander-in-chief today, were you?"

"No, sir," said the Captain, barely able to speak. He and the Sergeant were frightened and awed by their two visitors.

"I'll wager that you didn't ever expect to see me at all, at any time? Correct? That you would just go along in this pitiable forbidden place, running your own show like some feudal landowner."

The Captain did not answer.

"That's all very well," said Urko. "I understand what it must be like out here. And if it weren't for your prize, you could have done just as you planned. And if things work out to our, uh, satisfaction, you may continue."

"The General is very gracious," said the Captain.

"No, I'm not," said Urko, suddenly surly. "I just want results. I don't care how you live out here, as long as I get my results. And I'm here, and I want something, and if you want to see nightfall, you'd better supply me with what I want."

"The General is not gracious," said Zaius with some amusement, "but he *is* effective."

Urko turned abruptly to Zaius. "And which would you rather be?" he asked. Zaius only shrugged. Urko examined the Captain and Sergeant more closely. He turned and looked outside, into the hallway, where the guard had already relaxed again. "Your command could use some drill, Captain," said Urko. "Live your feudal dream, but don't let your troops become useless to you. If that happens, you will become useless to me. And when my officers become useless, they become dead."

"I'm sorry, sir," said the Captain, his words faint, "we didn't expect a visit from the Military Commander and the Chief Minister."

"Are you offering me that as some kind of an excuse?" roared Urko.

The Captain said nothing; his face showed intense humiliation.

"You're a detachment of gorillas," said Urko. "I expect you to bear some resemblance to my guidelines."

"Couldn't you postpone that discussion?" asked Zaius calmly. "I don't share your interest in drill and discipline."

"Drill and discipline keep you safe," said Urko roughly.

"Someday, let us get together about that," said Zaius, walking idly about the small office. "I'd like to know what you are keeping us safe *from*." He wearily shook his head.

"You know as well as I do," said Urko, through clenched teeth. "Otherwise, would you have taken this long ride with me today?"

"I'll concede that point," said Zaius. "But, Urko, we *have* had a long ride. It's almost noon, already."

Urko just looked at Zaius, without saying anything. He wanted to make the orangutan ask for anything he wanted. He wanted to prove that Zaius was, in fact, weaker than Urko. Zaius understood what Urko's strategy was, but he didn't especially care. Who could see this minuscule struggle of personalities? The Captain and the Sergeant? They were Urko's men already. What did Urko have to gain? Pride. Well, thought Zaius, pride is something I do not need. Urko can have all he wants. Someday he'll choke on it.

"My good General," said Zaius, "once we've dispensed with our ideological differences, and you've properly established yourself as the sole dictator of your forces, then I think we can get on with what we came here for. I'm tired. Let's get this over with."

Urko gave Zaius an ugly look, but turned away to face the Captain. "Bring the prisoner," he said.

The Captain nodded, then saluted, then said "yes, sir," unsure which, if any, response was proper. He was glad to get out of the office. When he left, the sergeant followed him, although there was no reason for the gorilla to go. He wanted to escape Urko's scrutiny as badly as the Captain did.

The long, cold night had stretched on, hour after hour. The discomfort was increased by the inability of Burke and Galen to guess what had happened to their friend. They awoke from light sleep at daylight, stiff and hungry. Galen went to the window. Sunlight cast light on the scene outside, but little warmth as yet. Galen huddled within the heavy leather tunic he wore. Burke, wearing only the rough homespun material of the humans, suffered more with the early chill, but he did not complain.

"Isn't it twenty-four hours yet?" asked Galen.

Burke joined his chimpanzee friend at the window. He looked up at the sky, then back at Galen. "Almost," said Burke. "It's been almost a day. A couple of hours yet, I think."

"He's not coming back!" cried Galen.

Burke thought about how Galen's outlook had changed

during the preceding months. Before Galen had met the astronauts he, like the other apes in the world, thought of humans as a lesser species of animal, something to be tolerated and used as slave labor. Humans could not have creative ability, for their intelligence was severely limited. Humans were needlessly violent. Humans were dirty. Humans were—the list went on and on. But in their mutual adventures, Galen had learned more and more about what humans could be like, if given the chance. And now, wonder upon wonders, Galen considered the two astronauts—the two humans—his friends. This alone branded Galen a renegade among his own people. He had few friends except the two humans who joined him in his travels.

Burke wondered how Galen felt now. Did he hope that Virdon somehow might be able to convince Zaius and Urko that humans presented no threat to the apes' way of life? Did Galen hope that the apes would welcome Galen back to his old life? None of that seemed at all possible; for one thing, Virdon and Burke wanted nothing more than the liberation of the human population, who were exploited as cheap labor by the overlord apes. Galen knew that; but Galen also understood that Virdon could never convince the ape leaders that ape and man could co-exist peacefully. There were too many shattered cities, too many examples of man's innate destructiveness, to lull the apes' suspicions. And, Burke thought, perhaps they were right. "We'll scrounge around for the stuff to make a battery," said Burke, avoiding the deeper questions, concentrating on the here and now problems that needed solving.

"I don't care about batteries!" shouted Galen. He picked up a shard of concrete and threw it against the wall in frustration. "I don't care about the knowledge you keep talking about. I care about what's happened to Alan!"

Burke was genuinely moved by this expression of a concern which, of course, he shared. He put his hand on Galen's shoulder and spoke gently, trying to reassure the young, still-immature chimpanzee. "I know," said Burke softly. "You've got company."

"Then let's *do* something," said Galen.

Burke looked around himself for a moment, thinking. "We've got about an hour to go. We'll use it looking for him. Is that all right with you? But if we come up empty— well, let's not get into that. Come on, let's get a move on." Burke steadied Galen's arm as the chimpanzee climbed over a large chunk of stone. Together they went out into the cool air of the morning. The ancient, dead silence of the city struck at them almost like a physical thing.

Not far away, down a few streets and across town about three quarters of a mile, in the headquarters of the gorilla garrison, the answers to Burke and Galen's unspoken questions were being formed. Zaius had seated himself, while Urko studied the map on the wall. The door opened, a hanging of cloth that one of the gorillas had placed across the open entry at Urko's order. Virdon stepped through, followed closely by the Sergeant and the Captain of the gorilla guards, each with hand guns drawn. Virdon limped, a fact that was not lost to Urko's keen, observing mind. Urko walked over to confront Virdon.

It was obvious that Urko was enjoying himself. He had been hunting Virdon, Burke, and Galen for a long time. They had not met often in that time. "Virdon," said Urko, drawing out the name with relish. "Good to see you again. You should be very flattered. We dropped everything and rushed here as soon as we heard that you were sighted."

"Captured," said Virdon flatly.

"Detained," said Urko, raising his eyebrows.

"Captured," said Virdon.

"Certainly," said Urko, laughing softly. "If you insist." Urko waited for Virdon to say something more, but there was only a tense silence in the room for a moment. "Let's not waste time, then, fencing with words, eh?" said the gorilla-general. "Where are the renegade ape and your friend, Burke?"

Urko waited for another moment, but Virdon still didn't answer. Urko, seeing that Virdon was still favoring his injured leg, took a step forward. Then, without warning, the gorilla kicked out at the injured leg. Virdon crashed painfully to the floor.

Urko studied the writhing human for a few seconds. Zaius, shocked by Urko's brutality, started toward Virdon, but stopped at Urko's curt gesture. Urko turned to the Captain and the Sergeant. "Help him up," he said.

Zaius stood off to one side, watching, still disapproving, while the Captain and the Sergeant quickly moved forward, dragging Virdon up to his feet again. He collapsed between them, and the two apes had to hold the astronaut upright.

Urko stepped very close to Virdon. They stared into each other's eyes for a long moment. There was nothing but pure hatred in the expression of either. "Now, simply, honestly," said Urko, "tell me where they are."

"I don't know," said Virdon. "That very well could be the truth."

"But it isn't," said Urko. "It never has been. You must have made contingency plans when you split up."

"Ah," said Virdon with a wry smile, "I knew we forgot something."

The Sergeant slapped Virdon for the man's insolence, as the gorilla guard had slapped Kraik the day before.

Urko reacted with anger. He turned to the Sergeant. "Never do that again," he said, growling. "*Never.* This is not just a human being. He is an astronaut." Urko shook his head. "Whatever *that* is," he muttered.

Urko was determined to learn the information he knew Virdon was concealing. "Where are they?" he shouted.

"I just told, you," said Virdon helplessly. "I don't know. Or would you rather that I made up some place, instead?"

Urko cut his answer off with a sharp gesture. "W*here are they?*" he said, his voice quiet but hard in tone.

"You know," said Virdon wistfully, "after being on this Earth for I don't know how many millions of years, this situation always goes on exactly like this. You ask me. I deny everything. You get mad. I get tortured. Either you get the information, or you don't. Or you get it and don't believe it. You'd think there would be something new, here. You'd think someone would solve the dilemma after all this time."

Urko stared at Virdon, saying nothing. An idea was forming. Something new. Just what Virdon wanted. Something new.

The city looked just as it had for the last two thousand years. Oh, every few months, some worn-out facade crumbled a bit more, tumbling down a crashing weight of stone and brick to the sidewalks and streets below. But these minor tragedies meant nothing. The city itself did not change. It was a skeleton, and its dead bones would remain throughout eternity as a grim reminder.

Burke and Galen walked the streets of the city silently. It was difficult to believe that this place had been such a vibrant, exciting center of human life. Its present condition seemed more like a stage setting rather than real life. But the overpowering drama and sweep, the vast scale of the disaster, at last convinced Burke. He shook his head. "A needle in a haystack," he said.

Galen glanced at his companion, puzzled. "Hm?" he asked. No matter how long they kept together, the humans always managed to drop in phrases from their past, idioms which Galen could not puzzle out.

"Nothing, nothing," said Burke apologetically. "It was just an old expression. It means something like—" He broke off suddenly seeing movement among the low hills of rubble about them.

A human scavenger came out of a building, evidently unaware of Galen and Burke's presence. The man walked innocently into the street, then stopped and froze in his tracks, staring at the astronaut and the chimpanzee in stunned surprise.

"Wait," cried Burke. This might be the opportunity they were seeking, to find clues to Virdon's disappearance. "We're looking for someone—"

The human suddenly turned and darted into the nearby ruins, disappearing from sight; he left Burke and Galen standing there helplessly. "My own people," said Burke disconsolately. "Human beings. If you can call them that."

"Have they changed so much from the old times?" asked Galen innocently.

Burke stared at him for a moment. "I don't want to answer that," he said. He looked around him, at the ruined buildings, at the timid, rarely spotted human denizens of the forbidden city. "In a haystack," he said helplessly.

The center of the gorilla garrison in the city had been taken over by Urko, Zaius, and their small entourage.

The Captain, who had always been in charge, felt a little disgruntled about the brusque way Urko had demanded and received every attention from the soldiers. After all, the Captain told himself, didn't this go against everything that Urko had written himself, concerning military conduct? But the one thing that the Captain was sure of was that he couldn't very well say anything.

Urko was planning a massive search of all the ruins in the extensive city, a search on a scale never before heard-of. The Captain had his doubts, and the Sergeant was exasperated—he knew who would have to do all of the leg-work—but neither gorilla said anything.

Urko gestured, and the two subordinate officers left the office. Urko and Zaius were alone, eating a meal. At least, Urko was eating. Zaius' food was untouched on the plate in front of him. He was deep in thought. Urko never noticed. Urko always ate with great appetite.

The meal progressed a little while longer, until Urko, too, had a thought. He jumped to his feet and shouted. "Captain!" he called. The Captain came into the small office from the hallway outside.

"Yes, sir," he said.

"Bring the prisoner back when I've finished eating."

"Yes, sir." The Captain turned and moved back to the hallway through the cloth hanging.

Urko gave no further thought to his plan. He went back to finishing his meal as quickly and efficiently as possible, taking not the least pleasure in doing it. In fact, if Urko could find a way of eliminating meals altogether, it would please him to save the time. Zaius watched him, thoughtfully.

"Look, Dr. Zaius," said Urko, "why don't you eat? You complained just a while before that you were hungry and tired. You need to eat. We'll be going to work soon. I'm starved."

Zaius waved away all of Urko's suggestions. "Are you planning to beat the prisoner again?" he asked quietly.

Urko never slowed the progression of food from his plate to his mouth. The idea of beating Virdon didn't strike him as unpleasant. "If necessary," he said simply, and quickly, in order to spoon in some more food before he was required to say more.

"You'll kill him."

"If necessary."

Zaius pushed his chair back from the table and sighed. Urko's methods were unarguable. He had no authority over Urko. Urko had no authority over Zaius. Technically, the President and Chief Minister of the Supreme Council could direct the actions of Urko and his men—but he could just try it some time! "If you kill him," said Zaius, "it would be too bad."

Urko paused, a spoonful of his food held between plate and lips. "You're mourning for a human?" he asked, in horror.

"No," said Zaius cryptically, "I mourn for Urko."

Urko put his utensils down and listened to what Zaius was saying.

"I mourn for you and the strong influence you have—you *had*—built up in the Supreme Council."

Urko laughed. He stood from his place at the table and began pacing the room, slapping a glove into his palm. "I'm not worried," he said. "My influence will go on growing stronger."

"Whenever you begin pacing like that," said Zaius, "it shows that you are nervous. You should know yourself better. But, anyway, your influence, such as it is, cannot be increased by killing humans. We're not concerned merely with the death of this prisoner. We must be more farsighted than that. We must consider the reactions to our deeds. We must make permanently sure that his dangerous ideas do not infect the domesticated humans. To this end, I believe we—"

Urko made a loud, raucous laugh. He had found nothing funny in what Zaius was saying, but the laugh served its purpose. It silenced Zaius for the moment. "I will make certain," said Urko, in his overriding manner. "Ideas die with the man."

Zaius shook his head doubtfully. "I sometimes wonder," he said. "If you kill a man, his followers make a martyr out of him. Then the problem is many times worse. In any case, eliminating Virdon is useless, if his companions are free to spread the poison. Urko, your prisoner—alive—is the surest way of capturing the other two." Urko was about to explode, but he controlled his anger. He stared at Zaius for a beat. "Why do I always have to take military advice from you?" he asked.

"Because sometimes your eyes are blind to your best interests," said Zaius simply.

"Or are they blind to *your* best interests?"

Zaius shrugged. "They could be the same thing."

"And now I see that the wise Zaius has his own plan for getting the information from the prisoner."

"I have been thinking about it," said Zaius quietly.

"And so have I. We will not kill the prisoner. We will do something else, instead."

"I am glad of that," said Zaius. "You are using your mind."

Urko paid no attention. A grim smile formed on his lips. "We will try… something new."

* * *

In the city streets, Galen and Burke continued to move up a street, still searching for any sign of Virdon. The people they met at rare intervals, without exception, refused to speak to them.

Their position was almost hopeless, and they knew it. But they would not stop.

In Urko's commandeered headquarters, Urko and Zaius were present as the Captain entered with the blonde woman who was captured along with Virdon. Arn was plainly terrified. She did not expect to live much longer.

The Captain threw her roughly into the room. She fell against the table, hurting one of her legs, but she did not cry out. Zaius went across the room to help her up.

"She was Tomar's woman," said the Captain scornfully. "He was a rebel. He isn't a rebel any longer. He is dead." Arn winced, but she wouldn't let these apes have the benefit of seeing her cry.

"All right," said Zaius, "Urko, if you have some kind of new technique, let's get on with it. So far, all I've seen are examples of the old technique, and I know those sickeningly well."

Urko stared at Arn judiciously. "When you capture a rebel it's probably better to kill his whole family," he said blandly. "Those around him are usually infected."

Arn was amazed by the ferocity of Urko's words. "Please," she begged, weeping, "I didn't mean to do anything wrong—"

The Captain of the gorilla guards caught up on Urko's technique. They would be rough on the woman for a while. He went over and forced Arn to stand upright. "Quiet!" he said.

"In this case," said Zaius, "it's as well you didn't kill her. She will serve a better purpose."

Arn had no idea of the conflict that the two ape leaders were engaged in. "What are you going to do with me?" The Captain took her roughly by the arm again.

"Come along," said the Captain viciously.

After Arn had been disposed of according to the agreement reached between Zaius and Urko, the Captain and his guards silently stalked through the same streets where they had last seen the boy, Kraik.

Kraik was hidden behind the rubble pile, scared now as he realized that someone was moving nearer to him on the street. He listened hard for another moment, then turned and ran off in the opposite direction.

As the poor boy turned to run, he careened right into the arms of a waiting gorilla who'd been stationed there some time earlier by the Captain. The gorilla grinned and picked up Kraik. The boy struggled, kicking and thrashing and swearing, but he was helplessly caught.

"Let me go!" screamed the boy. "I haven't done anything! Let me go!"

The Captain and two other gorillas rushed up toward the boy and his captor. The Captain stopped when he faced the still-screaming Kraik.

"Stop fighting," said the Captain in his oiliest tones. "You're in luck. As I see it, you have the chance to earn more food than you've ever seen before."

Kraik stopped his struggling, dangling helplessly in the gorilla guard's grasp at arm's length. "What do I have to do?" he asked doubtfully.

"It's very simple," said the Captain. "Just keep asking the right questions of the right people and tell us the answers."

"Are you sure that's all?" asked Kraik.

The Captain only shrugged.

The city's streets were silent, as always. They had been silent for thousands of years. They had been silent for a longer time than they had been filled with human racket. Therefore, according to some scale, the natural state of the city was silence. Human population had been an infestation, quickly and totally suppressed, although a few scavenging vermin still lived within the city's boundaries.

Burke and Galen moved through the oddly shadowed squares and open places among the fallen-down buildings, among huge mounds and piles of rubble. They studied a building across the street from their present position. Galen carried a couple of flat rocks in his huge shaggy hands.

Across the street from the fugitives was a large, solid-looking building, evidently built with a mind toward natural (or unnatural) disasters. It had weathered them all, and stood alone on the street as a tribute to the foresightedness of human scientists, a quality that was as rare as any other goodness in the human race. It was the Headquarters of the Scientific Institute, the main coordinating building of which the Institute the three fugitives discovered was only a subsidiary. Now it looked as though the Headquarters had been taken over by the gorillas. A uniformed guard stood outside. There was the flag with the three interlinked circles above the door. There was no sense in approaching the building from the front. Galen and Burke shrugged helplessly, but they said nothing. They moved away.

A few yards down the street, behind a protecting pile of debris, Burke spoke in low tones to his chimpanzee comrade. "As soon as I get into position," he said. Burke looked back in the direction of the Headquarters building. He was tense, worried, and helpless with his.

lack of information. But he hadn't yet given up. He was only waiting for an opportunity.

The opportunity came, as Burke expected that it would. As the gorilla guard looked the other way, Burke darted from behind the rubble pile, dashed across the street and pressed himself tightly against the corner of the Headquarters building. He was shielded from view by the large rectangular blocks that edged the corner.

Galen watched Burke's charge. He relaxed a little when he saw that Burke had managed to reach his goal unseen. Galen now used the two rocks to create a diversion down the street. The first rock landed in a pile of rubble, muffled somewhat by the loose dirt there. Nevertheless, the guard looked up suspiciously.

"Who's there?" cried the gorilla.

Galen tossed the second rock, and it hit the edge of a mound, making other large stones rattle and clatter down to the street level. The guard came out from his post to check on the noise. Now Galen ducked down, took a couple of rocks, and made clip-clopping noises. To the guard, it sounded as though a horse were riding away. The guard, thoroughly confused, stepped into the street. There was, of course, no horse. Galen clip-clopped less loudly, until he made the sound fade away altogether.

The gorilla guard was very puzzled at the disappearance of a horse that had never appeared, but, in his simple-minded way, shrugged the mystery off.

Burke, still hidden around the corner of the building, watched the scene tensely.

Once again, Galen, hidden behind the pile of rubble, started making the clip-clopping sound, very loudly.

The gorilla was determined to discover the source of the hoofbeats; he strode toward the pile of rubble. Just as he reached it, Burke darted out, around the corner, and made a diving tackle of the guard. The gorilla tumbled onto the pile of rubble. Galen jumped up and grabbed the rifle dropped by the gorilla, as Burke lifted the gorilla's legs, dumping the now-unconscious guard behind the rubble.

Burke twisted a piece of rope around the gorilla's wrists and knelt on the ape's chest, while Galen held the rifle on him. Slowly, the gorilla regained consciousness. His head hurt, of course, but he couldn't rub it, not with his hands tied. He looked around him warily, and was frightened to see two of the three enemies of the state they had been chasing the day before. The gorilla was more worried about what Urko would say, than about what this man and this renegade chimpanzee would do to him.

"All right," said Burke in a forceful whisper, "I'm not even going to give you the proverbial three chances. I want the truth, and I want it now. Where's Virdon?"

The gorilla shook his head and said nothing. Galen gestured for Burke to let him do the questioning. Burke assented.

"A man," said the young chimpanzee. "You'll remember. You were hunting the three of us. We separated. You caught a man. He was captured yesterday."

"Yes," said the gorilla, suddenly brightly. "He was brought in!"

Burke nodded toward Galen, who only shrugged modestly. "Now, what I'd like to know, and I remind you that your hands are tied up and that I've got your own rifle trained on you. Did they take Virdon into that building across the street? If so, which floor did they take him to? Which room?"

The gorilla studied the building for a few seconds, a frown on his face. He thought hard. "He's not there," he said at last.

Burke moved forward with a strand of strong metal wire. He put the wire around the ape's throat, garroting him a little. He tightened the wire, choking the ape slightly.

"You know," said Galen calmly, "my friend here has a passion for the truth."

"A human!"

Burke tightened the wire even more. The gorilla tried to loosen it with his bound hands, but couldn't.

"The truth!" cried Galen.

The gorilla was looking very frightened by now. "He was taken away this morning. I don't know where."

Burke was furious. He didn't want to have his plans frustrated so easily. "You're lying!"

The gorilla didn't know anything else to do in order lo convince them. Mere words had had no effect. There was nothing else to say. "The prisoner rooms are empty. You can see for yourself."

Galen put down the end of the rifle, sadly and a little hopelessly. "He's telling the truth," he said. "He believes that he'd be killed if he lied. No gorilla would be that smart, to lie anyway."

"What?" asked the gorilla, sensing a slur on his race.

"Nothing," said Galen.

Burke removed the garrote from around the ape's neck, but he left the gorilla's hands tied. "It's worse than a needle in a haystack. We're looking for a needle somewhere in a whole city, on a whole planet!"

Galen and Burke fell into a solemn thoughtfulness. After several possible suggestions occurred and were dismissed, Galen said, "They might actually have taken him back to Central City, instead of questioning him here."

Burke shook his head. "Yes," he said, "and they might not. Okay, we follow orders, Galen. We go with the top priority. Alan said that it was more important to go on than any of us being found…"

The Headquarters that were being used by the gorilla guards in the city resembled an old, medieval castle. Virdon's thought was that it had been a museum at one time, perhaps later converted into the main branch of the Scientific Institute. He would have given a lot to know the history of the world between the time he and Burke— and poor, dead, Jonesy—had blasted off and the time the apes came into power. What had mankind done? What advances had been made? That was what the machine in the Institute had been about to tell them…

Virdon was prodded into a large castle courtyard by two armed gorillas. His ankle seemed better, although he still walked with a slight limp. Around the perimeter of the courtyard, a couple of gorillas were standing sentry duty.

The apes marched Virdon across the courtyard, to a massive entrance closed by two iron-bound oaken doors. One of the gorillas opened the doors and shoved Virdon in, shutting the doors and locking them again behind him. The doors shut slowly with a loud creaking noise, and a dull, final thud. The rasp of the lock made the situation only that much more hopeless. Virdon was caught.

The first thing that he did inside was the initial reaction of any organism trapped in unfamiliar surroundings; he searched the area. He walked around the walls, studying the bare stone, the damp, chilly expanse of walls, the lack of decoration or ornament. He couldn't decide if this was the taste of the human builders, the results of subsequent lootings, or the imposed austerity of the apes. In one corner of the large chamber he saw the woman, Arn cowering. He went quickly to her.

He moved as speedily as his injured leg permitted. "Are you all right?" he asked. Even in the extremity of the situation, which, after all, was the one thing Burke, Galen and he had dreaded since the beginning—recapture—his primary concern was for this seemingly unprotected, yet strong, woman who had tried to warn him of the dangers he faced.

Arn said nothing. She only nodded, studying his handsome face.

Virdon was relieved. Arn presented him with a problem, someone to look out for other than himself. He was inclined to take chances, and with Arn to hold his behavior slightly in check, his odds for survival increased. Sure, he wasn't as impetuous as Burke or even Galen, but the possibility was there, especially when he had fallen into the stronghold of his enemies.

Virdon looked around in the gloom of the chamber, and he spotted Kraik, sitting huddled up in another corner. Virdon walked over to where Kraik sat kicking some stones from his path along the way. The astronaut tried to appear casual, but the presence of Kraik was becoming just a bit too coincidental. "Who are you?" asked Virdon softly, in order not to make Kraik withdraw into his sullen shell.

There was ho reply. Any question directed at Kraik, unless by an ape, drew this same reaction. Virdon waited a moment, then turned around and surveyed the room. There was Kraik, and Virdon, and Arn, all silently sitting a large distance apart from the others. "What's happening?" cried Virdon. "Why do they have us all here?"

Arn shook her head. It seemed evident that she didn't know. Kraik just drew himself closer into his protective ball in his corner. Whether the boy understood or not, Virdon knew that the information would stay locked within the boy's mind.

3

The castle courtyard had changed little in the few hours during which Virdon had been kept prisoner. He had examined the area minutely, and the examination boiled down simply to the simple facts: one, the gorillas had him, Arn, and Kraik locked in a room above the courtyard. Two, a pair of armed gorillas guarded the vast, locked gates that opened onto that courtyard. Three, there was no other way out.

So much for devious or sneaky ways around the obvious limits of the situation. Virdon almost wished for Burke's irrational turn of mind. Burke—or Galen, even—would think up something that used the gorillas' strengths against them, the apes. Virdon would only try hitting his head against the strengths, and ending up with a headache for his efforts. And Arn and Kraik were involved now, too.

Inside the castle, in the main room, Kraik was still cowering in his corner and Arn waited fearfully, unsure why she had been made a captive. She had committed no crime, other than to be found in the same area as Virdon. The apes and the humans of the forbidden city had derived an unusual truce; each side knew just how much the others would accept without rebellion, and neither apes nor humans looked for trouble. Arn felt that she had been treated unfairly, but she didn't have anyone to whom to complain.

Virdon walked around the large, spacious, once-grand hall in which they were locked. "No one here but us," he said to himself, a fact self-evident but somehow important. The knowledge tickled at his consciousness. He turned to the two captives with him. "Are you sure you don't know what this is all about?"

Arn only nodded sullenly. She hadn't spoken in all the time they had been locked in the high-ceilinged room. She was afraid to connect herself in any way with this stranger. Virdon glanced at Kraik. The astronaut had witnessed the transaction between the dirty waif and the gorilla Sergeant. Perhaps there was something more that might be gleaned from questioning the boy.

"You," said Virdon suddenly to Kraik. "Did they tell you why you're here?"

The boy didn't appear in the least bit concerned. He did not consider that he had sold out a fellow human being. He had only done what he had to do in order to secure himself the food he needed to live on. "I was caught stealing food," said Kraik. There was a tinge of fearfulness in the boy's voice, which might or might not have been genuine. It was difficult to judge just what part Kraik might play in the drama that was unfolding, and that fact made Virdon's job even more difficult. Could he trust this boy? Could he win him over?

"A human can be killed for stealing food," said Arn from her corner. The explanation brought silence to the cell. It was a harsh judgment, but it was one which the humans had always accepted. If it were true, then Kraik might fully expect to die. Virdon felt a flood of pity overwhelm him for the poor boy.

Suddenly, Virdon felt a cold shiver of fear run through him. He wasn't certain just what it meant; there was nothing about the circumstances that seemed any more threatening than other critical situations he had faced since coming to this planet of the apes. Or was it? Something tugged at his mind, some line of reasoning that would not speak clearly to him. He recalled the pity he had just felt for the boy; pity was an emotion that had grown extremely rare in this mad future. It was a feeling that Virdon and Burke had had to teach to the apes and humans who would listen to them. It was a feeling that sometimes put the astronauts at a disadvantage, making them act where less sympathetic individuals would run. But just as often, pity had won them friends and allies, like Galen, and it had often opened the door to love.

Still, wasn't there something wrong with this situation? Virdon wandered around the drafty room, trying to put his finger on just what it was that bothered him. "I don't know, I don't know," he murmured to himself. "Urko doesn't need an excuse to kill me. He's proven in the past just how anxious he is to do just that. Well, when he had the chance, why didn't he?" The question took possession of his thoughts for several moments, and he paced, oblivious to the words and actions of his two fellow captives. The answers he sought were not far away, he could sense that, but they still managed to elude him.

While Virdon paced painfully around the room,

pondering his unanswerable questions, Arn was also examining their place of confinement. She had lived in the forbidden city all of her life, and she knew it as well as any of the other starving humans. This was a good deal better than any of the apes knew the city. But this particular building was strange to her. The ape garrison had always held it off limits to humans. She had never been inside it before, and she was frightened. Human beings were often frightened by things they could not understand or things they had never seen before. "What is this place?" she asked, her voice hoarse.

Virdon's reply was automatic; he didn't really hear Arn's question. He was busily trying to find answers to his own problems. "This building was famous in my time," he said. "I remember seeing it. Built by a wealthy man. Oil money. He wanted to live like a sixteenth century baron or something." Virdon was carefully searching the walls, the fireplace, every possible place that might provide him with a clue to a way out of his current trouble. He searched with all the cunning that his knowledge and experience could lend him. He concentrated on his problem, but the room yielded nothing.

Arn walked closer to him. Her face was puzzled; she thought about his words, which had tumbled unguarded from his mouth. "I don't understand," she said.

The boy, Kraik, was also curious. He had heard something in Virdon's answer that he couldn't explain. "What do you mean?" asked Kraik, "in your time?"

Virdon was still moving slowly about the room, hoping to find something in it that he could use. He did not reply to his two cell-mates. His attention focused on the stairway. He started for it. Kraik followed after him. "Wait a minute!" cried the boy. "Where are you going?"

Virdon was jolted from his reverie. He turned to face the boy. "It's just a thought I had," he said. "I don't know what it means. But when Urko has a chance to kill me and get me out of the picture, and then doesn't do it, I want to know why. I have to figure out his game." Virdon spoke slowly and softly, staring over the boy's head at the cold stone of the wall opposite. With a shrug and a sad smile, the blond man turned again and continued up the stairs and into the hallway at the top. Kraik hesitated for a few seconds, then he, too, climbed the stairs, following Virdon. Arn remained below, watching.

Virdon walked slowly down the hallway, examining it foot by foot as he had the room. He eased himself past piles of debris that lay strewn about. A patch of light made him look up; above his head there was an unbarred castle window, high on the wall. Virdon piled wreckage below the window, and carefully pulled himself up to its level. He boosted himself up into a position where he could view the surroundings outside. He was suspicious—why would Urko imprison him in a room with access to an unguarded window? Virdon looked down.

He could see the ground at the base of the wall; there was the clean, unexpected green of grass and shrubbery below. The courtyard had apparently been a garden at one time, or the passage of time and the insistence of plant life had broken up the pavement that had once existed. Virdon did not know which. There was no movement in the area, no sounds.

Virdon was satisfied that no gorilla was around, walking guard duty in the courtyard. He could find no reason for that; still, he could find no reason not to take advantage of the situation. He straightened up on the window ledge and began to look for handholds or ivy vines, something to help him climb down.

While Virdon was occupied, a gorilla who had been concealed behind the shrubbery stepped quietly out, raised his rifle, and aimed it at Virdon.

Virdon did not see or hear his enemy. He continued his inspection of the wall. The crack of a shot rang out, followed instantly by the splintering of the castle wall less than a foot from Virdon's hand. Virdon ducked away from the shot instinctively; then he looked down to its source.

For a brief instant, the gorilla and the human being stared at each other. Virdon felt nakedly helpless, outlined against the window behind him. He saw the gorilla's finger squeeze the trigger; he heard the loud explosion; he heard the bullet as it spanged off the wall above his head. He could not move for a moment, paralyzed by the closeness of death. He could jump forward, into the courtyard, and fall a long distance; his ankle already was injured, and the fall would likely break some bones. He would be as good as dead, trapped by the gorilla guard. He could jump back into the corridor, but there, too, the leap would leave him helplessly injured. While he hesitated, two more shots in rapid succession hit around the window opening. Virdon turned, jumped, and caught the window ledge as he fell. He hung by his fingers for a few seconds, breathing hard. There were no more shots from the guard. After a while, Virdon let himself down, dropping heavily and awkwardly to the cold stone of the corridor. He favored his sprained ankle, and rolled away from the wall. Kraik rushed up to him.

"They could have killed you!" cried the frightened boy.

Virdon stood up and brushed himself off. He looked at the boy, and then up at the window. He stared thoughtfully. The scene with the gorilla just added to his confusion. "They could have," he said. "But they didn't. Deliberately. I was an easy shot. None of Urko's guards are so poor that I wouldn't have been nailed by one of those four bullets. That was very close range." He paused, thinking over the implications. "They want me here," he said. "They want me alive. And why was that gorilla hiding?" He thought some more, trying to add up all the pieces of the puzzle. Then, suddenly, as though someone beside him had whispered the answer in his ear, Virdon understood. "Sure!" he said. "It's got to be! A trap. And I'm the bait. I'm not the quarry at all."

"I never understand you when you talk," said Kraik. "What do you mean, a trap?"

Virdon answered exuberantly, finally glad to have the whole thing so clear. "Yes," he said, "a trap. For my friends, not for me. But it won't work! Urko's trap won't catch anybody. The trouble with these gorillas is that they think that everyone else thinks the same way they do. But not my friends!"

Kraik's brows came together as he frowned. "Why?"

Before Virdon could answer, Arn hurried into the hallway and up to Virdon and Kraik. "I heard the shots," she said worriedly. "Are you all right?"

Kraik nodded and Virdon said, "Fine."

"He tried to escape," said Kraik.

Virdon leaned against the wall. "I won't try again," he said, musing. "Not yet, anyway. I'll stick around and give a couple of pigeons more time to fly the coop." He stopped speaking; it was evident to his two companions that he was thinking about something private. Whatever it was, it brought a smile to his face. "Then maybe we'll find a way to fly," he said, his smile already fading away.

Again, both Arn and Kraik were puzzled by Virdon's cryptic remarks. They wondered where this strange man had come from, with his odd way of speaking.

Virdon gave them both reassuring smiles, but said nothing more.

There was a woman who bore a slight resemblance to Arn. The hair was cut differently and of a different color, and Arn had been starved a good deal thinner, but the resemblance could not be entirely discounted.

The woman was Virdon's wife.

In a deserted building not far from Virdon's prison, Zaius studied a picture of Virdon's wife and son. In the picture that Zaius held the human boy was about the same age and size as Kraik. Near him, Urko stood tensely, staring from a window. Zaius examined the picture for a few more seconds. "I wonder how they do this?" he said at last.

Urko, startled, turned around. "What?" he asked.

Zaius held up the picture. "This, of course," he said. "This picture that Virdon carried with him. I can't imagine how it was made. Those humans were able to do things that we cannot. And we have far more proof than this picture."

Urko slapped his gloved hand against the wall in agitation. "You waste time thinking about a stupid picture!" he shouted. "Zaius, he tried to escape!"

"Think, Urko," said Zaius mildly. "If you were ever taken captive—"

"Me?" roared the gorilla general. "Captive?"

"Think, Urko," said Zaius, "or is that asking too much? It you were ever taken captive, what would you do?"

"Escape," said the gorilla. As soon as the word left his lips, he hit the wall again. "He tried to escape!"

"But he didn't succeed." Zaius held up the picture again. "Here," he said, "I think that this will be the key to our problem. You'll see."

"I can't believe this," said Urko impatiently. "We have

him there, helpless, guarded. You agree with me that we'd be better off with him dead. Yet we don't kill him. I don't understand. I'm sorry I let you talk me into this."

Zaius laughed softly. "Urko, you can't be talked into anything unless you think there's a fair chance that you'll end up with ample rewards. You know that as well as I do. But I've studied the humans. They are extremely vulnerable when it comes to situations concerning their families. It's only a matter of time until Virdon will come to think of that woman and the boy as his own family. They certainly bear enough resemblance to the wife and son he left in his own time. He'll lower his defenses with our humans. Then he'll tell that boy things that all your tortures could never drag out of him."

Urko stared past Zaras' shoulder toward a blank wall for several seconds, thinking. Then he moved his head slightly and looked evenly into the eyes of the prime minister. From the gorilla's expression, Zaius could tell that Urko was not completely convinced about Zaius' way of doing things. It seemed that Urko was spending all of his energy just trying to keep his temper in check.

At the scientific institute, Galen and Burke had piled several crumbling wall sections together to make a flat surface on which to work. On this rough table sat a makeshift battery case, made from clay and mud. It was drying in the stale air. Burke was hard at work trying to assemble a battery from the materials they had scavenged together. The rifle they had taken from the gorilla stood against the table, near at hand.

Galen watched, not comprehending what Burke, was doing. The young chimpanzee was impatient. "How much longer?" he asked.

Burke did not look up from his labors. "I have to make the sulphuric acid," he said. "Then we'll put it all together and see if it will start that projector."

Galen wasn't satisfied with Burke's answer. He walked around the table, to the astronaut's side. "Then what?" he asked.

Burke still didn't look at his friend. "We find out where that hidden vault is," he said. "And we go there."

"And then?"

"We clean it out, and split," said Burke, without the urgency and doubt he felt inside.

Galen gave him a puzzled look. Burke did not see it. "I don't understand," said Galen.

"We get out of town," said Burke simply. "Leave."

"'Split' means 'leave,'" said Galen. "I will have to remember that. The language has certainly lost a lot since your day."

"A lot of things around here have," said Burke.

"But what happens after the vault?"

"We stash all that knowledge somewhere safe."

Galen kept up his questioning refrain. "After that?" he asked.

"I suppose after that," said Burke, looking up at last and smiling, "I guess we come back and find Alan."

Galen was very pleased by Burke's reply. It was obviously the answer he had been waiting to hear. "I was wondering how long it would be before we got around to that," he said.

Burke slapped the chimpanzee on the shoulder, then turned his attention back to the battery.

The castle room where Virdon had been confined seemed more cheerful to him. There was a fire in the fireplace, although it was not a roaring blaze. There was little to be used as fuel until he smashed up some of the furniture. Virdon walked to the fire and put another piece of wood on. After all, he told himself, it wasn't his furniture. Still, he felt a peculiar reluctance to break it up. Kraik watched him carefully; Virdon was aware that the boy had watched everything the astronaut had done during the day. It was very likely that Virdon was the first competent adult male human that Kraik had ever known. Realizing again what kind of a life the boy had had up until now, Virdon felt another welling of compassion for the boy. The blond man turned to him. "My name is Virdon," he said. "Alan Virdon."

There was a moment's silence. Then the boy, in turn, spoke up. "I'm Kraik," he said.

Virdon smiled. "Kraik," he said. "A good name. I'm glad to meet you, Kraik." Virdon, out of force of habit long suppressed in this hostile future, put out his right hand. But, of course, the action did not have the effect that Virdon expected. Kraik just stared at Virdon's hand warily. Then the astronaut reached over, took Kraik's right, hand in his own, and they shook.

While they did, Virdon explained. "Where I come from," he said, "when two men meet and want to be fiends, they do this. They shake hands."

"Why?" asked the boy.

Virdon looked down at Kraik for a few seconds, thinking. "That's a good question," said Virdon. "I'm not sure if I know the answer. Customs sometimes start way back and hang on after the reason is long forgotten."

"But when you know you don't know why you're doing something, why keep on doing it?" asked Kraik.

"Because after a while," said Virdon, "the custom gets a

value of its own. Because doing it makes you feel good or comfortable, even if you can't exactly explain why."

The man and the boy still grasped each other's right hands. Kraik tentatively shook hands again. Virdon nodded. "Perhaps, in the old days, when two new 'friends' met, they held each other's right hands so they couldn't hit each other with their weapons."

Kraik accepted this explanation for a few moments. Then he said in a solemn voice, "That's a pretty good idea, if the friend doesn't have a knife in his left hand."

Virdon laughed briefly. "You cover all bases, don't you?" he said.

Kraik looked puzzled again. "I don't know what that means."

"It isn't important."

"You've done that all day. 'Cover all bases.' All day, you've said things that sound as if they should mean something, but when I think about them, they don't,"

"It's a bad habit I have," said Virdon. "It's something that I just can't help. Never mind, though." The boy dropped his hand and nodded. Virdon started gathering some more scraps of wood for the fire, and Kraik followed behind him. "Do you have any parents, Kraik?" asked Virdon.

Behind him, the boy shook his head "no." Of course, Virdon did not hear an answer, and he straightened up and turned around. He started to ask again, but Kraik's repeated head-shaking stopped him abruptly. Virdon was about to continue the conversation, but instead he walked to the fire and tossed his wood in. He thought about how difficult it must be for a young boy alone in such a harsh world.

There was an uncomfortable silence in the room for several moments. Finally Virdon broke it. "Why were you put in here with me?" he asked. "That's the detail I can't understand. You're no threat to Urko. My friends don't even know about you."

"I don't know," said Kraik, "but I'm glad I'm with you." Virdon smiled and reached out to touch the boy's head. Behind him came the sound of the door creaking open. Virdon was startled by the noise and turned quickly. He saw Arn entering, carrying a bulging woven sack.

"We're in luck," she said happily. "Look what I found in a back room."

She emptied the sack on the floor. It was filled with food. Kraik immediately moved for it. That was the natural reaction for one who had to fight and steal for his meals.

Virdon watched him sadly. This is what the human race had become. This, is what domination by the apes had reduced the once-proud masters to. It seemed to Virdon that humans, despite all their faults, deserved a better fate.

Kraik hurried toward the food. He inspected it quickly and reached for what he had chosen. Virdon quickly closed the distance between them and grabbed the food away from Kraik before the boy could stuff it greedily into his mouth. "No!" said Virdon sternly.

Kraik's reaction was immediate and angry. He picked up a piece of wood and held it up before him, as a weapon. It was the only thing close to hand that he could grab quickly, as pitiful and inadequate as it was. But the boy's point was made; Virdon stared at him wordlessly. For a brief, tense moment it seemed as though Kraik were about to swing at Virdon, attacking the astronaut for the food. Virdon realized that the situation had become a crisis; more than food was on the line here, and he knew that he would have to proceed with caution.

"Take it easy, Kraik," said Virdon. "That's not going to solve anything. That's a lesson we never learn. But think about this, instead. If you eat all the food now, what about tomorrow? Maybe one of the reasons you and your people are in such bad times is because you and they never think about tomorrow."

Kraik sneered. His whole attitude had become contemptuous of the man he had so respected earlier. It was clear that this strange blond man knew nothing about life. Kraik felt that he, himself, knew more than Virdon. "I'm hungry now," he said. "I don't care about tomorrow."

"You will," said Virdon, "tomorrow."

Kraik thought about that idea for a moment, not easing his guarded position. After a while, Virdon could tell that the boy was beginning to accept what he was saying. Virdon relaxed just the slightest bit. "Let Arn portion out a little of it to each of us," said the blond man. "That way, we'll all be sharing the same. That's the way it should be. Then tomorrow we can really cook ourselves up a meal."

Kraik thought about that for a few more seconds. Then, slowly, he lowered his makeshift club and tossed it aside. Virdon took a step to him and smiled. He put his arm around Kraik's shoulders, showing the boy that Virdon felt good about it—almost as though he'd just taught his own son something.

Virdon and Kraik sat down on the floor beside Arn; the woman smiled at what Virdon had been able to accomplish. She began to portion out some of the food, watching Virdon's face. She wondered what emotions the strange man felt; she had no way of knowing that the situation was beginning to stir memories of Virdon's own family, just as Zaius said it would.

The day ended, and the sun disappeared behind the rows of buildings to the west. Outside the building that Urko and Zaius had chosen as their headquarters, a uniformed gorilla guard stood watching. He guarded the entrance to the building, and the flaming torch beside the door cast strange shadows on the scene. The gorilla did not have enough imagination to notice the flickering shadows. He had been ordered to guard the building, and that was all that was important to him.

Inside the building, in the sparsely furnished room that Urko had selected as his base of operations, torches on the walls dimly illuminated swatches of the floor. A good deal of the room was sunken in impenetrable gloom. Urko was talking to his Captain, instructing the subordinate in the precise orders which Urko had worked out to his own satisfaction. While this conversation continued, the two gorillas were interrupted by the arrival of Zaius. The orangutan administrator said nothing until Urko and the Captain finished their discussion.

"We start at daylight," said Urko.

"Yes, sir," said the Captain.

"I'll want all the soldiers you can spare."

"Yes, sir."

Urko turned away from the Captain. His voice was gruff and slightly weary. "That's all," said the gorilla general.

The Captain, still impressed despite himself to be in the presence of the supreme commander of the gorilla forces, saluted, turned, and left the conference chamber. When the ape had shut the door behind him, Zaius glanced at Urko, a quizzical expression on his face.

"Are you planning a war party?" asked Zaius.

Urko laughed mirthlessly. "A search party, Zaius, for the chimpanzee, Galen, and that nuisance of a human being, Burke. I don't care where he came from or what he knows. He's still a human being and deserves to be treated like one. You do it your way; I'll do it mine. Section by section, building by building."

Night shaded the crumbling edifice of the scientific institute. Through fissures in the ceiling, stars were visible. A chill evening wind blew through the chinks in the walls, but the man and the ape at work inside did not seem to notice these discomforts. The container for the battery still rested on the makeshift work table. Now, though, it was half-filled with clear liquid. A very weary Burke leaned against the bench, working with the copper tubing. He sighed deeply, put down the copper, and slumped down to the floor to rest for a few moments. Galen glanced at him, a worried expression on his face. Then the chimpanzee crossed to pick up the container. He almost knocked the stolen rifle down in his own fatigue.

"Don't touch it!" cried Burke. "That's sulphuric acid. It'd burn a hole right through your hand."

Galen looked at the container with greater respect. "Are you ready to put it together with the copper? Then we can see if it will work."

Burke staggered slightly against the work table. He rubbed his eyes. "In the morning," he said. "I'm beat."

Galen looked at Burke with an amused expression. "If you were to ask me, I'd say you were delaying."

"I can't think of a single thing in the world that would motivate me to ask you," said Burke.

"You're delaying," said the chimpanzee.

"Someone has to," said Burke wearily. He opened his eyes and glanced at Galen. Then, tiredly, he closed his eyes again. Galen smiled gently, slumping down beside his friend.

"Who knows?" said Galen. "Maybe he will be here by morning."

Burke opened his eyes again, glanced at Galen, and held up his crossed fingers.

Inside the castle prison, a fire was burning cheerfully. After a moment, Virdon joined Arn and Kraik by its side. He squatted down on the dusty floor and joined the other two in eating the hot meal that the woman and boy had finished preparing. They ate in silence for several moments. Finally Virdon turned to Arn. "It's very good," he said. "Thanks."

"Half of the thanks ought to go to Kraik," said Am. "He showed me some interesting tricks and things to do with old food."

"Thank you, Kraik," said Virdon.

The boy only nodded, wordlessly. He was busily eating, not taking time off to speak.

"It's very good, Arn and Kraik," said Virdon. "Thanks, again. I'm glad to hear that it was a community effort."

"I'm glad you like it," said Am.

"I want more," said Kraik.

Arn dished out a second portion to Kraik, then noticed that Virdon had stopped eating and was lost in thought for a moment. Arn could never tell what Virdon was thinking about when the man got lost in his private thoughts. "Something doesn't taste good to you, Virdon?" she asked.

Virdon shook his head vigorously. "No, no, not at all Arn This is a wonderful meal. It's amazing how hunger can make gourmet food out of the simplest things. I was just thinking about my friends. If they, have enough to eat."

He shook off the thought. It served no purpose to make idle speculations along those lines. Things would work out one way or another, and all the worry in the world would not change it. He went back to eating. Arn and Kraik exchanged glances.

"These friends," said Kraik, "where are they?"

"You're better off if I don't tell you," said Virdon.

"But I'd like to…"

Virdon stared over his bowl at the young boy for a few seconds. "Kraik," he said at last, "if the apes ever thought you knew, they'd tear you apart to get the information. That wouldn't be fair to you, or to my friends. I'll keep the information inside me, because I'm confident that, whatever Urko has planned, he won't get the information from me."

Kraik's expression hardened. "I don't care," he said. "I thought we were friends. I thought we could share things together. I've never had anyone like you before. I don't see what harm it could do if you were just to tell me where your friends are. Perhaps me or my friends could help them."

Arn interrupted quickly. She could understand the situation much better than the young boy. "He's trying to protect us, Kraik. It's not that he doesn't want you to know. But if you don't have the information, you can't be hurt by the gorilla guards. Can't you see that? *Us*. He's protecting us."

For a long moment, Arn stared at Kraik, hoping that her words would convince the hostile boy. Kraik could not meet her powerful, level gaze. He lowered his eyes. Then Arn glanced back at Virdon, with a growing sense of warmth. Everything about this strange man seemed honorable and upright.

"You are a very good man, Alan," she said softly. The words were difficult to speak; she had never addressed but one other man in such a way, in all of her life. "You are like Tomar was." Tears in her eyes threatened to spill out and run down her cheek. She fought them back.

Virdon heard her words with a rare, long-forgotten thrill of pleasure. "And you're a good woman, Arn," he said. "Like... His voice trailed off. He stopped himself and the line of thought that he had begun to pursue. "You're a very good woman," he repeated lamely. The two adults looked at each other for a moment, neither wishing to say anything further, each feeling their relationship building.

Another day began. The sun rose above the shattered buildings, pouring down its warming rays upon the few human and ape creatures abroad. Otherwise the city was deserted. Through the empty streets came the echoing clop of horses' hooves. Urko was personally leading several squads of gorilla' guards as they made an intensive building-by-building search through the city. As they proceeded, several men, haggard, starving, poorly clothed, were dragged as suspects from buildings and shown to Urko, who impatiently rejected them. He had no interest at all in these filthy creatures. There were only two individuals in the city whom he had any desire to meet. These poor creatures captured by the gorillas weren't the fugitives; they were permitted to scuttle away to safety.

Galen was hidden behind a mound of rubble, carefully looking ahead and off toward the searching gorillas. He watched them for another moment, then turned and retreated back into the rubble and hurried away from the scene.

Meanwhile, back inside the scientific institute, the first bright shafts of sunlight beamed down on Virdon, who was still curled up uncomfortably on the floor. He rose, stretched, and began the final preparations. He had almost completed the battery. He tested it and got a spark. It worked.

Burke did not hear the entrance of Galen, as the chimpanzee somewhat clumsily upset the piles of debris in the outer hall. Galen entered the work area and quickly moved toward Burke. It would have been obvious that Galen was bearing important news, but Burke was too concerned with his own success to notice.

"It works!" cried Burke exultantly. "After all these hours of frustration, I made the doggone thing work!"

Galen interrupted in an agitated voice. "We haven't got much more time," he said worriedly. "Gorillas are going into every building. They've started moving in this direction. We're sure to be discovered here. We'll have to think of something different."

Burke considered the problem. This was just the kind of incident that he had hoped might not interfere with their work. The gorillas always had a knack for disturbing them just on the verge of success. "The battery's ready to be hooked up," said Burke. "How much time do we have?"

"Not much," said Galen. "They know exactly what they're looking for. Us."

In the alcove, the projector machine stood on its pedestal in the niche. If the gorillas arrived first, the machine was as good as dead for all eternity.

Inside the castle prison, Virdon was seated in the warm glow from a shaft of sunlight. He was whittling a model airplane out of a piece of wood. Kraik was crouched down beside him, watching, fascinated.

"What are you doing?" asked Kraik.

"I'm whittling," said Virdon. "I used to love to whittle when I was a boy."

"Well, then, what are you making?"

Virdon held the piece of wood, out at arm's length, giving it a long, critical examination. He started trimming some of the bumps and ridges. "It's an airplane," he said at last. "A flying machine." Virdon held the plane and zoomed it through the air, near Kraik's head. The boy laughed.

"An... airplane?" asked the boy.

"Sure. We had them all the time in my day," said Virdon.

Kraik smiled to indicate that he didn't really believe this.

"I don't understand you again," said Kraik. "I understand the gorillas better than I understand you. Flying machine? Will it really fly?"

Virdon concentrated on his whittling. "Maybe," he said noncommittally.

"Can I have it?" asked Kraik.

"When I'm finished with it," said Virdon. "Maybe."

Arn moved close to the two males, watching Virdon as he worked on his project. She stood there with them, feeling a sense of warmth and fondness.

Virdon continued to work on the model airplane, concentrating on the toy to the exclusion of everything else around him. He did not see Arn's softening glance, or Kraik's fascinated stare. The airplane itself, being a reminder of Virdon's old world, brought him a warm and pleasant glow of the days he had been removed from.

"Did you fly yourself?" asked Kraik. "Did you ever really fly? Really?"

Virdon was amused by the vehemence in the boy's questions. They were tinged with disbelief but, yet, a kind of hopefulness. "Many times," said the blond astronaut. "I flew in an airplane probably more times than you went to sleep not hungry. There was a day when people used to fly everywhere. Instead of having to walk hundreds of miles, or steal rides on the backs of farmers' carts, people just boarded huge airplanes and flew for hundreds and even thousands of miles."

"And in those days," said Kraik, still not comprehending how Virdon's days were different than his own, "did the people have enough to eat?"

Virdon looked at the boy with compassion. This overwhelming search for daily food colored every thought the boy had.

The answer to the question was not simple. Virdon had to consider his reply carefully. He thought in silence for several seconds. "Not always," he said at last. "And not everyone."

Kraik shrugged. He had suspected that Virdon had not come from so far away, after all. "Like here, now," he said.

Virdon sighed. It would be very difficult to explain the differences in their eras; it would require an entire indoctrination about how the apes had not always been in power, and how human beings had governed the world. "No," said Virdon, "people in that time didn't have it as tough as you do now."

Kraik grinned proudly. "I don't eat bad," he said. It was obviously a sign of status among the people of the forbidden area. "If anybody can find food, it's me. I know this city like nobody else. If I hear somebody's got fruit or maybe sometimes meat, I sneak in the back way, or come up through a sewer, or crawl in a hidden window; I grab and run before anybody's even looking." He finished his speech with an insolent look of self-confidence, an expression that bordered on arrogance. He virtually dared Virdon to find fault with him.

Virdon did not want to find fault. He felt that it was necessary though to point out that there might be better ways to co-exist with the apes and the other humans in the city. "If we can get our hands on what's buried in this city," he said, "You nor anybody else will have to scratch and steal for food any more."

"Is food buried?" asked Kraik.

Virdon shook his head. "A lot of long-forgotten ideas that might be used to make this a nicer world," he said.

Virdon grinned at the boy. "There must be a million things you never dreamed of."

Kraik thought about Virdon's words. As before, there were elements that were totally above the boy's head. They bore no factual relation to anything in die boy's experience. "Could I have my own…" he said, stumbling on the words and the concept, "…'flying machine'?"

Virdon continued to whittle the airplane from the block of wood. The exercise was pleasant and restful. He had barely heard Kraik's question, and the answer did not come until the boy's words penetrated Virdon's conscious mind. "Oh," said the blond astronaut, "maybe."

Virdon stood up, holding the unfinished plane in one hand. He stretched and smiled at Arn, then walked toward the stairway. He slowly mounted the stairs, seeking privacy in one of the rooms off the corridor above. Arn followed.

Kraik stood where he was, watching Virdon and Arn as they left.

Virdon found the room he was looking for. In one corner was an old, small wooden box. He opened the lid and placed the nearly complete airplane model inside, for safekeeping. Arn came up behind him.

"Hello," he said to her. "I didn't hear you coming."

"I'm sorry to surprise you," said Arn. "He respects you, Alan," she said in a grateful tone of voice.

Virdon smiled and looked thoughtfully into the distance. "My own son would be about his age," he said softly.

"It's a remarkable thing," said Arn. "I've known him for several years. I'm sure that he never trusted anyone else before."

Virdon frowned. He thought about the different lifestyles that had molded Arn and his own son. "Never?" he asked. "He's never had a friend before?"

Arn shuddered. This wonderful, strange man had still a lot to learn about their lives. "In the city," she said, "no one has friends."

Virdon considered her feelings. "I wonder, though," he said. "He must have known his father or his mother."

"I would not recognize my own parents among those in this city," said Arn, without a trace of ill will. It was simply a statement of fact, accepted by all who chose to live in the forbidden area. "Even fathers—not all of them, but some—fight anybody for enough food to stay alive."

"That poor kid…" said Virdon.

Urko had a rough map of the city tacked on one wall. He stood near it, studying it, working on it, marking off sections. As Zaius entered, Urko turned from his work and smiled.

Zaius went up next to Urko and examined the map, with its bright colored pins stuck in ruled-off sectors. "How do the war games go, Urko?" he asked.

Urko grunted and turned back to his map. He did not bother to reply to Zaius for a full minute. He was irritated; whenever Urko and his allied soldiers prepared an intelligent search and seizure scheme, Zaius spoiled the atmosphere by referring to the procedure as a "game." Urko worked on his map while his anger cooled. "This is just in the event that I kill the prisoner before he tells me where the others are," said the gorilla. "It's a backup system. You would never have thought to provide for one. This is an example of gorilla efficiency and experience."

Urko turned back to face the President of the Supreme Council. "And Zaius," he said, "even if your way does not work, I intend to find Galen and Burke. And I shall kill them, too."

"I have no doubt about that," said Zaius unpleasantly.

In the scientific institute, the day progressed slowly. The niche in which the machine stood was partially blocked off by a makeshift wall, constructed of bits and pieces of fallen masonry. Galen approached with a piece of crumbling masonry which he added to the wall. As he finished doing this, Burke appeared with another piece of masonry which he, too, added to the wall. At all times, the two friends kept the stolen rifle close at hand.

Galen steadied the new pieces as the wall grew larger. He worked in silence until a question occurred to him. "If we cover this," he asked, "how will Alan know you made the, uh, the projector work?"

Burke laughed. "There are things you learn about someone when you spend a lot of times with him. Alan knows me like a book, and I have a feeling that I could guess his reactions in a situation, too. The answer is logic. Step One, he guesses we wouldn't cover it if there was nothing to hide. That brings him to Step Two. He uncovers it. He sees the new battery, he turns on the machine, and he learns the location of the vault. Step Three, logic tells him that's where we've gone."

Any further discussion was interrupted by the

terrifying clatter of horses' hooves not far away.

Galen stared at the wall of the institute. He listened with his superior hearing for a moment, then turned back to Burke. "Unless, of course," he said grimly, "Step Four, the gorillas catch us here before we can finish."

Burke snorted. "You're a real bundle of joy," he said.

Virdon, Kraik, and Arn were seated near the fire. Virdon had finished fashioning a pouch from rough cloth and leather thongs. "There you go," he said. "We'll work up a strap to hold it to your side, then you can carry your things in it."

Kraik looked at him blankly. "What things?" he asked.

"Oh, I don't know," said Virdon. "Not a baseball or a stick of chewing gum, not even crumbled up chocolate chip cookies…"

Kraik looked at Virdon uncomprehendingly, having no idea what the man was talking about.

"I'm rambling," said Virdon. "Where I come from, boys like to have pockets. Like this pouch, so they can carry whatever they want."

"This place you come from," said Kraik, almost afraid to ask. "Will you go back there?"

"I hope so," said Virdon with a faraway look in his eyes. "Some day."

"I think I'd like to see that place," said Kraik.

Virdon glanced at him with fondness. He reached out and tousled Kraik's hair. "I think you ought to pull your weight around here."

"What?" asked Kraik.

"Do your share of the work," said Virdon. "Go down to the cellar and collect some more firewood."

Kraik made a face. "I will," he said. "In a little while."

"That story you told Kraik," said Arn, "About what the world could be like. Was that true?"

"It was a hope," said Virdon.

Arn's expression changed. She was clearly disappointed. "Oh," she said. "Only a hope."

Virdon spoke quickly, wanting to reassure her. "It's not impossible," he said. "My friends and I found a place where there was a message. It told about hope for the world, for humans. Hope in the form of human knowledge."

Kraik looked disgusted. "What good is that?" he asked. "Can you eat it?"

Arn ignored Kraik's words. "How do you find this knowledge?" she asked.

Virdon thought for a moment. "Do you know that building not far from where you lived? It has big columns in front of it, and an arched entrance that's partly caved in."

"Is it made of crumbling gray brick?" asked Kraik.

"That's the one," said Virdon. "Didn't I ask you to get some wood?"

Kraik ignored the order. "I've been there. There's nothing inside, no food, no clothes, nothing."

"You're wrong," said Virdon. "There's a machine in that building, Kraik, and by now it may have told my friends how to find the knowledge that could change the world."

"A machine that talks?" asked Kraik, his credulity stretched to the breaking point. "You're making fun of me."

"If you don't get to work right now, I'll *really* make fun of you."

Kraik grimaced. "I want to hear more stories."

"Later," said Virdon sternly. "Do your job first."

Kraik started to protest again, but Virdon overrode him. "Right now," said the blond man. Resignedly, Kraik stood and went out.

For a few seconds there was silence. It was evident to

Virdon that Am, too, had her doubts and her questions, but she was working to overcome her shyness in asking them. "I like to hear stories about your world, too," she said.

"Compared to where you were living, almost any place would sound wonderful," said Virdon.

"When I first met Tomar," said Arn wistfully, "he lived on a farm with his brother. It was beautiful."

"Why did you leave?" asked Virdon.

"A woman goes with her man," she said. "Tomar wanted to reach other men, make them think the way he did, make them have hope. The apes killed him."

"He wouldn't have been really alive if he didn't have hope," said Virdon, realizing that Arn's dead husband had been one of the few humans in this world with the intelligence and vision to stand up against the apes.

Arn flared up momentarily. "Other men don't try to change the world. They live to hold a woman in their arms, to have sons…" Her voice trailed off; she seemed to be afraid of the depth of her own emotions. "I'm sorry," she said.

"Don't be," said Virdon. "Couldn't you go back to the farm?"

"I don't know," said Am. "I've thought about it. It's easier just to do nothing, though. And, when you're alone, maybe it's better not to go where you're always reminded that once you weren't alone…"

Virdon remained silent for some time, considering what his proper response should be. "You could meet another man," he said.

"Yes. I didn't think so, but now I do. Tell me another story, Alan."

There was a moment of quiet as they looked at each other. Virdon felt himself approaching an emotional brink that suddenly seemed dangerous to him. He withdrew with a conscious effort.

"What would you like to hear?" he asked lamely.

"Anything you tell me," she said.

Virdon recognized the dangerous terrain on which he walked with Arn. He moved away, so that he was not close enough to touch her. She watched for a moment, and then resigned herself to a less personal inquiry—if only for the moment. "Was there really a machine that talks?" she asked.

The conversation had moved back onto safe ground. "Sure," said Virdon. "And a machine that heats, and a machine that cools, and a machine that flies—like—" He had moved in the direction of the spot where he had left the model. He looked and stopped abruptly. The place where the plane had rested was empty.

Virdon glanced in the direction Kraik had gone, and the man shook his head. "I'll be right back," he murmured. Arn watched him curiously. Virdon left in the direction Kraik had followed.

Kraik sat alone in an alcove. He was resting on the pallet he used for a bed, examining the model airplane. He heard someone coming toward him, and quickly tried to hide the model. It was too late. It was Virdon.

"Why did you take it?" asked the astronaut.

"I didn't take anything," said Kraik.

"Listen to me," said Virdon, trying to control his voice. "We've got to have some rules about how we behave— you, me, Arn. Rule one, I guess, is we trust each other. All right?"

Kraik wouldn't look Virdon directly in the eyes. "Maybe," he muttered.

"We don't lie," said Virdon, "we don't take things

without permission…" He waited a moment for some kind of response from Kraik. There was a pause.

"I'm tired," said Kraik. "I want to sleep."

Virdon continued, more sternly than before. "Give me the model, please," he said.

"I won't!" cried Kraik.

Virdon extended his hand. "You don't take anything unless you're given permission."

Kraik deliberately ignored this. Virdon reached behind the boy and was about to take the airplane from where it was concealed. Before he could get it, however, Kraik grabbed the airplane and made a dash to get away. Virdon caught the boy, and held him firmly by the shoulders. He swung Kraik around so that the boy had to face Virdon. Kraik tried to pull away, to look away.

"Give me the airplane, Kraik," said Virdon calmly.

"Let me go!" cried the boy.

"Hand it to me."

"You made it for me," said Kraik. "It's mine!"

"It is not yours and it never will be unless you behave."

In a sudden fury, Kraik slammed the airplane to the floor where it broke into several pieces.

"There's your stupid airplane," said the boy, sobbing. "I don't want it!"

Virdon sighed and stretched his tense shoulders. "All right," he said finally, "you've made sure you won't get it."

"I hate you!" shouted Kraik. "I hate you!"

He ran from the room. Virdon looked after him, hurting terribly inside. He bent over silently to pick up the pieces of the shattered plane.

Several minutes later, outside, in the courtyard below the window through which Virdon had tried to make his escape, there was a strange scene. A sergeant, evidently doing sentry duty, marched his post in straight, military lines. But he saw something that made him stop, bewildered. A gorilla guard holding Kraik by the arm entered the courtyard and approached the sergeant. The guard saluted and presented Kraik, who tried to twist out of the ape's grasp.

"Here," said the guard disgustedly. "This creature wanted to see you. I can't imagine why you would want to see him, but as he was wandering about the restricted area, I thought it best to bring him to you. He says you promised him a reward."

"He did!" cried Kraik. "Let go!"

The sergeant bent down and gave Kraik an evil grin. "Well," he said to the boy, "What do you have to tell me?"

Kraik was silent, hesitant, frightened.

The sergeant grew angry. "Don't waste my time, human!" he shouted. "Do you know where the outlaw ape and human are?"

There was a long moment's silence. Kraik's ambivalence led him first one way, then another. Finally, he nodded affirmatively.

4

It was day, and the sunlight streamed through the high windows into the castle room. Arn and Virdon sat by the fire. Kraik entered and glanced toward them sadly; almost, almost he went to them, but he changed his mind and crossed instead toward his sleeping alcove.

Arn looked up and saw the boy. She stood up.

Kraik went into his alcove and went to his bed. He stopped short as he saw the model airplane, patched together again, on the bed. He picked it up gently and looked at it. Arn came in, and stood watching him for a moment. "He was very upset," she said softly.

Kraik turned around and looked at her, ready to cry.

"The 'airplane'," said Arn. "He was making it for you."

Kraik looked at her, at the airplane, and suddenly he could hold back his tears no longer. He was no more a self-sufficient, tough street urchin; now he was just a frightened little boy. He threw his arms around her, sobbing; "I... I told the gorilla," he said, choking.

* * *

Urko, the Captain, the Sergeant, and a squad of gorilla guards cautiously moved in around the scientific institute building. Urko expertly deployed the others so that there was no way anyone inside the building could possibly escape.

"You," called Urko, "see that no one gets out the back. You go with him. Sergeant, post troopers on both sides of the door."

Urko's orders were followed. Satisfied, the general signaled the others to follow him.

Urko, the Captain, and the other gorillas all came rushing into the institute's main room, where Burke and Galen had labored earlier. But Urko was furious to see that there was no one there. He did not notice that a section of wall that had hid the machine had been built up again, recently. The machine itself was nowhere in sight.

Back in the castle prison, Kraik looked at Virdon, although he did so from a sheepish, downcast posture. Evidence of recent tears, in the form of grimy tracks down his cheeks, marked the boy's face. Arn stood nearby.

"No, Kraik," said Virdon, "I don't hate you."

"I'm sorry," said the boy quietly.

"What will happen to your friends now?" asked Arn.

"They've been long gone from that building," said Virdon.

"Would they take the talking machine with them?" asked Kraik.

That thought suddenly worried Virdon. "No," he said, "but if my friends got it working, it could tell me where they are."

"It doesn't matter," said Arn. "You can't go to them."

"The apes might find that message," said Virdon urgently. "I've got to get out of here!"

Kraik spoke up confidently. "I know a way out!" he said.

Virdon looked suddenly toward the ceiling, as though to get a divine explanation from that direction. "Why didn't you say so before?" he asked.

"I kind of liked it here," said Kraik. "I had enough to eat, and the gorillas said they'd give me lots more if I helped them."

"All right, Kraik," said Virdon. "I can't promise you food, but will you help me?"

Kraik nodded.

Two gorillas had been left behind to patrol the courtyard. There was a knock from inside the castle door. One gorilla covered the second, as the latter unlocked the door. Kraik emerged from the castle. He said something to the gorilla but Virdon, who was watching stealthily, could not make out the boy's words. The gorilla nodded, and Kraik sauntered through the courtyard and beyond the wall. He was carrying a pack.

Beyond the wall, Kraik saw another gorilla guard outside. Kraik signalled the gorilla, and the guard moved to join the boy. "Did you get it?" asked Kraik.

The ape, confused, said, "Get what?"

"The gun."

"What are you talking about?" asked the bewildered gorilla.

"I told the Sergeant," said Kraik. "Virdon had a gun. I threw it out of the window."

"I'll show you," said Kraik.

He led the gorilla guard close to the wall under the window in the courtyard. The two patrol gorillas were ordered to watch the outside door. Alone with the third gorilla, Kraik indicated the shrubbery beneath the wall. He began his search. "It's here somewhere," he said. The guard joined him in looking for the fictitious gun.

From the window above, Virdon leaned out carefully, looking down. The guard was bending down, searching the ground. Kraik, too, was still looking.

Virdon climbed silently to the window ledge, then jumped, landing squarely on the guard. The gorilla went down with a grunt, stunned. A quick blow from Virdon's fist, and the guard was out of action. Kraik watched, delighted and impressed. Arn crawled out to hang down from the window by her fingers. Virdon reached up toward her, stretching his arms up, not quite able to reach her. "All right," he said, "drop."

She let go and fell. He caught her, and put her on her feet as Kraik gestured for Virdon and Arn to follow him.

Kraik led the way to a large shrub. He pulled away some foliage and debris to reveal a grate which covered a man-made drain. Virdon lifted the grate and all three people climbed down.

Back at Urko's headquarters, Zaius sat watching a furious gorilla general. "Was there *anything* at all in this place?" asked Zaius.

"Nothing," said Urko. "Not Galen. Not Burke."

"Are you sure?"

Urko, turned around, raging: "Of course I'm sure!" he shouted. "They were gone! If they'd ever been there."

"Just in the event Virdon should escape," said Zaius, "they would leave something behind. Something that would tell him where to go. Take me there."

Kraik, Arn, and Virdon emerged and entered the main room of the scientific institute. It was deserted. The three looked around cautiously.

"Where are they?" asked Kraik worriedly.

Virdon glanced around. "I don't know. It's possible that they—" He broke off as he noticed the temporary wall Galen and Burke had built to hide the machine. He crossed to it. The others followed.

"What?" asked Arn.

"They've hidden the machine," said Virdon. "Come on, help me with this wall." He started pulling the bits and chunks of masonry away.

Outside, Urko, Zaius, the Captain, the Sergeant, and a squad of gorillas were on their horses, moving through the streets at a quick pace.

After a few minutes of study, Virdon had the projected image of the Scientist on the wall, as before. "In the years to come," said the long-dead human scientist, "whoever finds our Institute—"

The wall hiding the machine had been partly torn away, exposing the machine, to which had been attached the improvised battery. Arn and Kraik watched the image with awe and near shock, while Virdon stood by the machine, watching anxiously.

The Scientist's voice continued. "We, the Scientists, greet you. The destruction of our world as we know it is imminent—"

Outside, there was the sound of approaching hoofbeats.

"—but our civilization's great advances must not vanish."

Virdon reacted to the hoofbeats now. He hit a control and turned off the machine.

Outside the scientific institute, Urko, Zaius, the Captain, and the other gorillas pulled their mounts to a halt in front of the building. They dismounted quickly and rushed inside.

Virdon, Arn, and Kraik were nowhere in sight. Urko and Zaius glanced around the room. Behind a pile of fallen masonry, Arn, Virdon, and Kraik huddled in the shadows, unseen by the apes.

"What are we looking for?" asked the Captain.

Zaius thought for a moment. "I don't know," he said. "Probably something you've never… seen… before…" His voice trailed off as he noticed something that piqued his curiosity. Quickly he hurried toward the broken, improvised wall, behind which the machine was exposed. He glanced at Urko. "You said there was nothing here," said Zaius.

Urko was startled. "It wasn't here before," he said. Zaius glanced at him with ill-disguised contempt. He approached the machine, studied it, probed it. Urko joined him. "What does it do?" asked the gorilla general.

Zaius ignored him. "One of these must be a control." He played with the buttons for a moment, then pushed one.

The Scientist's voice started up again. "We have therefore deposited the sum of all our scientific knowledge in a number of vaults—"

The Scientist continued to speak while the gorillas and the orangutan reacted with fear and dismay.

"What is it?" cried Urko.

"Witchcraft!" whispered the Captain.

"It's evil!" said the Sergeant.

Zaius, alone, was anxious to hear. "Quiet!" he shouted. "All of you! Quiet!"

"—which are located in various cities throughout the world," said the Scientist. Urko and Zaius watched, still awed and interested. "In this city, the vault is embedded in concrete in the lower level of the midtown railway station, at the gateway to track four."

From his hiding place, Virdon listened carefully.

The Scientist had one last wish for his listeners. "We bid you good fortune," he said, "you who find and use our knowledge."

The image faded, the sound ceased. The recording was finished. Zaius snapped off the machine.

"What is a railway station?" asked Urko.

"I've seen pictures of them," said Zaius. "We passed such a place when we rode in. A long, narrow building." Zaius and Urko led the way, as they all gathered quickly to move to the door and exit. The apes came out of the building, mounted their horses as speedily as possible, and rapidly rode back up the street.

A short time later, Virdon, Arn, and Kraik came back out into the main room. Virdon was miserable as he shook his head.

"I know the place," said Kraik quickly, "and I know a faster way to get there. The apes will have to ride through the city streets. They can't make very fast time, going around the trash heaps and things."

"How?" asked Virdon.

"I can go through places where buildings have fallen into the streets and no horses can pass," said Kraik.

Meanwhile, Urko, Zaius, and the gorilla squad rode up a street; they had to rein their horses to a stop as they saw the street ahead was impassable. Cursing, they wheeled their horses around and galloped off in a different direction.

* * *

At one end of the railway station a kind of cement door had been pried open. Inside the vault, Burke and Galen found themselves in a concrete storeroom. Several small campfires had been set from time to lime in the concrete vaults, and some of the seemingly endless reels of computer tapes that were stored on shelves had been unwound—some even tried as fuel for the fires. Galen examined some of the labels on the tapes, while Burke checked the huge computer dominating the underground vault to see if it could still possibly work.

"Could man ever have known this much, and done so little with it?" asked Galen. There was no reply from Burke.

Urko, Zaius, and the other gorillas galloped up another street, and found themselves obstructed once more.

Burke and Galen checked the computer and the endless reels of tape, oblivious to the converging forces around them. Finally, after a short search, Virdon, Arn, and Kraik stumbled into the vault.

"Alan!" cried Burke. "What happened to you? We thought you were dead." The dark-haired man noticed Arn and Kraik. "Who—?"

Virdon cut his friend off. "No time!" he said. "We can't stay here. Urko and Zaius are on their way."

"This place is a gold mine," said Burke.

"It'll be a cemetery if we don't get moving. Now!"

Burke and Galen saw the urgency in Virdon's face; then they turned and moved quickly to the door. Burke took with him the rifle he had been carrying. The four humans and the chimpanzee hurried up the street to the sewer opening. They climbed down it as quickly as possible and pulled the lid closed after them. For a time the street was still and deserted; then Urko, Zaius, and the others thundered into the street, past the sewer.

Inside the vault, Zaius and Urko were more stunned than they had been by the recorded image of the ancient scientist. Zaius moved among the objects, shaking his head. "Knowledge," he said. "Death. Destruction. In the history of our world, *their* world, one has been the same as the other." He turned to the gorillas, commanding. "Destroy everything in here," he said. "Burn this place to the ground."

The gorillas took a step to follow the order, but were halted by Urko. "Wait," commanded the general. "What is here would give us great power. The knowledge would be safe with us. We're not like humans."

Zaius laughed without humor. "What a reversal of our roles, Urko. Would we really be better off, or safer? Remember, once the knowledge here is set free, it will spread out of control."

"*I* will be in control," said Urko fiercely.

"You are now. You have weapons," said Zaius. "You have troops. But, suppose one of your officers here learns the secrets in there. He'll have the power to destroy you, to destroy the world. Would you risk that?"

There was a silent moment. Then: "Burn it!" shouted Urko. The gorillas hurried to comply. Urko turned to Zaius, as both were about to leave. "Virdon is no use to us anymore," he said. "I am going back to the castle and kill him."

There was a pleasant bridge over a babbling stream in the country some distance from the city. Virdon, Arn, and Kraik, along with Burke and Galen, crossed the bridge.

Burke still carried his rifle. On the other side, they all paused. Virdon looked quizzically at Arn. "Is that the farm?" he asked.

Arn looked off in the distance, to a pleasant, quiet farm. A few animals grazed, but no humans were visible.

For the moment, Arn didn't trust herself to speak. She nodded. Kraik looked around distrustfully. He was on unfamiliar ground, outside of the city.

"Tomar's brother—what was his name?" asked Virdon.

"Durlin," said Arn.

Virdon nodded to Burke and Galen, who immediately headed for the farm as Virdon, Arn, and Kraik watched them for a moment. Kraik looked around uncomfortably. "It's so quiet," he said.

"Peaceful," said Arn.

"You do feel all right coming back here?" asked Virdon.

Arn nodded. "Yes. It's different, now," she said. "I can't explain. Maybe because Kraik's with me, maybe because I'm not alone, inside myself."

"Why don't you stay with us?" asked Kraik, looking up at Virdon.

Virdon hesitated. He made no reply.

"He can't," said Arn.

"Why?" asked Kraik.

Arn shrugged, resigned to the situation.

Virdon looked at them both. "You'll like it here," he said. "You, too, Kraik. You'll get plenty to eat."

"Every day?" asked Kraik, unbelieving.

Virdon grinned. "If you behave yourself." He glanced off in the direction of the farmhouse. Burke and Galen stepped into view with Durlin, the farmer, and were evidently hitting it off all right. Burke signalled "okay" back to Virdon.

Arn, Kraik, and Virdon saw Burke's signal. The blond astronaut held out his right hand to Kraik and they shook. "There are two times to shake hands," said Virdon. "When strangers meet, and when friends say goodbye."

Virdon put his arm around both Arn and Kraik. "God bless you both," he said emotionally.

Arn took Kraik's hand and led him off toward the farm, leaving Virdon alone, watching. Burke and Galen moved away from Durlin, coming back toward Virdon. Durlin took a step to go with them but stopped. At that moment, Arn and Kraik moved into the scene. Burke and Galen smiled at the two and continued walking. Durlin embraced Arn, while Kraik stood by, still slightly uncomfortable.

Galen and Burke joined Virdon by the bridge. They watched until Arn, Kraik, and Durlin had walked out of sight. Virdon was deeply preoccupied. Burke tapped him gently on the shoulder to pull him from his reverie. Virdon nodded, and the three friends prepared to move off. Burke glanced at the rifle he carried, and shrugged ruefully. "Love to keep this," he said.

"Any ape that sees you with a gun, though—!" said Galen.

"Yeah," said Burke. "Instead of shooting at a target, I'd be one!" He chucked the rifle into the stream. Virdon paused for a final look at the farm. He showed satisfaction at Arn's safety, tinged with a small regret. He shrugged then, and gestured to the others that they all start off. They had a long way to travel.

THE HORSE RACE

5

Galen, Burke, and Virdon had no destination in mind. They rarely did. Sometimes in their travels they made friends who suggested others who might be hospitable. But more often, the three fugitives took their chances with luck and fate, keeping their eye open to danger and taking no unnecessary risks.

But sometimes, even caution was little defense against what the forces of destiny planned for them.

The road from Durlin's farm ran along pleasant, shady hills, through fresh fields and quiet forests. The skies varied from deep blue to black and stormy. The terrain changed from the soft floor of the woods to the stony, painful footing of a rocky hillside. But these things were details that the two humans and the chimpanzee gladly accepted as part of their burden. They were predictable and natural. It was only the actions and thoughts of human beings and apes that could not be relied upon.

* * *

Along a country road, dusty with the brown layer that spoke of too little rain in recent weeks, ran a ditch, shallow and choked with dead yellow weeds. The ditch was a drainage channel, but it had been a long while since any water had run off the road and collected there.

The road was being used on this particular afternoon. The sun beat down, almost directly overhead. The air was still and stifling. But none of those gathered along the side of the road seemed to notice, although the individuals, all apes, wore heavy leather garments over their thick, shaggy coats of hair. Two horses, one ridden by a gorilla and the other ridden by a chimpanzee, were racing along the road. The horses and their riders were decorated with colors; these were, in the case of the horses, ribbons woven through the manes of the beasts. Their jockeys wore matching sashes that crossed their bodies from shoulder to waist. The riders were not armed, and they crouched over the necks of the horses in familiar racing fashion.

A wooden platform had been constructed the day before to accommodate the simian spectators of the race. Behind it stood a country garrison of gorilla patrol guards. The viewing stand had been put together hastily by these guards of General Urko's army, and the unimaginative gorillas had not decorated it in any way. There were no seats. The platform was flat, raised, with a railing built around it to keep the spectators from falling. In the front, at the best place to view the race, stood Urko himself, along with the local prefect, a chimpanzee. They both squinted against the sun, trying to get a better view of the race. Just in front of them on the road was the finish line. Urko seemed very confident, and joked and boasted with the prefect and with the other gorillas, chimpanzees, and orangutans who had been invited to join him. Beside Urko, the prefect stood quite a bit more nervously. He did not share Urko's confidence and easy manner; in fact, the prefect was enormously anxious. The uniformed gorillas behind Urko were enjoying the respite from their military duties. One of these, named Zandar, was speaking in confidential tones to a chimpanzee; the chimpanzee pointed down the road, where the racing horses were raising clouds of dust. Zandar stopped speaking, checked his money pouch, and turned his attention to the race.

Behind the stands, almost unable to see the race at all, a small crowd of humans stood by quietly. Among them was a very tall, muscular black man, who was by occupation a blacksmith in the human settlement nearby. These humans were not permitted to gather idly and watch; they were guarded closely by an armed gorilla at all times.

On the spectator stand, Urko watched the nervous prefect almost as often as he turned his eyes to the thundering horses. He cast an amused smile on the prefect. "Relax," said Urko. "I don't understand why you're acting like this. You're an intelligent ape."

It was abundantly clear to Urko that the prefect would have liked to relax, but it was just as evident that the chimpanzee couldn't. "Yes, Urko," said the prefect unhappily.

"After all," said the general, "it's only a horse race."

"Yes," said the prefect, "with half my horses and half my land bet on the outcome."

"Think how rich you'll be if you win," said Urko.

"If," said the prefect, muttering to himself. He cursed his greed and the circumstances that had almost forced him to enter this foolish race. There was so much risk for the country prefect, and so little for the powerful

Urko. "If," said the prefect, louder. "If!" For another few seconds the prefect added up all of his wealth that he had put on the race. Then he tried to imagine what life would be like without it. That thought made him lose control momentarily. "*You* insisted on the race," he cried. "*You* made the arrangements. *You* demanded the bet! Have you ever lost a race to a prefect?"

Urko ignored the outrage of the chimpanzee, preferring, in the generosity of assured success, to forgive the prefect for his breach in manners. Urko had rarely been more supremely confident. "I will admit that I have been lucky," said the general. "But there's always a first time…"

The crashing hoofbeats drowned out his final words. Everyone's attention was drawn entirely back to the race. The two horses jumped a log barrier and pounded on toward the finish line. The gorilla-ridden horse, Urko's, was slightly in the lead. The two horses neared a spot in the road beside which grew a large tree. The horses sped closer to the tree, the prefect's horse on the tree side of the road. The prefect's horse was still a bit behind Urko's horse, but close enough to make the ultimate victor unsure in the spectators' minds. The prefect began to gather confidence, too. As Urko said, there was always a first time…

As the horses passed beneath the overhanging limbs of the tree, a gorilla hidden in the leafy boughs waited, carefully appraising the proper moment to perform his duty. He held one of the smaller branches, twisted back under tension. The gorilla was hidden from both the jockeys and the spectators by the foliage. At the critical moment, the gorilla loosed the branch which he was holding. It whipped away and down.

The freed branch slammed painfully into the face

of the rider of the prefect's horse, the chimpanzee. The poor jockey was almost thrown from the back of his mount. Frantically, the chimpanzee grabbed blindly at the horse's mane, trying to keep himself from falling to the ground and injuring, possibly killing, himself. The horse was confused and frightened as well, with the branch whistling above its head and the rider on its back sliding and kicking. The horse was thrown off its stride; in a reflex action by the chimpanzee, the horse pulled up and slowed. Urko's horse charged ahead, gaining an insurmountable lead. At last, the prefect's horse was brought under control. Its jockey, frustrated, still kicked up the horse again and took off in pursuit of the other.

The reactions of the spectators were mixed. Those who had bet on the prefect's horse were disappointed. To them it had appeared that some accident or faulty riding had lost the race for sure. Urko and the prefect watched and waited. Urko stared at the horses, almost oozing satisfaction with the way things were happening. "There!" he cried, pointing at his horse as it neared the finish line. "Ah, well, my friend. Better luck next year." The prefect watched the hoses approaching, his whole attitude eloquent of his sagging spirits.

The attention of all the apes was commanded by the two horses, as they closed the distance between them and the finish line. There was no talking among the spectators on the raised platform. They watched Urko's horse, with its commanding lead. The race seemed as good as finished, until the gorilla-ridden horse suffered an accident. The apes saw the horse break stride slightly, and then stumble. The observers with better eyesight saw a horseshoe skidding through the dust, and Urko's horse favoring its lame-leg. The distance between the two horses closed, as the prefect's jockey had never given up hope.

On the reviewing stand, there was a complete reversal of attitudes. Urko, who had previously been so sure of himself and arrogantly confident, now fumed helplessly. He was furious. The prefect looked off toward the horses, hardly believing what his eyes were telling him.

Urko's horse was limping severely now, unable to regain the quick pace it had set before, despite the cruel and vicious punishment it received from its jockey. The prefect's horse took advantage of the situation, passing on the outside of the lame horse and thundering by.

On the stand, Urko watched in a black, silent rage. The gorilla guards with him knew what kind of things happened when Urko worked himself into that mood. They were afraid. The prefect, meanwhile, was oblivious to Urko's anger; he was ecstatic. The prefect's horse crossed the finish line and won the race. A short time later, Urko's injured horse followed. The beast was pulled to a halt by its gorilla jockey.

The prefect couldn't contain his joy. He had won; he had put up most of his worldly possessions on the race, and he had multiplied them when it seemed a hopeless situation. He turned to Urko. "You were right," he said happily. "There *is* a first time!"

"Shut up," said Urko, growling.

While this short conversation took place, the two jockeys handed their reins to volunteer grooms. The gorilla came up to the raised platform. It was obvious that the jockey was frightened. "The horse threw a shoe," he said in a quavering voice.

Urko turned to the uniformed gorilla named Zandar. "Who shod my horse?" he asked.

Zandar thought for a moment, knowing the fate that

Urko had in store for the unlucky person. Still, there was no way to avoid Urko's command. Zandar pointed into the small huddle of humans, at the tall blacksmith. The man saw what was happening and began to back away in fear.

Urko seemed almost bored. "Kill him," he murmured to Zandar.

Zandar nodded briefly, then turned to the gorilla guards oh the platform. He whispered to two of them, and they in turn nodded. They went down the steps and into the crowd of humans. The blacksmith was clearly afraid. The gorillas grabbed him by the arms and dragged him away. Urko watched, frowning. He turned again to Zandar. "There are some things I want you to understand," said the general in a low voice. "First, have that animal shod for the next race. That will be in the village of Venta. Second, understand that if this happens again, I'll not only kill the blacksmith, I'll kill you as well."

Zandar stared at Urko without expression. "Yes, Urko," he said. He moved away to comply with the gorilla's instructions.

There was the sound of a long-handled shovel reaching into the heat of the furnace, shuffling the coals around. The man holding the handle of the tool scooped up a white-hot iron horseshoe and pulled it from the flames. He transferred it to an anvil, where he began pounding the iron into shape with a heavy hammer. The sound of iron on iron filled the small room. The smell of the furnace choked the air. It was a pleasant, honest, hard-working man who labored there, and the shop itself reflected these good qualities. The isolated blacksmith establishment was operated by a human named Martin, about forty years old. He enjoyed the ringing of the hammer on the anvil. He loved the tangy smell of the furnace. When he wasn't working, he missed the waves of heat that rolled over him from the banked coals. He hammered the horseshoe, his face dripping with sweat, his expression happy and serene. He was doing what he loved, and he was doing it well.

Nearby, Alan Virdon stood, soothing a horse tied to a post just inside the open front of the blacksmith shop. Pete Burke operated the bellows to heat the fire.

"It isn't necessary that you work for the little food I've given you," said Martin. "I know my hospitality is poor, but I'm a poor man."

Burke laughed. "In this world, is there any other kind?" he asked.

"It wasn't necessary that you give us food, either," said Virdon, smiling. "You could have sent us away hungry."

Martin was not accustomed to such generosity of spirit. He experienced it rarely; certainly never from the apes who ruled the province, and only on widely separated and memorable occasions like this, from his fellow humans.

Virdon led the horse to Martin, who had completed the horseshoe and was ready to fix it to the animal's hoof. Against one wall, in the shadow of the furnace, sat Martin's son, a boy of sixteen. His name was Greger. He sat with Galen; they conversed in animated tones. Greger spoke in a mixture of curiosity, respect, and veiled defiance. While he talked, he braided a whip out of lengths of leather.

"I've never in my life spoken to an ape before," said Greger, as Galen took the whip from him and braided for a few moments.

"Really?" asked Galen.

"Well," said Greger, "I mean, they've talked at me, and

given me orders, things like that. But never just like you and I are talking. Saying things you feel like saying."

Galen laughed. He could understand what the young human was thinking. "Would you believe that it was years before I talked to a human? Except for giving orders."

Greger shook his head. "Why should apes, give orders?" he asked. "Why must we obey?"

"There are two answers," said Galen. "There is my answer, and the one you'd get from the gorilla police. Mine isn't enforced, and the police have bullets behind theirs, so you'd better accept the police answer."

Suddenly, Galen stopped speaking. He looked up, a frown on his face. He sat motionless for a few seconds, listening. Then he cried, "Alan! Pete!"

Virdon and Burke reacted violently to Galen's call. They had come to rely on him in their travels. He had proven time and again that their senses were much duller than his; they needed the chimpanzee to warn them of danger. "Horses," he said softly. Greger and Martin watched. They, like the two astronauts, could hear nothing yet. Martin looked at Virdon; the blond man nodded. Just then the sound of hoofbeats came clearly to the humans.

"You'll be safe behind the barn," said Martin.

"Come on," said Burke, as the two humans and their chimpanzee friend hurried out of the blacksmith shop.

Along the narrow, tree-shaded road that led from Zandar's garrison to the shop, two mounted gorillas rode. One of the apes was Zandar, the other an armed patrol guard. They were not riding fast, because they led Urko's race horse, which limped behind them. They stopped in front of Martin's place.

Martin came out of his shop, wiping his hand on his apron. He raised one hand to shield his eyes against the sun and looked up at the two gorillas. Greger had moved to his father's side. Together, they waited for the apes to speak. Martin's attitude and posture were very deferential, but Greger's was less so.

Zandar dismounted and handed the reins of his horse to his gorilla companion. Then Zandar took the reins of Urko's horse and approached Martin. "This is General Urko's favorite horse," said Zandar importantly. "The animal has thrown a shoe. Otherwise, it seems to be unhurt."

Martin nodded. "I'll take care of him well, sir," he said.

Zandar laughed, but there was no humor in the sound. "Of course you will," he said. "If you want to go on living. I'll be back tomorrow. If you've done a bad job, I won't risk Urko's anger by telling him about you. I'll have you killed myself."

Martin's face paled under the threat. Shoeing a horse wasn't a difficult job, under normal circumstances. But even a workman with the experience of Martin could have doubts when presented with Zandar's threat. "Yes, sir," said Martin hoarsely.

Zandar turned, his business with the humans temporarily at an end. He mounted his own horse again; the two gorillas were about to ride off, when the patrol guard raised a hand. Zandar stopped, curious, while the guard addressed Greger. "There have been eyewitness accounts of a young human riding a horse near here," said the guard.

Greger stared at the guard unflinchingly. The youth knew the severe penalty for any human caught riding a horse. And Greger knew that, as the son of a blacksmith, he was a prime candidate for those charges. But his words were unwavering, and his voice strong as he answered. "A human riding a horse?" he said in mock surprise. "He must be crazy. Why would anyone take a chance on being shot, just to ride a horse?"

"Come along, Zilo," said Zandar impatiently. "We're wasting time bickering with these humans."

The guard prepared to ride off, but he had a final word to speak to Greger. "Perhaps this young human *is* crazy, as you say," said Zilo. "In any case, he'll be dead if he's caught."

Zilo nodded to Zandar, and the two gorillas kicked up their mounts and rode off in the direction they had come. Greger stared after them for a moment in silent thought. Then he took the reins of Urko's horse from his father and led the horse toward the corral. Martin, concerned over Zilo's warning, hurried after his son.

"Greger!" he cried. "It's just as I've been warning you myself. You've been seen. Worse than that, someone has reported you to the police. Son, how many times do I have to repeat it? It's death for a human to ride a horse. The next time, those gorillas might come here bringing me your dead body. What will I do then?"

Greger dismissed his father's worries with a wave of his hand. "Father," he said, "being seen is not being caught. There is no proof that the gorilla's report meant me. It could be someone else. Don't worry, Father. I'm careful."

Martin shook his head. He wished that he could get Greger to see how terrible the situation might become. It didn't seem worth it to Martin. He wore a worried expression and moved away from the corral, deep in thought.

Greger was at the age when he believed that he could govern himself without interference from parent or police. Of course, Martin was very rarely stern with the boy. Martin remembered what it had been like when he was that age. Still, it seemed to him that Greger was not as wise as the boy liked to think he was.

Martin approached the barn, behind which Virdon, Burke, and Galen were still hiding. He called out softly. "It's all right," he said. "They've gone."

Around the corner of the barn was a tall pile of firewood. Virdon, Burke, and Galen had crouched behind it. They had not seen the gorillas or heard the conversation. Now, at Martin's call, they stood up. Virdon and Burke walked toward Martin, with Galen behind.

Martin was still worried about his son, but these guests had become friends in the short time they had known Martin. The blacksmith did not want to burden them with his own worries, so he tried to suppress his concern. "The apes weren't after you," he said. "It was something about a horse that had—" Martin was interrupted by a shrill scream.

The cry had come from nearby, behind Virdon and Burke. They turned to look, and they saw Galen. The chimpanzee was on the ground, crawling toward them. He was looking over his shoulder at something; when he turned to face the astronauts, Galen's face registered terror.

Neither Virdon nor Burke could understand what had so horrified Galen. They ran toward him and followed his pointing finger. They saw an evil-looking scorpion crawling away from the pile of firewood, close to where Galen had crouched. "Look at that thing," muttered Virdon.

Burke was bending down, trying to get some coherent words from the frightened chimpanzee. "All right," said the dark-haired man, "What happened?"

Galen was still too much in shock to speak plainly. Burke knelt beside him, and Virdon joined him.

"What's wrong?" asked Virdon.

Galen was too weak to answer. He pointed, back in

the direction of the woodpile, then collapsed completely. Virdon stood and went to look again. The insect was gone. Virdon looked at Burke, and both men were becoming greatly alarmed.

"What is it?" asked Martin, who still did not know what the cause of the confusion was. He hurried to Virdon's side, by the woodpile. He had never before been concerned about an ape, but this friendly chimpanzee was evidently a companion of the two men.

"It was a tiger scorpion," said Galen at last. His voice was weak and barely audible. "I tried to get away from it without making any noise. I didn't want the gorillas to hear me."

"I should have warned you that there were scorpions near the barn here," said Martin regretfully.

Virdon hurried back to his friend. Burke looked up at Virdon, and suddenly the seriousness of the situation dawned on both of them. Burke ripped the leg of Galen's trousers, having a difficult time with the heavy leather. Virdon prepared to apply first-aid.

Galen tried to raise his arm, to make a gesture, but discovered that he couldn't. He only croaked out a couple of words. "No use," he said.

Burke looked frightened. He didn't like the tone of Galen's voice. "What do you mean, 'no use'?"

Martin answered, so that Galen would not have to use his little remaining strength speaking. "Without the proper serum," said the blacksmith, "the bite of the tiger scorpion is fatal. Always."

"You should have done something, Galen," said Burke. "We could have handled the gorillas easier."

At this point, Greger rounded the corner, attracted by Galen's scream. He arrived just as his father spoke and instantly understood the situation. "Your friend the ape is dead without that serum," said Greger.

"Where can we get it?" asked Virdon.

Greger was still unsure that two human beings could be friends with any ape. He didn't know whether he would want to help one, no matter how much the ape suffered. "Town," said the youth curtly.

"Okay," said Burke. "Hang in there, Galen."

Burke was ready to race off toward the town, which he didn't even know the name of. He was stopped by Greger. "It's five miles," said the boy. "By the time you got there and back again…"

Virdon spoke up. "Martin," he said, "I'm going to, uh, 'borrow' one of the horses."

"What?" cried Martin. The idea outraged and frightened him, for Virdon's sake.

"It's Galen's only chance," said Virdon.

Martin shook his head doubtfully. "You'd never get to the town without being seen."

"What other choice is there?" asked Virdon.

"My father is right," said Greger. "This chimpanzee is so important to you, that you'd risk almost certain death for him?"

"He is our friend," said Burke. "That ought to be enough."

"I've ridden before," said Virdon. "Maybe—"

"I'll take a horse and go," said Greger.

"No way," said Burke. "If any human takes a chance on riding for that serum, it'll be Alan or me. Galen is *our* friend."

There was a moment's pause. Greger looked down at the suffering Galen. "I'd like him to be mine, too," he said. There was no reply from Virdon or Burke.

"Believe me," said Greger, "I know a back way. I've done it before, you haven't. I can be there and back in no time. I'll bring the serum. You two probably wouldn't make it and Galen would die. Then you'd have caused two deaths for certain, and probably left the third to be discovered, not to mention the penalty that would fall on my father and myself."

There was a quick exchange of looks between Virdon and Burke. What Greger said made a good deal of sense. Neither of the astronauts had ever been to this town, while Greger said that he rode there often. Finally, bowing to the logic of the situation, the two men nodded their agreement.

Greger ran back to the barn to prepare a horse for the journey. Virdon and Burke lifted the now unconscious Galen. Martin led them toward the barn, where they could prepare a sick bed for Galen without the risk of being spotted by gorilla patrols. Greger had placed an old, cracked saddle on the back of a horse, and had mounted it. Without a word of warning or farewell, Martin watched his son walk the horse from the barn. The blacksmith turned to stare at Galen, and at the chimpanzee's two strange human friends. Martin heard the sound of the horse's hooves as Greger rode away. "If only he hadn't moved," said Martin. "If only Galen had remained still. The scorpion never bites if you just don't move." He spoke to himself, and received no answer or comment from Virdon and Burke, who hovered over Galen, unsure what to do.

Martin rubbed his eyes wearily. Outside, the sound of Greger's horse had died away. All was silent. The blacksmith thought about his son, and about the gravely ill Galen. He didn't know if his greatest concern was Galen's scorpion bite or the danger which now centered upon his son as a result of it.

* * *

Greger was true to his word. Avoiding the road and the settlements of the humans and poorer apes, he rode the horse across fields and through stands of trees on the way to the town. He ducked beneath low-hanging limbs and raced his horse through narrow streams. Soon he neared the village of Venta.

Because the area was horse country, although apes alone were legally permitted to ride them, the town had a feed and grain store, a saddlery, and other related shops on its main street. Some human workers carried sacks of grain from a cart into the feed store. Outside a livery stable, two apes were engaged in a spirited bit of horse trading. The saddlery displayed plain but functional equipment; the apes had little taste for decorative or non-useful items. As in every small town in the ape world, humans appeared on the streets only as servants or slaves of the ape masters. It appeared to Greger, however, that there was an abnormal amount of activity in the town for that particular time of day. He shrugged, putting the matter out of his mind. He had other things to do.

Greger stopped at the end of the main street and considered. It would be foolish to ride up to the doctor's office. He made a wide detour, heading back out of town a short distance. He did not dare go too far, because time was short; but he knew well the limits of safety.

Greger rode beyond the furthest building of Venta, back into a dark, wooded area. He directed the horse into a deep cut. The horse shied a bit at climbing down the embankment, but Greger urged it forward. He dismounted and tethered the horse to a tree, then hurried back toward town.

He ran as fast as he could; the distance was less than a quarter mile, but Greger was out of breath when he arrived at the doctor's office. That was good. It would make his story seem more believable; after all, he wasn't allowed to ride a horse. He would have had to run all the way from the blacksmith shop.

The clinic was a whitewashed building near the center of the main street. As Greger arrived, a bandaged ape was led from the entrance by a uniformed ape nurse. Greger knocked at the entrance door and waited. After a moment, the door was opened by another ape nurse in a blue smock.

"Well, human?" asked the nurse, looking, displeased at having been interrupted in her work.

"Excuse me," said Greger with mock deference, "but my brother was bitten by a tiger scorpion."

The nurse's expression did not change. Greger might just as well have announced that it was going to rain. "How long ago did this happen?" she asked.

"It wasn't very long at all," said Greger. "Minutes. As soon as it happened, I ran here."

The nurse looked at Greger for several seconds. She was plainly perplexed. "Are you telling the truth?" she asked. "If it has been longer, the serum will not help him. It costs money, you know."

"I am telling the truth," said Greger.

The nurse sighed. She had so much responsibility, and the humans only made her job more difficult and more complicated. "I never know when humans are lying or telling the truth," she muttered. "Ah, well, the prefect has ordered that the humans be kept healthy. Wait here."

Greger nodded. The nurse disappeared into the clinic. It seemed that everything was going well. The only problem would be whether the serum would reach Galen in time. Greger began to fret impatiently. He glanced down the street, fearing to see a gorilla guard that might be suspicious. He saw none.

At the end of the street was a small, open, sparsely furnished house. It belonged to the prefect of the district, a chimpanzee named Barlow. During the day, Barlow kept his official office hours in his house. Now, Barlow stood by a large window, staring out at the busy town. He frowned as he watched, evidently unhappy about something. One hand rested on the window sill, but the other tapped nervously against the wall. Behind Barlow, a door opened. At the sound he turned to see who had entered. It was his aide, a human named Dath, carrying a saddle.

The human bowed his head slightly in recognition of Barlow's authority. "Here's your new saddle, Prefect Barlow," said the aide. "It just came in."

"Fine," said Barlow. He came around his desk, toward Dath. He took the saddle from him.

It was a good saddle, an expensive piece of equipment that Barlow had ordered specially, all the way from Central City. He examined it, pleased at first; then, gradually, he became unhappy again. "It's no use," he said. "We have no chance of winning the race. Urko's horse will win as usual."

"It doesn't seem fair," said Dath.

Barlow stared at Dath bitterly. "Fair?" he cried. "When has Urko ever been fair? Look at the way he had me transferred here, from my native village. Urko has never been fair. He has no need to be. He is Urko."

There was a strained, uncomfortable silence in the office. Then Barlow spoke again, brooding. "And the stakes in the race!" he said. "Can you believe it? Half my horses, and half my lands, if I lose! And of course I'll lose!" Wearily, the prefect of Venta sat at his desk.

Greger still waited outside the clinic. He wondered for a moment if the nurse had forgotten him. He did not know what kind of routine was involved in getting the serum for humans. For a moment, he pictured how difficult it would be to explain to his father and the two strangers just why he came back empty-handed.

At last the door to the clinic opened again. The nurse stood there, holding a vial. "Here is the serum," she said.

"Thank you," said Greger. He didn't even wait for instructions, but dashed off down the street, toward the place where he had concealed his horse. He turned down a small alley and headed for the woods. The nurse stared after him for a moment, then shrugged and returned to her work. She didn't particularly care whether the serum saved a human life or not.

Zandar, accompanied by three gorillas, walked their horses slowly through the gloom of the forest. It was pleasantly cool and quiet among the trees. They stopped when Zandar raised a hand, near the mouth of a small arroyo. Zandar reined up and dismounted tiredly. "We'll make camp here," he said. "I suppose we could go on to the village and stay there, but I've learned from experience. There will be too many loud-mouthed humans there, for the races. Urko and his races. Sometimes I wish the whole thing was someone else's problem."

The gorillas began unloading their gear from the horses. One of the gorillas began gathering firewood in various sizes. Another set out to find a supply of fresh water. Zandar just sat on the ground, his back against a large tree. None of them saw Greger as he appeared above them, on a ledge overlooking the arroyo's mouth. When Greger caught sight of the gorillas, though, he froze. For a moment he panicked; then he forced himself to think calmly.

Greger remembered his father's warnings, and then he recalled how his father always taught him to be cautious. Greger decided to take things slowly and reason them out. He watched the apes as they prepared their camp. So far, Greger was in no immediate danger or trouble. He wanted to keep it that way. Greger's horse was tethered not far down the arroyo, at the closed end.

Greger thought and arrived at his decision. He tucked the vial of serum inside the waistband of his trousers. Then he looked up at the sky, as though there might be some help coming from that quarter. There was no more time to waste. Greger took a deep breath and moved as silently as he could along the ledge. He moved above the heads of the apes. They did not see or hear him. He stopped when he was directly above his horse. He looked down and measured the distance carefully, then slipped quietly into the arroyo. Some gravel fell with him, making more of a noise than the boy did himself. Then, worse, when Greger approached, the horse whinnied in recognition.

Several yards away, at the apes' camp, the noises broke through the stillness of the forest. The gorillas reacted; in the calm quiet, the sounds had the force of an explosion. Zandar and Zilo moved toward the noises, curious.

Zandar pointed, and Zilo moved to the other side of the narrow opening. Together they moved into the arroyo. Then, suddenly, Greger rode wildly out of the arroyo, right through the apes, scattering them. At the same time he let out a kind of war whoop as he rode by.

"It's a human!" shouted Zandar. "It's a human on a horse! Did you see his face?"

"I'm not sure," said Zilo. "It looked to me like the son of that blacksmith. The one I threatened."

"Should we chase him?" asked one of the other gorillas.

Before Zandar could reply, the fourth gorilla had retrieved his rifle and raised it. He aimed at the rapidly moving rider; it was a difficult shot, because of the distance and the trees. The gorilla fired, but the shot only tore through the thick foliage far to Greger's left.

"Mount up!" cried Zandar. "Ride after him! Shoot to kill!"

The apes scrambled onto their horses, checked their weapons, and spurred their mounts after Greger. The chase was wild and dangerous, for riding at high speed through a forest was an invitation to a broken neck.

Martin had a small hut between his blacksmith shop and the barn. There was only one large room, where Martin and Greger slept, ate, and rested after the day's work. Galen had been moved into the hut from the barn. He lay on Martin's bed, moaning deliriously. Burke sat by him, feeling the chimpanzee's pulse. Virdon paced the floor. Martin stood by the large open window, staring out, depressed and anxious.

Outside, the day was still warm and silent. There was nothing in the air to show the strain of the day's events; far away, crops grew. Birds wheeled in the sky overhead. Only the sound of horse's hooves made Martin watch the road anxiously. Would it be Greger? Or a squad of gorillas?

Greger, his horse limping, rode into the barnyard. Martin, Burke, and Virdon ran out of the hut to meet him. "You made it!" cried Burke jubilantly.

"Good work, Greger," said Virdon.

"Greger," was all that Martin could say.

The youth was still breathing hard from the chase. He slid off the horse and staggered a little. Then he reached into his trousers and handed the vial of serum to Burke, who dashed immediately to the house. Virdon remained outside only long enough to put his hand on Greger's shoulder and say, "Thanks. For Galen." Then Virdon, too, turned and ran toward the hut where the sick chimpanzee rested. Martin came nearer to his son and looked at him; on the father's face was gratitude that Greger had succeeded, safely. But Martin's expression changed when he saw what his son was pointing to.

"What's that?" asked Martin, although he knew very well what it was.

"A wound," said Greger. Martin was silent for a moment, very afraid to continue the conversation. He knew there was trouble here for them both.

"The horse!" said Martin finally. "What happened?"

Greger was still shaken by his narrow escape. He recalled the events of the last hour; it seemed to him that a great deal more time had passed than that. He felt that he had aged a full year in the space of sixty minutes. He knew that the details of the scene would only fret his father needlessly. "It's only a flesh wound," he said, trying to make light of the affair.

"I can see that," said Martin. "But the point is, for the horse to have been wounded, there must have been a great deal more happening. Now we *are* in trouble!"

Greger was impatient with his father, who always seemed to see things in their worst possible aspects. "It's not serious, Father," said Greger. "The bullet was deflected by the shoulder blade. The horse will be all right." He turned and rubbed the wounded area. The horse made a soft nickering sound. Greger managed a bit of a grin. "After all," he said, "just be glad they missed me."

"Who missed you?" demanded Martin. "Where? When?"

Greger just shook his head and began working over the horse's wound.

Inside the hut, Virdon had taken the serum from Burke and was preparing to administer it. He had poured the serum from the vial into a large spoon. Burke held Galen's shoulders and head up from the cot, to receive the medicine. Virdon put the bottle down and brought the spoonful of serum to Galen's lips. At first, the delirious chimpanzee had no idea what was happening. Galen believed that he was being threatened. He swung an arm weakly at his imagined attacker. Virdon raised the spoon and brought it back out of Galen's reach without spilling any of the serum. Burke held Galen's arms; with his free hand, Virdon forced open the chimpanzee's mouth, and then deftly, slipped the dose of serum down Galen's throat. Galen made a face, snorted, and swallowed. Almost immediately, the exhausted ape relaxed and went to sleep.

Burke let him lie back; the astronaut sat on the floor beside the bed, struggling to control his emotions. Both men watched the still form of the chimpanzee. Galen's face seemed peaceful. Virdon began pacing the room, thinking.

"Martin says the serum works within half an hour," he said.

"*If* it works," said Burke. "You know ape medicine."

"We've had experience with ape doctors before," said Virdon in agreement, thinking back over their long road since crashing in this strange world. "I suppose I'll go see if I can help with the horse." Virdon went outside, leaving Burke alone with Galen.

Virdon was a good deal more worried than he wanted to reveal to his friend. Ape medicine was an incomplete science; much of the knowledge that humans had discovered had been lost, and in the practice of medicine, the apes relied just as much on superstition and magic as they did scientific judgment. Virdon emerged from the hut, but he stopped in the yard as he saw the scene before him. Greger was working on the horse's shoulder, while Martin looked on, obviously worried, nervous, and fidgety. Virdon guessed that something serious had happened during Greger's journey, something the astronauts still knew nothing about.

Virdon decided that the best thing would be to find out just what happened. When the situation concerned horses, humans were immediately put in jeopardy. If that was the case, on account of Galen and the astronauts' worry for their friend, Virdon thought he ought to help wherever possible.

"Let me at that, Greger," he said. "I'm an old hand with horses."

For a moment Martin looked at Virdon sourly; he blamed the blond man for bringing trouble. Then Martin's common sense took over. Greger stepped aside and Virdon began examining the horse's wound.

Virdon felt a chill spread through him as he saw what had happened. There was a creased wound on the horse's shoulder, the path of a bullet. The bullet itself was still lodged against the horse's shoulder blade. As Virdon explored the wound, the horse flinched and reared. Virdon knew that the horse was in little danger; it was the implications of the wound that worried, him. For the bullet to be there, a gorilla had to have fired it. Virdon didn't like that at all. "Let's get this animal into the stable," he said. "I'll sterilize my knife and dig it out."

Virdon said nothing about how the horse came to be wounded. He felt that if Greger wanted to talk about that, he would. Virdon contented himself for the present with moving to the horse's head and taking the reins. He led the horse away, toward the barn. Virdon walked the animal slowly, with Greger and Martin following behind. Before the three humans could get the horse safely into the barn, there was the thunderous sound of horses on the road behind them. They turned to look; Virdon felt his blood run cold a second time as he watched Zandar and his companions, on Greger's trail, ride into the yard. No one said a word. Zandar got off his horse and handed the reins to one of the other gorillas. He walked to Virdon, who was still holding the reins of the wounded horse.

"Was it you riding a horse?" asked Zandar fiercely. "Do you deny it?"

Virdon would not be flustered. He had been in worse situations, and Zandar's aggressive manner did not impress the astronaut. He remained calm, thinking of bluffing through the situation. "I don't deny anything," he said. "This horse has been wounded. It must be taken care of."

With those words, Virdon moved as though to continue. He turned his back on Zandar and started forward, urging the horse toward the barn. Greger looked at Martin, but the blacksmith had nothing to suggest. The two humans followed Virdon for a couple of steps, until Zandar stopped them all.

"Halt!" cried Zandar. "Stop right there, or my guards will shoot you down where you stand. We have plenty of horses. A wounded horse is of no importance to me." Zandar turned to Zilo. "Arrest him!" he said. "Take him to the village. We'll have to make an example of him."

Zilo nodded. He was clearly pleased at having the chance to harass the humans. He gave Greger an ugly look. "I'll take the son, too," he said with an evil grin. "He's probably guilty, too. We have witnesses in town."

"You do not!" cried Martin. He was ignored.

Zilo jumped down from his horse and moved toward the humans, who still faced the barn. They had not moved since Zandar ordered them to remain still. The other two gorillas dismounted as well, and they seized Virdon. Zilo came toward Greger; the youth stepped forward, holding up a hand. "Let him go," he said. "I rode the horse."

The look on Zilo's face was terrible to see. There was an evil satisfaction, a fulfilled but horrible longing as he stared at Greger. "So it was you, after all," said Zilo. "I'm glad of that. I told Zandar that it was you. You may win me a promotion. What do you think about that?"

Virdon and Martin looked toward the boy. Their feelings were complex and painful. "Greger," said Virdon pleadingly, "don't do this just to save my neck."

"Please," said Martin. "He's young. He meant no harm. There was no other way."

There was a moment of silence. It was clear to both Zilo and Zandar that the situation had grown better, for the gorillas. Zilo realized that Martin had given the game away. He nodded to Greger. "His own father confirms it," said Zilo.

"Let the other go free," said Zandar.

Zilo and a gorilla dragged Greger and threw him on a horse. The two apes tied Greger's hands and ankles. Virdon was released. Zandar stood apart, overseeing the operation. Finally, Greger was a helpless captive, tossed crosswise across the flanks of the horse, unable to move his arms or legs. Zandar mounted and led the group away, pausing only for one last remark to Martin. "Thank you, old man," he said. "You will be invited to see the execution as part of the celebration, after the race." Zandar laughed. The gorillas wheeled their horses and galloped out of the barnyard. Virdon and Martin stared disconsolately after them. There was nothing they could do.

6

The excitement in the village of Venta grew. Business was concluded and humans and apes went home; the evening meal was eaten in a spirit of anticipation. The day of the race was approaching, and that was for many the high point in an otherwise drab daily existence.

Night fell, and Greger, now confined to the town's stocks, was alone in his miserable and hopeless gloom. The night was chilly; no one either cared or dared to take pity on the youth, and Greger passed a night filled with discomfort and sorrow. The next morning dawned, and once again the inhabitants of the village poured forth, eager and curious. Zandar, followed by his ubiquitous shadow, Zilo, swaggered down the single main street of the town. Wherever Zandar went, he was greeted by respectful citizens and humans. Zandar reveled in the recognition. He demonstrated his power upon the innocent bodies of human slaves. Zilo encouraged him and applauded him.

Zandar reached the stocks and stared for a moment at the imprisoned Greger, locked with his head and hands dangling through the wooden barrier. "Did you sleep well, human?" asked Zandar maliciously.

"Did you expect me to?" said Greger.

"That problem should cause you no further concern," said Zandar, stifling a yawn. "After the race, you'll have no problem sleeping. Ever again." The gorilla was pleased by his own wit, but he did not laugh. He waited for Zilo to do that for him. Zandar just stood by and accepted Zilo's appreciative praise.

At Martin's house, the atmosphere was anxious and tense. Martin himself was a grief-numbed man. He tried to work at his anvil, but his concentration was disturbed. His actions were almost reflexive, occupying no part of his thoughts.

From the hut itself, Virdon and Burke walked toward him. He did not notice them until Virdon spoke. "Galen is recovering fast," said the astronaut.

Martin looked up and nodded. It was evident that, as much as he liked his guests, he was not really interested.

Burke understood the problem. "We want to help Greger," he said. "We owe him that much."

"I could be petty," said Martin. "A small man would say, 'You got my son in this terrible trouble.' I admit, I even thought that last night. But there's nothing to be done."

"There is always something," said Virdon. "Not until Greger, you, Pete, Galen, and myself are dead is there a time to say that nothing can be done."

"If there was any way," said Martin, "anything, would I be standing here, working for the apes?"

"We can talk to the prefect," said Virdon. "Greger rode

the horse to save an ape's life."

"The prefect won't listen to a human," said Martin morosely.

"Then we'll try something else," said Burke.

Martin considered the words of the two men. He realized what good friends they were to him; a few days before, they had been total strangers. Now, they were virtually offering up their lives in an effort to help him. "I don't want you harmed," he said. "You can't help Greger."

"We'll just go into town and look around," said Virdon. "That would be the first step in any event. We need to gather information. We don't even know where Zandar took your son. Venta isn't a special production area, is it? We don't need special identification?"

Martin shook his head, unable to become enthusiastic over the astronauts' offer of aid. He had lived in the area too long, he knew what kind of trouble they were courting. "The new prefect, Barlow," he said. "He lets humans come and go freely."

"Barlow?" asked Burke.

Virdon looked at his friend thoughtfully; the name Barlow had registered on his memory as well as Burke's. Neither of them could place it immediately, however. Virdon was about to ask Martin some more questions, trying to pin down the identity of the prefect, but he was interrupted.

"Barlow?" came Galen's voice, unsteady but much improved. Virdon and Burke turned to see the chimpanzee walking slowly toward them. His movements were still a bit wobbly, but his expression and manner were cheerful. He had returned to his place as a member of their team.

Virdon walked toward Galen, happy that the ape was feeling better but still concerned for his recovery. "You're supposed to stay in bed. You remember what Martin said.

The serum has done its job, and the rest is up to your body. You should be resting quietly."

Galen looked scornfully at Virdon. "I am quiet," he said. "At least, I'm as quiet as I ever am."

"You were a lot quieter yesterday," said Burke. "After you passed out."

Galen ignored that. He turned his attention to Martin instead. "Was this Barlow the prefect at Cela before he came here?" he asked.

Martin thought for a moment. "Yes," he said, "I think he was."

"I thought so," said Galen.

Burke interrupted him. "I know what you're thinking, Galen, my furry friend. But we can talk to him as well as you can. You turn around, head back for the house, and climb back into the sack."

"You only think you know what I'm thinking," said Galen.

"I'm a match for any sick Galen any day of the week," said Burke.

"Barlow is my friend," said Galen. "He'll listen to me."

"We'll tell him we're delivering your message," said Virdon. "We'll say that you're too weak from the scorpion bite to come."

"A great idea," said Burke.

"A terrible idea," said Galen.

"Do you have something better?" asked Virdon.

"To make it more convincing," said Galen, "I'll come along and faint in his presence."

"Very funny!" said Burke, shaking his head. "Galen, I wonder how you got along without us before we met."

"As I recall," said the chimpanzee, "life seemed a lot less complicated."

"I'll bet," said Burke.

Martin had listened to their banter, and in it somewhere he saw a small glimmer of hope. "Is Barlow really your friend?" he asked. "Would he listen to you? Might he save Greger?" The note of pleading in the man's voice was terribly poignant, and his three guests were each moved by compassion.

Galen dropped the light tone he had adopted with Burke, and turned seriously to Martin. "I'll do what I can, I promise you that," he said. "You have to remember that we're fugitives. I don't know how much my request will be honored." Galen turned to the astronauts again. "Let's be on our way," he said.

Burke stared openmouthed. He turned to his friend but he couldn't say anything for a moment. Virdon felt the same thing. "He's stubborn as a… as a—" the blond man had difficulty coming up with a proper comparison.

"He's stubborn as an ape!" said Burke.

Virdon decided to give his argument one last try. "Galen," he said, "be reasonable. Venta is five miles from here. You're just not strong enough to walk that far."

"You have enough trouble when you're perfectly healthy," said Burke. Galen only glared.

"An ape of my wealth and position, with two human servants, doesn't walk," said the young chimpanzee. He adopted a snobbish air. Neither Burke nor Virdon understood what he was hinting at; the two men only looked at each other and shrugged. Galen continued. "May I borrow a horse, Martin?" he asked.

"Oh, yes!" said Martin.

"Fine, then," said Galen, still pretending to be a rich and bored ape from Central City. "You two walk. Maintain a respectful distance behind my horse. After all, even though I enjoy your company, I have to keep up discipline. You humans would be running all over otherwise. It would be chaos."

Virdon and Burke could only exchange looks. Galen loved to play roles; now, though, it seemed necessary. To the two astronauts, it was a tiresome repetition. Whenever Galen played a role, Burke and Virdon also played roles. And they were always the same roles. Slaves.

Some time later, Galen rode into the village on a horse, with Virdon and Burke following meekly on foot, as slaves. Virdon spotted something and gave a small nudge to Burke, who followed his stare. They saw Martin's son, Greger, locked cruelly in the town's stocks. Galen gave no sign that he recognized the youth, but that was consistent with the role that the chimpanzee was playing. As they passed, Greger saw them and recognized his father's friends. He almost called out to them.

Virdon could see that Greger, in his fatigue and loneliness, was about to spoil their deception. He felt sorry for the youth, but for the eventual success of their plan, there could be no connection between Greger and the ape and his "slaves." Virdon made a surreptitious gesture to keep Greger from attracting attention. Greger closed his mouth without saying anything, and Galen rode on, past the boy. Virdon and Burke followed, acting as though they had never seen Martin's son before in their lives. The three fugitives approached the house of the prefect; it had been described to them in detail by the blacksmith.

Inside, in the office, Prefect Barlow sat at his desk, working. Although the time of the race was rapidly drawing near, the prefect still had the daily routines to follow. The inner door opened, and Barlow, glad of the interruption, looked up to see who it was. His aide, Dath, entered.

"There's someone to see you, sir," said Dath.

"Who?" asked Barlow.

"He didn't give a name, sir."

"If he doesn't have an appointment," said Barlow, "I'm too busy."

Dath persisted. "He says he's a friend from Cela."

Barlow stopped his writing. The name of the prefect's home village brought a thoughtful expression to his face. He puzzled over the identity of his visitor for a moment, then gestured to Dath to admit the person. Dath stepped back through the doorway. "Please come in," said the human assistant.

Dath stepped aside as Galen, followed by the two astronauts, crossed the threshold into Barlow's office.

"Thank you," said Galen importantly. "That will be all. Prefect Barlow will want to speak to me in private." Dath understood what Galen meant, and closed the door on his way out.

Barlow immediately recognized Galen and the two humans. He was delighted to have a visit from them, and rose from his chair. He started across the floor toward them, a friendly greeting on his lips, but at the last moment he restrained himself. He waited for a few seconds until he heard Dath closing the outer door; evidently Dath knew when his presence was no longer required, and took the opportunity to go out on some errand of his own.

"It is better that your aide not know who we are," said Galen. "This isn't Cela, after all."

"Galen!" cried Barlow, confident that he wouldn't be overheard. "What are you doing here? You must be mad!"

"Of course," said Galen, smiling. "But nonetheless, I had

to see you. It was only good luck that you're prefect here."

"I see," said Barlow, a little of his enthusiasm dropping away. To the prefect, it was the same old story, one that he had experienced too often, first in Cela, then in Venta. He registered his disappointment that the visit was not purely social, that it had been proven once again that no one ever loved a prefect for himself alone. Barlow moved back behind his desk, behind the official symbol of his power and authority. He stood for a moment, uncomfortably shuffling papers on the desk, staring down at the petty matters that were his life. Then he looked up again at Galen. He sighed; then he sat down and folded his hands on the desk top. "I take it that you're in trouble again," he said.

"No," said Galen, "*we're* not."

"But a friend of ours is," said Virdon.

"Trouble follows you three," said Barlow. "Or else you drag it around. Who is it? What kind of trouble?"

"A human," said Burke. "For riding a horse."

Barlow rubbed his forehead and sat back wearily. The day had barely begun, and already he was faced with a difficult problem. It seemed that people always came to him expecting that he could pardon their friends and relatives from the most heinous crimes., "Oh, that one," he said finally, looking from Galen to Burke to Virdon. "I know the case. Yesterday, wasn't it? He's in the stocks now. That was Zandar's doing. I'm not one for locking someone up in those torture devices, myself."

"He's a good boy," said Virdon.

"I don't doubt it," said Barlow. "Young Greger. It's a pity that *he's* your friend." Barlow shook his head with finality. "There's nothing I can do."

"But he saved my life!" cried Galen.

"What do you mean, there's nothing you can do?" asked Burke.

Barlow looked at Burke silently for a long moment. He wished that the impetuous human could trade places with the prefect, just for an hour. "I meant what I said," murmured Barlow.

"Galen was bitten by a scorpion," said Burke. "He would have died if Greger hadn't come into town for the serum. It's that simple. He broke a law to save an ape's life."

Virdon came up to Barlow's desk. "He did it for one of your own kind!" he said. "It isn't as though Greger stole a horse to go joy-riding around the countryside. This case has too many extenuating circumstances to let the boy die."

"What do you want me to do?" asked Barlow. 'I'm helpless against Zandar,"

"If you explained the situation to Zaius—" said Virdon.

Barlow interrupted him. "Do you want me to appeal to Zaius on the grounds that Greger saved the life of an outlaw?"

Burke was becoming impatient. The meeting was not going as he had expected that it would. "You wouldn't have to tell Zaius that," he said.

"You don't know," said Barlow. "A case like this, I have reports, documents, things that have to be filled out and filed…"

"You could get around all of that if you tried," said Virdon.

"Don't you think I'd like to?" asked Barlow, with genuine anguish in his voice. "Do you think I enjoy watching justice and decency ignored in favor of order and paperwork?"

"Of course not!" said Galen. "Barlow, just be reasonable."

"Be reasonable," said Barlow in a soft voice. He stood up and went to his window. He looked outside. There were apes lounging along the dusty road. They were there every day, whether there was a race scheduled or not. The apes congregated together, with little to do except make trouble for the humans. And Zandar and the gorilla guards did nothing to stop them. The humans bustled about, trying to avoid any confrontations with the apes. Barlow sympathized with them; what a poor life they had to lead, a life of running and avoiding. Apes like Zandar just aggravated the situation, almost encouraging the others to treat the humans in more degrading ways. And the results of all their cruelty crossed his desk as statistics to be sent to Central City. Sometimes the job was more than Barlow could bear. Dath took some of the burden, but the difficult parts of the job could not be delegated. That was something that Galen and his two human friends would never understand; that despite Barlow's own private ideas, his public duty remained.

"There was a time when I tried to be reasonable," he said in a low voice. "Now I'm less reasonable. And more safe." He turned around and faced them again. "I hate it here," he said passionately. "I want to go home. There's a chance that I can—if I keep my record clean."

"Ah," said Burke bitterly, "I see."

Galen looked disappointed. "Is your job more important than Greger's life?" he asked.

Once more Barlow rubbed his weary eyes. How long would Galen and the humans press him? Why couldn't they understand something so simple that even Dath comprehended and felt pity? There was a point at which Barlow knew he was no longer the conscience of his world; he had reached that point long ago.

"It isn't a difficult thing for someone in your position," said Galen.

"I have some sympathy for humans," said Barlow with a great deal of ambivalence. "You know that well. But that is for humans when they behave and know their place. The young one is a fool. He deserves punishment."

"Death!" cried Burke. "For saving Galen's life?"

"No," said Barlow. "For breaking a simple but important law. It's a wonder the horse didn't kill him. Those laws are made to protect humans, also. Only apes know how to handle horses."

"I don't think you really believe that," said Virdon. "I've ridden horses since I was ten years old. That's just another one of your ancient ape bits of old wives' nonsense."

"Humans can't ride like apes," said Barlow. "It's been proven. It has something to do with skeletal structure or something."

Galen snorted derisively. "From what I've heard these last many months, Alan and Pete could have given you quite a long list of things that apes couldn't do. Where they came from, it was proven, too."

"If it makes any difference," said Burke, "I know personally that Alan is as good on a horse as anybody in this world."

Barlow's mouth opened, as he began to reply. Neither Galen nor his two astronaut friends had presented Barlow with an adequate answer to the prefect's challenge. But something made Barlow fall silent once more. He studied the men, thinking. Perhaps, he told himself, perhaps he could use these humans. His attention moved from Virdon and Burke back to Galen.

"I must be certain of some things first," said Barlow. "Before I make any kind of decision, you have to understand that I am in an extremely vulnerable position. Is he telling the truth?"

Galen smiled. "One thing that I came to learn early in our association is that my friends do not lie," he said. "Remember that they are not typical humans."

Barlow nodded distractedly. The beginnings of an idea were forming in his shrewd mind. He didn't have all the details clear as yet, and he was slightly frustrated and tantalized by the possibilities. He remained silent, and his three guests waited patiently. "Let me put it this way," said Barlow to Virdon, "I would be better able to judge things if you would be willing to prove your skill is not limited to talk."

"That seems reasonable," said Galen.

"I am a cautious ape," said Barlow.

Virdon remained still for a moment, studying Barlow. "How does this affect Greger?" he asked. "That was the reason we came here."

Barlow drew himself up, trying to look, like more of an official than a friend. "I am prefect here," he said. "I will handle this in my own way."

"There isn't much time," said Burke. "And Greger's not in your best accommodations, either."

"First, Virdon will ride my horse," said Barlow. "Then we'll talk about Greger."

Barlow, followed by Galen and the two astronauts, went out the back door and along a narrow footpath to a small corral. "That is my horse," said Barlow. "The brown horse with the black mane in the corner. Its name is Woda." Human handlers were working with the horse. Virdon saw that it was a high-strung animal, almost unmanageable. The handlers moved cautiously while putting a bridle on it. There was no saddle. Virdon studied Woda closely, his brow creased in a thoughtful expression. Burke looked first at the horse, then at Virdon. He was obviously worried.

Virdon spoke to Barlow. "He's never been ridden, has he?"

Barlow maintained his poise. He did not want to dupe Virdon into anything, because Barlow was an honorable ape. But, on the other hand, this was a situation out of which Barlow might be able to win valuable rewards. The prefect knew that he had to proceed carefully in order to satisfy both his desires and his sense of honor. "No," he said blandly, "he's a killer. No ape has been able to ride him."

Virdon laughed softly at Barlow's words. It had seemed in the prefect's office that this was to be a simple test of Virdon's riding ability. Virdon could hot understand why the test had to be with a killer horse. After a shrewd, penetrating glance at Barlow, Virdon turned away. His expression was disbelieving, and when he spoke, his voice was calm. "Forget it," he said.

Galen reacted with surprise. He had not expected his friend to avoid such a challenge as this. Barlow had the same reaction. The prefect frowned. "Then you aren't the great rider you say you are," he said. "That makes me unhappy." Barlow's half-formed plans seemed to die there.

Virdon turned back to face Barlow. The astronaut could sense that there was more involved here than the question of the human's riding ability. This test was part of some scheme of Barlow's, and Virdon decided that he could scheme as well as the prefect. "Give me one good reason why I should risk my neck on a wild horse," he said.

Barlow's mouth widened slightly in a brief smile. He knew that Virdon was much more clever than any other human the prefect had known; but nevertheless, he was surprised that Virdon had interpreted the situation so quickly. The time for bargaining had begun. "If you can ride him," Said Barlow, still hedging against making a commitment, "and break him, I may be very helpful to you."

"Here it comes," said Burke.

"Prefect Barlow," said Galen, "this young human may not mean anything to you, but he saved my life. Are you playing games with us?"

Barlow shook his head. "It isn't me who's playing the game."

Virdon looked at Barlow, and saw that the prefect was perfectly serious. The blond man was convinced that the ape was not merely using Greger as a pawn in some devious intrigue. Virdon looked at Burke, then at Galen. The astronaut and the chimpanzee shrugged. "Well," said Virdon, "let's find out what's going on. There's only one way to do that." He turned to Barlow. "All right," he said. "I'll give it a try."

Barlow smiled, evidently very pleased. "I'm glad," he said. "I had a feeling that you would."

"I had a feeling that you had that feeling," said Burke.

Barlow went up to the corral and called to the horse handlers. "Put a saddle on Woda," he shouted. The handlers nodded.

"I'll bet your workmen out there are happy about having to put a saddle on a killer horse," said Burke.

"They're good handlers," said Barlow. "They know how to protect themselves."

"Don't talk like that," said Galen. "It makes me worry for Alan."

"Don't worry," said Virdon, "I know what I'm doing, too."

"I hope so," said Barlow.

The handlers saddled Woda and brought the angry horse to the fence. Virdon climbed the fence and touched the horse's face, then the top of its head, letting Woda nuzzle his arm and get used to his smell. After a while, Virdon began to climb into the saddle. The horse reared; as Woda brought its forelegs down, Virdon slid into the saddle. Woda reared again, nearly unseating Virdon; the blond man was halfway on, but he forced himself into riding position. The handlers prepared to move away. Virdon made a final check of the saddle and bridle. He was all set.

"Let him go!" cried Virdon. The handlers backed away, and Virdon was alone on Woda. The ride was on.

Woda bucked and rolled, trying to dislodge the unpleasant weight on his back. Virdon, who had ridden unbroken horses many times in his childhood and youth, could almost predict what the animal would try next. He shifted his weight and grasped with his legs. Woda snorted fiercely, but Virdon would not be shaken off. When Woda realized this after a time, he stopped bucking and began running. Horse and rider sped across the corral, over the fence, and across the fields in a dead run.

"I don't believe it," murmured Burke.

"But you said that Alan was the best rider in the world," said Galen.

"I was just saying," said Burke. "I wasn't necessarily believing."

"Now you tell me," said Galen.

They watched as Virdon, using the reins, began to guide Woda around the fields, so that the run was no longer a blind, half-mad dash but a controlled gallop.

After a few minutes, when it became evident to those watching Virdon that the astronaut had the horse completely under his command, Burke, Galen, and Barlow were too astonished and elated to speak. As he flashed by the corral, Virdon managed a small smile of satisfaction; he was too busy to speak. Gradually, the exertions took their toll, and Woda slowed down. Virdon let the animal canter about the area, and then walked the horse back toward the corral. The handlers took the hard-breathing Woda. Barlow jumped down inside the corral and ran up to his horse; the prefect threw his arms around Woda's neck. "What a beautiful animal!" said Barlow.

"Have you asked yourself why none of the ape riders were able to do that?" asked Burke.

Barlow turned to Virdon. "That was good riding," he said. "For a human," he added, in a sly voice.

Virdon looked briefly at Burke. Burke just shook his head. "Thanks," said the blond man to the ape. "I'm glad you were watching."

"I don't think I ever saw a horse go so fast in my life," said Barlow. "It was really amazing."

"He is a beautiful horse," said Virdon, turning and walking toward the fence where his friends sat.

"Tired?" asked Galen.

"I'm a little winded," admitted Virdon. "But I haven't had a ride like that in years. It was terrific."

"I'm still amazed," said Barlow.

"Maybe that's because you've never seen a human jockey before," said Burke.

"Jockey," said Barlow, musing. "Why did you say 'jockey' and not 'rider'?"

"Because anyone can ride a horse," said Burke. "But a jockey knows horses."

"Exactly," said Barlow. "I was thinking much the same thing while I watched Virdon put on his excellent display. Now, I have a proposition for you. It ought to be clear that there are things that I want, and I'm perfectly willing to help you, if you'll help me. You know me well enough to realize that I'll stick to my word."

"Of course," said Galen.

"We're not questioning that," said Virdon. "What's the deal?"

"I've been challenged to a race," said Barlow, his expression becoming suddenly intent and serious. "I'm to put up my best horse against the fastest horse in this territory. I want you to ride Woda."

Barlow's announcement hit like a bolt of lightning. There was only stunned silence for several seconds, as the three fugitives considered what the prefect had said. Galen was the first of the three to speak up. "He can't ride in a race," said the young chimpanzee. "He'd be seen. Humans aren't allowed to ride."

Barlow knew that fact as well as anyone. He nodded. "Well," he said, his voice suddenly that of a person formulating a deception or suggesting a conspiracy, "I do have some influence with Zaius. Not a great deal, but enough so that he would listen to my request. I think that I could get him to make an exception, for a single race. What do you say?"

"Is that a deal?" asked Burke.

"As I recall it," said Galen, "a deal has two hands."

"Why should I say anything?" asked Virdon. "I'm not interested in racing."

Barlow held up a hand to stop Virdon. "Wait," he said. "I wasn't finished. Of course, I have something in mind to pay you back for helping me."

"What were you thinking?" asked Virdon.

"Ride Woda in the race," said Barlow, "and I will get Zaius to pardon your friend, Greger. If you win."

There was only a moment's hesitation. "I'll ride," said Virdon. "That's the deal that I expected."

"Just a moment," said Galen. "What if he loses? A good horse and a good rider don't guarantee a win."

Barlow frowned. "I know that," he said. "But I have confidence in Woda, and I have just as much faith in Virdon. I know what I've just seen, and I don't think there's a horse in the territory that could match it."

"What if there is?" asked Burke.

"In that case," said Barlow, "I won't be able to save Greger from Zandar. Your young human friend will die. But if Virdon doesn't ride, then Greger is certain to be shot anyway."

"Yes," said Virdon.

"If you could get a pardon for Greger if Virdon wins," said Burke, "why couldn't you get a pardon if Virdon loses?"

"Virdon's victory will be a wedge," said Barlow. "Something that I can use against Zaius. It's all tied up together. You don't have sufficient knowledge of the workings of the ape mind."

"That's for sure," said Burke.

"But I do," said Galen, "and I agree with Pete."

"You, Galen, don't have sufficient knowledge of the workings of the *official* ape mind."

"Meaning Zaius," said Virdon.

"And meaning me, too," said Barlow, smiling.

"Another thing," said Burke. "Alan, you'll be riding in a race with apes all over the place. And every one of them will be hating the idea of a human on horseback. That's looking for too much trouble in just the right place. I don't like that part of it at all."

"I said I'd arrange for permission," said Barlow.

"A lot of good that will do when a hundred apes start pointing rifles at him," said Burke.

"There will be protection," said Barlow.

"Who will protect him from the protection?" asked Galen.

"I've still got a feeling there's some kind of catch in this," said Burke.

"Remember the joke about why the guy played in a crooked gambling house, Pete?" asked Virdon. "Because it was the only game in town."

"Your jokes haven't improved any in the last few thousand years," said Burke.

Virdon laughed. "What I mean is, you're ignoring the main point. We don't have a choice. I have to try, I have to win. For Greger."

"That's it, precisely," said Barlow.

"Prefect," said Galen, "I hope Woda wins, of course, but I want your written promise that nothing will happen to Alan if he loses."

Barlow nodded. "I promise that I won't interfere in any way with his departure from Venta." There was no mention made of Zandar's potential intervention. But, as Barlow had explained, the prefect's jurisdiction over the gorilla garrison was virtually non-existent. Barlow, in what he thought was a gracious gesture, added to his statement. "The promise applies to all three of you, naturally," he said.

Burke was still dubious. "What about this ape he's going to race against?" he asked. "Will he cause trouble?"

"Why should he?" asked Barlow. "It's only a race."

As if to underscore the naive quality of Barlow's answer, Urko and a party of uniformed gorillas rode into Venta the next morning. Even the garrison of local patrol gorillas moved aside as the powerful general of the ape military forces rode by. It seemed to many who watched that Urko and his troopers made more noise and raised more dust than four gorillas on horseback ought to. There was not a citizen or slave of Venta who did not recognize Urko, and the word of his arrival spread quickly.

The day had only begun, but it was the day of the great race. The excitement that had infected everyone for the previous few days had grown to proportions that had the police and the prefect worried. From Barlow's house, runners with security orders kept entering and leaving.

The front door of the prefect's house opened again, and Galen, Burke, and Virdon emerged. They walked to the street, where Galen's horse had been tied. Galen was about to mount the animal when Virdon glanced down the street. "Wait a minute," said Virdon. He grabbed his two friends and stopped them. They looked in the direction the blond man indicated.

Urko, backed by his three hand-picked soldiers, were slowly approaching on horseback.

"It figures," said Burke. The three fugitives darted for cover around the corner of the house. Several tense moments later, Urko and the troopers rode past, not having seen the trio. Galen, Burke, and Virdon watched Urko go by.

"What's Urko doing here?" asked Galen.

"It could be an incredible coincidence," said Virdon.

"Somehow, I don't believe it," said Burke.

One of Barlow's handlers walked by, leading a horse to a watering trough. Galen stepped forward from his hiding place and spoke to the human. "You," he said imperiously. "Do you know who Urko is?"

"Yes, sir," said the handler. "Of course."

"I just saw him," said Galen. "Does he come to this town often?"

"No, sir. Only for something important. Like the big race."

Virdon had been listening, and the man's words made him more and more unhappy; with a sinking feeling he asked, "You mean the race with Barlow's horse?"

The handler smiled. "Is there any other race?"

Galen dismissed the handler, who led the horse on down the street.

"That Barlow's cute," said Burke. "*He* won't interfere in any way with our departure from Venta. He won't have to. Urko will take care of that!"

"I thought he was our friend," said Virdon.

"*His* friend," said Burke, pointing to Galen.

"We could leave now," said Galen.

"What about Greger?" asked Virdon.

"I said we *could*," said Galen. "I didn't say we should."

"Boy," said Burke, hitting his head with the palm of one hand, "are we ever boxed in! If Alan doesn't ride, Greger gets shot. Welcome to Venta and have a happy day!"

7

Barlow's stomach was bothering him. He had eaten a much smaller breakfast than usual, allowing Dath to finish the fruits and nuts that the prefect was unable to eat. Still, Barlow felt faintly sick. The feeling didn't improve any when Barlow went to his window and saw that Urko and his company had arrived, had taken rooms for their stay, and were walking toward the office of the prefect. Barlow stood by the window, almost hypnotized by the sight of the powerful gorilla swaggering along the street toward him. After a moment, Barlow shook off the effect and sat down at his desk, his face creased with a frown of deep concern. This was the day of the race, and everything about it made Barlow even more miserable.

The prefect of the village of Venta sat and waited for Urko. Barlow folded his hands, intending to stay in that position until Urko arrived. He did not move as he heard the sound of heavy footsteps outside. There was no knock on the door; it just opened, and Urko entered. The gorilla came into Barlow's inner office and stood, staring, for a moment. Then he spoke, "What's this I hear?" he asked.

"What do you mean?" asked Barlow, still sitting, still holding his hands folded in front of him.

Urko almost snarled. "You know exactly what I mean," he said. "Are you seriously thinking of using a human jockey in the race?"

"Ah," said Barlow. "Permission has already been granted by Zaius."

"We are a good distance from Zaius," said Urko, more mildly. "And permission has not been granted by me. What would you do if I said your human could not ride?"

Barlow stared; his upper lip was beaded with perspiration. "I would find another jockey," said the prefect.

Urko laughed. "Of course," he said. "And afterward you'd complain to Zaius. But that wouldn't do you any good. What could Zaius do to me? You're a bigger fool than I thought, Barlow. What chance will a human have against my rider? All Zaius has done is give you enough rope to hang yourself."

"We'll see," answered Barlow tightly.

"Who is this human who's crazy enough to ride against one of Urko's apes?" asked the general.

Barlow shrugged. "What difference dose it make?" he asked. "He's just a human."

Urko nodded. He looked around the room thoughtfully. "Has he ever ridden a horse before?" he asked in a casual manner.

There was a slight pause. "Yes," said Barlow. "He's quite good."

Urko gave the prefect a cruel smile. Barlow had walked right into Urko's trap. "Then you won't object if we raise the stakes a little, will you?"

Barlow perspired even more freely. His hands were still folded in front of him. His mind raced. He didn't see how he could avoid Urko's crafty maneuver. Barlow had already admitted that the human had ridden a horse, in defiance of Urko's own dictates. Barlow tried to stall, but he realized that would do no good. Finally, unhappily, he said, "How much?"

"*All* your horses," said Urko harshly. "If you lose, all your horses. And all your lands."

Barlow was stunned for a moment by the magnitude of what Urko was saying. If Barlow agreed, and lost, he would be reduced to the level of a propertyless human, without anything in the world but his personal freedom and his reputation as an honest ape. The idea of losing everything appalled Barlow, but there was no way to get out of it. "And if I win?" he said tensely.

Urko laughed at the very thought. Barlow and his human jockey, beating Urko's fastest horse, his most experienced rider? The foolishness of the idea made Urko expansive. He wondered what Barlow might be thinking, what greedy visions might be passing through that simple, country ape mind. "What would you like?" asked the general, prepared to be generous.

Barlow had reached the point in the negotiations which he both feared and longed for. This was the reason for the bargaining with Virdon and Galen. This was the reason that he was prepared to risk all that he owned in the world. He dreaded speaking, for fear that Urko would deny him. He summoned up the courage. "Transfer me back to Cela," he said, swallowing hard.

Urko laughed out loud again. Barlow had proven himself to be even simpler than Urko had estimated. With the opportunity to name great sums of money and property, the prefect would settle for such a trivial stake? It seemed outrageous to Urko. It seemed almost as though the prefect had spent too much time in the company of humans. "Certainly," said Urko. "If that's what you want." The gorilla turned his back on Barlow and walked to the door. Barlow watched him go, grateful that the interview was over; the prefect unfolded his hands, which were damp with sweat. Urko, shaking his massive, shaggy head, opened the door and disappeared outside. Barlow swallowed again. He had made a gamble so desperate that he didn't even want to think about it. He just wanted the race to be over.

In a field not far from Barlow's house, Virdon was putting Woda though some jumps and stretch runs, in training for the race. Barlow walked toward the man and horse, along with Galen and Burke. "Beautiful!" cried Barlow. "Beautiful! We're going to win!" The prefect paused a moment. "At least," he said, "I hope we are."

"*You're* going to win," said Burke sourly. "That was some deal you made with us. The world hasn't changed at all. Sometimes I have hope. I meet people, even apes, who are better than people I used to know. It's Alan who wants to get back so desperately. I wouldn't half mind settling down here. But then I always end up finding out that every dream has a lead lining. Barlow, this time, you're it. When Urko spots Alan on your horse, he'll kill him. And me and Galen, too."

Galen was equally as upset. He complained bitterly to the prefect. "I don't understand you," he said. "Don't you feel the least bit guilty about the way you tricked us?"

"Of course I do," said Barlow. "Absolutely."

"Well," said Burke, "I'm glad to hear it. What a big help."

"What could I do?" said Barlow in a whining voice. "I was forced into the race. My future depends upon winning it. Besides, I didn't know for certain that Urko was coming."

"Just like I don't know for certain that my head won't fall off," said Burke.

"I used to boast about honor among apes," said Galen sadly. "You've disgraced our race in front of Alan and Pete."

"That's all right, Galen," said Burke. "I've met humans like him, too."

"That's the problem," said Galen.

"Speaking of honor," said Barlow timidly, "I don't like to spread gossip, but I feel I should warn you. I've heard rumors that Urko's horse doesn't always win by fair means. A friend in Regego told me that Urko resorts to cheating, even if he's clearly ahead."

"Why is it that the news doesn't surprise me?" asked Burke of no one in particular.

"Was that designed to cheer us up?" asked Galen.

"I thought it was important," said Barlow. "After all, I was just trying to be helpful."

"You've already done a wonderful job for us," said Burke.

"I'm sorry," said Barlow. "I couldn't help it."

Burke sighed loudly. "Come on, Galen," he said.

"Where?" asked the chimpanzee.

Burke shook his head, laughing joylessly. "With all that Urko's got going for him, we'd better see if we can jiggle a few odds in our favor."

"What are you going to do?" asked Barlow.

"I don't know yet," said Burke.

"Be careful," said Barlow.

"What can happen?" asked Galen. "We could get

recaptured. We could get shot. That's what *will* happen if we *don't* do anything."

"We might as well take a chance or two," said Burke. "It will help pass the time."

The race course was actually little more than a rough lane going past a small grandstand; the stands had been built a few years before, when Urko began his circuit of racing. They were never used for anything but this yearly race. Right in front of the grandstand were two poles, which indicated the starting line and the finish line. More than half a mile away, out of sight of the grandstand, there was a large tree. The riders raced for the tree, circled it, and came back over the road. Near the two poles by the grandstand Burke was digging a deep hole in the ground. Galen watched to be sure that no one interrupted him; it was still well before the race was to begin, and no one was around. Galen looked like the overseer on some strange job; that was the way Burke and Galen had planned it, to fool any casual observers. While Burke dug, Galen busied himself carving notches in a wooden spool; the chimpanzee reclined on the ground.

"I really do wish that I could help you," said Galen.

Burke looked up from his labor and wiped his sweating face. "I'll just bet you do," he said without malice. "I can see how anxious you are to start shoveling."

"Really, Pete," said Galen. "But we must think of appearances."

"Yeah," said Burke. "Sure."

"If anybody saw *me* digging, they'd say, 'Why are you doing that? That's what humans are for!' Otherwise, I'd give you a hand."

Burke stretched the fingers on both of his hands; blisters

had formed on his palms, at the base of his fingers, from holding the shovel. His back hurt from lifting and throwing the dirt. His chest hurt from the heavy breathing he was doing as he worked. "Cut it out, Galen," he said. "You love it up there and you know it!" Burke leaned on his shovel and took a couple of deep breaths.

For reply, Galen held up his spool. "Well," he said, "I am contributing to the effort. I'm doing everything I can. Even if I don't exactly understand it. Your mind is every bit as devious as Barlow's. Do you think this is really going to help us save Alan?"

'Burke turned back to his digging. "You're getting warm, buddy," he said. "You're getting warm."

Galen was puzzled by Burke's words. "Warm?" he said, not able to find the slightest meaning in the word that had to do with their present situation. "I'm not the least bit warm."

"Then just keep cool," said Burke, throwing a shovelful of soil out of the hole.

"Is that another of your ancient human expressions?" asked Galen. "I wish there were some way you could warn me when you were going to use one. You know how much trouble I have understanding you and Alan sometimes." Baffled, Galen gave up trying to figure Burke's words out, and resumed carving notches in the spool.

Outside the village, at Martin's homestead, there was the loud ringing of metal on metal. In Martin's smithy, the man was shaping a horseshoe on his anvil. Virdon hovered nearby, watching the process critically.

"How is this?" asked Martin.

"Thinner, Martin, thinner!" said Virdon. He was becoming frustrated; he knew that Martin was, too. "A race horse must have thin, lightweight shoes on its feet."

"Urko's horses don't," said Martin. "And they always win. His horses wear the same shoes as any other horse."

Virdon jabbed his finger in the air to underline what Martin had just said. "That's the point!" said the astronaut. "That's where we have the advantage. In a race, every little bit helps. Even Urko understands that. We have to find our slight winning edge in places like this."

"I don't pretend to understand," said Martin. "But if it will help to save my son, I will do anything." He continued to shape the shoe to Virdon's specifications, and the astronaut bent closer to watch.

About a third of a mile from the finish line on the rural road, there was a rugged and rocky stretch. There was a jump across the race course, a kind of fence across the track, partly covered with foliage. Several gorillas, led by Urko, were making a tangle of vines just beyond the jump, where the horses in the race would land as they came over the fence. Urko supervised the operation, and he was a difficult taskmaster.

"Tangle them up," he cried. "Leave the way open at the side, though. Kagan will be told to ride my horse across there, where he will be clear of the vines. The human will be stupid enough to jump across the middle. I want to be certain that he falls." The gorilla general walked closer, inspecting the work. "More vines here!" he shouted angrily. "Make the tangle thicker!" Gorillas hurried to comply with his orders. Urko stood by impatiently, ordering his soldiers about viciously. After a while, the trap had been set to his satisfaction. Even then, Urko did not smile.

* * *

Near the grandstand, Galen was perched on a stump, fashioning something from a piece of wood, according to Burke's instructions. Burke came to the hole he had dug; he was carrying two large, heavy pails of water. He dumped the water into the hole, which was about half full. He put the pails down and took a deep, exhausted breath.

"Sometimes I question your judgment," said Galen. "First you had me make a spool with notches in it. Now I'm doing this. I'd think more direct action was called for."

"That's the difference between humans from my time and apes from this time," said Burke. "You apes have a lot of power, but you're not subtle. Maybe that comes from being bigger and stronger than humans. You think the solution to every problem comes in bashing someone over the head."

"It worked, didn't it?" asked Galen. Burke was silent. The chimpanzee wondered what the human was thinking.

"It worked," said Burke at last. His tone was sad and lonely. "I don't know why."

"I don't, either," said Galen. "But I think that it could help us here. Force, I mean."

"What are you complaining about?" asked the human. "I'm the one who's doing all the hard work."

Galen realized that Burke was under a great strain, and the ape was wise enough not to allow the situation to degenerate into a quarrel. That was the last thing in the world that they needed at this point. He busied himself with the little object he was carving. With a few more cuts, the block of wood began taking on a definite shape; Galen was making a fake scorpion.

In Martin's smithy, work had gone on until Virdon was satisfied with the strange, light shoes. Martin's face was blackened with soot, and sweat had run down, making little vertical stripes. He was now hammering the shoes to Woda's hooves. Virdon watched while Martin worked; finally, the blacksmith drove the last nail and stepped back.

"That's fine, Martin," said Virdon. "With those shoes, Woda will go like the wind and still have his hooves protected from the rocks along the race course. His legs won't tire as quickly as Urko's horse, because Woda won't have to lift as much weight with every step."

Martin looked at Virdon with a mixture of hope and worry. "I still don't see how you hope to beat Urko," he said. "His horses never lose."

Virdon put a hand on Martin's shoulder. "I can understand how you feel, Martin," he said. "You have every reason to be worried. I'm sorry that you've had to be put through this trouble; some of it we brought on you ourselves. But we're doing everything we can to overcome it, and we need your help. We'll do all right as long as you don't give up hope."

"Even if you do win," said Martin, "what's to keep Urko from killing you for daring to ride a horse?"

Virdon straightened the reins over Woda's head; the horse shied a little, and Virdon calmed the animal. "We don't intend to rely on his generosity or love for humans," he said, preparing to mount the horse. "I'm not about to ride up to Urko and see whether or not he shoots me. I know him too well for that. We have one or two tricks of our own up our sleeves."

"I know you are trying to help Greger," said Martin, "but if you trick Urko, surely my son will pay."

Virdon looked into Martin's eyes. The blacksmith was fearing for the life of his son, and a thousand doubts ran through his mind. Virdon sympathized; in the same situation, the astronaut knew that he, too, would question every plan that was devised. There was nothing that could satisfy Martin except a complete victory. "If all goes well," said Virdon soothingly, "we'll bail out your son and I'll be in the clear, too. Remember, Martin, that I'm staking my life on this." Virdon vaulted to Woda's back. There was no saddle, in another attempt to reduce the weight the horse had to carry.

"I am supposed to take Urko's horses to him," said Martin thoughtfully. "I could ask him if he would let me take Greger's place. Then you wouldn't be in danger, and neither would Greger."

"No, Martin," said Virdon. "That's a generous thought, but it wouldn't work. Urko doesn't make that kind of deal. Greger's only chance is my winning the race. And, more and more, I think I can."

"I pray that you're right," said Martin.

Virdon gave Martin a reassuring wave and rode Woda slowly out of the smithy. Martin was still deeply concerned about the safety of his son and of Virdon. After a few moments of thought, Martin went to the corral gate, taking off his blacksmith's apron as he walked. He hung it up on the gate, which he opened. Then he began to round up several of the horses inside.

In the woods outside of town, near the arroyo, where Zandar and his gorillas had made camp, Urko and several uniformed gorillas were passing the time by hurling lances at a square target on a tree. It was a game of darts for giants, and these massive apes qualified for that title. Among the gorillas playing were Zandar and Zilo.

"All right, Zandar," said Urko. "If you don't do better this time, I'll find someone else to run my errands."

Zandar only grunted in reply. He picked a lance,

aimed briefly, took a few steps, and threw. The lance hit the target with a chunking sound. "Almost dead center," said Zandar proudly. "Do better than that, if you can."

"Would you like to make a bet?" asked Urko.

Zandar suddenly lost the enthusiasm he had gathered when he saw how good his throw had been. He knew what happened to apes who bet against Urko. "No," he said. "Your temper will be bad enough if I beat you at lances. If you lost a bet along with it, well…" Zandar's voice trailed off. There was no need to finish the sentence.

"Don't worry," said Urko. "I won't lose." Casually, almost without looking, Urko flung his lance. It hit the tree and vibrated. The point of the lance rested just inside Zandar's, closer to the center. There were murmurs of praise from the gorillas who watched the contest. One of the gorillas took the opportunity to approach Urko. "Did you fix the tree on the back road, Moro?" asked the general.

"Yes, Urko," said Moro. "Just as in the last race. The branch will probably knock the human off Barlow's horse when I let it swing back."

"Good," said Urko. "Zilo!"

Zilo stepped forward. "Yes, Urko?" asked the patrol gorilla.

"When the race starts, you will be in place," said Urko. "I don't want you hurrying there in full view of the spectators."

"Yes, Urko," said Zilo. "How far from the finish line should I stand?"

"About fifty yards," said Urko. "Close enough to see well, far enough not to be noticed."

"Urko," said one of the other gorillas, "the human has arrived with your horses."

Urko turned and saw Martin tethering several horses nearby. Urko smiled to himself. He enjoyed startling humans almost more than anything else. He turned back to Zilo and raised his voice, to be sure that Martin heard. "If the human is leading when he passes you," said Urko, "shoot and kill him."

Martin reacted with horror; there was nothing, for him to do, nothing to say. Urko enjoyed Martin's anxiety.

"Of course," answered Zilo.

Martin's expression of fear deepened as the implications of Urko's scheme hit him. Virdon would be killed; but that meant the same for Greger. Martin finished tethering the horses, almost in a daze. Like a man sleepwalking, the blacksmith moved toward Urko.

The gorilla general and his soldiers had almost resumed their game of lances. "Since the human will be riding a horse, against your laws," said Zilo, "shall I shoot him even if he loses the race?"

Urko thought for a moment. "Zaius has given permission—foolishly—for the thing. Perhaps it's not important enough to kill the human if he loses. We do have the other young human, and he'll serve as an example."

Zandar, standing near, looked past the crowd of gorillas. "The blacksmith," he said.

"What about him?" asked Urko. "Has he finished his work?"

"Yes, sir," said Zandar.

Urko looked up, knowing precisely what his words had done to Martin. The gorilla relished the scene which he knew would be played out next.

Martin stood before Urko, his eyes cast down to the forest floor. He waited for Urko to recognize him.

"What is it?" asked Urko in his deepest rumble.

Martin was paralyzed for a moment. He only looked up humbly. He tried to speak, but he couldn't. Urko restrained himself; an evil smile almost broke across his face, but he maintained his stern expression. He eyed Martin suspiciously, pretending that he was unaware that the man was the father of the "young human." "What do you want, old man?" he asked in an irritable tone.

Martin was suddenly aware of the rash thing he had done. A human being never approached an ape for any kind of favor. And even an ape would think twice about approaching Urko. For a fleeting second, Martin considered running, fleeing the forest and the humiliating, painful circumstances. But there was nowhere to go. "Excuse me," he said in a low voice. "I am Martin. I have shod your horses for many years."

Urko knew all of this very well. He knew that Martin was one of the best, most skilled blacksmiths in the entire territory. But still Urko played his game of not recalling the human. 'I asked you once, human," said the gorilla, "what do you want? If I have to ask you again, you'll find yourself tied to a tree as a target in our lance game." The other gorillas laughed at this weak display of humor.

"Please," said Martin in an agonized voice, "I can be of help to you. I have also shod the horse that Barlow will race against you." This made Urko frown; the news was more interesting than what the gorilla had expected. There was a tense hush in the forest, while Urko waited for Martin to continue. "I know how to make sure you win," he said.

Urko gave Martin another scrutiny; this time, the suspicion in the gorilla's eyes was genuine. "Is there any doubt about my horse winning?" he asked. "I didn't have any doubt, until now. Tell me what you know."

Martin had reached a crisis. It was the most important moment in his life, and he knew it. He suddenly realized, though, what he was doing—he was standing in the forest, far from any friendly help, offering to betray a fellow human to their mutual enemy. But, Martin thought, it was a course he was forced to choose. Greger's life was at stake.

Urko had grown impatient. "Speak, human," he roared.

"Barlow's horse,'" said Martin, almost stammering in his fear and anguish, "Woda. It's a very fast horse. But I can fix his shoes with wedges under them that will pain him and slow him down. I know right where to put them. It would not be discovered until it was too late."

"That is very ingenious," said Urko. "I wonder why you have never suggested it to me in all those years you claim to have shod my horses."

"In those years," said Martin feebly, "you never seemed to need help. Barlow never had a horse as good as this."

Urko only grunted.

"Then you wouldn't have to worry about killing the rider," said Martin, hurrying on with his plea.

Urko spoke slowly. "Why do you want to help *me*," he asked in a contemptuous voice, "against Barlow, who pampers humans?"

Martin tried to speak and found that his mouth and throat were so dry that the words would not leave. He gulped a breath and tried again. "It's for my son, Greger," he said. He thought for a moment that he should leave it at that, but then realized that Urko might not know who Greger was. "He is the one who has been sentenced to die for riding a horse," he said in a hopeless rush of words.

Urko grunted once more. He knew perfectly well who Greger was.

Martin almost fell to his knees. Instead, he lowered

his head again. Speaking softly, almost inaudibly, he continued his plea. "I beg you," he said, as tears formed in his eyes, "he's young, headstrong, he didn't think. Let him go and I promise you he'll never ride a horse again." Martin paused; he realized that Urko didn't care whether Greger ever rode a horse again. His entreaty would have to promise something for Urko's benefit. "I will help you win," said Martin. "Greger will be safe, and so will the man who is Barlow's jockey."

Urko appeared to consider the offer. In reality, he was enjoying Martin's dilemma. He watched cruelly as his silence made Martin even more uncomfortable. Finally, Urko spoke: "Say nothing of this to anyone," he said casually. "If my horse wins, your son will go free."

Martin was almost as dumbfounded by this unexpected piece of good fortune as he was by the bad news he had heard before. He didn't know how to react. He just stood and stared at Urko.

"You will remember that you promised to help me win this race," said Urko. "Something about wedges under Barlow's horse's shoes. I don't care about the details. But you ought to get to work. There isn't much time."

Martin backed away from Urko, nodding and crying. "Thank you!" murmured the blacksmith. "Thank you!"

Urko watched Martin go, a look of scorn on the ape's face. When Martin was out of earshot, Urko gestured to Zandar. The gorilla came nearer his general. "As soon as the race starts," said Urko, "release the human from the stocks."

"At the start?" asked Zandar. "What if the blacksmith is lying?"

"What is done to a human who tried to escape from the stocks?" asked Urko with a smile of false innocence.

"But if I release him," said Zandar, confused. Then, suddenly, realization hit him. "Oh!" he said. "Who will know I released him?"

"When a human rides a horse," said Urko harshly, "he must die!"

"You said the human on Barlow's horse would be free if he loses," said Zandar.

"I think I was wrong," said Urko. "I'll settle the matter with Zaius later. In the meantime, if the human is winning, we'll kill him before he crosses the finish line. If he loses, we'll kill him afterward. It's only a question of when." Urko thought about the neat plan, and a rare smile of pleasure creased his hideous face.

8

In Venta, the carnival atmosphere had almost reached its climax. Apes and people mixed together in a large crowd; for one day out of the year, humans were tolerated—although grudgingly, and only at the order of Barlow. Emancipated for a few hours, the slaves made an elaborate festival out of the day of the race. The apes enjoyed watching the humans, and it all worked out rather well. Both apes and humans made their way toward the grandstand, where they could watch the start and finish of the race. There were banners, humans doing tumbling, acts, apes playing drums and pipes. Everyone in the village had forgotten the worries of the usual daily routines.

Everyone, that is, except Greger, who still languished in the town's stocks, watched over by a uniformed and armed gorilla guard. The ape stared at Greger in annoyance. After a while, when everyone else had gone to watch the race, the guard and Greger were alone. The street was otherwise deserted. "If Urko was only willing to get rid of you before the race," muttered the guard, "I'd get to see the horses run."

"I'm sorry I'm causing you so much inconvenience," said Greger in surly tones.

A lone figure appeared down the street. The gorilla did not reply to Greger; he watched the figure instead, his rifle held at the ready. His weak eyes saw that it was another ape. The gorilla relaxed his guard a little. The ape was Galen. The young chimpanzee hurried up to the gorilla. He paused and spoke. "Excuse me," said Galen, "but has the race started yet?"

"No," said the guard.

"Good," said Galen, "thank you." The ape started off toward the grandstand, then, as though a thought had just struck him, he stopped and turned back to the guard. "Perhaps you could tell me if I'd have time to eat my lunch before the start," he said innocently.

"You better eat fast," said the gorilla.

Galen thought to himself that the gorillas really weren't the most clever of the apes in the world. Their conversation was somewhat limited. "Well," said Galen, "in that case, perhaps I'd better not. I'd hate to miss the beginning of the race for the sake of some old vegetables. I could just as well eat after the race. Or even *during*—"

"Why don't you move along," said the guard. "You'll miss the whole thing, standing here debating with yourself."

"Yes, yes," said Galen. "Thank you." He started toward the grandstand again. Once more he stopped and turned back. "I can understand why that human isn't watching in the stands," he said. "But you—?"

"Guard duty," said the gorilla.

"I see," said Galen. The guard said nothing.

Galen stood for a moment as though studying Greger;

the human boy had made no sign that he recognized Galen. For a few seconds, Galen wondered if he did. Then he said, "Can the human get out of that thing?"

The guard looked scornful. "Not unless it's unlocked, of course. And I've got the key."

"Then what are you guarding?" asked Galen.

"Him," said the gorilla. There was another silence. Galen silently cursed the gorilla's stupidity.

"Why?" asked Galen.

"He's to be shot when the race is over."

"I see," said Galen, gritting his teeth. The gorilla just wouldn't see the point Galen was trying to make.

"You could shoot me now,", said Greger.

"Urko wouldn't approve of that," said the guard.

Galen knew that he was going to have to lead the gorilla to the proper insight, hand in hand, like he would lead a child through its lessons. "I commend you on your sense of duty," he said. "It isn't every guard who would miss the big race just to watch a prisoner who couldn't possibly get away."

"Thank you," said the gorilla.

Galen was about to give up. The gorilla was hopeless. The chimpanzee nodded and was about to start off. Just as he was leaving, he saw light dawn in the guard's expression. Galen thought that it was about time. "Wait a minute," said the gorilla. "What you just said. I can come back when the race ends. I don't have to stay here. No one would know."

"That's true," said Galen.

"Thank you," said the gorilla. Taking his rifle, he hurried away, toward the grandstand and the race.

Galen waited for the guard to go far enough away so that Galen might speak to Greger without fear of being overheard. The chimpanzee stepped up to Greger, who looked up gratefully. "You saved *my* life," said Galen softly. "You can be sure we've not forgotten you."

"I appreciate it," said Greger, "but there's nothing that you can do, or your friends."

"Barlow has arranged to free you if his horse wins the race," said Galen. "Alan is riding him and he won't lose. Don't be afraid."

"I'm not afraid," said Greger. "But my back hurts an awful lot."

Galen laughed quietly at the boy's remark; the human had more courage than most apes, including Urko. "I will see you later," said Galen. "After the race." He hurried away toward the grandstand, where Virdon and Burke waited.

The grandstand was filled to capacity. The crowd was excited and noisy. It was segregated, because even with Barlow's relaxed attitude toward humans, the different members of his little domain felt more comfortable with their own kind. Apes sat in the front section of the stands, and the humans were in the back. Barlow himself sat in the front row, nervous and worried. Beside him sat Zandar and his gorillas. There was a murmur through the crowd as Urko arrived.

"Well, Barlow," said Urko, "we've come to the moment of truth."

"Not quite," said Barlow mildly. "The moment of truth is at the finish line."

Urko granted. "In the matter of these races," he said, "I have come to look on the actual running as mere formality."

"It gives the day its tone," said Barlow, trying to appear unconcerned. He did not fool Urko. Both apes looked down toward the starting line, where an official stood with a flag, waiting to signal both the start and finish of the race.

"For this race," said Urko, "it's at the starting line." He appeared to have ignored Barlow's remark. That irritated the prefect, but he said nothing. Urko went on. "I learned a long time ago that I dislike losing," said the gorilla. "As a result, I make a habit of winning."

"That's a difficult habit to form," said Barlow. "After all, you're at the mercy of so many other factors."

"I try not to be," said Urko coldly.

"I thought the enjoyment of a race depended on being unsure of the outcome," said Barlow.

"For some individuals," said Urko. "But try not to worry about my enjoying myself. I expect to have a marvelous time. Ah, there are the horses."

Barlow was surprised by Urko's announcement.. He looked down the track and, sure enough, the jockeys were riding their horses up to the starting line. Barlow felt a queasy feeling. He thought there was more time before the race actually began. He would have liked to have postponed the whole thing indefinitely.

Urko's horse, which was called Tusan, was ridden by a gorilla named Kagan. Martin led Woda; the animal was nervous and prancing. Between the horses and the starting line was the water-filled hole dug by Burke. It looked like a broad puddle. Kagan steered Urko's horse around the hole.

Urko turned to Barlow curiously. "I see your horse," he said, "but where is your wonderful human jockey?"

The general's question made Barlow look down the track fearfully. Could it be that Virdon had decided at the last minute not to risk the danger?

"There's still the official call," said Barlow.

"It would be a shame to be disappointed," said Urko, echoing Barlow's thoughts. "I had so wanted to see a human matched against my Kagan. I will say your horse is beautiful. A little high-strung for my tastes, though. Perhaps badly broken."

"Woda is a very good horse," said Barlow distractedly, searching the track for Virdon.

"What was your jockey's name?" asked Urko.

"I'm sure he'll be here," said the prefect. "There's time. The race doesn't start for a little while."

"I don't mind if he doesn't appear," said Urko, smiling his mirthless smile. "I've no objections to winning by default." Urko's words did nothing to improve Barlow's depressed mood.

Martin led Woda past a small storage hut at the side of the grandstand, almost to the water hole which was filled with mud. Martin stopped, but Woda pranced around in obvious agitation. Martin took a deep breath; so much of his life would be decided within the next few minutes. He felt helpless.

Nearby, at the side of the hut, Virdon, Burke, and Galen stood together, out of sight of the crowd in the grandstand. They saw the pained expression on Martin's face. "I really pity that guy," said Burke. "I'd hate to have to go through what he's going through."

'I'd hate to have to go through what his son is going through, as well," said Galen, thinking of young Greger imprisoned in the stocks.

"I might remind you that our part isn't the most enjoyable, either," said Virdon, watching the movement of Barlow's horse with a critical eye.

"I'm glad it's you and not me," said Burke.

Virdon hardly heard. He was still observing Woda. "I

don't like the way that horse is acting," he said.

"I don't like anything about this race!" said Burke.

Martin heard the faint conversation of his three friends, but he did not turn around to acknowledge their presence. He knew that he had betrayed them, but he knew as well that his son's safety was more important. He felt guilty, but helpless. He had had no real alternatives. He looked away from Virdon and concentrated on steadying Woda.

Galen moved away a little and peeked around the corner of the grandstand, to make sure that everything was safe. All attention was focused on the horses. Galen looked back. "This is probably as good a time as any, Alan," he said. Virdon nodded.

"You better take off first, Galen," said Burke. "Get in position in back of the stands, and be sure you time things right. Roll that spool just as Alan rides past Urko."

"I hope you two have this worked out," said Virdon. 'I'm counting on everything to happen just the way we've planned. I wish we'd had time for a rehearsal."

"Don't worry, Alan," said Burke.

"I'll watch carefully," said Galen. "It's not that difficult; everything will happen right on schedule. I don't know how you can be careful, Alan, but… be careful."

"I plan to be," said Virdon.

Galen nodded and left. Virdon was still looking at Woda.

"What's wrong, Alan?" asked Burke.

"Look," said the blond astronaut. Burke followed Virdon's eyes. He saw Martin trying to calm the agitated horse.

"I don't know," said Burke. "You're the horse expert here. Woda just looks anxious to get going."

"No," said Virdon, "that's not it. There's something wrong with that horse."

"Something that could foul up the race?" asked Burke.

"I don't know," said Virdon. "I wouldn't be able to tell without examining the horse."

Burke looked at the animal worriedly. "There's too much at stake," he said. "If you have any doubts, let's call it off."

"How can we call it off?" asked Virdon. "Maybe Woda is just nervous. This is the first time he's been near a crowd. Well, we'll find out what's wrong soon enough. I'll see you after the race, Pete. You better hurry if you want to get your two dollars down on me."

"Look," said Burke. Virdon waited, but his friend said nothing more.

Virdon laughed and started to walk away. "Yeah," he said, "I know."

"Alan," said Burke. Once more, Virdon stopped and turned around. "Alan, be careful."

"You, too?" said Virdon, smiling.

"Yeah," said Burke, "me, too. What else can I say? That I'll miss your cooking if you get shot? Look, pal, you're the only other guy around here I can really talk to. I don't want to be the only ex-astronaut in the world. My booking agent says there's no market these days. No colleges, so no college lecture dates. I'd have to get a job as a slave or something. So, uh, be careful."

Virdon just shook his head and clapped Burke on the shoulder. Then, without saying a word, he hurried off toward the horse. He just couldn't say goodbye.

Virdon, alone, head down, walked to where Martin held Woda. Carefully, the man kept the horse's body between himself and the grandstand, so no one there could get a good look at him. Once on the horse's back, he tried to make himself as inconspicuous as possible, by hunching low over the horse's neck. Martin handed Virdon the reins.

Burke watched all of this, his stomach tight and painful from the nervousness he was feeling. He felt alone, but he knew that Virdon was feeling virtually naked and defenseless in front of Urko and a grandstand filled with hostile apes. Silently, Burke uttered a short prayer.

Virdon pulled back on the reins gently, but that caused Woda to whinny and dance even more. Virdon couldn't understand what was wrong; the horse had never acted that way before. Martin watched nervously.

In the stands, also watching, Urko was growing more complacent and arrogant, while Barlow became increasingly more unhappy. The two apes stared at the nervous horse, each possessed by his private thoughts, each the very opposite of the other.

Virdon and Woda moved around the mudhole. Virdon appeared to be trying to rein the horse away from the hole, but Burke and Galen knew better. Suddenly, the horse reared. Virdon was thrown, landing in the deep mud. There was an immediate reaction from the grandstand; the apes laughed hilariously, and the humans sat glumly.

Virdon knelt in the mud for a moment, evidently a bit dazed and disoriented. In the stands, Urko laughed delightedly. "He's a great rider, all right," cried the gorilla. "What a jockey, your human! He can't even sit on a horse!"

Virdon clambered out of the mudhole, covered with mud from head to foot. He was absolutely unrecognizable. He walked in a kind of stunned arc toward Woda, reaching for the reins. One of the gorillas shouted, "Put him in an oven and we'll have a clay pot by dinner time!" Virdon did not react. He stood beside his horse, getting his bearings.

Burke watched the show from his place of concealment

by the hut. For the first time, he showed some relief from the tension that had gripped him. He called out to Virdon in a low voice. "Great work, Alan," he said. "That'll do it! Terrific! Your own mother wouldn't recognize you now." He wished that he felt as confident as he sounded.

Virdon grinned, rather foolishly, as had been planned. Without wiping any of the mud from his body or face, he mounted the nervous horse again. The animal began to misbehave badly, rearing and twisting almost as if it had never been broken. Burke, although he knew little about horses, could sense that there was more wrong than simple nervousness.

Virdon felt that, too, from his place on Woda's back. There was something about the way Woda was acting that seemed suspicious to him. Woda sashayed back from the starting line. Near the shed again, Virdon arrived at a decision. He dismounted and led the horse backward by the reins. Virdon knew it was dangerous to interfere with the carefully plotted-out schedule. Still, he wanted to be certain that his horse had not been tampered with.

Kagan, on Urko's horse, watched the entire process. He was laughing heartily, as were many of the spectators, ape and human alike.

Virdon walked toward Burke, still holding Woda's reins. The horse was no longer rearing, but he was still plainly nervous. Burke ran toward Virdon. Martin walked toward them, his face blank and expressionless.

"What's the trouble?" asked Burke.

"Hold him," said Virdon to the blacksmith.

Martin took the reins and tried to calm the horse. Woda just wouldn't settle down. Virdon took one of the horse's legs and looked at the hoof. Burke stood by, silently, waiting for Virdon's decision.

"Oh, man," said Virdon softly.

"What is it?" asked Burke in frustration. "Come on, Alan, tell me."

Virdon just pointed. A metal wedge had been driven between the horseshoe and the hoof. "Here," said Virdon. "This is what's wrong."

"I don't believe it," said Burke. "Who could have done it? Woda hasn't been out of our sight all day. When we weren't with him, Martin was in charge. None of Urko's gorillas could have gotten near him." Suddenly, a light seemed to flicker in Burke's eyes. He turned abruptly and glanced at Martin. The blacksmith dropped Woda's reins, looking almost unbearably guilty. The man started to back away in fear.

Burke whirled away from Virdon's side and rushed toward Martin. Virdon caught Woda's reins as Martin turned to run. Before he could get away, Burke caught him and shook him fiercely. "Are you trying to kill Alan or your own son?" he cried.

"It was to save him!" said Martin, moaning.

A strange voice interrupted the scene. "Get ready for the start!" shouted the official.

"You're crazy!" said Burke.

"It was all that I could do," said Martin, once again close to tears. "It was the best thing for everyone. Urko has too much power. He makes you do what he wants."

Virdon wasn't listening to Martin's almost incoherent speech. The official had already called for the start of the race. Time was short. "Martin!" he said. "Give me some kind of tool to get these out! Hurry!"

Martin just stared dumbly. Burke had to shake him roughly to get a response. The astronaut was just about to slap Martin back to reality, when the blacksmith gasped.

"I... haven't got... tools..." he said weakly.

Martin shook his head despairingly. Burke released the poor man and rushed to help Virdon. "Here, Alan," said Burke, drawing the crude knife he carried. "I don't know if this will do you any good, but it's better than digging those wedges out with your fingernails."

"Thanks, Pete," said Virdon.

"I'm sorry," said Martin in the background. For the moment, neither of the astronauts paid him any attention.

Virdon still held Woda's hoof. "I think you'd better have a try at digging it out," he said. "I can hold the hoof steady and calm the horse."

"All right," said Burke, "but I don't want to get stepped on."

"You won't," said Virdon.

In the stands, Urko was becoming impatient. He couldn't see what was happening by the storage shed. "What's holding up the race?" he asked. He was just about to detail a gorilla guard to check.

Barlow, imagining all sorts of things, had worked himself into a genuine panic. "Races never start on time," he said. "You ought to know that by now."

"This one does," said Urko in a mean voice.

"Be patient," said Barlow.

Urko ignored the prefect. The gorilla stood up and shouted down to the official. "Start the race!" he cried. "No more delays!"

The official stood at the starting line. He was caught between the unusual situation with Woda and the anger of Urko. The official knew which was more to be feared. "Bring your horse to the starting line!" he shouted to Virdon.

Virdon and Burke were working on another hoof. "Got it!" said Burke triumphantly. "One more to go."

"That's it, Pete," muttered Virdon.

Burke wrenched the final wedge out and dropped it to the ground. "I got it," he said. "I don't want to do this again. Ever. Next time, we'll take the train."

"I promise," said Virdon.

The official stood with, his hand raised. Near him, a gorilla stood with his rifle aimed into the air, awaiting the signal to start the race. Kagan sat on Tusan at the starting line, poised for the race.

Urko was growing more furious in the stands. He stood up again. "I said start!" he bellowed.

The official was not prepared to disagree. "Go!" he cried. He dropped his hand, the gorilla fired the rifle, and Kagan spurred Tusan forward.

The crowd made a great roar as Urko's horse sprang forward along the race course. Behind the stands, Galen stood waiting for his cue, holding his notched spool and a length of string. He moved into place surreptitiously.

Virdon leaped on Woda as soon as he untangled the reins. Without a word, he kicked the horse onward to join the race. There was a cry from the stands.

Kagan was well past the stands, on his way toward the large tree that marked the mid-point of the race. Virdon, on Woda, approached the starting line. Barlow stood up and cheered the horse and rider. Urko glared, making no noise at all. In the stands, the apes shouted for Kagan and Tusan, the humans rooted for Woda and his nameless jockey.

Galen moved up closer to the rows of apes. He was not noticed by the humans as he moved among them. As he walked, he prepared his spool and string noisemaker, as Burke had shown him.

Virdon neared the first pass by the stands. Barlow was stunned a little at how much of a lead Urko's horse had.

Nevertheless, Barlow cheered. Virdon's face was covered with mud. A little of the drier mud flaked off as the wind whipped past.

Urko was peering intently at Woda's rider, trying hard to recognize the human. There was something tantalizingly familiar about the jockey. Urko cursed the mud which covered the man. Virdon drew even with the stands, and Urko leaned forward for a better view.

Just then, Galen made a nerve-shattering sound with the spool. Everyone, including Urko and Barlow, looked around. At the same instant, Galen sat down out of sight among the spectators. Seeing no one, Urko and Barlow returned their attention to the race. The diversion had worked. All that could be seen of Virdon was his back, as Woda ran away from the grandstand, after Tusan.

Urko settled back on the bench. He was still unsatisfied; he had had his curiosity piqued, and he was used to getting immediate answers. He rubbed his chin, trying to figure out what it was about the jockey that puzzled him. He decided that he'd have to wait until after the race to get his answers this time.

The race moved into a stretch of the course that was out of view of the stands. Tusan, Urko's horse, was still in the lead, but Woda was beginning to close the gap. Virdon urged Barlow's horse on. Behind him came the sounds of cheering, growing fainter in the distance.

Meanwhile, at the starting line, Burke caught up to Martin, who had wandered off in the general direction of his house. Burke grabbed the man again, shaking him. "Martin!" said Burke with genuine emotion. "Why? Why?"

"For Greger," said Martin simply.

"Alan's riding in this race to save your son!" said Burke, failing to understand.

"Urko has a gorilla there," said Martin, pointing. "The gorilla is to kill Virdon if he's winning. If he loses, he won't be killed."

Burke turned his head and saw Zilo, lounging at a point some distance from the finish line, with his rifle slung over one arm. "Oh, man," murmured. Burke. "There's just too much going on."

"You wouldn't understand before," said Martin in a dull voice. It seemed to Burke that the man was in a state of shock.

"I'm not sure I understand now," said Burke.

"I promised Urko that Virdon would lose if Greger was spared," said Martin. Suddenly, the whole thing was clear to Burke.

"Oh, no," he said. There was a lot to be done.

Kagan and Tusan were approaching the booby-trapped jump. Behind them, Virdon and Woda were coming on fast. At the jump, Kagan veered Tusan away from the middle, and they went over, clearing the tangle of vines. Virdon, unsuspecting, rode Woda over the center of the jump. Woda's legs were caught; the horse stumbled and Virdon was thrown.

The blond man scrambled to his feet as quickly as he could. He muttered angrily as he looked at the tangle of vines. It was a typical trick of Urko's. Virdon blamed himself for not being prepared for it. There was nothing to be done except climb back on Woda and take up the chase.

Near the grandstands, Galen had slipped away from the crowd. He moved off, staying out of sight. Burke hurried to join him, grabbed him by an arm, and quickly explained what Martin had said. Their plans had to be changed, and in a short time. Galen nodded in agreement. He took the fake scorpion out of his pocket; the object would play a new and more important role.

Zilo, the gorilla guard stationed to kill Virdon, still lounged at his post. He hefted his rifle, anxious to get into action. Burke and Galen walked slowly and silently as near him as they could get. Burke and Galen held one final whispered conference, with Burke pointing at Zilo; at last, Galen nodded that he understood. Burke left, and Galen remained, watching Zilo.

Woda was obviously the speedier of the two horses. Once again, the gap between them closed. Kagan looked back and was startled at how close Woda was. The gorilla urged Tusan on.

The horses neared a tree beside the course, with Woda on the side of the track nearer the tree. Tusan at this point was only slightly ahead of Woda. Just as Virdon reached the tree, a gorilla hidden in the branches above released a bent bough. The branch whipped at Virdon's face, but the astronaut's reflexes saved him. He was able to duck beneath the branch, but Woda was thrown slightly off stride and lost some ground to Tusan. Virdon didn't even look back over his shoulder; Urko had planned for this race well, and Virdon would just have to keep his eyes open.

The race course now crossed a stream. Tusan entered the water first, splashing water in a great shower. As Virdon and Woda came to the stream, water kicked up by Tusan splashed into Virdon's face, washing off a good deal of the mud. With one hand Virdon wiped the water out of his eyes. Woda inched closer to Tusan as both horses were slowed by the stream.

Coming out of the water, Woda was only half a length behind Tusan, closing even that small distance. Woda moved up alongside Tusan. Kagan tried to bump Woda, and Urko's jockey flailed at Virdon and Woda with his riding crop. Virdon, infuriated, caught Kagan's crop and threw it away. Then Woda finally passed Tusan. They circled the large tree and began the long, straight stretch back toward the grandstand.

The spectators were roaring as the two horses finally came back into view. By that time, Woda was leading Tusan by a good length. Urko had prepared his illegal tricks, thinking them sufficient; in the stretch there was nothing to hinder Virdon and Woda. Not until they passed Zilo, who waited impatiently with his rifle.

Barlow was on his feet, rooting Woda home in a rhythmic, hoarse cheer. Urko was furious; he couldn't believe what he saw. He looked toward Zilo and made a small motion with one hand. He couldn't be sure that Zilo saw the signal; nevertheless, Zilo was aware of what was happening. The uniformed gorilla raised his rifle.

Virdon was ecstatic as he neared the finish line. The exhilaration of the race had made him slightly giddy. He shouted into the wind. He talked to the horse. "Beautiful, Woda," he cried. "Beautiful. We've got it made!" It seemed to Virdon that nothing in the world could prevent them from winning the race and saving the life of Martin's son.

Zilo held his rifle at his shoulder and aimed. Behind him, Galen appeared and placed the fake scorpion on the other shoulder. Zilo didn't feel it. Galen shouted, "Scorpion! Don't move!" Zilo froze, knowing that the scorpions only stung a moving target. Zilo's eyes grew large, and he caught sight of the scorpion on his shoulder, though not clearly enough to see that it wasn't real.

The roar of the crowd grew louder. Virdon was winning by six lengths. Urko sat in the stands raging. Then his fury seemed to vanish instantly. The general of the gorillas stared in shocked silence. Virdon's face, no longer covered by mud, was clearly recognizable. Before Urko could say a word, Virdon and Woda crossed the finish line, winning the race to the cheers of the human spectators and the excited, shrill cries of Barlow.

Urko whirled toward the prefect. "Virdon!" shouted Urko. "Your jockey is the fugitive, Virdon!"

"Is that a fact?" said Barlow with feigned innocence. "He didn't mention it. All that I was interested in was his riding ability. He rides quite well, don't you think? Ah, well, it has nothing to do with our bet, whoever my jockey is."

Urko could scarcely contain his anger. He turned to the other side, where Zandar sat, growing uncomfortable in Urko's obvious fury. "Zandar!" screamed Urko. "Get the horses! Follow him! That man will be dead within the hour, or I'll find myself a whole new army!"

"Yes, sir," said Zandar uneasily, as he hurried out of the grandstand, followed by Urko.

Kagan, having lost the race, pulled up. Virdon, the winner, didn't stop to be congratulated. He knew what Urko would be doing, and he had made appropriate plans with Burke and Galen. Virdon kept riding, urging Woda past the grandstand filled with perplexed and curious humans and apes.

At the same time, the guard hurried from the grandstand back to his post at the stocks. Greger was still imprisoned there. The guard hurried up to the stocks and unlocked Greger, after first looking around to see that no one was in sight.

Greger was excited. "Did Barlow's horse win?" he asked the guard when he was free.

"Yes," said the gorilla, "you better run."

Greger joyously dashed a few steps down the street

of Venta. The guard lifted his rifle to his shoulder, aiming at the boy. Greger was still unaware of the guard's treacherous intentions. Just as the guard was about to pull the trigger, Burke came flying from between two buildings and threw a rolling block that cut the ape's legs out from under him. The guard went down, his rifle spinning off a short distance. The ape grunted, the wind knocked from his lungs. Greger heard the sounds, and stopped to look around. He saw the guard painfully scrambling for the rifle. Burke was on his feet, racing for cover, away from the guard. Behind them came the sound of horse's hooves. The guard regained his rifle and was about to level it at Greger when Virdon raced in on Woda. The blond man kicked the rifle from the guard's hands. "Greger!" cried Virdon.

Greger got the message and put himself into position as Virdon pulled Woda to a halt beside him. Greger made a vaulting mount onto Woda behind Virdon. The horse was goaded to gallop off, and Woda and his two riders disappeared down the main street before the guard recovered his rifle again. Urko and his gorillas had mounted in the meantime and were thundering in pursuit.

The chase lasted for a long while; Woda, faster than the gorillas' horses, was overloaded but still maintained a healthy lead. The marvelous animal didn't appear to be fatigued at all, even following the race.

Virdon and Greger rode until they came to a bridge. There they stopped and dismounted. Virdon slapped Woda on the rump, and the horse ran off across the countryside. Virdon and Greger hurried down among the rocks and hid beneath the bridge. Soon Urko and his gorillas rode by, stopped, listened, and heard the sound of Woda's hooves in the distance. With a signal, Urko led his gorillas on.

Urko rode for several minutes, at last admitting that he had lost the trail. The gorillas stopped on the country road, beside the thick brush that lined the way. Barlow was riding toward them, slowly. "Have you seen the fugitive?" cried Urko.

"Yes," said Barlow. "With you. When he won the race."

Urko gritted his teeth in frustration. "If I thought you knew who he was beforehand—!" he said.

"Could I dream a fugitive would dare to ride a horse under Urko's very nose?"

"I don't trust you, Barlow," said Urko. "Your reasoning is like the trail we've been following: full of circles. We've been chasing Virdon for almost an hour, and here we are back near your blasted village."

"I am an honorable ape, Urko," said Barlow. "I don't lie, I don't break promises—and I always pay my bets. When I lose."

"You'll be paid," said Urko grudgingly.

"I know," said Barlow. "I'm on my way to collect. I'm going back to Cela."

Urko glared. He signalled his gorillas again, and they all rode off. Barlow rode a short distance in the opposite direction, the direction in which he had been traveling. Then, when he was sure that Urko had ridden out of earshot, he reined in his horse. From the brush, cautiously, Virdon, Burke, and Galen appeared. Barlow, evidently, had been expecting them.

"I heard what you said to Urko," said Galen. "You don't lie. Well, perhaps not, but you certainly can tie the truth in knots."

"I also said that I don't break promises. Where are they?" asked Barlow.

Virdon made a sign. Martin and Greger came out

from the brush nearby. As the two approached, Barlow addressed them. "You two may come and live in Cela with me," he said. "You will be safe there."

"Thank you, Prefect," said Martin.

Barlow looked down at Greger. "But *you* are not to ride horses…" he said.

"Yes, Prefect," said Greger.

"…while I'm watching," finished Barlow. He smiled at Greger, started his horse, and moved off. Martin and Greger took a moment before they started after him.

"Thank you," said Martin.

Virdon and Burke nodded. There was nothing else to be said.

Greger looked at Galen. "You were worried once that I might not consider you my friend. You *are* my friend," he said.

"Friend," said Galen, smiling.

Martin and Greger waved and walked down the road, on the road to Cela. Virdon, Burke, and Galen watched them for several seconds in silence. While they looked on, Martin and Greger began trotting after Barlow's horse. Then, as though by unspoken mutual consent, Virdon, Burke, and Galen headed back into the brush and out of sight. They, at least, were still fugitives. On the planet of the apes, they might always be fugitives.

LORD OF THE APES

"The Tyrant"
based on the teleplay by Walter Black

"The Gladiators"
based on the teleplay by Art Wallace

Based on characters from *Planet of the Apes*

For the whole gang down at the Modern Sports Center.

THE TYRANT

1

It was late summer. The days were still warm, but there was a hint of coolness in the evening air that warned of an end to the pleasant weather. Far away from the bustling, cities, the changing of the seasons was marked more clearly, by the color of the foliage and the habits of the animals. In the country, one often felt closer to nature, at peace with oneself and with the world. The atmosphere encouraged contemplation and serenity. One went to the city for business, and to the country for tranquillity. This was often a mistake.

A narrow, rutted road ran among the trees, following the curving path of a small creek. Great limbs of oak and maple trees overhung the road, and the leafy ceiling made the pathway seem like a cool green tunnel. Birds twittered in the trees, and bees buzzed lazily among the flowering shrubs on either side of the road. It was a peaceful scene, and a deadly one.

The stillness of the picture was disturbed slightly

by the gentle clopping of a horse, its rider walking it slowly through the forest. A horse and rider might well fit into this pastoral scene, but the rider was of gigantic stature, carried a rifle over one shoulder, and had a bestial, grizzled expression—he was a gorilla. The huge ape wore the black leather uniform of his kind, although he had removed his gauntlets and stowed them in the saddlebags thrown across the horse's flanks. It was the standard uniform, worn throughout the ape empire by all police and military personnel, including the apes' commander-in-chief, General Urko. The approaching gorilla was Lieutenant Daku, a local police officer. He was the principal aide to Aboro, the local chief of police.

A fly settled on Daku's brow. With a gesture of annoyance he batted it away. The warm weather, the traveling, and his duties had made Daku more irritable than usual. He grumbled as he reined in his slowly walking horse. The horse snorted and came to a halt in the middle of the deeply rutted dirt road. Daku turned in the saddle and looked back in the direction he had come from. For a few seconds there was nothing to see. Then a wagon appeared around a bend in the road. Daku waved to the uniformed gorilla driving the wagon. "Come on!" shouted the lieutenant. The gorilla driver on the wagon flicked his whip at the single horse pulling the vehicle, but said nothing in reply to his lieutenant. The horse did not increase its pace. Daku watched and waited impatiently, muttering udder his breath. After a while the wagon had nearly reached the place in the road where Daku waited astride his horse.

"Can't you get that animal to move any faster than that?" asked Daku. Once more, the gorilla driver said nothing. Daku shook his head and gave his horse a light kick with his heels. The horse started forward. About a hundred yards further on, the road forked. Daku paused so that the wagon driver would be sure which fork the lieutenant had taken; Daku was not overwhelmingly impressed with the driver's intelligence. Without looking back, Daku urged his horse along the right-hand fork. The wagon followed him. Daku was gratified to hear the rumbling of the heavy wagon's wheels behind him. The driver had taken the correct way. Daku continued muttering to himself.

Not far away, four human beings and one ape were hard at work together; this was somewhat strange for this time and this world. The humans and the ape—a chimpanzee—seemed to be working together in harmony and friendship. The ape was not supervising or shouting angry instructions; instead, he was laboring as hard as any of his companions.

The chimpanzee, whose name was Galen, was an unusual individual in an unusual world. He had not been content to live his life according to the guidelines set down by the older and supposedly wiser apes. He had become interested in how the ape world had developed from its prehistory to its present level of sophistication. The apes in power controlled the schools and what was taught in them; Galen nevertheless had his private doubts. He became convinced that there was more to the story of the apes' dominance than what he had been taught. These doubts, and a restless curiosity that sought to answer them, caused a great deal of trouble for young Galen. He ignored the warnings of his loved ones. Galen's search for the truth took him, at last, too far; his actions could no longer be dismissed by the apes in power. Galen was branded a renegade, an exile from his own kind.

At this time, a remarkable event occurred. Two human beings from the twentieth century appeared among the apes of this far-distant era. Alan Virdon and Pete Burke were astronauts whose spacecraft had become trapped in a storm of powerful and unknown forces. The astronauts were buffeted through space by giant stellar winds of unimaginable proportions. Their craft was barely able to stand the stress. Only seconds before they lapsed into, unconsciousness, the men managed to trigger an automatic recall system, to guide the crippled ship back to Earth. This the rocket did—but somehow, due to the vortex of forces that had twisted the ship about like a cork on the ocean, when the astronauts found themselves on Earth, it was one thousand years after their original takeoff. They were on Earth sure enough; it was the right planet but the wrong year. It was not the planet they had known. It was a planet of the apes.

Virdon and Burke soon discovered that apes ruled the world and that humans had been reduced to a status only slightly above other animals. No official record remained of the time when human beings ruled the Earth. Yet once in a while, Virdon and Burke discovered scraps of their old lives, unofficial evidence that threw the highest ape leaders into a constant state of doubt and fear. For this reason, Virdon and Burke, potential leaders of a human slave revolt, were hunted across the face of the changed world.

It was a happy coincidence that brought the astronauts and Galen together. They had much to learn from each other, and all three shared a growing friendship and mutual respect. They also shared many adventures as they sought to avoid capture by the gorilla police and their leader, General Urko.

Galen, Virdon, and Burke were enjoying a quiet period

after their weeks of fugitive running. They were staying with humans of their acquaintance, two brothers named Mikal and Janor. The five of them were bagging grain. The grain had been harvested and the edible portions had been separated from the rest. In front of the farm's small barn, Janor and Mikal shoveled the grain from a large pile into gunnysacks; the astronauts and their chimpanzee companion closed and tied the filled sacks and stacked them in another pile.

"This is hard work, sure enough," said Janor, the older brother, "but it is much easier when you have friends to make the time go quicker."

Janor was large and extremely muscular. He was generally quiet and not easily aroused. To those who didn't know him well, he seemed docile.

He put down his shovel and walked over to the pile of bulging sacks. Janor walked with a limp, the result of an injury he had sustained years before.

"We're just glad to be able to repay you for your hospitality," said Galen.

"Hospitality that must be paid for isn't hospitality," said Mikal. He was a smaller man than his brother, but no less fit. His fiery disposition was the direct opposite of Janor's quiet nature.

"Well," said Galen, "what I meant was—"

"Wait a minute," said Alan Virdon. "Look." He stopped his work and pointed toward the road that ran past the brothers' farm. In the distance, coming around a gradual curve in the road, was a group of mounted gorillas, uniformed and armed with rifles. One gorilla evidently the leader, rode ahead; after a moment it became clear to the human observers that behind him trailed a wagon driven by an enlisted soldier.

Mikal turned to his brother Janor with an expression of disgust and hatred on his face. "Those are Aboro's troops, for sure," he said. He made no attempt to conceal his seething emotions.

Janor turned to Virdon, Burke, and Galen. "Quick," he cried. "Get into the barn. As long as our grain is out here, they won't bother going inside."

It didn't take the two astronauts and their chimpanzee companion long to understand Janor's meaning. They made for the barn's interior, stopped to take one quick look back, and then disappeared inside. Mikal and Janor knew that there was no use in pretending to work. They turned to face the oncoming wagon and rider.

As Daku, the police lieutenant, rode up, he pulled back tightly on his horse's reins. The animal made a grunting sound and pranced, but Daku's firmness on the reins held the animal in check. He contemptuously stopped the horse as close to the two farmers as he could, looking down on Mikal and Janor with scorn. He took a list from a saddlebag and consulted it for a moment.

"This, I suppose," said Daku in a bored and haughty voice, "is what one might call the farm of Mikal and Janor, humans permitted by the graciousness of the ape government to pursue their pitiable activities." He checked off the names on the list and turned toward the gorilla who had alighted from the wagon behind Daku.

"Shall I begin, Lieutenant?" asked the soldier.

Daku looked supremely contemptuous. Even though the soldier was another gorilla, a beast incomparably superior to the lowly humans in the farmyard, Daku could not restrain his natural impatience. "Yes, Hosson," he said to the driver, "you may begin. If you didn't begin, we would be here for the greater part of the day. And this isn't the most pleasant place to spend the greater part of the day, is it, Hosson?"

The driver was chastized. "No, sir," he said. "No, Lieutenant. I'll begin."

"Begin what?" asked Mikal; his voice was filled with its accustomed hostility toward the ape rulers.

Daku's eyes gave a quick flick toward Mikal, barely noticing the existence of the human. There was no attention paid to Mikal's reasonable question. There was no intention on Daku's part to answer. Instead, the ape leader returned his eyes to the list he held in his hands. "Begin loading the grain," he said to Hosson. "And don't waste half the day doing it, either."

"Yes, Lieutenant Daku," said the driver.

In silence the two farmers watched the beginning of this now-familiar drama. In silence they watched as Hosson ambled clumsily toward the pile of loose grain and the sacks of already bagged grain. There seemed to be nothing to do; that was the situation on the ape world, particularly where its human inhabitants were concerned.

Hosson walked over to the stacked sacks of grain and lifted one with a loud grunt. Even for the muscular gorilla, it was heavy. He carried the sack to the wagon and threw it in the back. Three more trips he made; three more sacks of grain joined the first in the gorilla's crude vehicle.

"All right," shouted Mikal. Janor tried to hold his impetuous brother back, but it was already too late. Daku's evil eyes jerked toward Mikal.

"That's enough!" Mikal shouted. "You've taken enough! How much do you want?"

"Well," said Daku imperturbably, "I have this list. And as much as this list says, well, that's how much I take. And, oftentimes, because of my special police powers, I can tell the list how much it says. If you know what I mean."

Hosson pushed Mikal roughly out of the way; there was a minor scuffle, but Mikal quickly backed off. Any show of force against an ape meant instant death. Meanwhile, Daku was urging Hosson to load more of the grain onto the wagon.

"No more!" cried Janor; even he at last realized the extent of the gorillas' thievery. "You have already taken more than you've ever taken before!"

"This time," said Daku evenly, hatefully, "we are taking it all."

"There'll be nothing left for us…" said Mikal, his voice trailing off into hopelessness.

In the barn, Virdon, Burke, and Galen watched angrily but helplessly. Many times in the past they had witnessed similar scenes of cruelty and savagery by the apes. It had been rare indeed that the three companions had been able to do anything to stop it. Now, the situation appeared beyond salvation. The two astronauts and their chimpanzee friend rested at full length on the floor of the barn's loft, peering down through a partially boarded-up window. They watched as Mikal hotheadedly stormed toward the gorilla soldiers, attempting to wrest a sack of the grain from the hands of Hosson. At this, Daku could control his arrogant contempt no longer. The human would have to be punished for his actions. From his place astride his horse, Daku drew his rifle, urged his horse closer to Mikal, and slammed the butt of the weapon against Mikal's head. Mikal collapsed immediately and lay on the ground without moving. There was a muffled gasp from Galen in the barn. From Virdon and Burke there was only worried silence. It seemed to all three that Mikal might be seriously injured, possibly even dead.

Still, there was nothing for lie three fugitives to do.

Janor moved a few steps forward toward his stricken brother, but stopped as Daku and Hosson both raised their rifles toward him. Burke half-raised his tall, dark-haired form from his hidden position in the barn until Galen placed a restraining arm on the astronaut's shoulder. "This is no time to be playing hero, Pete!" whispered the chimpanzee.

Below them, in the farmyard, Mikal had risen to his feet, stunned and somewhat dazed by the blow from Daku's rifle.

"Be thankful," said Daku haughtily. "I could have just as easily shot you both for attacking a member of the police."

"Why—" began Mikal angrily, rubbing the sore and bleeding area where he had been struck. His brother caught his arm and silenced him once again.

"Why didn't I?" finished Daku. "It didn't seem to me to be worth the expense of the rifle shells, at the time." The police lieutenant turned his attention carelessly away from the humans and back to Hosson. "Hurry it up!" he cried at the luckless soldier.

"I'm doing the best that I can, Lieutenant," said Hosson in a near whimper. "These sacks are heavier than they look."

"And you are weaker than you look," said Daku. "If that's the best you can do, maybe we should have had these human scum load their own grain onto the wagon, except that they could hardly be trusted."

"I'm all finished, Lieutenant," said Hosson.

"Wonderful," said Daku sarcastically. "I'm very proud. Once again we've demonstrated the overwhelming superiority of the simian race. My gorilla, Hosson, has accomplished what the two humans, working together, might have done in a quarter of the time."

Hosson tossed the final sack of grain onto the wagon. Left behind was only a scattering of loose grain, already beginning to disperse in the light breeze that blew across the courtyard. The remaining grain was too coarse, too unfit, and too unplentiful to be bagged by the brothers. The gorillas ignored it, but Mikal and Janor stared at it with almost unbearable sadness. It was all that remained of the labors of their entire spring and summer. And for the future…

Hosson leaped into his seat at the front of the wagon and gathered up the reins. Daku wheeled his horse around, his business completed, his mind already considering the next human farm, the next collection of grain.

"Move out!" called Daku. "We've got more farms to visit and the day is already half gone." He turned again and faced the two farmers, who stood dejected and helpless in their farmyard. Daku frowned. "I will be back next month," he warned.

"Next month?" cried Janor. It seemed impossible. What was left?

Daku eyed the scattering pile of grain significantly. "With luck," he said maliciously, "I have left you enough grain for one meal every two or three days!" His laughter was an evil thing to hear, and the three fugitives hidden in the barn did not miss the ringing notes of mockery which Daku failed to conceal. At last, the police lieutenant wheeled his horse around and followed Hosson and the wagon back onto the road.

As soon as the wagon and lone rider were out of sight, Virdon led Burke and Galen in a dash from their place of concealment in the barn. Their only concern was for the well-being of their friends; they gave no thought to being discovered by the ape patrol.

"Are you okay, Mikal?" shouted Virdon, as he crossed the distance between them.

Mikal turned to face his friends, his expression one of mixed anger and helplessness. He only nodded, one hand still pressed to the place where Daku had slugged him. "I'm fine, I guess," he said. "I'll live. Maybe." He looked around the farmyard. Burke, Virdon, and Galen gazed with him.

"They have left us only enough to starve on," said Janor, his voice heavy with bitterness.

"Surely the grain tax can't be this heavy—" began Galen.

"What tax?" asked Burke with heavy cynicism. "It looked like a plain, old-fashioned shakedown to me."

Janor nodded his head in agreement. "Aboro takes what he wants, when he wants it. He calls it payment for his protection."

Burke snorted derisively. "You'd think that after a couple of thousand years, they'd come up with a new name for that racket."

"People will be people," said Virdon sadly, shaking his blond head.

"Alan," said Galen admonishingly.

"Yeah," said Virdon, "and apes will be apes."

"Every farmer in the district must pay," said Mikal, spitting into the dust as a token of his hatred.

"Aboro..." said Galen. "Was that the gorilla on horseback?"

"No," said Mikal, "that's his lieutenant, Daku. Aboro is police chief of the district. He calls himself 'Lord of the Apes.' He has pretty much his own way out here in the far country."

"The rumor is that Aboro trades the grain for gold, but

so far there's been no proof. Even General Urko wouldn't stand for one of his underlings taking graft like that," said Janor. "Urko doesn't have any love for humans, but he knows enough to keep from getting us into a mood for fighting back."

"You're right, there," said Virdon thoughtfully. "The problem is how to get the apes working against each other without getting the humans caught in the middle."

"The humans *are* caught in the middle," said Mikal angrily. "We always have been, and we always will be."

"Not always," said Burke, but his voice was so low that only Galen could hear him. The curious chimpanzee's brow furled in thought, but he said nothing.

Janor walked to the well nearby and the others trailed after him. For a long moment each was lost in his own thoughts. There was a tense silence as Janor drew water and took a long drink. He offered the water around to the others. Virdon took the wooden ladle and drank deeply himself. Then he spoke.

"That wagon," said Virdon thoughtfully. "It had so much grain in it. A man could almost keep up with it, if he were walking fast enough."

Burke stroked his chin where a brown beard might have once been. "Yeah," he said in an excited voice, "I was coming to the same conclusion. A good runner could probably pass the wagon by."

"That's what I was thinking," said Virdon. "That's what you were thinking. That makes for a pleasant agreement."

Galen spoke up worriedly. "Not precisely unanimous, however," he said. "I fail to see how a race, even if one could be arranged through the woods and the twisting trails, would help our friends here."

"Oh, that's your trouble, Galen," said Burke, laughing.

"You just don't think human enough."

"Once again, for the thousandth time," said Galen, "I thank you humbly for that verdict."

"Anyway," said Virdon, "we weren't thinking of a race. We had more of, oh, an ambush in mind."

"Right," said Burke. "It amazes me how alike we think."

"We had the same basic training," reminded Virdon.

"Did they teach you deceit and cunning there?" asked Janor with some amusement.

There was silence for a moment. "Yeah," said Burke, "I guess they did." Everyone stared at him for a moment more; then all broke into amused smiles.

"All right," said Virdon briskly. "First things first. Any idea where Daku will go next?" He looked toward Mikal, who was still rubbing his throbbing head.

"Probably to Darog's farm," said Mikal. "It will take them about two hours' ride from here, particularly in the overloaded wagon that Daku's driver is leading."

"Good," said Virdon. "Now, are there woods the wagon will have to go through, like the ones around your farm here?"

"Yes," said Janor quickly. "The Great Forest. It's much larger, much denser. Why?"

"Because—" said Burke.

"Because," said Virdon, "that's where we'll be waiting for them!"

"We're coming with you!" cried Mikal.

"No!" said Virdon, his voice cold and commanding.

Janor protested the astronaut's simple decision. "But this is our fight, Virdon—not yours! We can't let you handle all of our battles for us. We have pride, we have anger, and we have our self-respect."

"Look," said Virdon forcefully, trying to convince the

aroused brothers, "if they catch us, well, we've been on borrowed time for quite a while anyway. We've been through this routine before, and I figure we must be getting good at it, or else we wouldn't even be here. But you two, you've worked hard for your farm. If they catch you, what happens?"

The answer came swiftly and chillingly from Mikal. "Death," he said in a sullen voice.

Burke took another drink of water and offered the ladle around again. There were no takers. "Our defense rests," he said.

The light which filtered down through the thick foliage of the trees was unlike the bright, warm sunlight that had bathed the three friends at the farm of Mikal and Janor. Burke, Virdon, and Galen had followed their scheme and secreted themselves in a part of the Great Forest, following the directions given them by the brothers. Virdon stood alone alongside the grassy lane that wound its way through the forest, a coiled rope in one hand. He stood unmoving, looking to one side. High above his head, Burke and Galen, only half-hidden by the leaves of a large tree limb, also stared in the direction from which they expected company momentarily. Suddenly Galen stiffened. His superior sense of hearing picked up a new and disturbing sound. "Someone's coming!" he called down to Virdon.

Virdon signaled that he understood, then made another sign that the two in the tree should retire further, to conceal themselves. Burke and Galen disappeared. Virdon stepped quickly behind another tree. There was a long, tense moment. Virdon waited, poised, his muscles almost aching. Then he, too, heard the sound. It was the noise of someone running. That was wrong. They were wailing for the distinctive clopping of horse's hooves and the creaking of a wagon. Then, just in Virdon's line of sight, into the small clearing the three fugitives had chosen, came Mikal. Panting from near exhaustion, he stopped and looked around. This was the area he had described in detail to Virdon. When the astronaut appeared silently from his hiding place, Mikal whirled in near panic.

"Mikal!" cried Virdon, almost angrily. "What are you doing here?"

"You know," said Mikal. "I've come to join you."

Burke had followed the whole scene from above and leaned out along the tree limb. He, too, was upset by Mikal's appearance. "No way, man!" he called down. "We've already been through all of that at least a dozen times."

Galen's voice joined them. "What about Janor?"

Mikal was slow in replying. "I told him that I was going into the village." There was another slightly embarrassed pause. "I had to come. This is our fight."

There came a warning sound from above. "Shhh!" murmured Burke from his place among the leafy boughs.

Everyone froze, Burke and Galen in the tree, Virdon and Mikal on the ground. They stood poised, listening, fearful. After a moment, the heavy noises of the approaching wagon broke the fragile stillness of the sunlit forest.

"All right, that caps it," said Virdon, grasping Mikal roughly by the arm. "Mikal, get up in the tree with Burke and Galen."

Mikal needed no second urging. He had decided to come and aid in the fight, but beyond that noble inspiration he had formed nothing in the way of a plan. From now on, he was at the mercy of his friends; at least they seemed to have some idea of a course of action. He climbed up the tree and out of sight among the leaves and branches. Virdon stepped back to his hiding place, out of sight. There was a long moment, during which the only sounds were the lumbering noises of the cart; then the steady hoofbeats of Daku's horse were heard. Suddenly, at the other end of the clearing, Daku appeared, on horseback as before, but this time not even cantering. He was so sure of his invincibility in this, his own realm, that he had dropped even the most rudimentary of precautions. Behind him appeared the wagon, Hosson the gorilla trooper on the wagon seat, holding the reins. Seconds passed as Daku, the wagon close on his horse's hooves, neared the spot where Virdon and the others hid.

Virdon leapt from behind his tree trunk, catching Daku entirely by surprise. The astronaut whirled his homemade lasso around his head and then let it fly. The rope's noose settled about the startled Daku's head and shoulders. Virdon pulled the rope tight and the lasso grabbed Daku's torso even more forcefully. With a single jerk, Virdon pulled the incredulous Daku from his horse.

Meanwhile, Burke and Mikal had dropped from their tree limb right on top of Hosson, knocking the driver from his perch onto the ground, where he fell stunned and unconscious.

"Need any help?" asked Burke.

"No," said Virdon, slightly out of breath, "it looks like this one is out cold."

Galen jumped down from the tree and climbed up onto the driver's seat, picked up the reins and began to turn the wagon around. "We'd better hurry!" he cried.

"Right!" answered Virdon. He turned to Mikal. "You see, Mikal," he said, "you weren't necessary in this battle. You could only have caused yourself trouble. From now on, I hope you follow your brother's example a little closer."

"You won't understand will you?" asked Mikal, eyes downcast; but his voice was filled with suppressed resentment.

"Forget it, forget it," said Virdon. "I didn't mean it to sound as harsh as it did. I just don't want to see you taking unnecessary risks."

"I'll have to decide whether or not they're necessary," said Mikal.

Virdon decided to change the subject. "We'll hide this grain in that cave you told us about. That's the next order of business."

Mikal only nodded, still unsatisfied with Virdon's reactions.

"You tell the other farmers that they can reclaim their grain as soon as it's safe," said Virdon.

Mikal clasped Virdon's aim. "We'll never forget you for this!" he said gratefully.

"Forget it," said Burke. "Saving the world is our business. We've decided to go into it full time."

Virdon clapped Mikal on the shoulder. He turned to see that Burke had run after the wagon, which Galen was already driving away. The two astronauts caught up to it quickly and both leapt aboard. Galen gave the reins another jerk and the wagon lumbered slowly away, back in the direction from which it had come.

Mikal stood in place watching his friends, thinking his private and somewhat confused thoughts. He didn't notice that, practically at his feet, the body of Daku stirred very slightly. The police lieutenant was regaining consciousness, but not yet moving noticeably. His eyes squinted as he looked after the wagon and his unknown assailants. His vision was blurry and out of focus. He could recognize nothing except the wagon, which seemed to be driven by an ape.

After a moment, Daku's vision cleared slightly. He still had barely moved, but his head had turned so that he could get a good view of the human who stood over him. Mikal still remained in place, watching his friends as they disappeared around a curve in the forest trail. Daku's eyes narrowed as he studied the human, one whom he recognized well enough. Then, slyly, the gorilla's eyes closed as though he were unconscious.

"There were three humans," cried Daku, "but the only one that I recognized was that troublemaker, Mikal. And I *did* recognize him. I've had dealings with him before."

Daku was standing before the large wooden desk of Chief Aboro, in the latter's headquarters office. The desk was highly polished and virtually empty of objects—a symbol of Aboro's authority and power. He called himself 'Lord of the Apes,' although in truth he was only a local official. But in this part of the ape empire, it was rare indeed for any superior officer to interfere with Aboro's supreme judgments.

Now Daku stood nervously before the desk of his chief. He knew that his story would not be received well. Nevertheless there was nothing else to do; Aboro would learn the truth, one way or another.

Aboro leaned over the bright surface of his desk, his leather uniform and the epaulets of his rank glistening in the desk's reflection. "So," he said, his voice deceptively soft, "two armed police guards—one of them my own trusted aide—allowed three mere humans—" (it is impossible to convey the huge amount of contempt which Aboro loaded Onto the word "humans")—"three mere humans, unarmed humans, to overpower my apes and steal a wagonload of my personal grain. Is that correct? Do I have the story principally as it happened, Lieutenant Daku?"

Aboro's voice grew gradually louder from the soft beginning, until at the finish he was virtually shouting, his words angry and voice deep with hatred. Daku shook nervously. He knew that he was in the gravest trouble of his career. His entire future depended on what happened in the next few moments.

"Exactly, sir," said Daku weakly.

"A wagonload that would have brought me ten kilos of gold!"

Daku shrugged, trying to appear calm. "I have explained, Chief Aboro, they surprised us—"

"Surprised?" cried Aboro, half-rising from his seat, his fists clenched, his face knotted with fury. "My first instinct is to have you taken out and shot! But that won't get me back my grain."

"No, sir," said Daku, thinking about his potential execution and not thinking about Aboro's grain at all. "Nor will that, however satisfying it might personally be for you, take care of your 'payments' in Central City this month," continued Lieutenant Daku after a, moment's hesitation. His inspiration might just save his life, after all. To Aboro, the ten kilos of gold was the important factor. Daku had made his point. He only hoped that Chief Aboro would agree.

Aboro frowned reflectively. "If the grain is not recovered," he said slowly, "and if the outrageous theft is not punished, the humans may very well refuse to make any further contributions to me."

"Rest assured," said Daku, calm now that the idea of his execution seemed to have been put at least temporarily to rest. "I will deal with Mikal myself. Quickly and harshly."

Aboro shook his head. Once again, his voice was fearsomely quiet. "I will take charge of this," he said.

Daku's mood changed instantly. He became immediately silent and respectful. "By all means..." he said lamely.

"Mikal will be made an example of," said Aboro fiercely. "But not before he has told us where he and his companions have taken my grain!"

The next day, under a bright sky and a warm sun, five uniformed gorilla soldiers rode at breakneck speed along a broad, rutted road through the rolling countryside: Police Chief Aboro, the self-styled 'Lord of the Apes'; his lieutenant, Daku; and three armed gorilla soldiers. Aboro led the way, his expression one of mixed expectation and hatred. The gorillas did not speak and they did not stop to rest their mounts. They rode as though the fate of their careers rested on the outcome of their mission. For the soldiers and for Daku, at least, this was painfully true.

There was a hidden cave; Mikal had mapped its location for Virdon, Burke, and Galen. The wagon which the three fugitives had stolen from the apes was backed up to the cave mouth as close as possible. Galen, Virdon, and Burke were working desperately to unload the sacks of grain quickly. Their main desire was to remove all sources of evidence as soon as they could. Finally, after a great deal of work and sweat, the last sacks were handed down from one of the three to the others, and deposited inside the cave. The three friends at last were able to straighten up and relax from their arduous task.

"That's a relief," said Burke.

"I'm glad that's all over," said Galen.

"It isn't all over," said Virdon simply.

"Have you noticed," said Burke to the chimpanzee, "that when Alan is in charge, the job usually takes three times as long to finish?"

"I've noticed that," said Galen. "I assumed that was another strange, inexplicable human trait."

"You may also have noticed," said Virdon with some humor, "that when I'm in charge the job finishes up in better condition."

"No," said Burke, "I hadn't noticed that."

"I have nothing to add," said Galen.

"All right, knock it off," said Virdon. "Let's hide the entrance."

All three began dragging branches and limbs, many heavy with leaves, toward the cave mouth. They were preparing to disguise the cave completely from view. Before this job could be completed, however, Pete Burke interrupted. "Hey, Alan," he said curiously.

Virdon looked over at his friend with a puzzled expression.

"We've been here before," said Burke. "About a thousand or two years ago, to be exact. I'm losing track. I mean, it looked a little different then, but…" He stopped, stood up straight, looked around the scene, then nodded his head in a definite manner. "See anything familiar about that mountain?" he asked.

He pointed toward a distant, pointed, oddly shaped hill. Virdon and Galen followed his gaze.

Virdon thought for a moment. "It *does* look familiar, I suppose," he said, "but—"

"No 'buts,' pal. That's Jennings' Nose!"

"That is what?" asked Galen, completely confused

and left out of his friends' conversation. "I beg your pardon, Pete?"

"Edwards Air Force Base," said Burke. "And our C.O. was a Major Jennings, and he had a nose on him you could hang laundry on!"

Virdon laughed. "One of the cadets named that hill after him, in honor of the similarity."

"Which," said Galen sourly, "I would imagine, your superior officer found less than amusing."

"True, true," said Burke. "Commanding officers haven't changed much in the last few centuries. It's a good thing that Jennings never found out whose idea it was."

Burke's smile vanished as Virdon chucked a small stone at him. Their merriment lasted a few seconds longer, but ended in a mutual sigh.

"Brings back memories, doesn't it, Alan?" asked Burke.

"Yeah," said Virdon, suddenly businesslike again. "Too many things do. Let's finish up." They turned back to their chore of camouflaging the cave mouth.

While Virdon, Burke, and Galen were having their short rest period, Aboro and his men were pounding toward them along the road.

At the very same moment, some distance away, Mikal and Janor were hard at work also, tending to chores inside their barn. Janor was mending the handle of the crude hand plow used on the farm; Mikal stood alongside him.

"I know I should have told you, Janor," said Mikal with a guilty expression, though his voice was ever so slightly defiant, "but it turned out all right. You should have seen the other farmers. If they could vote, they'd elect Virdon and Burke prefects!"

"Dead prefects, if the apes have anything to say about

it," said Janor unhappily. "Are you sure the gorillas didn't see you? You're sure?"

"Positive!" said Mikal. "There were only the two of them and they were both out cold."

Mikal's words were cut short by the sudden sound of hoofbeats approaching. The noise drew the attention of the brothers. They exchanged looks of apprehension; the horses sounded as if they were in the farmyard.

Janor and Mikal ran from the barn, but stopped short. There, before them, were five mounted gorillas, all with rifles drawn and pointed at them. There was nothing either human could do. Never before had either man felt so close to death. Aboro and his crew, swept down on them, their rifles never wavering.

As Aboro and Daku reined up, the two humans stiffened. It was their only sensible response. They stood their ground. The three gorilla troopers dismounted, covering Mikal and Janor with their rifles.

"Aboro?" said Janor with great respect. "What do you want here? Your troops already have all our grain. Ask your lieutenant, Daku."

"That is the grab which you took back and have hidden somewhere," said Aboro in a sinister voice.

There was a curt gesture from Daku, and a gorilla trooper moved into the barn.

"There's nothing in there!" cried Mikal.

"We'll find it," said Aboro coolly.

"And how we find it is up to you," said Daku in a threatening manner. The vicious gorilla officer gestured again, and a second trooper dismounted, hurried up behind Mikal, seized the bewildered man's arm, and twisted it up painfully behind his back. Mikal gave an involuntary cry of pain.

"Talk!" shouted Aboro, his expression calm and

confident, a complete contrast from the near-crazed face of Daku. "Who were the other humans who helped you in the grain theft? I'll have the truth, one way or the other!"

Mikal remained silent. It would take more than a twisted arm to make him reveal the names of the other farmers who had had their stolen grain returned. The gorilla twisted Mikal's arm further. Mikal grimaced, tears forming in the corners of his eyes. Still he said nothing.

"This goes beyond stubbornness," said Daku with disgust. "This is the kind of stupidity we have come to expect from humans. It would be so easy for this creature to spare himself—"

Daku was cut off by a wave from Aboro. The police chief was not interested at all in his lieutenant's speculations. "He will talk. Then he will be shot." There were a few seconds of sickening tension. "Take him," said Aboro without raising his voice further. "In fact, take both of them."

For the first time, Janor reacted to what was happening in his farmyard. He didn't believe that active resistance could be of any benefit—and against five armed gorillas, he was probably correct. But now things had taken an unexpected and drastic turn. He leapt for the gorilla who was holding Mikal; with one sharp swing of his arm, Janor had knocked the burly beast to the ground. "Run, Mikal!" cried his brother.

Mikal took one quick look at the situation and knew that it had become desperate. He had no idea what to do, and his brother's words activated him. He began running toward the woods. The gorilla whom Janor had flung to the ground rose to one knee, aiming his rifle at Janor. Quickly, the farmer kicked out, just as the trooper was about to fire. The barrel of the rifle jerked away, as the shot fired. The noise of the explosion in the quiet country yard startled both Aboro's and Daku's horses, which began to rear. The two ape leaders had all they could do to bring their beasts back under control. Janor swung his huge fist again and hit the trooper on the jaw, then grabbed the rifle. With one mighty clout, Janor brought the rifle's stock down on the side of the trooper's head. He flung the rifle aside and, like his brother, began running for the woods.

The sound of the shot and the subsequent fighting had aroused the curiosity of the trooper who had been dispatched to search the barn. He came running out and spotted Janor sprinting for the woods, one of his comrades lying injured on the ground, and his two leaders still having difficulty managing their horses. Without waiting for orders, the trooper took his rifle and aimed at the back of the fleeing Janor. He fired one shot, then another. Janor appeared to be hit by the second; he crumpled to the ground, where he lay motionless.

Mikal, meanwhile, had been aware of all the battle sounds behind him. The sound of the shots, however, made him stop his headlong flight and look back toward their farmyard. His expression changed to horror as he realized that his brother had been hit. "Janor!" he cried.

Aboro had finally quieted his horse, which stood placidly beside the body of the fallen gorilla trooper. Calmly, almost without emotion, Aboro drew his pistol from its holster, raised it, aimed, and fired.

The shot split the silence that had reformed over the countryside. Mikal heard it at the same moment that he felt a horrible pain. He spun around as though he were a puppet jerked on a string. He fell dead, shot cleanly through the chest. Aboro's expression did not change. He slowly returned his pistol to his holster, giving some though to the old maxim that said if you wanted something done, you had to do it yourself. Nevertheless, the circumstances here at the human's farm were an empty victory for the proud gorilla who called himself 'Lord of the Apes.' There were apparently two more humans eliminated, but the precious grain that Aboro desired had not been found. There was little more to be done. Aboro kicked his horse and started it walking toward the road. He glanced back over his shoulder to his subordinates. "Burn this farm to the ground. That and the death of these two criminals might teach the other humans."

Daku, on his steadied horse, watched as the two troopers lifted the unconscious body of the third gorilla soldier to his horse. Janor and Mikal lay where they had fallen. All else was stillness. The late summer noises of the woods and the farmland returned to lend a false note of peace to the scene.

A few moments later, that scene was disturbed one last, fearful time. The barn and the house that Mikal and Janor had built and protected so jealously became first smoking torches in the mild breeze, then leaping, raging blazes that drove the apes away from the heat and smoke. The outlines of the buildings became lost in the turmoil of the conflagration and then the wooden structures succumbed. With loud crashes, the final remnants of the brothers' lives fell to the ground. Everything was smoking ruin. Aboro allowed himself a small, contented smile. Then the apes rode away on other business.

Virdon, Burke, and Galen were cautiously making their way up over a rise on their way back to the farm. They had worked hard that day, but their labor had been well-rewarded by the gratitude of the farmers. Now, though, Alan Virdon, who was taking his turn leading the others, stopped, puzzled. He raised an arm to halt his friends; then, without a word, he pointed ahead of their path.

Smoke in thick ugly clouds was rising above the ridge. From their vantage point the astronauts and the chimpanzee could see nothing else. But their imaginations were working furiously. Without the need for an order, the three ran over the ridge and down toward the farm. At once, everything was visible to them. The smoking farm buildings, now nothing more than blackened ruins, and the two bodies lying in the clearing told the entire tale.

"Oh, no; oh, my God, no," whispered Burke. Virdon and Galen were too occupied with their own thoughts to add anything more.

They increased their pace and in a little more than a minute were at the scene. Virdon and Galen knelt by Janor; Burke examined Mikal. Virdon looked with some degree of expertise at the wound Janor had suffered. There was a nasty-looking crease along Janor's forehead above one eyebrow. Unexpectedly, as Virdon held Janor's head, the farmer gave a groan. He wasn't dead. Virdon's expression turned to one of shock, then joy. "He'll be okay," said the blond man to his ape friend. "We'll make sure of it. The bullet only grazed his thick skull here, the lucky devil."

Janor gave another groan and tried weakly to sit up. Virdon restrained him gently. "Don't try to move yet, Janor," he said. "We really don't know the extent of your injuries."

In a weak voice, Janor gasped, "M-Mikal..."

Virdon looked over his shoulder, where Burke was tending Janor's younger brother. "Pete?" he called.

Burke looked up, caught Virdon's eye, and, with a grim expression, shook his head. Mikal was dead.

Janor did not catch any of this byplay. He had fallen,

wounded, before Aboro had so coldbloodedly murdered Mikal. "Where is my brother?" he asked.

"I'm sorry, Janor," said Virdon simply.

Janor's face did not change expression for a moment, as though Virdon's quiet apology were too difficult to understand. Then, slowly, the burly man changed, as hopelessness twisted his features. This emotion was quickly replaced by a desire for vengeance.

Much later, the grave had been dug. Mikal's body had been interred without even the comfort of winding sheets or coffin. The dirt and the sod had been carefully replaced, but nothing, not the slightest mound, marked the spot. Janor was on his knees at the grave's edge. Virdon, Burke, and Galen stood behind him, their eyes downcast, their hands folded in front of them.

Janor's hand traveled absently to the crude bandage he wore on his head. "I blame myself, Mikal," he said, as though there were no others present. "It was I who caused them to shoot. It was I who told you to run, when I should have known those apes would never let you escape. I caused your death."

Virdon reacted sharply to Janor's words. He realized the frame of mind that the farmer was working himself into. "That isn't so, Janor!" he said urgently. "They would have shot him anyway. And you, too. You know that."

Janor, still kneeling, turned a little towards his three friends. But he looked as though he had not heard Virdon's words. "Did you know when Mikal was very young I played a game with him?" he asked. "A game where he was all grown up and free, where humans, were equal to apes. That game turned into a dream, and like a fool I encouraged that dream. A hopeless dream. A dream that ended here."

"Janor," said Virdon softly.

Janor again appeared not to hear the astronaut, so caught up was he in his memories.

"Janor," repeated Virdon.

Janor turned and saw the three fugitives, their expressions full of sympathy. Nevertheless, he turned back to the grave without a word to his friends. "I promise you revenge, Mikal!" he cried in a voice suddenly grown hard and cruel. "I promise you Aboro's life in exchange for yours! At least I can give you that much. At least I can try to make it up to you."

Janor bowed his head for a moment. Neither Virdon, Burke, nor Galen said anything, although Janor's words worried them deeply. Then Janor gave a deep sigh and rose to his feet, turning again toward his friends. His face was still angry.

"You have been good friends," said Janor slowly. He did not have the quickness of mind that his dead brother had always shown; it was difficult for Janor to speak his thoughts. "But now I must do what has to be done. Alone."

Burke pushed forward slightly, reaching to take Janor's arm. The farmer avoided him.

"What are you thinking, Janor?" asked Burke. "Are you trying to make sure that this time you get yourself killed, too?"

"I will gladly die if I can take Aboro with me."

Galen raised a hand and spoke. "There has to be a better way," he said. "Janor, you haven't done much thinking about this plan of yours. It is too soon, too soon after Mikal's death. You should take time, cool off, be thoughtful about what you want to do. It will gain you nothing, or Mikal nothing, or the other human farmers nothing if you waste yourself in a foolish act. Aboro may be police chief here but he doesn't run the district. Go to your prefect. He'll see that justice is done."

"*Ape* justice!" cried Janor with utter contempt. There was so much hatred in the word that even Galen felt included. "You've seen ape justice at work already, right here. Do you think things will be any different anywhere else? Have they ever been?"

"Yes, Janor," said Virdon, remembering some of their previous adventures, "sometimes they are."

Janor chose to ignore Virdon's remark. "Laws are for apes, not humans. If I went to Prefect Augustus, he'd throw me in jail and I'd wind up back in Aboro's hands. Do I have to paint a picture of what would happen to me then?"

"Augustus?" asked Galen with some surprise. "Did you say that the prefect of this district is named Augustus?"

"Yes," said Janor. "I have never had much to do with him, but he is like all apes. All apes are alike."

Galen flinched. "I'm truly sorry you feel that way, Janor," said the chimpanzee. "But my point is that Augustus is my cousin. More accurately, he's my third cousin, on my mother's side. We grew up together. We played together and went to school together. The last that I'd heard of him, he had some minor post in Central City. Well, well." Galen looked quickly at the members of his group. "Augustus is sure to help us."

"Where apes are concerned," said Janor, "none of them is sure to do anything, except hurt humans whenever possible."

"I really hate to remind you," said Burke with a trace of irritation in his voice, "but the fellow who has just been trying to help you is an ape. A chimpanzee, and a regular nice fellow."

Janor was silent for a moment. "I apologize, Galen. I hope you can understand my feelings today."

"That's all right," said Galen.

"Look," said Burke to the chimpanzee, "about this cousin of yours, Augustus. Aren't you taking a lot for granted? A lot of time has passed since you were children together. And your own situation has changed as much as his, though not for the better."

Galen laughed softly. "I know Augustus as well as anyone in the world. I know that his personality will not have altered. Augustus has a highly developed sense of justice. You can trust him believe me."

"I trust no ape—except for you, Galen," cried Janor. "I think it's just foolishness for me to place myself in the hands of my greatest enemies. There's only one thing that apes like Aboro understand—death!"

"Look at it this way," said Virdon. "If you try killing Aboro and, successful or not, you are identified, the apes will make an example of your whole village and every farm in the district. Their revenge will be too hideous to imagine."

There was a long pause while everyone present tried to imagine that unleashed flood of hatred which Virdon had called merely "hideous." The word was actually mild, compared with what the three humans and the chimpanzee knew would happen. The scene at Janor's farm would be repeated dozens, scores, hundreds of times across the entire district.

"Please," said Galen in a pleading tone, "give us a chance, Janor. Just one chance. There is justice for humans. You'll learn. Have we done anything to destroy your confidence in us? Will you not accept our advice now?"

There was another pause, while Janor considered Galen's proposition. It was evident that Janor was deeply moved by the still-fresh memories of his brother's death, by his desire for revenge, and by the arguments of his friends. Finally, simply, he said, "Very well."

Virdon, Burke, and Galen relaxed visibly. The moment of crisis had passed.

"Until sundown tomorrow," said Janor. "More than a full day. That is how much time I will give your 'justice.' But at sundown tomorrow if Aboro is still free, I will come looking for him—to bring him *my* justice." Janor pounded a fist into his open palm and looked around the group. No one said a word.

2

The village of Hathor resembled many other villages in its district. Wooden houses, shops, and official buildings lined the dusty street. Apes of all three varieties traveled back and forth on business of their own. Humans, most on errands of their ape masters, hurried by with concerned expressions, careful not to disturb any of their ape superiors.

On this day, there was quite a large number of humans about, watched closely by two or three gorilla police who patrolled the village. Into this quiet but subtly tense scene strode Galen, as though he were not a famous fugitive ape, a renegade hunted far and near across the entire landscape of the ape empire. Behind him, their eyes downcast as though they were obsequious servants, walked Burke and Virdon. It was a disguise they had adopted many times in the past.

Galen stopped abruptly. "There," he said. "That is the District Headquarters."

"Okay," said Virdon. "Pete and I'll mingle with the

other humans. But we'll keep as close to your cousin's building as we can."

Galen smiled, gave a half-wave, and continued on toward the headquarters building. Their plan had begun.

Inside the prefect's office, Augustus, a chimpanzee like Galen, was working furiously at his cluttered desk. He muttered to himself as he scribbled across page after page of work. Suddenly, there was a knock on the door. The sound irritated Augustus slightly, interrupting his work and his concentration. Without raising his head, he said, "Yes, yes! Come in, come in!" His voice was harried, preoccupied, and just a little pompous. The door opened, and Galen entered.

Augustus still hadn't looked up. "Yes, yes? State your business, please."

"I wish to report a theft," said Galen. He was half-grinning, anticipating the moment when Augustus would recognize him. "Two apples stolen from a tree belonging to a human farmer. The culprits were seen running from the scene. Two chimp teenagers approximately fourteen years of age—"

At this point Augustus looked up, and his mouth opened in surprise. He dropped his pen from his shaking hand. "Cousin Galen!" he cried.

"Cousin Augustus," said Galen happily. "Or rather, should I say 'Prefect' Augustus?"

Augustus rose from behind his littered desk and came around to meet his cousin. The two relatives clasped hands joyfully in the middle of the office.

"This is a… surprise," said Augustus.

"You mean something closer to shock, don't you, cousin?" asked Galen. "I'm sure you get simple surprises almost every day."

Augustus nodded soberly. "I will confess that I hadn't expected you to walk in and—" Augustus broke off suddenly, his expression becoming worried. "Galen," he said, "what were you thinking of, coming in here? A fugitive, with two humans?"

"We must have a long discussion about all that another time, cousin," said Galen wearily. "But right now—"

"I always told you that your impulsive nature would one day land you in trouble."

"That's funny," said Galen, smiling. "When you were lecturing me about being impulsive, you never mentioned that time when I allowed myself to be caught by that human farmer so that you could make good *your* escape."

Augustus laughed aloud. "True, true," he said. "You never once held that against me." The prefect sighed. "Those were the days, eh, cousin Galen? Carefree, happy."

"Yes," said Galen, "not like now. Which is why I am here. I need your help, Augustus."

Augustus slapped his cousin's shoulder and returned to his seat behind his desk. When he spoke, there was a trace of humor in his voice. "Somehow I didn't think you had come in here to give yourself up," he said.

Galen went straight to the point. He knew that Virdon and Burke were vulnerable outside. "It's your chief of police, Aboro. Are you aware that he is robbing the district's farmers on a very regular, monthly schedule?"

Augustus looked stunned. "No!" he said.

Galen nodded his head forcefully. "I assure you that it's true. We've watched him in operation. What he does with the grain he takes I have no idea, but he is rapidly reducing the farmers to absolute poverty! That says nothing about the methods he's using, which are turning the humans of your district into fearful, mindless slaves of Aboro's terror tactics. And just yesterday he brutally murdered one of them for daring to defy him, while my two friends and I watched him burn their farm to the ground."

Augustus shook his head through all of Galen's speech. This information was new to him and very difficult to accept. "I'm finding this all hard to believe, Galen, as much as I trust you."

"There is proof," said Galen. "The dead man's name was Mikal." Galen went on to tell Augustus everything that had occurred during the tragic hour the day before.

Meanwhile, as Galen tried desperately to convince his cousin of the true situation, Virdon and Burke lounged outside the prefect's headquarters, trying to appear as inconspicuous as possible. This was difficult for two humans not on any apparent business.

"Do you think his old cousin turned against him, Alan?" asked Burke worriedly. "Arrested him, maybe? Maybe we should check—"

"Oh, oh," said Virdon. As Burke turned inquiringly, Virdon gestured down the main street of the village. The two men watched for a few seconds as two mounted gorillas, uniformed in black leather, armed with pistols and rifles, rode slowly into town. As they drew nearer, it became clear that the apes were Aboro and his lieutenant, Daku.

"Yeah," said Burke. "Oh, oh. Trouble."

"There's not a whole lot we can do now," said Virdon.

"Mainly disappear," said Burke.

"Out of sight," said Virdon. "I'll have to warn Galen." Burke moved around the corner of the building and Virdon hurried through the front door.

Not more than half a minute later, Aboro and Daku, having seen nothing, suspecting nothing, casually dismounted in front of the prefect's headquarters. They tied up their horses at the hitching post there, surveyed the street with the air of habitual lords among underlings, and swaggered toward the building.

Augustus was still having his debate with Galen while all of this was occurring. It was so strange to him that he was laboring to understand. "If what you've told me proves to be accurate," he admitted at last, "I can promise you that Aboro will be severely punished, Galen."

"Thank you," said the chimpanzee. "That's all we were looking for. We promised Janor justice."

Both Galen and Augustus turned in alarm as Virdon burst through the door. "What—?" began Augustus, but Virdon, panting, cut him off with a wave of a hand.

"Is it Janor?" asked Galen. "He promised us more time."

"Gorillas!" cried Virdon, almost panic-stricken. "Heading this way! No time!"

Augustus was, of course, astounded to be addressed in this manner by a human being. Galen introduced the man. "This is my friend, Alan Virdon," he said.

Augustus didn't answer. He was an intelligent ape and he was already reacting to Virdon's words. He hurried to his window and looked out onto the street. "Aboro!" he cried. "He mustn't find you here."

"That's a vast understatement," said Galen angrily.

"Quickly!" said Augustus. "Behind the curtain. Both of you. It's not much, but there's no time for anything else." He indicated the green curtain drawn over the back part of the office, giving the prefect a small private area in the rear. Virdon and Galen were no sooner behind it, the curtain falling back into place hiding them, when the door of the office opened and Aboro strode in, followed by Daku.

Augustus rose from his desk again. He was evidently. very nervous and ill at ease. "Well, well," he said weakly.

"Aboro. How... I... well, this is a surprise. I hadn't expected to see you until your monthly circuit. Come in, come in."

Aboro laughed. The sound made Augustus even more uncomfortable, because he had no idea in the world why the police chief should be laughing. "As even you can tell, *Prefect*," said Aboro, emphasizing the word in an ugly manner, "I already am in." Aboro gave another grumbling laugh. "As a matter of fact, I am in, and you are out. Am I not correct, Lieutenant Daku?"

"Yes, sir!" cried Daku. "Just as you say. A very neat turning of words."

"What do you mean?" asked Augustus.

Aboro walked up to Augustus' desk and reached inside his leather uniform. He came out with a brown parchment document which he slapped down on the desk, spilling several other papers to the floor. "Read it," said Aboro in a commanding voice. "Even you should be able to understand it."

Augustus was beginning to shake with suppressed rage; this was no way for a mere chief of police to speak to the prefect of a district. Augustus picked up the official-looking paper, unrolled it, and began to read. "It is from the Supreme Council itself," he murmured to no one in particular.

"Read further, Augustus," said Aboro languidly.

Augustus looked up at Aboro, for the first time feeling a sense of trepidation. He gazed back at the parchment. "'To Prefect Augustus, Greetings'," he read. "'Know all apes, by these present, that reposing special trust in our loyal servant, Police Chief Aboro, you are herewith recalled to Central City. After reporting to the Supreme Council, you will be reassigned to the province of Dorvado. Also, in accordance with this change of status, we herewith appoint the aforesaid Aboro new Prefect of your District, with all rights and privileges which appertain to such a promotion, all to be effective as soon as possible, with a minimum of delay.'" Augustus finished reading the paper, but he stared at it in mute fury for several seconds. Aboro stared, waiting for some kind of reaction. Finally, Augustus looked up, evidently shaken to his core. "This cannot be!" he said. "I have done an exemplary job here. I have not been given one inkling that they were displeased with me."

Aboro laughed again. "That is not the point at all, friend Augustus. As far as your, work here, it has not proven so difficult, has it? I mean, I don't doubt that even a human could be trained to fill your functions. Any mouse can shuffle papers. It takes strength, however, to govern a district. Govern. That is the key word, and that is where the Supreme Council may feel you have fallen down."

Augustus was still stunned by the implications of the order. "But Dorvado!" he said plaintively. "That is a wild, mountainous place—"

Aboro sighed, wishing that he could be far from this tedious, boring chimpanzee. He much preferred the simple, brutal ways of his fellow gorillas. "The Council probably feels that you can do less harm out there," he said cruelly. Then he swaggered to the door. He put one hand on the latch, then turned back to face the prefect. "I am in no hurry to move into this office, Augustus. I am trying to be reasonable. Still, the situation demands an orderly transfer of authority. Anytime within the next two hours or so will suffice." Then Aboro was gone, and the smirking Lieutenant Daku followed. The door slammed behind them.

"That's pretty incredible," said Virdon, emerging from his hiding place.

"I'm sorry, Augustus," said Galen.

"I can do nothing for you, now, cousin. You heard," said Augustus. Galen nodded.

"Dorvado," mused Virdon. "That's like Siberia."

"Where?" asked Galen. Virdon didn't reply.

"I can only offer advice now," said Augustus. "You and your human friends get out of this district as fast as you can. Aboro is vicious."

Virdon was giving thought to another aspect of the matter. "Isn't this a little unusual?" he asked. "I mean, I thought that gorillas were pretty much reserved for military and police duties. That has been our experience."

Galen nodded. "Administrative positions have always been filled by our kind."

Augustus stroked his chin thoughtfully. "I must give Aboro credit," he said regretfully. "It must be that he has powerful friends on the Council."

Galen stepped forward and grasped his cousin's shoulder in a solicitous gesture. "I am truly sorry, cousin, not only for the failure of our plans, but for what this means to you. My good wishes will be with you." Augustus couldn't answer. He was still too shocked.

Pete Burke entered from the rear of the building; it was evident that he had heard everything that had transpired in the previous few minutes. "Well," he said, "it was a good idea. Even if it didn't work." Burke's attempt at lighthearted humor fell dismally flat.

The day passed slowly. It was warmer, and the weather was still pleasant as they traveled through the woods toward a forest clearing. Burke led the way this time, followed by Virdon, and finally by a weary and panting Galen. They were all deep in conversation, trying somehow to loosen the knot of trouble which seemed to bind them.

"That's got to be why Aboro's been trading grain for gold," said Burke. "He bought the job of prefect. He bribed someone or some group on the Supreme Council. They just don't go handing out administrative posts to obvious crooks like Aboro. The Supreme Council has some pretty good minds on it, after all."

"Bribable minds, if you're right," said Virdon.

"Anyone can be bribed, if the price is right," said Galen.

"Not that any of this information helps our situation, any," said Burke, vaulting over a large fallen tree trunk. Virdon hurdled the massive obstacle, and Galen climbed slowly and painfully over it.

"Maybe it does," said Virdon. "Galen, aren't there laws against corruption, bribery of officials, things like that? There must be. This can't be the first time this has happened."

"There are very strict ones," said Galen, wheezing and trying to get his breath back. "If we could find out who Aboro's been in touch with in Central City."

"Nothing to it," said Burke with his accustomed cynicism. "All we have to do is walk back to Central City, ask Zaius for an appointment, and then ask everybody to take a lie-detector test. Who knows? It might be Zaius himself who was taking the bribes."

Galen made a frown of concentration. "I would stake my reputation on Dr. Zaius' integrity."

"Right now, pal," said Burke with a short laugh, "in Central City, your reputation is about as good as ours."

"Must you remind me?" said Galen, with mock displeasure. "By the way, what is a 'lie-detector test'?"

"That's where a lot of police like General Urko stand around and ask questions," said Burke. "If you sweat a little, it means you're lying."

"I don't even need the questions," said Galen. "Just thinking about Urko makes me nervous."

"Janor's only given us a little time," said Virdon, breaking into the light banter of his friends. "I'm glad that he understood how the situation has changed, and I'm glad that he gave us another day. But that still leaves us only until tomorrow night to finish this entire business."

There was silence as the three companions considered what those few hours would bring to each of them, separately, to Janor, and to the humans of the district. It was a heavy responsibility and there were no easy answers.

A small procession was wending its way through the quiet country lanes of the' district surrounding Hathor toward the center of the town. Leading the parade were two mounted gorilla troopers, uniformed as usual, with special shiny metal decorations to mark their important assignment. They were heavily armed with rifles more sophisticated than the ones used by the local police officers. Behind these troopers rode General Urko, the mighty, almost all-powerful military ruler of the ape empire. His horse was a gigantic black stallion, the most impressive beast that Urko's staff had been able to find in all the realm. Bringing up the rear were two more gorilla troopers. They wore the expression of disdainful superiority that naturally attached itself to all who spent too many hours in the presence of General Urko. The lead troopers stopped in the road, on the edge of the village of Hathor, and, turning their horses slightly, waited for Urko to canter toward them.

"Yes?" demanded General Urko.

"District Headquarters, sir," said one of the troopers respectfully.

Urko looked in the direction that the gorilla was pointing; he saw only the typical dry, dusty main street of a dry, uninteresting, rural farming village. There was normally nothing in such a place to interest a personage of General Urko's magnitude. He didn't even make out which building the trooper was indicating. But that didn't matter. Urko had other thoughts on his mind. "Ah!" he said in his deep, rumbling voice. "Aboro will be surprised and delighted to see me."

The two troopers turned their horses to lead the way into town but, after a grunt from their commanding officer, they gave way. Urko himself would lead his triumphal entry into Hathor.

A few minutes later, one of Aboro's troopers, who was seated in a crude chair in the office of the prefect, sprang to his feet as the outer door was thrown open with a horrendous crash. Urko's troopers entered quickly, their rifles drawn unnecessarily, producing the desired effect. Aboro's man was shaken and stood quaking in the center of the room. The general's troopers flanked the door; a moment later Urko himself entered. Without looking from one side to the other, Urko spoke. "Announce me to the prefect!" he cried.

"Yes, sir!" said Aboro's trooper in a broken voice. The trooper ran into the back private office, from which all the noise of the general's entrance must clearly have been heard. There were murmured voices, but no distinct words were audible to Urko. The general didn't care; he knew what was happening back there. The thought of it made him smile slightly.

The trooper reappeared a few seconds later. "Please come in, Commander Urko," he said. His voice was even less under control.

Urko stepped through the curtain, tossing it aside as if it irritated him. If it irritated him enough, it was clear that the general would merely rip it down. Aboro rose and came forward to meet his superior officer.

"Urko!" he said in a less-than-pleased voice. "What a pleasant surprise! What brings you to Hathor?" In the back of Aboro's mind was the unpleasant suggestion of just how similar this situation was to the scene he had enacted with Augustus not so long before.

Urko, Aboro, and the ever-present Daku were alone in the private office, shut off from the eyes and ears of the gorilla troopers in the outer chamber. Urko needed no great audience, however. Aboro would be enough. "Well, *Prefect*," he said, giving the word the same contemptuous underlining that Aboro had used with the dispatched Augustus. "Since I was in the district on a tour of inspection, what better time to come by to offer my congratulations on your appointment! I was amazed and delighted to hear of it."

"I am honored, Urko," said Aboro nervously. "Honored, indeed! Oh, this is my aide, Lieutenant Daku." Urko merely threw the subordinate officer a glance, nodding once. '

"A great honor, sir," said Daku.

"To think that my old friend is both Prefect and Police Chief of this important district!" said Urko, pacing the narrow office area. "I don't recall that you were ever noted in the Police Academy for your administrative skills."

"Anyone can learn to shuffle papers, Commander," said Aboro, trying to regain his composure and his easy, seemingly bored attitude. He was failing at that. "We can always hire chimps for that, can't we?"

Urko let out a booming laugh. "True enough," he cried, "true enough."

"Would you care for something to drink?" asked Aboro.

Urko nodded that he would, indeed, care for something to drink. Aboro went to a small cabinet and took out a wooden decanter. He poured two cups of purplish liquid, quite evidently leaving out the inferior Daku. He handed one of the cups to Urko, and raised the other in salute to the general. "To your health, old friend," said Aboro.

"And to yours," said Urko.

After the toasting was completed, Aboro returned the cups and the decanter to the cabinet. "And now," he said, turning back to the general, "is there any way I can help you?"

"Well," said Urko, removing one of his leather gauntlets and slapping it against one of his leather-clad legs, "there is always the matter of the human astronauts and the traitor, Galen."

"Yes," said Aboro, "I have been receiving reports about their movements from your office for some time now."

"Any sign of them?"

"None," said Aboro. "You'll find them somewhere else. My district is under the strictest control."

"I know that," said Urko, and both gorillas understood that the general's words were less a compliment than they sounded. Urko shook hands with Aboro again. "If we don't meet soon, before I return to Central City, again my congratulations on your appointment," he said.

"I appreciate this, Urko," said Aboro, still somewhat confused by the general's meaning and intentions. "It is a great honor for me."

Aboro and Daku stood at attention as Urko nodded absently, turned, and sauntered through the curtain into the outer office. Aboro then gestured to Daku, who went and peered out, making sure that Urko and his troopers had left the headquarters building. Daku turned and gave a quick nod. Aboro took a deep breath and moved past his lieutenant into the main room and his official desk. Aboro collapsed in his chair. Slowly he let out his breath. "I'm just as glad to see the last of him," he said softly. "Even back at the Academy you felt like he was seeing right through you." He put his feet on the desk, disturbing piles of Augustus' unfinished work.

"You realize that his visit has... *confirmed* your appointment," said Daku slowly.

"How do you mean?" asked Aboro suspiciously.

"Well," said Daku thoughtfully, "first and last, Urko is a policeman, a good one. He was sniffing around here. I know him that well. If he had any idea you'd 'bribed' your way into this post, he wouldn't have left so quickly. No, he's satisfied and that means we're—I mean, *you're* in total control of the entire district."

Aboro nodded, slightly more satisfied. "You're probably right as usual, Daku. As long as I continue to make my payments to Central City, I'll be left alone to amass my own personal fortune!"

The two human astronauts and their chimpanzee friend had made a temporary campsite, a place to rest and formulate their plans. Things had happened so quickly that their schemes and ideas had to be scrapped and rethought almost hourly. Virdon leaned against a rock, carving a kind of long swagger stick from a short branch with a penknife. Burke squatted nearby, tacking together two strips of red cloth. Galen paced before them, somewhat nervous, adding little to the constructive activity of the other two, showing his apprehension.

"It'll work," said Virdon. "I'm convinced of that. *If everybody does his job.*"

Burke turned to Galen with a grin, indicating the material he had been working on. "Your disguise," he said. He got up and placed the red collar around Galen's neck. Galen took a deep breath.

"Are you scared?" asked Burke.

"I can't believe how often the two of you come up with the most' insane plans. Every scrape we get into involves the most complicated, ridiculous bit of playacting to get us out alive. And it's usually me that has to perform. But this is the absolute limit."

"Are you scared?" repeated Burke.

"Chimpanzees are *never* afraid," said Galen. "We sometimes feel anxious… apprehensive…"

"That's what I mean," said Burke. "You're scared. Well, so am I. Good luck."

Virdon handed Galen the swagger stick. Galen accepted it gravely and nodded, then started to turn away. "Galen," called Virdon. The blond man understood that the chimpanzee was walking into a desperate situation, and that, although as courageous and loyal as anyone the astronauts had ever known in either of their worlds, Galen could still be filled with doubt.

Galen turned back to look. "Fingers crossed," said Virdon. He held up his crossed fingers; Galen stared curiously. After a moment, he did the same.

"I'll never understand," said Galen to himself. "Sometimes I learn so much from these humans. Sometimes I have to pretend that they know what they're doing."

Virdon and Burke watched Galen walk slowly away. They looked at each other and nodded.

In Hathor, little more had been done in the District Headquarters office since Aboro's visit from General Urko. The general had been correct in his estimation of

Aboro's administrative abilities. It was clear, though unimportant, to Lieutenant Daku that the day-to-day affairs of the district would soon begin to suffer. It was just as clear, and more important, that these affairs would pass into his control. Lieutenant Daku was looking forward to the increase in his own power.

Once again, the front door of the building flung open. Daku looked up, startled. Was this Aboro's unlucky day? Was this General Urko again, checking up, as Daku had hinted before? No, no, it wasn't Urko; Daku saw that in an instant. Still, he wondered who beside that powerful leader would have the effrontery to burst into the office in such a fashion.

One of the gorilla troopers was resting in one of the chairs. When the front door banged open, the trooper jumped to his feet, fumbling with his rifle, which was tangled among the legs of the chair. The trooper's frantic movements and Daku's angry words were both halted by an imperious gesture from Galen. Yes, this was Galen, but a chimpanzee few would recognize. This was not the somewhat timid, curious, friendly ape whom the astronauts had grown to admire and respect. This was a new role for Galen—and Galen secretly loved playing roles, as much as he complained to Virdon and Burke about the necessity to do so.

Galen marched into the center of the room, arrogant, swaggering, a natural bully with natural authority. "Inform the Prefect that Octavio is here to see him," he said in a voice as loaded with disgust as he could make it. He looked at neither the trooper nor the lieutenant. His attention was on his swagger stick, which seemed in almost certainty to be used against the skulls of both gorillas unless they did as he said, immediately.

The gorilla trooper moved up behind Galen and spoke diffidently. "You have an appointment?"

The ridiculousness of the question made Galen swell up with tremendous indignation. "'Appointment'?" he cried. "Octavio needs no appointment to see some insignificant prefect! Do as you are told!"

The gorilla hurried through the green curtain into Aboro's private office. He returned immediately, explaining that the prefect must have stepped out temporarily. The trooper looked very worried.

"Is there something that I can do for you?" asked Lieutenant Daku.

"Who are you?" asked Galen, as he might address the lowest creature on Earth.

"I am Lieutenant Daku," said the gorilla. "I am the prefect's aide."

"You will address me as 'sir,'" said Galen, pushing the circumstances as far as he could, beginning to enjoy it.

"Yes, sir," said Daku.

"Tell your master that Octavio, Private Secretary to Dr. Zaius of the Supreme Council is here," said Galen. "I will wait in this chair. It will be well if you seek out your superior, rather than make my stay overlong. This village of Hathor has wearied me already."

Daku nodded, unable to speak. He was visibly impressed. He turned and went back through the green curtain. Galen could plainly hear conversation in the inner chamber. Evidently Aboro was in, after all, and the gorilla trooper had lied, waiting to see who Galen presented himself as being. Now the identity of "Octavio" was important enough for Aboro to make a sudden "return." Daku reappeared shortly and gestured to Galen. "This way, sir," he said.

Galen followed him through the familiar green curtain. As he expected, Aboro was seated at his small desk in the private area. For a moment, the two apes stared at each other, sizing each other up. Then Aboro rose, nodding to Daku to bring up a chair for Galen.

"Uh, won't you have a seat?" asked Aboro, completely bewildered and unsure of the seriousness of the visit.

Galen accepted the chair, but said nothing for a moment, slapping the swagger stick instead against one leg. The silence grew uncomfortable.

"Is this an official visit, Octavio?" asked Aboro.

Galen coughed into one fist. He looked idly about the narrow room. "You might say so, you might say so," he said, clearly not wanting to give Aboro any premature indication of what was planned for the new prefect. "Dr. Zaius has had his eye on you for some time, Prefect Aboro. You *are* Aboro, aren't you? I assume that you are, as I assume that this village is Hathor. But so far from Central City, all the towns look so similar. Have you noticed that? And the prefects! How similar they are, also!" Galen was intensely pleased to see the anger start in Aboro's eyes at these words. Nevertheless, the prefect kept his fury under control.

Aboro stammered for a moment. "I... yes! I'm Aboro," he said angrily. "What do you think I'm doing behind this desk?"

"I have no idea and as little interest," said Galen in supremely bored tones. "To continue: Dr. Zaius has had his eye on you for some time."

"So you said," said Aboro. "In what way do you mean that?"

"I mean simply that you have attracted the attention of a considerably busy ape," said Galen.

"I am deeply honored," said Aboro.

"We shall see," said Galen ominously. "Dr., Zaius also knows all about your clumsy attempts to bribe his subordinates!"

This revelation fell like a bombshell in the prefect's small office. There was shocked, stunned silence for a long while. Aboro looked at Daku, who only shrugged helplessly. There didn't seem to be anything else to do other than allow this emissary of the Supreme Council to make his accusations, his threats, and his departure.

"He... knows?" asked Aboro lamely.

Galen's voice was even firmer. "Everything," he said. "He knows *all* that goes on around him. That is why he is the head of the Supreme Council, and not some bumbling fool like Urko. He knows much that goes on behind his back, as well. He made you Prefect, Aboro—even though Zaius' subordinates think that they did. He closed his eyes to your bribery for one reason, and one reason only. Because he had already earmarked you for greater things."

This declaration had much the same effect as the previous one, but for totally opposite reasons. Once again, Aboro was speechless for several seconds.

"Greater things?" asked Daku, trying to keep the conversation proceeding. He saw greater things for Aboro as meaning, at the same time, greater things for Daku.

"Greater than Prefect?" asked Aboro in a whisper.

Galen smiled and smacked the stick against his leg a few more times. Then, with a bored expression, he stood and walked slowly back and forth. "It is no secret," he, said. "I am giving away no confidences." He drew nearer to Aboro, and lowered his voice. "Still, there are apes who know of these things, apes who will learn, and apes who must be kept ignorant for a time. Do you understand my meaning?"

Aboro nodded. He jerked his head in Daku's direction questioningly.

"Let him stay," said Galen generously. "He may have a part in this." Daku smiled. "Now," said Galen seriously, "the basic story is this. In Central City, of course, Dr. Zaius has long had his differences with General Urko. You, as a gorilla, and I, as a chimpanzee, are well aware of these differences. Too often has Urko acted independently of the Council, going over Dr. Zaius' head, ignoring the authority of the Council and Dr. Zaius. Zaius bided his time, until he found the one leader who would be the perfect replacement for Urko." Galen stopped meaningfully.

Aboro looked at Daku and licked his dry lips. He wondered if he understood Octavio's words correctly. Aboro looked back at Galen. "The thought of higher office than this has never even crossed my mind!" he said.

"Of course it hasn't," said Galen. "Perfect. That is one of your chief recommendations."

"Besides," said Aboro, "Urko and I are friends of long standing. I have never even thought of replacing him."

"Of course you haven't," said Galen. "But now, you just might." Galen walked toward the curtain, stopped, and turned. "Think over the implications of what I have shared with you. I shall contact you again tomorrow morning."

Aboro's lips tried to form words, but failed. Galen nodded brusquely and left the office. Aboro looked at Daku, who could only wipe his sweating brow and collapse into the chair which Galen had vacated. Aboro sat down heavily behind his desk.

Outside the office, Galen's reaction was no less severe. The mental and emotional strain of his act caught up with him. He leaned against the outside of the closed door, absolutely spent. He panted a little and shaded his eyes with one hairy hand. He let out a long, slow sigh of relief.

While Galen recovered his wits, Aboro and Daku were doing the same inside. Daku faced his superior officer over the narrow table of the back room. "*General* Aboro," said Daku, with a note of suspicion in his voice. "*Commander* Aboro. Very impressive."

Aboro was euphoric. "Imagine the great Dr. Zaius knowing of me all the time!"

Daku's voice was slow, still not completely convinced. "According to Octavio, yes," he said. "But who is this Octavio?"

"Why, Zaius' secretary!" said Aboro. "You heard him—"

"Yes," said Daku. "We heard him. But we have only his own word that he is who he says he is. He brought no identification, no written word from Zaius."

There was a pause, as doubt crept info Aboro's mind. "Daku!" shouted the Prefect. "Get off a heliograph message to Central City. Let us find out if Octavio is, as he claims, from Dr. Zaius!"

3

The wooded countryside was peaceful; the great turmoil which occupied the residents of Hathor did not extend beyond that village's limits. And, in truth, this was the case elsewhere, too. The ape empire was loosely knit. One town was isolated from another, not only by geographical distance, but by custom, laws, and sometimes language as well. In the woodlands, there was never anything but peace, unless human beings ran through on furtive errands of their own or mounted apes crashed through on mighty missions of government.

Now, as afternoon edged slowly toward evening, Virdon and Burke made their way through the brush. Leaving Galen to play his part in the village of Hathor, they had departed on their own assignment. Virdon stopped suddenly; without a sound, Burke halted behind him. Virdon parted the shrubbery in front of him and peered out. He gestured to Burke, who leaned over Virdon's shoulder to take a better look.

Not far away, at the top of a small rise, stood a heliograph tower. The apes, hating all the technology which represented their earlier domination by mankind, had developed this system of sending messages by reflected light from mirrors mounted high on towers. It was an ingenious system, and it criss-crossed the empire, linking all the outlying districts with the Central City. The structure itself was rickety looking, built with a crow's nest aloft. A gorilla guard patrolled the base perimeter of the structure; his companion, another gorilla patrol officer, lolled on a stool high above in the crow's nest.

"Pete," whispered Virdon. He gestured to Burke, his hand indicating the ape in the crow's nest. Burke nodded his understanding.

The gorilla guard at the base of the tower had not yet heard or seen anything suspicious. He leaned against one of the supports of the tower, sleepy, bored. Nothing ever happened so far from the city... After a while, he began his slow patrol again. He took his time marching around the structure. As he disappeared around the corner of the heliograph tower, there was a loud rustle from the bushes on that side of the clearing. There was a muffled cry, and then the solid thunk of the guard being struck by a heavy object. There was the sound of the guard's body falling to the ground. Then, once more, there was silence.

Virdon bent over the fallen guard, checking to make certain that the gorilla was entirely unconscious. Then, laboriously, the blond astronaut began dragging him into the brush, out of sight.

The guard in the crow's nest heard something, he thought, but he couldn't be certain. He looked over the railing, but he saw nothing unusual. He sat down again and tilted back in his chair. Burke climbed the tower silently;

when the guard looked over the railing, the astronaut had had to press himself tightly against the rough wooden beams of the tower. Now, though, he knew that he was relatively safe. He tried to make his voice a good grumbling imitation of a gorilla's hoarseness as he called, "Halt! Who goes there? Stand right there!"

The gorilla guard in the crow's nest got to his feet and unslung his rifle. He peered down toward the ground, but he could see nothing, not even Burke as he clung to the shadowy dark timbers that formed the base of the tower.

"Gorak?" called the gorilla from the top of the tower. "What is it?"

Burke once more disguised his voice as best he could. "Humans," he called.

That was the signal for Virdon to begin thrashing about in the underbrush again. The noise was clearly audible to the gorilla guard this time. "Hold on," called the ape in the crow's nest. "I'm coming down!" The gorilla swung a leg onto the outside ladder that led down to the ground and began the tortuous climb. He grasped the rungs tightly, fearfully, as his rifle swung back and forth. The gorilla guard was very frightened of heights, although that was something he could never tell his commanding officer.

Burke was on the ground level now, standing beside one of the broad base timbers. "Stand still!" he cried in his best ape voice. "Hold, or I'll shoot!"

"Just a second," called the gorilla. "I'll be right there. Hold them off until I can help."

Burke looked up and watched. Just before the gorilla came within reach, Burke slipped around the corner of the tower. As he disappeared from view, he heard the heavy sound of the gorilla jumping to the ground.

"Gorak?" called the gorilla.

"I got him," answered Burke.

The gorilla guard needed to hear no more. He dashed around the base of the tower. There was another sickening thunk and the crash of another gorilla body to the ground.

"Not bad," said Virdon.

"Two for two," said Burke.

The astronauts dragged the second gorilla to a spot near the first. Then they took time to tie and gag both guards securely. Virdon examined their handiwork critically, then finally gave a satisfied nod to Burke. "Okay," he said, "we're all set down here. These guys aren't going anywhere for a long time."

"After you?" asked Burke.

"Thank you," said Virdon. The blond man started up the ladder toward the crow's nest, followed immediately by Burke. The climb went smoothly and quickly; there were no other gorilla troops anywhere nearby. The two men were confident, yet Burke voiced the only negative thought that had occurred to him.

"You know what I've been scared of?" he asked.

"Yes," said Virdon, anticipating his friend's fear. "That we got here too late and the message was already relayed."

"How did you know what I was thinking?" asked Burke.

"How many times in the last few months have you thought anything at all that either Galen or I hadn't already thought of?" asked Virdon. "No, seriously, it was a possibility that I've been worrying about for a while."

"Hey, look!" cried Burke, pointing far into the distance, where the blue-green of a range of hills was split by the lightning flashes of a heliograph. All else in the panorama was still and serene, grayed by distance, but the bright reflections from the giant minors drew all the attention of the two humans.

"All right," said Burke to himself, figuring the time scale in his head. "That has to be from Aboro's headquarters, assuming that Galen's act went off according to schedule. If that's the case, then we got here just in time."

The two men watched the heliograph winking its coded message for several seconds in silence. The system was clumsy and inefficient, dependent on the time of day and the weather, but it was the best that the ape leaders could devise—or would allow.

"Can you read it, Pete?" asked Virdon.

Burke stared with his eyes squinted. "'...requested on Octavio, an aide to Dr. Zaius. Inform Prefect Aboro of status immediately,'" he said. "That's it. I think they're repeating the message a second time. Yes, I got it."

"I'm glad your code-reading is better than mine," said Virdon.

"The important thing is that Galen pulled it off," said Burke. "He did it. At least well enough to make Aboro go through the trouble of checking. He was at least that convincing."

"We're not out of the woods yet, Pete," said Virdon, seriously.

"Doggone it, Alan," said Burke impatiently, "why is it that every time we accomplish something, make some really great heroic play, you have to turn to me with that long face and tell me we're still hanging around in the Valley of Doom? Why don't you ever give us credit for our success?"

"I do," said Virdon. "And I will—after we've made sure of it this time. We still have a long way to go. You better acknowledge that message before they get suspicious."

"Oh," said Burke. "Yeah. Right. I'm sorry. I forgot."

While Virdon watched anxiously, Burke studied the

mechanism of the heliograph mirror, finding that it was operated on a simple shutter mechanism. He worked the shutters in a brief coded message, then waited.

Across the valley, from the distant hills, came an answering flash. "'Acknowledged,'" said Burke. "They bought it. They swallowed Galen, and now they've fallen for us. How are we doing?"

"Close," said Virdon.

"Close, but?" said Burke.

"Yes," said Virdon soberly. "*But...*"

"You always have that 'but,'" said Burke. "I can always predict it."

"That's what's kept us alive, enough times," said Virdon.

"Well, anyway, so far, so good," Burke replied.

"I'll grant you that," said Virdon, relaxing a bit.

"One of the interesting things about that message is that Aboro is prefacing his name with a new title these days," said Burke. "He's calling himself 'Lord of the Apes.'"

"I can think of a few apes right off hand that would dispute him," said Virdon, gazing out toward the now-darkened heliograph tower in the distance. He looked up at the position of the sun, just past noon, sliding down into afternoon. "It'll take an hour or better for the relays to get the message to Central City," he said musingly. "Another hour back. We'll give it two hours and then heliograph the confirmation."

"Like clockwork," said Burke.

"That's what it is," said Virdon. They both stared down at the peaceful forest below and wished that their lives were as free as they pretended.

Inside Prefect Aboro's office in Hathor, the gorilla chief

was pacing his floor. He was consumed with anxiety and curiosity, and he knew the limitations of the transmitting equipment. There was nothing to do but wait; but that didn't mean that he couldn't bother his subordinates every few minutes, just to relieve his own tension.

"Any word from Central City yet, Daku?" he asked as his lieutenant entered.

"We should hear from them very soon, I estimate, sir," said Daku. There was a short pause. "Aboro," said the lieutenant slowly, "suppose this Octavio is an imposter? It could be some kind of trap or plot against you. You should be giving thought to that."

"Believe me," said Aboro, grinning evilly. "I have, I have. In that case, Octavio will be executed before sundown."

The time passed as slowly in the crow's nest as it did in Aboro's office. There was nothing for Virdon and Burke to do to pass the time. But the time did pass, eventually. Virdon studied the position of the sun, which was just beginning to dip behind the taller, of the forest's treetops. "As near as I can figure," he said, "it's been a good two hours. You might as well go ahead, Pete."

Burke nodded, saying nothing. There was no need for any further discussion; all conversation had been used up many minutes before. Burke went straight to the heliograph mirror, took hold of the shutter handle, and shuffled the shutters in the proper code. Then he stopped and waited.

Far away, a similar heliograph tower watched as a message was flashed toward it. This tower stood on the outskirts of Hathor. One of Aboro's troopers waited at the base of the structure, in order to get the message to the prefect, as quickly as possible. The tower received its message, then flipped a quick reply, not realizing it was asking for Burke's fiction.

"All set, Alan," said Burke. "Let me have it."

"Take your time and get it right," said Virdon, getting set to dictate the message. "'Octavio, Assistant to Zaius, on official business. Extend courtesy. Signed, Supreme Council, Bron, Acting Secretary. For Prefect Aboro only."

Burke's hand flipped the control handle, and the mirror beamed its coded dispatch toward Hathor.

Some time later, Aboro's voice was heard in his office, reading from a transcribed copy of the message, delivered by his trooper. His voice was intended to be noncommittal, but Daku could read the trace of excitement in Aboro's tone. "…on official business. Extend courtesy. Signed, Supreme Council, Bron, Acting Secretary. For Prefect Aboro only."

"That seems to clear up any doubt," said Daku.

Aboro just stood staring across his office, the paper forgotten in his hand, his eyes unfocused, dreaming of previously unreachable horizons. He, Aboro, General and Commander of all gorilla army and police forces in the entire ape empire! Unbelievable!

"So Octavio is really who he says he is," said Daku, again trying to break his superior's daydreaming. Daku had his own plans, and Aboro might need some careful guidance in the more delicate moments from now on. Urko had said himself that Aboro wasn't the best at making plans…

"Which means that one day soon I shall be *Commander* Aboro!" whispered the prefect.

Daku smiled. Aboro was beginning to think practically

again. The two gorillas shook hands solemnly, marking the occasion.

Less than an hour later, Galen was ushered into Aboro's office by Daku, who was going out of his way to act like the subservient and unctuous aide he was supposed to be. Aboro sprang to his feet when he saw the chimpanzee. "A pleasure to see you again," cried Aboro, almost out of his mind with anticipation. "Ah, Octavio, won't you have a seat?"

Indeed, Daku had already led Galen to a chair, and Galen was already sitting. Aboro didn't seem to notice.

Galen laughed softly, into one palm. He looked at Daku for a moment, then turned back to Aboro. "What is this odd preoccupation of yours with *chairs*, my dear Aboro? It seems that every time I'm in your presence, I'm being urged from one seat to another. If I stand, I'm practically pushed back into a chair. I assure you, I'm quite comfortable, and very skilled at maintaining that comfort. That is a talent one acquires in Central City. One, I'm sure, that it will not take you long to learn." He smiled meaningfully.

"Yes, Octavio," said Aboro, almost dizzy with disbelief. He could barely understand the significance of what Galen was telling him.

"Just remember, please, my dear Aboro," continued Galen, "I am quite capable of sitting down without an invitation. Now, have you been thinking over what I mentioned to you earlier?"

"I… yes, I have," said Aboro weakly.

"I thought so, I thought so," said Galen, laughing softly to himself as though there were some private joke between them. It was just the sort of thing a pompous bureaucrat would do. It was the kind of thing that made

Galen so valuable to the schemes he and his astronaut friends devised. "And of course you checked on my credentials at the same time."

Aboro looked with horror at Daku. "Who could have said anything about that?" cried the prefect, his innocence wounded for the first time.

Once more Galen laughed. "Don't look so guilty!" he cried in mock delight. "In your shoes, I would have done the same thing. Well! I would have been very disappointed if you hadn't!" His tone changed immediately, from one of light bantering to a cold, businesslike voice. "Have you reached any conclusions?" he asked.

"About—?" murmured Aboro.

"Your old friend," said Galen, beginning to show some impatience at the verbal game they were playing. "It should be obvious that nothing can be done about you until *something* has been done about him."

Aboro nodded his agreement.

"I expect that you have a suggestion or two?" said Galen lightly, leaving all the responsibility in Aboro's lap, so the prefect would realize that he was being tested.

"Why can't the Council simply... dismiss Urko?" asked Aboro.

"My dear Prefect!" cried Galen, half-rising from his seat. "On what grounds? Even the Supreme Council needs evidence. I was hoping you could provide that. Besides, Urko and Zaius are the Supreme Council, in effect if not in fact. It would be most, *most* difficult to get Urko to agree to his own dismissal."

Aboro paced nervously. It was obvious to him that the pleasant future he had painted for himself would not be achieved without a great deal of effort and danger. Aboro did not mind danger—when it was aimed at someone else. "I'm not sure I understand," he said.

Galen heaved the sigh of an adult trying to explain something to a particularly dense child. "I will continue then in words of one syllable," he said. "Dr. Zaius wants— no, more—*expects* you to provide him with the evidence he needs to discredit Urko, to dismiss the general, and, shortly thereafter, to offer Urko's vacated position to you. This is not so much a test of your abilities, which Dr. Zaius already appreciates, as a kind of bond and pledge of your loyalty. You will understand how your actions will ally you closely to the policies of Dr. Zaius in the future. This is what he stands to gain from the transaction."

There was a pause, while the vast ideas which Galen had communicated were absorbed by the reeling brain of Aboro and by the greedy mind of Daku. Then, patiently, Galen continued. "For instance," he said off-handedly, "consider the possibility of incriminating Urko by discovering contraband evidence in his own home. Evidence such as illegally possessed gold. Perhaps, as a hint, the same gold that was used to bribe Dr. Zaius' subordinates."

Aboro nodded. The idea made much sense and was the kind of scheme to which the prefect was attracted. He had arranged similar seizures in the past, although of course on a much smaller scale. "But how would you get the gold into Urko's home?" asked the prefect.

Galen looked at the ceiling as if expecting some kind of help from that direction. "Not I," he said. "*You.* I've passed my examinations, many times over. It is you, Aboro, who is being given this opportunity. You will prove your loyalty to Dr. Zaius by planting the evidence yourself."

There was another thoughtful pause. Aboro wasn't pleased with the idea at all. There was too much personal risk. There didn't seem to be any escape clause in case of failure. "Too risky and too unsure," said Aboro. Then, with decision, he announced, "I have a better idea."

Galen cocked a curious eyebrow.

"I have always favored direct action, Octavio," said Aboro.

Galen had a fear of what was coming. He tried to hide his concern. "Direct action?" he asked.

Daku paced along behind his master. He, too, understood what Aboro was hinting at. He had been party to many of Aboro's previous dealings. "Yes," said Daku. "It will be much *safer*. Then you will truly be 'Lord of the Apes.'"

Galen was still pretending that he wasn't precisely sure what Aboro and Daku were talking about. "Just what are you suggesting?" he asked.

"Daku," said Aboro, ignoring the false Octavio in his excitement, "who is that human you've used before?"

Daku thought for a moment. Although Aboro himself never directly involved himself with the details of these matters, Daku was expected to recall all the pertinent information. "Amhar," said the lieutenant at last. "From the village of Loban."

"A human?" asked Galen.

Daku toned to Galen with a look of mock surprise. "You wouldn't expect us to think another ape could possibly do the job. Amhar is a professional."

"A professional... what?" asked Galen.

"Killer!" cried Aboro. "Apes do not murder other apes, friend Octavio, even though apes may plan the removal of other apes. The actual foul deed is left to someone of the lower order."

Galen reacted violently. This was not the way the

conversation was supposed to have proceeded. "But that's terrible!" he cried. Then, realizing that his reaction was incorrect, he recovered. "I mean," he said more calmly, "that's rather a more drastic solution than Dr. Zaius—"

He was cut off by Daku. "The advantage is that the solution is very permanent. There is no chance that Urko might recover his lost influence to use against the prefect at a later time."

"Very good, Lieutenant," said Aboro. "Daku, arrange a dinner party for Urko here tonight. We may as well get this entire charade finished as soon as possible."

"And Amhar?" asked Daku, anxious to be certain that he understood all of Aboro's intentions. The two gorillas stood very close together, almost completely ignoring Galen as they planned out the details of their plot.

Galen walked casually toward Aboro's desk, where he saw a clutter of papers. Among them, though, was Aboro's official seal. This was something that Galen realized might come in especially handy. While Daku and Aboro talked, the chimpanzee lightly picked up the official seal and slid it into his tunic without arousing any suspicion from the two plotters.

"I have a special plan," said Aboro. "Have this Amhar— you'll recognize him, won't you? I've never seen him before—have him here an hour before Urko arrives."

"Well," said Galen, "this isn't the way Dr. Zaius expected matters to be settled, but nevertheless it appears you have everything in order for General Urko's... dismissal... or what was it you called it?"

"Removal," said Aboro simply.

"Yes," said Galen. "In any event, if all goes as I hope, I can safely promise a radical change in your personal situation. This is definitely assured."

Galen smiled at Aboro, indicating that he wished to leave the rest of the tawdry details in the hands of the gorillas. Aboro nodded and indicated that Daku should show the chimpanzee out of the office.

In the small clearing, Burke watched as Virdon melted a piece of wax over a folded letter. A small pool of hot wax dripped on the folded edges of the parchment. Then Virdon pressed Aboro's seal into the wax. Behind them, Galen paced, nervous as usual.

"I just don't like it," he said unhappily.

Virdon looked up from his task. "Who does?" he said. "This matter has grown very ugly. But who could have foreseen those gorillas coming up with the idea to use a professional killer?"

"Yeah," said Burke distastefully. "And by candlelight dinner yet."

"Wait a minute!" said Galen excitedly. "There's something we've forgotten. Janor! He won't wait!"

"Let's cross that bridge later, Galen," said Virdon.

Galen muttered something, but the astronauts couldn't hear. The two men stood and began pushing their way through the brush at the side of the clearing. Galen hesitated a moment; then, his expression changing from consternation to determination, he followed his friends.

The afternoon sunlight glinted on the black leather uniform of Daku as the gorilla rode on horseback at an easy canter through the wooded countryside. He was too engrossed with his own thoughts to notice Virdon, Burke, and Galen lying in wait for him on a rock outcropping beside the road.

"Daku," said Galen in a hoarse whisper.

"Most of it depends on you, Pete," said Virdon. "You're playing the lead role."

"Don't remind me," said Burke.

Daku rode on, unsuspecting of the trio who waited for him to get near enough. Virdon gathered himself as Daku's horse passed almost directly beneath his position. As Daku reached the point in the trail that Virdon had marked, the astronaut rose to his full height and launched himself downward at Daku, knocking the gorilla from his horse. Galen ran toward the excited animal and gathered the horse's reins, soothing the beast. Meanwhile, Burke was on the stunned Daku with ropes and a gag, rendering Aboro's lieutenant helpless. Virdon removed Daku's pistol from its holster.

"Come on," cried Virdon, "let's get off the road. Quick!" Virdon and Burke dragged Daku off the road and in among the brush alongside the trail. Galen stood patiently, calming Daku's horse.

The gag was put in place around Daku's mouth, and Burke finished tying Daku's hands behind his back. Once done, Burke went to the horse, took the reins from Galen, and saddled up. Virdon stuffed a small pouch and the letter into one of the saddle bags.

"Good luck!" cried Virdon. "We won't be too far behind you."

Burke gave a wave as he spurred the horse; in a few seconds he was riding furiously down the road in the same direction Daku had been heading before the gorilla had been ambushed.

Burke's thoughts were confused, partially by the speed and urgency of his mission, partially by the importance and danger of their actions on this day. Rarely in their travels together had Burke, Virdon, and Galen joined in such a devious yet momentous scheme. All Burke could hope for was good luck, good planning, and the fewest number of new surprises. He didn't want any more unplanned emergencies ruining what was already a hazardous undertaking.

He rode as fast as the poor trail allowed him. He saw the barricade in the road only a few seconds before he would have run directly into it. His teeth clenched and a few words passed through his lips as he reined in the horse. There, in the middle of the trail, was a temporary barrier and three of Urko's own elite guards. All three stood with their rifles pointed directly at him.

"Well," said one of the gorillas.

"A human riding a horse," said one of the others.

"A punishable offense, I believe," said the third, and the three gorillas broke up in laughter. Burke wondered how moronic a situation had to be before a gorilla would laugh at it.

"Halt," said the first gorilla. Burke only shrugged. He brought the animal to a reined stop. As the gorillas stepped forward, Burke quickly turned the horse and stormed past the surprised gorillas. The tactic might have worked, except for the two squads of gorilla guards who rushed into the road from the concealing brush. Burke had to swerve; the horse reared. It was all that Burke could do to control the animal. The gorillas all had their weapons pointed at him.

"Okay, okay," said Burke.

"Get down," ordered one of the guards. He waved his rifle imperatively. Burke obeyed, standing there with a look of worry and concern on his face.

A few moments later, none other than General Urko himself walked about his private camp in front of his command tent. Urko had a very contented smile on his face "So," he said, "my very dear, very old friend Burke.

Burke stood before Urko, his hands tied behind him, guarded by two gorillas."

"What a great pleasure to meet again after all this time!" said Urko in a terrifyingly cold voice. "A very great pleasure!"

4

The gorilla troopers, the hand-picked guards of General Urko, went about their tasks. Some fed and watered the horses, others waited for the guttural commands of their leader. A good many gorillas still held their blunt rifles on Pete Burke, although the human was bound, helpless, and presented little threat of escaping or harming Urko.

The gorilla general was engaging in one of his favorite pursuits: drawing out each moment of victory, savoring the circumstances in a greedy way that only made each second more of a torture for his victim. "I'm curious, Burke," said Urko, as he paced back and forth before his captive. "I thought you were cleverer. You've demonstrated an aptitude for quick thinking in our previous encounters. At least, I thought you were cleverer and quicker than *our* humans."

Burke refused to be baited by the gorilla commander. He had a strong sense of pride, and no thinly veiled insults from Urko could make Burke forget his own heritage. "I got news for you," he said insolently. "I'm even cleverer than your gorillas, Urko. Not that it takes any real brains to accomplish that. This bunch must be out on a punishment tour. Are you leading them, or are you just part of the chain gang?"

Urko's eyes flashed at Burke's contemptuous remarks. Still, the general looked around at his troopers. They did not seem to have earned such spectacular sarcasm. "My guards are picked for several qualities, as you know," said Urko in a tightly controlled voice. "They must have loyalty. They must be strong. And they must be obedient. Intelligence can be a hindrance, beyond a certain point. But I can assure you, every one of these guards is capable of following any order I might give." There was a massive threat implied in that final statement.

"In my present condition," said Burke, "and noticing that I am, in fact, outnumbered, I am not surprised."

"You have an odd sense of humor for one so near to death," said Urko, unable to understand just what made this human so different from the pitiable humans he usually dealt with. He stopped pacing and faced Burke squarely. "You must know that the penalty for a human who rides a horse is to be shot. It occurs to me that we've been through this before."

"Maybe I like to live dangerously," said Burke with a small smile. "But if it makes you happier to know, I got separated from my friends last night. One of your famous patrols was after us again. By the way, I wish they'd either catch us or give up, already. All of this is starting to get on our nerves. Anyway, I split from them and 'borrowed' this horse. I was using it to try to catch up with Virdon and Galen."

"You 'borrowed' the horse?" asked Urko. "Where?"

"Does it make a difference?" asked Burke, shrugging.

Urko was persistent. "Was his owner riding him at the time?"

Burke adopted a casual attitude. "Come to think of it," he said slowly, "he was. He's probably got himself quite a headache."

Urko was silent for several seconds, his expression thoughtful. He knew Burke, and he knew that the three fugitives would not likely split up except under the most unusual circumstances. Lacking any understanding of the present situation, Urko turned his attention to the evidence at hand. He examined the horse Burke had been riding. "It's a handsome animal," he said, musing. "It's obviously a horse that belongs to an official." He thought for a while longer, then raised his voice to one of the guards waiting nearby. "Any identification in the saddlebags?"

The guard came to attention at the sound of Urko's voice. He made no reply. He was as silent as a statue, a statue of a very well-drilled, well-disciplined soldier.

"Well?" asked Urko impatiently. "I didn't ask for a demonstration of your training. I want an answer. Now."

"We haven't yet checked the saddlebags, General," said the gorilla in a slightly timorous voice.

"You haven't checked them," said Urko quietly. Then his expression changed to a snarl and he roared, "Why not?"

"We were waiting for an order, sir," replied the thoroughly frightened soldier. "We did not know if that was what you desired."

"Do you have to order them to blink, too, General, sir?" asked Burke mockingly.

"I am surrounded by incompetents!" cried Urko, slapping a gauntleted fist against a leather-clad thigh. "Check them now! Instantly!"

"Yes, sir!" cried the guard, who hurried off to comply with General Urko's wishes.

Burke turned to watch the operation. Urko stared sullenly. The first guard ran to the horse, while another guard held the reins in case the animal should shy away. The first guard rummaged for a moment in the saddlebags, finally coming up with the wrapped bundle and the folded letter which Virdon had placed there.

"We're getting some place at last," muttered Urko.

"If only you'd let me give you some advice," said Burke. "We humans were in the same place about five, hundred years before I was born."

"I could give *you* some advice, Burke," growled Urko.

"That's the kind of talk that's making me hunt you and your friends from one district to another."

"Is that why?" asked Burke innocently. "I thought it was just a parking violation."

Meanwhile, the guard had run up to Urko with the contents of the saddlebag. Urko removed the wrapping from the bundle. The bright sun glittered, off a small but hefty bar of pure gold. The flickers of reflected light gleamed in the polished leather of Urko's uniform and shone in the deep, dark wells that were his eyes. "Gold?" he asked. "This interests me."

"If I had known about that, I might just have run off and bought myself a farm somewhere," said Burke.

Urko was not really listening. "Humans cannot own farms," he said curtly.

"Not in your world," said Burke. "But your world can't be the *whole* world."

"Be quiet, Burke," said Urko gruffly. "Well, well. This makes everything so much more enjoyable. Here," he said to the guard, "put this gold in my tent. Wait, let me see that paper." The guard handed Urko the letter, took back the gold, and hurried toward the general's private tent.

"It seems to be an official thing," said Burke, trying to needle Urko even more by pretending innocent helpfulness. "There's a seal on it."

Urko didn't notice Burke's tactic, so engrossed was he in the matter. "I *know* what it is!" he said. He inspected the seal for a moment. "Hmmm. Prefect Aboro's seal."

"Aboro?" said Burke. "Isn't he that gorilla who has that terrific collection of jokes about you and—"

Urko had ceased paying any attention at all to Burke. Eagerly, he ripped open the sealed letter, totally ignoring Burke's opinion that Urko was tampering with the mails. Urko unfolded the parchment. He read it through quickly, then read it again. For a moment, it looked as if Urko were about to crush the letter in his huge hand, but he did not. There was a silence. Then Urko looked up at Burke with narrowed eyes. His voice was filled with hatred. "You say you knew nothing of this letter?" he said.

Burke shook his head, his eyes wide with innocence. "What do you think I was doing last night?" he asked. "I was in a hurry, remember? I didn't think about riffling around in the saddlebags on the horse! I just wanted the horse. I had one of your patrols on my tail. Besides, what do I have to do with ape letters?"

Urko was buying nothing, neither Burke's protestations of good faith nor the possibility that the human was telling the truth. There was a great deal at stake; when the game became so important, Urko became cautious. That was how he had made his reputation and his career and it was how he kept them both intact.

"What indeed?" pondered the ape general. He raised the parchment letter again and read aloud. "'To Amhar of the village of Loban. Urko dinner tonight at nine. Be here one hour earlier for final instructions. Aboro.'" The message obviously upset Urko. Being a gorilla and of a similar temperament to Aboro, Urko was fairly certain that he knew what those "final instructions" would be. Fortunately, though, the letter had been intercepted. If what Burke said was the truth, then Urko had managed to save his own life and had detected an important traitor in his chain of command. If Burke was telling the truth.

The entire situation was too deadly, too filled with danger to permit a quick decision. Yet time was running out quickly. General Urko realized that he had come to one of the major crises of his life. And he had very little idea of how to continue. "Kronak!" he called.

Another gorilla guard stepped forward and saluted. He placed his rifle smartly on the ground, its butt pressed next to his boot. "General?" he asked.

"Does the name Amhar mean anything to you?" demanded Urko in a surly voice.

Kronak the guard was silent for a moment, thinking. Like the others of his kind, his memory was slow and dull. Then he answered. "Yes, General," he said. "There is a human known as Amhar who is believed to be a hired killer."

Urko stared at Kronak, but made no sound. He waved the gorilla guard away before the subordinate could see that Urko was clearly displeased and worried. Kronak went back to his duties, and Urko stared into the distance, lost in thought.

"Sounds like this Aboro's planned quite a dinner for you, Urko," said Burke in a light voice.

"Silence, you," snapped Urko.

"Yes, sir," said Burke. "I understand that you need time to consider these latest developments."

Urko began pacing again, his face twisted in a frown that displayed varying emotions as his thoughts changed. From the look on his face, none of those thoughts could have been pleasant. "All right," he said, more to himself than to anyone nearby, "it must be that Aboro is summoning this human on another matter altogether." He slapped the letter.

Burke laughed quietly. "I don't understand how someone as sharp as you are can keep coming up with the wrong answers, Urko."

"What is the right answer, then, human?"

Burke spoke casually. "Maybe it's just that Aboro wants your job."

Urko glowered at Burke with an expression of pure hatred. "There is more here than you can know," said the gorilla chieftain. "You don't have the facts in the matter."

"Neither do you," said Burke. "Otherwise, you wouldn't be jumping around like a frightened rabbit."

"I have had gorillas shot for repeating insults lighter than that in my hearing," said Urko.

"Maybe that's why this Amhar is dining with Aboro before you get there tonight," said Burke.

"One thing that you don't understand, human," said Urko through clenched jaws, "is that there is a bond of honor among gorillas. Among all apes. That is what sets us apart from human beings. That is what makes us superior. We are creatures of intellect, strength, and integrity. It would take a human mind to devise a scheme as odious as the one you suggest."

"Oh, come on!" said Burke. "Let me ask you this. Weren't there gorillas ahead of you in the chain of command at one time? Or were you born a general?"

"Of course, there were gorillas more important than me," said Urko.

"And did they all retire? Did they all die natural deaths?" asked Burke.

Urko was close to strangling Burke. The rage mounted in the general until he could barely control it. But the truth was clear to Urko and Burke; the situation that Urko faced was possibly fatal for the gorilla general, and that matter took priority. Urko tried to make one last effort to dismiss the matter from his own mind. "Aboro is an old friend!" he said. "One of my dearest companions from childhood. And gorillas do have depths of loyalty that your filthy human mind could never understand."

"Anything you say," said Burke wearily.

Urko looked up at Burke again, with an evil smile, creasing his ugly face. "But we've strayed from the main subject, haven't we, Burke?"

Burke gave Urko a puzzled look.

"The subject of your punishment, of course!" said Urko, almost laughing aloud. He turned to one of the waiting apes and gave the order in a hard voice. "Take him out and shoot him!"

"Hold it!" cried Burke, suddenly galvanized, realizing that his delaying tactic had failed and that more drastic action was called for.

Virdon and Galen were nearby, as they had promised, watching the entire scene. It had played almost exactly as they had planned, up until the moment when Urko disregarded the note and ordered that Burke be taken away and killed. That had very definitely not been in their plans. From their place of concealment along the camp's perimeter, they could hear every, word spoken between Burke and Urko.

"The whole thing's backfired," said Galen.

"You are so right," said Virdon grimly, taking out a pistol; he checked to see that it was loaded, then lifted it and aimed it directly at Urko's chest. Suddenly, however, he stopped dead. The gun wavered slightly in his grasp.

"No one has told me to 'hold it' in a good many years," said Urko dangerously. "The last time, as I recall, the unfortunate ape who said those words died rather suddenly. A lack of communication between his heart and his brain. A bloody one."

Burke was too deeply involved to be put off by Urko's grim memories. "Let's you and me make a deal," he said.

Urko sneered. "A deal with a condemned human?" he said.

Burke sighed. "I am about to be killed, right?"

"Correct," said Urko. "You're just starting to come to your senses. How tragically late for you."

"My point is that I have nothing to lose," said Burke. "If I can offer you enough to keep me alive, I have everything to gain. I can be a lot of help to you, Urko. Maybe you've never seen that before, but it's true. Look, you're not all that sure about Aboro, never mind all that stuff you were telling me about loyalty among apes. Don't bother to answer, let me talk. Suppose he does intend to have you killed? You'll never know unless you let him meet with the hired killer."

Urko stared. Some of what Burke said was sensible enough. Mostly, though," it sounded to the general like the half-mad ravings of a doomed human. He had heard that kind of nonsense often enough in his career. "And of course I am foolish enough to allow that and give Aboro a chance to have me killed," he said. "*If* he is planning all this, which frankly I still doubt."

Burke knew that he had begun to win an advantage,

that his arguments were beginning to have an effect on Urko's reasoning. Urko was the most intelligent of his gorilla comrades, but even so the general was slow to change his ideas. Burke had to press on. "Maybe you doubt and maybe you don't. But I'll bet you never get another good night's sleep until you find out the truth, once and for all!"

Urko took up his pacing once more. There was so much to consider, and Burke was just an annoying complication. "And so, human," said Urko, staring at the parchment in his hand, "I send on this message and allow the killer to meet with Aboro? Is that the foolish idea you're suggesting?"

"No, Urko," said Burke, beginning to sound slightly exasperated at the gorilla's lack of imagination. "You allow *me!*"

There was a stunned silence. Urko could only look blankly at the agitated prisoner. In the shrubbery around the edge of the camp, Virdon and Galen heard Burke's words and were equally surprised. They were dumbfounded by the dark-haired astronaut's quick thinking and a little unsure about what he meant to do. Like Urko, they could only listen and hope to discover his plan.

Burke continued talking, not letting Urko voice an objection, not letting the gorilla leader have a few moments to dismiss the whole situation, have Burke killed, and take his entire entourage back to Central City. After all, if he could have Augustus transferred to nowhere, he could have Aboro sent less than nowhere just as simply, and the whole question would be easily settled. Burke didn't want Urko to have the opportunity to make that decision. "I play Amhar!" he said. "And all it costs you is my freedom. You can see how I stand to gain. What have *you* got to lose?"

Urko grimaced. "You for one," he said.

"You've done that before," said Burke.

"If you're trying to convince me of something," said Urko, "you're going about it the wrong way."

"My point is that our paths, thanks, to your diligence, seem to cross at fairly regular intervals," said Burke.

"Once ought to be enough," said Urko.

"Aw, admit it," said Burke with a forced laugh. "You'd, miss the thrill of the chase."

"I have other things to chase."

"Look," said Burke, "nobody but you knows you've caught me. You and your guards, that is. And *they* won't open their mouths if you tell them not to."

"That is the first true thing you've uttered," said Urko. He looked around again at his gorilla troopers. They all remained at their stations, their rifles unslung, their expressions empty. They existed only to fill Urko's orders.

"It's the second fact," said Burke. "The first was that you'll never rest easy again until you know that letter means nothing or you have your proof against Aboro."

It was clear that Urko was weakening quickly. The silence this time was filled with his muttering growl. Burke couldn't make out any specific words, although the rhythm of the phrases sounded to the astronaut like curses. It didn't make any difference. The solution to the matter would come quickly enough. "And for this peace of mind you're granting me, you want what? Your freedom again? No perpetual guarantees? No official pardons?"

"I don't think you'd honor them, anyway," said Burke. At Urko's darkening glance, the man hurried to explain. I mean, I respect your devotion to duty too much to think that you'd just forget about me and my buddies."

"You are right again."

"And if I'm right so often lately, maybe you ought to give some genuine consideration to my plan," said Burke. "Let me loose after I pretend to be your killer. And give me a couple of hours start. That's all I'm asking. Just fair sport, Urko. You could have me hogtied again by tomorrow night, if you work fast."

Urko took a deep breath and let it out slowly. He looked over his shoulder at his troopers. "Go on, find something to do," he ordered them. They hurried away, leaving Urko alone with Burke. Even after the gorillas left, the general said nothing for quite some time, studying the human closely, as if he hoped to discover the truth or falsity of Burke's claim somewhere on the man's face. Through all of this, Burke did his best to remain passive and calm, although a few drops of perspiration ran slowly down his forehead, maddeningly along the bridge of his nose, and with demonic, ticklish slowness to his chin.

"Very well," said Urko. "We'll keep that rendezvous with Prefect Aboro, just to prove you wrong. Then I will have you shot."

Burke was about to make a remark about how often he had heard Urko threaten to shoot him. But he caught himself in time and his better sense kept his mouth closed.

Virdon and Galen in the nearby brush let out their long-held breaths in collective sighs of relief. Virdon turned to the chimpanzee and whispered, "Good old Pete! He could con the pearl right out of an oyster! Come on."

Together they backed away into the denser underbrush.

Behind the gray hills in the distance, the orange ball of the sun was beginning to light flames which, later, would reach into the sky as the brilliant dying embers of sunset. The valley which comprised the district governed by Aboro was already beginning to darken in the first faint touches of dusk. One bright star hung low in the sky. The sounds of daylight birds and animals were fading with the light. Night was coming quickly on.

Activity in the valley did not cease with the daylight, however. Gorilla patrols still continued their angry pursuit of whatever they decided might be a human crime. The humans themselves were just beginning to hurry home from their laborious daytime occupations to share a few hours of peace with their families and neighbors.

On the road to the village of Hathor, a slow-moving wagon rumbled its clumsy way among the rustling trees. The wagon was half-filled with supplies and was drawn by an ox. An old human of about sixty years, his hair sparse and white, his face covered with rough stubble, sat on the warped seat and drove his lazy animal. Beside him sat another man, dressed in a dark cloak pulled over his head to shadow his features.

"You know," said the old man, "it's good to have you along, stranger. These trips I make are lonely, taking supplies out to the ape outposts. Weeks go by sometimes without me seeing so much as one other human being. Those that I do see from time to time never have much time to talk, what with all the work their ape masters give them. And the last creature in the world you want to try to talk to is one of those uniformed gorillas. You know what I mean?"

The other figure made no response. A sudden bump jerked the cloak from the man's head. In the dim light of the setting sun, Janor pulled the garment back over his grim features. The old man rambled on and on, oblivious to the fact that he was being ignored, that Janor had much weightier problems on his mind. Janor had plans to make, or, rather, a variety of different schemes to choose from. He had given the matter thought all day, and he hadn't yet decided which way would best suit his need for revenge. Outwardly, though, an observer would never guess the murderous content of Janor's thoughts. He seemed to be just a stoic, silent man, no different than many other docile humans.

"You say you have business in Hathor?" asked the old man.

Once more, there was no response from Janor. He stared straight ahead at the dusty road. Beneath the cloak, surreptitiously, absentmindedly, he slid his finger along a knife blade. It was a short, stubby knife, not very sharp, but it would do the job he had planned for it.

"Well," said the old man, "with luck we should be there soon after dark."

There was not the slightest reply from Janor.

"Yes," said the old man, "it's good to have somebody to talk to every once in a while. Does the soul good."

The wagon rumbled on into the gathering darkness, its two occupants lost in their private worlds.

The town of Hathor had settled down for the evening. The bustling humans had returned to their shabby homes. The gorillas lounged in eating places or stood guard duty at their posts. The ape citizens had long ago closed up their shops. All was peaceful in the town of Hathor. But for a few lights burning in huts along the village's main street, everything was now in darkness. All, that is, except the headquarters of Aboro, which was ablaze with light from within.

Inside Aboro's place, the sparse and cold atmosphere of the prefect's office had been transformed into a festive scene. A table had been moved into the middle of the outer office. The desk and other office equipment had been pushed back. Chairs had been set around the table, an expensive tablecloth had been laid; candlesticks placed at either end of the table, and the finest ape made earthen dishes had been set. Aboro paced nervously around the table, examining each detail. A human servant was placing the last of the table settings when Aboro's nerves got the better of him. "All right!" he cried. "It's finished. It looks fine. Stop fussing with it. Get out of here." The frightened human gave Aboro a quick look and then almost ran out of the prefect's building. Aboro was not relieved. He stared at the table and listened to the quiet settle down around him. He wished that the night's events had already ended.

Beyond the prefect's building, the main street of Hathor quickly fell into total blackness. There were four more huts between the house of Aboro and a small intersecting alley. One of these huts had light streaming through an open window. The light was not as bright or intense as the light coming from the prefect's building. The other three huts were dark. There was movement between two of these darkened huts. It was difficult for anyone—gorilla guard or scurrying human servant—to see the movement in the night darkness; from the well-lit interior of the prefect's house, all of the outdoors was featureless.

As the moving figures approached the relatively dim light from one of the huts on Aboro's block, however, the forms of Virdon and Galen might have been recognizable to anyone who knew them. They glanced out quickly into the main street and then ducked back into the shadows. They carried objects with them which they held hidden in the darkness. Virdon adjusted the leather loops fastened on the ends of three wooden poles. Galen did the same with a single pole he carried.

"Keep your eyes open for Pete," murmured Virdon in a low voice. "He should be along here any minute."

Galen didn't answer for a moment. He had been thinking about something that would upset their plans. "He will," said the chimpanzee finally, "unless Urko changes his mind about letting him go. He could just as easily have Pete executed."

Virdon realized for the first time that this was definitely a possibility. "Yeah," he said, but he quickly dismissed the notion. It would do no good to worry about theoretical difficulties. They had had enough genuine ones to bother them already.

"Alan!" said Galen excitedly, pointing back toward the main street.

"What is it?" asked Virdon. "Pete?"

"No," said Galen. "Look."

Virdon strained to see what Galen was indicating. The astronaut's eyesight was not nearly as keen as the ape's, but soon he saw what Galen meant. The hooded figure of a man moved along among the shadows of the huts across the way. From the way he sought the darkest patches of the street, it was clear that the figure did not want to be seen. With his definite limp, he was easily recognizable as Janor.

"Janor," whispered Virdon.

"Yes," said Galen. "That was what I feared most. Both for him, and for Pete."

Virdon grabbed Galen's arm and the two bolted off

into the darkness between the huts, carrying their leather-strapped poles. They ran as quickly as they could without making any noise, keeping low to avoid any stray beams of light from the apes' huts. They raced ahead, parallel to the main street, in a desperate attempt to cut off Janor before the enraged farmer could put his plan of vengeance into action.

Meanwhile, Janor, unaware that he had been spotted by his two comrades, continued on his course directly toward the house of Prefect Aboro. He took his time, being careful, but he did not linger in the shadows. The powerful emotions that controlled him now would permit no dallying.

He allowed himself to pause when he came to a point at the end of one of the small block of huts along Hathor's main street. There was no more protection for him further on. He would have to cross the street to the same side as his goal and proceed in the shadow of three or four darkened buildings. With the fire of pure hatred in his eyes, he moved across the narrow lane that served as Hathor's chief thoroughfare. He took his knife from his belt in preparation.

Janor moved stealthily toward Aboro's headquarters, his mind a raging, confused mixture of emotions. His eyes, however, were steady. They were fixed on his goal, and nothing near him distracted his attention. As Janor passed one of the wooden buildings near the prefect's office, two hands reached out suddenly from the black, curtained doorway. Virdon clapped one hand around Janor's mouth; with his other hand he grabbed the wrist of Janor's knife-wielding hand. While Janor struggled and tried to cry put, Virdon dragged him into the building.

Once they were inside, it was clear that the shop was

a crude blacksmith shop, the type owned by apes but worked by humans. Galen watched the two humans struggle, praying to his half-forgotten gods that they didn't arouse too much attention or make too much racket among the tables, benches, and tools of the shop. There was a horse in a small stall near the back of the building and it was already beginning to make small, nervous whinnying sounds. Galen could only look on helplessly, his eyes riveted on the knife.

"Janor!" whispered Virdon hoarsely. "It's Virdon! Listen to me! You've got to give us more time."

The huge farmer easily pulled free from Virdon's grasp, pushing the astronaut aside. Virdon landed heavily and painfully on the hard-packed dirt of the floor.

"No!" said Janor. "My last offer was more than fair. Your time is up. It was up at sundown, as I said. You've failed. Aboro will die tonight! Now!"

"I admit it," said Virdon. "We didn't accomplish our plan before sunset. But we had other problems."

"That makes no difference to me," said Janor.

"An hour," said Galen. "Just give us one more hour."

"No," said Janor firmly.

Janor started out of the blacksmith shop. Virdon, still on the floor, lunged for Janor's legs, tackling the large man. Janor fell backward, twisting, landing on Virdon's back. For a moment, the wind knocked, out of him, Virdon couldn't breathe. Janor raised his hand, hesitated, then drove the knife into the dirt of the floor, only a few inches from Virdon's shoulder—a warning. The two men wrestled briefly, although it was always clear that Janor was Virdon's superior in strength. Slowly, they lifted themselves to their knees; then they stood, still struggling. Kill Aboro," said Virdon, panting, "and you'll be throwing your own life away."

"We've been through this before," said Janor. "It's impossible to argue with you. You don't understand."

"Don't sacrifice yourself, Janor," said Virdon.

"My life is mine to give for Mikal," said Janor.

Janor hurled Virdon aside one more time. Virdon crashed through the shoddy back of the stall. He raised himself painfully to his elbows, gasping for breath. "And will you sacrifice Burke's life as well?" he asked.

Janor only stared, not comprehending what Virdon meant.

"In a few minutes," said Virdon, "Pete's coming with General Urko himself. You want justice? Then help us all get it."

Janor studied Virdon, scarcely believing what the man had told him. Some of it sounded simply insane. Pete Burke, arriving with General Urko, as though the office of Aboro's were the scene of some lukewarm cocktail party instead of the intended setting for murder. Janor glanced back at Galen, then again at Virdon. For the moment, there was nothing that he could say.

At the edge of the village, where the main street tackled off into the dusty country road that ran through the forest, there was a small clearing. Not far from this end of the street was the headquarters of the prefect. The lights from within beamed through the boughs of the trees, casting strange shadows. Five riders approached slowly, walking their horses, attempting to make as little noise as possible. The five were General Urko, three of his omnipresent troopers, and Burke. They pulled to a stop at Urko's command, dismounting in the clearing and tying up the horses to trees.

"My men will surround the building," said Urko in a growling whisper. "I will be listening outside. You had better not have any tricks planned."

"Don't worry," said Burke. "After all I've gone through just to get this far, I'm fresh out of tricks." Nevertheless, the astronaut secretly hoped and prayed that his friends, so long out of communication, had come up with a few of their own. Burke walked slowly and quietly to the door of Prefect Atroro's quarters. He paused a moment, collecting his thoughts. Then he knocked three times. There was a pause, and then the door was flung open. "I am Amhar, sir," said Burke.

Aboro stood looking at him for a few seconds, his pistol in his hand. "Inside," he ordered.

Not far away, General Urko and his troopers watched as Burke entered the building and the door closed behind him. Urko moved his head slightly and made a small gesture. The gorilla troopers had been briefed and understood what their leader meant. They left their place of concealment and scattered to take positions around Aboro's headquarters.

Inside, Aboro was still tense. Suddenly, a thought occurred to him. "Where is my aide, Daku?" he asked.

Burke shrugged. "He delivered your message and left," he said.

Aboro nodded. He did not need Daku any more that night. Indeed, it might be well not to need Daku any more, *ever*..." That was a thought Aboro would have to pursue later. "He told you the price?" he asked.

"Yes," said Burke in a sullen voice. "He said I would be well paid, *after*."

"Have no words on that account," said Aboro. "Let's make the arrangement now, if it worries you. Fifty kilos of gold and safe passage to another village. You can mingle with other humans until the search is over. And, after this, there *will* be a search, I can promise you. The murder of Urko will not be lightly passed over."

Urko stood just outside the building, listening at an open, curtained window. He was invisible to the individuals inside, but everything they said was clearly audible to him. He stiffened at the mention of his name. It seemed that Burke had been telling the truth. Urko resisted the impulse to burst into the building and arrest Aboro then and there. There was more he wanted to hear.

Virdon, Galen, and Janor were slowly making their way through the sleepy town, trying to reach a small stand of trees where they could take refuge. When they reached their position, Virdon gave signals to the other two. They fanned out according to his plan.

Urko's first trooper was positioned behind a slender tree near Aboro's headquarters. While he waited, he thought that he heard a sound from nearby. He turned in that direction, his rifle unslung and held at the ready. Virdon slipped closer, behind the wary ape, and quickly dropped the leather loop on the pole over the gorilla's head. With a strong yank, Virdon pulled gorilla backward into the brush.

Behind Aboro's building, the second trooper waited in his position. He heard the sound of the first gorilla being dragged away and reacted. He turned and saw Virdon wrestling the unconscious gorilla out of sight. The second trooper started in that direction stealthily; he reached the area and stopped. He looked about cautiously, his rifle raised. Suddenly, he heard the sound of a soft whistle behind him. He spun around. There stood Galen with a sheepish expression on his face. Before the trooper could do anything, Janor stepped out from behind a tree to the rear of the trooper, dropped his loop over the gorilla's head and yanked him back, slamming the gorilla's head into the tree trunk and knocking him unconscious.

"When do you want the job done?" asked Burke.

"Tonight," said Aboro. "You will be hiding..." The prefect turned to indicate the green-curtained alcove. Burke nodded. "In there," said, the prefect. "When I raise my glass in a toast and say, 'A toast to General Urko,' that will be your signal to enter and fire."

At this point, Urko could stand it no longer. He had heard quite enough to convince himself that Burke was telling the truth. He slammed the door open and, pistol in hand, burst in.

"Urko!" cried Aboro in a strangled voice.

"I didn't want to believe it," said Urko. "But it's true, isn't it, Aboro?"

"Urko," said Aboro, stricken almost dumb with panic, "I can explain."

"Can you now?" said Urko.

Virdon, Galen, and Janor were sneaking up on the last of Urko's three guards, moving silently like commandos. Virdon dropped the loop over their quarry's head and quickly subdued the ape. Motioning Galen and Janor out of sight, Virdon raced noiselessly to the door of Aboro's building. Then, pausing to gather his energy and his resolve, he, too, slammed the door open and stormed in, a pistol extended in his own hand.

"Drop your gun, Urko!" shouted Virdon.

There was a pause; then Urko's pistol clattered to

the floor. The ape general half-turned to see what this interruption meant. His eyes narrowed as he recognized his adversary. "Virdon!" he exclaimed.

Virdon ignored the ape, and turned to Burke. "We've been tracking you all over the countryside!" he said. "How'd you wind up here, with him?"

"It wasn't my idea, buddy," said Burke, obviously relieved to see that his friends had been able to improvise his rescue. "I would have been plenty satisfied to go along with our original plan. But this hairy Napoleon had to mess things up, like usual."

"Well, tell me all about it later," said Virdon. "Let's get out of here."

Burke sidled past his friend, moving cautiously by the chagrined Urko. Virdon covered the other man's escape; then he, too, edged out of Aboro's place and slammed the door behind him. Burke and Virdon raced through the sheltering darkness toward the clearing where Galen and Janor waited for them.

"I'm glad to see you Pete!" said Galen, his voice choked with emotion.

"I'm glad to see me, too, old buddy!" said Burke, laughing.

"You're something else," said Virdon.

"The next time," said Burke, shuddering, a little, "you can be something else. I'll let you play the starring role, and I'll stay in the audience." All together, they moved out quickly, disappearing into the deeper night beyond the village of Hathor.

The next morning saw Urko leading his guards, recovered but aching, and the rest of his entourage away from the District Headquarters area. All the apes were mounted on fresh horses, including, in the middle of the armed pack of guards, Aboro and Daku, their hands bound behind their backs. Their expressions were hopeless. Urko turned to survey his former friend. "You could have had a great future, Aboro," said Urko, shaking his head. Then it occurred to Urko that "a great future" was what the former prefect's murder plan was intended to insure. Once again Urko turned and glared wordlessly at the traitor. The parade passed a small crowd of humans, for whom this was the greatest entertainment in some time. In the midst of this crowd, and therefore unnoticed, stood Virdon, Burke, Janor, and Galen. They watched the procession move away from them.

"So much for the 'Lord of the Apes,'" murmured Burke.

"Thank you, Virdon," said Janor softly. The burly farmer turned from the blond astronaut to Burke. "And you, too, Pete. And Galen. I owe you much more than my life."

Galen stared at the diminishing spectacle of Urko's party, as it rode further away. "The Supreme Council will have to bring Augustus back as Prefect," he said. "And this time he'll be able to appoint an honest police chief."

Janor nodded, then turned back to Virdon. "I didn't want to believe your way would work," he said. "There was such a hurt inside me. I thought the only way it could be healed was to inflict hurt."

"We understand," said Virdon.

Burke shouldered his pack, filled with fresh supplies. He handed another pack to Galen. "Well," said Burke, "I guess we'd better be moving on."

Galen spoke; he sounded disappointed. "Oh, do we have to?" he asked. "I was looking forward to staying on for a while."

"Believe me," said Burke, "we've got to go."

"Give me one good reason," said Galen.

"Gorillas!" said Burke, gesturing with one hand.

Galen looked in the indicated direction, only to see two of the town's gorilla troopers heading their way, nonchalantly, more or less on patrol, but clearly without any notion of apprehending the fugitive trio.

"Better not ask for trouble," said Janor.

Galen looked at Burke. "Humans are always so convincing," he said. "They really shouldn't be, you know. That's what we are taught." Galen smiled and followed Virdon and Burke as they headed in the opposite direction from the gorillas. They turned once to wave at Janor. Then, shouldering their packs in preparation for a long day's march, Virdon, Burke, and Galen turned their faces westward.

THE GLADIATORS

5

There were many villages along their route, and sometimes Virdon, Burke, and Galen were able to stop their fugitive running for a few days and rest at the home of a sympathetic human. The sight of two humans traveling with a friendly chimpanzee, though, was often enough to force the trio to make a quick exit from the premises of a suspicious human. There were more than enough people around who might try to earn extra food or privileges by turning in the astronauts and their chimpanzee companion to the local police authorities. Still, Virdon, Burke, and Galen managed to plot their course westward with a minimum of trouble.

The summer was coming to an end. Already the leaves on the trees had turned from green to a variety of colors. The air was taking on a crispness at night that was refreshing after a tiring day's journey, but that same coolness promised only the inevitable slide into deep winter. The three travelers wanted to be well west and south by the time the first snow fell. In their situation, constant exposure to the cruel winter could be as deadly as a bullet from a gorilla's rifle.

One morning, not far from a small village called Kaymak, the three friends found themselves pushing through a large area of dense underbrush. The work of crossing the tangled jungle had made them weary, although it was still early in the day. Virdon, leading the others, almost stumbled as his foot became caught in a mass of tough roots. He managed to recover his balance, but he paused and looked around. Behind him, Burke leaned against one of the gnarled trees that grew in the area and Galen sat down on a boulder, panting from near exhaustion. Virdon muttered something, but his words were inaudible to the others. He took out an animal-skin water container which he carried slung over one shoulder, untied the mouth of the bag, and drank long and deeply.

"Let me have some, too," said Burke, coming up to take the improvised canteen.

"Sure," said Virdon. "This place here is really something. It'll take us all day just to get across that clearing." The blond man pointed. Burke, still drinking, nodded. He finished and gave the canteen to Galen.

"This is where they must be." There was a large wall map of the western part of the North American continent, constructed of several sheets of dark, parchment-like paper. The details of the map were only roughly sketched in, and there were vast areas of the country that were left entirely blank. In one particular area, near the west coast, there was a cluster of five villages. A leather-gloved hand hovered above that place on the map and with an angry blow struck it.

The hand remained on the map for a few seconds, as though to pin down its elusive quarry. Then General Urko spoke again, reading from a report, "'reported at Radec and Slonk and possibly sighted at two more hamlets in the vicinity. Two humans calling themselves "astronauts."'" Urko crumpled the report and threw it across his office. Near him stood another uniformed gorilla, Urko's current top lieutenant, an ape named Jason. "And that renegade chimpanzee, Galen, has been seen with them," said Urko. "That proves it. They're heading for the sea." Once more he indicated the cluster of five villages, each about twenty miles from the next.

"Are you sure, Urko?" asked Jason.

Urko turned to face his aide. His expression was the same mask of hatred he wore whenever he thought about the three escapees who so constantly eluded his grasp. He scowled at Jason. "I'm sure of nothing!" he said, with great intensity. "These reports are next to useless. They come in days, weeks late. They are prepared by country apes who don't even know what they're looking for or what they're seeing. My patrols let those three slip through their fingers time after time. I'm sure of nothing except that they are a dangerous threat to our security and they must be caught. I must study the settlements in that area." He turned to the map once again, and Jason looked over his shoulder.

"General Urko," said the aide, "are these villages primarily human settlements?"

"In this area, yes," said Urko. "There is very little manufacturing or trading done here. The majority of the population is human. Tenant farmers. Each village has a garrison of gorilla guards and an incompetent prefect."

Jason smiled behind Urko's back but dared to say nothing. He waited for Urko to devise his plan of action.

"I want you to go out there, Jason," said Urko at last. "I want you to alert every prefect. Give each of them full descriptions. The three of them will show up sooner or later. Tell the prefects that all strangers—all strangers— are to be arrested on sight; this office is to be notified. No travelers are to be allowed to leave any area until they have been checked out by me or by one of my representatives. Do you understand?"

"We'll find them!" said Jason, with the kind of enthusiasm a junior officer forces into his voice when he feels just the opposite about an order.

"Finding them has not been the problem in the past," said Urko, with the greatest scorn and malice. "Disposing of them after I've found them has given me a great deal of trouble. I want to end that. Take troops from the main garrison, collect those three criminals, and bring them back here to Central City, unless they try to escape. Of course, even Dr. Zaius has granted that prisoners attempting to escape should be shot."

"Yes, sir," said Jason. He turned to leave, believing that his briefing was over. He crossed the chamber to the door, but before he could open it, Urko's voice stopped him.

"Jason," said the general.

Jason turned to face Urko, puzzled, wondering what he had done wrong. "Yes, sir?" he asked.

"I expect them to try to escape. Have I made myself understood?"

Jason smiled. This was the Urko he had grown to know and fear. He was glad that the general's wrath was directed away from himself and at the three unfortunate fugitives. "I understand, sir. Their treacherous corpses will lie where they fall, until the weasels and the buzzards take care of them."

"Fine, fine," said Urko, his mind already moving on to other matters. "Now, get out of here and get going." He looked at another report and dismissed Jason with a wave of the hand. Jason turned to the door again and left.

As Jason checked his supplies and mounted his horse giving orders for his gorilla troopers to do the same, Virdon, Burke, and Galen came to a rest stop in a wooded area many miles away.

"We don't need a rest yet, Pete," said Virdon, although there was not the slightest trace of reproach in his voice.

"I'm leading this excursion at the moment," said Burke. "And even if Iron Man Virdon doesn't need a rest, maybe some of the rest of us do."

Virdon only nodded. Actually, he was glad for the stop, too. He was only more concerned for their safety. He knew only too well how precarious their position was. He would have been happy if they could have traveled without resting at all, without stopping to look for food or water, without sleeping. He sighed.

"It's getting cooler," said Galen.

"It's getting on to winter," said Burke. He looked at the trees around him. "It looks to me like autumn is almost over."

"It's going to be a hard winter," said Galen.

Burke pulled the thin, homespun shirt closer to his slender body. "We're going to have to find something warmer," he said. "Like Miami Beach, for instance."

Galen didn't understand Burke's reference, but that didn't make much difference to the chimpanzee. He had come to learn that he wasn't expected to understand about half of Burke's references. He let this one pass in silence. Then he changed the subject slightly. "I think this will be an exceptionally hard winter," he said.

"How can you tell?" asked Burke.

"The hair on my face," said the chimpanzee. "It's growing in thick. That always means that the winter is going to be heavy and cold."

Burke laughed. "Do you really think that the hair on your face can predict what the winter is going to be like?"

Galen looked offended. "Of course," he said.

"That's nonsense."

Galen seemed about to become angry, but he controlled himself. "How do you know that autumn's almost over?" he asked.

"Just look," said Burke. "Look at the trees."

"If the trees can predict the seasons, my hair can do the same," said Galen huffily.

"The leaves on the trees aren't saying a word about what kind of autumn we're having," said Burke.

"But you use them as a sign, because it's the same every year," said Galen. "And the same is true of my hair. It's right, year after year."

"Alan," said Burke, "will you explain to this genius why he's sounding like a total idiot?"

There was no reply from Virdon. Both Burke and Galen looked in silent appeal to the blond astronaut, but he seemed completely lost in thought. He stared past his friends, unconsciously fingering the smooth metal disk that he wore on a thong about his neck.

"Oh, oh," said Burke, recognizing the signs. "He's back home again."

"Uh," said Galen, respecting Virdon's loneliness, knowing that Virdon occasionally slipped into long, melancholy reveries concerning the wife and children he had lost by hurling through time into this fearful future. Burke and Galen left Virdon to his thoughts. Burke sat down and began whittling a stick. Galen started looking for something edible among the trees and bushes of the area. After about twenty minutes of silence, Galen returned, carrying a number of strange looking pieces of fruit in his arms. They were round and lumpy, about the size of a small grapefruit, pink in color, with a peel like a banana that split along three seams. He put some of the fruit down near Burke. "It's good," said the chimpanzee. "I was lucky to find it."

Galen then put some down by Virdon, who smiled up at him but made no move to pick up the fruit. "Thanks," said Virdon.

Galen sat down, took one of the fruits, and peeled it. Burke watched him with interest, then did the same. "I've never seen one of these before," he said. "What do you call them?"

"They're opers," said Galen. "Didn't you have them where you came from?"

"No," said Burke, "but I'm willing to try one." He took a bite and chewed thoughtfully. "It's kind of odd," he said. "It has a sort of mushy consistency, like a banana." He chewed some more. "It is good. Feels like a banana, tastes sort of like an orange. It must be some kind of mutation, obviously subtropical. But if the compass and the sun aren't loused up, we're somewhere north of what was San Francisco. We should be eating apples and pears." He took another bite, staring up at the bright blue sky that glittered through breaks in the foliage above. "Whatever turned this world upside down produced at least one good thing," he said, looking at the fruit in his hand. Then he grinned up at Galen. "No offense, Galen," he said."

"It's nothing special, Pete," he said, not understanding

Burke's apology. "It's just an oper."

Burke finished the fruit and peeled himself another. "In our time," he said, speaking with a mouthful of oper, "we'd call it a banorange or something, and we'd have singing TV commercials, and billboards, and weekly specials at the supermarkets. And you don't even know what TV, billboards, and supermarkets are. But you have these, and if you didn't know what they were, I'd be going hungry right now. I'm grateful, Galen."

"I don't understand, Pete," said Galen, wondering about Burke's unaccustomed seriousness.

"I mean," said Burke, "that you fit in this world, and we don't, no matter how long we stay here. I see this fruit in my hand, and the only thing I can think about is that there would surely have been a Banorange Bowl along about New Year's every year, with a contest to pick Miss Banorange, and a parade, and two football teams that couldn't make it to one of the better bowl games."

"Now I don't understand," said Galen.

"Call it a draw," said Burke. "Right, Alan?"

Virdon, still lost in his own thoughts, glanced at Burke, hardly having heard any of the preceding conversation. He was still fingering the metal disk on the cord around his neck. "Hm?" he said. "I'm sorry, Pete, I wasn't listening."

"I know," said Burke.

"So say it again," said Virdon.

"I was only thinking that anybody who believes a magnetic disk is going to get us back home is strictly off his rocker," said Burke. He laughed briefly, more to let Virdon know that he wasn't completely serious. But, in a way, he was; unlike Virdon, Burke had left no family, no ties in the old world. He was content to try to build a new life in the new world. He wasn't satisfied with the ape world, but then he hadn't been satisfied with the human world, either. All he needed was peace and freedom to pursue his own happiness—and that had been a rare commodity in both eras.

Virdon realized that he had been fingering the disc, and removed his hand with a quick, embarrassed smile. He was glad that his friends permitted him his quiet moments of memory, because it was possible that in those moments were his final visions of everyone and everything he had loved.

"Try an oper," said Burke. "It's good."

Virdon picked up a piece of fruit, glanced at it thoughtfully, then looked back at Burke. "It's our only chance, Pete, and you know it. I don't care how you ride me about this disk, it's our only chance. With it, maybe we go home. Without it, for sure, for absolute *certain*, we never do."

Burke was a bit afraid to answer, knowing that almost anything he said would only start the same old argument they had carried on since their arrival on the planet of the apes. "If you say so," he said flatly, obviously trying to humor Virdon.

"I *do* say so!" said Virdon vehemently. "All the details of our flight are recorded here," he said, tapping the disk. "It can tell us when, maybe how and where, we hit that time warp. If we run it through a computer, reverse the direction, then—"

Burke had had enough. "What computer, Alan?" he asked. "Where? Behind that tree?"

"No, Pete, no," said Virdon wearily. "We've been through parts of what the apes call the Forbidden Zone. We've seen places we used to know. There's been evidence that somewhere, somehow, our entire civilization didn't disappear overnight. We just have to keep looking."

"I do keep looking," said Burke. "About once a minute, over my shoulder, for gorillas. That's all that has me worried right now."

"There's got to be…" said Virdon, defeated, letting his voice trail off. He struggled to get his mood under control. After a moment, he looked up at Galen. "Do you know this area, Galen?" he asked.

"Not very well," replied the chimpanzee. "Our study of geography was limited, and my education was somewhat rudely interrupted."

"Are there any settlements near here?" asked Virdon.

"I'm not sure," said Galen, "Tell me where we are, and I might be able to make a guess. But heading in the direction we're going, west, there's just a large ocean. Between here and there are possibly a few farming communities. Certainly nothing large enough to have one of your computers." The ape shuddered; he recalled previous adventures during which Virdon and Burke had shown him examples of the ancient, forbidden human knowledge. Galen had seen millenia-old human machines operate in ways that even the intelligent and logical chimpanzee thought almost magical. The one thing that these adventures had had in common was danger. Each time they had been observed and nearly captured by gorilla patrols, whose duty it was to keep the Forbidden Zone off limits to apes and intruders.

"We'll search until we—" began Virdon, but he broke off. He was startled by the sound of crashing in the woods some distance away.

"Listen," said Galen.

"I can hear it, too," said Burke.

They all froze, listening intently. The sound was of

something being thrown around in the underbrush; a few seconds later came grunts and yells of pain. "Humans, I think," said Galen, using his more acute sense of hearing. Virdon glanced at the others, then swiftly and quietly moved in the direction of the sounds. The others followed.

The three went stealthily through the woods toward the noises. There was clearly the sound of a struggle, now, punctuated with more cries and grunts. Virdon, Burke, and Galen came to the edge of a clearing and cautiously peered out.

The clearing was a natural open area in the woodland, dotted with occasional rocks and small boulders. A path through the woods ran along the far side of the clearing, opposite to that where the fugitive trio was hiding. In the center of the clearing, two men were involved in a violent struggle. Both men were of amazing size and physical strength. They were both well over six feet tall, broad-shouldered, extremely muscular, and powerful. The elder of the two seemed to be in his late forties; as he had passed through his younger years and approached middle age, he had not allowed himself to grow soft in any way. His face was badly scarred, almost disfigured. His nose looked as if he had broken it and then had had it reset by an incompetent doctor. The younger man was in his early twenties and showed a quickness that the older man could not match. It was clear to the hidden observers, however, that the younger man was not the dedicated battler that the scarred veteran was.

The fight between the two men was fierce, but it was fought without weapons. The entire conflict was carried on with their bare hands alone, though brutally and without pity. First one, then the other was knocked to the ground. Neither seemed able to achieve a lasting advantage, however. Each managed to regain his breath and position before the other could close for the final blow.

"What do we do?" asked Galen.

"We watch," said Burke softly. "We have the best seats in the house, we don't know the champion from the challenger, we don't have any idea who the good guy is, or who the bad guy is. Until somebody comes along with a scorecard, I suggest we mind our manners."

In the clearing, the two men were locked in an almost motionless pose. They had grasped each other in the grip of two wrestlers trying to bring each other to the ground. Neither would give way. Their muscles bulged, and the hidden trio could hear both men panting and grunting with effort. Finally, there was a sudden movement by the older man, and the youth crashed to the ground. This time the boy did not move, lying as if stunned. The older man stood over him, then reached down as though to strangle the defenseless boy.

"I just changed my mind," whispered Burke. He burst from his hiding place and ran into the clearing, startling both Virdon and Galen.

"Pete!" called Virdon, but Pete was beyond replying; he had suddenly decided that the fighting was within bounds, but that the older man's effort to murder the dazed opponent was not, no matter what the original quarrel had been.

Burke rushed at the unsuspecting wrestler and knocked him off balance. Roaring with anger, the huge fighter turned to face Burke.

Virdon couldn't control himself any longer, either, once he saw what kind of trouble his friend had gotten himself into. It was evident that Burke would be no match at all for the gigantic older man. Virdon, cursing under his breath, maneuvered himself within the edge of the clearing, in case Burke needed immediate help. He was of half a mind to let the impetuous astronaut take a bit of a beating first, though.

The younger man, still on the ground, his head beginning to clear, looked up and saw his former antagonist struggling with Burke. The younger man raised himself to his knees, trying to shake off the effects of his beating.

Burke and the older man had joined in combat, and Burke was being soundly beaten. The older man's experience seemed to offset Burke's more sophisticated techniques; still after a few solid punches to his body and a near-miss to the side of his head, Burke landed his first blow, a crushing shot that sent his foe staggering backward.

The youth watched this and jumped to his feet. He charged into the battle, but to both Burke and Virdon's great surprise, the young man tackled Burke! This was in spite of the obvious fact that Burke had been trying to save the young man's life. Together, the two former opponents faced Burke, who stepped backward, unsure of what he had rushed into.

Virdon was in the same predicament. For a few seconds, he was too surprised and confused to understand. Then, before he could make any judgment, the two giants were cooperating in beating Burke into unconsciousness. Virdon rushed in, charging the older man, who had stepped away momentarily to allow the younger man a clear shot of Burke's unprotected body. Now it was two against two— the two astronauts against the two massive men.

Galen was still hidden in the underbrush, watching worriedly. He had even less of an idea of what was happening than the astronauts, but he attributed that to the insanity customary when dealing with most humans.

From the other side of the clearing, above the noise of the battle, the sharp-eared ape heard something that made him even more concerned, however. There came the distinct sound of horse's hooves. As soon as he convinced himself of the approaching horse, Galen rose and called out, "Pete! Alan!"

The horse was coming closer. To Galen it was obvious that its rider, necessarily an ape, was coming along the narrow trail that cut into the opposite side of the clearing. Virdon looked quickly over his shoulder at Galen's concerned call. "What?" he said, panting from his exertions. He ducked under a wide roundhouse swing from the older of the two fighters.

"A horse!" cried Galen.

"Let's move," muttered Virdon.

Quickly, both men disengaged from the battle, rolling suddenly out of reach of their huge antagonists. The astronauts got to their feet as swiftly as possible; the two giants, however, did not want to let them escape. Virdon and Burke shoved them aside, Virdon with a forearm across the throat of the younger man, Burke using the same forward blocking skill he had displayed as a college football player. Then, once clear, the astronauts raced madly for the cover of the underbrush and disappeared from view just as a horse and rider stepped into the clearing on the trail.

The rider was a chimpanzee of late middle age, wearing the insignia of prefect on his tunic. He reined in sharply and sat for a moment, watching the two giant men in the clearing. His gaze was cynical and clearly one of an ape accustomed to command.

Both of the large humans were panting from their exertions—from their own fight and their abbreviated battle with the astronauts. The chimpanzee dismounted and walked toward them. His expression changed to one of compassion. He was not an evil ape, not one that plotted in secret, like Aboro, or lusted for power, like Urko. He was merely a local prefect, and these two men were known to him. When he spoke, there was a tone almost of friendliness in his voice. "Training hard, I see," he said.

"Let's keep moving," said Burke softly, from his prone position behind a large bush.

"Wait," said Virdon. "I'm dying to find out what we just went through."

"'Dying' may be the word, Alan," said Burke.

"Quiet," said Virdon. "You started it."

"We were training well," said the older man to the chimpanzee. "We have been training hard, Prefect Irnar, all morning, until two humans, strangers, not from the village, attacked us suddenly. Then, just as suddenly, they rail off. I don't know what they wanted."

The chimpanzee, Irnar, did not appear to be concerned. After all, the mere doings of humans were below his notice. Such a thing was for the gorilla police to attend to. His duties were purely administrative, not really concerned with chasing and apprehending every renegade human that crossed his district. Besides, the gorilla garrison guarded their power jealously and might look at any action by Irnar as trespassing.

"They were probably outlaws passing through the territory," said Irnar. "Some of them are no better than wild animals. We have police and an army that are supposed to protect us from these humans. I'll have the patrols watch for them." Irnar grunted, dismissing the entire incident from his mind. "Well, now," continued the prefect with keener interest, "the more important question, Tolar: Is he ready yet?"

The older man, addressed as Tolar, stepped back from the younger man, looking at him appraisingly. Irnar's face was creased with a frown of concentration. "Almost," said Tolar. "Dalton is almost ready."

Irnar smiled. "Good, good," he said. "You've done a good job teaching him. I can't tell you how anxious I am to see him in action. If he shows half as much ability as you, Tolar, I will be greatly pleased."

Tolar stood still, quietly proud and pleased by the ape's compliment.

Virdon, Burke, and Galen had seen enough. There was no longer any reason for staying nearby, where they might easily be spotted and captured. It was certain that Irnar would not listen to any explanation from the astronauts with sympathy. And as soon as it was discovered that Galen was traveling with two human outlaws, their identities would be known. That meant one thing: they would be back within the clutches of Urko in a matter of days.

The fugitives moved as quietly as they could while they were in the immediate area of the clearing, trying not to disturb the brush and making as little noise as possible. With Burke leading them, they broke into a sprint through the forest after about fifty yards. As they ran, Virdon suddenly became aware that the magnetic disk was missing from around his neck. He stopped suddenly and Galen almost ran into him from behind.

"Hold it," called Virdon. Burke stopped and glanced back, startled. "Wait. I have to go back."

"What?" cried Burke. "What are you talking about? We have to make tracks."

"The disk," said Virdon simply. "I dropped it."

Burke's shoulders slumped. "Alan!" he said. "We can't risk going—" He never got the chance to finish, his sentence, because Virdon had already turned and was running back toward the clearing. Burke looked helplessly at Galen, who only shook his head. There was nothing to say and nothing to do but follow their friend, hoping that they would stay out of trouble.

Virdon arrived at their previous hiding place and peered out through the undergrowth into the clearing. Tolar was holding the reins of Prefect Irnar's horse, while the chimpanzee himself stood a few feet away, glancing at Dalton.

"I expect to be proud of you some day, young man," said Irnar to Dalton.

The young man wore an unreadable expression. "Yes, sir," he said.

"You will be, sir," said Tolar with a touch of pride, in his voice. "My son will give you everything you expect."

Irnar grunted, then walked toward his horse. "All I can say is keep training, and keep me informed."

"I will, sir," said Tolar. He handed the reins to Irnar.

Virdon watched and listened. He would have to wait until Irnar rode off and Tolar and Dalton left the clearing before he could begin searching for the disk. He was prepared to wait all day and all night, if he had to. While he watched, he was joined by Burke and Galen.

Irnar shook out the reins to his horse and was about to mount, when something attracted his attention. He bent down and stared for a few seconds, then reached down and picked up the shining metal disk on its leather thong.

"Guess what," said Burke.

"Oh, no," said Virdon, groaning. "Maybe he'll drop it again."

The astronauts were not to have that kind of fortune. Irnar straightened up, holding the thong and disk out at arm's length. He looked at it with great curiosity. "Strange," said Irnar. "Very strange, indeed."

Almost instinctively, Virdon moved as though he were going to rush out and recover the disk. Galen reached out quickly and grabbed Virdon's arm. With a crestfallen expression, Virdon, usually so cautious, realized that he couldn't move. He could only watch, his expression tense.

Irnar put the disk into his pocket, mounted his horse, and, with a few final farewell words to the giant humans, rode off along the trail, out of sight. Tolar and Dalton followed on foot. Burke, Virdon, and Galen watched in unhappy silence.

Less than a minute later, Virdon slammed his fist into the layer of dead leaves on the ground. "I've got to get it," he said.

Burke said nothing for a short time. His thoughts ran through several different emotions before he replied. His answer was simple. "You're not serious," he said.

Virdon, very clearly, *was* serious. "You know how I feel," he said. "I'm getting it back, Pete. I don't know how, but I'm not leaving without it. I don't care about the danger. We don't have a chance without that disk. You two can go on without me, if you want. We can meet somewhere away from here."

Burke was clearly frustrated. "Don't talk nonsense, Alan," he said. "We'll either stay together or leave together. None of this splitting up. But we have to talk this out, first. I mean, what difference does it make? even if we *found* a civilization that was able to interpret that disk, somebody would still have to be able to build a spacecraft, they'd have to guarantee that the reversal process would work—

something that's only your pet theory, up until this point, Alan—and even then, we'd end up back in the twentieth century again." He said this last as though there was nothing in the twentieth century that made it any more attractive than where he was. "Do you think we'll ever find a tiny pocket of humans who have hung onto all the facilities we had? I mean, a Houston control, and a Florida launch site, and a worldwide network of tracking stations, and all the rest? We'd need all that, don't you think?"

"I'm aware of all of that, Pete," said Virdon, obviously not willing to pay proper attention to the logic of Burke's arguments. "But it's all beside the point."

"I don't think so, Alan," said Burke angrily. "I think it *is* the point. But I'm not going to persuade you."

"Alan," said Galen, "as much as I understand how you want to return to your own time, I can't figure why you want to walk into this unknown risk. We don't have any idea what we're going to meet here."

"I can't just forget about that disk," said Virdon. "It's hope… home. I can't forget it."

There was a crude hut standing along a dusty country road. Behind the human habitation were a few fields, some filled with brown husks of the summer's corn crop. Near the hut was a well. The human farmer was drawing up a wooden bucket from the well. A horse stood a few yards from the well; on its back sat Jason, the lieutenant of General Urko. The human filled a dipper from the bucket and handed it up to Jason. "Very few soldiers come this way, sir," he said.

Jason ignored the human's remark. "How far to the nearest village?" he asked, reaching down and taking the dipper. He drank from it.

"Half a day," said the human. He looked up at the sun, getting an idea of the hour. "You should be there by morning."

Jason finished drinking the water and tossed the dipper to the ground disdainfully. Without acknowledging the human's directions or aid, Jason turned his horse and rode off, joining his troopers who waited on the road. The human glared after him with annoyance, picked up the dipper, and wiped it clean on his rough shirt.

It was night. A gibbous moon cast stark shadows on the uneven, ground outside the village of Kaymak. The village itself was mostly dark, its business of the day completed, its human inhabitants too poor and too weary to continue any entertainment much later than sundown. A few lights shone, but these came chiefly from the barracks of the gorilla garrison and the homes of the few ape inhabitants. At the edge of the village, where the main road became a narrow country track, there stood a large structure built of stone, instead of the more common rough-cut logs. In the darkness, it was impossible to tell what might lie within those damp stone walls.

Three figures ran quickly across the ground from the road to the shadow of the stone structure. Virdon, Burke, and Galen pressed themselves against the solid rock walls; the three were invisible to any eyes that might be turned in their direction. They held still for a full minute, surveying the area. Virdon gave a signal to the other two and they hurried away again.

They ran as fast as they could, Virdon in the lead, followed by Burke and then Galen, until they reached the safety of the shadow of the first of the village's huts. They pulled up there, breathing hard from their exertion.

About twenty yards away stood a corral where the

horses belonging to the gorilla garrison were kept. A gorilla, rifle in hand, stood guard at the corral's gate. He yawned, clearly sleepy and bored. The horses whinnied nervously in the corral and the gorilla jerked upright, alert once again. He looked around in all directions, but he saw nothing; he leaned against the gate and yawned again. The two astronauts and Galen peered from behind the corner of the hut around which they had hurried at the sound of the anxious horses. Galen indicated the gorilla guard, then pointed up the road toward a well-lit house. "That gorilla is the only trouble I see," whispered the chimpanzee.

"Yeah," whispered Burke, "but he's enough for now."

While they watched, the gorilla turned completely around, resting his rifle on the ground, his two arms on the top wooden rail of the corral's gate, and his head on his arms. If General Urko had seen that gorilla, the unfortunate trooper would have been dead before he could scoop his rifle up again.

Galen, Virdon, and Burke took advantage of the guard's inattention to slip down the road and hide near the lighted building that had attracted Galen's interest. In front of the hut was a flagpole; the trio could see a pennant with some insignia sewn on it flying from the pole; it was illuminated by light coming from the open windows of the hut.

"That's a prefect's house," said Galen, indicating the insignia on the pennant. "That chimpanzee we saw talking to the two humans was wearing the same emblem. This is his house."

"You're sure?" asked Virdon.

"Alan," said 'Galen impatiently, "every once in a while—rarely, I admit, but every once in a while—I can contribute something to the success of our journeys Sometimes we come up against things that I know about even better then you. I was born here, remember?"

"I'm sorry, Galen, I really am," said Virdon softly.

"All right, Alan," said Galen. "I understand. Wait for me here."

"Listen, Galen," said Virdon. "Wait a minute. There's no reason for you to risk your safety on my crazy account. The disk doesn't mean a thing to you. Let me go get it."

"Do you have a plan?" asked Galen. "Or are you just going to walk into a strange prefect's house in the middle of the night and ask for it?"

Virdon began to reply, then fell silent. "No," he said finally, "I don't have a plan."'

"Then let me go," said Galen. "The disk is important to you. You're my friend."

"I know that, Galen, and I appreciate it. But still, I can't ask you to endanger yourself for me."

"I never heard you ask," said Galen. "That prefect is a member of my species, Alan. I'll have a better chance with him alone."

Burke had followed the conversation with great interest. He, too, had wondered what they were going to do when they reached the village. He had hoped that Virdon had formed a more definite scheme; he was disappointed to learn that this wasn't the case. "He's right, Alan," said Burke. "But I don't think it's worth the risk. Do *you* have a plan, Galen?"

"No," said the ape. "But I don't really need one. I can travel with complete freedom, as long as my true identity is a secret. I can just drop in to the prefect's office, say hello, tell him that I'm passing through, and maybe learn a little. It all doesn't have to be done tonight, even though that would be best."

"Galen, it's impossible to argue with you," said Burke.

Would you do it for me," asked Galen. He turned to Virdon. "I'll get your disk."

Galen stepped out into the road and walked to the front door of the prefect's house. He knocked boldly on the smoothed timber of the door. After a moment, the door was opened by Irnar. "Yes?" he said.

"Good evening," said Galen. "I'm sorry to bother you so late, but I have a small problem, and I thought you were the proper ape to notify."

Irnar's brow furrowed in a frown. "Yes, yes, of course. Come in," he said, and Galen followed the prefect into the house. The door shut behind them.

Burke and Virdon watched all of this anxiously. After they saw the door close, they both let out deep sighs, neither of them until then realizing that they had been holding their breath. "Keep your fingers crossed," said Burke.

The horses in the corral whinnied, somehow still aware of the disturbing influence of Virdon and Burke nearby. Virdon glanced in that direction. "Horses," he said thoughtfully. "Maybe we shouldn't just be hanging around here, doing nothing. We could be putting ourselves to work, too. If Galen gets in trouble and this thing blows up in our faces, we'll all have to get out of here fast."

"I'm glad you still have that devious mind of yours working;" said Burke, nodding. They both headed back toward the corral.

The interior of Irnar's office was a combination work space and living room equipped with a desk, bookshelves with a few large books, and a locked cabinet, as well as a few chairs and a number of plants and flowers in odd, handcrafted pots. Irnar sat in a chair behind his desk. He had been listening to Galen's story, and he looked at the young chimpanzee quizzically. "You say you were thrown by a horse?" he asked. "Where?"

"Out there, somewhere," said. Galen, pointing off in a vague direction. "I've been walking for miles. Believe me, I was absolutely delighted when I saw your village."

Irnar still studied Galen with a hint of suspicion. "And what were you doing on that horse? 'Out there'..."

"I'm engaged in scientific exploration," said Galen smoothly, falling into another role, a task at which he was becoming very skilled. "I'm searching for artifacts of past civilizations."

Irnar grimaced. "Don't we have enough trouble coping with our own?" he said dryly.

"I wasn't exactly sure that we had one," said Galen.

Irnar glanced at him; his eyes narrowed for a second. Then, suddenly, to Galen's great relief, the prefect burst into laughter.

"I think I'm going to like you, young chimp," said Irnar. "Yes, I think I'm going to like you very much, indeed. Would you care for something to drink? You must be thirsty after your long walk!"

"Yes," said Galen, "thank you."

"Fine," said Irnar. "And I think I will join you." He stood up from behind his desk and went to a wooden cupboard. On a shelf built into the upper part of the cupboard was a collection of bottles and glasses. Irnar searched among the bottles, looking for one in particular. "You know," he said, his back turned to Galen, "it can be a rather isolated and lonely life here."

Galen nodded, not thinking that Irnar could not see the nod. He did not answer. He was already looking around the room, searching out the prefect's personal effects, separating them from Irnar's official belongings. Galen wondered whether Irnar would be more likely to keep the disk with the personal or the official. Then, something directly in front of him attracted his attention. Galen shifted slightly in his seat and looked around a stack of papers. There, only a few feet from him, was the disk, on Irnar's desktop.

Irnar's voice continued, as he clinked a couple of glasses and unstoppered the bottle he had been seeking.

"This is just a village of humans, after all," he said sadly. Once again, Galen only nodded, his whole concentration on the disk. "A small garrison of gorillas," said Irnar, finishing his pouring. "But what company are a dozen gorillas?" he asked.

Galen couldn't take his eyes from the disk. He didn't dare do anything to attract Irnar's attention; if he were caught trying to swipe the disk, it might permanently ruin any attempt to get it back and lead to the fugitives' recapture. Galen knew that he had to play this coolly.

Irnar turned around again, carrying the drinks back to the desk. Galen's eyes were still on the disk. The prefect kept up his complaint. "You know how crude and uneducated gorillas are. Oh, I have nothing against them, actually. But, truthfully, they have no understanding of beauty or culture." His voice was full of distaste. "Oh, just a moment," said Irnar. "I have something that will go well with these drinks."

The prefect bent down and opened a lower drawer. While he was occupied, Galen shrugged and almost gave in to the temptation. He reached out slowly to pick up the disk. As his hand neared the object, Irnar rose again, bringing with him a box of dried fruit. "I almost forgot I had these," he said, putting the box on the desk. Galen drew his arm back quickly, unnoticed.

"Do you know," said Irnar, "I've been prefect of this village for twenty-five years? Would you believe that? Twenty-five years, and this dusty town of Kaymak is all I have to show for it. I used to hope for a promotion to District Prefect, but I've long since given up that dream. Here, have a drink and some fruit."

"Thank you," said Galen, his eyes fastened on the disk.

"Were you traveling alone?" asked Irnar.

"Yes," said Galen, after a brief hesitation.

"Twenty-five years," said Irnar musingly. "It's been that long since I was your, age." He raised his glass. "To companionship," he said.

Galen would have liked nothing better than to grab the disk and flee the office, but he knew that was impossible. Instead, he raised his glass in a toast.

Virdon and Burke moved swiftly along the side of a building, coming to the corner from which they could watch the corral. They looked toward it. Nothing had changed there. The gorilla guard still napped with his back toward them.

"Whew," said Burke softly. "Are you ready, Alan?"

"Just a second," said Virdon. He reached down and picked up a length of wood that he could use as a club. "I am now," he said. "Let's go."

"There is little enough to keep me amused," said Irnar. "Intellectual stimulation, that's what is chiefly lacking this far from Central City." He indicated a rather crude painting that hung on one wall. A flickering lamp nearby made moving shadows over it, so that it took on strange, almost surreal qualities. Galen saw that it was a portrait of Irnar. "Rather nice, isn't it?" asked Irnar. "One of the humans did it, if you can believe that. Some of them are surprisingly talented. Even artistic, although none of them comes close to what the sophisticated apes in Central City create."

Galen's mind was on the disk, and he spent little time examining the portrait. "A human painted this, you say? How interesting."

Irnar poured himself another drink and walked up to the painting. Galen's eyes flashed back to the disk. Once again he was stopped before he could take it; Irnar laughed softly, turned again, and sat back down behind his desk. "As a matter of fact," said the prefect, "I have a theory." To Galen's horror, the older chimpanzee idly picked up the disk and swung it on its leather cord. "Put fifty humans in a room," said Irnar. "Give them all pots of paint and brushes. Give them enough time—oh, years and years, of course—and eventually they'll duplicate every masterpiece that has ever been painted." He laughed again at the wild idea he had just expressed. Irnar seemed to enjoy his own sense of humor greatly.

"What is that?" asked Galen.

The prefect tossed the disk into the air and caught it. He looked at it for several seconds, then grunted. "I found this only recently. I wonder if this could be one of those artifacts you're looking for."

Galen tried not to appear too eager. "I don't know," he said in a carefully controlled voice. "I'd have to examine it, possibly give it a few tests."

Irnar looked at it closely again, tossed it into the air, and caught it. "No," he said, "I don't think it's an artifact. It's much too new. If it belonged to an ancient civilization, it would be all corroded. And I found it lying in the grass near here. I've picked up genuine artifacts over the years. Some of them are fascinating."

Galen was almost hypnotized by Irnar's disk-tossing. "Are you a collector?" he asked.

"Only an amateur," said Irnar. "One finds strange things. For example, our ancestors must have been excellent metal-workers. Very advanced in some ways that have been lost to us. And yet, the use to which they put their talents was primitive. I have a weapon I found, evidently a war club. Beautiful workmanship, but the thing would be so inefficient in combat." Irnar stood and went to the cabinet, holding the disk in one hand. Galen was almost going out of his mind with frustration. The prefect opened one of the doors in the lower part of the cupboard. He reached in and brought out a battered golf club. He carried the ancient artifact back to his desk and passed it over to Galen for the young ape's inspection.

"Hmm," said Galen. "I've never seen anything quite like this." The metal of the golf club was pitted with age. To Galen's more knowledgable eye, the thing was clearly of human manufacture, from the time of Virdon and Burke, rather than from any of the apes' ancestors. Galen had as little idea of what the golf club could have been used for as Irnar had.

"The quality of that metal is higher than anything we could produce today," said Irnar. "A lost art. Interesting. But I dare venture to surmise that it was a pitifully inadequate weapon."

"Yes," said Galen, "it is interesting." He handed the golf club back to Irnar. "That disk you're holding seems to be made of the same material. May I see it?" Galen extended his hand across the desk.

Irnar glanced at Galen quizzically. "You seem especially

eager to see this," said Irnar, swinging the disk on its thong. Any particular reason? I don't think I want to sacrifice part of my collection in the interests of your science."

"Just curiosity," said Galen carefully.

Irnar smiled, walking back to put the golf club away. "That's, certainly characteristic of us chimpanzees," he said. He closed the cupboard door and returned to his desk. Well, let's both try to restrain our curiosity until a later time." He opened a locked drawer in his desk, tossed the disk in, shut the drawer, and locked it. Galen felt a sinking feeling, although he knew that all was not yet lost.

"You'll stay overnight, won't you?" asked Irnar.

"I'm… not sure," said Galen, wondering about Virdon and Burke and whether he ought to extend their stay in Kaymak. The longer they remained, the more vulnerable to detection and capture they became.

"Of course you will," said Irnar. "The chance to talk to someone interesting doesn't come to me very often. Now that I have you here, I insist that you accept my hospitality, at least tonight. I wouldn't dream of your leaving. Let me find you a place to sleep. Let's see. Where can we make you most comfortable?"

Near the corral, the napping gorilla had entered a deeper level of unconsciousness, thanks to the club wielded by Virdon. Virdon and Burke dragged the guard to one side, out of sight. Virdon picked up the ape's rifle when he and Burke returned to the gate. Burke unlatched the wooden bolt that held the gate closed. "Shouldn't we tie him?" asked Burke.

"Nobody'll find him," said Virdon. "He won't be moving for a while." Without further discussion, the two men entered the corral.

* * *

Irnar was reading a note on his desk. Galen waited patiently. "After all," said Irnar absently, crumpling the note when he reached its end, "this isn't Central City. Our accomodations here are simple. Come."

Galen followed Irnar across the office to the door. Irnar started to open the door. He turned thoughtfully back toward Galen. "There's so much I'd like to discuss with you," he said. "So many aspects of culture that—" He broke off at the sound of unusually loud noises coming from the corral.

"What were you saying?" said Galen, hoping to cover the neighing of the disturbed animals.

"Shh," said Irnar, listening intently. Again there came the anxious whinny of several horses.

Virdon held one horse by its lead. The animal evidently didn't like being roused in the night and was unused to humans. It made so much noise that Virdon grew worried. "Come on," he whispered, "or you'll wake up the whole village." He grabbed the lead of another horse as Burke led a third horse toward him. Burke now carried the rifle in his free hand.

The horses reared and whinnied as the two men struggled to lead them out of the corral. Suddenly, out of the corner of his eye, Virdon saw Burke react, startled by something. Virdon's view was blocked by one of the animals. He could hear Burke's anxious voice. "Oh, oh," said Burke.

Virdon moved forward for a better view. Directly in front of them, just beyond the corral gate, were three gorillas, each with a rifle pointed directly at the astronauts.

Behind the gorillas and to one side stood Irnar and Galen.

"Out here!" cried the prefect. "Both of you!"

Burke and Virdon had no choice but to drop the reins of the horses. Burke dropped the rifle to the ground. Covered by the weapons of the gorilla guards, they moved out of the corral toward Irnar and Galen. Virdon and Burke looked at Galen, who could do nothing but stare back. It would have been very unwise for either humans or the young chimpanzee to show signs of recognition.

"They're not from my village," said Irnar to Galen. "I can assure you of that." His voice was angry and outraged. "I never have this kind of trouble from my humans." He turned suddenly, inspired by a thought, to look at Virdon and Burke. "Of course!" he said. "The two outlaws Tolar saw!"

There was no response from the humans. Irnar shrugged. "Your audaciousness has quite disappeared now, hasn't it?" Again there was no reply. Irnar turned to one of the gorillas. "Put them in the cage!" he ordered.

The gorilla stepped forward, prodding Virdon with his rifle. With one last, hopeless glance toward Galen, the two men were marched away by the gorillas.

Irnar and Galen watched them move away. Irnar smiled at Galen. "Well, now," said the prefect. "As long as we're here, perhaps you'd like to choose a horse. I'd like to give you one, but you know that even a prefect has his expenses. But my price will be minimal, for such a friend as you."

"Thank you," said Galen in a dull voice. He was still watching his friends being led away. Irnar, who had already turned toward the horses in the corral, did not notice Galen's behavior.

6

The countryside had returned to its peaceful state, despite the intrusions by humans and apes. Virdon, Burke, and Galen had not changed anything in their passage from one village to another except, perhaps, the lives of a few, individuals they met along the way. The countryside, however, was untouchable; as soon as the transients disappeared, the wooded, rural scene smoothed itself with silence and tranquillity.

Just as surely, though, that atmosphere was broken by other intruders. The next to pass along the dusty track that led to the village of Kaymak was Jason, the gorilla aide of General Urko. He paused near a stream, bending down to hand his canteen to one of his troopers. They were all taking a short rest break on their journey. While Jason idly watched his subordinate filling the canteen in the stream, he ate a fruit which would have been as foreign to the astronauts as the opers. Jason was totally oblivious to the beauty of the countryside around him. To a certain extent,

Prefect Irnar had been correct about the barbaric nature of the gorillas. But in another regard, Jason was admirably well suited to the area and his task. He was a strong and forceful ape, a resourceful leader, like most gorillas proud of his ability to take care of himself anywhere in the ape empire. Irnar would have been greatly uncomfortable on a journey to the nearest village, twenty miles away; he would have had difficulty finding fruit and fresh water. Jason had nothing but contempt for the softness of the chimpanzees and orangutans, the two varieties of ape who ruled the empire. The gorillas, to Jason's delight, *enforced* that rule, and to him that was a good deal more satisfying.

He threw the core of the strange fruit to the ground, wiped his mouth on the back of his leather-gloved hand, and took the filled canteen from his trooper. Without saying a word, he slung on the canteen and gave his horse a firm kick. Once again he was oh his way; his guards followed behind.

The cage to which Prefect Irnar had referred the night before was a wooden structure attached to one of the buildings that formed the gorilla garrison. Three of the walls of the cage were solid, built of heavy hardwood planks fitted closely together, unlike the usual open, airy construction that the apes favored. The fourth wall, composed of heavy bars, faced the main street of Kaymak. The floor of the cage was covered with straw. It was reserved for special prisoners; normally, the occasional insolent human was imprisoned within the building itself, which was far more comfortable for the inmates and less of a humiliation.

Virdon and Burke, fast asleep, were sprawled in the straw. Slowly, as from a bad dream, Virdon stirred and awoke, unable for a moment to recall where he was. That was a situation that happened often, for the very good reason that he did not remain in one place long enough for it to make an impression on him. Then, with unpleasant suddenness, he remembered. He looked through the bars toward the street; what he saw there startled him.

Gathered in the main street of Kaymak, staring back at Virdon through the bars of the cage, was a mass of people. Men, women, children of all ages and sizes regarded him soundlessly. On one side of the crowd stood a gorilla guard, armed with a rifle. He, too, stared at Virdon with mute boredom.

Virdon was puzzled and somewhat troubled. He had seen many strange sights since his advent in this world, but this was without precedent. He could understand being caged. He could understand the gorilla guard. But Virdon couldn't understand the silent, almost expectant expressions of the humans who watched him.

Next to him, Burke moaned in his sleep. Virdon reached over and shook him awake. "Pete," he called. Burke opened his eyes, glanced at Virdon, and closed his eyes once more. Virdon shook him again. Burke looked up at him, and the blond astronaut gestured toward the street. Burke looked and, as Virdon had before, reacted with a muffled, startled cry.

"All right," said Burke. "I give up. What's going on?"

"From the look of things," said Virdon, "*we* are."

Burke just stared for a moment at his friend, but there were no answers coming from Virdon. Both men got to their feet and went to the bars, looking out at the villagers of Kaymak. "What are they going to do to us?" Virdon asked them. "Do you know?"

There was no response at all from the humans, who

continued to stare at the trapped astronauts. The gorilla guard seemed calm and totally unconcerned. There was a touch of tension in Virdon's voice when he spoke next. "Look," he cried, "we're not your enemy."

There was no response from the crowd.

"You don't seem to be getting through to them," said Burke.

Two familiar figures pushed their way through the crowd and came near the bars. It was Tolar and Dalton.

"Look who's here," said Virdon.

Tolar and Dalton did not acknowledge Virdon's words. Like the other inhabitants of the village, they stood and observed the two men in the cage.

"What's going to happen?" asked Burke. "Don't you know?"

Tolar, several inches taller than Burke, stared down at the bewildered astronaut. Then, slowly, almost ritualistically, the huge man bent down and gathered up a handful of dirt. He held the dirt in his hand after he straightened up, looking Burke in the eye, his expression neutral. Without warning, he threw the dirt in Burke's face.

This action brought the first reaction from the crowd. A chorus of "Ahhhs" rippled through the mob. Burke jumped to the bars angrily, reaching out with one hand, blindly trying to grab Tolar as he rubbed the dirt from his eyes. "What do you think you're—"

"Quiet!" said the gorilla guard in a menacing voice, for the first time making his presence known. The ape intervened swiftly, moving toward the cage, brandishing his rifle. Burke hurried back away from the bars as the gorilla stood there threateningly.

"Are you all right, Pete?" asked Virdon in a worried voice.

Burke had regained his composure. "You know how long it's been since I've been this unpopular?" he asked. "The third quarter of the Ohio State game, my junior year."

"Quiet!" roared the gorilla.

Tolar stood patiently watching the reactions of Burke and Virdon. Strangely, he ignored the intervention and presence of the gorilla guard in a way few humans did in that oppressive empire of the apes. This fact was not lost on Virdon, but he didn't know what to make of it. Tolar treated the gorilla as though the ape did not exist. Tolar seemed uninterested in Burke's reaction, also, although he watched, like the remainder of the crowd. With a disdainful wave of the hand, Tolar turned deliberately and then walked back among the villagers. The mob parted for him; Virdon noticed that they all wore expressions of admiration as they turned to follow him with their eyes. Then, slowly, the crowd broke up and the humans of Kaymak wandered off, as though their presence were no longer necessary. All of this only served to confuse Virdon and Burke further. The only thing they were certain of was that none of it promised anything good for the astronauts.

Irnar took a large, heavy book from one of the shelves and opened the front cover thoughtfully. He turned the pages, not really looking at the printed words on them. Behind him, Galen was looking worriedly from a window, toward the cage.

"These books are my closest friends," said Irnar.

"Um," said Galen. "Yes." He wasn't paying attention to the prefect's words.

Irnar walked toward Galen with the book. Galen was still staring out of the window. "The prisoners," said the young chimpanzee. "What will you do with them?"

Irnar ignored the question. "I found this in an abandoned underground shelter many years ago," he said.

Galen, in turn, ignored Irnar's remark. "What about the prisoners, sir?"

"Why should you care? They're only human."

"They breathe," said Galen. "They walk. They talk."

Irnar laughed cynically. "You sound like a revolutionary," he said. "They're humans, my young friend. The only animal on this Earth that makes war on its own kind."

"I know," said Galen, "but—"

Irnar broke into Galen's protest with a curt gesture. "Man is by nature hostile and aggressive. You certainly can't dispute that, even with your limited experience, can you?"

Galen bristled somewhat at the mention of "limited experience." He was certain that he had seen a good deal more of the world than this prefect who had been relegated to the village of Kaymak for twenty-five years. "Yes," said Galen. "I mean, certainly, you're correct there, but—"

"Listen," said Irnar, breaking in again, evidently beginning a lecture on one of his favorite topics. "War and revolution. Destruction and murder. That was always the natural outlet for man's aggression. It still would continue today; but we can no longer allow that, can we? We, the apes of the world, have a responsibility as man's natural superiors to guide him away from self-destructiveness, a trait which often endangers ape lives and property. Man must be kept docile and unwarlike. But that is a difficult problem, one which even the Supreme Council in Central City has admitted it has failed to solve. But the solution may be simple enough—merely find a less dangerous outlet for man's hostility. Do you see? Do you understand what I mean?"

"What does that have to do with—"

"They're thieves," said Irnar, continuing on his well-worn track, ignoring Galen's reactions. "They're vandals. And these two prisoners are just perfect examples of what I call the human impulse. 'The human impulse.' Very good term for it, I think. And the prisoners. Finally, they will serve a noble purpose, despite themselves."

"What do you mean?" asked Galen.

There came the sound from some distance away, a mournful note like someone blowing on a ram's horn.

"Come," said Irnar. "I know you'll find this interesting." Taking Galen's arm, he led the young chimpanzee to the door.

Virdon and Burke stood in the cage, just out of reach behind the bars, even though no one had tried to harm them after Tolar's dirt-throwing of the morning. The gorilla on guard had not moved nor shown any further interest in the prisoners. Irnar moved across the street, still guiding Galen by the arm.

"I still would like to know what you meant by 'noble purpose,'" said Galen.

Irnar laughed loudly. For him, the day was going along in a familiar and pleasant fashion. "Was I really that pompous?" he asked. "Did I really say that? 'Noble purpose'? I can't believe it." The two chimpanzees came near the cage. "You know my fondest wish? To spend the rest of my days here as prefect, with my humans, my books, and my plants."

Irnar stopped as they came up to the cage. He wore a studious expression as he examined Virdon and Burke through the bars. Galen stood behind Irnar, also looking at them. As had been the case the night before, none of the trio dared show any sign of recognition. Irnar turned to the gorilla. "Which one?" he asked.

The gorilla grunted and turned to look at the astronauts. He took a good deal of time making up his mind. With a short gesture he indicated Burke.

"Good," said Irnar. "It was Tolar's choice." There was a slight pause while the prefect considered some matter unknown to Galen or his human friends. "All right," announced Irnar finally, "it's time."

The gorilla nodded. Irnar picked up Galen's arm and their conversation as though the trip to the cage had never been made, as though they had not interrupted a pleasant stroll from the prefect's house. "A small ambition, I know," said Irnar, "but its fulfillment would afford me great pleasure." They continued down the main street, the elder chimpanzee talking endlessly, the younger thinking, plotting hopelessly.

Meanwhile, the gorilla, his rifle held at the ready, approached the cage. "Get back," he growled. "Both of you."

Virdon and Burke stepped back further from the door. The gorilla opened it and gestured to Burke. "You," said the ape. "Come." Burke looked at the gorilla, but didn't move. The guard gestured angrily with his rifle. "Come!" This time Burke exchanged helpless glances with Virdon and started toward the open door of the cage.

A villager with a ram's horn stood outside the stone building on the outskirts of Kaymak. He wore a bright sash, the emblem of the official herald. He raised the horn to his lips and blew another mournful note.

The herald's call was hardly needed. Already, the entire population of Kaymak was heading into the stone amphitheater, talking among themselves, laughing, and carrying on in a festive manner. The calls of the ram's horn cut through the noise of the crowd, but did nothing to silence it.

On one side of the amphitheater was a marked-off practice area. Tolar and Dalton were wrestling with each other here, much as they had been in the clearing when Virdon, Burke, and Galen had first discovered them. Both of the large men were perspiring freely; their struggles were punctuated with gasps for breath.

Irnar and Galen approached them around the corner of the amphitheater: "Here are my prizes," said the prefect proudly. 'I'm sure you will appreciate what I am doing here. Perhaps, when you return to Central City, you might indicate to your urban friends that we in the outlying districts sometimes solve their problems with direct action, the sort they're afraid to take. Ah, Tolar!"

Almost immediately, Tolar and Dalton stopped wrestling, and walked toward Irnar, their heads bowed in respect. "Prefect," said Tolar.

"Tolar, are you ready?" asked Irnar.

"Yes, sir."

"And your son?" asked the Prefect.

"Soon."

"Not today?"

"Please, sir," said Dalton hurriedly. "Not yet."

Irnar glanced at the youth quizzically. "Why?"

Dalton was uncomfortable. "I… don't think…"

Tolar hurried to interject. "His stomach, sir," he said. "His stomach is… not feeling good."

Irnar's eyes narrowed. "I see," he said quietly. He took a long look at Dalton. "All right. Not today."

"Thank you, sir," said Dalton.

Irnar only nodded, again taking a thoughtful glance

at the younger man. Then the prefect turned and walked away. Galen, still puzzled by all of this, glanced from Tolar to Dalton to Irnar; then he hurried to catch up to the prefect. As the chimpanzees left, Tolar, tense with suppressed anger at his son, came up beside Dalton.

"When will you stop disgracing me?" he asked.

"I'm sorry, Father," said Dalton, confused. "I... don't think... I like the games."

Tolar grew angrier. "The games are not to *like*!" he shouted. "They are to *do*!"

Irnar and Galen approached the entrance to the amphitheater. There was no one else around; the villagers had all taken their places inside. "The father is a fine human," said Irnar reflectively, "but the son seems to be a problem. He doesn't have the proper appreciation for the games."

"What are these games?" asked Galen.

Irnar, with his customary concentration on his own thoughts, ignored Galen's question. "His attitude will change," said the prefect. "It will change with his first kill."

"'First kill'?" echoed Galen. "What *are* these games?"

Irnar gestured. "This way. Follow me."

Galen glanced briefly at Irnar, then entered the amphitheater, more worried than ever. As he entered the stone building, not knowing what to expect, he paused, startled as he looked around.

He saw the bare ground of an arena and then the rough-hewn rock benches that surrounded the arena, benches on which all the villagers were seated and waiting eagerly and anxiously. Galen, vaguely troubled, looked at the assembled humans.

Irnar turned and came back to where Galen had paused, wearing a smug smile. "I said you'd find it interesting," said Irnar.

After another few seconds, Irnar led Galen to the Prefect's Box in the amphitheater, which was situated directly opposite the entrance. Galen looked around him with concern and interest. The humans buzzed with excitement, but the young chimpanzee could sense that the energy was only barely controlled.

Men, women, and children surrounded Galen. All seemed very tense and full of anxiety; they sat murmuring to each other. Every once in a while an impatient human would shout, "Come on!" It occurred to Galen that never before in his life had he been in the midst of so many humans in so close an area. His sensitive nostrils were filled with their vaguely unpleasant odors. He felt oddly fearful. "They seem so tense," murmured Galen.

Irnar was pleased to see that Galen seemed suitably impressed by the spectacle. The sight of a stone amphitheater in a village as remote as Kaymak was a wonder in its own right. "They're waiting for blood," said Irnar. "It's their nature. Human nature."

Not all humans," said Galen, shaking his head.

"*All* humans," said Irnar in his lecturing voice. "And I give it to them here, in the arena, normally, with a challenger from the village. They work off all their aggression here. And after the game, they live quietly and peacefully—until the next game." He smiled. "That's the secret, my young friend. All the human hostility in my village is used up right here. Nowhere else."

There came a final note from the herald's ram's horn.

"It's time for me to go through the usual nonsense," said Irnar, sighing. "But they seem to expect it. And it does seem to help." Irnar rose from his seat, raising his arm high above his head. The villagers in the amphitheater fell silent when they saw the prefect standing in the Prefect's Box, his arm raised for their attention. "Welcome to your games, humans of Kaymak!" cried Irnar. "Welcome to your hero, the greatest fighter of Kaymak. Welcome to Tolar!"

As if on cue, Tolar strode proudly into the amphitheater. His fellow villagers went wild with their welcome. They shouted, jumping to their feet. They screamed Tolar's name. They clapped and whistled. Tolar was, indeed, their hero. He was the very personification of what little remained of human dignity and pride.

Some distance away, in the cage, Virdon moved closer to the bars, his curiosity and anxiety piqued by the distant screams of the crowd.

Tolar strode directly to a point below the Prefect's Box, bowing his head to his village's master. Irnar produced a ceremonial sword and held it high above his head in a ritual gesture. "All honor to the man who will challenge death," said Irnar in a loud voice.

Once again, the crowd screamed its approval. Irnar had worked out the mechanics of the pageant on his own; he had found exactly the right psychological triggers for his own purposes. He knew how to use them well. He brought the sword down suddenly, and the screams stopped. "Bring in the opponent!" shouted Irnar.

Four gorillas marched in, surrounding Burke. This time, the reaction of the humans was vastly different than it was to Tolar. They rose to their feet again, yelling insults, threats, and imprecations. Galen watched Burke, totally dismayed. Burke was marched to a position directly beside Tolar, below the Prefect's Box. The gorillas then departed. When they reached the entrance, they split into two pairs. Two of the gorillas stood guard by the entrance. The other two mounted into the stands, crossing toward the Prefect's Box. En route, they passed Dalton, who sat in the stands, watching impassively. While all around him people were standing and booing Burke, Dalton sat ignoring the tumult.

Burke and Tolar stood before the Prefect's Box, neither having moved at all, Tolar stood proud and straight. Burke was puzzled, still wondering what everything was all about. He had not been told.

Irnar raised the sword again. The shouts and catcalls stopped. There was dead silence. "The game will begin!" he cried. "To the winner... life! To the loser... death!" On the word "death," he brought the sword down sharply.

In that instant, the amphitheater fairly rocked with the mad screams of the villagers.

In that instant, Tolar suddenly whirled on Burke, who had just caught an inkling of what was happening. "Hey!" he cried to Tolar, recalling the uneven fight in the clearing. "Now wait a minute!"

Tolar jumped for him and knocked him down instantly. The crowd sighed, a slight disappointment that the match would be ended so quickly. But there the fight just began. Realizing that he was fighting for his life, Burke tried nevertheless to stay on the defensive. In the clearing, neither he nor Virdon had wanted to kill. Both astronauts had been well-trained in many sophisticated forms of hand-to-hand combat that would have defeated several antagonists like Tolar simultaneously and fatally. Now in the arena, Burke still had no desire to kill. The decision to stay on the defensive could cost him his life, he realized after a short while. Tolar was much bigger and stronger, with greater endurance and stamina. Burke could keep Tolar from getting a final advantage, at least for a while. But, sooner or later, Burke would tire. And then his reflexes would slow and he would make a mistake. Just one mistake. That would be all that Tolar would need.

The action in the arena was fast, desperate, and exciting, although Burke's tactics and methods looked strange to the villagers. They shouted encouragement to Tolar. Dalton watched tensely. Galen was worried to the point of distraction, but helpless. Irnar was evidently bored, judging by his frequent yawns. "They're like children, aren't they?" he asked Galen.

Tolar jumped at Burke, fully confident now. Burke sidestepped agilely and chopped down with the side of his hand, hitting Tolar just behind the ear. This was a move completely unknown in the ape world. It was something Tolar could not be prepared for; all of his previous opponents had simply tried to wrestle. Burke's karate blow sent Tolar spinning into the dust. Tolar lay stunned. Burke stood waiting.

The reaction of the villagers was stunned amazement. Never before had Tolar been even close to defeat. It had been dozens of games since any opponent had even sent Tolar sprawling, as Burke had done. All at once, the crowd found its voice and directed another volley of insults at Burke.

Tolar got to his feet and charged again. It was a clumsy run, motivated by the huge wrestler's desire to recoup his image of being undefeatable. He wanted to crush Burke in one powerful lunge. Again, nimbly, the astronaut moved to the side, like a bullfighter performing a *veronica*, and clubbed Tolar on the side of the head. Tolar went down again, shaking his head. He panted, resting on one knee in the dry dust of the arena. Twice more Tolar charged, and twice more Burke made the champion look almost foolish, so easily did he send Tolar crashing to the ground. The charges came ever more slowly, as Tolar grew wary and just a bit frightened. Burke, too, was frightened; he knew his own limits, and he wondered if he could wear Tolar down before the exertion of the battle wore *him* down.

The spectators, as fickle as any crowd ever was, began to change in response to the fighting of Burke, which looked to the people of Kaymak crazy but effective. A few voices cheered when Tolar was knocked down for the third time, and a great many more shouted their approval on the fourth knockdown. The humans wanted and demanded a hero and a champion; it was becoming clear to the combatants that the man didn't necessarily have to be Tolar.

Dalton, sitting among them, was aware of this, also. He watched in almost unbearable tension. He had never seen his father treated like this in the arena. His aversion to the games was overcome by his concern for his father.

Irnar watched, also concerned for his champion. He wondered how it would affect his village to have the long-time hero defeated by a common thief and criminal. As he watched, Tolar struggled to his feet, circled around Burke, and tried to grab hold of the astronaut. Burke placed one foot behind Tolar's right foot and gave a quick shove with his shoulder. Tolar fell heavily to the ground, not badly hurt but deeply humiliated. He sat in the dirt and looked up at Burke, desperation on his face.

The main street of Kaymak was deserted as Jason and his troopers rode into town. The roaring of the crowd in the amphitheater filled the air, but for the moment Jason ignored it. He pulled to a halt outside the prefect's house, noting the flagpole and the signal pennant which flew from it. Jason told his soldiers to wait while he himself dismounted and glanced around, puzzled by the emptiness of the town and by the screams coming from the amphitheater, which he now listened to curiously. He shook his head; another outlying village, another town full of mad apes and crazier humans. He strode up to the door of Irnar's house and. knocked. There was no reply. He opened the door and entered.

The main room was empty. "Irnar!" called Jason.

"Prefect Irnar!" He was answered only by silence and the muffled sound from the arena. With an expression of displeasure, Jason turned and left the house.

As Jason emerged from Irnar's home, he glanced around again, puzzled and increasingly annoyed. There was another roar from the amphitheater. Coming to a quick decision, Jason strode off in that direction.

Tolar was in very bad shape, shaky and bleeding from cuts over his eyes. Burke kept backing away from him, not wanting to hurt Tolar any further, but Tolar refused to give up—of course, to do so meant death, but there was a look in Tolar's eyes which said that surrender meant far worse things to him than death. He forced the fight to Burke, and the astronaut had no choice but to send Tolar down again. This time, Tolar did not move at all.

The villagers watched, suddenly silent once more. Then, from various parts of the amphitheater, voices cried out, "Throw the sword! Throw the sword! Throw the sword!" Over and over this was repeated; more and more people took up the cry.

Virdon could hear the roaring; the longer it lasted, the more uncomfortable he grew. "What's happening?" he demanded of the gorilla guard. He might have asked the inanimate stones in the ground, for all the response he got.

Galen watched, not sure if Burke's seeming victory were much better for their situation than a defeat. Irnar lifted the sword and threw it out into the arena. The crowd screamed. "It's not how I would have had it," said Irnar to Galen, "but it may all work out for the best."

The crowd took up a different chant now. "Kill him! Kill him! Kill him!" echoed in the arena as the humans stood, screaming insanely and waving clenched fists. Burke stood over the inert body of Tolar; the sword fell at his feet and, almost instinctively, he bent down to pick it up.

Tolar opened his eyes weakly, looking up at Burke. There was frustration and humiliation on his face, but not fear. Burke stared down at him, holding the sword. They regarded each other, oblivious of the pandemonium around them. Burke did not move.

The frenzy of the villagers grew. "Kill him! Kill him!" they screamed, while the eagerly awaited climax to the game was delayed by Burke's hesitation. This was the moment they had come to see. It did not matter to them whether Burke killed Tolar or the other way around; it was as Irnar had said: they had come to see blood. Dalton was the only spectator still sitting, except for Galen and Irnar. The youth remained quiet, surrounded by the shouting people, his vision cut off by their standing bodies.

While this scene formed, Jason entered the amphitheater. He was stopped momentarily by the two gorilla guards at the entrance, but, with a curt and contemptuous glance, he silenced them. The villagers were making so much noise that his questions had to be shouted. The guards shouted an answer and pointed in the direction of the Prefect's Box. Jason followed their gaze and saw Irnar. He did not acknowledge the directions from the gorillas—after all, they were rural police, inferior in all ways to his own troopers from Central City—but headed into the stands and around the amphitheater toward Irnar.

The villagers' emotion mounted further as they screamed for the kill. Burke, suddenly understanding what he was expected to do, turned away and threw the sword to the ground. The villagers were momentarily appalled; then they shouted their anger and rage at Burke. The insults they had hurled at him before were remembered and amplified. Dalton watched, too stunned and afraid to stand, unable to see the action, only partially aware of what was happening. He tried to understand the change in their screams. While all of this was happening, Jason was making his way slowly through the furious crowd, clubbing his way among the uncaring humans, whose attention was focused on the two men in the arena.

"I don't understand," murmured Knar. He was fascinated by Burke's reaction. Galen was about to reply when some commotion nearby attracted his attention. He looked off to one side; he was not certain of what he saw through the mass of people there. He squinted his eyes just a little and waited. A second or two later he was sure. He saw the uniformed gorilla moving through the crowd. Galen was shinned by what he saw; Jason was well-known to him. General Urko's chief aide was well-known to almost every ape in the empire. And, Galen knew surely, he himself would be well-known to Jason.

The villagers screams were even louder, although that seemed scarcely possible to the suddenly frightened Galen. As he watched, the humans began moving down through the stands, into the clear central area of the arena. It appeared that a riot was about to begin.

"No!" cried Irnar, worried. He waved to the gorillas that stood to either side of his box. "No! Stop them! Stop them!" The gorillas moved forward to follow the order.

As the villagers swept down toward the arena, Jason had

more difficulty getting to the Prefect's Box. He pushed and clubbed with his fists, but it was all he could do to prevent himself from being carried along with them.

Galen took the opportunity to slip away from the Prefect's Box. He saw that Jason was momentarily blocked and Irnar's attention was elsewhere. Galen moved away from Jason, down toward the arena and the crowd.

Dalton stood now, unable to maintain his tense paralysis any longer. The crowd swept around him. He was completely fascinated by what was happening; he felt an unpleasant sense of disgust.

Burke and Tolar both were menaced by the approaching crowd, Tolar for his defeat, Burke for his refusal to carry out the execution. The humans still chanted, "Kill him! Kill him! Kill him!" Burke, almost hypnotized by the chant, fearful that he might at any second be torn apart by the mob, stooped to pick up the sword. His expression was slightly dazed.

Galen pushed through the crowd and reached Burke's side. "Galen!" cried Burke.

"No time!" answered the chimpanzee. "Urko's lieutenant is up there! He'll recognize us!"

Burke looked up toward the Prefect's Box. Jason was talking urgently with Irnar, whose expression was startled, then angry. They both started to make their way down toward the arena. "Come on, then!" shouted Burke over the screaming mob. He and Galen tried to push their way through, Burke in the lead. He used the sword threateningly, almost cutting a way forward. Meanwhile, the gorillas were trying to rush people out of the arena, shoving them toward the entrance. "Out!" cried one gorilla, brandishing his rifle. "Everybody out!" He fired the rifle into the air. Near him, humans, frightened by this threat, hurried to comply with the ape's direction. A stream of villagers started pouring out of the amphitheater. The gorilla moved away to help channel the remainder of the humans. Burke and Galen slipped by him as he turned. Another gorilla started toward Burke; the astronaut hurled the sword at the ape. While the gorilla ducked, Burke and Galen hurried out of the arena among the other townspeople.

They emerged, panting and bruised. "Virdon," said Burke.

"No time!" said Galen, wheezing slightly. "Later!"

Inside the arena, Irnar and Jason were trying to shove their way through the crowd toward the entrance. Jason walked ahead of the prefect, roughly hitting the humans, clearing a path. As the two apes came out of the amphitheater, they looked around in frustration. Burke and Galen had escaped.

7

Jason stood at the window of Irnar's office, staring out at the street with great annoyance. Behind him, Irnar paced nervously. In all of the twenty-five years he had been prefect of Kaymak, no one of Jason's importance had ever visited him. And now, the official visit had to happen on the worst day of his entire career. From the window came indistinct crowd noises; they faded slowly. After a moment, the door opened and a gorilla entered. Irnar looked up at the ape. "Well, Morko?" asked the prefect.

"We've finally managed to clear all the humans off the street," said the gorilla, panting a little, obviously exhausted.

"Any damage?" asked Irnar. "Any injuries?"

"Nothing serious," said Morko. "One of my troopers was slightly hurt. I've never seen the humans so—"

Jason interrupted the report of the rural officer. "What did you say?" he cried, as though he couldn't believe what he had heard. "A trooper hurt? By a human! Don't you have rifles?"

Irnar tried to soothe Jason's outrage. "My orders are that weapons are used only as a last resort. You may go, Morko."

"I don't like this," said Jason in a dangerously quiet voice. The gorilla trooper gave him an anxious look, then left Irnar's office. Jason turned on Irnar in angry incredulity. "Your reports always described this as a peaceful village!" he said.

"It was!" said Irnar, protesting. "I mean, it is! The game wasn't brought to its proper conclusion, that's why they—"

Jason had heard enough. Everything about this rural village and its prefect sounded to him like sheer lunacy. "Games!" he shouted, slamming his fist on Irnar's desk. "You don't govern with games! You govern with this!" He raised his gauntleted hand, fingers open, and slowly closed it again into a rock-hard fist. "And you don't allow two important prisoners to escape! I've never seen such incompetence!"

"I don't believe that I can be held responsible for their escape," said Irnar coolly. He had had enough of Jason's attitude; he was angry enough to forget just how powerful Urko's aide was.

"Well, then," said Jason acidly, "who can I hold responsible? You bring him in here, because I have some plans for him."

Irnar ignored that. "I had no way of knowing that chimpanzee and the horse-thief were important prisoners, not until you came." Irnar was showing signs of irritation and anxiety. He was swinging Virdon's metallic disk on its thong as he spoke. The habit annoyed Jason.

"Must you play with that thing?" growled the gorilla. Irnar caught the disk and stared back angrily at Jason. The silence grew very tense. Irnar's resolution failed him first and he looked away from Jason's angry eyes. He opened his desk drawer, and dropped the disk into it.

Then he closed and locked the drawer.

"Is that all right?" asked Irnar in a dull voice.

"Thank you," said Jason dryly. "Now let's see the one prisoner you *haven't* lost. Not yet, anyway." He turned and started for the door. Irnar looked at Jason's back, his thoughts filled with disdain for the gorilla's crude manner and self-pity for having gotten involved in the entire sorry situation.

On the opposite edge of town from the amphitheater was a thick stand of trees that began only a few yards from the last hut in the village. The small forest ran on a couple of hundred yards, with only a narrow, grass-covered trail through it. In a clearing at the farther edge of this woodland stood Tolar's house. The structure was a rather primitive wooden shack, crude even by the standards of the rural humans. Not far from the house, about halfway between the building and edge of the woods, stood a well. Dalton was at the well, drawing up a bucket of water, which he transferred into another bucket. He turned and carried the water toward the house. He did not realize that, as he labored, he was watched by two pair of eyes, one pair human, the other chimpanzee, staring out from the shelter of the woods.

Hidden by the underbrush, Galen and Burke watched Dalton enter his house. For a moment longer the two held still. Then they crawled back a short distance and crouched among the trees.

"I don't understand your thinking, Pete," said Galen.

"Trust me," said Burke.

"But what makes you think they'll help us? Until now, we've been nothing but enemies to them, particularly you. You attacked them in the clearing, you were held as a criminal in the cage, and you fought Tolar in the arena."

"I could have killed that man," said Burke, peeling the bark from a twig and staring into the distance. For a few seconds he did not speak. The events of the day had been a heavy emotional drain on him. "The crowd wanted me to," he said finally, a trace of sadness in his voice. "He owes me *something*, don't you think?"

Tolar had made a separate sleeping area for himself by putting up poles and draping heavy, dark material over them. Now his quarters were even darker, for he had covered the window with the same thick fabric and closed the crude shutters over the outside. Tolar lay on his rough bed, his eyes wide open in the gloom, staring into the darkness that covered him. He heard the door open and Dalton enter, but he did not move. Dalton pulled back the hanging material that separated Tolar from the rest of the living room, and light flooded across Tolar's body. Still, Tolar didn't turn, didn't acknowledge in any way his son's presence.

"Father?" said Dalton. "Fresh water from the well?"

There was no response from Tolar. There was not even a flicker in the man's eyes to indicate that Tolar had heard his son speak. Dalton looked at his father for a moment, troubled. Then he made a decision and crossed to Tolar's window.

"You should have some light in here," said Dalton.

"Leave it closed."

"But, Father," said the youth, pulling back the dark fabric.

"Do as I say."

"This darkness is unhealthy."

Tolar's breath was exhaled in a sudden burst. "The

dead have no need of light," he said bitterly.

"And the living?" asked Dalton, pushing open the shutters.

"He disgraced me, Dalton," said Tolar, his voice filled with recrimination. "Why didn't he use the sword? Why? It is something I cannot understand. The man was no coward."

Dalton couldn't answer immediately. He, too, wondered the same thing. When he did reply, his words were hesitant. He was trying to express ideas he had not thought out fully. "I'm… not sure, Father," he said. "I think…" He broke off, grappling with concepts entirely foreign to what he had always been taught. "I keep remembering things Mother said. Secret things she'd tell a small boy because she couldn't tell you. About violence and killing and what is right and wrong. She tried to make me understand that there are other ways to prove one's manhood."

"Your mother could know little of that," said Tolar.

"Perhaps more than either you or I," said Dalton.

Tolar dismissed the idea. "I'm a dead man who breathes," he said, "and he did this to me."

"He spared your life, Father," said Dalton. "Can that really be bad?"

"Without honor, a man should not live. He took my honor and left me my life. You think that could be good, Dalton? Did you hear the people of our village, our neighbors, yelling for my blood? Do you think I can walk among them now?"

Dalton, more confused than ever, didn't know how to answer that. His father was indeed humiliated in the eyes of the people of Kaymak. More importantly, Tolar was humiliated in his own eyes. Dalton's arguments meant nothing to his father. Instead, Dalton turned and silently left the sleeping area, letting the drapery fall closed again. Tolar continued to stare silently up at the ceiling. Dalton went into the main room. He stood there, alone, by the window; he stared out, confused...

Virdon, his back to the street, was leaning against the bars and thinking. He had grown tired of pacing the small cage like a wild animal. Suddenly, he was hit with a staggering blow to the back of his head. He cried out and tumbled forward as someone prodded him in the back. He rolled across the cage and came to a stop against the solid wall, rubbing his head. He got to his feet, facing his attacker, breathing heavily.

Jason and Irnar were opening the door to the cage. The door swung open and the two apes entered, under the watchful gaze of four armed gorilla guards. Jason held a rifle, with which he had just hit Virdon; now he walked menacingly toward him while Irnar looked on, somewhat dismayed at the gorilla's unnecessary viciousness. "Where did your friends go?" said Jason in a surly voice. "Where is your meeting place?"

Virdon held himself upright, although the pain in his head made him dizzy and sick. He glared up at Jason. "When you questioned me before, I told you that there wasn't any meeting place," he said. "If you didn't believe me then, you won't believe me now."

"I don't believe you now," said Jason.

"And there's no way I can possibly persuade you that I'm telling the truth, so I won't even try."

"I might be persuaded," said Jason roughly, "if you told the truth."

"There isn't any meeting place," said Virdon.

"You'll tell me where it is, or I'll—" Jason raised

his rifle and turned it, preparatory to giving Virdon another clout with the butt end.

Irnar raised a hand. "Jason," he said, "I don't approve of this method of interrogating the prisoner."

Jason ignored Irnar's objection. "I'm not very much interested in your approval," he said to the prefect." Then he turned back to Virdon. "I'm giving you good warning. I have had a good deal of training, and I can promise you that you'll talk before much longer. The condition you'll be in at that time is entirely up to you."

"I forbid this!" cried Irnar. "I'm still prefect in this village, and you're under my jurisdiction."

Jason turned sharply, glaring at Irnar for a moment. "You don't have any jurisdiction, you clumsy country chimp! Talk to Urko, if you have any doubt about who has precedence here. You'll be lucky to get out of his office with your head on your shoulders. I won't hear any more of your empty threats, Irnar. I advise you to enjoy your title, *Prefect*, because you will no longer have it, once I make my report." Jason turned and stalked out of the cage.

Virdon glanced at Irnar. "Thanks," said Virdon.

Irnar whirled to face the astronaut. He gave a cry of anguish, seeing his peaceful future vanishing, his one dream of contentment ruined. "Why did you ever come here?" he shouted. Then he turned and left the cage. The door was locked again by one of the guards.

Moving quickly, Burke and Galen ran from the woods, raced across the open area, and reached Tolar's house.

They listened for a few moments, but there was only silence. The two looked at each other. Burke shrugged.

Inside the house, Dalton sat alone in the main room. Tolar had not stirred or said anything further. The dark drapery remained undisturbed. The youth stared at it, lost in thought. He was startled by a knock at the door. He glanced in that direction, puzzled, wondering who it could be. Tolar and Dalton had received few visitors, despite the father's previous glory. With many broken, confused thoughts spinning in his mind, Dalton got up and went to the door. He opened it and was even more surprised to see Burke. Galen stood to one side, out of sight.

"Can we come in?" asked Burke.

Dalton hesitated, turning to look at the somber barrier his father had erected. Finally Dalton nodded and stood away from the door. Burke entered; when Galen followed, Dalton reacted with even greater astonishment. For a few seconds, he could only stare at the young chimpanzee.

"I want to speak to your—" said Burke. He broke off when he saw the way Dalton was responding to Galen's presence. "Oh," said Burke, "this is my friend, Galen."

Dalton was confused. "Friend?" he asked. "An ape?"

"Don't let his appearance fool you," said Burke.

Galen smiled, understanding what the young wrestler was feeling. He was not at all insulted. "Oh, yes," he said. "It's quite possible. Hello." Galen held out his hand to Dalton.

"Hello," said Dalton, more out of reflex than social grace. Hesitantly, though, he held out his own hand.

The young man and the young ape shook hands. Now, suddenly, Dalton smiled broadly, as though he had made a great discovery. It was, indeed, merely a confirmation of something he had always suspected. "Yes," he said. "It is possible, isn't it?"

"Look," said Burke, "we need your father's help. Yours, too."

"What kind of help could we be?" asked Dalton curiously.

"Our friend's in the cage," explained Galen. "We have to get him out."

"No." Burke, Galen, and Dalton turned to see Tolar, who stood in front of the dark curtain. "No," said Tolar again, this time more forcefully. He was very tense and angry; his hands were clenched at his sides and his face had flushed a deep red color. He glared directly at Burke.

"You have disgraced me," said Tolar in an anguished voice. "We will not help you disgrace the prefect, too." He turned to Galen with a touch of deference. "We are loyal citizens here," he said, not knowing Galen's relationship to Burke.

"Listen to me for a moment," said Burke, not yet understanding Tolar's reluctance to help them. "My friend's a human being. He'll be taken back to Central City and Urko will have him killed."

"He's a stranger," said Tolar. "We owe him nothing. He is a criminal. We have no debt to him."

"You owe *me* something!" said Burke hotly. "You owe me your life!"

Tolar walked across the room until he was very close to Burke. He looked into the astronaut's eyes as he had before throwing the dirt in Burke's face, as he had in the arena. On each occasion Tolar's reasons had been different, but his expression had been the same, the same as it was now—determined and proud. He spoke, and his voice was tight and filled with bitterness. "For that I tell you to leave my house!" he said.

"No, Father!" said Dalton sharply, almost without thinking.

Startled, Tolar whirled, staring at Dalton in shock.

"He'll stay," said Dalton. "And if I can, I'll help him."

There was a long moment of silence as the man stared

at his son, not knowing what to say. The youth was only a little smaller than his father. They were nearly matched in strength; only Tolar's vastly greater experience allowed him to defeat Dalton in their practice wrestling matches—that, and, of course, Dalton's natural reluctance. But now, with Dalton asserting himself, Tolar was at a loss. "So," he said finally, "you are taking on the authority of father."

"I am sorry," said Dalton, anguished. The situation was very difficult for him. He had never contradicted his father in this, way before. "You have retired to your bedroom. You said that you were no longer among the living. Well, this man's friend *is* among the living, and he needs help."

"This is your decision?" asked Tolar.

"I can't turn them away," said Dalton.

Tolar looked, from Dalton to Burke. Slowly, his proud demeanor almost visibly altered. His shoulders slumped slightly, and he turned slowly and went back through the curtain, into his sleeping area.

Jason was making use of Irnar's desk, writing his report. He barely glanced up as Irnar entered the hut. Jason continued to write. Irnar glared; the implicit insult of Jason's working at Irnar's own desk and the omitted acknowledgment of Irnar's presence were clear enough.

"The approach you were taking with that man would not have worked," said Irnar, attempting to be firm with Jason. The gorilla didn't bother to reply. Irnar pressed on. "Some men do not respond to force. I have made a study of human behavior. I have had a good long time to observe them."

"You'll have your opportunity to tell Urko all about your studies," said Jason contemptuously. "It will get you nowhere. Urko doesn't share your tender concern for humans."

"My way is practical," said Irnar. "It controls humans with the minimum effort and cost."

Jason gave a short laugh. "Yes, yes, of course," he said. "That's precisely what I'm putting in my report. I saw an example at the arena."

"The people reacted that way because they need a death to finish off their games," said Irnar. "They didn't get it."

Jason put down his stylus with exaggerated calm. He looked up at Irnar; his expression was ugly. "I'm very, very sick of hearing about your games, Irnar!" he said.

"But it's true!" protested the prefect. "Human nature! "Violence! Aggression! Hostility! My way keeps them from—"

Jason interrupted the flow of Irnar's arguments. "You're raving," he said. He was about to add something, when he suddenly slapped the top of the desk. "I'm such an idiot!" he cried. "*Your* way," he said, in response to Irnar's questioning stare. "Your humans want a death. We should let them have the prisoner."

"But I thought your orders were to capture the two humans and the chimpanzee and return them to Central City?" said Irnar. "Don't you have to keep him protected until Urko can question him?"

"Officially, yes," said Jason, letting his voice trail, off meaningfully. Irnar looked at him for a long moment, then grinned.

"You needn't send in that report, either, Lieutenant," said Irnar.

Jason looked up with a good deal of distaste. "I am General Urko's lieutenant," he said slowly. "At least, sometimes I am described that way. More accurately, I am his aide de camp and his military liaison officer on detached duty. My own rank is colonel. Even a raw gorilla recruit would know that from the insignia on my uniform."

"That's beside the point," said Irnar excitedly. Jason's expression indicated that he did not agree, but the prefect went on anyway. "I have a feeling that I may be able to stay on as prefect. You're going to see how my theory works." Jason only nodded doubtfully.

Curtains were drawn over the windows in Tolar's house, protection in the unlikely event that someone from the village approached the house while Burke and Galen were still there. Tolar had retired to his separate quarters. Galen sat by one window, the curtain drawn back just enough so that he could peer out. Dalton and Burke were seated by the fireplace, in which a fire had been built to chase the sharp coolness of the evening. Burke whittled on a stick and Dalton added another bit of wood to the fire. "Humans more important than apes?" Dalton asked incredulously. "There really was such a time?"

Burke shrugged. "I was there," he said.

"What happened?"

"I don't know," said Burke, staring into the fire. "That's something we've been trying to learn since we got here. Information, history... all of that seems to be jumbled and scrambled and lost. But I can guess. War. Killing. Men destroyed each other. Themselves."

"But the arena," objected Dalton. "You didn't kill my father. And you could have. You were *supposed* to."

"I had no reason to kill him," said Burke.

"It's the way of the games," said Dalton. "Ever since I can remember, that has been the way."

Burke repeated his statement quietly. "I had no reason to kill him."

Dalton looked at him for several seconds, touched by Burke's sentiments, yet troubled. He rose, his inner feelings in conflict. He went to the window beside Galen and looked out. Then he glanced back at Burke. "In your time, did all humans feel this way about killing?" he asked.

"It depended on the war," said Burke. "But there were always some who wouldn't kill for any reason. Conscientious objectors. Pacifists. Whatever label people stuck on them, they all meant pretty much the same thing; that these people figured human life was just too special."

Dalton glanced at Galen. "Do you understand this?" he asked.

"I've never understood the need to kill," said the chimpanzee. "It's a thing for humans."

"My mother was a... 'pacifist,' I think," said Dalton.

"Do you remember her?" asked Burke gently.

"Of course," said Dalton. "I was young, but she told me things. Father doesn't understand, but I try—"

"Wait a minute," said Galen, raising one hand.

"No, really," said Dalton, misunderstanding. "I sometimes think about what my mother—"

Galen was listening intently. He cut off Dalton again. "Horse," murmured the chimpanzee. "Someone coming." He moved quickly away from the window.

"Hurry!" said Dalton. Burke looked at Galen for a moment. There was nowhere to hide in the cabin, with the possible exception of Tolar's shutoff area. But it was not likely that Tolar would let the fugitives hide there. They ran for the back door. Dalton watched them, concerned for their safety. In a few seconds, he heard the sound of a horse walking. The sound stopped; a short time later there was a knock at the front door. Dalton opened it. Irnar entered, and the young human nodded his head respectfully.

"Prefect," said Dalton.

"How is your father, Dalton?" asked Irnar. Before the youth could answer, Tolar pulled back the drapery and appeared. "Ah," said the ape, "Tolar. How are you?"

"I am ashamed, Prefect."

"No, no," said Irnar. "I won't have it. The champion of Kaymak all these years. Such a glorious career."

"All careers come to an end," said Tolar. "Mine should have, but didn't. Not in the way I deserved."

"No," said Irnar musingly. "But it was the man who fought you, he should be ashamed. Not you."

"Yes," said Tolar. "I…" His voice trailed off. He glanced at Dalton, a mixture of emotions running through him. He hesitated, then looked back at Irnar. "Prefect," he said, "I—"

Dalton could guess what his father was about to say. He wondered if Burke and Galen had remained close enough to listen to the conversation and to run if it became dangerous. "I think you should lie down, Father," said the youth.

Tolar looked at his son. "I think he should know—"

Dalton interrupted. "There's nothing for him to know," he said. "The prefect needn't be bothered with every detail of our lives. It is nothing."

Irnar's eyes closed slightly. He glanced from one human to the other. "I am concerned for your welfare," he said. "What is this 'nothing'?"

"My father's disgrace," said Dalton smoothly. "You cannot imagine how much it troubles him."

Irnar shook his head. "I knew it would," he said. "Your father is a most proud man. But, Tolar, it will be forgotten. Your shame will be washed away, I promise. The games tonight will make the people forget."

Dalton gave Irnar a quick glance. "Tonight?" he asked.

"Yes," said Irnar, turning to Dalton and smiling. "The torches will be lit and you will bring honor back to your family. *You* will fight the friend of the man who disgraced your father. And this time there will be a death. Is that understood? I want no error. There will be a death." With that, Irnar turned and left the house.

A moment later, the back door opened and Galen and Burke entered, standing just within the doorway, disturbed, looking at Dalton.

Dalton was stunned by the prefect's announcement and stood staring into space as Tolar came to him, proudly putting his arm around his son's shoulder.

8

The cool dusk was marked by the first faint flush of stars. In the west, the sky was still bright red where the setting sun had burnt it. Virdon sat on the floor of the cage, pushing the straw around idly. He was slumped disconsolately against a wall; after the clout he had taken from Jason's rifle, he had not come near the bars. His attention was aroused by the sound of a key being placed in the door's lock. He looked up.

Morko, the gorilla guard, was opening the door. Behind the gorilla stood Irnar. There was a second gorilla standing guard near the prefect. Virdon looked at them without much interest. Irnar entered the cage and walked over to the man. He looked down at him with a sense of compassion. "I'd like to speak to you for a moment, if I may," he said.

"It's your town," said Virdon, shrugging.

"I can understand your hostility toward me," said the prefect. Virdon only looked at the floor in silence. "You say you are from another time, I hear," continued Irnar.

"You and the other human. This is what Jason told me."

"Yes," said Virdon.

"Is it better than now?" asked Irnar.

"It's different. And it's home."

"Yes, I can understand that. As this is home to me. And that's the reason I—" Irnar broke off sadly. "I'm sorry you ever came to my village. Any of you."

Virdon answered flatly. "No sorrier than. I am. We had no choice. From the moment you picked up that magnetic disk and put it in your pocket, I had to get it back."

Irnar looked at him in surprise. "It was that?" he asked. "That little thing? That's why Galen came to—? I wish he had simply, told me. I'd have given him the thing with my blessing. It meant nothing to me. Instead, that disk has caused us all an untold amount of grief. So foolish."

"You can still do it," said Virdon. "Just give me the disk and let me go."

Irnar shook his head sadly. "Give you the disk? So that you can be free to search for your home, while I lose mine? I'm sorry. Truly. But the time for free choice is past."

"It never is," said Virdon. "Not for intelligent minds."

"Sometimes," said Irnar, "there comes a time for action."

"Not unreasoned action," said the human.

"What happens now is not the result of whim,"said Irnar gruffly. "I can assure you of that."

"What happens now?"

There was no answer from the prefect. Irnar signaled the gorilla guards that he was finished and left the cage. Morko locked the cage again and walked off with Irnar, leaving the second gorilla to stand sentry duty.

Galen and Burke moved stealthily along the street. There were still a few people about, but these were concerned only with getting to their houses and supper. No one noticed the chimpanzee and the astronaut as they moved closer to the cage, walking in the shelter of the huts' shadows. One of Jason's gorillas crossed the street ahead of them. They took refuge against the side of a building, peering around. "It's impossible," said Burke under his breath.

"It's possible," said Galen, unaware that he was voicing Burke's unheard sentiment. "How can we do it?"

"I don't know," said the astronaut. "But it has to be before night falls. And we can't swing it alone. You're the one who came up with the plan to—" Burke broke off thoughtfully. "Wait a minute. I'll be back as soon as I can." He turned and ran, leaving Galen alone, worried, and watching.

Some time later, Burke arrived at Tolar's house, out of breath from his run. He rushed up to the house and opened the door. He burst into the main room, which was unoccupied. "Dalton!" cried Burke. There was only silence. "Dalton! Tolar!"

He hurried to the drapery that shut off Tolar's bedroom, opened it, glanced in, then went back out to the main room. His idea was in jeopardy; he had not counted on the house being deserted. He looked around in frustration, trying to plan his next move.

There was a small graveyard near the edge of town. The markers stood in rows like sentinels. Near one particular grave, a huge figure was kneeling. It was Dalton, alone. He was lost in thought; anguish and helplessness showed on his face.

After a while, during which Dalton was lost in solitary meditation, another figure approached, from behind, standing there for a moment, watching the thoughtful young man. It was Tolar. Dalton was as yet unaware of his father's presence.

"I loved your mother very much," said Tolar finally.

Dalton glanced up at Tolar, then looked at the grave. "What would she tell me to do?"

"A man is not a woman," said Tolar. "Even if she were alive today, she could not do your thinking for you."

"She said there was no honor in killing," said Dalton.

"She said. But she loved me, Dalton. And she would never have noticed me, except for the games… I would have been nothing, except for the games."

"That's not true, Father," said Dalton earnestly. "You would have made some other life for yourself."

Tolar stared at his hands and shook his head. "Doing what?" he asked. "Have you not lived well, because of my success?"

"How many have *you* killed, Father?" asked Dalton.

"The prefect created the games. They brought peace to the village. That is a blessing."

"That is beside the point," said Dalton. "Do you even know? How many men have you slain?"

"As many as I have fought," said Tolar impatiently. "As you will tonight. In the arena, it will all look differently."

"But I have no reason to kill him," said Dalton, remembering Burke's words.

"It's the way of the game," said Tolar.

"Is it?" asked Dalton, not believing it for a moment any longer.

The last traces of the sun's rays were vanishing, and the sky was turning from dark blue to black as Dalton arrived at the house of the prefect. Inside, after Irnar admitted the youth, there was an uncomfortable silence. Irnar studied Dalton, not quite sure what to make of him. Dalton was rather uncomfortable at suddenly doing this rash thing.'

"I wanted to talk to you, Prefect," he said.

"I know that you have a strange reluctance about fighting in the games," said Irnar pensively. "Strange for the son of the great Tolar."

"That is possibly my mother's influence," said Dalton quietly.

"It *is* the nature of man to kill," said Irnar. "That is something that has been demonstrated to the satisfaction of every scientific investigator."

Then why didn't the stranger kill my father?"

"Perhaps there is some unknown explanation," said Irnar. "These strangers are fugitives and criminals, after all. They are desperate. Perhaps the stranger accepted a bribe, or something of that sort. Not that I'm trying to implicate Tolar, you understand. But possibly there was some illegal contact with another inhabitant of our village. Who knows? Who can tell the ways of humans?"

"I don't believe it," said Dalton.

"What exactly do you want from me?"

It was difficult for Dalton to get the words out, but it was something he had to do. "Prefect," he said, stammering, "I… I think the games are wrong. I think maybe that killing is wrong."

Irnar completely lost his patience with the young man. "Not in the games!" he cried.

"Always, my mother said. Always. I never understood until now, Prefect. But the stranger didn't kill, and now I know that my mother was right." He paused for a moment as he gathered his courage. "Prefect, I'm not going to fight."

Irnar stared at him, amazed at Dalton's impudence. "I order you!"

"I can't," said Dalton, his sudden courage used up. He felt weary. "It's wrong. And I have to tell the others in the village. I have to make *them* understand that it's wrong, too."

"You'll do no such thing!" shouted Irnar. "You are directly attacking me and my system of government. You are being rebellious. Be careful what you say, Dalton."

"The people have to know what has been shown to me," said Dalton. "They have to know that the games are wrong, that killing is wrong—"

Irnar was incredulous. In a fury, he rushed to fling open the door and call out. "Sergeant!" he shouted. "Sergeant! This human has broken curfew!" He looked at Dalton. "That's all I need…"

Tolar's main room was no longer deserted. The huge human paced across the floor, raging. Near him stood Burke. Tolar was nearly out of his mind with hatred.

Burke watched and listened carefully; somehow he had to get through to Tolar.

That seemed unlikely, in Tolar's present frame of mind. "Destroyer!" he cried. "Destroyer of me! Destroyer of my son!" Tolar stopped his frantic pacing, breathing heavily. He turned to face Burke. Tolar's hands clenched and unclenched, and he flushed with anger. Burke backed away a step or two, warily, as Tolar slowly moved toward him.

"Easy, Tolar, easy," said Burke in his most conciliatory voice. He was trying to avoid setting the man off entirely. The one thing he didn't need was a rematch of their battle in the arena. "Just relax, Tolar, just—"

Tolar had other ideas. "You tell him killing is bad! What have you done *but* kill? You killed my honor! You killed my son's manhood! You—"

"Wrong, Tolar, wrong," said Burke, frightened by Tolar's intensity. He raised his hands as though to ward off the man's savage emotional outburst.

Tolar had had enough debating. With a snarl he leaped for Burke, his hands outstretched to catch and twist the smaller man's neck.

The door opened and Galen ran in, sizing up the situation as quickly as possible. Burke was going, into a defensive crouch, his knees slightly bent, his arms hanging loosely at his sides. "Tolar!" cried Galen. "Tolar, don't!" Tolar stopped at the unexpected interruption. He momentarily halted his advance on Burke to see what the voice behind him meant. "Tolar!" said Galen, "Your son! He was arrested! He's been put in the cage!"

There was only stunned silence from Tolar. He didn't know how to deal with this latest and most unexpected turn of events.

"Tolar!" said Galen, trying to stir the man to positive action. "Your son's been arrested!"

The news finally penetrated. Tolar tried desperately to understand. "Dalton? In the cage?"

"Yes," said Galen. "Because he was against the games."

Tolar's anger and outrage grew. He forgot the fury he had felt for Burke, now that it was turned in a new direction. "In the cage? My son?" His voice became almost a scream. "*My son?*"

Virdon once again had company in the cage. This time, however, it was neither Irnar nor Jason. It was Dalton, and the young human was a prisoner, also. Virdon was trying to catch up on the activities of his friends, whom he hadn't seen since much earlier that day. "Did they have any kind of scheme or plan?" he asked.

"No," said Dalton. "At least, none that I heard."

Virdon chewed his lip while he thought. The situation in Kaymak, as peaceful as the village had appeared to be, had turned into one of the most perilous the three fugitives had ever experienced. "If they're smart," said Virdon, "they'll just take off."

Dalton didn't understand Virdon's words. "Take off?"

"Go away," said Virdon. "Leave. An expression from my time."

"In your time," said Dalton. "If there had been no killing then, men might still be important now. That's true?"

Virdon glanced at Dalton. In all of his travels about the ape empire, Virdon had met very few humans or apes who understood that simple truth. "It's possible," said Virdon after a moment.

Dalton thought for several seconds. "It could still happen," he said. Virdon looked at the young man, realizing that there was more depth to Dalton than he had first guessed.

Two gorillas stood on guard outside the cage. One of the apes nudged the other and pointed down the street. "Look," he said. His companion looked and saw Tolar striding down the street toward them. His bearing and quick pace indicated that he was in a dangerous mood.

"No closer," said the first gorilla, raising his rifle as Tolar came near them.

"I want to see my son," said Tolar, his voice almost a growl.

"Nobody sees the prisoners," said the guard. "And no humans are allowed on the streets."

"He's my son," said Tolar. "I want to see him!"

He stepped even closer. The other gorilla moved up, confronting Tolar with another rifle. "Don't do it, Tolar," said the second gorilla. "You were a great fighter. Go back to your home."

"Please," said the man. "All I ask of you—both of you—is a little pity. Pity on a poor human, whose son has been condemned to—" By now, he had gained the attention of both apes, who had known and appreciated his superior talents for many years. They listened to him in a way that was generally reserved for their ape friends. Tolar had won a grudging amount of respect, even from these most ungenerous gorillas.

It was while Tolar was speaking that Burke and Galen leaped out from their hiding place. They both attacked the first gorilla, knowing that neither of them could tackle a gorilla one-to-one. Together they dragged the guard to the ground.

The second guard turned toward them with a roar. Tolar struck him on the side of the head, sending the ape to the ground with one blow. He dove for the gorilla even as the ape tried to get to his feet. Tolar clasped his hands together and clubbed the gorilla unconscious. The human got to his feet, not even breathing hard. He looked toward Galen, Burke, and the first gorilla.

The gorilla was struggling with Burke. Galen had rolled away from the conflict. It was clear that Burke was having difficulty at close quarters with the massive gorilla. Tolar jumped in, grabbed the ape, and knocked him out with two punches. Galen quickly bent down and got the key to the cage.

While Galen hurried to the cage, Virdon and Dalton anxiously encouraged him. Galen unlocked the door and the two human prisoners both hurried out.

Dalton rushed to his father's side. "Father, I—"'

"I don't understand you," said Tolar, "and I never will. But no one should put you in the cage for that."

"I don't think that I could ask more from you than tolerance," said Dalton. "I don't expect to have your approval."

Burke came over to them. "I hate to break up this reconciliation," he said worriedly, "but we'd better move, and *now*."

"What are we going to do?" asked Dalton, who, like Virdon, was in the dark about any plans Burke and Galen might have formulated. Before Burke could answer, a shot rang out; a cloud of dust was kicked up near their feet. The small group looked down the street to see a sergeant of the gorilla garrison with his rifle pointing directly at them. He was preparing to fire again. Once more the crash of the rifle split the air as the four humans and single chimpanzee jumped for cover. The bullet bit into the floor of the cage. The gorilla sergeant ran toward the escaped prisoners.

Burke led the way as they rushed away from the sergeant in the direction of Irnar's house, by way of the back alley along the huts' rear sides. Once more the rifle shot was heard, although the "gorilla was being left further behind every second.

The gunfire aroused the curiosity of Jason and Irnar, who were arguing in the prefect's living room. They rushed outside, Jason drawing his pistol as he did. The four humans and Galen suddenly appeared in front of them, dashing across the street toward the astonished apes. "Stop!" cried Jason. "Stop, before I shoot!" Burke raised a hand and the party came to a halt. They hesitated in front of the prefect's house.

Tolar pushed his way to the front, coming close to Jason. He was intentionally blocking the gorilla's view of the others. "No! No!" he cried. He turned to look over his shoulder. "Run! Now!" Jason fired. Tolar was hit at close range but he would not be stopped. After hesitating another moment, the others ran off down the street, Jason turned to fire at them, but Tolar, badly wounded, blood covering his chest and abdomen, grabbed him. The human and the ape struggled wordlessly, Jason still holding his pistol.

The gorilla sergeant came running up on his short legs. He raised his rifle, then lowered it. Irnar grabbed the gorilla's arm and silently shook his head. The sergeant looked up at Irnar, clearly puzzled, unable to understand why the prefect was preventing him from aiding Jason.

Tolar and Jason still battled, grunting and panting from the heavy task of trying to control the weapon. Tolar's grasp on Jason's wrist tightened. The pistol fell to the ground with a dull clatter.

"Now, Prefect? Shall I shoot him?" asked the worried sergeant.

"No," said Irnar.

"But—"

"No," said the prefect again, coldly.

The villagers were drawn out by the commotion, as well. Disregarding the curfew, they gathered in a mob around the struggling pair in the street.

Tolar scrabbled for the pistol. Jason pushed him aside, sweeping up the pistol as Tolar staggered toward him again. The human wrapped the gorilla in a tight bear hug. The pistol fired, and after a moment Jason slumped in Tolar's hold. The human moved his arms apart, no longer supporting the gorilla's dead body. Jason fell into the dust at Tolar's feet, shot fatally through the chest. Tolar turned, his eyes filled with pain, and looked toward Irnar. The man reached out one hand beseechingly; then he, too, collapsed to the ground, dead.

Irnar stared at the scene impassively for a long moment. He knelt beside Jason's body and saw that the gorilla was dead. Then he glanced toward Tolar's bloody corpse, feeling a genuine sense of loss. "Nobly sacrificed, my friend," he murmured.

The sergeant moved to kneel beside Irnar. He made a quick examination of his own. He was shocked when he looked up at Irnar. "He's dead," said the gorilla.

Irnar was calm, secure in his superiority and greater intelligence. He was also pleased that everything about the matter had been tied up, more or less neatly, by this unexpected turn of events. There was the matter of the escaped prisoners, but only Jason and Irnar knew of the importance of Burke, Virdon, and Galen. As for Dalton, he was imprisoned merely for "breaking curfew," and no humans had actually seen the young man in the cage. "Umm, yes," said Irnar. "As you saw, he died a hero's death, fighting a crazed human."

"But I could have—"

Irnar raised a hand calmly. "Sergeant, your bravery is not in question. I will see that you are properly mentioned in my official report."

"Thank you," said the sergeant, confused but willing to be honorably cited.

"We must not let unfortunate incidents like this interfere with our normal routines," said Irnar. He made a gesture of dismissal to the gorilla, then glanced up. Around them, watching, were the human villagers of Kaymak. There was an audible "ahh" passing through the crowd, a collective sigh. This was the climax they had been denied in the arena.

Tolar and Jason were the deaths they had needed to witness.

The next day, Virdon, Burke, Galen, and Dalton were walking along the trail that led to the. clearing where the fugitives had first seen the youth and his father wrestling. They moved silently through the late autumn woods until they reached the clearing. Gradually, from the distance, the sound of a galloping horse grew louder. Galen heard it first, but soon the others could make it out as well. Virdon stopped them. "Someone is in a real hurry, riding that fast along a trail this bad. Come on," he said. They hurried off the path, into the underbrush where they could be out of sight. They hid themselves and waited. After a few moments Dalton grew nervous. The horse's hooves were coming closer. He made a decision, rose, and started out into the clearing. Virdon tried to grab one of the young man's arms. Dalton looked at him. "No," he said quietly. "Please, no."

Virdon let the young man go. Dalton stepped out into the clearing; the others remained where they were, watching him.

Dalton waited as the sound of the galloping horse was almost upon him. Suddenly, Irnar emerged from the trees, into the clearing. He pulled his horse to a halt when he saw Dalton who walked up to him.

"What of my father?" he asked.

"He was a brave man," said Irnar simply.

Dalton studied the prefect's face. "And the games?"

Irnar sighed deeply. "I'm afraid they died with him. Perhaps there is a better way to govern."

"There must be," said Dalton.

There was a long moment, of silence as they looked at each other. "Tell your friends that I have never met them, and they have never met me," said Irnar.

"Yes, Prefect."

Irnar reached into his pocket, extracted something, and handed it to Dalton. "And wish them good luck for me," he said. He suddenly wheeled his horse around and rode back down the path. Dalton stood watching him go and then glanced down at the object in his hand. Resting in his palm was the magnetic disk on its leather thong.

Later, after some walking through the woods guided by Dalton, the party stopped at a fork in the trail. "You sure you won't go with us?" asked Burke.

Dalton nodded. "There's so much for me to think about. So much I still don't understand," he said. '

"It could be dangerous here for you," said Virdon.

Dalton paused, thinking hard. "That isn't important," he said. "What *is*... important... I think... is that killing should stop." He paused again, having difficulty articulating his feelings. "People should know that. Killing should stop. Well, I guess I won't be seeing you. Good luck."

"You never know," said Burke. "We may pop back in on you sometime."

"I hope so," said Dalton. He turned and walked off in the direction of his home. Virdon, Burke, and Galen watched him go.

"A beginning, I guess," said Burke.

"Who can tell?" asked Virdon, smiling. "The world seems to be able to use all it can get." He pointed off down the right fork, which Dalton said went on almost due south. With an audible sigh from Galen, the three fugitives shouldered their packs more comfortably and continued their march.

ABOUT THE AUTHOR

A winner of the Hugo and Nebula Awards, George Alec Effinger was the author of *What Entropy Means to Me* and *Schrodinger's Kitten*. He died in 2002.

For more fantastic fiction, author events,
competitions, limited editions and more

VISIT OUR WEBSITE
titanbooks.com

LIKE US ON FACEBOOK
facebook.com/titanbooks

FOLLOW US ON TWITTER
@TitanBooks

EMAIL US
readerfeedback@titanemail.com